THE BROKEN REALM

KINGDOM OF THE WHITE SEA BOOK TWO

SARAH M. CRADIT

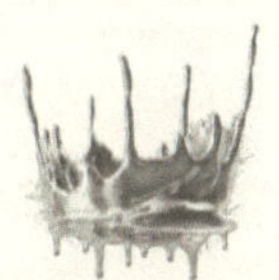

Cover Design by Regina Wamba of ReginaWamba.com
"Garden of Truth and Temptation" Art by Alexandra Curte
Portrait Art by Lauren Richelieu (Marsh's Portrait by Alexandra Curte)
Map by The Illustrated Author Design Services
Editing by Emily A. Lawrence of Lawrence Editing

Publisher Contact:
sarah@sarahmcradit.com
www.sarahmcradit.com

Complete character guides by location can be found at the end
of the book. These are spoiler-free and include only
information that is true at the start of the book.

You can find a complete list of content warnings on my
website: sarahmcradit.com

OWLING SEA
N
W
E
S
MIDNIGHT CREST
ICEBOLT MOUNTAIN
MIDWINTER REST
WITCHWOOD CROSS
WHITECAP
NORTHERLAND RANGE
FOREST OF LYCANA
WULFSHEAD HAVEN
9
TORRIN'S PASS
6
WESTPORT
EASTPORT
DUNWOODE
1
DARKWOOD RUN
SALTHILL
WULF'S NECK
7
MAYKE
SALEEN
ASGILL
2
DRUMAIN
BY THE SEA
TERMONGLEN
RUSHWOOD
WHISPERING WOOD
12
VALLEYBROOKE
EVERLEIGH PIKE
STREAMSTOWNE
EVERHART THICKET
WILDWOOD FALLS
PARTH
RESPLENDENT RELIQUARY
5
THE SEPULCHRE IN THE SKIES
10
BRIARHAVEN
THE SEVEN SISTERS
GAP O' EVER
GREENFEN
RIVER RUSH
WINDWATCH GROVE
PINE BLUFF
WHITEWOOD
OLDCASTLE
FIONN'S PASS
3
OAK HILL
WHITE SEA
EAST DERRY
IRON HILL
BLACKPOOL
STONE MAWR
NEWCARROW
4
SANDYMOUNT
GREENCASTLE
GOLDTHORPE
SANDYCOVE
LEECASTER BAY
11
HORNSEA
PORT WORTHING
CAMP ATONEMENT
GREYSTONE ABBEY
WHITECLIFFE
8
CAMP RESTITUTION
1.) NORTHERLANDS
2.) HINTERLANDS
3.) WESTERLANDS
4.) SOUTHERLANDS
5.) EASTERLANDS
6.) ISLE OF BELCARROW
7.) DUNCARROW
8.) WASTELANDS
9.) WULFSGATE
10.) LONGWOOD RUSH
11.) WARWICKTOWN
12.) WHITECHURCH
KINGDOM OF THE WHITE SEA

PROLOGUE

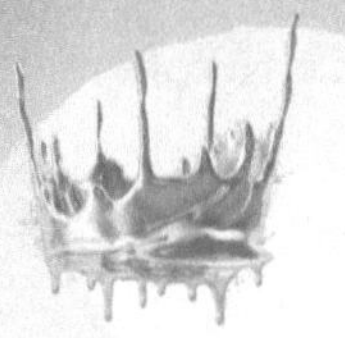

Assana Rhiagain moved through the dreary halls of Duncarrow like an unmoored ghost. There'd been whispers intended for her in those first few days. They all wondered about the replacement bride, the girl whose only value was in securing her father as the key sycophant of the king. Some took great pleasure in their anticipation of the pain she'd endure at the hands of King Eoghan. Others reflected on this same thing with resigned sadness. Pity. The pity was the worst of all. She'd rather they all exalted in their joy over her painful marriage than direct toward her even a grain of sympathy.

The whispers had since moved on, redirecting their focus to the latest court intrigues. The Right of Choosing and a consolation prize would-be queen were no longer so interesting when measured against Asherley Blackwood's moonlight flight, prompting a rare display of the king's righteous fury. They looked to him to set the tone of their own emotions, and he didn't disappoint. For *this*, he'd finally left his bedchamber, stomping through the barren halls of Duncarrow in his nightshift, roaring like a vexed dragon. Assana supposed they were all surprised his voice could carry like that at all. His cruelty had always been louder than his words.

Asherley had taken with her the male heirs of the Southerlands and Northerlands. Asherley herself had been among the king's pawns, and so her escape meant the loss of his leverage with the three Reaches who had failed to deliver as promised at the Right of Choosing.

Something else had been stolen as well, though no one knew precisely what. Only that it was of great importance to the king.

That left only Assana. Assana, burdened by her questions. Assana, laden with the weight of the many betrayals painting her short life.

No one looked her way now as her bare feet connected with the damp stone. She was no longer worth the height of their emotions on either end of the pendulum. She was hardly worth Eoghan's time, and his supposed need of her was the reason he'd dragged her to Duncarrow.

Asherley's escape had been supplanted by yet *another* event that stirred the busybodies into a frenzy. This one was a hit closer to home, but not for the reasons others must have assumed.

Assana approached the rear of the keep and started the long, winding climb up the crumbling stairs. Every few steps the stone had decayed away altogether, and if one wasn't attentive, they might find themselves careening through the gaps to their death. Assana was aware of everything, in a place where it all meant her harm, so she nimbly lifted her skirts and stretched her legs to dodge the holes where the stairs should be.

No one ventured here without proper business. That didn't mean the guards had questions for her. They seemed surprised, perhaps even relieved, to lay eyes on someone who wasn't one of them. Visitors were not a common occurrence.

"Lady Assana," one said, nodding. He and the other guard scrambled to their feet. He didn't address her as queen. As Eoghan had said, so many times now that it no longer bothered her, she was not a queen. Only a woman bearing Rhiagain blood could be a queen, and even a Rhiagain queen would never be regent.

She didn't return the nod. She still had some of her dwindling dignity left. She was still a Quinlanden. Still among the fairest of all families, in all the Reaches.

They knew who she'd come for. *They*, who all had her defined, fitting neatly in the boxes designed, assumed they knew everything about her. That there could be no greater depth beyond the turbulent waters at the surface of her bearing.

Not that they were wrong, but it was two, not one, she'd come for.

But first.

The guard paused outside the cell. "I can't let you in, Lady Assana. Not without the king's authorization."

"I have no wish to go in," she snapped back. "Merely open the window where you pass his dinners."

"That I can oblige. With pleasure, my lady." The guard fumbled with the massive ring of keys, sweating through the effort. She sighed, loudly and forcefully enough for him to understand where it was directed.

He found the proper key at last and slid it into the lock. Pulling back the small metal window, he said to her, "You let me know if he gives you any trouble."

Assana rolled her eyes at his soft, rotund belly and layers of hard-earned jowls. Only at night did the guards bring in the tougher men, because no one dared attempt an escape in the daytime. "And what would you do, if he did?"

The guard's face fell. "Just the same, my lady."

She almost felt bad. But he was surely no different than the others, who whispered behind her back, who had reduced her to the worst of herself as well. She would take what little power she still possessed, even if it came at a cost to others.

Assana approached the makeshift window separating prisoner from freedom. The man on the bed across the room looked up, and, Guardians bless him, the hope in his face almost brought her joy. Had he only been someone else; someone she loved, and who loved her in return, she would've reveled in knowing she was doing good. But she hadn't come to intervene on his behalf. She wouldn't, even if she had that power.

"Assana! Oh, thank the Guardians!" he cried out, grasping at her through the window. She stepped back, beyond his reach, never taking her eyes off him. "My blessed child!"

"Father." Assana ground her jaw.

Aiden brightened with relief. "Oh, I knew you would come. You've at last talked sense into your husband, the king. I had no doubt."

"I've done no such thing," Assana said. "Had I tried, they would've been words wasted upon the air."

Aiden's face lost some of its unbridled enthusiasm. "You haven't come to release me?"

"No."

"I don't understand your hostility toward me, Assana." Aiden dropped his hands to the small ledge at the base of the window. "I made you a queen."

Assana laughed. "I am no queen. And you know this, for he told you so himself, in front of all the court, before throwing you in here."

"Your cursed aunt has him heated, that's all." Aiden's cheeks flooded with dark red anger. "Asherley will pay a heavy toll for what she's done."

"You already took the head of her husband," Assana replied.

Aiden ignored her. "The king has calmed by now, surely. Weeks have passed. No man has a temper that long."

"You perhaps don't know King Eoghan as well as you thought," she said. Assana took a single step closer, staying clear of the reach of his hands. "You will die in here, Father. Not because he's angry at Aunt Asherley. But because he's afraid of you. You brought him Rowanwen, and then the Westerlands, but though he is young, he is no fool. He knew those gifts were not for him."

"Reckless girl," Aiden hissed. "Are these the things you whisper in his ear, in the bedroom?"

"In the bedroom, he prefers the ministrations of a mother's touch, I'm afraid. I'm surprised your own spies didn't uncover this... proclivity of his. You would've done better to send my mother in my place."

Aiden pressed his forehead to the small gap. "You will find a way to reach him, Assana. You'll appeal to his better sense, remind him of all I've done, and will do. Or I'll have you cast into the sea, like Eoghan cast Darrick, years ago."

Assana sighed. It turned into a yawn. "I have to go. I have a more pressing matter."

"Go? What could be more pressing than aiding your father through this terrible misunderstanding? We have not done all these things to see it end in the sky dungeon of Duncarrow!"

Assana whistled at the guard. He hobbled over, set to the tune of the clinking keys as he again fumbled for the right one.

"Assana!" Aiden called, as the window closed. "Assana, do not forget who you are!"

"I haven't, Father," Assana whispered and beckoned the guard to follow her farther down the corridor, to the end. There was but one cell past the bend of the tower, and if rumors were true, it hadn't been opened in many years.

"That one?" The guard hesitated. He seemed almost scared. "Have you perhaps the wrong cell?"

"Is this not the cell of Oldwin the Sorcerer?"

"Yes, but—"

Assana silenced him with a hard look. "Open it."

TAINTED BLOOD AND BARBED TONGUES

I

TORRIN'S PASS

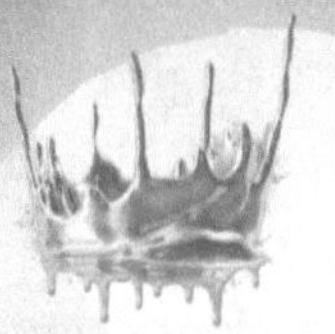

Christian loaded the last of the crates into the wagon. Aylen was only half a beat behind, stretching and snapping the canvas over the top. He helped her secure the rope ties, and within moments, the contents of the wagon vanished under the dark cover. A fresh layer of snow dotted the top, further sealing their efforts.

"Is it enough, do you think?" Aylen asked. She crossed her arms, regarding their work with a troubled frown.

"It has to be. We can't risk making weekly trips."

"The bows will be an improvement from the swords. The scholar will know how to hunt. And Pieter is old enough that your father must have provided some training, right?"

"I think you underestimate the women in that camp," Christian said with a short laugh. "But you're right. You can't hunt with a sword in the Northerlands. They'll eat better with the proper tools."

"Have you seen anything? Any visions?"

"No," he said. "Not about that. My gift has been inexplicably quiet lately."

Aylen frowned. "I put some toys in this time. They aren't much, but..." She sighed. "He's just a boy. He's never had anything of his own. I know these aren't essential to survival, but in a way, perhaps, they are."

Christian kissed her on her temple. "You were right to put them in. His mother will appreciate that most of all. No one is more aware than she is of what he's been denied."

"It doesn't seem possible, Christian. All these years, and no one knew they were there? Not a single person tried to help them?"

"Maybe they did and were punished for it."

"Do you think..." Aylen turned her head away. "Lord and Lady Dereham knew about Darrick and Anabella. We read the scrolls. Their entire courtship happened here, at Wulfsgate. Your mother even advised Anabella on the matter. Isn't it also possible they knew of their marriage?"

Christian had wondered about this, too, but there was no good to be found in losing oneself in speculation. His parents had nothing to do with Anabella's kidnapping. They were as shocked as anyone to learn that she lived, that she had a son with the rightful king. "I don't think they knew of the wedding, or they would've had a weapon against Eoghan long ago. Even after reading Anabella's words, though I believe her, none of it seems real. Steward Weatherford thought his daughter had been lost in a storm, like so many others of the Northerlands. There was no reason to suspect something more sinister."

"I suppose you're right." Aylen pulled her fur hood back over her face when the wind kicked up. "The kingdom will not take well to this news. To what Eoghan did."

"No," Christian said. Ahead, he saw his father, on Sorcha, returning from a patrol. Alric lingered behind on his smaller pony. "Though we will trust to our betters to decide when and how that news is to be spread."

"Has Lord Dereham given any indication? Any at all?"

Christian didn't answer. He didn't have one. Much had changed since he'd been a boy, running around the Wintergarden, chasing after his younger siblings. Though, perhaps it hadn't changed, so much as he'd been too young to realize the wisdom in Wulfsgate had even then rested with the lady, and not the lord. It would be his mother who decided what to do next, and while she was cunning enough to make her husband believe the idea was his if she wanted to, there was a crushing cruelty in her, and that, too, had been a surprise.

He eyed the cart. This run included less food than the past one. They had to make room for fresh clothing, blankets, furs to withstand the cold weather. There were bows and knives for hunting and dressing. There had also been a request for vellum and ink, though this left him anxious. They wanted, they said, to send them back with letters. There was risk in this, but Christian found he couldn't deny either the writer or the receiver of these letters. To be safe, he'd run it by his father, who'd rightly reminded him that those taking refuge in the cave were not their prisoners.

It didn't ease Christian's fears, though. If they were discovered, it would bring the entire kingdom down around them. It would bring war to the Northerlands.

Christian and Aylen had taken on the responsibility for these trips. They told others that Aylen's father was ill, and there was a need for the two to cross the pass to tend to him intermittently. It wasn't necessary to cross Torrin's Pass to reach Witchwood Cross, so they claimed to be picking up furs from Steward Weatherford in Whitecap along the way. And they did both. They would stop in Whitecap and pile the furs into the now-empty wagon, and then continue on, crossing the pass at the northern end, to dip into Witchwood Cross for a visit with Aylen's father, Steward Wynter. Yet, by the time they returned home, it was already time to make the trek once more. Exhaustion had set in, and Christian forced himself to disregard it.

Lord Dereham approached, his mare's hooves crunching through layers of snow from past storms. Only in springtide would some of it melt away, revealing the crushed green of the ground. "All ready, then?"

"It would seem so," Christian answered. His eyes traveled to his uncle, Alric, who was slower to join them. He rode a pony, he said, because he'd been atop a horse when that bear, years before, had dragged him from his mount and taken him away to be feasted upon. The horse had run off. A pony, he claimed, would have no such disloyalty.

This was one thing that hadn't changed at all. Alric had always seemed to exist in another realm altogether, in body and thought. He made a strange match with the spirited Earwyn, and their only son, Balfour, had been sent to Oldcastle, to university, before he was old enough to say the word. Christian heard his mother say that this had been Earwyn's doing, so that the son didn't become the father.

"You have the weapons? It will mean less exposure for you. For them."

"We do."

"Good." Holden squinted his eyes against the sun penetrating through the hazy sky. "Don't linger in Witchwood Cross. Your mother has a feeling that news is imminent."

"Lady Gretchen has always had keen instincts," Aylen said, and Christian wondered if it was only he who noticed his father flinch.

Alric at last pulled up on his pony. He settled to a stop, lingering just behind Holden. "Don't forget, the veil is thin in the pass. If you aren't paying the air around you fair mind when you approach the pearapple tree, you might step through."

Christian and Aylen exchanged a look. Holden closed his eyes, his patience spent before he could conjure it, as it often was with his only living brother.

"I've told you not to waste your breath on nonsense about veils."

"You wouldn't be so cross with me if you'd stepped through, to Beyond. If you'd returned with me, when I asked, so I could show you."

Holden's face blossomed into red fury. He balled his fists tighter around Sorcha's reins. Many who knew Lord Dereham said he led with emotion, but Christian wondered if any of them had witnessed the tremendous restraint he employed where his brother was concerned. Alric had always been different. Christian couldn't recall a time where his uncle seemed normal. But there were few things that marked him quite so much as his claim to have been to The World Beyond the Sea, that indefinable realm or realms that existed beyond the shores of the kingdom. What made it worst of all was that Alric believed his claim, and this magnified his already legendary lunacy.

"More like to come across a snowbeast," Holden muttered.

Aylen stepped forward and rested a hand upon Alric's forearm. "We will practice utmost caution, Sir Alric."

Alric dropped his head, smiled. "You put an old man's mind at ease, Lady Aylen."

THE TREK out of Wulfsgate was no simple affair. Since news landed of Lord Quinlanden's betrayal, and the escape of Lady Asherley from Duncarrow, the town existed in a perpetual state of restless anticipation. Lord Dereham had barred all entrances and exits from Wulfsgate except the southern one, and that one was heavily manned, some travelers waiting days to come in, or out. Aylen felt an especial guilt when the guards guided them to the front of the line, ahead of some who had been waiting for many ticks of the sun. If those hiding in the caves were not counting on them for survival, she would have refused the special treatment, subjecting herself to the same treatment as all the others.

She'd known no town of the north to be so fortified. There were always guards, of course. But under normal occasion, only enough to maintain the gates, to watch over the keep. In the past month, all men, and boys old enough to wield a sword, had gone to carrying them. Farmers had been mobilized to soldiers. Even a visit to the market was tense and wrought with worry.

Wulfsgate wasn't unique. Holden had called upon the stewards of all Great Families to follow his lead or risk conquer from The Deceiver—what they'd all taken to calling Aiden Quinlanden after his cowardly seizure of the Westerlands by murdering Lord Byrne under the cover of night. It was evident, he'd said, that the king was in support of The Deceiver's actions, and thus no one was safe. They could only rely on themselves to protect what was theirs.

Aiden's men hadn't come. The last word of him was that he'd sailed to Duncarrow to present his gift of the Westerlands to the king. He'd been there since, plotting, spurring even more terrified rumors of a coming onslaught. Between Lord Quinlanden and King Eoghan, they had armies large enough to subdue the Northerlands and Southerlands without significant effort. Aylen didn't know what they were waiting for, but she was grateful for each day that the Reach had strengthened their skills in battle. Blacksmiths, armors, and bowyers worked by moonlight to supply the endless demand.

You couldn't ride more than a hundred feet without seeing men of all ages practicing their swordplay in the snowbanks. Fathers, teaching sons. Old men, handling steel for the first time in many years. Women, too. In the Northerlands, toughness wasn't reserved only for men. Aylen herself had no fear of her sword, Witchwind, and had skill to spare.

She wished she could tell them what they would soon fight for. That Darrick Rhiagain yet lived. And what was more, he had a son.

But to protect Darrick and Stefan, there was no choice but to preserve these secrets to the hearts of the few sworn to safeguard them. It seemed especially unfair to keep father from son and wife, but within Darrick and Stefan existed two distinct weapons against the usurper king. Holding them at opposite ends of the kingdom did more than preserve their lives. It preserved the future of the entire realm.

Torrin's Pass was one of the few navigable paths across the long stretch of the Northerland Range. The uneven road was treacherous for anyone unfamiliar with its steep inclines and sharp switches, and even, sometimes, for those who were. But when they'd all huddled by the fire in the keep, whispering their plan, Aylen hadn't hesitated to raise her hand when this assignment was presented. Someone had to take the risks, and she was the only healer properly authorized to perform this gift. As part of their banishment from the Sepulchre, she was given permission to heal, in service. *We came here to serve,* she told Christian. *Only the Guardians know what they've been through. What injuries may have befallen them on their way to safety.*

This was their second trip through the mountains to visit the refugees. When they'd departed for the first trip—the day after the messenger brought news of those convening in the cave—Gretchen had thrown herself at Holden's feet and begged to go see her Pieter. It was a terrible thing to witness. Holden had reminded her she had no business in Witchwood Cross, and her joining them would only draw unneeded attention. She'd relented, but Aylen saw the slow death begin behind her eyes and so, later, she'd gone to Gretchen's chambers and asked what she could bring on her behalf, for Pieter.

Gretchen, in a haphazard flurry, gathered some sweaters and his chronicle. She'd looked Aylen in the eye and said, *you'll under-*

stand, one day, when you're a mother. The destruction of your soul if one of your own is taken.

Gretchen hadn't meant the words with malice, but they'd cut Aylen anyway, who had always seen herself one day tending her own brood. But Christian was single-mindedly against having children. He'd joined the Sepulchre to be rid of the expectations of family. She'd known this before she married him, and nothing had changed since. It was the only wedge between them.

I will make sure he knows how you yearn to hold him once more, Lady Dereham.

Aylen remembered this as the cart began the slow approach down the narrow, steep side path that led to the system of caves. Christian dismounted Sun and led the horses and ponies by hand. They bucked, fighting the decline, but he whispered softly into their ears and their angst eased some.

She spotted Pieter's thatch of red hair behind some bushes. "Christian. The signal."

Christian sounded the series of whistles, and Pieter jumped out, thrashing through the snow as he bounded toward them.

He threw himself into his brother's arms, and the two men stayed this way long enough for the beasts to grow restless again.

"How are things inside?" Christian asked.

"Lady Blackwood and the princess argue constantly. Day and night. They've argued since we ported, weeks ago. I wonder if they'll ever stop," Pieter said. He glanced back toward the caves. "Stefan wants to play all day. He's run Ransom and me ragged with his demands. I tried to tell him there are no pirates in the Northerland Range, because you need *ships* for piracy. But he doesn't believe me. He says I'm lying to him."

Christian smiled at Aylen. "We perhaps have some relief for that, courtesy of Aylen. Something else to grab his attention."

"And don't forget, Stefan has never had friends before. He must be so happy to have some now, even if they are older and have outgrown their imagination," Aylen said.

Pieter nodded at Aylen. "And, eh, Anabella, she's afraid."

"Afraid?" Aylen pressed.

"For her son. For Stefan," Pieter said. "She has these nightmares. She sees the king take him away from her." He lowered his voice. "She sees the king take her son's life."

Christian shook his head. "The king will not find them here. Our men are manning all ports. We will know if anyone who shouldn't be here attempts to land."

"They could come through the Hinterlands."

Aylen smiled. "They'd not fare well there, I'm afraid. Men who veer from the path in those lands rarely find it again. Even if they took the Compass Road, Salthill is a veritable barricade these days. The Northerlands are well and truly cut off from the kingdom, Pieter."

Pieter didn't look convinced. "We aren't as well guarded up here. We have only one man. Ransom would say two, but he can hardly pick up Scholar Edevane's sword without wincing."

Christian tousled his red hair. "You forgot to mention Pieter Dereham, the most fearsome wulf cub of the Northern Reach."

This elicited the grin Christian had been after. "Did you at least bring me a bow?"

"Perhaps."

Pieter brightened. "No more rabbit traps, then. We'll eat true meat again." His smile faded. "It isn't easy being so close to home but forbidden from returning."

"I know," Christian said. "I wish it were different. Mother misses you so." He clapped a hand over Pieter's shoulder. "But you know why this isn't possible right now. There's no way we could keep your presence secret, and secrets grow longer legs the more who possess them."

"And why can't Mother or Father come here?"

"You say you are not well guarded. But that isn't true, Pieter. The absence of others is what protects you. They stay away to keep you safe."

"I have a letter for you, from your mother," Aylen said, slipping the vellum from inside her coat. "If you'd like to write one in return, I'll be happy to take it to her."

Pieter turned his head to hide the budding tears. He nodded. "Right. Sure."

Christian turned to Aylen. "Shall we? Our friends have been waiting long enough."

WYAT EDEVANE JOINED Christian in unloading the cart. Asherley and Assyria oversaw the exercise, peppering the men with their questions and demands as they eyed each addition to their cache. Aylen used the opportunity to pull Anabella aside.

Aylen remembered Anabella from childhood. Anabella was a few years older than she was, but they had been occasional playmates as young girls, when Steward Weatherford would come to Witchwood Cross to trade his furs. But the woman standing before her was not that girl, and Aylen wondered how many transformations she'd endured before coming to this point.

Anabella had been malnourished when Aylen came to her weeks earlier. She'd healed her to the best of her ability, but there were some things beyond her power.

Aylen rested a hand on the woman's arm. "How have you been since we last saw one another?" Anabella had put on some needed weight, and there was again color in her pale cheeks, but the light in her eyes remained dim.

Anabella directed her gaze out of the cave, toward where Stefan played in a small grove of trees. They were at the timber line here; any higher, and the caves would not have been the seclusion they needed. "I'm so grateful to be free, Aylen. I'd never want anyone to think otherwise."

"Of course not."

"But there's somehow more pain in knowing Darrick lives, and is out there, somewhere, than believing he was dead all these years." She hung her head. "I shouldn't say such things. I know this."

Aylen moved closer, wrapping her arm through Anabella's. "As women, we're expected to keep our counsel far too often. You say what you feel with me. It stays between us."

Anabella's smile was weary, but grateful. "I want him to know his son, as I have. He isn't even aware Stefan exists."

"He knows now. Our messenger to the Southerlands returned right as we departed to come to you. We have nothing in writing, as Lord Warwick felt there was too much danger in this falling into the wrong hands, but they delivered the message."

Anabella closed her eyes. Exhaled. "He will understand why I can't come to him, then. Of course he will."

"I read the scrolls. The ones you wrote at Duncarrow," Aylen said. Anabella looked up. "I hope you don't think that's an intrusion of your thoughts. When Asherley passed them to us, Gretchen felt we should all commit them to memory, because we can't know the lengths Eoghan will go to in order to protect this truth from the kingdom. They entrusted me with seeing them locked somewhere safe. For when the time comes for the kingdom to know the truth."

Anabella watched her in silence.

"I never met Prince Darrick, but I know him through your eyes now. A little, anyway. And I know he wanted more than anything for you to be safe, especially once he knew his own safety was in peril. Now that he knows your son, his son, is out there, he would want this doubly so." Aylen unlinked their arms and took her hand. "He survived these years on the memory of you. You gave him something to live for. Everything to live for. You mustn't forget that, when your strength threatens to falter."

Tears rolled down Anabella's cheeks. "Can I ask you something, Aylen?"

"Anything."

"Do you trust these women?"

"Lady Asherley and Princess Assyria?"

Anabella nodded.

Aylen breathed out. "If I'm truly honest with you, I don't know them well enough to answer. Lady Asherley has a reputation for being ruthless, but fair. She wants to see this kingdom restored to better days as much as anyone. I know nothing at all about Assyria. No one does beyond Duncarrow. But they have both surrendered their freedom and their lives to protect you."

"I know."

"What troubles you?"

Anabella cast an eye over her shoulder. "I know I should not expect their kindness. But they treat me as if I'm a child, like Stefan, and not an equal. They tell me nothing. When I ask, they dismiss me."

"Lady Gretchen tells me Lady Asherley is one of the few in this kingdom she would trust with her life." Aylen waved at Stefan when he jumped up to show the Snowbeast he'd built. "Perhaps it would be helpful to remember that when faced with the decision to be caught or to leave Pieter and Ransom behind, she couldn't leave without them. Even if it meant that the entire plot to extricate you and Stefan from Duncarrow could fail."

"I suppose you're right," Anabella replied. She smiled at Stefan and wiped at her tears. "I swear to you, I was never this emotional during my years in captivity. You probably have trouble believing that."

"Not at all," Aylen said. "I think you are very, very strong. A weaker woman would not have survived and endured what you did. And look at him. Your son. His color has returned. He's added weight to his bones. To see him now, you wouldn't know he'd ever gone without."

Anabella sniffled into her dress. "You're right. I need to remember this, when I am lost to my emotion."

Aylen planted a kiss on her cheek. "No, Anabella. You need to do nothing at all except breathe in the crisp mountain air of your homeland and exult in watching your son finally explore the world of his imagination."

"Nothing? Nothing at all?" Asherley asked. She'd made no threatening gestures; had not said the words with malice. And yet, Christian still had the instinctive urge to take several steps backward.

"Not yet," Christian replied. "We had hoped for more direction when our messenger returned, but Khallum felt it wasn't safe. My mother expects he'll send his own instead. She thinks it could be any day now."

"Your mother? Does your father still have his balls in his possession?" Assyria demanded, hands splayed against her hips.

The princess was a stunning woman in her middle age, her red hair flaming against the clear icicles dangling from the top edges of the cave. He'd heard about the Rhiagains and their golden red manes, but he'd never seen it with his own eyes. This wasn't Pieter's red, or Lisbet's. This was a color from another world. It made him uncomfortable, for reasons he couldn't identify.

"Holden has his balls when Gretchen grants them to him," Asherley replied, without looking at Assyria. Christian sensed there was something between them. Some burgeoning rift. "And what of the Westerlands? Any news of Byrne?"

Christian forced himself not to look away. "Not yet, my lady."

"And my children?"

Christian had brought with him to Wulfsgate the news of young Hollyn's demise at the Sepulchre. But, as with Byrne's tragic end, and Lord Quinlanden's assumption of Westerland command, Gretchen felt it was best to keep this from Asherley for now. They couldn't risk her flying into a grief-stricken rage and storming back to Quinlanden-occupied Longwood Rush. "I'll let you know when we do."

"At least Emberley had the good sense to come to Wulfsgate," she muttered. "You should bring her on your next visit."

"I don't think that would be wise."

"Your mother does the thinking for the Derehams. Ask her."

Christian winced. "Do you have any other requests? For supplies, that is? We expect a return in another fortnight, if the weather holds."

"No," Assyria answered for them both. "We have all the dried fruits and meats we can stomach. What we require is direction. A plan. We cannot hide here forever, Lord Dereham. You cannot be so naïve as to believe your border lockdowns will last. And why should they? By their very nature they have drawn the king's eye. He is not very wise, but if he has Aiden Quinlanden, that cunning dog's cock, he will have made this connection. Why would one tighten their borders without reason? Without cause?" She leaned in closer. Her clear, soft skin smelled like ashes from a spent flame. "We didn't rescue my brother and his son for them to hide in exile. The kingdom must know they exist. That they are alive."

"And why..." The words left Christian's mouth before he could think better of them.

"Why *what*, Lord Dereham?"

"Why are you here? Why does this matter to you? You're a Rhiagain. A Rhiagain still sits upon the throne."

"The wrong Rhiagain," Assyria replied.

"And yet you could have left this all to Lady Blackwood. To Edevane, and the others who aided you."

"Be mindful of your neck. She slit their throats. These others you speak of," Asherley said, with a swift, subtle glare at the princess.

"My reasons are my own," Assyria countered. She was so close now her breath burned his lips. "And my plans will be my own if the lords of this kingdom cannot produce them first."

2

THE RAMBLINGS OF A SWINDLER

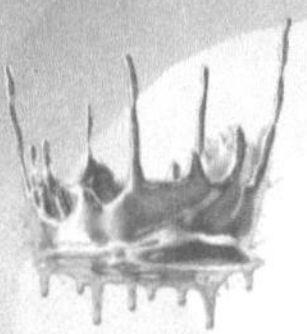

Jesse hadn't expected to lay eyes upon the decaying main road leading to the heart of Greystone Abbey again. Upon their last visit, he'd decided the earth would soon reclaim the wood and stone, resisting even the will of the steadfast James men; that the small village, hanging on by pure stubborn resilience, was already in the throes of its final exhale.

Lady Blackwood was the only thing keeping the James men and their stretch of land from being relegated to a completed chapter in *The Book of All Things*. She had a soft spot for Easlan James—some might say, a blind spot. She rewarded his loyalty with unchallenged placement among the Great Families. Those who didn't understand this seemingly unwise choice from a woman otherwise known for her great cunning hadn't known Easlan James. Many said that he'd been blessed with great fortune to have the favor of Lady Blackwood. Jesse understood, as Asherley herself must also, that it was the other way around.

The loyalty of all the Westerlands was being tested. Quinlanden men swarmed the larger towns and villages, ready to shut down anyone rising in defense of the Blackwoods. This Jesse and the others had discovered upon their attempt to return young Brook to his home in Windwatch Grove, just across the River Rush from Longwood Rush.

But their path had never strayed far from the Whitewood. It was in Parth, at the same Tavern at the Middle of the World where they'd sought refuge weeks before, that the news of the realm reached them.

Lord Byrne Warwick, murdered by Quinlanden.

Lady Asherley Blackwood, escaped from her captivity on Duncarrow, whereabouts unknown.

Lord Quinlanden, in Duncarrow, plotting with the king.

Every Blackwood child, missing.

The Westerlands under siege by Quinlanden.

Esmerelda had paled at the news. If this had happened in the Westerlands, it could happen elsewhere.

The Westerlands are not safe for us, Ravenna had said, but in her eyes Esmerelda showed she was thinking the same as Jesse. *There is one place.* She knew it, even though she'd fought him until she was breathless over leaving the Hinterlands. Ryan wouldn't know where to find her. He'd have no warning of the inexplicable danger awaiting him when he encountered the Medvedev. *What then, Jesse? We send him from one prison to another?*

Jesse didn't have the answers she sought, but Ryan wouldn't want his wife and child in peril, and so he did the only thing he could.

They'd taken the unpredictable passage through the forests, careful to avoid even the outskirts of towns where the Quinlanden men might be scouting. And when they at last arrived back in Greystone Abbey, Easlan James greeted them without surprise.

You're only the first, Jesse. More are coming.

What do you mean? Coming here? Why?

I've received raven after raven from the stewards of the Westerlands, until ravens were no longer safe. You know the silent war between East-

erlands and Westerlands has brewed, unchecked, for many years, and now this over-reach from Quinlanden is beyond bearing. They will not stand for it and will defend their Reach, and their lady, to the death, if it comes to it. Quinlanden has men, but there's more to winning a war than swords.

And they're coming here? To Greystone Abbey?

Look around you. Remember why you came here. Did you see any of The Deceiver's men on your ride in? No, and you won't. They won't come here. To them, we are forgotten, a relic of yesterday. A true Westerlander would not disregard us so. The stewards cannot leave their lands without drawing eyes upon us, but they're sending their trusted advisors and emissaries.

Jesse, thinking of Esmerelda, of Ravenna, of how he could protect both their secrets when the swarms of men arrived, had considered where else to take them when Easlan laid a hand upon his arm.

Take them to Dungarde Keep. It isn't what it once was, but it's secluded and safe. We don't live there anymore. We've made the tavern our bed and hearth for years now, ever since the wife's promise was spent, and Kaslan and I only return to feed and tack the horses. You'll be protected there. I'll house the others in the inn, and at the other properties abandoned when our people left for Newcarrow. None but Kaslan and I will ever know you have a refugee princess on one arm and a sorceress on the other.

Thank you, Easlan. I am indebted to you beyond what I could repay.

I don't keep score on favors, Jesse. You'll remember this, and do for another, when the time is right.

What do we do about the boy? Can we get word to the Ashenhurts? That their son is safe?

He will not be safe until we drive The Deceiver and his men from our lands. Until then, I've a need for an assistant to help keep up with the sweeping and stocking, and a palette in the back for when his day's work is done.

. . .

A HOWLING wind ripped across the insufficient plain that Dungarde Keep sat upon. The trees on all sides of the exposed land compressed the foul air, whipping it into a tempest that sent anything not tethered flying. The horses sang their discontent from the stables. Everyone talked about the storms that passed through the Northerlands in midwinter, but Jesse recalled Easlan James telling Jesse's father, Hamish, that one didn't need snow to sunder the land and tear roofs from foundations.

He pulled his cloak tight as he dismounted, stabling his own horse with the others, who were still kicking up their protests. "Shh," he said gently. "Easy now, lasses. These stables are stone. Your home isnae going anywhere today."

The storm had darkened the skies. He started toward the keep, but then paused and turned back toward the far edge of the forest.

Jesse found Esmerelda at the waterfall. It spilled into a pool of freshwater that she'd been using both to replenish their water-skins and wash their clothing. No one had suggested she be the one to do these things. She'd decided this on her own, daily retreating to the water's edge. She told him she couldn't abide stillness in herself, but there was more she wouldn't say, and to press her would open doors better left closed.

He'd just returned from an exhausting afternoon at The Long-Trodden Mule. More men from across the Westerlands had arrived, the trusted commanders and aides of the stewards. His job was to show them around, introduce them to the resource cache and where they'd stay while in Greystone. There'd be another meeting that night to discuss the findings of their network of spies.

Jesse hadn't planned to be pulled into the resistance against the king. As a Southerlander, he was bred to loathe the crown, but his life and work were affected little by who sat upon the throne in

Duncarrow. As long as he could provide and be useful, he had no qualms worth following through on.

But he had no other repayment for Steward James' kindness. For allowing the women to remain hidden in the small keep in the clearing of pines, safe.

Jesse knelt next to Esmerelda. Her obsidian hair was pulled back off her face, tied poorly with a ribbon. Rogue hairs annoyed her, and she spent her free hand batting them away, peeling them back off the sweat matting her forehead.

"Can I help?"

"You have more important matters, I'm sure," she said, breathless, as she dunked one of his shirts once, twice, and again, wringing between each cycle.

"I'm done in town, for now. I came to check on you."

"That was unnecessary."

He reached his hand over and steadied hers. Her mouth trembled—in anger, in sadness; he could never distinguish between the two with her these days—as she eyed the audacity of his touch.

"There's a gathering tonight. Some emissaries have returned. There may even be some coming from the Southerlands."

"Spies, you mean." She returned to her animated dunking, wringing.

"I've no care what they call them. There could be news from home."

"I have no home."

"We may have news of Ryan. Of..." He hesitated. Esmerelda didn't know Ryan had gone to prison, not on a false charge, but a rescue mission. So many times he'd almost told her, but each time, something within him bid him to pause. It wasn't his secret to tell.

"If he has escaped, then he'll be on a fool's errand now."

It was painful to watch the way she assaulted the linens. He reached down to help. "Ryan will find you, whether you're in the

Hinterlands, or upon a ship in the White Sea. He would find you anywhere."

"He's a freebooter, not a Magi," she hissed, taking the linen back.

"Esmerelda, it wasnae safe there. You heard what Brook said, about his friends."

"Brook doesn't have Medvedev blood! *You* do." She touched her belly. "And I do, within me."

Jesse dropped his head. "You were there. You witnessed how they responded to my claim. They didnae believe me, or care. Something is wrong there. Something that isnae ours to fix. Ravenna was right when she said we can help the others better if we aren't in danger ourselves. We cannae help them at all, or ourselves, if we're taken captive as well."

"Ravenna." Esmerelda sneered at the word.

Jesse didn't understand Esmerelda's enmity toward the sorceress. He'd been just as adamant about leaving the Hinterlands behind. "The Medvedev took her own love away. She suffers too. She'd never have left if she didnae think she was better served to aid him from elsewhere."

Esmerelda looked up. "Suffers? She seems quite adjusted to life at your side. Her Dereham lad is a distant memory."

Jesse opened his mouth to respond to this claim, but then closed it again. He didn't know where this was coming from, but it was better to leave it rest. "My only charge is to protect you and your child, Esme. There is nothing else. Do you understand? Do you believe that?"

Esmerelda pressed her lips tight in her anger. She nodded.

"Aye, ye should. For I'd rather be enjoying an honest ale at my own hearth in Sandycove than choking down the piss water that passes for it here. Do ye know how much effort I spend feigning my love for it, so as not to harm poor Easlan's tender heart?"

Esmerelda tried hard not to smile, but one tickled the corner of her mouth.

Jesse tucked a stray hair back from her face. "Your child changes everything. I'd have faced down the entire Medvedev guard if not for your bairn. You're both safe here. We'll stay until I know there's a better, safer place for you both. It's what Ryan would want, and when we know he's safely returned from the Wastelands, we'll find a way to send him word."

Tears beaded in her eyes. She returned to her laborious scrubbing.

"You'll see him again," Jesse said. He pushed himself up off the damp grass. "I promise."

RAVENNA RAN her hands over the bow mounted above the hearth. The wood, smoothed once by the hands who crafted it, and many times by the ones wielding it, felt like raw power. She'd never had occasion or need to hold one, to pull back upon the string and feel the command in the resistance before releasing it, delivering, if her aim was true, a clean death.

They didn't eat meat at The Rookery. The sorcerers of Midnight Crest consumed the greens, fruits, legumes, and grains from the covered gardens behind the kitchens. It had been an adjustment for her when she'd dined with the Derehams in Wulfsgate, tables filled with crisp boar and glistening venison. She'd once snuck a taste of the venison and it turned her belly. But weeks on the road with Drystan and the girls had left her with no choice but to consume what was available, or dwindle away. Now, she rather enjoyed the earthy richness of a freshly taken elk-kind. Even rabbit, though too lean to be filling, made her mouth water now.

Another sign she was moving further away from herself.

"You fancy a hunt?" Jesse asked.

Ravenna's face flushed in tandem with the surge in her chest.

She withdrew her hand. "I don't think I could take a life." She remembered the acrid scene of the burning flesh of the brigands. Their animalistic screams that started hopeful and ended otherwise. "I was only curious."

"You could if you were hungry enough." Jesse pulled the bow from the hooks. He gripped the center of the arch in the carved wood and drew back the string with ease. His head fell to the side as he pretended to find something to aim at. He released it and handed it to her. "I could teach you."

"No need," Ravenna said. "I spent some time in the woods, gathering some foods that were familiar to me. I never should have let myself become accustomed to meat."

"You don't eat meat at..."

"The Rookery," she finished. "I'd never tasted it before my training with the men of Wulfsgate."

Jesse nodded slowly. She pulled the questions from his mind.

"You want to know how I came to love a man, and not one of my own."

Jesse laughed. "I cannae say a word about love, sorceress. I've never known it myself."

"What you do for your brother is love."

"Aye. But it isnae the same."

"What happened with Drystan wasn't intentional," Ravenna said. "By the time I realized it, it had gone too far."

"And Lord Dereham wouldnae allow you to wed his son?"

"It wasn't Lord Dereham. I didn't want to end up plastered frozen upon the side of Icebolt Mountain for treason against my blood."

Jesse's eyes widened. "They have you train with men, but would kill you for bonding with one?"

"Yes. Exactly that." Ravenna glanced toward the window. She could see Esmerelda in the distance, taking her fears out on the poor linens. She would have liked for them to be friends. Ravenna had even tried at the task, attempting to engage her on the return voyage from the Hinterlands by asking about Ryan and her life in the Southerlands. But Esmerelda blamed Ravenna for turning them back south. Ravenna *had* been the one to push them to depart the Hinterlands, but she suspected that the Medvedev's inexplicable fear of her would not last once the shock dissipated. They would return, with others, and there'd be enough of them to overcome whatever they feared in her. When that happened, they'd be captive in a place unknown, bound with magic unknown. At least free they could plan to help Drystan and the others.

Our cause is not yours! Esmerelda had hissed at her, growing weary of Ravenna's attempts at kinship. *I came to take refuge with my husband's people, and now we are forced to abandon this for your whims!*

I wouldn't ask you to abandon your cause. Only to realize how futile it becomes if you are a prisoner of the same peoples you believed would shelter you.

They might have done so. Because of you, we will never know.

Neither of us has to leave behind our causes, Esmerelda. We only have to be wiser in pursuing them.

There is no 'we,' Ravenna. Only you, and whatever you've done to Jesse to make him follow you.

There was no use in insisting Ravenna had done nothing at all to Jesse. Whatever confused feelings Jesse harbored, they were his own. She'd seen glimpses into his dreams of her... his flushed, feverish face when he'd wake, struggling to make sense of them. But she hadn't sent the dreams.

"Ravenna." Jesse shifted, holding his hands crossed over his torso. "I've made a decision. I should have told you sooner, but I've been running between here and the Mule, and—"

"You're staying. Until the child is born."

He cocked his head. "How did you know?"

Ravenna tapped her temple. "I don't intentionally read your mind, but sometimes I can't help myself."

Jesse blushed. Likely recalling a few things he'd prefer she didn't take from his thoughts. "Right. Aye, Esme and I are staying. She's safe here, and there may be nowhere else in the kingdom I can protect her right now." He swallowed, nervous. "She's carrying my brother's son or daughter."

"You don't need to work so hard to persuade me of your motivations. I understand them well enough," Ravenna said. She stepped around him and leaned in to whisper, "Would you like me to stay with you? Is that where this is going?"

Jesse took a step back. "You should do what your conscience compels you. As I am."

"I wasn't asking about your conscience."

"I would help you rescue Drystan and the others. But it may be months before I'm free of this duty. I cannae ask you to wait months."

Ravenna thought of her own dilemma. Drystan's imprisonment was only part of it. It was too early to be certain, but if there *was* life growing within her, she had few options in protecting the child from the grasping hands of others. The Derehams would never let her keep from them their future heir, no matter how unwilling Drystan was to embrace his birthright. And she equally couldn't spend her life in Wulfsgate married to a Dereham, so close to her ancestral home, flaunting her treason, gazing perpetually over her shoulder for the rest of her life. Her sins would catch up to her.

No, there was no future in the north with a child of Drystan Dereham. Or anywhere, if the Derehams believed he was the father.

"Ask me. I can always refuse," Ravenna whispered. She shouldn't enjoy the pronounced ebb of his throat as he watched her mouth move; as he remembered how she looked, lying beneath him in the world of his dreams. She didn't love him as she did Drystan, but she needed him, and though she was still beginning to understand the strange plan formulating in the back of her mind, she needed him to need her.

Jesse inhaled a deep breath. The heat rising off him was palpable. "I willnae ask that," he said, quickly recovering the hitch in his voice. "But you are welcome to stay, for as long as you need. Your secret is safe, as are you."

Ravenna eased off. "I'll stay, for now. Until I have my own plan," she said. Leaning on the tips of her toes, she pressed her lips to his cheek. She lingered like this long enough for him to shift in place. "Thank you for your aid, Jesse. You have no reason to help me. I won't forget that you did."

A crash startled them both. Esmerelda dropped the basket of wet clothing at the door and bolted up the stairs. Ravenna tried to speak, but Jesse had already gone after her.

Jesse perched at the corner of the bar, watching through the smoke as the Long-Trodden Mule slowly filled with unfamiliar faces. The men were representatives of the Great Families of the Westerlands, sent in the stead of their stewards. Jesse and his father, though from a Great Family themselves, seldom broke bread with men like this. He was more at home in the company of the merchant class. Theirs was a language he understood. Judicious with words, loud in intention. They needed no history between them to fall into familiar routines, of drinks and fun. No one cared who you were, what name you bore, what standard you had stitched into your armor.

These men filtered in quietly, bursting for *something*. Some knew one another, or had done business in the past, but they had never gathered to huddle over the future of their Reach. There was a low, nervous energy that passed through them, bouncing from table to table, a series of thoughts unspoken.

He waved at little Brook, who swept the floor with a sense of purpose, tongue wedged between the corner of his lips. Brook brushed his hair back and returned the greeting.

Kaslan leaned forward next to Jesse, arms spread over the bar. "Never expected you'd be part of plotting a war in the Westerlands, did you?"

Jesse almost laughed. "No. And I willnae *be* in a war, should it come to that. I'll help here, how I can."

"So you say. Wait till the promise of bloodlust spills through your veins."

"We talking about me or you now?"

Kaslan chuckled. He pointed at a table of solemn men sitting together, each occupied with different distractions to avoid engaging each other. "They'll say they have no fight in 'em. For some, might even be true. But men are men, Jesse. We're born to the sword, and most prefer to die to it."

"There's been no war in our lifetime, or our fathers'."

"Aye." Kaslan's eyes twinkled. "So we agree. We're due."

Jesse grunted. "Spend a year fighting the White Sea with a Strong man. That'll satisfy your craving for war. My grandfather and his father before him paid their sacrifices to the sea, and I expect that'll be my end someday, too. There's a reason our skills are in such high demand."

Kaslan stretched his jaw in a grimace. "I'll pass on that one, friend."

"The emissaries. Did they all return?"

Kaslan turned to him. "Didn't you hear?" Jesse shook his head. "They already heard their reports. There was nothing new."

"How can that be?"

"The Deceiver's men are everywhere. Makes you wonder who's guarding the Easterlands."

"Nothing from the Southerlands?"

"'fraid not. Lord Warwick declined to provide any aid or wisdom to the cause."

"Why are we here then?"

Kaslan grinned. "We have a special visitor. Lady Blackwood's seer arrived this evening. He has a vision to share with us all."

Jesse ground his jaw. "We're here to entertain the ramblings of a swindler?"

"Wouldn't have pegged you for a non-believer. Not after what you told us about your mother."

"Isnae about believing," Jesse muttered. "You should fear for the Westerlands if it's come to this, Kaslan. It isnae a *mage* who will save your Reach."

"This is about the mage in your bed, I think," Kaslan teased. "She cross you? Leave you wanting?"

"There's no one in my bed but me," Jesse countered.

Kaslan jumped out from behind the bar. "Yet." He winked and skirted off before Jesse could correct him. But what would he have said? He didn't want or need the distraction of the bewitching sorceress from the north. She invaded his dreams without consent. She'd driven a wedge between him and Esmerelda, doing nothing other than existing in the same space. He didn't want her in his bed. Nor could he wipe the fantasy of it from his mind.

He'd been away from home, and a life he recognized, for too long. That was the only explanation he could conjure for how she had affected him. His will and desires had never been so disconnected.

Jesse had hoped she would rise to his offer to leave, but her response earlier implied she had, inexplicably, something else in mind. Something he desperately hoped she hadn't seen in his own troubled thoughts. He would stem it before it could sprout leaves and twine itself even further into the safety of the small estate in the woods. He had no other choice. Though he'd espoused confidence in Ryan's mission outwardly, he was all too aware of the risks his brother took to restore the crown. There was always a fair chance he'd never return to see his deeds in action. Now there was a child, and if the father did not or could not return, the bairn was all they'd have left of him. It took little for a pregnancy to turn poorly. He knew it all too well, from watching his mother decline after losing several bairns.

Jesse had no control over the Guardians and their intentions, but he could protect the body and soul of Esmerelda Warwick, and that meant keeping her—and himself—from dwelling on matters that had no place.

The energy in the room shifted. The din of awkward conversation turned to the excitement of anticipation. Easlan James emerged from the room behind the bar with another man, and though Jesse had never seen him before, he knew he was looking upon Joran Rosewood. The Enchanter's silver hair was thinning in his twilight years, but fell in patchy waves over his matching robes. He was an eyesore, practically glowing against the dingy browns and grays of the Mule. Easlan held him by the arm, and soon, Jesse saw why. Joran leaned heavily on a walking stick.

"Anyone who has had the pleasure of visiting Longwood Rush will recognize our friend, Joran Rosewood. Joran was born a man of the Easterlands, but he has lived, and will die, a true Westerlander."

The room hummed with reverent respect for the elder man. Jesse wondered what he'd done to earn it. Lord Warwick kept a healer in his keep, but had never paid mind to soothsaying. *An imprecise fool's weapon,* he'd said. Jesse had never known a seer, or been privy to their predictions, but it seemed to him that in a world of finite outcomes, one could say almost anything and have a fair chance at the truth.

"My greatest and truest appreciation to you, Steward James. As Lady Asherley has always valued your loyalty, now I, too, find myself on the proper end of it," Joran replied. Easlan released his arm and stepped away. Joran faced the gathered men. "There are things you must know, you, who are also among the most loyal of Lady Asherley. The sacrifice she made, for all of us. And though she may hang me later, as she was wont to threaten when I did not tell her what she wished to hear..." The men laughed in understanding. "I will tell you nonetheless. I believe it is what she would wish me to do, in her extended absence, which I assure you, is for the realm and none other."

A small figure bumped against Jesse's side. He whipped his neck around. He recognized the worn cloak from Easlan James' closet. He leaned down and peered inside it to see two very familiar green eyes.

"What are you doing here? It isnae safe," he whispered.

"You said there could be news from home. News of Ryan," Esmerelda replied. She kept her head bowed. He didn't suppose she could see a thing from beneath the massive hood meant for a man twice her size.

"I was wrong," Jesse replied. "Seems your father isnae interested in revolution unless it suits himself."

"This surprises you?"

"He wants the aid of others, he'll need to be ready to provide some when they ask."

Esmerelda made a *pfft* sound. "Did ye not hear? Isnae another man alive been wronged by the crown such as the great Lord Khallum Warwick has."

Jesse chuckled under his breath. "Ye do sound like him. Best lower your voice, though. Even in the back of the room." He pointed. "That's Lady Blackwood's seer."

"She has a seer?"

"Aye. He's made a rather theatrical entrance. Says he has news to share from Lady Blackwood herself."

"So he's seen her? He knows where she is?"

Jesse tapped his head. "*Seen* her."

Esmerelda clapped a hand over her mouth, laughing.

He nodded ahead, where Joran had stepped upon a stool to be seen. As if anyone could miss him in his silver glory.

"When Lady Blackwood departed for Termonglen, to the event that has thrown our kingdom into chaos, she did so knowing she would not be returning to the Westerlands or Longwood Rush for a long time. Perhaps ever."

Shock rippled through the men. "Lady Asherley would never abandon us!" one called out.

"She has far from abandoned you," Joran continued, smiling, as if he'd anticipated and been further empowered by the question. "A fortnight before The Right of Choosing, I came to Lady Blackwood. I came to her with a vision. A terrible vision, of the highborn children of the realm in chains, dragged back to Duncarrow."

Men whispered the names Ransom, Pieter.

"They believe him already," Esmerelda said.

"I bade her send her children away before they could meet this fate. And send them, she did. She scattered her four babes to the corners of the realm where they could not be poisoned by The Pretender's cruel grasp."

This revelation was met with some skepticism. The men struggled to believe she would send her children away, unprotected, with no way to get news of their fates. But Joran was undeterred. "If faced with seeing your children taken or delivering a new fate, a better one, you would do as she did. She was right to do it. All but her eldest yet live. Many of you know how ill Lady Hollyn was before she left her home, and it should come as no shock that the Guardians finally deemed her promise spent. We beseech the Guardian of the Unpromised Future to protect her in death, as her mother did in life."

The men repeated the words, solemn. Esmerelda bowed her head lower. Jesse rested a hand on her lower back.

"The children departed with other children, little ones you all know, from your own towns. Children of Great Families. They are all safe. I have seen them, as only a seer can," Joran said. "I cannot reveal their whereabouts, as they will not remain secure the more know where to find them."

"He's lying," Esmerelda said, leaning close to mask her voice. "Gabi isn't safe at all. Who knows where Emberley and Brandyn are, or the others with them. Does he even know about little Brook Ashenhurst sweeping the floor in the back?"

Jesse grimaced.

"But... I tell you now, her son is coming to Greystone Abbey. Where he, her heir, will join with us, and will help reclaim the Westerlands from The Deceiver's men. Brandyn is on his way to us now. He has left his comfortable life in the Sepulchre to serve his family and this Reach."

Easlan James smiled, regarding the surrounding men with pride. He enjoyed their renewed energy as they cheered the news; news that would not have reached them had he not found the means to deliver. Jesse was happy for him, after years of being relegated to the steward of the forgotten. His moment had arrived where he had something of value to offer his peers, other than his stalwart loyalty.

"And when Brandyn doesn't show?" Esmerelda murmured. "How will the seer explain that?"

"Once Lady Asherley could rest soundly in knowing her children were not in danger of The Pretender's cruelty, she made peace with her own mission. She knew The Pretender would take her, in place of her children, and she was not afraid." Joran's hands shook as he looked around, training his eyes across the sea of men. "She was not afraid, for she knew the key to saving this realm could be found only in Duncarrow."

"She go to kill the king, then? Seems she forgot to do it before escaping," a man asked, and others around him laughed.

Joran didn't even crack a smile. "There are secrets that can bring upon one a fate worse than death. Your lady of the Westerlands knows this. She left her hearth and home to discover this secret, to weaponize it against this kingless crown. She lost her husband, our beloved Lord Warwick, for standing tall against his many repressions. Can any of you say the same?"

"He's a persuasive man," Esmerelda whispered. "Do you suppose any of what he says *is* true?"

"Only he knows," Jesse replied. His heart raced. Was the truth of Darrick's fate the secret Asherley Blackwood discovered? If Eoghan knew his brother lived, then neither Ryan nor Darrick were safe.

Joran rattled a long sigh. "I am old, and I am tired, and I have said what I came to say. All except this, which is most important of all."

Joran's face was deathly serious as he regarded the gathered men; the last stand of the Westerlands. "If Asherley Blackwood fled Duncarrow, we can be certain it is because she obtained what she went there for. Your leader has not abandoned you—she has put in motion a plan that will *save* you."

THE MOON WAS the only light on their trip back to Dungarde Keep. They rode in silence until they left the better part of the main road, switching to the path that took them up into the foothills and the keep.

"I'm sorry about your cousin. That's no way to learn of her passing on," Jesse said.

Esmerelda dropped the hood back. "I didn't know she was so sick. Aunt Yesenia wrote not so long ago, after she'd gone to Longwood to visit with Uncle Byrne. In her letter she said Hollyn was improving."

"It could've been a lie. Joran's words."

She shook her head. "No. These men are loyal to the Black-woods. He may mix his tales in with the truth, but he wouldn't lie about that. Not to them." She rolled her head back and inhaled the night air. "I don't trust the seer, but I can't help my hope that he isn't lying about Brandyn. How I'd love to see him again, especially now. He must be so afraid, after what happened to his mother and father."

Jesse winced at the thought of yet another pulled into the secret of Esmerelda's survival. But he would not deny her the comfort of family, should the boy actually show up.

As they passed into the thicket of trees that would lead to the last stretch to the keep, he found the words he'd been meaning to speak to her for hours. "I want your only worry to be caring for the bairn in your womb. So I'll tell you this once and hope the words are enough to ease you. Ravenna has no sway over me. She seeks her own refuge, for her own reasons. I cannae deny her that, but it has been only you, and me, for months, and when at last we see Ryan again, it will be you, and him, and the bairn, and none of this will have mattered."

Esmerelda turned to him. Her emerald eyes glowed in the moonlight. "Pay me no mind. The bairn has driven me to madness, that's all."

When Jesse didn't respond immediately, Esmerelda scoffed. "Not going to correct me? Ply me with reassurances?"

Jesse smiled in the darkness. "I said I would protect ye, Princess, not lie to ye."

3

DRUMMOND'S COCK

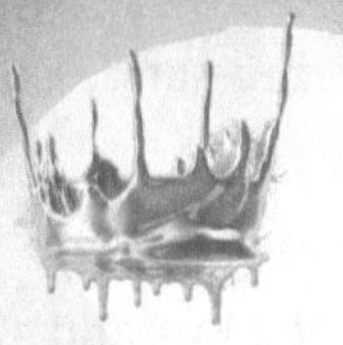

Darrick stretched his legs into a sprint for the last hundred yards. Law paced him and together they ran toward the beckoning white cliffs and that monstrous statue that before he'd only seen from the sea. Carved from an immeasurable amount of stone, Drummond Rutland, Erran's ancestor, towered over two hundred feet into the sky. It was the largest shrine in the kingdom. Even the vainglorious Lord Quinlanden and his kin did not have a monument so massive.

Darrick paused at Drummond's feet—the soles of which were even taller than Darrick—and doubled over to catch his breath. Law was right behind him, decidedly less winded.

"Better," Law said. "Quicker. And soon, further."

He'd put on weight. It felt strange to no longer feel the hard cut of his ribcage when he braced himself. His belly no longer concave. But other effects lingered. Many of the muscles below his abdomen had atrophied. Willing them back to life had been a feat, one led by the exacting ministrations of Samuel Law twice daily.

Law handed him the waterskin, and Darrick downed a generous gulp. As he opened his eyes again, he witnessed the morning sun breach over the horizon. He once feared this sight. It left an eroding sensation deep in his belly, of dread and resigned despair. The familiar clench seized his bowels, but nothing followed. He was remembering how he'd viewed many things, before they'd all been taken.

There were worse places to convalesce. It was said Whitecliffe was the most beautiful town in all the Southerlands, and, standing at the top of the miles and miles of jagged alabaster cliffs, the sea lapping upon the glimmering sand, Darrick was willing to wager this truth.

"They call him Drummond's Cock," Law said, leaning his head back to regard the scale of the Rutland ancestor.

"I can't tell if that's a compliment or a slight," Darrick said. "He is massive."

Law smiled. "When a man sees fit to raise something to heights larger than need necessitates, it is said he may be doing so in compensation for an absence elsewhere."

Darrick's mouth parted in a curl of amusement. "Right. And Steward Erran. What does he call it?"

"I rather think he's embarrassed by it."

"Why not have it removed?"

Law turned to him. "For the same reason we will restore you to your rightful place as king. There is comfort in tradition for many. Those who sail past may jest about Drummond Rutland and what did or did not dangle betwixt his legs, but it is a beacon of familiarity. A landmark of hope, one might say, in a world ever changing. Even those who claim they would return to a time before the Rhiagains would not raise their hands to see it done."

"How hated have we become?"

"Quite," Law replied. "Your brother is a less polished replica of your father. He has his cruelty, but not his cunning. Not his head for politics. Even Khain grasped the value of compromise and concession."

"My father was an old man by the time we came of age," Darrick said. He watched the glare of the rising sun glisten off the waves, creating a sea of shimmering dots. It was almost blinding. "He'd already raised two daughters to maturity. He needed us, but had nothing left to give."

"He had you, and you had nothing to learn from a man like that," Law said. "He didn't foresee a day where it would be Eoghan rising into his place."

"You perhaps give him more credit than is deserved." Darrick took another drink from the skin. "I believe my father had a hand in Eoghan's betrayal of me. If not directly, then in planting the seed that took root. He could have undone the plans my father laid for the Right of Choosing, but yet, he pushed forth. Had we not already forced our will upon the Reaches with the Epoch of the Accordant? Had we not already taken their ancestors, swept our fist across their beloved histories? We'd made our point. To ask for their children was madness."

"You were, of course, right."

"Even I didn't foresee the degree of chaos that followed."

Law clapped a hand on his back. "Well, we are not seers, are we? We are men of reason, who take what we know of the world and apply what wisdom we have to determine expected outcomes. It is enough that you were right. That you'd have put a stop to that madness, had it been you ascending the throne. And your future ascension will no doubt curtail future madness Eoghan has devised."

"And are we closer to a plan? Has there been word?"

"Lord Khallum reminds us we've waited five years to see you free, and it will be a sliver of that to see you restored. But our patience will win this. Impulsiveness will sink it. There are many layers, and we are privy to only some."

Darrick nodded. He looked away, again, toward the sea. He had no skills to captain a ship capable of sailing north, but perhaps he could chance it. He could put down anchor at Eastport, as his wife had weeks earlier... as his *son* had. He was a father. Anabella had survived, and she had carried his son in terrible conditions. Had grown him, fostered him, sheltered him from the fate that would've awaited him had Assyria not stepped in.

He'd given up believing she'd deliver. His faith in her hadn't wavered as much as his faith in her power at Eoghan's court. When Darrick and Eoghan were born, taking their first breaths as their mother took her last, Khain had demanded his older daughters take the place of the mother and raise them to men. Correen had been assigned Eoghan, and Assyria, Darrick. He'd always known he'd gotten the better deal in that exchange. Assyria was tough, but loyal. Strong. Others would have said she had a man's intelligence, but Darrick didn't subscribe to such antiquated views on women. Assyria was capable in her own right, and much of who he'd become had happened under her careful but serious nurturing. When she'd come to him that night on the cliff, it was only his fear that had driven him to doubt. Once washed away, his faith in her had been doubly restored. She would do as she promised, if she could.

But while Darrick languished under the unforgiving heat and dust of the Wastelands, Assyria had fed and protected his wife and son. He would spend a thousand years in the Wastelands to know they were safe. Now they were free.

"You're contemplating the difficulty of commandeering your own ship and sailing north."

Darrick laughed. "Was I so transparent?"

"A Southerlander prefers the view of the land from the sea." Law slipped the waterskin back in his trousers. "Also, those are the thoughts I would have, were I you."

"I know I must be patient. Only I... I never expected to see her again. Now that she is free, and I am free, I struggle against my own iron will to go to her. To take into my arms the son she had held tight for both of us, for five long years. To take from her the incredible burden she's carried."

"I may hold you back from doing so, Prince Darrick, but it isn't because I don't understand the desire."

"I haven't asked you, Law. Are you a married man? Children?"

"Aye," Law responded. "One son and four beautiful daughters. They're all married and starting families of their own. All except my son." He reached his hand into the soft ground and dug up a handful of dirt. He stood again and then let the dirt seep through his fingers. "We had hope he would've wed Lady Esmerelda, Guardians bless her."

"Guardians bless her," Darrick repeated. "What a terrible loss." He would never betray Ryan's confidence; that Esmerelda yet lived and awaited him to come to her.

"A shame about Hamish's lad," Law said. "A death sentence, for a lass whose promise is already spent."

"He isn't dead," Darrick said, more forcefully than intended. "The Guardian of the Unpromised Future will find himself disappointed should he come to collect. We'll rouse him yet."

Law didn't look convinced, but he nodded. "You'll be famished after that run, and I've some business with Steward Rutland. Shall we?"

THEY WERE HOUSED in the old keep. The new one, so grand it could be seen from the sea, much like old Drummond, had been built under Erran's grandfather. The castle, as they called it, was so grand, it was, Darrick thought, a vision of what a court under a competent and princely king should represent. Not the crumbling, grimy rocks of Duncarrow and a castle devoid of light and joy.

But the smaller keep, nestled back toward where the forest began, was no beggar's quarter. It was here that Erran's wife, Mariel, tended to the men who streamed in from nearby towns and villages, sick, destitute, or simply without name or aim. She had a tender heart, one Erran rightly let loose upon those who could most benefit. He'd gifted her the keep when she'd finished bearing children, and it had become her new child. One of her daughters, Agnes, aided her. Agnes wouldn't have a family of her own. The hunch in her back decided things. Many of the maids tending the lost souls in the old keep were daughters unfit for the marriage bed.

Although Darrick came and went for his daily exercises and sunshine—Godfrey, he was known by, when others asked for a name—his quarters were separate from the others. While most men languished in rows of cots, he and Ryan had a private room on the top floor. He assured the men that he needed no special treatment, but they insisted it was less for his station and more for safety. A false name wasn't enough protection against prying eyes and curious questions. Mariel's patients were transient; it would be nigh impossible to control the spread of information if one came upon even a whisper of the truth.

Law had left him at the entrance to the keep. Darrick continued on inside, flashing kind smiles at the ladies who bustled about with their pails and rags. He wound up the stairs at the back, leaving the noise and bustle of the infirmary below behind. By the time he reached the door to his room, there were no sounds at all, save the low rumble of snores from Hamish Strong, perched at the bedside of his son.

Hamish stuttered back to life. He wiped the drool with the back of his meaty hand, struggling to regain his bearings.

"Don't trouble yourself, Steward Strong. You need your sleep. Guardians know, you've had enough stolen already."

"Oh, aye, uh, I dinnae need sleep, your... Prince Darrick. I jus', ye see—"

"It's all right. When have you eaten last?"

Hamish exhaled. "Oh, aye, I dinnae. But dinnae fuss yerself, sire." His belly jiggled when he gave it a hard pat. "Reserves to spare."

Darrick smiled. "None the same. I can sit with him for a spell while you find some food."

"Oh, I donnae know, he's my son and my responsibility."

"And he's my friend and brother. It would be my honor."

Hamish flushed purple. He bowed his head and used the bed to help him stand. "If ye say it is so, well, I cannae argue against brotherhood. I willnae be long."

"Take the time you need. Grab a better sleep than the chair can offer you, too, if you wish. I'll not leave him, Hamish."

Hamish nodded. As he left, he muttered something that sounded like, *good lad.* Darrick smiled.

When he was gone, Darrick settled into the chair left warm by Hamish's colossal frame. He looked down upon Ryan, who had never seemed so at peace. He didn't appear to be sleeping, or even dead, only completely, serenely still. There was color in his face, but it was a false hope, for he'd lost mass since arriving in White-cliffe, not gained it. Darrick felt if he traced his finger over his cheekbone, it would feel sharp and uninviting.

"Just us again. I daresay that I never foresaw a day where I'd miss your crazed ranting, but here we are, and here I am, missing it all the same."

Ryan gave no sign he knew Darrick was there. No twitch of understanding. He hadn't expected one, but he'd held to the hope that this time might be different.

Darrick's memory of their escape from the Wastelands hadn't been fully restored to him. Once they'd taken the herbs, a strange dizziness had come upon him, and his next recollection was of jostling around in the back of a wagon. The decaying stench of moldy wood, mixed with the lingering remnants of rotting cabbage. Something wet, sticky, pressed against his cheek. Days, it must have been. Days lost. From what he knew of the herb, meant to bring a man near death but just shy of it, he might never possess knowledge of the events following their "death." Of how they came to be escorted out of the wretched lands that would have killed them, had they not found another way to use death to their advantage. He'd whispered for Andy with no response. He'd even called him Ryan in his delirium.

When he was next conscious, he was no longer being jostled along an uneven road, but was still, lying against something unrecognizable at first. Fresh linens. Behind his head was a pillow; a *real* pillow, not straw bundled together. He heard voices; men he didn't know. A strong smell. Bone broth, he'd learn later, when a young woman ladled the hot relief into his mouth.

You are safe. Be well.

He remembered those words. So curious. Did she know who he was? Or was it simply something she said to all the men she tended? *You are safe. Be well.*

"Who are you?" were his first words spoken. The bustle of energy in the room shifted, and all the voices from before swarmed around him. *He's awake. He lives.*

"They call me Missy," she said. She patted a damp cloth around his face.

"Missy. Curious name."

"It isnae my name. Tis only what they call me."

"I see. Missy."

"And yours, sir?"

"Godfrey," a man said, answering for him.

"Godfrey," she repeated with a smile as she wrung the cloth in the basin. As Darrick drifted away, he heard her soft voice say, "What a stately name. Like a prince."

When he awoke next, Missy was gone. In her place were two men. He didn't know if this was fewer men than before. The same ones, or different. So much of the world was in pieces.

"He's waking," one of them said.

"I am awake. Unless I'm dead, and this is the Unpromised Future?"

"Welcome back to the kingdom, Your Grace." This was who he later learned was Erran Rutland. "We have never been so invested in a man opening his eyes."

Law gathered at his side, speaking, about the future, about all they would accomplish. But all Darrick remembered was the sound of Hamish's cries as he waited for Ryan, too, to wake and join in their joy.

They'd done it. Those were the words Darrick grasped to, for the first time, after a week of delirium. He was free. They were free!

But only he was free.

Ryan was in a new prison; one they'd not yet figured how to break him from.

Now, weeks lost to it, hope was waning.

If he will not wake, why does he not die? Law had asked Missy.

I know not, but there's a fire in him that isnae so easily extinguished. He is at war with the darkness.

Who will win?

I cannae say, sir. I pray it is him. I beseech the Guardians each night, as I do for all men I look after.

Can't we bring in a healer? An Enchanter? Darrick had asked when she'd left to refill her basin with clean water from the stream.

It isnae a risk we can take, they'd said, but what they meant was, *it isnae a risk we can take for the one who will not be king.*

And anyway, they said his body was healed. It was his mind refusing to return to them.

Darrick leaned close to Ryan and whispered, "Did you know... well, yes, you probably *do* know, but it sounds like something you would say. That statue? They call it Drummond's Cock. Is that your handiwork? I can see you spreading that around the Reach with glee."

Ryan remained impassive.

"Ryan, I will not, I refuse. I abjectly refuse to believe the Guardians have weighted my life to be worth more than yours. We both know how you love a good jest, but you have to know when a joke has run its course, brother. It's time to wake up."

Would he have done it, had he known this outcome? Darrick toiled over this subject daily. Would he have sought his freedom at the price of Ryan's life? It was an impossible quandary. The kingdom, for his friend. One life, against many. A question with no answer; none that left his soul anything but restless.

He wrapped his hands through one of Ryan's and brought it to his mouth. Pressed his lips against Ryan's still warm flesh. "Esmerelda is waiting for you. Your beauty with the emerald eyes and fire on her tongue. If nothing else stirs you, draw deep upon the memory of her in your arms. Your joy doesn't have to be what it is for these men who conspired to send you in and bring me out. Yours can be as simple, as powerful as love."

A bright light flashed outside the window. He'd been so consumed he didn't notice the darkening skies, or the din of fresh rain peppering the earth.

"Please find your way back to us," Darrick pleaded. "You are my true brother, the one the Guardians should have sent me." He bowed his head. "If the cost of my freedom is your life, it will not be a debt I'm capable of paying. Nor will it be one I can live with. We are both only men. No matter what the others may say, my life has no more value than any other."

Darrick looked up just as lightning struck. "And this belief has brought the kingdom to its knees for too long."

4

CRIMSON AND GOLD

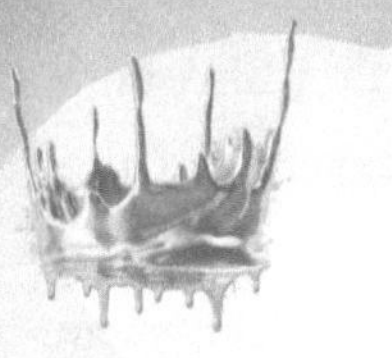

Drystan summoned all of his willpower to keep his face expressionless as Valen observed with scrutiny his dressing of the deer. The initial tear from his knife wasn't the worst part, or even the several jagged attempts following. It was removing the entrails, still warm, that threatened to do him in. The residual warmth reminded him that this animal had lived, and only moments ago. That *his* hands had taken this life, and there was still some left as the force left the deer's carcass not immediately but gradually. This power over life and death terrified him. It left him hollow and afraid, as if drowning.

Valen taught him first to hunt. It was probably best he'd started there, and not with the ritual of tending to the aftermath. Drystan couldn't explain why delivering the fatal blow with an arrow was easier than sifting through the carcass, but Valen suggested the kill was less personal. To bury your hands in the body of another was a task designed for intimacy, whether animal or man.

Drystan simultaneously wished Valen away and desired his approval. He couldn't explain this either. The man's claim—that he, and not Holden Dereham, was Drystan's father—was both preposterous and intriguing. When a man lied, he did so with purpose, and there could be no gain in feigning himself as Drystan's father. If true, it removed Drystan as an heir to Wulfsgate and made him nobody. Nothing. Valen had abandoned the house of Sylvaine, and they'd given Rushwood to another.

If not true... to what end was the telling? To stir trouble in the house of Dereham? This was the question Drystan couldn't draw an answer from, and Valen himself would never say, if so. Unless Valen, or Ash, or whatever he called himself, had qualms with Holden, or even Gretchen, the claim seemed meaningless.

Unless it was true. The only way to confirm was beyond his grasp. If he could look into his mother's eyes, he would see her truth. She was the only path to the answer, and the path was closed.

Ravenna could probably pull the truth from Valen's mind, but the way to her was also shut, likely forever. Perhaps it had been shut even before they'd departed Wulfsgate. She'd made her choice, or fate had made it, but it was her own to make. His wounded heart would make peace with it, eventually, or maybe never, but had no power to change it, and his acceptance of this gave him hope Ravenna wasn't the only one who'd changed since leaving home.

"You don't have to be so dainty with it, Drystan. It won't bite you," Valen said. A sickening slosh sounded as he buried his hands next to Drystan's. They wrapped around the ribcage and he shook; the deer flopped around as if in the throes of an episode. "Don't think about the blood on your hands. It can be washed in the stream. Think instead of the task at hand and completing it with expedience and care. We cannot take too long or the meat will go to rot and our bellies will stay empty. The Medvedev gave us more land to roam so we could serve ourselves, as they will not."

"I know," Drystan muttered. From the corner of his eye, he saw

Lisbet pass through the meadow, accompanied by those two sons of the chieftainess, with their violet hair and accusing eyes. If Drystan were a more capable guardian of his sister, he would have objected to their taking her away daily for questioning, challenging them to solve the matter by sword. But he was not. She came back each day, weary, with the same explanation of her time away. *Yseult asked who we are. Why we are here. Who sent us. What we want. That's all. And I gave her the same answers as I did the day before. And then she released me.*

Things were better now, though they remained prisoners. For almost a week they'd toiled in the magic cages, and then they'd been moved to their own section of the vibrant and peculiar forest, with a durable tent made from the animals roaming the land around it, and a bountiful stream in which to fish, wash, and draw water. It was still a cage, only a larger one. The magic barrier stretching farther, but still there.

It means they do not yet trust us, but also don't believe we're an imminent threat, Valen explained. Drystan was coming to the same place with Valen as Lisbet had been all along. Questioning. Distrustful. Even disdainful. *What troubles them most is that men understand their world is off-limits. To venture into it anyway is bold, and a sign of intent. They struggle to believe that we had no intent, other than the seeking of asylum.*

Valen had led them there, knowing this. Drystan didn't bother pointing it out. He'd only respond in vague, veiled words that created questions and answered none.

Then there were times Drystan felt his animosity toward Valen was unfair. The man had saved his life. Saved Eavan's and Lisbet's. He'd taught Drystan things even his father hadn't bothered with, like how to properly hold and swing a sword, and now, how to kill and dress his own meat. The instructions traditionally passed from father to son.

"Better," Valen said. "We'll skin the fur as well, I think. Though

Yseult was generous with her own furs, we're still in the throes of midwinter and the Hinterlands is not immune to storms."

"Does it snow here?"

"Yes, in wintertide, and late season storms in midwinter aren't rare, either. It surprised me to see the land so green when we entered the Reach."

"Magic?"

"Could be." Valen went quiet.

"Maybe it has to do with what Eavan said. What Kian told her. About the Quinlandens enslaving Medvedev."

Valen looked surprised at Drystan's words. "Why would it?"

"Eavan said the Drumain and the other clahnns are all going to fight back, to protect the Saleen. What if they cleared the land because they're preparing to march?"

"That's what Kian told her," Valen said. A tearing noise sounded in the air as he worked at the fur and flesh. "We must remember they are our gaolers, not our friends."

"You don't believe him?"

"I believe that Aiden Quinlanden reached too far this time, and that he'll answer for it. But the clahnns of the Hinterlands have existed for hundreds of years in peace... separately. Their history isn't for us, but what we do know of them tells us that there was a division, long before men populated the kingdom. They separated into clahnns, and have remained so ever since. There is love between them, kin to kin, but there's no amity. No alliance."

"My mother says men find alliance in common foes."

"Your mother has always been wise, but men aren't Medvedev."

"No, but..." Drystan paused, thinking over his words. "Surely men have overstepped with the Medvedev before. What did they do then?"

"Minor violations. Not at this scale. Not thousands of Medvedev subjugated at our hand."

"How? That's what I can't understand. How, when their magic is so much greater than ours?"

"Than ours, yes." Valen's knife separated meat from bone. "But there have long been rumors of the abilities of the Rhiagain sorcerers, who aren't from this kingdom. Immortal, they say, with magic unlike ours, in kind and power. There are two in Duncarrow, or were."

"Not even the Medvedev or Ravenwoods are immortal."

"Hand me the longer knife, Drystan. Thank you." Valen grimaced. His muscles swelled under his tunic as he tugged at the meat. "When Aiden Quinlanden laid Rowanwen at the king's feet, they say it was not without reward."

"Another sorcerer?"

"I assume that's what Kian meant when he referred to Aiden's magician. An army the size of Lord Quinlanden's doesn't come free, not even for a king. I can't think of any other way to subdue the Medvedev magic than through a stronger magic, which doesn't exist in this kingdom as far as I'm aware. Not even from your beloved Ravenna."

"Have you met a Rhiagain sorcerer?"

Valen paused his butchery. "No. But their existence isn't speculation, only the extent of their magic, which has gone the way of legend."

Drystan sometimes got the sense that Valen enjoyed his inquisitiveness, and other times, like now, that he wished Drystan would learn to quash it.

He buried the rest of his questions and returned to helping Valen finish up work on the deer.

MANY WERE NOT aware that the great Whitewood wasn't named for the pale, peeling bark of its stalwart inhabitants, but one very specific tree. Only the elders in the town of Whitewood, which perched at the edge of this same-named forest, even bothered to remember such a trivial fact.

Storm told Brandyn this as they waited at the base of the massive ghost arboria.

"And why would *you* know or care about such a thing, then?"

"My father is the steward of these lands. It befits him to be in possession of all number of facts he can use to regale the guests who pass through."

Brandyn cracked a small, humorless smile. "He tell this to any Quinlandens?"

"Truth is, we received very few guests here in Whitewood. They're much more enamored with their holidays at Wildwood Falls, or the rolling valleys of Windwatch Grove. Our position on the wrong side of the Seven Sisters keeps us safe, but also painfully isolated."

"Capture by Quinlanden men would be painful. I'd much prefer isolation."

"Don't trouble over it. Even the few who actually listened to my father's words over the years wouldn't know the location of The Ghost Queen."

Brandyn judged her from his peripheral. "That's really what you call this thing?"

"Trees aren't 'things,' Brandyn. They live, same as you or me, though their lives are quite different obviously. And if you hadn't noticed, men traded cleverness for clarity when they named this world."

Brandyn didn't give a fig about a tree. He had more pressing matters on his mind. He'd never seen so much crimson and gold in the Westerlands. It sank his heart into his boots. How fast Lord Quinlanden had settled and taken root in a land that was not his own. He had to have been planning this treachery long before the Right of Choosing. But how had he foreseen circumstances would develop there that would leave the Westerlands absent of their leader and ripe for takeover? That would leave Brandyn's father vulnerable?

A seer, no doubt. One better than him.

Most of the ride from Briarhaven, and the Sepulchre, had taken them through the Easterlands. They'd doubled the time needed for their voyage to keep even farther from the path than the last time they'd passed this way, with Hollyn—which now seemed an entire lifetime ago. They'd mercifully had no trouble, but as soon as they crossed into the Westerlands, they had to disappear deeper into the woods. Banners of crimson and gold, flying high into the sky, set to the sounds of hundreds of hooves, were an immediate assault to the senses. And so far from even the main roads, which meant the towns would be swarming with them.

We won't know if we can make it into Whitewood without capture until it's too late, Storm had said, reading his mind. *And I can't enter even without you. I've been missing too long. Quinlanden will have figured out by now that I've been with you.*

We have to do something. We can't stay here, and we have nowhere to go. I won't go back, not until I've restored my mother's lands to the Blackwoods.

That will not be so easy hiding in the woods. But I have an idea.

Storm's idea had been to send a raven into Whitewood with a coded message. Brandyn wasn't keen on this. Anything coded could be deciphered, and with as many men as Quinlanden had milling about on sentry in the Westerlands, it was a significant risk. But she insisted their code was different. It was, she said, not actually code at all, but a message written with the innocence of childhood.

When I was a girl, my father was a busy man. But when he had time for me, it was at this remarkable tree, The Ghost Queen, that we would meet. We would see who was fastest to the stream, and we marked our times upon the bark. Although he could've shouted across the keep to get my attention, he sent me a raven, simply saying: a prince requires his princess for a quick game. And I would know precisely where to meet him.

That still sounds like subterfuge. Especially now.

That's why we must wait. Days, weeks. Until my father can come safely. Until the suspicion has passed.

Twelve days they'd camped beneath The Ghost Queen, with no news, no return message. They took turns on watch, but after so long without direction, Brandyn's sleep was no longer restful. Storm had to force him to eat, which he did, but only because he couldn't organize a rebellion if he was dead.

"Did you hear that?" Brandyn asked. His hand moved to his bow.

Storm rose to her feet, slowly. Making a fist, she knocked it against the bark in a strange pattern.

"What are you doing?" Brandyn hissed.

"Quiet."

The next sound came from the forest. A whistle, following the same pattern Storm had beaten upon the tree.

Storm smiled. "My father."

"These you can eat," Eavan said, opening her palm for Gabi and Meadow to see. "You see here? The dark lines that pass through the center of the nut? You look for that, and you will live." She opened her other palm. "These have no dark line. You eat these, at best you'll be stricken with flux for days. At worst, you'll be read the dead-given rites, though I daresay you won't be around to hear them."

Meadow's eyes widened in fear. Gabi reached forward and took one of each nut. "How many would make me sick?"

"I would not chance a single one," Eavan replied. "You aren't considering it?"

Gabi tossed aside the safe one and examined the other. "Well, it looks so harmless, does it not?"

Eavan emptied the piles into the grass and reached for Gabi's hand. Gabi quickly moved it away.

"And how do you even know such things?" Gabi challenged. "You're no Medvedev."

"Gabi," Meadow warned.

"What? My question is fair. And aren't you supposed to be an expert in flora? What say you about these nuts?"

"These lands are foreign to me. We should listen to our elders."

Eavan flushed bright pink. "I'm eighteen. Hardly an elder."

"You didn't answer my question," Gabi said. "Why should it be you we trust to determine the safety of our food?"

"Gabrianna," Eavan replied with a heavy sigh. "Your mother would want me to look after you here."

"You say this as if we're on holiday!"

Eavan frowned. "Of course we're not on holiday. But we must make the best of what the Guardians have given us. I have no power here, but I did spend several childhood summers in these woods, upon the exclusive invitation of Yseult herself, and what I know, I learned from Kian."

"Kian. Who wishes us dead."

"If he wished you dead, you'd be dead."

"Oh, right. It is only *you* he wishes dead."

Eavan snaked a hand out and slapped her. The moment of connection shocked her as much as it did Gabi, and she immediately wished she could take it back. "Gabi... forgive me. I don't know what came over me."

Gabi dropped the nut and clutched her face. "It is *your* father who has marked us as enemies! How could you not know? How could you not have seen thousands of Medvedev, *thousands?*" Gabi jumped to her feet. "Your father killed *mine.*"

Eavan fell back upon the grass in defeat. She'd pondered this to the point of exhaustion. The question wasn't how she hadn't seen it, but why she hadn't cared. Of course she'd seen the Medvedev milling about in the woods beyond Whitechurch. And part of her had even wondered about how positively odd it was for them to be there at all. But such was the business of men, not girls, and so she'd left it for other amusements, which were more suited to her.

Kian had said nothing to her since revealing the truth of her father's terrible machinations. Even the news of her uncle, Byrne, had been kept from her until she was reunited with the others. She'd been so shocked to see Gabrianna here, but the terrible news that Eavan's father had killed Gabi's quickly stilled that shock.

Somehow, that was even more difficult for her to accept than what he'd done with the Medvedev.

Her father had taken a life. With his own hands. His *brother*, in the eyes of the kingdom's laws. And then he'd taken the Westerlands, which was not his, any more than the Medvedev were. He was now an enemy to all his peers, his actions an aggressive declaration of war.

Backed by the same king she'd nearly wed.

"Let us see if Lisbet has returned," Eavan said, gathering her skirts with a strained smile. "Perhaps this visit has been more illuminating than all the last."

Mason Wakesell nodded to his wife, Jasmine. She lifted her hands above her head and then let them fall down to her sides in an arc formation. She turned to another angle and did the same, repeating this until, at last, she dropped her arms and smiled.

"We will be safe here. For now," Jasmine said, adding the last with a light frown. "I could do with some practice."

"Your mother knows magic?" Brandyn whispered.

"The Blackwoods aren't the only in the realm who find reason to hide it," Storm said.

"But what if she's discovered? She could be put to death!"

"Your mother knows," Jasmine said to Brandyn. "In fact, I would say there's very little Asherley Blackwood does *not* know. Wouldn't you?"

He nodded. "And I... I would never tell."

Jasmine laid a hand against his cheek. "I know, little one." She looked at her daughter. "What a gift it is to see your face, to know you're all right. You had us so worried."

"Of course I was all right. Father trained me well."

Mason grinned from one corner of his mouth. "I told your mother as much."

"I wish you'd not waited to return for such volatile times, but that would be to misunderstand your intentions, I believe. You've returned *because* of these things, haven't you?"

"We've been careful, Mother," Storm said. "We took our time in getting here, though we saw no Quinlanden men in the Easterlands at all on our path. Only when we entered our own Reach did the crimson and gold make itself known."

"Hmph," Mason said. He placed a hand on each sword. "A bold traitor, he is, leaving his own lands sparsely tended. He must think so little of us that he does not fear us taking it."

Jasmine smiled sadly at Brandyn. "We are so very sorry about your father, dear. Lord Byrne was a good man, even measuring him by the standards of a Westerlander. We all loved him, as I know you did."

Brandyn pressed his tongue to the top of his mouth to quell the quick storm of emotion. He nodded. "I will avenge him, Lady Jasmine. And all others who have and will fall to protect the Westerlands. I will avenge us all."

"Of course you will." A dark pall fell over her face. "But you will not do it from Whitewood, I'm afraid."

"They're really here now, too?" Storm asked, defeated. Brandyn, too, felt the sinking sensation at the confirmation. "Here, on the eastern side of the pass?"

"At first, they stayed to the towns close to Longwood Rush. But when they lost communication with The Deceiver, they spread their tendrils farther," Mason explained. "If you ask me, they do it from fear, not power."

"What do you mean, lost communication?" Brandyn asked.

"Lord Quinlanden has been on Duncarrow nigh a month," Jasmine said. "His men didn't expect him gone so long, but what concerns them is that the ravens bring no response. He's gone silent, and no one knows why."

Storm grinned. "And how do you know this, Mother?"

Mason shook his head. "You know quite well how your mother knows this. We can't know what it means, but the king has been allied with The Deceiver since the springtide. Longer, perhaps, we don't know. But his men are restless. He has one... a Mads Waters. Frightening man, lacking a conscience, so others more acquainted are saying. It was that one who ordered more knights from the Easterlands and spread them south, to cover more land."

"So they're everywhere," Brandyn said, sighing.

"Not everywhere..." Jasmine said. "There is much a foreigner would not know about our Reach. Such as places beloved to us and forgotten by others."

Storm watched her mother. "I don't understand."

"Greystone Abbey," Brandyn said. "That's what you mean, isn't it?"

Jasmine smiled as she nodded.

"Everyone has sent men to Easlan James," Mason replied. "Rebellion stirs in the neglected town, and Quinlanden's men are none the wiser. It will all begin or end there."

"It will end with Lord Aiden's head on a pike, and my family back where they belong."

"We would all help you see it done. But we are powerless here.

They've already executed a dozen of my men, good men, for failing to reveal your whereabouts. This is why, we believe, Waters has infiltrated all the key cities. He knows you're a child, who will have no destination as enticing as ones familiar to you."

Brandyn's eyes closed. "And yet, that's exactly what I did. Returned home."

Jasmine tucked his hair behind his ear. "No. You returned to reclaim what is yours, Brandyn Blackwood. You did what any heir would and should do. And you *will* reclaim it, with the help of all those loyal to your mother and her kin. But it won't be from here."

"You believe we should go to Greystone?" Storm asked.

"I believe it is the only place in the kingdom you can be both safe and also positioned to stir the rebellion."

Storm bowed her head. "I had thought... we had planned... Brandyn could pretend to be Shadow, and we could be safe *here*."

Jasmine pulled her daughter in for a tight embrace. "My dear. It was a wise plan. You couldn't have known how determined the men of crimson and gold would be to see Brandyn's head next to his father's. But there are too many in Whitewood, in all the towns and cities, who would recognize him on sight. Many would not be clever enough to hide that recognition. Others would trade their lives for Brandyn's. We all live in this fear, now. Not all are as brave or as loyal as we are."

Mason patted his daughter on the back. "You will need to practice the same caution when you travel to Greystone Abbey. Shadow was a fair choice for a cover, and we can spread a rumor that Shadow has been seen alive, in case you are apprehended. It may or may not save you, Lord Blackwood, but every moment of peril comes down to fortune and chance. Does it not?"

Brandyn nodded. He looked off into the woods, into the sea of white bark and lush undergrowth. He was weary of travel. He'd trade all the food left in his satchel for even one night in a bed.

But he trusted the Wakesells. There had been few Great Families as loyal, and he'd seen that reflected in Storm as she made difficult, brave choices to protect him and Hollyn.

There was also the vision that had come to him while they awaited Storm's parents. He'd seen the ruins of a town once great. The face of a man who his mother would raise up and protect until her dying breath. Joran had been there too, though this made little sense, as Joran hadn't been seen since Byrne's death. Brandyn's visions were still difficult to read. He'd left in the middle of vital instruction from Magi Christian, and he was unsure now of what he could and couldn't trust.

There was another he saw. One whose face was covered, but her magic was strong. A sorceress, though unlike any he'd studied with or under at the Sepulchre. Hers was a magic unfamiliar; perhaps forbidden. Why she was there was as unclear as her identity.

If the Wakesells would send them to Greystone Abbey, the very place Brandyn had seen in his vision, then there was no other destination. They must go.

Jasmine passed a satchel to Storm. "Food, and two new water-skins. Even if you double your journey, it should be enough to keep you both sustained until Steward Easlan can resume care of you. You will tell him, too, that we'll send more men as we're able."

Brandyn thanked them both and let Storm say her goodbyes.

In his mind, he was already traveling the path ahead.

LISBET SAT before the imposing chieftainess, as she had every day for weeks, and answered the same questions they'd asked her each day. She'd even come to feel relaxed in the small thatched room with no dressing or adornment, or at least no longer afraid. The fresh dirt on her knees as she lowered herself to the exposed ground reminded her she was yet alive.

"Who are you?" Yseult demanded.

"I am Lisbet Dereham, eldest daughter of Lord Holden Dereham and Lady Gretchen Dereham."

"Who sent you?"

"No one. I sent myself."

"Why did you come?"

"Idealistically, perhaps foolishly, in search of a place where I could be free from being wed to a cruel king and my brother could be safe to follow his heart."

"What do you want?"

This was the only answer Lisbet had changed since the first time asked. Early on, she'd answered that she wanted her freedom. That answer felt wrong now, though she didn't know why.

"I want for you, Chieftainess Yseult, and the others to know that neither I nor any with me knew of the atrocities undertaken by Lord Quinlanden on others of your kind. That we're united in our horror of it." Lisbet paused. She didn't know if she should say the next words. She was afraid of them, but also compelled to speak them into life. "That we would join you in avenging the Saleen and righting the wrongs perpetrated."

Yseult, who had already bored of the scripted conversation and prepared to dismiss Lisbet, paused the waving of her hand in midair. She looked left and right at her sons with a disdainful smile, which they both returned in mirrored kind. Kian's, though, faded when his mother looked away. As he watched Lisbet.

"And what could you, Lisbet Dereham, bring to this retribution that would be of any value to the Medvedev?" She laughed. Her sky blue hair, piled into braids atop her head, shook with the rest of her. "You, girl, not even a man."

Lisbet's heart beat so hard she felt it behind her eyes. She'd never stayed this long. Exchanged so many words. "I... don't believe you look down upon women at all, Chieftainess. You draw these words, instead, from a disdain unique to man, that they can't see the gifts women alone can bring to war, to battle, to politics. Values you do not share."

Kael muttered something that she couldn't hear. The hawk on his shoulder screeched.

Yseult raised a hand, this time to silence her son. "I have no disdain for the feminine strength. But do not compare yourself to me and mine. We are dissimilar in more ways than are immediately obvious to someone with your limitations."

Lisbet bowed her head. "My apologies. That wasn't my intent."

"Your intent remains unclear to me."

"We are not your enemy. We would very much like to be your friend."

"We require no friendship from men. It brings us nothing beyond strife."

"Your offer. Friendship," Kael said. Unlike his mother, he didn't bother adjusting to the cadence of men, for Lisbet's sake. "Bonds you offer. Not freedom."

"It's true, I'm your prisoner, and I understand why you wouldn't trust any offer made under such conditions," Lisbet said carefully. "But with all your magic, can none of you see into our hearts, to our intent? Can you not see that we came, as I've said, foolishly, but with an idealistic belief that we, too, could live in peace?"

"Our peace is not your peace," Yseult replied. "The men of this kingdom are fallible and unwise, but most possess the prudence to stay far from our forests. I cannot say the same for you."

"The folly of youth," Lisbet said with a nervous smile. "We are all, all of us, children."

"All except the one with the eyes of ash and many names."

"He saved our lives," Lisbet said. "But he's not one of us. We don't claim him."

"You should. It is for him I spared your lives."

Lisbet swallowed the hard lump in her throat. "Of course. And we thank you."

"I require not your gratitude, only your truth." Yseult waved her hands. "We are done."

KIAN TOLD his brother he would escort Lisbet back on his own. Kael was dubious of this offer, but Kian's objection was about Yseult, and the need for someone to escort her to her home. She was frail that morning, when just the day before, she'd been full of life. Lisbet didn't understand the sudden shift. She was afraid to ask.

When they were free of the small gathering room, aimed again toward the forest, Kian said, "It is unwise to provoke my mother. She has no trust for the world of men."

"She once welcomed them into her lands."

"A mistake she has come to regret."

It surprised Lisbet to hear him speak in the parlance more familiar to her, as his mother did. Kael never had. "I wasn't trying to provoke her. I don't know the words she wants from me."

"Only those she has asked for."

"But they don't seem to be enough. She asks them, daily, and clearly isn't satisfied with my answers."

Kian navigated her away from tripping over a tangle of brush. "Your answers have changed."

"Only because I feared she didn't find them satisfying!"

"Then you choose your words according to what you believe she wishes to hear."

"That's not what I meant," Lisbet said. "My words are true. I haven't lied to her. But still she doesn't believe me."

"You think she doesn't believe you?"

"If she believed me, she wouldn't ask me the same questions every day!"

Kian smiled to himself. "You have much to learn."

"Of course I do. I'm only fourteen. I have no guile or malice in my heart. Only love."

"No one has only love in their hearts, Lisbet," Kian replied. "Not even a child fresh to the world."

Lisbet continued on in silence. The Medvedev hadn't been unkind, but nor had they let them go. They'd given them a bigger prison, one she might have enjoyed without the invisible boundaries reminding them of their limitations. But that was not freedom.

She didn't know why she'd been chosen by Yseult to speak on behalf of them all. And was she not as shocked as the Medvedev must have been to see Gabrianna Blackwood and her friend Meadow show up as well? She couldn't speak for them. She could hardly speak for herself.

But the Medvedev had not been surprised. Gabrianna had told her about the strange encounter with Kael in the cave. The lost days following.

"The boy. Brook. He is not dead. Not by our hands."

Lisbet almost tripped at the sudden resumption in conversation. "What?"

"The kin of Meadow. He escaped and ran off. Joined other men, and from there, we know nothing of him. You may tell her."

"What men? Do you know who he went with?"

"Yes."

"But you won't tell me?"

"No."

"Is there any other news you can share? Of the kingdom?"

"The news of the kingdom is of no matter to us."

"Kian," Lisbet said. "When I asked if you had the magic to look into our hearts. None of you answered."

"Our magic is our concern, not yours."

"But you must possess it. How else would Kael have known Gabi was coming to the Hinterlands? To you?"

Kian said nothing. They were drawing close to the magic barrier, though she couldn't see it with her own eyes.

Lisbet ceased walking. "Look into mine."

Kian stopped several paces ahead. "I will not."

"But that means you can. You didn't say, 'I cannot,' only 'I will not.'"

"Only men seek to interpret words in such a way."

Lisbet laughed. "Your mother asks the same four questions of me daily. Is that not what she's doing? Interpreting my words?"

Kian grabbed her roughly by the arm and dragged her forward. "Heed my advice on my mother or abandon it at your peril." He pushed her through the barrier.

Lisbet pressed her hands to the invisible wall. "I thank you for concerning yourself with my peril, Kian of the Drumain."

Kian huffed and turned away.

5

THE COUNSEL OF OLDWIN

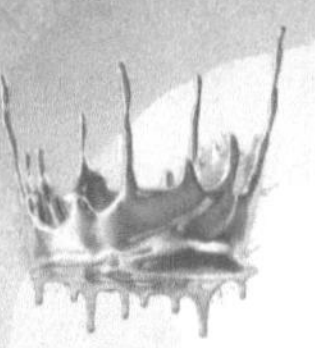

Eoghan Rhiagain slumped in his chair. His ass hung in precarious balance at the edge of the velvet, legs spread so wide his feet no longer had respectable purchase on the floor. His arms he let dangle at his sides. They were utterly useless anyway. Everything in Duncarrow was. Everyone.

Once an hour, upon the hour, Correen appeared at his chamber door, requesting audience. He had none to give her. He may have needed her once, but it was Assyria he'd wished would guide him, as she had lovingly taught Darrick. And now Assyria had revealed herself as a traitorous bitch, which made him desire Correen's presence less, not more. In the absence of a more competent mentor, Correen's failures burned especially bright.

She liked to slip her outrageous opinions in when he was otherwise indisposed, so he'd be less able to argue. Over breakfast, as his mouth was stuffed with pastry. During his bath, where there were ears not suited for such conversation. She was most passionate, for some reason, about him establishing a true court, with counselors and merriment. None of the men had ever suggested such things. But he had no men he trusted.

The sun crested low upon the horizon. When he'd first sunk into the chair, he'd watched a fresh light illuminate the world. He'd been there that long. He could stay longer. He frequently did.

No wisdom afforded him had prepared him for how little joy he'd take from running the kingdom after seizing power from his brother.

Eoghan had considered this over the intervening five years since he'd had Darrick thrown to his death. About *why* he'd done it. Darrick's reign would have undone everything their father had put in place. It was reason enough, even without the fear that Darrick might dissolve the entire monarchy once it was within his right to do so. And it was true also that he loathed his twin brother. Darrick was the embodiment of goodness, of strength and aptitude, and there was nothing, no one, in all the kingdom who reminded Eoghan he possessed none of these things as Darrick did.

But Eoghan hadn't wanted the kingdom. He'd wanted his brother dead, and the two, unfortunately, couldn't happen in exclusivity. Assyria and Correen were not fit to rule. There was no one else.

He'd hoped for another ten years with his aging father, and, instead, Khain died so soon after Darrick that Eoghan had no time to proffer more than minimal counsel.

Word had reached him of his beloved Hollyn's death. With it, the rumor a Rhiagain had given her the disease that killed her.

His only accomplishment as king had been to craft an event meant to gift him four wives in order for him to have the one he most wanted, and instead, he'd lost the only one he wanted, and been left with the daughter of the man who would style himself an ally, but was truly a traitor.

It was almost amusing. The only lord of the kingdom who had ever shown meaningful fealty was also his enemy.

Oh, how Lord Quinlanden had argued that point! Pandering, begging, and all the while, that look in his eyes. One Eoghan recognized all too well. *He thinks I'm a fool. He thinks he can control me, as all the others have. That I have no sense or cunning of my own. That I possess none of what made Darrick so great.*

And, like all the others before him, he will find himself wrong.

IT HAD BEEN in the throne room—a room Eoghan had used less than five times in his reign—that Aiden had laid the head of Byrne Warwick at Eoghan's feet and declared the Westerlands property of the crown.

"All the kingdom is property of the crown, Lord Quinlanden," Eoghan answered. Correen tried to whisper something in his ear, but he swatted her away.

"Yes, Your Grace, but as we are all too aware—"

"You will refrain from referencing you and me as one, regardless of topic."

Aiden's face changed; perhaps he was seeing the first sign that all wasn't as he'd expected to find it when sailing to Duncarrow. "Yes, sir. As *I* am aware, the crown has ultimate authority for all the kingdom, but the riches of each Reach are preserved within."

"As is the burden of maintaining said riches, and the population. A burden the crown does not want. Hence why we follow the King's Decree, which gives the Reaches their freedoms at the expense of a fair tax."

"Of course, sir. What I offer you is the whole of the Westerland wealth, *without* that burden."

Eoghan's nose twitched at the foul stench of Warwick's rotting head. What he wouldn't give to see the Blackwood bitch witness the fruits of her own treachery. But he would deal with her later.

Assana was as still as steel at his side.

"And how, Lord Aiden, do you propose that to be possible?"

Aiden's grin was foul. "Why, with you as king, anything is

possible. You can demand what is yours and leave the problem of maintaining to your subjects, who have little choice in the matter."

"You believe this is how I should run my kingdom."

"Sir."

"And so by that reasoning, I should take, too, the Easterlands. Demand her resources, give nothing in return."

"Sir, as your ally—"

Eoghan turned to Assana. "Wife, I would ask your opinion on a matter. Do you have opinions?"

Assana bowed her head. Her hands gripped the oak of the chair. "I am possessed of some, Your Grace."

"What do you make of your father's decision to deliver to me something I did not ask for, and then to tell me how I should make use of this gift?"

"Your Grace, if I may—" Aiden raised a hand.

"You may not," Eoghan replied, still looking at his wife. "I am asking my wife."

Assana's voice shook. "I can't pretend to understand the business of men, husband."

"Pretend. That is what I'm asking you to do."

Aiden laughed nervously. "Your Grace, as the queen has said—"

Eoghan spun his head toward the Lord of the Easterlands. "Your daughter is not a queen. She is only a lady of the realm, ranking even lower than my sisters, one of whom is a barren block of ice, the other a bold traitor. Only a Rhiagain can be a queen." He returned his focus to Assana. "Go on."

"I..." Assana stumbled for words. Eoghan wanted to slap them from her mouth but feigned an encouraging smile, or they'd be there all day. "I would be most worried, Your Grace, about the war that may follow such a gift."

"The innocence of a child!" Aiden called out. "With respect, Your Grace, Assana will bear you children, not great wisdom."

"As it happens, Assana and I are united in this wisdom," Eoghan answered. "You say you took the Westerlands for me. But you did not *ask* me if I wanted the Westerlands. You did not *ask* me if the death of Lord Warwick was something I desired, or part of my own greater vision in leading this realm. His family already loathes us. Did I ask for war? I did not, and yet, by your actions in the Westerlands, and the loss you have wrought upon the Southerlands with Warwick blood spilt, you have invited this very thing."

Aiden's resolve cracked. It was a beautiful thing to witness. First, the fading light in his eyes, then the shaking hands that had never seen a day's labor. Eoghan relished in this. So few had witnessed Eoghan in a brilliance he occasionally possessed and even more rarely had occasion to employ.

"For you, sir."

"For yourself," Eoghan corrected. "For a future where you see a Quinlanden, and not a Rhiagain, sitting upon this seat. A future that will never come to pass."

"No! Never! That has never been my aim, sir. I look only to bring honor to your house."

"Then where is the ship?"

"Sir?"

"The *ship*, Quinlanden, bearing the traitors of this realm."

"I know not—"

"While you were occupied serving your own needs, Princess Assyria and Lady Blackwood commandeered a vessel they used to bear themselves, and both the Dereham and Warwick boys, away. I want to know what your men have done to find it. Was it not these men you swore to me when you laid Rowanwen at my feet?"

Aiden's shock was a solace. "I know nothing of this, sir. I had hoped to lay Lord Warwick's head at his wife's feet."

"I thought you knew all, Lord Quinlanden. Is that not what you said to me, when you beseeched me before the Right of Choosing to inform me that the other lords of the realm were preparing for treason?"

"I cannot know all. But I have always, and will always, share with Your Grace what I do know, and act in accordance with what is best for Him and this realm."

"You believe me a fool, and have acted in accordance with *that.*"

Aiden prostrated himself lower, looking squarely at the floor. "I know you are the most glorious king the realm has ever seen, sir. I would aid you in that glory."

"Even I know there's little truth in that. Get up."

Aiden scrambled back to his knees.

"*Lord Chancellor.*" Eoghan grimaced. "You reach too far. You have overplayed yourself, Lord Quinlanden, and as my father always said, you must cut away the rot before it can spread, or it will overcome you." He nodded at the guards, who leaned in and seized Aiden's arms.

Aiden whipped his neck back and forth in horror. Eoghan wanted to smile at this, because he so enjoyed besting the man who thought his wisdom superior to all, but the fall of Aiden Quinlanden was instead another reminder of how alone Eoghan was. The most powerful man in the kingdom, with no one he could trust.

Eoghan rose. He turned to Assana, who stood with him. "I could send his head to your mother. Would she like that?"

"Assana!" Aiden cried, thrashing with futility. "I'm your father!"

"She very much would," Assana replied, calm.

"And you? Would you like this?"

Assana turned her eyes down, thinking. With a light sigh, she said, "Yes, though I think that may be too light a punishment for his crimes against you."

Aiden howled in anger.

Eoghan nodded. "I'm listening."

"To sever a head is to deliver a moment of pain. To leave someone toiling, head intact, for the rest of their days in a cell is to deliver a lifetime of agony."

At this, Eoghan did smile. He'd not married the woman of his heart, but, perhaps, he'd wed one of like mind. "The wife of the king has announced her sentence, and the king agrees."

Eoghan's scant memories of Oldwin painted the enigmatic sorcerer as a whisper in the shadows. Always there, rarely seen in full view. He'd been the only man King Khain trusted implicitly, and the court rumor was that this trust was founded in a love beyond what men were permitted to have between one another.

Eoghan himself had seen nothing to give legs to such a slight against his father, but it was also said that Khain's love for Oldwin was what prevented him from executing him when the time came to exact his punishment.

But this was where Eoghan and his father were different. Khain had banished the man for speaking his truth and failing to see others. Eoghan understood that magic was capricious, and that to punish one for what they didn't see was to cut oneself off from what they could. Assyria used to say, don't sever your toes because they are ugly, for there are other beauties one can possess but only one way to balance.

The guards pushed Oldwin through the double doors of Eoghan's chamber. He heard him coming, the loud echoes of chains dragging the floors.

"Unlock his chains," Eoghan commanded.

"Your Grace?" one guard asked, voice quaking. The fear of this court, this kingdom, sustained him. Protected him. But it came at a cost. Not one here would ever speak plainly, for fear of being thrown into the White Sea.

To be fair, there was a precedent for this.

"If I was not certain, I would not have said it," Eoghan replied.

"But, sir, the sorcerer—"

"Possesses magic? Yes, as sorcerers do. No great secret there. Had he the power to break from the sky dungeon, he would have. He isn't that kind of sorcerer." Eoghan chided himself for wasting so many words on a guard, but he was not only saying them for the faceless man asking him petulant questions.

When Assana broached the suggestion about bringing Oldwin back into court, he'd at first slapped her for speaking out of turn, and then tore the idea to pieces, searching within his own words for a good reason *not* to do precisely that. He needed counsel. This, he'd never openly admit, but he was not unaware of his own failings. He would kill any man bold enough to point them out—or have them killed, as his precarious, weakened muscles were incapable of wielding a sword—but it didn't mean he was oblivious to them.

A seer didn't see everything. But what Oldwin *had* seen had been a boon to Khain.

It could be a boon to Eoghan.

"Now leave us," he said.

The guards both wore panic at the suggestion, but neither asked what they wanted to ask. Instead, they did as bidden, and, bowing, exited the doors.

"Should I leave as well, husband?" Assana asked.

Eoghan began to nod, but then thought better of it. It had been Assana's idea to return Oldwin to the king's side. It would be her downfall if this failed. "No. Stay."

She bowed and stepped to the side. As she dipped into the shadows, he caught a glimpse of the purple at the outside of her left eye. Perhaps he'd gone too far this last time. He hadn't realized he had the strength capable of it. Once she was with child, he would need to practice more caution. His father taught him that, if nothing else. *Your hands belong on your wife. Women know no other way but the fist. But not when she grows life. When a child grows within, the vessel is sacred.*

Oldwin had served Khain, and Fynne before him. And if the word of both men could be trusted, he'd served all the kings before them, too. Had been, they said, on one of the ships that crashed against the rocky shore of Duncarrow, hundreds of years past.

He looked no older than forty, despite how he hunched forward, thinning hair greasy and matted. A good bath should fix that and make him once again fit for court.

What court? He heard Correen's mawkish voice say in his head.

"Wife. Give the man some wine."

Assana nodded and flitted to the small table in the corner. She tilted the decanter, pouring two glasses, which she handed to both men, taking none for herself.

Oldwin sniffed the garnet liquid.

"If I wanted to poison you, I'd not sully my own chambers to do it."

Oldwin looked up. His crystal blue eyes were startling. Had they always been so clear? "Forgive me, Your Grace. Only it has been far too long since the rich scent has tickled my nose, and I wish to enjoy the moment."

Eoghan almost smiled. "You may sit."

"I have been sitting for too many years, Your Grace."

Eoghan lifted both hands in a shrug. "Do you know why I've summoned you?"

"Your wife has shared little with me."

It pleased Eoghan the sorcerer didn't refer to Assana as queen. Already he understood this world, small but powerful, his forebears had built upon the rocks of Duncarrow, better than Aiden or any other man of the kingdom. "My wife already possesses more wisdom than her father. And, I am learning, even women can have fair ideas, despite themselves."

Oldwin grinned. "If you look to women for council, you most definitely have need of my service."

"I have no need of anything," Eoghan snapped. "Yet I can see the wisdom in having one who shares my blood, who understands the world we have come from and not the one we landed in and have attempted, and often failed, to turn to our ways."

"Most of the men who came before you understood it wasn't necessary to subjugate the kingdom, only to subdue them."

"I have no intentions of subjugating anyone! Save for a few bearing certain names," Eoghan said. He paced the chamber floor, annoyed with Oldwin's familiarity with his words. For a man who had spent years in a cell, he was perhaps a little too comfortable here. "But if Aiden thought himself capable of besting me, there will be more who share this belief."

"You were right to imprison him."

"I don't require your approval."

Oldwin bowed his head. "Apologies. I speak from many lifetimes of serving the Rhiagain kings, and those who failed to address threats against their crown lived to regret it."

"Many lifetimes," Eoghan muttered. He hadn't decided if he believed in the man's immortality, but his father certainly had. Khain spoke of knowing Oldwin from when he was a small boy, and his father, too, had been raised with him. He didn't like to think about it. It disconcerted him. "Then why do you not suggest I have him killed?"

"He may be of better use to you alive. For now."

"What kind of use?"

Assana spoke up. Her voice squeaked like a tiny mouse. "His men don't know he's dead. They will be all over the Westerlands, keeping them in line. They will do so until he commands them to stop."

"Hmph," Eoghan said. He should chide her for speaking out of turn. It's what his father would have done. But his father had also left all of Eoghan's rearing to the hands of two cunning women, and if he'd learned anything from that experience—aside from his father's disdain for his own sons—it had been that women, though not as useful as men, could, occasionally, bring something unique to a situation.

"Your wife is right. She must get her head for the business of men from her father. Even if he is a traitor."

Assana lowered her eyes to the floor.

"And? Is that your counsel, Oldwin?"

"There are more reasons than one to keep them in line. You executed their lord, for committing no crime."

"For a seer, you see very little, apparently. Aiden conceived of that foolishness all on his own."

"And that will not matter in the eyes of the kingdom. When Aiden laid Rowanwen at your feet at springtide, he became your man. They will believe he acted under your command."

Eoghan's mouth parted in horror. This was what he'd been afraid of when Aiden rolled Lord Warwick's head across the stones. "Well, he did not. Though Lady Blackwood deserves that and more for what she's done."

"Word will have reached the kingdom that she has escaped. Her men will rise to serve her. To avenge her." Oldwin set his wine glass aside and folded his hands. "Let Aiden's men do the labor of guarding and watching the Westerlands."

Eoghan turned toward the window. "You still see some, then."

"Stone walls are not enough to quiet the voices I was born with. I will die with them."

"My father nearly killed you for them."

"I informed your father of every vision I received from these voices. But I could not share the ones I never had."

Eoghan spun back around. "So you saw nothing of the boy, Dain, living and thriving? Nothing at all?"

"I regret I did not," Oldwin replied. "But I was gifted a vision of him much later, once your father had already decided my fate."

Eoghan took several steps closer, but stopped. The foul scent rolling off the sorcerer turned his belly. "And did you share what you saw with him then?"

"How could I? He left me to rot. Had he visited me, I would have."

Assana sprang to life when Eoghan snapped his fingers and pointed for her to refill the man's wine.

"You will tell me now, then, what my father never heard."

Oldwin accepted his wine and emptied half the glass before speaking. His tongue traveled across the residual drops on his lips as he searched his thoughts. "It is true. Dain yet lives, or he did, when last the voices spoke to me, which has been some years now, at least where he is concerned."

"And what did they say? These voices?"

"That Dain knows not who he is, or where he comes from. He was raised in ignorance and will remain in ignorance. That secret died with your father and with the servant who failed to kill the boy when he had the chance."

"It didn't die with anyone. You know it. I know it. Now my wife does."

Oldwin smiled. "You could kill us to protect it. That remains an option."

"I yet might," Eoghan replied. "You say Dain bears a new name. What is it?"

"That I have not seen, or heard. I have not had news of him in years. It's possible he died, just much later than your father intended."

"Do you believe that?"

"I believe we must always be prepared for all outcomes," Oldwin said with a wide grin. His yellowed teeth sent chills through Eoghan. "He may be dead. We should proceed as if he is not."

Eoghan nodded. Something about the old sorcerer unsettled him. He didn't want him standing there anymore, boring holes with his eyes and his ancient judgment. But he could see what his father could not: Oldwin's usefulness was not yet spent.

"Your prior chambers have been turned into a pile of cobwebs and old furniture. You may make the arrangements to have them restored as you please."

Oldwin bowed low. "Your Grace."

"There is one more condition of your freedom. I command you to tell me something that no one else in Duncarrow knows. No small thing, either. Something... something you have never shared with anyone else. No meaningless dangle, either. Something of importance to you."

"A man is not so easily parted with his secrets, sir."

Eoghan laughed. "You are no man, Oldwin. Tell me, if you value freedom and service again. Or don't, if lifetimes in the sky dungeon suit you better."

Assana wore the anxious look of a cornered animal. Oldwin's failure would be her own.

Another man might ask her to leave. Letting her stay was no matter of love. It was rather a reminder that she had brought this man to him and was responsible for his words, his actions. She would've possibly fared better by leaving. It would depend on what Oldwin said next.

"Ilynglass." He almost sighed the word. "Does that name mean anything to you?"

"No. Should it?"

"It will now. Ilynglass is where the Rhiagains come from, Your Grace. The world left behind when we arrived on these shores and Carrow Rhiagain named them for himself. He nearly named this hunk of rocks Ilynglass. Had he, things may have been very different for the Rhiagains, who were accepted as kings and gods only for the unique magic, magic so different from the men of this kingdom. For the mystery that arrived with us that fateful day. It was me who advised Carrow to keep it hidden in his heart. To bury it away and create, in its place, a mythology of our choosing. And while there are others who once knew this, they are all long dead. All but me."

"Ilynglass. What a lovely word. I've never heard another like it," Assana whispered.

"Never speak it aloud!" Oldwin said. "Never share it beyond this room. This crown is woven together by what the kingdom does not know about us. To discover such things is to unravel it all, and once apart, it can never again be put back together."

ASSANA EXHALED as Oldwin departed the chambers, decidedly more free than he'd entered them. She'd gambled on the sorcerer. Had he failed the test with Eoghan, she would've been the one standing at the cliff's edge, whispering goodbye to the remnants of her short and disappointing life.

But Eoghan seemed pleased. Something else, as well. Relieved. He'd been burdened by the expectations of kingship, lacking the experience and wisdom to combat his shortcomings. She'd seen this desperation in him. The idea of restoring Oldwin had been born of it.

Assana would need to watch the sorcerer carefully. Eoghan might not have picked up on the lie, but she hailed from a family of professional prevaricators. Whether the lie was the beautiful word itself, Ilynglass, or the matter of its secrecy to others, Oldwin's first act of service to his new king had been deception.

Eoghan might fall for it, but she would not so easily be trapped in the wily creature's web.

She prepared to dismiss herself, but Eoghan stopped her.

"Your father," he said. "You haven't once asked for mercy on his behalf."

"No, husband."

"I'd like you to tell me why." He was once more the petulant child, stumbling, demanding. The one who'd left her painted with bruises, in his confused cruelty of failed lovemaking.

"I am wife to the king first, before all else," Assana said, treading the space of her words with great caution. She didn't trust the easy way he'd dealt with her on the matter of Oldwin.

"Yet you are also his daughter."

"I am my mother's daughter," Assana said proudly, before she could consider whether the words were the right ones. "And my father needs to remember his place in this kingdom. He'll do so better from a prison cell."

Eoghan let her words wash over him. He looked away, nodding.

With a raise of his hand, she was dismissed.

6

THE FLAME

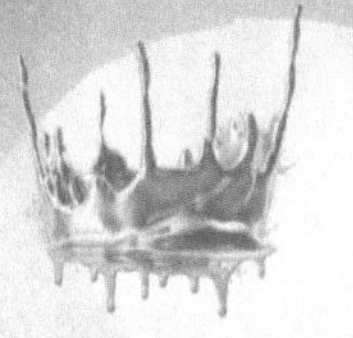

Light pink petals rained on Ember's face as she reached the peak of her desire. She twined her fingers through Marsh's soft hair, pressing his face down as she climbed over the edge of her pleasure and came undone.

She fell back against the lone lump of grass protruding through the snow, looking up at the cherries strewn about the tree, struggling for breath. Marsh's grinning face beamed up at her with pride.

"Where did you learn *that*?"

"I don't suppose you'd believe I was born with such instincts?"

"I would not."

Marsh wiped his mouth on the back of his hand and settled back, sitting on his heels. "The armorer's kid. Angus?"

"Argus," Ember said.

"He evidently stays quite busy, and his business isn't with the chain mail."

Ember laughed as she searched around for her clothing. "How does something like this even come up in your interactions? Armor boy, can you craft me a helmet, and while you're at it, lessons on your expertise in pleasuring ladies?"

Marsh scrambled to his feet. He picked stray bits of clothes from the grass of the Wintergarden and dropped them by her. He no longer winced in pain at simple tasks, thanks to Aylen's healing of his arm the bear had mangled. It was as if that strange night had never happened now, at least to Marsh. "Better you don't know." He reached for another piece, but stopped, frowning.

"What is it?"

"That Ravenwood boy."

"Alasyr," Ember said, though the confirmation was unnecessary. It was always Alasyr. If he wasn't circling Wulfsgate Keep, he was hovering. And always, it seemed, wherever she was. He never took a day off. If she didn't know better, she'd think he was stalking her, like prey.

"I'm tired of it. I'm going to say something."

Ember reached for his arm. "No. Don't. He's just angry, is all."

"He isn't the only one!"

"You would have your own anger if your sister, Lyria, disappeared. And you might direct that anger at those you felt were responsible."

Marsh stopped glaring at the raven and looked down. "And are they? The Derehams? Responsible?"

"Everyone wants someone to blame for their hurts, Marsh. It isn't always so tidy. Would you say Drystan is responsible, for loving her? That takes from Ravenna any power over her own choices. Or Lord and Lady Dereham for not seeing it and stopping them? I'd say they've had their share of things on their mind lately."

Marsh pointed. "Someone should tell *him* that."

Ember pulled herself up with his hand. She kissed the corner of his mouth. "Fine. I will."

"What? No, I didn't mean you. Stay away from him, Ember. He's dangerous."

"You've seen what I can do. It comes from the same place."

Marsh twined his fingers through hers, tightening. "I'm serious."

Ember unlaced the bond. "I am too, Marsh. Alasyr lingers because he has unsettled business. And while I would love to forget the world and disappear with you in the Wintergarden forever, I must remember I have my own." She looked back toward the raven. "He reminds me of that. I see his tenacity and I wonder how I've lost mine."

Marsh pulled her in for a kiss. "You haven't," he whispered through their joined lips. "You are still the same Ember."

Ember pressed her forehead to his and then drew away from the embrace. She peered over her shoulder at Alasyr, who perched upon a branch, waiting. "If that's true, then I have to prove it. I came here for direction, and all I've done is linger with you. Don't look at me like that. I've enjoyed every second, you know I have. But that isn't why we've come here. To languish. I've let others decide whether I should see my mother. I didn't come here for anyone to tell me what I can and cannot do."

"What are you saying?"

"Go on. I'll meet you inside. I have something to say to the raven prince, and then you and I will prepare for a trip over the pass."

Asherley pulled back the string on her bow. The arrow's tip followed the raven dancing across the sky, controlled by her focus, restrained only by her curiosity. The raven came to a fluttering halt upon a snowy branch. White dust shimmered, disappearing into the void of the forest floor far below.

Her fingers twitched. Which Ravenwood was this? It wasn't the first to circle the air above Torrin's Pass, and as she had more sightings of them, she could no longer pretend it was coincidence. Their position was compromised now, depending on what motivated the Ravenwoods.

None had revealed their true form. She'd heard that, when a Ravenwood died, their raven form disappeared and they were as a man again. Releasing the arrow would be one answer to her question, then.

"Are you going to kill that bird, Lady Asherley?"

The small voice of Stefan stayed her hand. "No, little one. I was only practicing my aim."

"Sir Wyat is teaching me to shoot."

"I know he is. Is your aim improving?"

Stefan shrugged. "I still can't hit anything."

Asherley dropped the bow to her side and knelt down. "When you are king, you will have many men eager and willing to fire their own arrows at your pleasure."

Stefan's face contorted as he considered this. "Mother says we must learn to do for ourselves."

Asherley stood again, eyes returning to the raven. She couldn't lose sight of the little spy. "Your mother is very wise. A less clever woman would not have kept you both alive in that dungeon, all those years. She's right, Stefan. Learn to do for yourself, so that when you choose to have others do for you, you know that command comes not from ineptitude but authority."

"I don't know what that means."

"You will." The raven cawed, flapping its wings. Taunting. "Now, go. I'll be back inside shortly."

She turned to watch him scamper off, and when she returned her gaze to the branch, the raven was gone. She regretted not loosing her arrow. It might not provide answers as to why the Ravenwoods had been spying on them, but it would've quelled the awful sense of being powerless against it.

There was no worse feeling to Asherley, and she'd built the whole of her life around avoiding circumstances where she had no choice but to surrender her power. Even in Duncarrow, she'd been in control of her destiny. She'd never doubted her sway over the king, only the potency and immediacy of her charm. She'd *chosen* to go away with him, seeing a future where the truth that would save the kingdom could be found only at Duncarrow. Finding that truth had empowered her further, but somewhere on the voyage away from those rocky shores, she'd lost her control.

Assyria was calling all the moves. It was Assyria who picked Eastport as their destination. Assyria who ordered the ship and contents sunk into the sea to keep the Rhiagain men off their trail. Assyria who turned on those who had been most loyal, her servants, and slit their throats with her own hand.

Assyria who was now, Asherley suspected, plotting behind their backs with Lord Warwick.

Scholar Edevane was the one who led them to the cave, deposited into a blind turn deep in Torrin's Pass. So high only the ravens could spot them. His name wasn't on Eoghan's list of traitors, for though he'd served Darrick Rhiagain with loyalty, when Darrick was sent to the Wastelands, Edevane returned to his home, and his life as a scholar of Oldcastle. His name slipped away from the tongues that would tie the men together, and he garnered great respect for his commitment to the Resplendent Reliquary. All the while plotting with Assyria, biding their time. When he rode into Wulfsgate requesting an audience with the Lady of the Northerlands, his strong reputation had made it no challenging matter to gain entrance.

Since then, Gretchen sent her son and daughter-in-law to deliver supplies, but they, too, awaited direction on the matter of Darrick. Asherley understood Assyria's impatience to move, to take action, but also feared it would be what got them all killed.

She ducked into a patch of bushes and drank from the vial

Aylen had brought her on the first trip. Asherley had no cause to think she was with child, but nor did she have any intention of allowing such horrors to sneak up on her. *Drink the first vial in its entirety right away. Then, two sips from the second vial every evening, for a fortnight, and the matter is settled.*

It wasn't the same root women used in the Westerlands. The vile, bitter taste of the boiled leaves turned her stomach. But she'd grow no Rhiagain in her womb.

But Aylen had brought questions with her as well. *I must ask... not for my own curiosity, but for the sake of your life, Lady Blackwood. Is the man you are trying to rid from your body's memory a Rhiagain?*

The man is King Eoghan.

Aylen had tried to hide her shock at this, but failed miserably. *I see. Well, I ask because in my studies at the Sepulchre, I came across a rare and terrible disease, a fatal one, passed by some Rhiagain men to women they share intimate relations with. I wish I could tell you there was a cure, but there isn't. Not beyond Duncarrow, that is. It is not... it is not for certain that one will be afflicted by it, but it is almost for certain that one will eventually succumb to it if they do.*

Asherley read into the woman's whispers then, and she saw how and why the Magi had come upon such knowledge. She fought her tears as she heard Aylen's memories of Hollyn's final moments; Aylen's refusal to leave her side until the very last.

I am fine, Lady Dereham. I've had no illness other than my own restlessness. And you must let go of your guilt for not being able to save Hollyn. Forgive me, also, for reading your whispers. I know you'd take this secret to your tomb, but I would not be denied the honor of embracing the woman who cared for my eldest daughter until her last breath.

Asherley knew Hollyn was dead before reading Aylen's whispers. She sensed the loss of her own blood kin, the void where Hollyn's force had once lived in her heart. But she'd resigned herself to this loss long before it came to pass, and she had three other children, and a husband, to keep safe. Ember was in Wulfs-gate, which was precisely where Asherley had hoped she'd go. Brandyn was safe at the Sepulchre. It was only Gabi still lost to her, but she still sensed the vibrance of her youngest burning bright.

Ember, her mirror. The flame of her heart. She'd led them all. It should have always been Ember to lead when Asherley's promise was spent, and now, she'd decided, it would be. Byrne would understand why she changed her mind and returned the Wester-lands to a woman's rule. He knew Ember's fire better than anyone.

"Ignore the ravens," Assyria said.

"There are no ravens."

"Not anymore. You scared them off."

"I haven't harmed a single one. They are my blood."

"I know," Assyria said. "That's how you see it. To them, you are the progeny of a defector."

"Hmph." Asherley tightened her jaw.

"I may not possess your ability to read whispers, Lady Black-wood, but I know the look of a woman conflicted."

"Your powers of observation are without match, Princess."

Assyria grunted a laugh. "You question our alliance. You've questioned it for a while."

"We are both eager for action," Asherley said. "But you're ready to risk the lives of everyone for it, and I am not."

Assyria turned to face her. "You are cunning and clever, Lady Blackwood. I admired you from afar for many years before meeting you, and I was not disappointed. I see a woman who, like me, knows her power is not limited to what a man would give her. But if it were not for me, Darrick would be dead. You would still be on Duncarrow. Anabella and Stefan would be wasting away in the sky dungeon, or even dead, for Correen had already planted this seed in Eoghan's mind, and it was taking bloom. Your control of my brother was a delight to watch, but for all your hold on him, you had no power. I put in years, and you, days. My years earned his trust, and that trust allowed me to secret us away from that wretched place."

"I would deny none of that."

"And yet?"

"And yet, I fear your recklessness will not always lead to such successes. The Rhiagains have kept their world as small as Duncarrow. There, you are a god. Here, you are reviled. This world is not your world."

Assyria ran a finger through Asherley's dark hair. "Fear will bind you, Asherley. It will utterly stifle you, until there's nothing left but the memory of what you could have been."

"Spare me your pretty words. I fear very little, and you know it."

"You fear for the lives of those you don't even know. Who is Anabella to you? Ransom? Scholar Edevane?"

Asherley spun on her. "Nothing at all until you decided you needed me. And that is a curious thing, is it not? That for all your years with the king and his trust it was a lady of the realm you required to actually see it through?" Asherley shook her head. "But now? Now, they're my charge, and I have no choice but to concern myself with their fate."

"I have spent years of my life protecting Anabella and Stefan. They were never nothing to me. Remember that when you let your mind wander on my intentions," Assyria said before returning to the cave.

"What are you doing?" Alasyr demanded. "I have no desire to speak with you."

"But you do. Obviously." Ember crunched through the snow, keeping her distance but narrowing the gap. She wrapped her arms over her chest, tucking her gloved fingers under her arms.

"I do *not*."

"What other explanation could there be for your relentless stalking of me?"

"My being here has nothing to do with you. I've told you my reasons. Is it my fault you're incapable of grasping them?"

"You have," Ember said. "Your sister. Who isn't here."

"Not here, but they know where she is."

"Do you think if the Derehams knew where she was, they wouldn't have brought their own children home by now?" Ember asked. "They live with their worry, too, but they don't charge up to The Rookery demanding answers."

"One cannot charge The Rookery. There is only flight."

"Whatever."

Alasyr pressed his lips tight in anger. He pulled back whatever response he had for her and changed direction, nodding behind her. "Your lover is watching."

"Seems only fair, since you've been watching us."

"Rutting like beasts in the garden for anyone to see. Hardly my fault for seeing it."

Ember grinned. "You should try it."

Alasyr sneered, diverting his eyes. "Whenever I see you, it becomes ever clearer what foul things happen when you mix our pure blood with the sludge of man."

Ember took a step closer. "Your lot tell other Ravenwoods they'll lose their magic when they leave. But we all have it. Me. My sisters, and brother. My mother. Though I never met my great-great-grandmother, Rhosyn, we still speak of her power."

"Fly away, then. Show me."

"What if I did?"

"Then do it, and stop speaking in mysteries."

Ember hid the burgeoning frown. He'd presented a conundrum she hadn't solved yet. It was known that the closer to Midnight Crest, the more potent the magic of one with Ravenwood blood. Rhosyn herself was clipped from flight in the Westerlands, but upon return, on a visit to Wulfsgate, again found her wings.

So where was Ember's? If she could only find her raven form, she could fly to her mother and wouldn't need the Derehams.

"See?" Alasyr grinned, pleased. "Your blood is tainted. Unclean. What you have is an abomination, not a gift."

"Your life must be very sad, Alasyr Ravenwood, if your delights are limited to the deficiencies of others," Ember said. "Is there really nothing else that brings you joy?"

"Ravenna," Alasyr replied, head raised in defiance of her charge. "Ravenna brought me joy. All of it."

Ember nodded sadly. "What a burden she must have borne for you, then." She pointed behind her. "I have my own problems to contend with now. Goodbye. Or, as the Northerlanders say, 'I'll see you at first snow.'"

"It always snows. How would one know the first?"

Ember laughed. "Perhaps the expression doesn't mean what I think it does, then."

"Careful," Gretchen warned. "Your father is back from his ride with Alric."

Christian stifled a sigh. "I don't like keeping things from him."

"You know why we do."

"Why *you* do." Christian leaned against the hearth. "I understand you've been unhappy with some of his choices."

"In particular," Gretchen said, "the one involving selling your sister away like cattle. There's also the matter of his witlessness causing your brother to be taken away to Duncarrow in chains."

"But Pieter is safe now."

"Your father gets no credit for this."

Christian grimaced. "I don't like it, either. Had I been here, I would have tried with all my power to dissuade him from sending Lisbet."

"And your pleas would have fallen upon a man with no ears to hear. Holden is as stubborn as he is a fool." Gretchen pressed her lips tight. "I love your father, Christian. But his foolishness could be borne when it didn't put my children in danger. I cannot forgive or look past that."

"But he's already agreed to you and your way of doing things. He's accepted your leadership on recent matters. As the lord of the Northerlands, that's no small thing. It isn't right to cut him out entirely." He paused before saying the next. "And to do so may make him less than amenable to continuing an arrangement he has no legal obligation to hold to."

Gretchen turned away. "You've been away a long time, Christian. A lot has changed here."

"Some has changed. He has not. You have not." Christian wanted to approach his mother, to afford her some small, warm gesture, but the ice between them was still melting. "I offered him Iceborne. He wouldn't accept."

"Did you really expect him to?" She laughed. "You think I'm stubborn about your future, but it's your father who cannot accept truths."

"Still, I won't lie to him."

"Did I ask you to lie?" she said into the darkness.

"I don't know what you're asking."

"I ask nothing of you," Gretchen hissed. "I know better."

The words stung, and she seemed to know it, because she turned immediately, apology burning in her eyes. "Forgive me, Son. I didn't mean it."

"You did," Christian said. He feigned a smile. "It's all right, Mother. I understand why you feel as you do. I deserve it."

Gretchen shook her head. "I once thought so, but as I look

around me, at what has become of our family, I find myself instead envious of you."

"Of me? You know I'm on banishment from the Sepulchre, my home?"

"Wulfsgate is your home," Gretchen said. "Whether you choose it or not. And though I know you may not recognize the world you left, you must trust me when I tell you that your father will, despite his best intentions, impair our efforts and put many lives at risk."

"So you intend to send another scout to Khallum, then? And not wait for him to send his own?"

"You and Aylen said yourselves; the situation in the cave grows tenuous. Khallum may be content to wait, but they are not. And I fear what will happen if the two groups come out of accord."

"Aylen says it's not Lady Blackwood, but Princess Assyria who struggles with inaction."

Gretchen laughed with a light sneer. "Lady Blackwood struggles too, I assure you, she just possesses a deeper wisdom to prevent poor decisions from risking everything she's worked for. And when she learns what befell Byrne, what little patience she possesses will implode."

"We haven't said a word."

"It isn't what you say. It's what you think."

"I know, Mother. You told us about the whispers. We've been cautious."

Gretchen's suspicious gaze lingered on him longer than he liked.

"It's done. I already sent the scout," she said. "So tell him, if you like. He's too late to stop it."

His mother left the room before he could think of what to say. Almost right away, someone else joined him.

Emberley.

"Wipe the fear off your face, Christian. I don't care about the scout. Who would I tell?"

Christian downed the last of his mother's wine and set the glass down a little too hard on the table. "I know your mother is a reader of whispers, but it's impolite to listen in on conversations that don't include you."

Ember shrugged. "It's not my fault the two of you couldn't control your voices. I didn't come here to talk about Lady Gretchen sneaking around behind Lord Holden's back. I came to talk about my mother."

"I told you I'm happy to bring her a note from you, or any other gifts, as we've been doing. Leave them with Aylen." Christian made toward the great hall, but she was right behind him.

"She doesn't want my notes. She wants me."

Christian stopped, halting unintentionally near the great woven tapestry of Torrin's Pass. He hoped she didn't see the flicker of familiarity and guilt. "What she wants is for you to be safe. And you are. *Here.* Give her one less thing to worry about."

"Hmph," Ember said. "Do you know my mother? I do. Well. Has she asked after me? Asked to see me? Don't lie."

Christian sighed and turned his head to the side.

"So you can take me with you next time you go, or I'll ask my new friend Alasyr Ravenwood to scour the whole of the Northerlands and tell me where I can find her."

Christian's mouth dropped. "You are not actually friends with Alasyr Ravenwood?"

"Now you're interested."

Christian leaned in, lowering his voice. "Ember, you're a wise girl. So you should know, there's no good that can come from befriending him. He's after revenge, not companionship."

"He seems to think I can aid him in both regards."

"He asked you to seek revenge on his behalf?"

"No," Ember said after a long silence. "Nor would I help him.

But it suits me he thinks I might. Because I *will* ask for his aid, Christian, if you will not offer your own."

Christian looked ahead and behind him to ensure no one else had joined them in the long hall. "If I say yes, you tell no one. Not Marsh. Not your new sorcerer friend. Definitely not my mother. She'll be furious once she realizes."

"You have my word."

"And you bury every bit of sorrow for your father somewhere deep, somewhere even your mother cannot go with her reading of whispers, because she doesn't know he's dead."

Ember's brows lifted. "No one has told her?"

"No one has told her. No one *will* tell her, until it is safe to do so," Christian said. The fire died away from his words, and he softened. "I know she's your mother. You're still a child. This must be hard for you."

The look Ember gave him could've melted the snow in the tapestry behind him. "I'm not a child, Lord Dereham. But my sister was, when she died. She had the sense of a babe. My mother knew it, and that's why she chose me to lead us out of danger. She knew Hollyn was dying. And now that Hollyn is dead, it will be me, just as it was me who delivered the others toward safekeeping, who will look her in the eye and deliver that truth."

7

THE ROOKERY

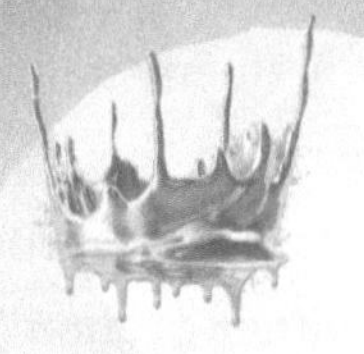

Alasyr Ravenwood thundered through the starlit halls of The Rookery, chaos resounding in every knock of his heavy boots against the dampened stone.

He had never, in all his life, felt such powerful *rage*. It had so many sources he knew not where to best direct it. Ravenna. His mother, father. The Derehams. That *girl* with the tainted blood and barbed tongue in Wulfsgate.

How was he the only one who still concerned himself with Ravenna's fate? The search for her, if one could call it that, had been haphazard and brief. How quickly the conversation had shifted from finding her to repudiating her. All efforts were now on preparing Ryandyr to take her place. Ryandyr! She was a child, and Ravenna was... was...

Alasyr leaned over the balustrade and launched a silent scream into the howling wind.

"Your anger will first consume you. Then destroy you."

Alasyr froze at the sound of his father's voice.

"I see you take flight and soar down to the world of men, in search of answers. You'll find none, Alasyr. Only pain."

He tried to speak, to defend himself, but it was as if his mouth was bound with rope.

A cold hand settled between the blades of his shoulders. "Ryandyr will make a fine High Priestess, and you will cast your lot once more. I cannot say for sure whether the magic is so fickle, but I've always believed it prefers the brothers to the men less closely related. It certainly helped me."

Alasyr grimaced without turning. He found his words. "Do not worry after me, Father. I will do my duty."

"You wish you could perform this duty with Ravenna."

Alasyr didn't trust his father. He trusted his mother even less. Whatever faith he had in either of them was thrown aside at their quickness to abandon Ravenna. "I wish Ravenna was still here, and that her leaving hadn't torn us apart."

"Torn us apart?" Argentyn dropped his hand and laughed. "She has torn only herself apart, with her childish whims. We know where your sister is, just as you do. She chose that fate for herself, and there is no returning from such a choice. That is our way. She knew this."

"You know where she is?"

"I know with whom she has gone, and that is enough for me."

Alasyr half turned. "Why allow such a slight from the Derehams to go unanswered?"

"You know why." Argentyn stepped forward and wrapped his fingers around the damp stone edge. "I will not toss aside an alliance that has aided us for centuries for your sister. For anyone. Nor will your mother. And I daresay, neither will the Derehams. We have both lost our heirs, and are doing what's needed to rectify that. We are, for once, united in something."

"So you would not take her back, if she returned?"

Argentyn's cheekbones flexed as he swallowed. "Not unless she was dragged wounded and dying from the lair of a wulf to refute what I know to be true."

"But what if you and Mother are wrong? And she didn't leave willingly?"

"We've discussed this, Alasyr. It is not wrong for you to love your kin, but dwelling on the actions of a traitor will tempt you to be one as well."

"Father, that is not—"

Argentyn's smile was ice. "Channel what remains of your love into looking forward. For Ravenna ceased to exist when she chose life with man over a life of greatness."

Alasyr dropped his eyes. "Yes, Father."

ADYNORA STROKED the silver hair of the midnight goat. Her jeweled fingers were a symphony of shimmering sounds as she ran them down the long, groomed mane of the only four-legged creature native this high in the Northerland Range.

Ice encased the Courtyard of Regents. It was like this most of the year. The trees had only several short weeks to bloom and show the world their gift of life, and then they again retreated, lying dormant beneath the long-reigning hand of winter, until at last their time came again. There were over a hundred ice-covered trees painting the courtyard. Despite this, it was the warmest place beyond the keep. Someone once told Varinya the thick ice created an insular barrier against the icy wind and snow. One of the men. She'd paid him little regard.

"You lead with fear, with such suppositions," Adynora said. Her dark hair sparkled against the canvas of white. Varinya had never seen a woman more beautiful than her mother. And now, living in the glory of her beloved First Death—a retirement, men might call it, though men retired not in their prime but in elder age —she could revel in its absolute precision.

"You know that is *not* my intent, Mother," Varinya replied

smoothly. "I have faith in Ryandyr. She's my daughter, as Ravenna is."

"Was."

Varinya bit back a sigh. Repeating the word came with a bitter taste in her mouth. "Was. And I know Ryandyr will make a fine High Priestess. It is only the magic of firstborn daughters I wish I understood better."

"Varinya, magic is not for us to understand. That is at the core of its nature. How could we worship something that we could grasp within our minds? We are meant to have faith in it, not to dissect it and define it in the space of the words we are granted."

"So you're not worried then? That she will not experience the visions, because she was not first?"

"I am not," Adynora said. She ran her palm along the soft chin of the goat. "For it was magic that prepared Ravenna and it will be magic that prepares Ryandyr."

"Of course. You're right." Varinya nodded, eager to show her mother she was only making discussion, not experiencing doubt. "Is there precedent for this? Have you heard tell of any firstborns who defected?"

Adynora leveled a strange gaze at her daughter. "You tell me. You've seen our histories, same as all firstborn daughters."

Varinya sputtered. Closed her mouth. Adynora had caught her amidst a conundrum lacking answers. The gift of a vision of their histories was bestowed only upon the firstborn daughter of the High Priestess, and it was through these women that their past lived on into their future. Through them, and them alone.

But Varinya had never had her vision.

She dared never even think of this terrible truth, for if her mother were to know this, there would be horrifying consequences. She'd faithfully lied when Adynora asked her if she had at last seen the histories, almost two decades earlier.

Yes, mother.

And?

And they are glorious.

Yes, daughter. That they are.

And that was all. No discussion, comparing of stories, examining of pasts. Adynora seemed just as keen on moving on, pleased with the confirmation, desiring nothing more. They never spoke of it again.

Varinya had let Ravenna tell the same lie, except Varinya couldn't hide her doubt at her daughter's deception. Perhaps it was her own failure, which she had hoped would die with her. It terrified her she might have passed this defect on to Ravenna, who had such promise. Ravenna had a fire in her that burned hotter than it should, but that fire had stirred something in Varinya, too. It had melted the icy prison encasing her heart, keeping it safe, and she'd loved her daughter, beyond what was allowed.

And now Ravenna was gone. Driven away by more than the promise of forbidden love, of that Varinya was certain. Ravenna had seen reflected in her mother's eyes a terrible failure and had fled in horror, knowing if she stayed she might be cast out, anyway.

There was no way now to tell her that Varinya would have never allowed that to pass. Had there been no other choice, she would've beseeched Ravenna and confessed her own awful truth, and bade her tell the same lie. For Varinya had reigned well as High Priestess. Visions or no. Ravenna would have done do the same.

The worst agony of all was the face she had to wear that wasn't her own. The one who didn't miss Ravenna, who had effectively and succinctly cauterized her love. Who didn't agonize, night after night, over a way to bring her home, to make it all right.

"My darling," Adynora said. "I'm almost grateful I can't read your mind right now. But please don't trouble yourself with questions lacking satisfying answers. As the High Priestess, you have done your duty by Midnight Crest and the Ravenwood heritage.

You have delivered us four daughters, which is fortuitous in the present condition we find ourselves. And all of this is to earn the right to our First Death. Your First Death *is* your life, Varinya. Your reward; perhaps the only one you will ever have. It is your right to live, to be forgotten, to be a Ravenwood of your own choosing, and not the one chosen by magic. You spend these years preparing, and I am sorry for you, that Ravenna has prolonged what should have been yours in short order. But Ryandyr will make a fine High Priestess. And when she is delivered of her first daughter, you will join me, and there's much more we can discuss that isn't suitable for a former High Priestess to share with a current one."

Varinya looked up. "I look forward to that day, Mother. Where we can speak without the tethers of duty."

"Oh, my child. We will always have some tethers of duty. Such as the one in your heart still holding fast to Ravenna." Adynora looked off to the side with a light smile. "Argentyn will tell you that your love should die, but we know better, don't we? But there is no more you can do for Ravenna, Daughter. She has made her choice, forcing you to make yours. If magic is kind, Ravenna is happy. You may never know, and you must be satisfied with that."

"I understand, Mother. I have accepted it. It is only understanding it that eludes me."

Adynora laughed. "Why do you think the magic bids us intermarry? It is not *only* to protect the potency of our blood. It is so we are not foolish enough to think our hearts worthy of guiding!"

Varinya grinned despite her aching heart. "Yes, I can see the reason in that."

"Think no more on it," Adynora said. She rose, clucking at the goat, who disappeared beyond the trees of ice. "Ryandyr is your future. *Our* future. And I look forward to the day when you can join me in First Death and we can speak of those things you would like to say to me now but cannot."

Varinya released a painful breath when her mother disappeared back inside The Rookery. She felt as if she'd been holding it in her entire life.

She had years ahead yet before she could ask her mother the questions she needed answers to. And had Adynora asked these same things when she at last greeted her own First Death? Was it only then that Varinya could finally question the magic that held their world together so neatly?

If Varinya's dangerous suspicions about the visions were true, then their entire world was a lie. All of it. If no one had seen their past, then perhaps there *was* no glorious history of the Raven-woods. These visions were the fabric that held their delicate lives together; that predetermined leadership pass through the women only, and never the men.

Varinya prepared to stand and greet the rest of her day when two bony hands clamped down on her shoulders. She sucked in a hard, inward breath.

Argentyn's cold lips dribbled kisses across the back of her neck, as she tried desperately not to shudder.

Ravenna didn't know how fortunate she was, having a brother she loved. She may have turned her nose at having him in her bed, but there was a fondness that was beyond measure of value. Alasyr would have been a fine companion for her.

They'd wed Varinya to the same brother who'd found his plea-sure in torturing her, and once her husband, she exchanged her cries for smiles.

She held all the power in Midnight Crest, and none of the joy.

There was not a single person she could confide these things to.

Not even herself.

Alasyr waited until his father was long gone before taking flight. The path was almost too familiar now. He knew precisely where the wind would catch under his wings and float him across the air, and where he needed to dip below the clouds to begin his descent into the world of men.

He swooped in on the approach to Wulfsgate, nearing the vast and aptly named Wintergarden. He wished he wasn't so fascinated with the trees that bore vibrant fruit in midwinter, or the benches and gazebos beckoning the curious to come sit a spell and marvel in these wonders.

On the last bend, a lone figure came into view.

The girl.

He dropped in lower and settled upon the branch of a great, sprawling oak.

Watching.

8

RUSH RIDER

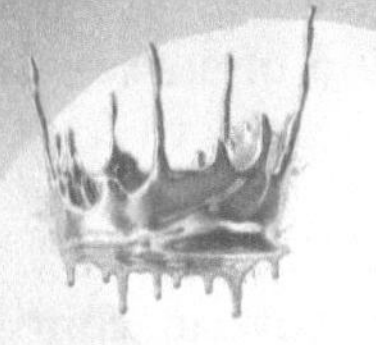

Corin Quinlanden spread his hands across the splintered cedar. He appeared to be greeting the world at the start of his day, as he did on more ordinary mornings, but this was not an ordinary morning. He had one eye on the rising sun, and the other on the insidious figure of the sorcerer Mortain.

Mortain went out to address the Medvedev each morning—he had his routine, too—but there was no peace in such a gesture. He raised his hands above his head and began whatever it was he did to renew his magic's hold. Because he did this every day, Corin had deduced that it was a necessary thing to maintain the unnatural control he had over the Saleen soldiers. He wondered how long it would hold without this daily ritual. If Mortain were to become detained.

Mads Waters watched the sorcerer with one hand upon his sword, ready to slice it through the flesh of anyone who dared disrupt. With him, a hundred other guards redirected to protection of the sorcerer for this short morning spell. A hundred guards not manning the keep of Arboriana.

"And? Has he started?" Yesenia asked from the lounger.

Corin turned. "Just now."

"Good. A half tick, then. Where is your brother's wife, anyway?"

"I'm here," Maeryn replied, appearing as she often did, as if unfurling from some nearby shadow.

"Guardian's cock," Yesenia hissed with an exhale. "Were you there all along?"

"No," Maeryn said. "Yes. Somewhat."

"Somewhat? What kind of answer is that? You either were, or you were not."

"My apologies, Lady Yesenia."

Maeryn pretended to cow in contrition. Corin knew better. There was nothing contrite or cowing about Maeryn Blackwood, peculiar though she was. But she and Yesenia had never gotten on. At first, he tried to understand the odd and sometimes blistering tension between them, but like many nuances of women, it fell beyond his comprehension.

"Lady Yesenia." Yesenia frowned, drawing a tight line with her lips. "*You* are the predominant lady of this house, Lady Maeryn. I ask only that you consider not sneaking around and planting your-self in dark corners unannounced. And now we've wasted precious seconds dealing with it." She turned her attention to her husband. "Tell her what you know, and quick."

Corin resisted the urge to return to his balcony to monitor Mortain. It was only during these brief morning rituals that the three dared be in one room together, alone. Only in these few minutes where Mads' eye was on the Medvedev and not the three prominent nobles of Whitechurch. Even Corin's own chambers with Yesenia were no longer private at most hours. Mortain stashed his guards everywhere. In every room, closet, corner. And that was only the keep. Corin hadn't been allowed into the city to witness the restrictions imposed upon the citizens, but he'd heard the main gates were under strict lockdown, allowing none in or out without special authority. Only those by air, the ravens, could enter and leave, and he had no doubt they intercepted every single one before final delivery.

Their gaolers didn't dare throw the lords and ladies of the Whitechurch into a prison, but they were prisoners nonetheless. Even Aiden, in all his cruelty, had never behaved this way toward his people. Corin didn't know if the orders came from his brother, or if Mads and Mortain had taken these measures on their own authority. They couldn't know because Aiden had gone silent from Duncarrow. Their last news of him had been the reports of his ship at port upon arrival to the island of the king.

"We must be cautious with our loyalties here," Corin began. "For we may be asking a man to give up his head if caught delivering truths to us."

"But you have heard? From Aiden?" Maeryn asked. She watched him in the most curious way. It made him feel as if he was standing before her in the nude.

"Not from Aiden," Corin replied. "But I have heard whispers repeated back to me. And at last I understand better why it seems my brother has fallen into Beyond."

"And? Is he dead?" Maeryn asked, stopping just short of licking her lips.

"I fear not," Corin replied. "But it would be more true to say no one knows whether he lives or dies, and that is the problem."

"The problem?" Maeryn repeated.

"Mads and Mortain have sent raven after raven to Duncarrow. None have been returned. Not from Aiden, and none from the king. Utter silence. And if others knew this, it would diminish the hold they have over both Reaches. They're doing all they can to keep this truth silenced."

Maeryn slinked against a tall chair across the room, sliding slowly down. "He's done it then."

"Done what?" Yesenia asked. Her dark hair flowed in soft

waves over the back of the chaise. Corin swallowed a lump back in his throat. The Epoch of the Accordant had chosen his wife for him, but he'd chosen her every day since. Twenty years had passed, and she was ever more of a blessing to him each day. Even now, with the guards running the Reach, and their futures far from certain. When they no longer had the power to protect each other.

"He's killed my sister!" Maeryn practically shouted. "He isn't ready for the kingdom to know is all. Eoghan will help him cover it, or defend it, branding her a traitor."

Yesenia sighed. "Aiden is a monster, but he isn't foolish enough to add your sister's murder to his crimes. He will be fortunate if he isn't the victim of some revenge for what he did to my brother. He's betrayed not one but two Reaches. If he hadn't fled like a coward, we'd be listening to the cleric recite the dead-given rites."

Corin placed a hand on his wife's shoulder. "One day, Yesenia. I will help you do it."

Maeryn rolled her eyes. "You both so easily forget his alliance with The Pretender. He is *protected*. He can do as he pleases. Do you think he would have dispatched of Byrne had Eoghan not blessed it?"

Yesenia glared in response. "I have a different take. Sister."

Maeryn waved a hand. "By all means. Sister."

"I don't think Eoghan blessed my brother's murder at all. I think this is yet another instance of Aiden overreaching his authority and overestimating his value to the crown. So no, I don't believe he's there, scheming and conspiring these long weeks. I think Eoghan is weary of him and has done something about it."

"If that were so, Eoghan would proclaim that for all the kingdom to know. It would be his men here, not Aiden's."

Yesenia smiled bitterly. "But don't you see? Aiden can yet be of use, even as a prisoner. Why waste his own men, when Aiden's are still perfectly useful? When it was Aiden, and not Eoghan, who determined the way to subdue the great Medvedev for his purpose?"

Maeryn smirked, but her eyes betrayed her. She realized the wisdom in Yesenia's supposition. Aiden was too vain, too consumed with the belief his way was the only way, to leave his men without guidance. If he was scheming with the king, he would want them all to know. It would be yet another flex of his presumption of power.

"I'm afraid it's time," Corin said, exhaling. "If there's word, we'll again send for you, Maeryn. If there is not, then we'll again meet in a fortnight." He stepped across the room and took both her hands in his. She shivered, but squeezed back. "You aren't alone. We yet lack the wisdom to make the change the Reach deserves, but when we do, we will."

"I only wish for a future where a fair and just Quinlanden sits upon the throne of the keep," Maeryn whispered. She slipped away without saying goodbye to Yesenia.

"I don't trust her. Nor have I ever liked the way she looks upon you," Yesenia said when Maeryn was gone.

"She's Blackwood, through and through. Don't let her adaptability fool you. She's done what was necessary to survive in Aiden's world." Corin turned. With a grin, he added, "And there's not a woman alive who could turn my head away from Yesenia Warwick. Shall I show you, before our guards return?"

Clarissant Tyndall stood at the door to the Round Room, named so by her husband, Griffath, for the simple reason that the room was cylindrical. But it wasn't a room at all. It was once an old cistern that Griffath had stripped and turned into a place of business, separate of the keep, at the edge of the Tyndall lands. Close enough to the falls to form a natural barrier of sound, keeping words both in and out. The men of crimson and gold swarming

Wildwood Falls tried to keep Griffath from retreating to his favored place, but Clarissant had charmed them with distractions; enough for him to slip away for the most urgent of matters.

Not with magic. The bane of Clarissant's life was that she wasn't born a magic dealer. But she'd learned her own form of witchery, studying with the type of women who were not welcome in Great Cities of the Westerlands. It was not the same, but she valued it more, for she'd worked through her sweat and tears for every ounce of power she wielded.

"Griff," she said from the entrance. She was the only other person with a key to the Round Room. "The Rush Riders have returned. Arturo is among them."

Griffath looked up, weary. His brother, Rhydian, was on his feet before the words were out of her mouth.

"Did you guide him here?" Rhydian asked. "To us?"

"I did," Clarissant replied, but was looking at her husband. Griffath's exhaustion settled into the lines of his face; lines that seemed to appear with Aiden's men. More scratched their way along his flesh when these same men raped their daughter, Lyria. And again when young Jonah returned home, beaten close to death.

Rhydian's soft smile put her at ease. She had little use for the Reliquary, but Rhydian seemed born to have a place in its ranks. He was both assuming and servile; docile and a force. He was hardly three decades into his life but was a Grand Minister of the Reliquary, a role usually reserved for men closer to death than birth. He was the highest ranking clergyman in the Westerlands, and in the kingdom was second only to the Archminister. He spent some of the year at the Resplendent Reliquary, and the rest at Longwood Rush and traveling the Reach, serving in the name of the Guardians. But when news of the betrayal of Byrne reached his ears, he'd ridden directly for Wildwood Falls, and had been a stalwart presence at his brother's side since.

"He has news of Marsh," Clarissant said carefully. "He wanted to share with all of us together."

Griffath's face crumbled. "He's dead, then."

Clarissant shook her head. Now she did look at her husband's brother for strength. "I would have seen that in his eyes."

"And I would have never made you wait to hear such a terrible truth." Arturo's deep voice called from behind her.

A swift wind passed by Clarissant as Rhydian flew by and landed in Arturo's firm embrace. "Brother," he whispered, and there was something else, something she heard but was not meant to as they lingered overlong in one another's arms.

Arturo broke away and nodded at Griffath. "Steward Tyndall."

"Rider Blackfen. Your travels were fair and without incident, I hope."

"They were. Mostly." He leaned his longbow against the wall. "I won't make you wait longer for news of your son. He's safe in Wulfsgate. He arrived there with Emberley Blackwood."

"Wulfsgate!" Clarissant declared. "Marsh is in the Northerlands?" She looked at her husband in her astonishment, but he, too, was making sense of this strange news.

"Indeed," Arturo replied. He removed his metal bracers, and then his plate, chest armor, setting both aside. He sank into the chair across from Griffath. "I cannot say how they got there, or why they chose the destination, only that they're both well and safe. Lady Dereham has sworn her men to protect their safekeeping."

"Lady Dereham?" Griffath asked. "And what of the Lord of Wulfsgate?"

Arturo smirked. "The lady *is* the Lord of Wulfsgate."

"Guardians," Clarissant whispered. "I'm relieved he's safe, as he would not be here."

"And he has served Lady Ember well. At least one of the Blackwood children is now safe, thanks to him," Arturo said. "Pride should accompany your relief."

"Yes," Griffath said, slowly exhaling. "He brings honor to our house."

"Are there men of crimson and gold in the north yet?" Clarissant asked.

"Not as of my travels there. The Northerlands have closed all borders, land and sea. The only ones allowed in or out do so on special permission from the Derehams, of which I was able to obtain, through great effort. I asked Lady Dereham to allow the children to remain in Wulfsgate, presuming they are most safe there with these precautions in place. Lady Ember in particular is in especial danger in the Westerlands. If the winds don't change, she may be our future Lady of Longwood."

"Yes," Rhydian said. "You did right."

"Did you see him? With your own eyes?" Clarissant asked.

"Aye. I did. And Lady Ember. Lady Blackwood's sister, Lady Earwyn, resides in Wulfsgate, as you know. She looks after them. I delivered your words to Marsh, and he was grateful to receive them. He wished for you both to know he's well and asked that you not worry after him."

Griffath sucked in both lips. Clarissant recognized her husband's attempt to stave off tears. The veins at his temples throbbed in response to this effort.

"Thank you. For finding him. For delivering our words to our boy."

Arturo bowed in his chair. "If we could safely usher Lyria and Jonah there, I would escort them myself."

It was Clarissant's turn to fight tears. "They will all die for what they've done to my children. I will see it done myself."

"And I will aid you, when the time is right," Arturo answered. "But I fear I'm not long for staying in Wildwood."

Rhydian shifted back and forth on his feet. "Where will you go next?"

"Greystone Abbey." He looked at Rhydian. "And I would like you to join me."

"It is true, then," Griffath said. "Easlan James is collecting men."

Arturo nodded. "It is the only place in the Westerlands where Aiden's men aren't lingering like flies on shit. Any Westerlander knows Greystone Abbey and the men running it are essential to the Westerlands, but Aiden didn't trouble to educate himself before sneaking across the River Rush to mark himself a traitor."

"I will go," Rhydian said. "I can travel freely. Even Aiden would not dare assail a man of the Reliquary."

"As of now, the Rush Riders can move unmolested as well, as long as we're not traveling in numbers and formation," Arturo said. "I don't expect this to remain so for long."

"Are all the Great Cities sending men? And the Lesser?" Griffath asked.

"Most," Arturo said. He looked at his hands. "Some fear the consequences of standing against the crimson and gold. Others wonder at how Asherley could abandon them."

"Abandon them!" Clarissant cried. "A true Westerlander would never question Lady Asherley's faithfulness to her people!"

Arturo nodded solemnly. "And yet, she's not here. Her lands are overrun with fear and self-preservation." He rocked forward and launched to his feet. "Others, like us, would see the fear ended."

"You leave now?" Griffath asked. "So soon?"

"Every moment wasted is a moment we condone this lawless subjugation."

"What if we sent Jonah?" Clarissant asked, her hopefulness outweighing her sense of reality.

"We'd not make it beyond the town gate," Rhydian said. "I

know his suffering pains you. As it does all of us. But he would not survive if marked a traitor."

"And you? Will they not wonder at the Grand Minister of the Westerlands gone missing?"

"My role often requires travel. If they ask, I've returned to the Reliquary."

Arturo replaced the armor he'd shed only moments before. "We must go. One more thing. There're whispers among the loyal that Joran Rosewood is in Greystone. And another... someone else of great magic, whose name has not been revealed. I don't know if either fact will be important to our cause, but we will take what help we're offered. We will take back our Reach."

Clarissant kissed him on both cheeks. "We *must* or there will soon not be a Reach to take back."

KHALLUM OBSERVED, with a mix of anger and indifference, the miners storming the shores beyond the keep, fists raised to the sky, angered voices carrying across the sea breeze. He had half a mind to remind them they were squandering what little energy remained to them. It wasn't his fault they were starving. Not his fault that the ratsbane Quinlanden had murdered Khallum's brother and then launched the kingdom into a chaos that wasn't quite war, but could be. It would take so little to topple the careful orchestration of agitated guards and closed borders.

He'd closed his borders, as well. He had no other choice. Both the Westerlands and Easterlands were under the control of the king now. Most of the Southerland food imports came from the Westerlands, but he could trust nothing coming across the Reach thanks to The Deceiver. They subsisted now on what they could bring in from the sea. Only in the borderlands were heartier foods growable, but the Southerlanders were not farmers. They'd left that to their neighbors, and now they were paying for it.

They wanted war, the miners. Khallum had war in his blood, and he'd enjoy, all too well, the weight of a claymore in his hand as he swung it upon the skull of a Quinlanden or Rhiagain grunt. But, for once, he had something within his grasp that not even war could supersede. More than he'd known he had when he sent Ryan Strong into the Wastelands to bring Darrick Rhiagain home. He had not only the father but also the son. But both their lives were in precarious balance, counting on what meager shelter they had in exile. He didn't think many Southerland men were loyal to the crown after all the abuse their Reach had suffered under the Rhiagain reign, but he wasn't certain enough to stake everything upon this faith.

Everyone awaited his direction, and he had none to give. His fear of action shamed him, how it had brought him straight to his knees. Asherley and Assyria. His men in Whitecliffe. The ones dying below him, before his very eyes. They all looked to him, and for what?

"You stand here for hours as if your presence alone will change their empty bellies," Gwyn said from behind him. It surprised him she'd entered the Hall of Warring. She was the only woman who could enter without special dispensation, and she rarely abused this privilege. But he'd given her cause to worry once more; he'd failed to adequately ease her mind on the uncertainties ahead.

"That isnae why I stand here."

"What will you do?"

Khallum bristled at the question and loaded an appropriate response. But his anger wasn't for her. "I've yet to decide." He grunted and added, "I cannae resume trade with closed borders. I have no money coming into the Reach without minerals going out. If I halt mining production, I'll have none for when trading resumes. Either way, the miners starve."

"Aye, husband. You've no control over what others put in motion. But what of your own plans?"

He tightened his grip on the balustrade, stained white from the years of bird shit. "Speak plainly. I've not the spirits for anything less."

Gwyn appeared at his side. She wrapped her shawl tight against the assaulting sea wind. "Go to Whitecliffe, Khallum. There's nothing you can do here, but there's power in seeing your work before your eyes. What *you* put into action. The freedom you alone will deliver the realm. And yes..." Gwyn pointed at the emaciated mob. "These men, as well. They cannot know what you've done for them, but they will. And those strong enough to survive to see it will revere you beyond any king this kingdom has ever had."

"You think I should go to him? And draw eyes upon Whitecliffe?"

"Your men will tell the people of Warwicktown you're meeting with your men about The Deceiver. About The Pretender. That you're rallying."

"You've it all laid out, have ye? Think ye know what's best?"

Gwyn shook her head. "I'm only the mother of your children. You are the father of this entire Reach. A man of action. A *Warwick*. That man doesn't stand by and watch his world dissolve into chaos. He reaches into that chaos, commands the center, and makes it his own."

Khallum closed his eyes, rolled his shoulders forward, and pressed his exhale into the briny air. "I cannae fail at this, Gwyn. There isnae another plan."

"Then donnae let mere men do a lord's work. You belong at the side of the king." She turned to him. "The *real* king."

THE GUARDIANS
DON'T MAKE
MISTAKES

9

THE LAST STAND OF THE WESTERLANDS

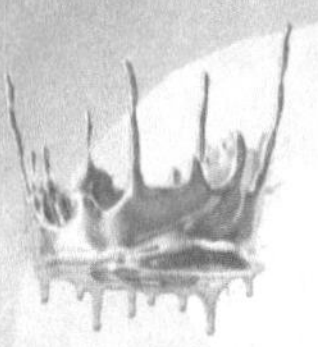

Ravenna's smooth hips designed the perfect movement, arcing under his hands as she slid herself over him in full, agonizing strokes. Riding with such beautiful dexterity, as if she'd spun this skill from centuries of practice. The way she pulled him closer to finish, his undoing, and yet stilled him, drawing out both their pleasures, was a magic of its own kind.

Somewhere in him screamed a denial, but it never touched his lips, and as she rolled forward, her dark hair tickling the beads of sweat dancing upon the flesh of his chest, he spilled so hard within her he feared they might both fly from the bed.

He struggled for words through ragged breaths. Now he *had* to find them. This couldn't go on. He'd sworn it would never, ever come to pass in *this* way. But ahh, her mouth was upon him now, reviving him once more, and oh, Guardians, had there ever been anything so soft, so wonderful, so...

Jesse awoke with a violent start, hearing Ravenna's smooth voice in two places at once. She was humming some soft whisper against his cock, but she was also standing at the end of his bed, calling his name in escalating urgency.

One reality faded away as the other took solid form. Ravenna was telling him to wake, quickly, that they had visitors. Jesse propped himself upon one arm, trying in futile desperation to clear his mind before she could read it. With his other, he swiped in awkward moves at the sweat that painted him everywhere now, not just his chest. What he needed was a dip in the river beyond the keep, but that would have to wait.

Ravenna watched these strange ministrations with a curious look, saying nothing. She waited for him to gift her with his full attention, and then began again, with a touch of exasperation.

"Kaslan is downstairs, and he's brought visitors with him."

"Who?"

Ravenna didn't answer. Instead, she turned and left him, but he didn't miss the tiny smile playing at the corner of her mouth.

She knew.

When she was gone, Jesse fell back against the bed, arm over his eyes. Spent. Ashamed. On top of it all, he'd slept longer than the others, and the day was already getting ahead of him.

But he could ruminate on his failings as a man later. He had business downstairs.

He dressed quickly and made his way to the main floor, where the small room was now full of life. He didn't recognize the newcomers, but he didn't need an introduction for the young man wrapped in Esmerelda's arms.

Esmerelda laughed through her tears as she held the boy tighter. "I can't believe it's you. That you're really here, all the way in Greystone. You must tell me everything, Brandyn! Everything!"

Ravenna stood at Jesse's side as they watched the reunion unfold. He didn't like the way she sidled up to him, as if they were allied in yet another thing. "It seems your seer wasn't wrong in his predictions, after all."

"He isnae my seer," Jesse muttered, but his frown quickly melted into something warmer, for he hadn't seen Esmerelda experience real joy in so long he'd forgotten what it looked like on her.

"There's much to tell," Brandyn said, breaking the embrace. He wore a very serious look, far too pensive for a child his age, and the smile for his cousin was forced. For her sake, it seemed. "But there are others who should hear it, too. Steward James insisted I should come here first." This time, when he smiled at Esmerelda, it was real. "I'm glad he did."

"Call me Kaslan, Lord Blackwood. Steward James is my father."

Brandyn nodded. The room came alive with introductions. Then it was Brandyn's turn. He gestured toward the girl standing by the hearth, who'd said nothing yet. She was older than he was, almost at the point in her life where she'd be standing by a husband. "This is Storm Wakesell. She's been my companion through everything, through all, and I would ask you to treat her with the same respect and brotherhood."

"I know her," Kaslan said. "The Wakesells don't look down upon us as some of the others do."

"Loyalty makes a man. Not a name," Storm said.

"Aye," Kaslan said, flushing.

"Storm, your family. Where are they?" Ravenna asked.

Storm looked at Brandyn. "Whitewood isn't safe for any who would see Brandyn back where he belongs. Where his father belonged before The Deceiver took our lord's life in the cowardice of moonlight."

"They've sent men to us here," Brandyn said. He looked at Jesse with the words, but stayed close to Esmerelda as if he, too, felt a responsibility for her. "They've all sent what they can."

"Aye," Jesse said. "We've seen them come from all over the Reach. More every day, it seems."

"My father will aid, if we ask him. If we tell him there's a proper resistance brewing out here," Esmerelda said, brightening.

"No one knows, as he does, what it is to see your own land taken by another. And Uncle Byrne was his brother."

"We've asked him. Again. He'll send none," Kaslan said, avoiding her eyes.

"Yes, but that was before. Surely..." Esmerelda said, her words trailing into a whisper. Her eyes were wide with a whirlwind of emotions. She looked at Jesse, but he had already known this truth and kept it from her, to keep her mind at ease. "He has always said that the Reaches must be united in only one thing, and that is the protection of their lands and ways."

"Aye, but no one came when your father asked. When his grandfather fought the Rhiagains," Kaslan explained. "And now he's returning the favor."

"Your father did," Jesse said.

Kaslan waved his arm around. "Lot of good we are in Greystone. Until now, that is."

"Kaslan," Brandyn said. "Can you take us back to your father's inn? I have much more to share, but it will be easier if I only have to say it once, for everyone."

Kaslan nodded. "Lord Blackwood."

Brandyn's eyes glassed over as he looked away from them, out the window and toward the field beyond the keep. "I am Lord Blackwood now. Though, it was not the way I saw it coming to pass." He turned to Ravenna. "But I did see you."

Ravenna recoiled. "Me? What did you see?"

"I saw another wielder of great magic, but not my magic," Brandyn said. He looked up at her. "But as you stand before me, I see kin. You're a Ravenwood, aren't you?"

Ravenna paused, then nodded.

"All the way out here?"

"My story is long as well, Lord Blackwood."

"When we all left Longwood Rush, my sister Emberley was on her way to your people. Did your paths cross?"

"They did not, but it seems a lifetime ago that I left Midnight Crest. I was traveling with Drystan and Lisbet Dereham, and Eavan Quinlanden. We got separated in the Hinterlands, and then I came across Jesse and Esmerelda."

"My other sister, Gabi, was headed to the Hinterlands, with two companions."

Ravenna looked at Esmerelda. "We didn't come across Gabi, but we rescued one of her companions. Brook. Steward James is caring for him at the pub, for now."

"Only Brook?"

"I'm afraid so. He told us his sister, and yours, were taken by the Medvedev."

"Taken?" Brandyn repeated. "They came to them for aid!"

"Aye," Jesse said. "So did we, but what we found was anything but. We fled here after they accosted us."

Brandyn's eyes widened. "You really do have quite a story to tell."

Ravenna nodded. "But mine will stay within these walls only, as Esmerelda's will. No one can know who we are, or that we're here."

"But has any harm come to Gabi? Did Brook say?"

Jesse answered for her. "We suspect they've taken her wherever they took Ravenna's companions. But we know nothing beyond that."

"I don't understand. None of this makes sense."

"Aye. We share that feeling. I know you may be thinking of rushing off to save them—"

"No, Jesse," Brandyn said. "I could, and then what? Bring her back to a Reach in turmoil, tell her she has no home anymore? We have work to do here first."

"Let's have at it, then," Kaslan said, leading the way.

· · ·

"Esmerelda."

Esmerelda dropped the basket of linens near the door at the sound of Ravenna's voice. Even if they weren't all crowded together under one roof, she'd know it anywhere, from its lyrical, otherworldly sound. If she didn't know what she knew about the Ravenwoods being from Beyond, she might think they were instead Guardians themselves. Witnessing Ravenna's effortless beauty, her grace and perfection was a gift, though not to her.

Esmerelda had been raised to know her own beauty. It was her singular value, beyond the command of her name, and though she wished to be known for more, she'd embraced it, for what has value also has power. As a woman in the Southerlands, even a Warwick, she had all the power of a bird screaming from a gilded cage.

"I have washing to tend to, before the men return."

"The men will be awhile. Let them do their business, and we can do ours."

Esmerelda pointed at the basket. "That's what I intend to do."

"You spend your days washing so exhaustion will find you at night," Ravenna said. "And you have no one to share your fears with. Or, so you think. But you can share them with me."

Esmerelda nearly snorted, then remembered how indelicate it would sound. On the heels of that reminder, she recalled that there was no one here to make this observation, but the moment had passed, and to do it now would be not only indelicate but strange. "With you?" She picked up the basket again, determined to be far from this conversation, from Ravenna. Her thoughts about the sorceress were wrapped in complexity, but most reflected her own shortcomings. Her jealousy, for one.

The sunlight was coming over the eastern edge of the forest. Enough light now for her to see her work. When she'd once tried to start her labor before the sun's crest, she'd discovered later all the dark stains in the fabric still there when the light arrived.

A year ago, that she'd be this concerned about linens would have been a jest to her.

Ravenna scooped the basket from Esmerelda's arms. "I'll help you, Esme. I have some things I'd like you to hear. You don't have to talk, if you don't wish to."

"My name isn't Esme."

"Jesse calls you that."

Esmerelda flushed. She pushed past the sorceress and made her way toward the lull in the river's rush, the hidden pool at the base of a small waterfall, near the forest edge. There was no sense in telling the sorceress to leave her alone. Ravenna knew nothing of boundaries, or respecting another's wishes. If she did, she would've left them in the Hinterlands.

Ravenna dropped to her knees and started the washing. "Drystan wears a necklace. One I gave him."

"Now you have your men wearing jewelry, do you?" Esmerelda muttered as she pulled one of Jesse's shirts from the basket. He'd been wearing the old wardrobe of Easlan James, from when Easlan was a younger man, a fitter one. He looked like he belonged in them. Like a lord.

"A pendant," Ravenna went on. "Bound by magic. I told him what it was when I gifted it to him, and he wore it willingly. A tracker."

"Oh, aye? A tracker? *Love*," Esmerelda quipped.

"Did you know you slip into speaking like Jesse when you're cross?"

"Like my father," Esmerelda corrected. "Like salt and sand."

"But your mother was from elsewhere, was she not?"

"The Northerlands," Esmerelda answered. But Ravenna would already know that, for the Derehams and Ravenwoods were notoriously close. It was one of only a few things her mother and father ever crossed words on. Khallum believed the Derehams were more loyal to the Ravenwoods than the realm. Gwyn insisted it was more complicated than that, that only a Northerlander would understand.

"Lord Dereham's sister."

Esmerelda preserved an ounce of power this time in keeping her counsel.

"I know Lord Dereham. He's a good man, if unsure of his leadership. Drystan is like him in this way. Neither were meant for the seat at Wulfsgate, but your Guardians had other plans for them."

"This cannae be what you came here to tell me." Esmerelda ran her fingernails down a dark spot on Jesse's shirt, pulling out the stain.

"This tracker," Ravenna went on. "I could stand at the Courtyard of Regents in Midnight Crest and he upon the fiery shores of the Wastelands, and I'd still detect him. The magic knows no range too far."

"You trust him that much, do ye?"

Ravenna ignored the jab. "I tell you this so you understand the magic has no limitations. No limitations in this kingdom." She paused her washing. "When he was taken by the Medvedev, I lost sight of him. I can no longer sense him at all."

Esmerelda cooled her blood, conscious now of her speech. "Perhaps your magic is not as strong as you think it is."

"This magic is bigger than me and my capabilities. It's an ancient magic. I know it's worth. That is not in question."

Esmerelda laughed. "So you think he went Beyond?"

"I don't know what Beyond is, any more than you do. I know he went where we cannot go, not without a Medvedev to extend invitation. I know we could wander the rest of our days in the Forest of All and never find them, unless they wished for us to."

"Jesse could have."

"He has their blood, but not their wisdom. Their experiences. He's not one of them, not in their eyes. Do you not understand that they'd have killed him?"

Esmerelda threw the shirt against the bank. "You want to know why I'm always cross with you, Ravenna? It's because you always say things... things like this, as if you know all, as if *only* you could know a thing. But you don't know! You don't know Jesse, or what the Medvedev would or would not have done. You can only guess, as I can, but now we will never know the truth of it, for we are here, and they are there, and that's precisely how you seem to want it."

Ravenna regarded her with eyes that nearly glowed. Esmerelda's eyes were often said to glow, too, but they lacked the unsettling intensity of the sorceress', and she felt that, too, was another thing separating them. "Say what you mean."

"You need me to? Or can you pull it from my head?"

"I could. But that would make me no better than you think of me."

Esmerelda did snort this time. She enjoyed the sound of it. It was the sound of her father and his men. Of strength. "You've distracted him. Spelled him. I see how he looks each morning when he wakes, as if his thoughts are no longer his own."

"Whatever Jesse feels—"

"Whatever Jesse *feels*? So now there are feelings between the two of you?"

"That isn't what I meant. There's nothing between us. I have no power over him."

"You tell me of this magical tracker that can keep your lover in line, and then in the next breath insist you have no power over another man?"

"My magic doesn't work that way," Ravenna insisted. "I can't control a man's thoughts. If I could have... I... I think I would have persuaded Drystan not to love me to begin with. I'd have spared us both this pain."

Esmerelda laughed. "You make no sense to me."

"I should think you, of anyone, would understand how

conflicting it is to be in the middle of a love that's forbidden," Ravenna charged. "Would you not have swayed Ryan's thoughts away from you, to save him?"

Esmerelda's hand fell to her belly. "I didn't know my father would send him to that terrible place."

"Nor could I have known that Drystan would be taken prisoner. But we are, you and I, both of us in denial if we claim we didn't know it would end poorly for them both in some manner."

Esmerelda stumbled over a response. Ravenna's words angered her, for they struck at the heart of a conflict that had been burning in Esmerelda's heart for some time. Though she had been given everything as a Warwick, she'd been given what others determined were her needs, never what she desired. And she had wanted nothing before, until she'd fallen in love with Ryan Strong. The Guardians couldn't deny her the only thing she'd ever asked for, no matter how unlikely, or impossible. Even as a woman, she believed there must be some equity in the eyes of the Guardians.

Even as Ryan was taken away in chains, she held fast to the hope that the trials ahead were the cost of their eventual happiness. She ignored Jesse's naysaying, his stalwart reminders that the Wastelands were no place for a man who wished to survive.

"There's a storm brewing. We'll finish the wash later," Ravenna said, standing. "I had hoped you and I could be friends. I still hope for it."

"I already have a friend, Jesse," Esmerelda replied as she gathered the wet linens. "I need no others, and if you look upon me as fondly as you claim, as a *friend,* then you will do as a friend would do and leave Jesse alone. Leave me alone. Leave us and return to whatever fate you and your magic will design next."

STORM STOOD with Jesse at the back of the bar. She perched at the edge of the long counter, hips cocked, wearing the same look as most of the men. She seemed more like them than the young woman she was, lacking entirely in the awareness she didn't belong. But Brandyn had made himself clear. She was to be wrapped into the brotherhood, as one of them.

"The two of you. You've seen more than enough on your way to us," Jesse observed.

"I can't speak for what Brandyn has seen. But I've watched a boy become a man."

"He's eleven."

"Twelve," Storm answered. "He turned another year during our travels." She frowned. "Or so we believe. Time is strange now."

"Your blade. The one you cannae take your hand off. It's good steel, but you willnae need it here."

Storm pulled it from its sheath, regarding the curved metal in the dim light. "There were two of them, not so long ago."

Jesse's mouth parted. Recognition passed over his memory of the night they'd spent in Parth. The group of children gathered at the corner table. The melee that followed. "It was you. Who killed those men at the tavern."

Storm grinned. "You were there?"

"I wanted to help, but I had to keep low, for reasons you now understand."

She slipped the blade back in its sheath. "I didn't need your help, anyway. I had it all well in hand."

"Did they come after you? I didnae stay to see the matter resolved. I was afraid for... for her. I had to get her to safety. If I'd known who ye all were—"

Storm waved a hand. "You did what all men came there to do. To not be seen. I would've done the same. Yeah, they came after us. Regretted it, too."

Jesse chuckled as he watched her. "I imagine they did."

A hush fell over the room. Easlan and Brandyn moved to the center of the candlelit room, as Easlan had the night he brought

Joran Rosewood to sing his predictions. Well, he'd been right about this one. Jesse couldn't deny it. The old man held court alone in the corner, in a swath of silver and white, wearing a satisfied grin he'd earned, Jesse supposed.

"Since that eve that Joran shared his secrets with us, we've seen more men join us. Men from all over the Reach. Men of the Reliquary. Men of the Sepulchre. Rush Riders." Easlan landed his eyes upon Arturo Blackfen, who stood tall in the corner next to his impressive longbow. Jesse had met Arturo the day before, along with his traveling companion, a high-ranking member of the Reliquary called Rhydian Tyndall. "And now, the lord of our Reach has come to us, just as Joran said he would. And he would say some things to the men who have gathered to take back what The Deceiver has stolen."

Low, anxious energy rippled through the room. These men were cautious. Excited, for a Blackwood to be returned to them. Nervous, for that Blackwood was a mere child.

Brandyn stepped onto the chair. Even raised up, he was a smallish boy. A final born, as the saying went in the Southerlands, when describing the child who'd gotten the last pickings of what the mother's body had to offer. But where he lacked in size, he made up for in intensity. Storm had said she'd watched this boy become a man, and it was in Brandyn's eyes that Jesse saw a glimmer of that.

"My father was murdered." Brandyn didn't ease into his speech. He spoke plainly, with an anger that had settled into all of their bones, taking root, festering into something newly awakened. "Murdered in his home. The work of a traitor."

A fresh vigor replaced the pall of before, and now the men were ramping up. They sat straighter, awaiting his next words.

"You call him The Deceiver. My friends in the Southerlands would call him a ratsbane. I call him a coward. And soon, I will call him a dead coward. To his face. As I hold his head aloft, bloody hair gathered in my fist."

"He's clear in his purpose," Jesse said to Storm as the men swelled in their gathered vitality, stomping, applauding.

"He has no choice."

Brandyn stepped higher, climbing atop the table. He, too, seemed to gather energy from the room, growing bolder with the strength of the men who had served his mother, and now would serve him. "They say my mother has escaped The Pretender. And I say, whatever she has planned next will bring this crown to its knees." He looked around the room, pausing to regard each man. "But we can't wait for her. She wouldn't wish for us to be idle, while she plots in the shadows. She didn't send her four children into the wilderness for us to do nothing, while our Reach is commandeered by the filth of betrayal."

"Do they also teach them the gift of language at the Sepulchre?" Jesse asked.

Storm grinned.

"She sent us knowing there would be a moment in which we would all be called upon. Ember is safe in the Northerlands, but she is not idle. I see that is news to some of you, but not to others." Brandyn looked at the Rush Rider, Blackfen. "I have seen it, in my mind's eye, the magic of my mother's kin. And you have confirmed it."

Blackfen nodded. "I've seen your sister, and her companion, Tyndall's eldest, with my own eyes. The Northerlands aren't idle either. They do what is necessary to move their part forward."

"With closed borders and their fighting men locked behind them?" a man asked.

"Have you considered, Sir Carlisle, that a locked border may be more for protecting what lies within, than keeping men out?" Brandyn asked.

Sir Carlisle looked confused about whether that was a true

invitation to respond, or merely an attempt to call him to account. "Themselves, you mean."

Brandyn smiled. "What the Northerlands protects is not for us to know. Trust in them to know their part in this, as you trust in the Blackwoods to know theirs. They are our allies." He surveyed the crowd once more, and as he did, as his eyes again fell on each man, their spines more erect, their pride clearer, he, too, seemed to grow stronger. "We will first take back our lands. And when the Westerlands is ours once more, we will step forth and join with the other Reaches in taking back our kingdom."

The roar this time was louder, shaking the unsteady timber of the Long-Trodden Mule. Even Jesse couldn't deny the stirring within him at the sight of this young but powerful child standing amongst handfuls of those most loyal, rising them to his side, the growing resistance of the Westerlands. He remembered Byrne Warwick, who had been a good man. Who had been loyal to both the land of his father and his wife; a good husband and father. What had happened in The Westerlands could happen in the Southerlands. Had happened before, from a crown who thought more of themselves than the Guardians did.

"I see it in your eyes," Kaslan said, sliding in beside him. "I see you coming alive."

"It's too dark in here to see anything," Jesse countered. He felt Storm grinning at the other side of him.

"They would follow him. Will follow him," Kaslan said. "He's naught but a pube, but they will. Mind me."

"As they should. He's their lord now."

"And you'll be with them. I see it now."

Jesse watched Brandyn as he told his story, the tale of all he'd encountered after leaving his home and venturing out into the kingdom toward a new fate. "I told your father I'd help how I can, from here. But more than that, I cannae do. I've another task, one that may not seem to you to be as important as the fate of your Reach, but is everything to me."

Kaslan clapped him on the back. "We'll see, now, won't we?"

JESSE LEFT his boots by the door. He hung his jacket over the bench, then checked the waning coals in the fire. They'd die on their own soon, with no help from him. The women must have retired long ago.

He made his way up the stairs, fighting off an exhaustion that seemed to start all the way in his bones. Every time he stood amongst the last stand of the Westerlands, he was filled with a heaviness that wasn't his to carry, but settled into his marrow without invite, taking root. He had his own burden to bear, but he would bear this one, too, it seemed.

Jesse paused just outside his door, listening. His room wasn't empty. The sound was almost imperceptible.

Hand on his sword, he gave the door a light press, careful not to push hard enough to make the wood creak. Moonlight spilled across the bed, lighting the answer. His hand fell away.

Esmerelda slept huddled in a ball atop his blankets. With a sigh, Jesse sat down at her back and rested a hand on her shoulder. It was then he heard the crying and realized she wasn't asleep at all.

"I had a terrible dream," she said, breathless. Her voice cracked with the remnants of a long night. "About Ryan."

Jesse squeezed her shoulder. "Dreams are only that."

"I saw him, in the darkness. He couldn't find his way back to us. He's lost, and... I don't know how to tell him. How to find him. I'm afraid for him."

Jesse didn't know the words she needed. Anything he thought of saying stayed in his head. It had always been like that for him. "No matter what darkness Ryan finds himself in, he'll find his way out. He has every reason to fight." He let his free hand hover over her belly, swelling through the fabric of her nightshift. "More than even he knows."

"What if he can't?"

Jesse stood and peeled back the quilt. "Go on, then. The fire is dead, you'll catch a chill."

"I'm sorry. I woke, and I didn't want to be alone."

"And you won't be."

She slid under the blanket, looking up at him. "I ask a lot of you. I know this."

Jesse joined her in the bed. His heart surged at their closeness, his thoughts bouncing in and out of the shadows of his intentions and his concern for her. Ryan would not want him to leave her in such a state, he told himself, while also feeling as if there was no separation great enough to still his pulse, which raged inexplicably faster and higher with each pass of his skin over the soft bed.

"Rest, Esme. The morning will look much different. It always does."

IO

LOUDER, FOR YOUR FATHER

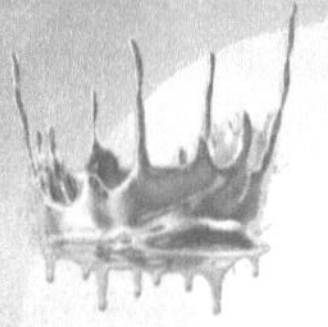

Oldwin no longer wore the harrowed mantle of a man who'd spent the better part of a century in a prison. His countenance unsettled Eoghan just the same. Eoghan decided if he did nothing else, he would need to learn to hide this from the old man. He also needed to stop thinking of him as an old man, for this was an increasingly confusing moniker that told very little of the true story of the creature. Oldwin looked no older than forty, even if he had, so they said, lived the equivalent of many lifetimes. Eoghan didn't want to believe this could be true, for if it was, there were implications far beyond his reasoning. But he couldn't deny the subtleties about Oldwin that stirred thoughts of a time long before. His manner of speaking. That, though he didn't actually carry a smell, Eoghan's mind associated Oldwin with the cloying scent that might assault you if you opened a room that had been closed for far too long.

They were scheduled to visit the Isle of Belcarrow, to stir inspiration amongst the Rhiagain Guard and Knights of Duncarrow, but the sea was too choppy for a voyage by ship, and so they'd postponed the visit. Eoghan was outwardly disappointed at the news, declaring his regret at not being able to pay homage to the men who kept peace in his kingdom. Secretly, he was most relieved at not having to stand before men who were twice him physically, and perhaps in other ways, too. Men he was supposed to inspire, but he knew would snicker and sneer when his back was turned.

He also had no suitable answer to give the inevitable queries about their idleness. He had no intentions to deploy more than what he already had. The irony of needing a guard of this size on an island kingdom with no outside enemies was one he was afraid to question for fear he was missing something substantial. Certainly he could never turn them against his own people. Those conscripted came from the Reaches.

"Better that this will wait for another day, Your Grace," Oldwin said as they walked back toward the keep. Eoghan struggled to keep his pace. The sorcerer stepped as if he had legs twice as long as his body. Eoghan couldn't complain about it without exposing his own weakness. "For they will be awaiting news of war. News from you."

Eoghan curled his upper lip at the corner. "They have been trained for war. They will always want it."

"They will want direction, is all. News reaches even the isle of war of what has transpired in the kingdom. They will want to know their role, which only you can decide."

Eoghan paused as a foul wind nearly ripped him off his feet. He pulled his cloak around his head, then felt silly for it, for how it must look, but it would betray his feelings if he removed it now. "It is not the crown who desires for war."

"Whether or not you desire it, it may be upon us."

"All credited to that fool in the sky dungeon. It is good I left him to rot, for who knows what other damages he would've wrought if left to his own choices."

"He's done damage enough already, I'd say," Oldwin replied. He stepped in front of Eoghan to keep him from sinking his ankles into a puddle. Eoghan didn't thank him. He needed Oldwin to understand his place. They were not equals.

"The Westerlands will do nothing with the Quinlanden Guard placed within their cities."

"And the Quinlanden Guard will maintain their position only so long without word from their lord."

Eoghan paused. A hard snap from the crossed swords of the Rhiagain flag catching in the wind made him momentarily furious, but he recovered. He was learning to control his emotions better. "Then we send word."

Oldwin grinned at his back. "A most prudent choice, sir. Though we must also consider the fate of the Westerlands in longer terms as well. Their lord is dead, and their lady is a fugitive of the realm. Even if she's apprehended, she cannot reign."

Eoghan agreed wholeheartedly, but detested when the sorcerer said what he was thinking before he could. This seemed to be a frequent occurrence, which confirmed to Eoghan he'd been right to free this man to give him counsel. He didn't have to like him to appreciate the necessity. "They have three children who could restore order."

"Not while their mother lives."

Yes, Eoghan had been thinking about this problem a good deal. Aiden's treachery was subdued, but Asherley and Assyria must be brought to heel. Assyria he would imprison, for she was blood, and he would not be the king who executed his own sister. Asherley he had no such restraint for. Her head would go on progress throughout the kingdom, reminding all of the price of betraying a Rhiagain crown. Of the chaos she tried to bring to innocent lives.

But they had to find them first. The Southerlands seemed the most willing to harbor enemies of Eoghan, but he'd sent the Rhiagain Guard into every town and village, and there'd been nothing reported. He'd even given them leave to do as they wished in order to elicit the answers required, and still nothing of use. The only sightings of the ship had been heading north. But if they were in the Northerlands, then Eoghan would have to find and bide his patience. He couldn't enter those lands, even if they hadn't closed their borders. But Assyria had taken Anabella and Stefan not to wither, but for some great plot yet to be revealed. If Eoghan had no patience, Assyria had even less. She would not be idle long.

They would leave the Northerlands, or wherever they were, and when they did, Eoghan had men at the ready.

"Permission to speak without restraint, Your Grace," Oldwin said, breaking him from his stream of thoughts.

"Seems to me you already do."

Oldwin's face was hard as granite. "I saw, from my cell, you enraptured by the Blackwood girl, before you even left Duncarrow to meet her acquaintance. I saw how it would end." Eoghan awaited the sorcerer's condolences, but none came. "I saw her death at the Sepulchre, and I saw the Dereham heir's wife learn what killed her."

Eoghan spun around. "What killed her?"

"It was you that killed her, sir, however inadvertent."

Eoghan had heard this, that it could be some rare ailment only a Rhiagain could pass, but if that were so, all foreign brides brought to Duncarrow would have been recipients of this foul disease. "Rumor only."

"Not rumor. The Magi call it the Virulent Spindle in their trite spirals of notes on us. On all they do not know about the Rhiagains. But we call it Fornicus Mortem. Around half of Rhiagain men carry this disease. You have it. Darrick did not. Fornicus Mortem didn't exist in the kingdom until we brought it with us. And because it doesn't exist here, their medicine cannot assuage it, and the healers cannot address it. Only we know the cure."

A hard surge of blood rushed into Eoghan's face. "You know the cure? We could've saved her?"

"To save her, I would have had to have been free. I was not free while Hollyn Blackwood drew breath, so no, we could not have."

A fire burned deep in Eoghan. Rage had always led to frustration, for he had no outlet for the anger. No power with which to see it turned to action. His frail limbs fought with the flame of his agitated mind. "You kept this to yourself, knowing I could've pulled you from your cell much earlier, and brought relief to an innocent girl. She died, for love of me."

"I see your anger toward me runs deep, but anger is no replacement for rational thought, sir. Even had I called for you, you would not have come. Your need of me began when Lord Quinlanden ran afoul of the kingdom, not before. I hadn't the power to convince you of my usefulness until you determined on your own that it was necessary." He dropped his eyes to the side. "Or your wife determined."

"You don't know that!"

Oldwin's face twitched. He seemed as if a grin was waiting to break through. "I do know that. Just as I know that when you speak of innocent girls dying, this means nothing to you, for I've seen your treatment of your own wife, another innocent girl. I've seen in your heart what you would have done to the other wives, had their actions not stolen the opportunity."

"Speaking as you wish does not mean I will tolerate insubordination!"

Oldwin was unfazed. He stood patiently, waiting for something.

"Now you are absent of things to say?"

"I have nothing more to say on the matter of Hollyn Blackwood. She is the past. There is only the future now. I'll ensure we deliver Lady Assana of the elixir needed to keep her from meeting the same fate, and that will be that. But, as you have solicited my counsel, I would provide some to you, if you would still allow it."

"Go on then, say it!"

Oldwin folded his hands over his dark robe. "Lord Warwick's

daughter, Lady Esmerelda, is not dead. She's in hiding."

Eoghan's eyes widened. "Not dead? How can that be?"

"Many who take their life in the Southerlands employ the sea to that end. Women, particularly, who lack the courage to fall on swords as a man might. Many never return to land. It is their way. A way that is convenient if one wishes others to believe they've surrendered their life to the sea."

"I will have Warwick's head, too!"

"Warwick," Oldwin said with a small grin. "Does not know."

Eoghan's mind turned over this truth, wondering how he could weaponize it. "What an unexpected turn of events, Oldwin. I suppose she feigned her death to escape me then, is that it?"

"For love, they say," Oldwin said, with a light sneer. "As only a woman would."

Eoghan felt a very brief pang of sympathy for Esmerelda Warwick, whose actions were not so very different from his own when he devised a way to marry Hollyn. But this empathy ended at the realization that these same actions had contributed to the chaos of The Right of Choosing, and all that followed. In her way, Esmerelda was responsible for the grief swirling around his fragile world.

"Let Warwick's belief of her death remain so," Eoghan said. "He has earned no relief from us."

"If she were to fall into our hands, she could be so much more."

"Yes," Eoghan said, considering. The wind died down, but a fresh rain peppered the earth, and them. He hated the rain. Wanted to go inside. But Oldwin was fickle in his revelations, and it seemed he had more to say. Eoghan wouldn't interrupt that.

"I have not seen her in some time. If her location becomes clear to me, we will send the Knights for her."

"What else would you have me know?"

"A Ravenwood has flown The Rookery."

"What care have I of a Ravenwood?"

"Sees herself as another Rhosyn, it would seem."

"And is she? Will she, like Rhosyn, form yet another house that loathes me?"

"I know not," Oldwin said. "But have you never wondered why your father, and his before him, have left the Ravenwoods to roost? Why none have ever ventured farther north than Wulfsgate?"

"Some sort of agreement, he told me. An armistice of sorts. It is why I haven't sent men to destroy Dereham's Reach, inch by inch, blockades be damned. Not all in this kingdom is ours."

"It is so much more than that," Oldwin said. "The Ravenwoods and Rhiagains have a shared past. They, shall we say, came from where we did."

"Ilynglass?"

Oldwin didn't answer. "We have a common ancestor. And we cannot harm them, while they cannot harm us. To even attempt it would be to invite utter destruction."

"A common ancestor," Eoghan whispered. Had his father known this? Why would he not have shared it? Eoghan had been young and not ready to rule, but when his father knew he was dying, he should have prepared him better. The opportunities had been there. He should have conspired in his knowledge, so that Eoghan was not left floundering at the head of a bloodline he knew nothing of. "Do the Ravenwoods know?"

"If they have paid homage to their own past and protected it, I should think so."

"Do we have reason to fear them?"

"We have reason to leave them upon their perches," Oldwin said. "Yet, if the wayward bird were to find herself upon our shores, we would maintain our innocence in the matter."

"I see," Eoghan said. A Ravenwood. Here. He'd never seen one with his own eyes. He'd never considered that he might want to. But now it was all he could consider. All he could think about. A Ravenwood. His bride. Uniting a past to bring it into the future.

"I'm rather glad I cannot read your mind," Oldwin said.

"Yes. Be glad of it. For you have given me a gift and you do not even know it!"

Oldwin's slithering grin had Eoghan thinking the sorcerer knew exactly the gift he'd given, and Eoghan was again left wondering if he'd shared what he'd shared more for his own greater design than Eoghan's benefit. But what the man revealed was too valuable to put pause to it, and so he had no choice but to see where it took him.

As if understanding this very thing, Oldwin said, "You have asked me before of Dain. I have seen more since we last spoke of him. I believe he lives."

"I swear to you, my father taught me to hunt," Anabella said, grimacing as her arm trembled at the pull of the bow.

"You'll find no doubt with me. I haven't met a Northerland woman who couldn't catch her own supper," Wyat replied. He braced himself behind her, holding the wood just below where her fist shook. "It isn't your skill in question. Only the body out of practice."

Her practice was not the worst of it. Anabella's waning strength in the sky dungeon had come with more than a wasting frame. She found even lifting the water pail to be too much most days. But each was better than the last, and when she at last came before Darrick once more, she wanted his eyes to behold the Anabella he'd left all those years ago in the Wintergarden, not the one who'd suffered high in the sky dungeon.

"That's enough for today," he said, easing her fingers off the bow when she refused to release it. "I sense your frustration, but it won't serve you. I see your strength improve daily, even if you do not. You must trust me."

Anabella tried not to laugh. "Trust you? I trust very few,

Scholar Edevane, and you are among them."

"Wyat," he said softly. "There's no point in titles here. Not yet. And if you trust me, trust I would not lie to you. You are getting better, and will only continue to. Our bodies are as resilient as our minds, when we set ourselves to the task."

"Thank you, Wyat." She dusted her hands on the apron of her dress. "Can I ask you something? I know, perhaps, it isn't prudent for me to ask this, and you are of course welcome to tell me that. But until very recently I thought my life would soon end, and it may still, if we cannot find a way to move forward, so I find myself not wanting to leave questions unasked and words unsaid."

Wyat nodded. "Ask me anything."

"When Darrick was... when we thought they'd killed him. How did you make it out with your own life? Eoghan knew you were loyal to his brother. You were his best man."

Wyat dropped his eyes. He set the bow aside and leaned against the snowy tree. "I should feel shame in what I did, what I had to do, those days after Darrick was taken away. If Assyria hadn't gotten to me first, I would've run, but she did find me, and she told me what she'd done, sending Darrick to the Wastelands. I was astounded. I hadn't even considered that something like that could happen, that *she* was capable of it. So I stayed, knowing there must be some task left for me in service to my prince. With my heart in my throat, I swore fealty to Eoghan, though I knew I'd die upon my sword before ever having to prove it in any meaningful way."

"There is no shame in the choice you made. You are no ally to anyone dead," Anabella replied.

Wyat looked up. "I'm not ashamed. For I knew there was still a way I could serve my prince, my friend, through you. It was never Eoghan who had your meals sent. He'd never known enough about his own court to question that it would have taken a royal order, or the order of one serving the royal court, to feed any prisoner. Even

Oldwin was fed upon the prevailing order of his old master, Khain. There was so much Khain could have told his son, and didn't. At times, I think that was intentional, though I cannot guess why."

"It was you who sent our food?"

"And Assyria, when I left Duncarrow."

"What made you leave?"

"Once I'd convinced Eoghan of my loyalty, I returned to the Reliquary. You see, Anabella, a lie cannot be so easily held when it is always present to inspect. I knew the truth of my deeper intentions would eventually be laid bare, and I couldn't help you or Darrick if I was dead, or imprisoned."

Anabella wrapped her shawl tighter. "I was most surprised to see you upon that ship."

"Because you thought I was dead?"

"I thought Eoghan had them all taken from me. Darrick. My father."

Wyat smiled. "I visited Steward Weatherford once each year you were gone. More would have drawn attention. But it was enough to ensure he still had the fire within him to go on. I couldn't tell him about you, but I could be sure of his health, so he would be ready for the day he could witness his daughter returned to life and crowned queen."

"I was certain Eoghan had him killed when they took me," Anabella said, breathless from the fierce wind sweeping over the pass. "I was so relieved when Lady Dereham sent word to us here, that he lived and thrived. Still the best furs around, I imagine."

Wyat frowned. "There's something else you want to ask me, but you're afraid."

"How do you know this?"

"They train us to see intentions at the Reliquary. It's not magic, though some may say it is a form of it," Wyat answered. "You needn't fear anything with me, Anabella. I am perhaps the only one here whose loyalties are clear."

Anabella sighed. She looked past him, toward the cave, where her life was consumed by the escalating tension between the two women who had conspired to rescue her and her son. Only out here, in the biting cold, could she be free with her thoughts. "It is that very thing that troubles me. I could never be more grateful for what they've done for me and Stefan, for all they risked to do it. But I also cannot help but worry."

"Because they're ever at odds."

Anabella nodded.

Wyat glanced back toward the cave. "You're right to worry. I worry as well."

Anabella's heart sank. "I had so hoped you'd have more reassuring words on the matter."

"I won't deceive you," Wyat said. Men of the Reliquary wore their hair close cropped, but his had grown longer in his adventures to rescue her. Its gentle waves were a comfort, just as the void of the mountains beyond were a comfort. Anything that was not a prison was a relief. "I believe they're both well intentioned. But they are not in accord."

"I fear for what happens when their disagreements become more."

Wyat turned back to her. "You're going to suggest we leave. You and I."

Anabella sighed, looking away, a new shame rolling over her. To abandon those who had risked all for them was the ultimate form of ingratitude. But it was not for herself that these thoughts had taken over, but for Stefan. Little separated him from a role as a prince in exile and one as a pawn to be positioned at will.

"The men after us will be looking for more than three travelers. Perhaps if we break away..." Anabella's words scandalized her, but that didn't slow her from saying them. "If we leave, then even they are safer without us. They argue about what to do with my son, but if he's not here to quibble over, then they can move forth toward whatever ends they had before he was in their hands. Lady Blackwood has an entire Reach to return to. Assyria... well, I confess, I know nothing about her. She's an enigma to me."

"She's an enigma to all, even her own blood," Wyat said. He ran his hands down over his face. A damp sheen lay upon the trail he'd left. "If we *were* to leave..."

Anabella's pulse did a hopeful leap. "I'm not completely mad for the suggestion?"

"I may be mad for entertaining it," Wyat said with a long exhale. "But I, too, worry of what brews between them and threatens to boil over. Mostly, for what it may mean for you and Stefan."

Anabella stepped closer, dropping her voice even lower. "But where would we go?"

"Mama!"

Anabella and Wyat both jumped at Stefan's voice.

"What is it, darling?" Anabella welcomed him into her arms as he looked up at her, excited.

Ransom appeared behind him. "I believe we may have a problem."

"You TOLD me before you didn't know whether Dain lived or died," Eoghan said through gritted teeth. He'd grown increasingly weary of the sorcerer's parceling of information. How satisfied he looked as he doled out what he shared, and when. What to keep close to his bony breast.

But there was no one else. No one else with his knowledge. Knowledge that was immeasurably valuable to Eoghan.

"When the treachery of your father's Lord Chancellor was revealed to us, that Dain had not been killed, I beseeched the Guardians of this kingdom for wisdom, for *anything* to help Khain understand how we could find him. I debased myself in prayer to higher powers no Rhiagain has ever believed in. For the crown."

This entire kingdom believes in them, you fool. Eoghan nodded in impatience.

"But the magic does not come on command, Your Grace. Though... when one's mind has spent enough time on a matter, the visions can sometimes follow. As you and I have discussed the fate of your elder brother, I've been fortunate enough as to have been gifted with another sight."

Eoghan's arms lifted his robe to his sides. "And?"

"I see him in a clearing in a wood. A man still young with life, but graying at the temples. He is waiting for something."

Eoghan winced as a wave crested the tall rocks beyond the gravelly courtyard. "How thrillingly vague, Oldwin. That could be anyone. Anywhere."

"It was once said that to look into the eyes of little Dain Rhiagain was to look into the eyes of Beyond. I would know these eyes a thousand years from now, just as I know them now. It was, after all, I who condemned them to die, even if the task wasn't completed. I know you regret that you never knew your brother."

"I regret that my father's Lord Chancellor lacked the spine to do as his king commanded," Eoghan replied. He leaned his head back so that he could meet the sorcerer's eyes, no matter how unsettling the effort. "And that you couldn't have foreseen it and prevented this predicament we now find ourselves enmeshed in."

"That is not how magic works," Oldwin said once more, and Eoghan mimicked him.

"Yes, yet one more thing I'm forced to take your word for, aren't I? For I know nothing of it myself, and I am at your mercy."

Was it Eoghan's imagination, or was Oldwin suppressing a grin?

"You have again given me life. I would repay that, in sharing what I know."

"Then tell me how a nondescript man in a clearing in the woods is of any use at all to us!"

"Your Grace, it is the beginning. It is confirmation of what we suspected, and we can find power in that. For we know of him, but he does not know of us. This kingdom is only so big, and even a forest can reveal much. For, there is nowhere in the Northerlands where the ground is not inundated with snow right now, so it cannot be there. The Southern Reach is a realm of sand. That eliminates half the kingdom."

"We are still looking through the eye of a needle, Oldwin."

"For now."

"And how can you be sure he doesn't know of us? Of who he is?"

"If he knew he was the heir to the kingdom, do you not think he would've come to reclaim that?"

Eoghan twisted his lips. "Unless he doesn't want it."

"He knows nothing," Oldwin said, his clipped words tinged with a confidence he didn't further explain. "Your Grace, it's growing colder, and this wind is not hospitable to your constitution."

Eoghan tensed under his robe. There were few things more offensive than the reminder of who he was by others. But neither could he deny the dogged chill permeating straight through to his bones, or the ache that might leave him bedridden for days if he didn't address it. "I have matters to tend to, so we will return to the keep," he said. "But I must know. They say you have been on these shores since Carrow Rhiagain washed up. That you were with him."

Oldwin folded his hands over his robe and nodded.

"But you cannot be so unique, can you?"

"I don't understand the question, Your Grace?"

"If there are two of you, you and Mortain, there must be three. There must be more."

"Sorcerers?"

"I won't quibble over a name, Oldwin. Whatever you believe you are."

Oldwin's eyes shifted to the left ever briefly. "If any others made it to the kingdom, I am not aware of it."

Eoghan was certain the sorcerer had just lied to him.

"STEFAN, can you go collect firewood? We'll need more for tonight," Anabella asked. She knew now—one of many things she was learning about her son, now that he had been introduced to a world bigger than her and four walls—that he didn't respond well to any request of him that led to his exclusion. But to give him a task that proved his usefulness was to win his heart.

When he was out of sight, Anabella and Wyat turned to Ransom.

"Both women are completely mad."

Wyat was the first to speak. "I believe they'd both agree with you, and with pride," he said. "But I assume you're not here to repeat what we already know."

"You've heard them. Always arguing. Nay an hour can pass that they aren't at each other's throats, clawing for the top. It only gets worse."

Wyat and Anabella exchanged a look.

"That's nothing new," she said to Ransom. "Has something happened?"

"It's not what has happened, but what will if she isnae stopped."

"Assyria," Wyat whispered, just as Anabella started to ask who.

"Aye, Assyria," Ransom said. He spat upon the snow at his feet. "She's madder than a seabird coated in mine dust. She'll listen to no one!"

"Tell us what she's done."

"Not what she's done, but she will do, if no one stops her, as I said," Ransom said. He looked at Anabella. "You'd think she's the mother o'yer son, not you, miss. She's got her plans for him."

"What plans?"

Ransom threw a glance at the cave. "Unless ye want her to take your son and leave—"

"Take my son!"

Wyat steadied Anabella with his hand. "You're certain? She said this? Said she would do it?"

"Aye, and nothing stopping her. She willnae listen to the reason of Lady Blackwood, and who else is there? Us? She's scarier than most men of the Southerlands, and I suspect there's magic in her, as there is in all Rhiagains."

Anabella had seen no signs of magic in Eoghan, or even Darrick, but that didn't mean Ransom was wrong. Had that not always been both the mystique and the fear surrounding the Rhiagains? How what they knew of them could never match what they did not?

"We could take him with us," Anabella whispered when Ransom was gone. "Return him to his father, where he belongs."

"He won't be safe in Warwicktown any more than Pieter would be safe in Wulfsgate. They're fugitives of the crown. Even with our borders closed, there will be spies. There always are."

"Let Lord Warwick decide where he should be. He's his father. He'll have places a man can go where no one will find him. Just as Torrin's Pass has protected Pieter."

"I don't think we'd make it all the way to Warwicktown. Especially if Assyria intends to go there herself. The father and the son, together. She's said it more than once," Wyat said. He eyed his bow, still leaning against the tree. "I would not forgive myself if I couldn't protect you and Stefan."

Anabella laid a hand on his arm. "Wyat. He's my son, and *I* must protect him, as I have for all his life. But if it eases your heart, there is no one else I'd trust to join me. No one but Darrick himself."

Wyat paced the patch of snow under the tree, casting furtive glances toward the cave. "There may be a place we can go. But if we do... if we leave, we must ride hard. Hard enough that we'll be sick from it. Hard enough that, trail or no, there'll be no catching us."

Anabella felt a new hope swell within her. It was bigger than her fear. "Just tell me. Tell me when."

He turned to face her. "Tomorrow."

EOGHAN CLOSED his eyes as the iron door swung closed behind him. The sound was satisfying. He knew it would keep any of his enemies at bay when they stretched beyond what he could bear. One, only a cell away, called for him, but it would remain unanswered. He might order the lord's food intake halved. Not that it would change anything, for any remorse found in suffering was born of circumstance, not truth. There would be no redemption for Aiden Quinlanden, only the potential for future use.

He stepped lightly over the stones that had never been washed, not in five years or more. Grime coated them, enough that he nearly slipped. He wondered if *she* had known the right spots to step; the ones to avoid. She must have. The old wooden desk, the one which had not been made level and had never been fixed, rocked as he ran his hands over it, as she once had. He felt the grooves in the soft wood where she had pressed her quill, writing the letters that had sustained him, angered him, immersed him. Ah, to imagine her saying these words to Darrick. He had soiled his nightshift with every read and reread, knowing that it would never again *be* to Darrick that the words were said and then now it was he, *he,* the true king, the one who had emerged from hardship to overcome and rule, who was hearing them.

He'd never wished for Anabella's death. No, that wasn't entirely true. In those early days, he'd fantasized of performing the task with his own hands, strangling the life from those beautiful eyes with his cock buried deep within her. A seed for the dying, for the dead. Perhaps he'd continue when her body had gone cold, even, leaving a message for the Guardians. When finished, he would simply toss the boy into the sea and be done with it. The last of his worries washed away.

But that errant anger had been what washed away instead. As he sniffed at the filthy sheets no one had bothered to send to washing, that still smelled of her, Eoghan thought of how calm he felt, suckling at her breast, the hard, fearful beat of her heart lulling him into a fugue. Sometimes his cock would rise from beneath his pants, and he would tend to the ministrations that his body demanded, ignoring her rise of disgust as the white stain spread over his hands, his clothing, sometimes her bed.

But never, not once, had he taken Anabella. Now that she was gone, and no longer his, a remorseful pride came over him at his tremendous restraint. For there had been nothing stopping him, save his own willpower. Nothing stopping him from burying himself in her night after night, while her son watched as he suckled his thumb in the corner of the cold chamber.

His hand felt for the crumbled vellum in his robe. *Isa. My beautiful.* Not his name for her, but he'd stolen it, forcing her to sign her letters with a name that would forever remind her of her dead husband.

Your Grace, my thoughts are often with you. How I long for your presence. For your lips upon my breasts, so that I may feed thee and see thee grow strong.

Eoghan shivered. She'd never meant the words. She'd bartered with them, for her life, for her son's life. But their power over him was no less potent, even now.

"I'm here, Your Grace." Assana's voice cut through his reverie, but his anger stilled before it could take over. He'd called her here. It was as if he'd known only the presence of another could combat the loss of himself to the ghosts of his past.

Eoghan lifted his hand and waved his fingers toward the meager bed. "If you cannot produce a child bearing my blood, you are of no use to me."

"Your Grace." Assana moved tentatively toward the bed. He could almost read the questions brewing within her. Why here? Why now? Was this some trick?

"On your knees."

Assana fumbled through the removal of her clothes. As she prepared herself, Eoghan recalled once more the warm milk that spilled over his tongue as Anabella's hair fell over his face, a blanket of protection from the world. Anabella had taken that. Asherley had taken that. Assana would have this for him, in due time, but he had to swallow his disgust of her and do his duty by her to get there. As he had done his duty when he sent Darrick to his death. As he had done his duty when he imprisoned the traitor in the next cell over.

Eoghan climbed upon the bed behind her. His erection was born of every drop of milk he'd had from the women not his mother. Every last nourishing drink. They were all there, kneeling down to deliver to him that which he most needed, Asherley, Anabella, every milkmaid in the keep who had serviced his needs over the years. Assana screamed as Eoghan drove inside her, imagining her covered in milk, filled with milk, milk spilling from her privates, from her mouth and ass.

"Louder, for your father," he commanded, grunting his satisfaction into every aggressive thrust, grinning through his victory that, at last, he had found the manner of which to deliver a future to his house and crown.

II

THE QUARRELS OF OUR PAST

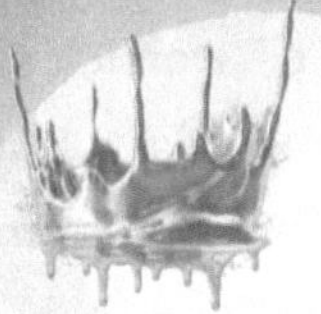

"Your Grace!"

Khallum lowered himself into an inelegant bow, his feet performing an awkward dance as he reacted too late to the moment he hadn't prepared for. He'd never bowed in his life, not for any Rhiagain at least. At first, he hadn't realized he was looking at Prince Darrick at all. He could've been looking at any man in the kingdom, any laborer from the smithy's forge to a spinner from a clothier. Dressed in the threads of a commoner, as was wise, but it gave him a pause he felt the urge to apologize for. He'd met this young man before, once, when he was a lad on progress through the kingdom he was destined to serve.

"You needn't bow to me, Lord Warwick. I'd not be standing here if it weren't for your determination."

Khallum rose. Now, he could regard the man better. He was tall and comely. He reminded Khallum of someone, though he was too flustered to place the recognition. Though he hadn't seen Darrick fresh from Camp Atonement, the skin melting from his bones, he could almost see it now, in his eyes, where the last five years lived. To look at him now, Khallum wouldn't have known the man's trials, only his resilience, which radiated from Darrick Rhiagain as if a color he was painted with.

But it was something else that had caused his eyes to pass over the prince in search of the real one. Khallum realized he'd been looking for the gnarled form of the brother, of pitiful, broken Eoghan, and not this strapping, princely man standing before him now.

"It has only been five or so years since I met you last, but it may as well have been a lifetime," Darrick said when Khallum couldn't find the proper words. Here, at last. Darrick Rhiagain, in the flesh. Not a dream, or a whim, but a real man, of blood and bone, of honor. Alive.

"Aye," Khallum said. His voice cracked, and he pounded the base of his throat. "You speak true on that, Your Grace."

"Darrick." His smile was half-hearted. "Or Godfrey, when the ears are listening."

"I could never. No matter what I might think of your brother or forebears."

"Ryan did." Darrick looked down at the Strong boy. He ran a hand over his forehead lovingly. "And will again."

Khallum checked the door to be sure Hamish wasn't lingering. "What are they saying, about young Strong?"

Darrick lowered his eyes. He brought his hand back and lowered himself into the chair next to Ryan. "They say we're fools to look for his waking. I say they don't know the man I served with. They didn't see the flesh beat from his bones, or the fire in his eyes as he spoke words that would take food from his belly. They didn't see the man who swallowed the herbs knowing well that he may not come out the other side of it. Knowing he may die for his realm, to save it."

Khallum sighed as he watched Ryan. Slow breaths, rising and falling, but nothing else to show the spirited boy who had chased seabirds in Sandycove was still within. The whip of a lad who had deigned beyond his reach, but had done so for the fire of love burning hot within him. He wondered if Ryan even knew Esmerelda had gone to the Guardians.

He'd never wanted this. Only to slap his hand and remind him of his place. Not this. "He was your friend, then."

"He *is* my friend, Lord Warwick. And my friend he'll remain, for I have hope where others have surrendered theirs. I have hope enough for all of us."

"There isnae harm in hope, till there is."

Darrick nodded. "And if it were me upon that bed, there'd be no shortage of it, I presume." A more serious look passed over his face. "I must ask you to relieve me of a curiosity I've had since Ryan first told me you'd sent in him to find me."

Khallum grunted. He shifted his boots on the wood. "Aye. If I can."

"The Warwicks have good reason not to love a Rhiagain. Why put this effort into restoring one to the throne instead of seeing it all undone and let the Reaches rule unto themselves, as they once did?"

Khallum expected this question, though not so soon in their acquaintance. "What ye say is true. We've reason, and so do others, even if they've not the belly for the same hatred we've grown in salt and sand. But the Rhiagains were nay the first to think themselves worthy of ruling all in the kingdom, only the ones who made it work. Before the Rhiagains, there was more than unrest. There was war, war with no winners. For even a battle won isnae a victory when they never end."

Darrick nodded. "You believe if you pulled Eoghan from the throne with no replacement that there would be war."

"Aye. War from those who have seen how good a crown looks upon a Rhiagain and might ken it would look well upon them as well." Khallum cleared his throat. He had a powerful urge to send the snot careening into the wall, as he would in his own keep, but he was standing before a man who would be king. "Things were well under the reign of Fynne the Good. I ken they could be well under you."

"I hope to prove you right, Lord Warwick." He nodded again, his thoughts once more seeming to be elsewhere. "My wife and son. Have you any new word?"

Khallum had sent the Dereham scout back without a message of his own, because he distrusted any message delivery in the kingdom. And then he'd received Lady Gretchen's message about the growing unrest in the cave. If Gwyn had been the one to plant the idea of coming to Whitecliffe, it had been Gretchen's worries that solidified it. If the situation with the young prince was compromised, then it was once again down to Darrick Rhiagain alone. Khallum could no longer leave the matter of the future king to others.

But he would not trouble Prince Darrick with such things. "Your wife and son fare well. They grow stronger, and are eager to join you, when the time is right."

Darrick smiled, looking off to the side. "I never in all my dreams imagined I would see her again, but a *son*?" He shook his head. "I once told Anabella that not all that lacked explanation should be disregarded as magic, but I may have been wrong. Only magic could've delivered me such a gift."

"I know you're eager to be reunited."

"I want more for them to be safe, and far from harm."

Khallum's belly turned. The prince was being charitable. He'd not mentioned Khallum's failure to act, when it must be all he could think about in this agonizing convalescence, so far from where the action should be. "There's no place more safe than the Northerlands, right now, if Dereham's borders hold. But I ken we didnae spring you from prison for safe, did we?"

Darrick laughed. "No. We did not."

"My hesitation... my..." Khallum stopped short of saying *fear*.

"My delay, Your Grace, Darrick, is only due to recent events in the kingdom. What Lord Quinlanden has done, as I assume my men have kept you well informed on."

Darrick nodded. "His treachery regarding Lord Byrne will be paid tenfold. But what he has done to the Medvedev is even beyond my imagining. Has anyone deduced how he's managed such an unfathomable feat?"

"It is said he has a Rhiagain sorcerer in his employ."

"Does he?" Darrick pondered this. He seemed to go somewhere else.

"Do you know about that, Your... Darrick?"

"The great sorcerers of Ilynglass," Darrick said, as if he was talking more to himself. "I've known a few. Oldwin toils in the sky dungeon at Duncarrow, or did when I was there. There is also Mortain, and I remember there were two others my father spoke of, though they weren't around when I was growing up. Spies, I always thought, though he never said that. Lysanor and Isdemus. There may be more. I don't know. Those who might are dead."

"Ilynglass?" Khallum repeated.

"It is said that's where the Rhiagains come from. Before Carrow washed upon the shores of this kingdom."

Khallum wanted to know more, but there'd be time for that later. "Mortain. That's the one. The one The Deceiver has in his employ."

Darrick nodded, sighing. "Yes, I could see that, then. But why now?"

"It is true then, of the sorcerers? That they are..."

Darrick again turned to check on Ryan, this time running the damp cloth over his face. "Who can say? But my father insisted Oldwin looked no different when my father was a boy than he did when my father was old and dying. He says Oldwin served his father, and his father before him. It defies explanation, but many things do."

"If The Deceiver had one? Could a sorcerer truly subdue them all? As powerful as the Medvedev are?"

"Our magic isn't your magic," Darrick replied. "I can't pretend to know how magic works, but I know that when we came to your kingdom, we brought with us a kind the kingdom had no defense against. Though should not also the reverse be true, that those of you native to these lands must have magic we cannot defend either?" He shook his head. "It isn't true what some say, that Rhiagains have magic. It's the magic of sorcerers to be feared. There are few, but they have never needed numbers for power." He dropped the cloth in the basin. "Yes, I believe it's possible. What you ask."

"How do we stop this madness?"

"I don't have the answer," Darrick said. "Even Rhiagains don't understand their magic. Only another sorcerer would."

Khallum snorted. "Aye, and the lot of good that does us, when we've none?" He remembered himself, his quick fire fading. "Your Grace."

"Lord Warwick, you've been right to give pause to action rather than storming into the Easterlands with no eye to the risk awaiting you. But Mortain is one creature, not many. His magic may have been enough to enslave the Medvedev, but his power has limits, as all things do. If the kingdom knew of Quinlanden's crime against them, they would not accept it."

"You think I should spread word of this treachery?"

"I do."

Khallum leaned back against the wall. Maeryn Blackwood had trusted him with this secret, but he'd never considered why it should be one. Or had that been her motive all along, to deliver this knowledge to one with the power to see it answered? The one with the fire and mettle to do what others would not? "I confess, I'd not given this the thought it deserves."

"Aiden is in Duncarrow with my brother. He's been out of communication, they say, and so his men are under command of his officers. Without leadership, they will fall apart, and his officers will only provide enough of that for so long." Darrick looked at Khallum, meeting his eyes. "I think the reason Aiden has sent no word to his men is because Eoghan has imprisoned him."

Khallum's mouth parted. "And why would you think that? Your brother is who *ordered* the attack upon my brother, upon the Medvedev. Who else would have given him the sorcerer to do as he pleased?"

Darrick rose to his feet. He moved to the tiny window at the other side of the room. "I don't think Eoghan ordered any of those things. He wants obedience, not war. He wants others to worship him, not loathe him."

"Too late for tha'."

"If Eoghan gave Aiden use of Mortain, it was in gratitude for laying Rowanwen at his feet. Eoghan must have thought... must have believed he had subdued Quinlanden himself with his acceptance of such a gift. He wouldn't have realized that the act had empowered him, not stilled him. Lord Byrne's murder would have horrified Eoghan, as we can only take such a thing as an act of war."

"You have a soft spot for him? After what he did?"

"I have nothing but contempt for Eoghan," Darrick said, turning away from the window to look again at Khallum. "But I won't let my anger get in the way of what I know to be true. Eoghan is no conniving monster. He is weak, and he is foolish, but that is not the same. He'll be horrified by the guards patrolling the Westerlands, inciting rebellion from those loyal to Lady Blackwood. He'll be lost for how to deal with it."

"I donnae ken what ye mean for us to do. Ally with the ratsbane? That cannae be what you're implying?"

"No," Darrick said. "I have something else in mind."

. . .

HAMISH WAITED until Darrick's steps faded into echoes at the base of the spiral staircase. He'd thought Khallum might join the prince, so that Hamish could again be with his son, but Khallum lingered in the room where Ryan convalesced. If he wanted to be with his son, he'd need to face Khallum as well.

"Lord Khallum. Forgive me, it's only that I want to be here. When he wakes, ye ken."

Khallum sat in the rickety chair half supported by the wall. He watched Ryan. "Hamish. My old friend. I've been waiting for a moment where we could have a word."

"A word? Have I displeased ye, sir?"

"No, not that, it's only... now that I've seen Ryan with my own eyes, I know what he's done to bring this gift to us, and I want ye to know my gratitude. But I also *need* you to know, it was never this I wanted."

Hamish flushed. The sensation traveled all the way to his fingers and toes. He'd always been the man in the room short on the right words, but it most aggrieved him when he had no proper response for his lord, who had done right by him, better than another might have. Khallum had never forgotten their friendship as children. He kept the other men from silencing him when he had the words to say.

But Khallum was apologizing, even if he'd never say the precise words, and Hamish would be expected to accept it as it was.

"I did... I wanted to punish him, for kenning he could have what wasnae his," Khallum went on. "For assuming himself upon my Esmerelda. But I didnae send him in to hurt him, Hamish. I had faith in yer boy, and he did what we sent him to do. He saved us. He may have saved this entire realm."

"Aye. I never doubted him," Hamish managed. His eyes burned. He didn't need these words from his lord, for he'd known Khallum's love for him was not tinged with vengeance. He'd never been angry that it was Ryan who'd been sent, and not someone else's son. "He's my son. My true blood, through and through. My only son."

"I'll nay disagree that Jesse is more his ma, but he's still your son and a fine man."

Hamish shook his head. He hadn't ever planned to make this confession, but he needed Khallum to wear another look than the guilt-laden grief painting his sorrowful face. "Ye know how I loved my Yanna. I didnae care what others said, 'bout her. Tha' she didnae belong. I never let a word hit me any deeper than the flesh."

"Salt and sand," Khallum whispered. "Not all are born to it. It is a way of life. Yanna understood our way. She was one of us."

"Aye, she did. She embraced it, as I once embraced her when I learned of the man who had harmed her." Hamish bowed his head. The words were harder, even, than volleying the appreciation of apology. "Who had *befouled* her and taken her very honor."

"What are you saying, Hamish?"

"Yanna was already with child when I married her. Aye, I knew it. Before that, even, for when I met her, her belly ware already swole. She'd said I needed to know what I was askin'. What she *was* now that he'd done what he did."

"Jesse," Khallum said. He exhaled, looking away. "He's nay your son at all, is that what you're saying?"

"He's my son in all ways tha' matter, my lord. I'll nay tell him, ever, for it doesnae concern this or tha', nae does it? Jamesan is my son and my heir. Doesnae make a whit of difference who sired him. I reared him from a bairn."

"Do you know who his father is?"

Hamish shook his head. He blubbered the unwelcome snot into his fist. "I nay asked. For if I knew of the name of the ratsbane who'd harmed my Yanna, I would've taken his heart out with my teeth, and I'd ha' been no good to anyone. Ye ken?"

Khallum's eyes were wide as he nodded. "I ken."

"So as ye see, Jesse is my heir, but Ryan is my boy. My baby."

Hamish's lower lip trembled with his hard breath. "I'll nae survive hearing the dead-given rites read over him, Khallum. It'd be the end of me."

Khallum pushed to his feet and approached Hamish. He laid both hands upon his shoulders. "Ryan took the herbs knowing the risks. He took them, knowing the reward. And there isnae a better way, as I see it, to honor his sacrifice than seeing his work through to the end. Will ye see it done with me, brother?"

Hamish lowered his head and sobbed. Nodded.

"Aye, ye will. For there's none as beloved to me as my Hamish Strong," Khallum said. "And I cannae think of a better way to wake Ryan from his wee slumber than having the ratsbane's head upon a pike in Sandycove for all to see."

Gathering at all was a risk. They had to be prudent with their time. If they let their words linger well into the night, there'd be whispers. Whispers of what Khallum Warwick was doing by moonlight with three of his top men and one of Stewardess Rutland's convalescents.

Darrick chose to say nothing. He didn't give his reason for volunteering his silence, but Khallum understood. Darrick trusted him to lead them forward into this plan, even if Khallum himself wasn't certain it was the right way. But Khallum's men would follow Khallum before they would follow Darrick, no matter what they'd risked to rescue him.

"We haven't long," Khallum said. He stood by the fire. Hamish lingered by the stone wall, their lookout. Law and Rutland hovered across from Khallum, stealing glances at the prince sitting upon the log in silence. "So I'll say this but once. And if ye donnae want a part in it, then so it is, for the lot of you have already delivered more than I could ask for if it were to come to pass again. But if you're in, we leave before first light."

"You've led us fair thus far, Khallum," Law said. "We'll see it done, whatever you ask now."

"Aye," Rutland replied, his face lit only be the flickering flame. "As he said."

Hamish knew already. He'd been the first to know, for it was but a small show of faith for the man who had sacrificed his son for this cause. He kept his eyes divided between Khallum's small band of men and the perimeter.

"He's recovered here long enough," Khallum said, with a nod in Darrick's direction. He dared not say his name,; not out here, in the dark, where even Hamish couldn't catch every wandering ear. "He's ready to move."

"Move?" Law asked.

"As he and I see it, we've two problems standing between us and restoring the crown. Both caused by The Deceiver."

"Aye," Rutland whispered.

"Until answered, any effort of ours willnae last long," Khallum went on. His hands were shaking. Shaking! His hands never shook, not before his men, who he had no cause for nerves with. He buried them in his leather vest. "We must snuff out The Deceiver's hold upon the Westerlands. They've solicited our aid. There's a cabal of men, gathering, ready to fight."

"I thought we'd decided this was not our fight, my lord," Law said. "As the other Reaches have always reminded us."

Khallum ground his teeth. He'd made this very argument. Believed it still. It rooted around like shards of glass in his soul. That the Warwicks had asked so many times, and had been told it was their own fight, their own problem. But it was always the fight of the realm, when one was under attack. For one was never enough. "We must put aside the bad blood of the past, Law, much as it aggrieves me to think of these past slights. If the Westerlands falls, we fall with it. The realm will descend to chaos. And if we donnae rise to see this prevented, when we have... when we have *this...*" Khallum pointed his hand at Darrick. "Then we're naught but fools! We donnae deserve victory if we would put it second to the quarrels of our past."

Law and Rutland both nodded, each considering this in their own ways.

"What about the bairn in the north?" Law asked.

Khallum hadn't shared his concerns about the situation in the Northerlands, even with his own men. "He is but a bairn, and 'tis a man we have here, with us, *ready.*"

"The Westerlands, then," Rutland said.

"Aye, the Westerlands. To where they've gathered the vestiges of their rebellion. A place I dare not say aloud. But we cannae travel as we are, men. We cannae allow our presence to draw Aiden's eye."

"Some may remember his face," Rutland said with a nod at Darrick. "Our secret may not stay so for long."

"Aye," Khallum said. "It's a truth that must come out, and he knows the risks of sharing it now. But the men of the Westerlands have no friend in Duncarrow. They will join with us, after we've restored order in the Reach. As will the others in the kingdom, when they receive the ravens we sent earlier this day."

"What ravens?" Rutland asked, frowning.

"We begin this war by spreading the horrors that befell the Saleen at the hands of The Pretender and The Deceiver. This truth belongs to the kingdom, and now they shall have it. Will only make the other truths easier to swallow, when the time comes, I ken." He looked at Hamish. "Your place is with your son, Hamish. But I will send for you, to lead the Warwick Guard to the Westerlands, when the time comes."

Hamish nodded.

"I'll have word sent that we've traveled north. It will not stay the attention of spies for long, but perhaps long enough," Law said. He kicked at the coals, roaring the flame back to life. "It will be nothing for us to travel as common men. Rutland and I are quite versed in the efforts by now."

"Aye, ye making a joke, Law? 'Tis a first, it is," Hamish said with a laugh. Law's lip twitched.

"Should we send word ahead? That we're coming?" Rutland asked.

"Nay," Khallum replied. "Ravens fall into enemy hands too often these days for them to be trusted with our secrets." He glanced at Darrick. "And I've so few joys in life now that I'll take the one coming to me when these men see who we've brought them."

12

THE BLACKWOOD BANNERS

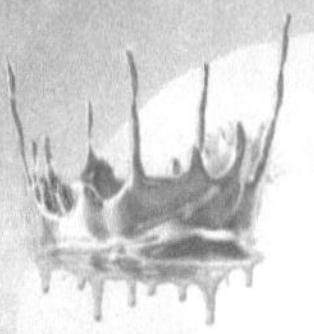

The tavern reeked of old wood stained with the ale and sweat of the men who had moved on for the evening. Kaslan busied himself behind the bar, tidying after the departure of fifty or so who had just shuffled out, returning to the abandoned shacks they called home until theirs was again safe.

The few who lingered behind were what Easlan had lovingly begun calling The Blackwood Banners, the men most trusted with words spoken by moonlight alone. Jesse had become one of these men without meaning to, these bannermen of Brandyn, who the young heir drew counsel from and gave trust in return.

Both James men were in this group, as the recognized leaders of the gathering, but so was the enigmatic Rush Rider, Arturo Blackfen, and his unusual choice in companion, the highest man of the clergy in the Westerlands, Grand Minister Rhydian Tyndall. Jesse trusted less the presence of the Enchanter, Joran Rosewood, but Brandyn was blind with love for his mother's principal confidante. Some whispered it was a way to feel close to his mother again.

"This tavern won't be big enough, men keep arriving as they

do," Easlan remarked. He leaned against the bar in his black coat, watching the others from beneath the wide brim of his hat. "Standing room only, as it is. Even the ale's running dry."

"I'll make more," Kaslan said. "I can wake earlier than I have been, double the barrels."

"They'll drink faster than you can brew. They've already run through our stores in the cellar."

"Doesn't mean I can't try."

"Trying isn't enough, Kaslan. We're here for more than trying, or I should hope."

"Then what do you suggest, Father? We bail water from the streams and have an uprising when we serve that instead?"

Jesse felt the sting of the backhand his own father would have sent for speaking to him that way. But Easlan gave no indication of irritation at his son's insolence. His eyes were fixed, already, on the near-empty room, where the ghosts of the resistance lingered. It was as if he could still see them all, their bodies hot with readiness to move, to see their world restored as the tips of their swords. "We've lingered to discuss what comes next. Sent our spies who haven't returned to us, and may never. Greystone has been a fine enough gathering point, but we won't save this Reach from our sad corner of the map. And it won't remain a haven forever."

"More will come, Steward James," Brandyn said. He stepped forward, his face lighting under the metal crown of the candlelit chandelier. "They come slowly, to keep eyes off their travels, but they would all come, every last one, if they could do so safely."

"Young Lord Blackwood, by the time they did, this would be a land fully under Quinlanden rule. Perhaps irreversibly so."

"You think we should go to battle now? As we are?" Kaslan asked. His eyes passed around the room with a bemused grin.

"That's why I asked some of you men to stay a spell longer this eve. It's what I'd like to propose for discussion."

"An old refrain," Joran muttered to himself. "One without answer."

Kaslan was aghast. "But we have perhaps fifty men. Not more than seventy. We'll show up to a battle and gift them with a rout."

Brandyn looked at Arturo. "In your travels, Rider Blackfen, what have you seen?"

"There's nowhere now that Quinlanden's men are not stationed in numbers larger than ours. Nowhere but here, and as Steward James says, it's only a matter of time now."

"And the Easterlands?" Brandyn asked.

"It seems impossible he's left enough for its defense, from the numbers I've seen here. But that would be a dangerous assumption without confirmation."

"I have also heard this," Rhydian replied. "If it is so, then the Guardians have willed it."

"Grand Minister, begging your pardon, but the Guardians work for the Rhiagains these days, in case no one told you. Forgive me if that leaves me absent of faith in what they've willed and not," Kaslan said.

Rhydian was unruffled by Kaslan's words. "The Guardians existed long before the Rhiagains. What they have forced upon us is a structure of that faith, not faith itself. The Guardians don't answer to anyone, and they don't make mistakes. If the Easterlands is undefended, then this is the work of the Guardians."

"I suppose we should just let them fight this war then, aye?"

"There doesn't have to be a war if we can find the heart."

"Eh? The heart?" Kaslan scrunched his face. "What nonsense is this?"

"The heart is in Duncarrow, languishing in some delight or another while his men await his word," Easlan said. "Without the heart, the body is weak. Weaker each day. When the heart returns, so does the strength."

"They don't lack in strength, I assure you," Arturo said. "They grow restless without word from their lord, but this has only led to further attacks upon what should be out of limits for them. They've crossed the bounds of decency that we have always followed. They're attacking sons, raping daughters. And they'll do worse, if left without the master to bring them to heel."

"It's that evil doer. Mads Waters," Joran said, breaking his silence. "Oh, he's a foul one! Aiden may be a cruel boy, but Mads provides the meals that feed the cruelty. He sees an opportunity, he takes it! He *has* taken it!"

Kaslan rolled his eyes at Jesse from across the dim room.

"Then we come for Mads," Brandyn said. "If the heart is in Duncarrow, we take the hand."

"He'll be surrounded by men to prevent this very thing," Arturo said.

"After what he did to my father, he should have one eye cast over his shoulder until his last breath leaves him," Brandyn said. "Where is he now?"

"Whitechurch. He hasn't left."

"How many men?"

"I cannot say. I haven't left the Westerlands, for fear of being denied a return."

"The Deceiver is in Duncarrow, and his dog is in the Easterlands, so who's directing these men who have taken our home?" No one answered. "No one knows? Is that it? What say you, Joran? What future have you scried for the Blackwoods that you haven't shared?"

"Lord Blackwood, you know I would tell you if I'd seen anything."

Brandyn smirked. "As you were always so faithful to my mother."

"My lord, I don't believe I know what you mean. I was *always* faithful to Lady Blackwood."

"Then you forget that I, too, am a seer, Enchanter Rosewood, and even in my inexperience I've seen more men coming. Men of importance. A seer of your great wisdom and practice must have seen so much more."

Perhaps the young lord was wiser about Joran than he seemed, Jesse thought.

Joran fumbled with his bony hands, rolling them over the silver fabric of his robe, looking distressed. The seer might have a genuine gift of magic, but his acting was also something to behold. "Nothing clear, I'm afraid, and as I know they've taught you at the Sepulchre, we are to nourish a vision until we have clarity, not seek to scry the meaning without the full picture."

"Lord Blackwood, you said men of importance." Jesse stepped away from the bar, toward the small cloister of men. "Did you see who? Or from where?"

"No," Brandyn said. He looked so small in his leather armor, but his thoughts were bigger than all the men there. He wore the weight of his family, his entire Reach, upon him, a task Jesse had no envy for. "But Magi Dereham... that is, Christian Dereham, Lord Dereham's son, promised to stir his father to our cause. The Northerlands are our allies. The Southerlands, too, though they've refused our invite. And I struggle to believe that Lord Quinlanden doesn't have men in his own Reach who would disavow what he's done."

"And did you see numbers? Will we get many more?" Jesse pressed.

"I don't know. I'd hoped Joran would."

Joran cast a pitiful look at his hands.

"Numbers against time," Easlan interjected. "Do you think that The Deceiver's men will grow weaker as we grow stronger? Time provides strength for all. We can act with fifty, or five hundred, but the five hundred will come at a cost, for our enemy will have used the time same as we have. If they haven't already defeated us."

"You can say this because you haven't seen them with your

own eyes, Steward James," Arturo said, stepping out of the shadows. "Ahh, but I have. I put a sword through the one who defiled Lyria Tyndall, and Rhydian carried her brother, Jonah's, broken form to be mended by his mother. And those are highborn children. What of those less fortunate left rotting, discarded, in the beds of cabbage? What of those homes burned and razed to the ground? Our strongest defense, my brotherhood, the Rush Riders, are scattered throughout the kingdom, searching for allies, finding mainly seclusion and fear. You present a stirring cause, Easlan, one I'm all too eager to join you in, if I could push all I know and have seen to the back of my troubled mind. But I cannot. We will crush The Deceiver with our cunning, not our count."

"Well, we must do *something!*" Kaslan cried. He slammed both palms upon the bar. "We have toiled here for weeks, promising these men action. They drink our ale, sleep in the cold beds of the men who left us for better ventures. Father is right, it will not be the watered down ale that drives them to madness, but the lingering! The nothing!"

"And what do the Guardians say, Grand Minister Tyndall?" Joran asked, his words tinged with the same dripping cynicism others leveled upon him when he spoke of magic. "What do they advise?"

"As you know, they're not a beacon for answers, only strength. They prompt men to find within them the solutions needed, rather than stepping in to see the tasks done themselves."

"Hmph. You may as well beseech the air, for all the good to be done from that."

"Cunning," Jesse said, repeating Arturo's word from a moment ago. "Seems we're not in short supply of *that*, so why not discuss how to employ it?"

Easlan James scoffed in disgust. "Cunning is for women, Jamesan. With their vials of poison and their tricks of magic. We are men, and there will be war, and if none of you have the belly for it, then I'll lead it myself, lead it for Lady Blackwood, for all of us, even if all that awaits me at the end of this cursed path is death!"

He slammed through the doors leading to the kitchens, Kaslan not far behind.

"Well," Brandyn said. "Perhaps things will look clearer for us all in the morning."

"I KNOW MY WAY. I donnae require an escort," Jesse said as Arturo rode at his side, aimed toward the woods, and the keep. Arturo's horse sat a foot taller than Jesse's. It was bred for speed and for war, and for, as Jesse heard tell of it, the precision that could come only with a true bond with the one riding. Arturo would know his horse as well as himself, as the horse would know him the same.

"You and I see things through common eyes," the horseman said. "Easlan is right, the men are clamoring for war, and soon, we'll have a problem to contend with, if they aren't given it. But what they want more than war is their land and freedoms restored. Their families no longer in fear. If we can do that before they go mad with unrest, we will be better for it."

"You look to the wrong man for answers," Jesse said, as they came upon the end of the main road and the start of the forest path. "I have none. Even if I did, this isnae my fight."

"Ah, yes, you're just a trader's son, all salt and sand, no care for anything but," Arturo said. "Or not. I know which I'd stake my gold on. Fair evening."

Arturo's horse spun without being ordered, and they headed back toward town.

"IT'S TOO SOON," Gretchen said. She poured herself a second glass of wine from the jug. It was good wine. The last from the cask rolled out at her second wedding to Holden, the one thrown by the locals in Wulfsgate welcoming her to her new home. Dunwoode's finest. She'd been saving it. For what, she couldn't say, though it seemed to her the birth of her first grandchild might be an occasion worthy.

Now, she saw no point in waiting for any such occasion to pass. Nothing was certain, not even her own feelings on matters she once thought decided.

"Gretchen is right," Holden said, nodding her way as if this agreement made up for all the arguments that came prior. "You brought enough provisions to tide them for another month, and another trip so quickly after your last will draw questions. They will wonder why you didn't just stay with Aylen's father, rather than subject yourself to the precariousness of the dangerous pass. No, we'll keep to the schedule we discussed."

"It's more than that," Gretchen said, ignoring him. It felt good to ignore him, for him to know the slight was intentional. The balance of her love for him slid closer to hatred each day. But these little rebellions, these pulls for power, helped stave off the utter darkness of a failed marriage little by little. Her marriage was saved in a thousand tiny cuts delivered by her tongue and intentions. "As you both have told us, the situation on the mountain grows volatile. Lady Blackwood and Princess Assyria await direction that we cannot give, and every time we remind them of that, we upset the delicate stability of their living situation."

"Why again are we waiting for Lord Warwick? Can we not decide for ourselves how to break this stalemate we have here in the north, and how to proceed with the matter of Stefan Rhiagain? He's our guest, not Khallum's," Christian asked. He watched her with the same look Holden often gave her, but there was something more in Christian's eyes that kept her from worrying over it too much. His questions were meant to elicit conversation; this was the instructor in him, and why, she was loath to admit, he must love it so.

"Khallum Warwick should not decide the actions of the Northerlands," Holden added. "They arrived on our shore, not his."

"Inaction is your weapon of choice," Gretchen replied. To her son, she said, "The kingdom lacks unity. You were here when that Rush Rider, Blackfen, told us about the state of things in the Westerlands. We may think this isn't our fight, but it is, just as it was ours when the Southerlands called for aid and those before us ignored their pleas. The king will only benefit from our discord now, and we should not deliver him that gift so easily."

"When will we send men to aid the Westerlands, then?" Aylen asked. "As Rider Blackfen said, they're all gathering now. They won't abide Lord Quinlanden's men on their lands much longer."

"It's not enough to send men into a cause lacking direction. When they have a way forward, they can be certain the Northerlands will join them," Gretchen said.

"And our men are still at practice. Theyre improving, but more is needed," Holden said.

Gretchen sighed before she could stop herself. "If you say it enough, perhaps it will be true. Let a man decide for himself if he's capable of defending what he most cares about. His answer might surprise you."

Holden shoved himself out from the table and stormed from the room.

"Mother," Christian said.

"Don't look at me to explain your father's insecurities."

"You goad him. Endlessly. You never have a kind word. You can't let a thing he says go without answer."

"Your father is a fool and a coward," Gretchen said. "I won't apologize for making it known."

"He *knows* how you feel about him. Is it necessary to grind your hatred of him into his flesh like glass?"

Gretchen closed her eyes and focused her breath through a long exhale. "I don't hate your father."

Christian threw his hands up. "Then I fear for the man you truly do hate."

"I will eventually overcome my anger for what his obedience to The Pretender drove your brother and sister to do," Gretchen replied. "But his pride will recover. Drystan and Lisbet are still lost. Our kingdom lies on the brink of war, and we have one of the keys to unlock all of that. Khallum has the other. For that, we must remain in alignment. But understand, Christian, Aylen, that I will not rest idly forever. The Westerlands won't survive it. We might not, and my children will never be safe until Eoghan Rhiagain is no longer king."

"Father said you called off the search party for Drystan, Lisbet, and Eavan," Christian countered. "Forgive me, but I cannot understand that. They could be home with us now, part of this very conversation, even. With our borders closed, they *would* be safe."

"I called them off because they had better chances out in the wilderness than they did in the hands of Eoghan Rhiagain," Gretchen answered, tempering the venom for the son who was building to the levels of the father. She didn't want to feel this for Christian, now or ever. Anger at his choice, yes, but never this. She sighed. "But as it is, I agree. Things are different now. And your father doesn't know this, but I've sent them out once more. They've found their trail, but it goes cold just before the Hinterlands, and our men won't enter the Forest of All."

Christian gasped. "You think they're in the Hinterlands?"

"They must be. And if they are, they're either safe, or they're dead," Gretchen said plainly, looking away from the shock on her son's face. "No, they're not dead. I would know if it my own babies had gone from this world. And they have Ravenna with them. Her protection kept them safe up to that point. I have to believe it will continue to do so."

"What do we do, Lady Gretchen? For now, while we wait?" Aylen asked. Her calming voice was solace upon the charged conversation that consumed their words and thoughts, day after day. "How can we continue to be of aid?"

Gretchen placed her hands over Aylen's. "Ember has lost her father and sister, and been denied her mother. She is forbidden from her own home, and she may never see her other siblings again. With the kingdom on the brink of war, I feel as if I've not been able to give her the attention she deserves. It would be a great service to me, and to Lady Blackwood, if you could help ease her through this."

"Ahh, thank you," Jesse said, accepting the mug of tea from Esmerelda. She returned to the chair by the fire and curled her legs up under her, wrapping both hands around a belly now betraying its truth.

"I tried something new tonight. See if you like it."

He settled into the chair across from her. "How do you feel?"

"Tired," she said, sighing the word. The dim light of the fire showed only hints of the darkness under her eyes,. But he'd seen these changes in Esmerelda when he'd return home in the evenings. She'd always be there, waiting, with his tea and an ear for what little he had to say.

"You seem troubled," she said. She pulled a quilt from the back of the chair and wrapped it around her. "More than usual."

Jesse nodded. He brought the steaming mug to his face and let the warmth wash over him before drawing a sip. "I've told you how the men grow restless. Tonight, they brought it to discussion. I'm afraid no one can agree on how to move forward. Fight. Sit. Wait. No matter what we do, there willnae be accord, though, of that I am certain."

Esmerelda dropped her head to the side, regarding him through the bleary eyes of one who should have turned in hours ago. "And what do you think should happen?"

The way she looked at him was a far cry from the disdain he saw in Easlan's eyes, not even a tick of the moon earlier. She wasn't making conversation, or entertaining his need to get his troubles out; she thought he might have answers, and more, that they'd be worthy of considering.

Her faith in him left Jesse feeling emptier than he had been in a long time.

"I... I don't know, Esme, but I cannae help but think of where we'll go when the Abbey is no longer safe for you."

"Maybe you have it all wrong, Jesse. Maybe we're exactly where we're supposed to be. My father always said the Guardians don't make mistakes."

Jesse half-chuckled. "I heard a man say those very words tonight."

"There's comfort in them," Esmerelda said, stifling a yawn. "Even if they turn out not to be true."

"These men would bring battle to their doorstep."

"It would be hard to blame them, after what's been done against them. After what happened to my uncle."

"It is their right, and I cannae say a word against it. I haven't. I won't. But I can't protect you here, if they do."

Esmerelda dropped the blanket and moved toward him. With a slight kneel, she leaned in and kissed the top of his head. "Release your worries to the stars for the evening. The problems of the kingdom won't be solved tonight, but the problem of your sleepless nights might." She stepped back and smiled, and an invisible hand fell softly over his eyes as the gentle lull of sleep beckoned. Esmerelda took the blanket and laid it over him. "I told you I tried something new. Consider it a small cup of my gratitude."

CHRISTIAN WALKED with his wife in the Wintergarden. Each step revived old memories of the two of them playing here, before there was love between them, when the joy of imagination was bigger than the potential of any future bond. It was painful to remember how happy he'd once been in Wulfsgate. But the memories of Aylen from that era were the source of his youthful joy.

"How do you think Brandyn and Storm have fared?" he asked her as they stepped under the winter blossoms of the cherry and plum trees. He didn't ask the question often. The lack of answer concerned him. "I didn't expect them to send a raven, but hearing nothing at all has me wondering if we shouldn't have brought him here with us."

"Have you not seen anything? Anything at all?"

"Nothing," Christian said. "But I think... I hope, if he were in danger, I would know it. My visions seem most closely connected to those I care about."

"But you've seen nothing of Drystan or Lisbet, either."

Christian shook his head.

"Perhaps it doesn't work that way, then. The other Magi would tell us visions are a random gift of magic, with no reason. Some even believe that the magic is a gift from the Guardians them-selves, and that faith and mysticism are intrinsically linked. If that's true, it explains why you were sent the vision of Brandyn and Storm in peril. It was something you had the power to act upon."

"Do you believe that?"

"I don't know," Aylen said, with a dreamy look. "Nor am I sure it matters. We get what are given, nothing more."

"I worry for my mother. Her hostility will eat her from the inside out."

Aylen stopped. "Christian, I feel I need to say something to you. About this."

"You know you can say what you feel with me."

"I, too, have sympathy for your father and how she speaks to him. I've witnessed her do it before his own men, and that is wrong," Aylen said. "But... I also understand what lies behind her words."

Christian folded his hands over his torso. "How do you mean?"

"I have a great respect for your father, as does my father," Aylen went on. "But he doesn't seem ready for what's coming. I find myself in solidarity with Lady Gretchen on most things, though her methods are only driving further enmity where we need amity."

"I see."

Aylen folded her arms. "You're cross with me."

"No, I—"

"You say I can speak my mind, but I have, and as it doesn't match your view on things, you're preparing to tell me why I'm wrong."

Christian stepped forward. He wrapped his gloved hands around her shoulders. "Aylen. That's not it." He kissed her. "That's never it. Not with us."

Aylen relaxed some. "It better not ever be. Our marriage wasn't some contract beyond our control. I *chose* you."

"As I chose you. And I promise you. Your mind is your own, no matter what mine is thinking," Christian assured her. "We're not in disagreement here, anyway." He sighed. "The truth is, I know my mother is right. But, as you said, it's her methods. A leader must inspire, not separate, and if she sees herself as the leader of this, as it were, then she needs to consider that she will *need* my father at her side, if not in deed then in body. Most of his men won't follow a woman. She may be the power, but he is the face. She's pushing him to break from her, and I'm terrified of what that might bring."

Aylen nodded, considering his words. He loved this about her, that she didn't vie for her chance to speak, understanding when to listen and when to talk. He tried his best to be the same for her.

Christian dropped his voice lower. "And... what troubles me all the more is, I see so much of my father in me. It's why I couldn't stay... why I couldn't..."

Aylen cradled his face. "I know why, Christian. I know your fears. But you're wrong. You are very much like them both. You are what Lady Gretchen should aspire to be if she desires to be the one leading the Northerlands through whatever is to come."

Christian brought his forehead to hers, and they remained that way until a distant sound drew their attention.

"Is that Ember?" he asked as they both watched a bundled form storm through the perimeter of The Forest of Lycana.

"She's hunting, she said, when I saw her leave the keep earlier," Aylen replied, but there was something else she wasn't saying.

"You seem unsettled."

"About Ember, yes."

"Why?"

Aylen watched the young woman until she was out of view before speaking. "Your mother asked me to look after her, and I'm happy to oblige. I've already been spending time with her, and I'll give more of myself, as much as needed."

"But?"

"I know you agreed to take her with us across the pass next time. You said she seemed very mature for her years, and very aware of herself and what she's asking for. And I see it in her, too. But I see something else, something that terrifies me."

"What do you see?"

Aylen looked at him. "I see a fire burning deep within her, and when it erupts, it will consume her and everyone else who follows."

13
WHAT HE DOES IN THE SHADOWS

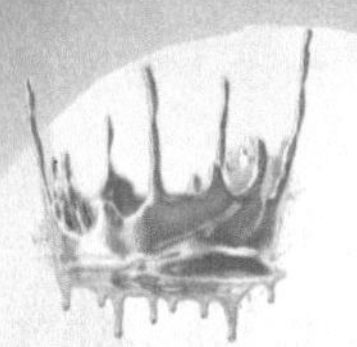

Argentyn darted down the stone halls with furtive glances every few steps. He didn't want to be seen, and Alasyr wanted to know why. Nothing made sense anymore, not since Ravenna left. The secrets and lies from those closest to him drew a tight circle around his heart like a vise, squeezing so tight he couldn't breathe.

Alasyr gingerly removed his boots as he drew closer to his father, cautious of any sound that might give him away.

Before Ravenna ran off, Alasyr hadn't cared at all about the High Priest's strange winged jaunts to the land of men. Ravenna had always been curious, too. It was natural to wonder about those things that were different from your own world, even if many Ravenwoods frowned upon paying such trivialities any mind. When Alasyr wasn't angry at them all, he understood that curiosity himself. The world of men had always been a mystery, one that intrigued him even if he reviled it.

But where before Argentyn had made his journeys only seldom, he now daily took to the skies. Sometimes he'd leave both morning and night. He must have known how unusual and suspicious it was, for he only turned to flight once he was certain he was alone, always retreating to the far edges of the castle before making his transformation.

Alasyr froze and pressed himself against the cool wall when his father stopped. With an inward breath, he rolled his head slightly toward the corner, and his father again came into sight.

Argentyn looked left and right, his cheeks flushed with nervous excitement. Seemingly satisfied, he looked toward the sky and then erupted into feathers and night, soaring up and out.

He quickly disappeared behind the darkening storm clouds. Snowbolts tonight, then. If his father felt pulled to go out in weather like this, then whatever was ahead for him must be important. Something even the threat of death couldn't keep him from.

Alasyr cast a nervous glance at the sky. Determined not to lose his father in the burgeoning storm, he quickly shifted and aimed himself toward Wulfsgate. Though this was not where they were going, he was sure of it. Not if prior trips were any indication of Argentyn's intentions.

It was late. The morning sun would crest beyond The Rookery soon. His father had never been so reckless with his trips, and Alasyr needed to know what it meant. He saw the arc of his father's wings riding the wind ahead and dropped back. If caught, he'd be punished. It was possible, even, that his father might sacrifice him against the side of Icebolt Mountain to protect whatever secret he didn't want others to know.

Alasyr passed over the Forest of Lycana. In the distance, Wulfsgate slept. Within its walls rested that strange girl who was like him, but not at all.

His father flew on, aiming himself higher as he had the last few times Alasyr had tailed him. Up the mountain, toward the pass. Icy air whipped by Alasyr, flipping him sideways, threatening his stability. He pressed on, fearful of losing sight of his father and being lost in a storm.

Alasyr had to arc back when the clouds cleared. At last, his father returned to view. He was perched upon a tree near the cave where the men and women had been hiding for weeks. Raven-woods had been talking about it since they arrived, several having spotted them right away on their flights. It was good that the sorcerers had no interest in men, for it was not a secret amongst the sorcerers of Midnight Crest.

Alasyr found a nearby tree to land on. He was too high to see any detail in what had his father's attention, but the huddled figures of two adults and a child walking horses down the path and away from the cave left him curious as well.

Where would they be going in the middle of the night?

Nowhere good, Alasyr thought, and in the next breath wondered why his father would have known this would happen and when, why he was interested in whatever had transpired amongst the group of exiles that had nothing to do with them.

The three figures disappeared from sight down the pass. Argentyn didn't follow. His raven's head was fixed on the cave, where those who hadn't slipped away still slept.

Alasyr felt the air change above him as another raven glided down toward where Argentyn perched. He hopped a few branches to get closer, but had no better view of who the new raven was. He could tell only that it was not his mother, for her form was larger than her husband's, and this raven was smaller. It was the first time he'd seen anyone join his father in his secret jaunts.

A dark feeling passed over Alasyr. They were up to something terrible. Alasyr's own magic was not as strong as some, but as an empath, his sensitivity to the intentions of others was so heightened it sometimes left him breathless. If he'd been in his priest form, he'd be doubled over from the force of this sensation.

It was this same magic that told him that, though she was

descended from traitors, Emberley Blackwood herself was true of heart.

He couldn't stay here. His desire to be left out of whatever machination his father was planning was greater than his curiosity.

Alasyr again took to flight, speaking silent entreaties to the wind that his father and his companion hadn't spotted him.

HE HADN'T INTENDED on stopping in Wulfsgate. When he'd aimed himself away from the pass and his father's designs, he should have bypassed the town altogether. But he remembered something from his harried flight to follow his father, and a new curiosity, this one safer, took over.

Alasyr landed upon a branch and watched Emberley Blackwood try to murder a deer with her mind.

He jumped to the forest floor, unfurling into his priest form. "What *are* you doing?"

Ember stumbled backward, the crunch of icy leaves atop snow piercing the night. "You shouldn't be here. These woods are dangerous at night."

"Counsel I don't see you following," Alasyr countered. He stepped closer. "Where's your man?"

"I have no man."

"How you love to be contrary. The one you rut with in the Wintergarden when you think no one is looking."

Ember grinned through her annoyance. "I know *you're* always looking, Alasyr. I only hope you enjoy the performances, which have become at least somewhat for your benefit."

Alasyr snorted. "You didn't answer."

"He's sleeping. As you should be. As I plan to be, once I've done what I came to do."

He again moved closer and realized it was the nearest he'd ever been to her. Her pale skin sparkled in the moonlight, nostrils flaring with whatever hard energy she'd brought with her to the forest that night. He supposed there was a familial resemblance, but he couldn't forget what she was, and what she wasn't.

"You were trying to kill that deer. With your mind."

"I was not," Ember lied poorly.

"You were. I saw you. Why?"

"You saw wrong." She tapped the bow hanging over her back. "I was trying to kill that deer, but the proper way."

"I don't believe you."

"I shan't miss a wink over it."

Alasyr pointed eastward. "There are men hiding in a cave in Torrin's Pass. Do you know?"

Ember's impertinent smile died on her face. She was silent for a moment, but when he tried to read her thoughts, to understand this silence, he found he was blocked. "Yes. I do know, and if I find you've told anyone else, I'll kill you." It was her turn to step closer, and Alasyr reflexively stepped backward. "You don't look nearly convinced I'll do it, but that deer is only alive because I can't kill unless threatened, it seems. That deer has caused me no harm. But you... I could kill you, if you opened your mouth and shared what you just told me with another."

Alasyr swallowed a gulp of cool air. It relieved him to feel the tingle of his wings at the ready. "It isn't me you need to fear, half-blood."

He didn't give her a chance to respond. He erupted into a swarm of feathers and was gone.

Ember watched Alasyr Ravenwood disappear into the thick, dark clouds, moving across the night sky. He wasn't her friend. He wasn't her enemy. But he was *something*, and all she really wanted him to be was her ally in her quest for self-discovery. If there was anyone who could help her realize her powers, it was him. Yet he also seemed to be the last one who'd ever be inclined to do it.

He'd broken her focus. No, the deer wasn't going to die. She hadn't even wanted to kill it, only to understand it, to see if she could connect with it as she had the bear, but this time without harm.

The deer was gone now, as were most creatures that had been roaming the area before Alasyr dropped down. She could move on and find another place to practice, but a whisper of orange light tinged the horizon, and she didn't want to do this in the daytime, when others might find her and question her. Aylen in particular was interested in her behavior, and Ember had no answer for her questions. She'd chosen the dead of night to avoid specifically this, and she'd evaded Aylen, but not Alasyr.

And what *had* he been doing, prowling around in the night? He'd come from the east, and the pass, so his revelation about the exiles was connected in some way, but why was he there at all? Why there, and why now?

If Alasyr knew, there must be others who knew. Other Ravenwoods, and why were they there, watching her mother and the others? What were they after?

Ember's attention was torn to her feet when the ground beneath her shifted. It happened again, but this time it wasn't one sensation but many, like a rolling tremble. She gasped as the surrounding trees swayed in an invisible wind, the branches picking up momentum as they bowed low, whipping the air around her, nearly swiping her from her feet.

Then she felt it. That slow burn from within, the hot meld of fear and rage and helplessness travel from her belly and outward, radiating in fiery darkness toward her fingers, toes, her neck and face. Ember opened her mouth as if to expel it, but then closed it once more as the sensation shifted from one of abandon to one of power. The building flame was almost soothing, though there was nothing calm or complacent about this, this tempest swirling, vying to break free. Her whole self swelled with it.

Ember closed her eyes just as the flame burst out from a thousand points. The world was alive with a vibrance of spectacular light, and light was life, it was love, it was power, it was... it was everything.

Ember wanted to be who she was in that moment every day for the rest of her life. Even that would not be enough.

But then it stopped. The flames within her eased. The sensation that her limbs were swollen with power waned until they were just arms, just legs. Her hair no longer fanned in the wind of her own creation.

Ember dropped to her knees, gasping for breath. She wheezed inward, drawing hard gulps of air into her aching lungs. She pressed her palms to the forest floor, but recoiled at the charred sensation that met her palms.

She opened her eyes. All the snow had melted away. As far as her vision could travel in the dark of night, she could see what remained of the forest. Branchless trees, a dark, barren floor covered in soot, singed in the aftermath of whatever she'd just done. Dying. Dead. Another wind would turn them to ash.

Ember turned and ran.

14

DISGRACED LORD

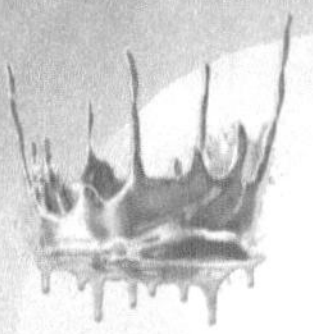

Eoghan huddled under the cloak that was fit for a man much more filled into his skin. He'd chosen it intentionally. Anyone could visit a prisoner. So seldom did it happen that the guards were all too happy to let a man pass without more than a fleeting glance. Only on Eoghan's orders could a cell door be opened, and after the debacle with Lady Blackwood, the guards they had now were fresh from the Isle of Belcarrow, trained for more than resisting slumber and sharing kingdom gossip. The corpses of those who had failed still lined the rocky shoreline of Duncarrow as a reminder that no matter how mundane their job, there would be no abiding miscarriage of duty.

But Eoghan had no desire to have Aiden's cell opened. He may not allow anyone to make a point of his physical shortcomings, but it didn't mean he wasn't aware of them. Lord Quinlanden was a vainglorious man, but he was also the man who had bested Byrne Warwick. These guards were operating at greater attention, but they were untested. Eoghan's foolish choice to open a dangerous man's cell would not be what prompted the occasion for them to find their worth.

He also wanted privacy. An unknown man of the court might get an eyebrow raise, but the king would have every ear trained on his words, both said and unsaid.

The guard opened the small window to Lord Quinlanden's cell and backed away. Eoghan waited until he heard him return to banal conversation about the latest kitchen scandal, and then turned to face the disgraced lord.

"Your—"

"Silence," Eoghan barked, slicing through Aiden's attempt to name him. "I shall talk, and you shall listen, and for every word that I did not ask for, you will sacrifice your meals for a day."

Aiden's mouth parted. It snapped closed. He was a man of pride, but he still had some sense. The harried loathing in his eyes could have been enough to kill Eoghan, had Aiden been possessed of an ounce of magic.

"You have sent word to your men in the Westerlands and Easterlands today. I had the ravens dispatched this morning."

Aiden's anger faded to confusion. "Bu—" his word died away before he could complete it.

"Good. You learn quickly, even if you are a fool. The ravens were sent under your seal, but they were my words. I've instructed them to be at ease, to maintain position but not seek to act. That to incite war in the Westerlands would go against all your designs."

Aiden appeared to be fighting off physical pain as his lips blubbered in helpless flaps.

"Let me see if I can anticipate your questions. You want to know why I would allow them to believe you are alive and still directing their moves? That one should be easy. They are loyal to you, though I cannot pretend I understand why when you are loyal to no one but yourself. I cannot be so certain of their loyalty to me if they learn you are my prisoner. I have a plan for that, but first you will want to know why I wouldn't let my men—yes, they are my men now, even if they do not know it—sack the Westerlands and bring it to heel. Because, though you may think very little of my shrewdness on matters of politics, I can see what you cannot. That a war upon the Westerlands would not end there. You cannot see the loyalty the Northerlands and Southerlands have upon their sister Reach, for you yourself have never known such loyalty. Once Lady Blackwood is brought to me to answer for her crimes, I will restore another Blackwood to the seat at Longwood Rush, one who will swear a loyalty to me that her mother never would. Ah, be cautious, Lord Quinlanden. Your belly will be pained at your inability to keep your words behind your lips. Oh, and I regret to inform you that I've had the men you brought with you executed. It was no longer prudent to pack them all into cells not meant for their number, and the kitchens grew weary of preparing so many meals."

Eoghan glanced back toward the guards, but they were engrossed in their own conversation. "And then, lastly, you may be wondering after the future of your own Reach. At the appropriate time, when the thirst for war in this kingdom has died away and order restored, your brother, Corin, will assume your position as Lord of the Easterlands."

Aiden's pained expression had become unbearable to watch. "You may speak now."

"You cannot do this!"

"There's nothing I *cannot* do except best you in a battle of height, but if you are suggesting I *should* not do this, then I will advise that you choose your words very carefully."

"My son, Cian, is my heir, he is—"

"*Your* heir. His loyalty is to you. I will have a Quinlanden in that seat who serves me and only me."

"My brother is not half the man you need in that seat."

"Then he's still twice the man you are."

"But the Medvedev, Your Grace! I brought them to you!"

"Mortain answers to the Rhiagains alone. It will not be any

trouble for me to have the enslaved redirected toward my own efforts."

"Your efforts? What efforts? If you don't intend to take the Reaches, what other reason could there possibly be for having them at all? What good is power with inaction?"

Eoghan pulled the hood down over his eyes to hide anything Aiden might read in his face. He didn't know what to do with the Medvedev. It would be nothing to order them released, and yet... and yet... "That is all I've come to say. You are now fully apprised."

"But why, Your Grace? Why tell me this? Why tell me any of it?"

Eoghan leaned in and hissed. "I want you to know what your treachery has bought, so that you may ruminate upon your losses in the endless hours that count for days up here, until I have at last decided your promise spent."

Emberley's sudden, furious cries slammed Gretchen into consciousness.

She strained against the relentless combination of the first sliver of sunlight coming through her window and the desperate sounds that hadn't come on gradually. Sitting, one hand over her eyes, Gretchen tried again asking Ember what was wrong, but the girl was in a fugue, unable to do anything but follow the racing sound of her nonsensical words.

Gretchen at last pulled herself from the bed and reached for Ember's arm. "Emberley. Be still."

Ember regarded her with the wild eyes of a hare in a trap. Her chest rose and fell in ragged beats under her leather armor, the bow she was inexplicably wearing at this hour hanging half off her.

"Yes. Like that. Breathe."

The sounds coming from Ember dissolved into small, desperate cries. She looked at Gretchen, in some battle with herself, unable to speak, unable to do anything but gape in confused fear.

Gretchen led her to the bed and sat her down. There was so much about this situation still beyond her understanding. Ember, donning the gear of a hunter. Ember, with the char of dying coals dusted over her, from her face to her boots. Ember, who looked as if she'd seen the ghost of her father.

"You came to me for a reason," Gretchen said gently. She ran her hand over Ember's cheek, taking the dark grime with it. "Perhaps you'll feel better if you tell me what it was."

"I... I... it's... you see..." Ember buried her face in her hand and released a scream. When she again looked up, she was calmer, though looked no more at peace than she had moments earlier. "I came across Alasyr in the Forest of Lycana."

"Is that where you've come from? Looking as you do?"

"He'd come from the pass. He knows."

"He knows?" Gretchen repeated. "What does he know?"

"Do we have more than one secret in the pass, Lady Gretchen?"

"I don't understand. He told you this? What did he say? What did he say exactly?"

"He asked if I knew there were men hiding in the pass. I said if he told anyone, I would kill him. And then he said it wasn't him I needed to fear."

Gretchen's hands fell away from Ember. "I see."

Ember shot to her feet. "We have to warn them! Don't you understand? That's what Alasyr was trying to say to me. He wasn't goading me, he was warning me!"

Gretchen nodded. She inhaled for what felt like the first time that morning. "We'll wake the others and discuss what needs to be done."

"Brother."

Eoghan cringed at the pitch of Correen's nasally voice. She could never simply say hello, or even proffer a compliment on his complexion or choice of dress for the day. She was always after him for something. Always *nagging*.

And after the time he'd spent alone with the slippery Aiden Quinlanden, he felt in dire need of a scalding bath.

"What is it now, Correen?" he replied without turning. "Don't tell me. This is about the court again, isn't it?"

"You're aggravated with me. You wish I would stop bringing this up, that it's all I ever come to you with."

"Yes, you do, and yes, I wish that."

"And I will, when you take heed to my counsel. You always followed my wisdom as a boy, and I cannot see why you won't do it now, for I have lived twice what you have. I remember how things were, not only under our father, but our grandfather. What is a king without a court? Without merriment? Without a council?"

"Merriment is a word that sounds foreign on your tongue. Do you even know the meaning?"

"If Father were here—"

Eoghan spun around. "But he is *not*. And there are no rules that a king must do what those before him did. What good is merriment? What do I care if others around me experience joy? Why should it be incumbent upon me to provide it?" He lowered his hood. "As for council, I would first have to trust enough men to fill one."

HOLDEN SHIELDED his bleary eyes against the assault of moonlight spilling across his vision intermittently as Gretchen paced his bedchamber. She'd started in on him when he was still half pulled to slumber, but that didn't mean he'd missed anything, for she was going on and on, echoing the same words over and over in repetition.

"There. Stand there," he murmured.

"What? Do what?" Gretchen demanded. She whipped her gaze back to him.

"Nothing." Holden grimaced through closed eyes and propped himself up against the dense wood of this bed. "Sit down. Your pacing has my heart ready for battle."

Gretchen could have struck him dead with the look she leveled on him. He was often grateful she didn't possess that power. He might be a disappointment to her, but he'd live to disappoint her another day.

In the end, she sat. Agitated. Fidgeting.

"Start over, my dearest. Slower this time, so that your words may wash over me like a fresh spring morning."

"Do I seem as if I'm in the mood for your ill-timed humor?"

Holden's attempt at a smile faded. "There was a time when it would calm you."

"If there was, my memory is no longer capable of conjuring it."

Holden waved a hand. "Fine. What is it that has you so harried at this early hour?"

"Our allies in the cave have been compromised."

"They what? Compromised how?"

"Their position has been discovered."

"By whom?"

"By the meddling Ravenwoods. Oh, I *knew* that wasn't the last we'd seen of that slippery Varinya!"

Holden was just then grateful that his wife had stopped paying mind to the little changes in him, for she'd certainly missed the flush in his cheeks at the mention of his first love. He'd take the memory of her ivory skin brushing over his to his tomb, and Varinya would never tell another. They'd never taken things as far as he had so desperately wanted, but it was love that stilled his passion for the young raven whose future had already been decided. Gretchen wasn't the only one who'd brought the ghost of an ill-fated past into the marriage.

"How do you know this?"

"The Ravenwood boy, Alasyr, told Emberley."

"He told her? Are they friends now?"

"No! Of course not."

"Then how did this conversation come about?"

"Does it matter? They *know*, Holden. They know."

"If the Ravenwoods know," Holden said, measuring his words with caution, "then I would counter it makes our allies more safe, not less."

"More?" Gretchen stammered, nearly choking on the word. "More safe? They are more safe with enchanters who can fly this news anywhere in the kingdom?"

"To what end, Gretchen? The Ravenwoods rely on our alliance for survival. Spreading this information beyond our borders would invite the very last thing they want."

"Our secret has spread. That makes it no longer one."

Holden leaned closer to his wife. He forced himself not to cringe at the way she recoiled. He often wondered if it was one or many moments that had led her to this derision of him, but he knew how to spot a lost cause and regaining her respect had been lost for many years. "There are many things you're wise on, Gretchen. Even I cannot deny this, and I would not, for you have earned your place here, as my equal. But the relationship shared between the Derehams and Ravenwoods is more ancient than you or me, and while you tolerate it, you have never understood it. Never. You turn your nose when you face the north. You cannot even say their name without a light curl in your lip. They are safe, because of us. We are safer, because of them. This is our way and will always be our way. If the Ravenwoods have spotted our allies in the cave, then they are either curious, or helping to ensure it remains a secret to all who would bring us harm."

"Hold—"

"No, Gretchen. I will grudgingly defer to you on many things, but not this. Not this thing you cannot understand and have never tried to. We will not send warning over the pass. It will only lead to more problems. We stay to the course we plotted together. That is all I'll say on the matter."

Holden enjoyed the contortions on his wife's face as she mulled over the way he'd taken back some of his authority. He relished more the slow realization falling over her that, this time, she would not be getting it back.

For this time, she was wrong.

"Does he know?"

"He thinks he knows. He knows very little. He knows less than his forebears."

The face peering back from the water nodded. "He's like a child, is he not? But a child answers to their parents. He answers to no one."

"His whims can be brought to heel. But only if he stays in the dark, where he belongs. Where his forebears lived most comfortably."

"And you are keeping him in the dark?"

"He suspects I parcel information like sweetmeats, giving him enough to slake his appetite and no more."

"Then he's not a complete fool."

"Let him have his suspicions. He knows nothing. He wants what I know, badly enough that he's willing to overlook it. He understands that is the price."

"For now."

"Yes. For now. I will consider what needs to be done when he grows weary of it. As I did with his father."

"You were fortunate with Khain. You couldn't harm him, but

you didn't need to. The illness took care of that."

"I deserve more credit than that, do you not think? He begged me to heal him. I denied him that."

The face in the water shimmered in annoyance. "I have no care of the fate of a man long dead. The time is upon us, as was long foretold, and if we cannot see this plan through to the bitter end, then we will not again have such an opportunity."

"It will happen. We have seen it. We know the way. I have no care what the boy king does or does not know. His knowledge will change nothing."

"Pray that his suspicions do not impede with us drawing the three from their veil of safety."

"*She* protects them."

"She knows we look for them. But I cannot see the fourth. You must also keep looking for this one, searching your own visions."

"I have, to no joy. It's as if there's an enchantment over him. Over all of them. If not for your link to the Saleen we would not have known the three had passed the Drumain veil, nor even of their existence. Would not have known of a fourth."

"If there is an enchantment, it comes from the very same who so carefully crafted their existence."

"But they are beyond our detection."

"Yes, and? They created the four without a whisper of premonition from either of us. Neither of us saw the boy live, taken away, and grow to make more of himself, more of—"

"Is this, also, the work of our brother and sister? Have they at last returned?"

The face in the water darkened. "Two can never again be four. They saw to that decades before with their treachery. Should they return, their removal will take precedence over more important matters."

"Knowing now what they are capable of, they may already be here."

15

TWO SEALS

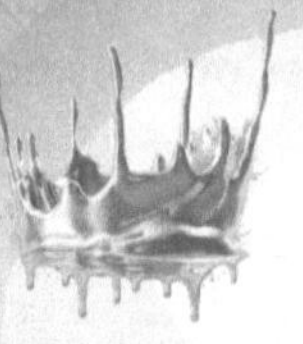

Corin read the words four times. He even re-rolled the vellum and approached the scroll with fresh eyes, to ensure what he'd read wasn't a sleight of magic, or his own fears manifesting some new strange reality.

"Yesenia." He stood behind his wife. The steam from her bath rose forth and tickled his nose. She only murmured in response, and he realized she'd fallen asleep.

He dropped down beside her. Her obsidian waves fell into delicious curls against the cypress basin. "Yesenia. My love. We've talked about this. You could drown."

Her sleepy smile made him reconsider telling her about the message. He yearned to drop into the warm water beside her and take her in his arms, be lost to the delightful sound of her giggles against his ear as he let his hands search out her favorite places. She wasn't afraid of pleasure. Of giving or receiving. He hated the Rhiagains for many reasons, but his animosity softened when he remembered they'd given him the gift of Yesenia Warwick.

"I won't drown. I'm a Warwick. One with salt and sand, remember?"

"There's no salt in this bath except you."

"Why do you look like that? As if you've eaten plums by accident?"

Corin winced at the memory of the last time he'd mistakenly eaten a dish with the wretched fruit inside. He'd been at the privy for days. Yesenia's amusement at the event seemed to have no end. "We have to talk."

Yesenia slid upward, alert now. She looked around and then leaned toward him. "Here? There are ears."

Corin unrolled the vellum slowly, carefully. He held it out for her to read, and then, when she at last looked up, wearing the same startled expression he must have when the words settled into his mind, he pressed a finger to his lips.

"But this makes no sense," Yesenia hissed, in a low whisper. She read the words again before handing the scroll back to him. "Can this have really come from the king?"

"It bears his seal," Corin said, voice as low as hers. "It seems we were right after all. Aiden overplayed his favor."

He again looked down upon the words.

Your brother has caused me great displeasure, and is not fit to rule the Easterlands. It is my command that, at a time of my choosing, you, Corin Quinlanden, second eldest, will take his place and assume this role. For now, these words are for you alone, and if shared, your life, and that of your wife and son, will be forfeit and I will pass the mantle of leadership on to someone more grateful for the gift. For the present, I have made the request that your guard be eased and you be allowed to proffer leadership in your brother's stead, though all military command will come from me alone.

"When it was delivered, I saw no guards in the hall."

"That doesnae mean they aren't there, Corin."

"I love when you speak to me as your brother would."

Yesenia gave him a playful smack. "And what if this is a trap? What if we're being led?"

"Whether his words are true, the offer is a trap," Corin whispered. "Because I can serve The Pretender no more than I can serve my brother. And what of Cian? Does he really mean to pass him over? And if so, are we expected to sit back and allow it?"

"A dilemma indeed." Yesenia nodded. "I wish it were safe to send this to my brother. He deserves to know what's happened in Duncarrow. That both our enemies have been weakened."

"The raven wouldn't make it out of the castle."

"Aye." Yesenia sighed, slipping again into the water. "What do you think he's told the others?"

"The others?"

"If the king sent us a raven, when we were not expecting one, surely he's also sent one to those who have been? Those awaiting Aiden's word? And if he has, we need to know what he's told them."

Corin exhaled into a light gasp. "You're brilliant. Of course he has. Now, how do we get our hands upon one?"

Mads waited for the sorcerer to complete his morning routine. He didn't know what foul magic the creature employed, and didn't want to. His job was to protect Mortain in these fleeting, fragile moments where he was most vulnerable. When that daily task was done, he wouldn't need to even speak to him again until the next morning.

He didn't like Mortain. He didn't need him. Lord Quinlanden knew this, and Mads suspected his lord felt the same, for he grew very solemn whenever Mads broached the subject. Mads thought his lord was afraid, even, though Aiden would die before admitting such a thing.

But Mads needed the sorcerer now, for something was wrong. Very wrong.

"There," Mortain said with a dusting of his hands and a light smile, as if he'd just tidied his room. "Now. What leaves you with this constipated look you offer me?"

Mads bit his tongue, not responding as he'd most like to. Not once, nor even twice, but three times Lord Quinlanden had chided him for his lack of respect toward the sorcerer, and though his lord wasn't here now, Mads was leading in his stead and would act accordingly. "I'd like your outlook."

"Hardly a cloud, and that wind is *so* delightful."

Mads sighed inwardly. "We've at last had word from Lord Quinlanden."

Mortain's eyes twinkled. "Have we? Now that is a pleasant surprise! And why do you not look as if this pleases you?"

"Something is wrong. Read it for yourself." Mads thrust the scroll at Mortain. "Perhaps you can use your... whatever it is you use to ascertain the problem."

"Ah, let's see. 'All is well in Duncarrow. The king is a most pleasant host and I could never thank him enough for offering of me all the delights of court. So much so that I have lost the thread of time, and been remiss in my communications home.'" Mortain regarded him over the vellum. "Seems pleasing enough."

"Read on."

"Here we are. 'I regret that we still have much to discuss, and so my return will be further delayed. I leave you with the following command. Leave your men in position, but stay their hand from violence or an eye to battle. Their presence should inspire peace, not fear, and if I hear of any going against this order, their decision will be treated as treasonous. Until I'm with you again, be my eyes and mouth in this matter. Lord Quinlanden.' I don't see what has you so twisted about, Waters. This all seems perfectly reasonable to me."

Mads gaped at him. "Reasonable?" He gestured wildly toward the Medvedev, wandering about the forest in an enchanted daze. "Before he sailed for Duncarrow, he was crying war! He was building an army, one bigger than any before it, and even that was not enough! Now he wants peace?"

"Perhaps his time with the king has been illuminating," Mortain said lightly, his deep red robe swimming around his bony wrists as he gestured at nothing. "Even with an army such as ours, there's a time for war and a time to stay the hand."

"This was your idea!"

"One of my very finest," Mortain said with a bright smile. "But I am patient, and so it seems, is your lord, as he has seen the prudence in easing off for now. And so we will follow his direction."

Mads' cheeks flushed with incredulous frustration. He couldn't believe it, any of it. Not his lord's words, not this devious sorcerer's easy acceptance of them. None of it fit in with the man he knew Aiden Quinlanden to be. "Then I'll sail to Duncarrow and hear him say the words myself."

"If I were Lord Quinlanden, I would take that to mean you don't trust in his leadership."

"He knows I trust him. But I cannot help but wonder—"

"Then trust him," Mortain said. With a swish of crimson, he spun and left him.

Clarissant Tyndall hovered at the door of the Round Room, one eye to the outside and one to the inside. For the moment, the crimson and gold was not their concern, but it would be. But it *had* come to them, in another way, in the form of Stirling Oakenwell.

"You cannot speak with him!" she cried to Griffath when he mounted his horse, headed for the Round Room. "If he's deceiving us, we are lost! If he's a traitor, then we are equally lost!"

"Look around you, Rissa," Griffath had said from atop his horse. "Do you see anyone come to save us? Do you see the men at Greystone returned, with a plan to end this?"

"They need time is all, time for—"

"Time they take is time The Deceiver takes as well. If my brother were here, he would remind us that the Guardians don't make mistakes. Oakenwell's defection is a gift, one we would be fools to turn away."

Clarissant didn't like for her husband to see her cry, but she wouldn't look away from him, either. "If this puts our children at risk of further pain..."

Griffath's gloved hand reached down to caress her cheek. "If I detect even an ounce of deception from the man, I'll have his head before he can finish his words. Now come, wife, and hear what he has to say yourself, for I trust your counsel on the matter."

So she had. She'd followed, both listening to the words within and straining for the signs of any without.

"I know you have no reason to trust me," Oakenwell was saying. "I would not, were I standing where you are."

"Then why should I?"

"Because I'm showing you what neither Lord Quinlanden nor the king would ever want you to see." Oakenwell slapped a roll of vellum onto the desk. "Read it yourself, Steward Tyndall. Quinlanden is ordering peace, you'll see, but those are not his words. You can be certain of it."

Clarissant loved her husband for the deeply skeptical look he gave Oakenwell as he unrolled the vellum and read.

"Sounds more as if your lord has lost his courage. Perhaps he at last realizes that razing an entire Reach isn't the quick work murdering a man in his nightclothes was."

Oakenwell dropped both hands onto the desk. "Tyndall. There is no love between our Reaches. There never has been. When this is over, there will not be then, either." He pulled back, pointing at the vellum. "These are the words Mads Waters will have received as well. It is our responsibility to deliver the orders, he and I."

"So deliver them and leave our sons and daughters alone."

"But these aren't Aiden's *words*, don't you see? These are the words of a man under duress, a man whose mind is not his own."

Griffath laughed. "Oh, that you think I would care about the distress of Aiden Quinlanden."

"You should. For if they aren't his words, then whose are they?"

"Why does it matter?"

"It *matters* because there's something even more foul happening in this kingdom than any of us envisioned. I don't believe these words of peace, and neither will Waters. If Waters believes our lord has been compromised, he'll do as he believes Aiden would want him to. Aiden is volatile, but Waters, unrestrained by a reasonable master, is something else entirely. The worst is yet to come for the Westerlands."

"Why are you here? What do you want from me?"

"I've come to you because I have heard you, of all the Blackwood stewards, are the most reasonable."

"The most gullible? The one most willing to walk into whatever trap you've laid?"

"This is no trap. Not from me." Oakenwell slipped the vellum back into his satchel. "And if you're not interested in my aid in seeing this madness ended, then I'll find another."

Griffath sighed, closing his eyes. "You're his best man, Oakenwell. You expect me to believe you've defected, seen the error of his ways, after all this time?"

Oakenwell leaned in. "I was loyal to Aiden's father, and I have tried to be loyal to the monster who replaced him. But the Easterlands deserves better. They deserve a man who draws his fealty with love, not threats. Not unnecessary wars. Lady Blackwood knew my true heart, that I was an ally long before Lord Quinlanden took the head of Lord Warwick and thrust us into this terrible place."

"How convenient for us both that she's missing and cannot confirm this."

"Steward Oakenwell," Clarissant said from the door. Both men turned in surprise. "You ask for our trust, but must provide some in return. Tell us something that The Deceiver would not want us to know. No small thing will do."

Oakenwell looked at her, then back at Griffath. "You think what he did to Lord Warwick was an abomination, but that's nothing, nothing compared to what he's done to the Medvedev, and what they'll do to you, on his command."

16

IN DREAMS

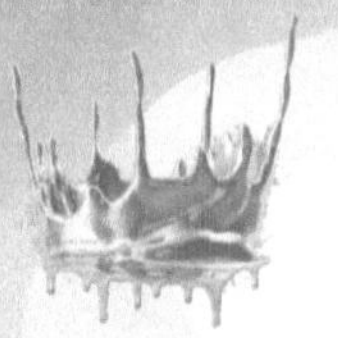

Drystan watched his sister set out for her daily interrogation. He and Valen had been washing their knives at the stream after an early hunt when he glimpsed her walking by, Kian on her heels, her red hair like a flame against the emerald and sapphire of the waking forest.

He set his frown to the glare of the rising sun. It cut a hard line between the trees, setting the plum-colored leaves into a spray of colored light on the forest floor. A breeze sent some floral, pleasing scents their way. He'd been here long enough to know precisely which flowers they'd come from. The ones in question were shaped like bells, with tiny arms and feet, like the little people of myth that his nan used to speak of. But it was their color that first caught his eye and still held it, even now. A pink so vibrant, so unlike anything else he'd ever seen, and yet it was exactly like every other strange flora populating the Hinterlands.

After all these weeks here, Drystan was no closer to under-standing their captors. He should be grateful they'd been given this freedom to roam and hunt and prepare their own meals, to sleep in piles of soft furs. But he knew also that a nicer prison was still a prison. Until they understood their crime, there'd be no leaving it, either.

"Why haven't they released us? Why do you really think we're still here?"

Valen didn't look up from his rigorous scrubbing. "I don't know, Drystan."

"If they thought we would do them harm, we'd still be in those cages, but we're not. We're all but free, even if we're not free at all. If we tried to leave, the magic would stop us, but I'll bet we could walk for quite a spell before that happened."

"Perhaps."

"None of it makes any sense. We're not a threat. We've committed no crime against them. So why keep us?" Drystan said. "As I think about it, all I can come up with is that they keep us because they need something from us."

Valen stopped washing. "The Medvedev need nothing from man. They never have, and never will. There is no... no *gift* we possess that is greater than their own."

Drystan noted the subtle but clear shift in Valen's tone at his last question. Valen was attempting to silence him, but that soft push back only made him want to press further. "Does everything have to be about magic? We roam the kingdom freely, and they do not. We have access to things they do not."

"Things they do not *need*. Look around you." Valen waved the knife as he gestured around. "Would you ever want or need for anything if this was your home?"

"It is our home, right now," Drystan reminded him. "Possibly forever, if we cannot figure out why they keep us. As lovely as it is, I have needs beyond what they've given us."

Valen sighed in agitation. "Is this not what you wanted? You and Ravenna? To be free?"

Drystan recoiled. "Do you see Ravenna? Because I don't. I don't think I'll see her ever again, if I'm being honest with myself, and I no longer find any point in self-deception."

Valen returned to his work, but not before Drystan saw the flash of anger in his eyes. "No, I don't expect you will, either."

"Did you know? That she would leave me?"

"No."

"You hesitated when you responded. You did, didn't you? Did you see what I should have seen all along, then?"

The tensing started in Valen's shoulders, flexing at the curve of his neck, traveling out through his limbs. It was as if he was exercising some great restraint. "You and your questions."

"Why are you angry with me? You once welcomed my questions. It was you who first fed my curiosity, and now you want to kill it."

"Did I say I was angry?"

Drystan nearly laughed. "I don't think giving voice to a thing is needed to draw attention to the obvious." Whatever humor in him was quickly extinguished by a sudden sense of sadness. "Have you tired of me already? Is that what's happening?"

Valen dropped the knife on the blanket and jumped to his feet. He rushed to Drystan and took him by the shoulders. He gave him a gentle shake as he said, "You are my *son*. I could never tire of you. Forgive me."

It was Drystan's turn to withdraw. He'd avoided, intentionally, any talk of father and son with this man, no matter what the truth might be. It was too much when his life had already been turned on its head. He had to hold on to what he knew to be true, not what might be. "Then what's wrong?"

Valen dropped his head. "I don't know why they keep us, Drystan. I truly don't, and, like you, the not knowing gnaws at my heart and leaves me gutted and hollow. I came along to protect you and the others, and it's as if I've been neutered. I'm powerless here, in a way I've never been, not even when I stood back as your mother was married off to a man she didn't love. Even then, I still had power. The understanding that I have no power here, not anymore, has been most difficult for me."

"I thought Yseult was your friend?"

"As I, too, thought. Perhaps it is friendship that has stayed her hand from something more final. I don't know. You may not know this, but man has before strayed from the Compass Roads, wandering into the forests not meant for them. The Medvedev judge the purity in their hearts, and if their intentions are innocent, they allow passage. Often it's children who find themselves lost in these forests, having run from home, as you did. Gabi told us that her sister, Emberley, would have passed through these woods on her journey north, and we can only assume she made it through, for she's not locked away with us. But if Emberley's heart was judged to be true, why not Gabi's? Why not Lisbet's? Or yours? There's no sense in any of it. In all my voyages here, she has never done anything like this, even when I'd overstayed my welcome and was cast out."

"Then we should ask her! Can we not do that, Valen? Simply ask what has changed, and why she keeps us?"

Valen shook his head. He dropped his hands back to his sides. "That isn't Yseult's way. It isn't our place to ask the questions when we're in her lands, but hers."

"Like she's doing with Lisbet?"

"Yes. Like that."

"But Lisbet says Yseult asks her the same questions each day, and she gives the same answers."

Valen sighed. "I don't know what's in Yseult's mind, Drystan, but I'll tell you what I do know. I, too, was on the other end of Yseult's questions, and it was not until I gave her my truth—the one that is known deep within, and only there—that she at last released me and treated me as kin."

Drystan let this roll over him. "But... if it's only known deep within, how could Lisbet know what Yseult wants from her?"

Valen's shoulders dropped as he exhaled. "She will first have to surrender herself."

Eavan sent Gabi and Meadow off to pick berries for their breakfast when she saw Lisbet and Kian in the distance. Lisbet walked a pace ahead of Kian, which piqued Eavan's suspicion. Before when she'd seen them walking to visit Yseult, he'd kept Lisbet fastened at his side, his distrust for her most obvious in every step, every hard glance and stiffened pivot if she should veer even slightly off course. The only bond between them had been gaoler and prisoner.

Now Lisbet walked ahead of him, no longer measuring her pace but moving with sprightly vigor. Kian's pace had slowed, gained a more casual feel. His hands were no longer at the ready to bind her, lest she run, but instead, shoved inside his vest, elbows bent at lazy angles. He might as well be whistling into the wind, gazing longingly at the deer-kind frolicking in the woods.

But whatever was or was not happening between Kian and Lisbet was the least of her concerns, she thought, as she turned toward the stream and heaved the last of the prior night's supper.

Lisbet knelt in her usual spot, preparing for the usual questions. The hard-packed dirt from the floor of the hut no longer made her knees ache. She'd been coming long enough to form protective callouses, which were not unlike the ones formed around her heart to keep the fear away every time she came before the chieftainess.

"Who are you?" Yseult demanded.

"I am Lisbet Dereham, eldest daughter of Lord Holden Dereham and Lady Gretchen Dereham."

"Who sent you?"

"No one. I sent myself."

"Why did you come?"

"Idealistically, perhaps foolishly, in search of a place where I could be free from being wed to a cruel king and my brother could be safe to follow his heart."

Lisbet resisted the urge to tap her thigh in impatience for the final question, *what do you want*, ready to return and aid Eavan with the making of breakfast. This refrain had been old for weeks, but she understood it was necessary, even if Yseult's reasons were beyond her comprehension. The sooner they finished, the quicker she could get on with her day.

"Lisbet Dereham, why did you come?"

Lisbet's impatience froze. "I... I'm sorry, Chieftainess, if my voice did not carry, but as I said, idealistically, perhaps foolishly—"

Yseult held up her hand, and Lisbet stopped speaking. Both sons turned sharply toward their mother, looking as surprised as Lisbet felt.

"I have grown weary of false answers. I am older now, and have not the time I had before to endure them," Yseult said. "I see your weariness in me as well. You think I am an old fool, asking aimless questions to tire you."

"I don't think that."

"You seem afraid to think, Lisbet. One who is afraid to think is not alive."

Lisbet shifted her knees on the soil. She suddenly didn't know what to do with her hands. She wondered what must be written upon her face that the chieftainess would seize upon and use against her. "I'm not afraid to think. If I was, I'd be the king's wife right now."

Kael made a clicking sound, like a snicker. Kian silenced it with a twitch of his fingers.

"Fleeing is not thought. Fleeing is action," Yseult countered. "Lisbet Dereham, why did you come?"

"I've told you—"

"LISBET DEREHAM, WHY DID YOU COME?"

The force of Yseult's commanding pitch sent Lisbet backward, landing on her hands. She scrambled away reflexively. "I was afraid! For myself, for..."

The pressure in the air diminished as fast as it had appeared. "Who were you afraid for?"

"For Eavan, for—"

Kael moved as if to come apprehend her, but Yseult stayed him. "She will answer. Who were you afraid for, Lisbet?"

"My brother!" Lisbet cried. Tears burned her eyes, but she didn't know where they'd come from. "For Drystan!"

Yseult settled back in her wooden chair with a smile. "Yes."

"I don't understand you!" Lisbet sobbed. "I already told you I left for my brother!"

But Yseult had more questions to ask. "Why were you afraid for your brother?"

"He was in love with the wrong woman, and I feared for his life."

"Why were you afraid for your brother?"

Lisbet gasped for breath amidst her tears. "I don't know what you want from me!"

"Why were you afraid for your brother?"

"Because he loved her! Ravenna. And... and I knew he would never leave her, even if they killed him!"

"Why were you afraid for your brother?"

"Because he's a fool with all heart and no sense, like my father!"

"Why were you afraid for your brother?"

"He has so much more to give than he knows!"

"Why were you afraid for your brother?"

Lisbet rolled forward. She was now on all fours, but found she had no desire to return to how she was before. She had to extinguish the desire to crawl toward Yseult and wind herself around her feet in submission, like a tamed wulfling. "Because I love him. And he can't see what I see."

Yseult paused. "What do you see in your brother?"

"Greatness." Lisbet crawled forward despite the screaming within her to halt. Her tears landed in the dirt, creating small drops of mud, which her knees sluiced through as she moved toward Yseult.

"What do you see in your brother?"

"I see him saving us all." Lisbet inched closer.

Yseult reached her hand down and pet Lisbet, running her hands over her hair. "And where did you see this?"

"In dreams," Lisbet panted, and then she gave in to the darkness.

WHEN LISBET AWOKE, she was lying supine upon a soft bed of pelts. She strained against the light streaming in through a nearby door, and when she tried to sit, her body resisted. A cool hand ran down her brow, and she craned her neck back to see it was Yseult soothing her.

Nothing about this made sense. How she got here. The tenderness from a woman who had spent weeks mired in her distrust. She couldn't see them, but she sensed both Kael and Kian in the room, too. From Kael she felt a charged anger, and from Kian, kindness. Maybe something else from Kian, also, but she was too exhausted to read him.

Yseult settled onto a stool fashioned from a log. "At last we understand one another, Lisbet Dereham."

Lisbet's voice croaked. "I understand less now than I ever did."

"You are beginning to recognize that which is known deep

within you, and nowhere else. Something has awakened within you. Do you feel it?"

Lisbet nodded, for she *did* feel it, even if she couldn't identify it.

"You have seen your brother in your dreams."

The tears again. Lisbet wanted to fight against them, but they seemed to be a part of this, whatever it was. "Yes, I have."

"What have you seen?"

"They are only dreams."

"What have you seen?"

"I saw... I saw him swallowing his fears. I saw him facing down great evil." Lisbet was shocked by the words, as if she was speaking of someone else's experience, though she knew, she knew it was her own. She remembered this dream now. She must have buried it, and Yseult had helped surface it.

"Where?"

Lisbet shook her head. "I don't know. Not home. Not here."

Lisbet flinched in anticipation of Yseult's insistence she remember where, but it didn't come.

"That wasn't a dream. It was a vision. Sit."

This time when Lisbet tried to sit, the effort came with ease. She pulled herself up and let her feet fall over the side. She was now face to face with Yseult, but she didn't dare allow herself the indulgence of taking her measure. "It cannot have been a vision, Chieftainess. I have no magic in me. Only my brother, Christian, does."

"There is a magic waking all over the kingdom," Yseult said. "The long slumber ends."

"I don't know what that means."

"It wasn't a dream. It was a vision. Your brother is here for a reason."

Lisbet rubbed at her bleary eyes. She saw now the brothers, perched at different corners of the room. Dark and light. "But it was Eavan's idea to come here, not mine."

"Your path would have led you here either way," Yseult said. "For Drystan was always meant to be here, when the magic awakened."

"What do you mean, awakened?"

Yseult's hawk sounded like a cry.

"The Four Sorcerers have anticipated this moment for hundreds of years. The subjugation of the Saleen is but one sign of this. Placing the boy king upon the throne is another."

"We didn't know about Lord Quinlanden's treachery, I swear to you."

"We know you did not. But you have strayed from what matters. It is your turn to ask a question, and there is only one that matters."

Lisbet's heart threatened to jump from her chest. She wanted to place both hands over it, for it seemed to her everyone in the room could see its erratic jumps against her flesh. "Who are the four sorcerers?"

Yseult placed a hand upon her brow. It was almost loving. "No, that is not the question. For now, enough. More, when ready." She'd returned to her more natural speech, as if extinguishing a light and returning Lisbet to darkness.

Yseult left the dark room, and Kael followed. Kian lingered to escort her, and when Lisbet was sure the others were far away, she asked him, "What was that? What happened?"

Kian smiled. "You at last answered her with your truth, and now we can begin."

THE ONE BEATING MOST SWIFTLY TOWARD YOUR DESTRUCTION

Jesse grasped for his clothes, tripping over the chair and the bedpost. His head was a mess of moments from his latest dream, moments he needed to be well rid of. Esmerelda's draught had bought him precious sleep these past nights, but once there he'd been trapped by these images of Ravenna, these enticements he hadn't asked for and didn't want.

If only that were true. He wanted her well enough. But it went no further than a physical response to her undeniably enchanting presence. Whatever relief it would offer him wouldn't be worth the cost.

Anything you want, it's yours, she'd repeated as she gazed down upon him. As she moved in steady, torturous rhythm.

Ravenna's voice, this time real, cut through the morning fog. "You've been having more interesting dreams."

Jesse tugged his pants up over his hips. The leather of his belt stung his hand as it whipped inward from the force of his efforts. "And you think it's acceptable to violate the thoughts of others where you come from?"

"Mind reading isn't always intentional. Sometimes it's inadvertent."

Jesse pulled his vest over his shirt. "This isnae the first time you were standing here when I woke, wearing that same smile, so it seems rather intentional to me."

"And you're rather defensive about your own thoughts. You seem to spend a lot of time running from them, and not just the ones of me."

He searched around for his sword belt. "They're not my thoughts. I have no control over my dreams."

"Dreams can be a way of working out our greatest desires and fears."

Jesse stopped fumbling with his sword and looked at her. "I neither desire you nor fear you."

Ravenna looked down and laughed. "Now *that* isn't true."

"What I fear," he said as he finished dressing, "is that I've brought Esmerelda to a place that has become a danger to her and her bairn. I fear the Westerlanders cannae come to an agreement on what to do, and that will be the end of them. Those are fears, Ravenna. Genuine fears. I donnae fear some rogue dreams of you that will never be naught but."

"Your care for Esmerelda is inspiring."

"She's my sister. My brother's wife, if not yet in the eyes of the law. I've a duty to her, one I take to heart."

"It's more than that. I can sense it."

Jesse scoffed at the suggestion she seemed to be making. "Your intuition needs some adjusting. I've never touched her."

"The way she looks at you, I don't think she'd mind if you did."

"And which is it, then? Am I in love with you, or in love with her?" Jesse shook his head and brushed past her, into the hall. "Only a fool would suggest such a thing. She isnae mine."

"She's not Ryan's either. Wasn't that the point of leaving? So she can belong to herself?" Ravenna called after him.

He ignored her. Jesse needed a word with Easlan James in

private, without the other bannermen present, but first he needed something else more.

Brandyn gave Storm the slip.

They shared chambers at the inn. Easlan James had fallen all over himself, concerned Brandyn wouldn't find the rooms there up to his standards—but equally unwilling to let him stay elsewhere, where someone could do to him in the night what they'd done to his father—but it was better than the accommodations on the road and he didn't care about that the way they all thought he would. He was a Blackwood, yes, but he was also a Warwick.

What he cared about was not having had time alone with his thoughts. Storm was his friend, and his self-proclaimed body-guard, but there were things he had to do for himself. Hardly twelve, he'd been thrust into leading both a Reach and a rebellion, and he'd had no time to settle into either role. There were men counting on him. Families. Futures.

Storm had insisted, with the backing of the James men and the other men they were calling his Blackwood Banners, that he could never be left without protection. As she trusted no one else as much as herself, that meant she slept little, and when she did need it, she'd built a trap against the door designed to wake her with any fussing.

Brandyn carefully deconstructed the trap from the inside, lifting and moving the piles of wood to the rise and fall of her snores. When done, he whispered a wordless apology and left.

He peered over the balcony, down into the empty, open room of the tavern. It was here he'd seen the first crack appear in the resolve of the men sworn to protect the Westerlands. It didn't fracture his own trust in them, though. Even Jesse, who wasn't one of them but had just as much passion as the others for seeing the end to Quinlanden's power grab.

But that was the problem. Passion. He, too, had that passion, and it came to him mostly in the latest hours of the evening, when he fantasized of taking his blade to Aiden and a thousand of his men, one by one, as he commanded them to remember the face of Byrne Warwick while the blood left their traitorous bodies. As he spat on them for daring to even step one filthy foot upon their lands. He dangled their wives and children on ropes, payment for what they'd done to the women and children of the Westerlands.

He knew these fantasies would be his undoing if he indulged them too long.

They'd all lost, and had more to lose. Few more than Brandyn himself, who had neither blood nor home anymore. But he didn't trust his capacity for making decisions when he couldn't shake those losses, and this was true also of his men.

All save one.

As Brandyn descended the steps, the corner of the pub came into view. As expected, so did the hunched figure of the man he'd come to see.

"Lord Blackwood." Joran straightened, brushing stringy silver hair back. He ran his fingers down his robe as if wrinkled, though they both knew the silken strands that crafted them could never be defiled in such a way. "It is quite early. We didn't expect you for another two ticks or so."

Brandyn looked around the empty room. "We?"

Joran chuckled. One fist tapped the table in nervous staccato. "Steward James rises with the sun, his son too. I suspect Blackfen never sleeps at all, and Tyndall has probably made a deal with his precious Guardians exchanging rest for fealty."

Brandyn pulled out a chair and sat across from him. "You really don't like the Reliquary, do you?"

Joran sucked in a breath with a guilty, harried look. "Oh, I suppose it would seem that way to you, wouldn't it? You, still so fresh an Adherent. Would that the Sepulchre and the Reliquary could live in harmony, for we are not so different. But they see us as cheap tricksmen, and we see them as too high upon their thrones to understand us, or the kingdom, at all."

"Do you believe in the Guardians, Enchanter Joran?"

"I very much do. It's their earthly agents I've little trust for."

"And you? Do you sleep anymore?" Brandyn studied the old man's face, wondering if it was only his imagination that there were now more lines than before. More darkness in the deep crescents under his eyes. "Or is it coincidence you know the patterns of others?"

Joran looked down at his hands. "Your men would bring ruin to the Reach, and they'd do it with love, my lord." He again looked up. "For they all love you, as they love your mother."

Brandyn slowly nodded. "That's why I've come to see you, Joran. No one knows my mother as you do, and her counsel right now is what I most need."

Joran brightened. "It would be an honor if that were true, but it is your father who knew her best. The light to her darkness, I called him, though never when he was around."

"My father is dead."

Joran sighed. "Yes, Guardians bless him."

"I need you to tell me what you saw that made my mother hand herself over to the king."

The sorcerer shrugged. "Nothing you would not already know, Lord Blackwood. I saw the Warwick and Dereham boys in chains, and though you were not with them in that vision, your mother believed you could be, if not protected. I saw also the cruel display the king made upon the dais with his new Quinlanden wife, the young Assana, and your mother did not want that fate for your sisters. Thus, she went to Ember and told her what she needed to do."

"So it's true. It was my mother who sent us away. It wasn't Ember's idea at all."

"Yes."

"Why not just tell us that? Why not send us off with proper goodbyes at least?"

Joran ran his finger along the old wood. "Well, I suppose she was afraid of knowing where you'd go, that someone might pull it from her mind, the way she can from others. She was clear with Ember, that Ember was to decide where you all would go, Ember alone, who would know until she delivered your orders to you. There was no better way of protecting all of you than her complete ignorance of your whereabouts."

Brandyn nodded. He didn't have to like it to understand it. "But why would she want to fall into the hands of the king? That's what you told the men. That it was part of her plan."

"I'm afraid that part has less clarity. Your mother and I had the same vision, though we equally saw very little. We both saw the dark halls of Duncarrow, your mother moving through them, freely but not free. We both felt her secret thrill as she discovered something that would bring the king to his knees and restore our kingdom to what it should be."

"But what? What was she sent to discover?"

Joran, arms upon the table, lifted his palms in a sort of shrug. "That was our dilemma. Neither of us saw more than that. But your mother was convinced that it was no happenstance we'd both seen this same thing. And so, I can only believe, Lord Blackwood, that she found what she went to Duncarrow for, and this is why she left, to protect it."

Brandyn leaned back in his chair, looking up into the metal candelabra above. "We need to know what she knows."

"Impossible, until she returns to us. Or unless the magic sees fit to gift us with more visions on the matter. I would wager money on neither of these things happening quickly."

"Then I need to know what to do, Joran. Here. With these men. I need to know what my mother would do." He rocked forward again. "I say again, that no one *living* knows my mother as you do. What would she do?"

"Oh, well, this is hard to say for sure. You know your mother, she—"

Brandyn leaned in. "Joran. I'm asking *you*. What would my mother do, if she were me? Right now? How would she guide these men?"

The expression on Joran's face shifted. He was no longer the blubbering old man whose mind was half gone. "Your mother was never one for war. She knew that even a war won was a war lost. For can it be called a victory if the cost is the loss of the men and lands we so love? No, your mother was a mistress of subtlety, dispatching those who would trouble her quietly, in the shadows. Tidy dealings. What they said about the heart was not wrong. But they were wrong about the identity of that heart."

"The heart isn't Lord Aiden, you mean."

Joran shook his head. "No, Lord Blackwood. Aiden is only a hand. He is the face the heart wants you to see. And there are other hands, other faces. There are even more hearts, equally dangerous. But without the heart, there can be no faces, no hands. There can be none of this."

"If he isn't the heart, then who is? The king?"

Joran dropped his voice. "The king is *nothing* compared to the heart. The king is yet another pawn, another hand. The king's father understood this, and he imprisoned one half of the heart, for he was incapable of killing him."

"You mean... the sorcerers? The Rhiagain sorcerers?"

"Yes, but they are no Rhiagains. And where they come from, it was Rhiagains who served the sorcerers. Where they come from, Rhiagains were nothing."

"How do you know this?"

"Before I served your mother, I was an Elder Magi."

"Why would you give that up? That's an even greater honor

than serving in the kingdom, even in a great house like my mother's."

Joran nodded. "I went to the Head Magus with my concern about the great sorcerers of Ilynglass. Yes, that's where they come from, though none have successfully found its location or returned to it, that we know of. They don't realize we know even that much about them, but a name matters not, only what a name means. I told the Head Magus that they were few, but they were powerful, and they were *patient*. I told him they were waiting for their moment, and by the time we realized it, it would be too late."

Brandyn's jaw went slack. "Wow."

"And for that, he said I had overstayed my time at the Sepulchre and would find my honor in service."

"He didn't share your concerns?"

"He thought me a foolish old man nearing expiration." Joran looked down at the thin layer of skin covering his bones, rolling his hands in the dim light. "He is not wrong. But nor was I."

"How many are there? Sorcerers?"

"I know of four. One is in the sky dungeon at Duncarrow, imprisoned by Khain when he was still living. Two disappeared from our knowledge before you were born. The last..." Joran sighed. "The last was given as a gift to Lord Aiden when he laid Rowanwen at the king's feet."

Brandyn gasped inwardly. "The heart."

Joran nodded. "The one beating most swiftly toward your destruction, anyway."

RAVENNA WATCHED him leave the small keep, headed not for town but the river that ran through the forest. She had a strange urge to grin, but the weighted sadness within her overpowered it. She was almost used to this now, existing in these strange polarities. Good. Bad. Night. Day.

She didn't recognize the woman sparring with him about his dreams and desires. She didn't think she'd changed so much since leaving her home, but even if she had, did it have to be to *this*, to someone who was all cunning, no heart? If she were Jesse, she would've asked herself to leave long before this morning, but now there was little chance he wasn't thinking this very thing, and searching for the way to see it done while still maintaining his honor. She'd disrupted their delicate balance. Not once, nor even twice.

Honor is a creation of man. Only men would need their own word to compel them to do the right thing. Her mother's words. She'd said them without irony, though there was plenty to be found in them just the same. Honor. Duty. They could call it anything they wished, but there was no other way to live as a Ravenwood without embracing their way of life. There was no other way at all.

If she'd only stayed and done her duty. Lain with the eligible male sorcerers by the greenlight fires, one by one, kept her mouth shut and her eyes to the future she was destined for. Counted her blessings, even if she didn't see them that way.

But she wasn't destined for that future. Not anymore. There was no going back to Midnight Crest, even if she didn't have the child of a man growing within her. Now she had to do all she could to ensure it wasn't the wrong man assumed to be the father, and she had little time remaining to her, if any at all, to grasp firmly to this deception and make it work. It was the last gift she could give Drystan, though he would likely never know it.

As for Jesse, she'd ask nothing of him once her child was born. This careful veil of deceit was more than she deserved.

Even as Ravenna opened the door and made her way down to the river, it felt like it was someone else's hands pulling the old wood, someone else's feet making the steps. She could neither explain her actions nor put halt to them.

She saw Jesse's clothes scattered on the bank before she saw him. He burst through the water's surface, shaking his head as he whistled through the shocking cold. While his back was turned, Ravenna eased out of her own dress and then slipped into the icy waters.

"Guardians! Ravenna, you cannae just sneak up on a man like that," he cried when she swam up to his side. "If I'd had my sword—"

"Here? In the water?"

"What are you doing here?"

"Does it matter why I'm here, or that I am?"

"Ravenna, I donnae have the mind for—"

Ravenna wrapped her arms around his neck and kissed him. His lips stiffened, but she felt his soft groan vibrate against her mouth, and she knew she could have him, then, there, that very morning, if she only had the courage to see it through. The dark, not the light, guiding.

Jesse gently pushed her off. "No matter what you've seen in my head, in my dreams, this isnae going to be the way of things between us. I donnae have... I've other priorities. You're beautiful. You know ye are, you donnae need me telling you. But there's a war brewing just beyond this forest, and I need to sort myself out, sort out what to do about my brother's bairn."

"Jesse?"

They both turned at the sound of Esmerelda's voice. Her confusion at the scene unfolding, at what it might or might not mean, put a dagger through Ravenna's own heart. Esmerelda might not yet know how she felt about the brother of her dear love, but Ravenna had seen it, and it could only end in heartache for them all. It didn't lessen her guilt at what she was herself trying to do, but she told herself she was only sparing Esmerelda that eventual pain.

Jesse swam away from her and up to the bank, where he looked up at Esmerelda. "Only rinsing off before I go into town. I need to have words with Easlan. Just he and I, without the others. About what I told you the other night."

"I see," Esmerelda said, but she was looking at Ravenna, not Jesse. "You won't have eaten yet, then. I can warm some bread for you."

Jesse smiled. "Donnae fuss yourself, Esme. I can find something at the pub."

"And she? She rinsing off, too?"

"That? Well. Eh—"

"Esmerelda, come join us!" Ravenna called, hanging onto the grassy edge of the opposite bank. As the words flew from her mouth, she knew they'd come from her conscience; not that other thing inside her that had guided her to this moment.

"It looks cold," Esmerelda said, but now she was looking at Jesse, awaiting his word on the matter. "This isn't proper water for bathing, not with the skies as they are. I could've warmed some water for the basin, you know."

"I was just getting out," he said.

Esmerelda seemed torn between some better sense and a potent desire to not be left out of whatever was happening. She bound her arms tight around her. "What about my clothes?"

"You donnae have to come in here, Esme. It's freezing, and—"

"Not too cold for the two of you, aye?"

He started in on an objection, but something changed his mind, for instead he said, "It's not so cold, really. If you wanted to come in, you'd be all right." Jesse turned back toward Ravenna. The look he wore was stronger than a hundred daggers. "We'll turn our backs while you change."

"All right," Esmerelda said. "Turn around, then."

"I thought you were getting out?" Ravenna whispered as she swam up beside him.

"You're the one who invited her in. She shouldnae be in here alone, or at all. These currents can be fierce, and she'll catch a chill."

"She wouldn't be alone. I'm here."

They both turned at the splash. Esmerelda hovered near the bank, one hand wrapped in the tall grass, the other around her chest. Her jaw trembled as she shivered.

"You... l-lied," she accused through chattering teeth.

Jesse laughed. "That's what my father used to do when Ryan and I had too much hesitation in us. He'd say, 'oh, 'tis nay so bad,' and we'd believe him, every time."

Esmerelda twisted her shaking mouth into a grin as she clutched the riverbank. "Ryan has done that to me a few times."

"Come on," Jesse beckoned. "Let go. I willnae let ye get whisked off down the current."

"I never learned to swim properly."

"I've got you, Esme."

Ravenna cut off the sigh forming at the back of her throat. A swell of anger caught at the back of the clipped sound, but it wasn't Esmerelda she was angry at, but herself. For contriving this. For failing at it.

Esmerelda half jumped into the current. A small, nervous giggle erupted as she found her footing. Jesse's smile as he watched her, a mix of protectiveness and of a joy belonging to the two of them in their shared moment, reminded her of Drystan. A sharp pain jabbed at her, but it wasn't the agony of missing him, but of missing herself. Who she'd been, which was not who she was now. She missed who she was, but she missed more who she was supposed to be when she set off to find herself. It was not this... not this woman of hollow motive and shallow needs; not one reduced to the games girls played, not women.

"Almost there. Just step carefully. Some rocks are sharp," Jesse said. Ravenna let herself into his head, ignoring the voice reminding her it was an invasion, that she wasn't supposed to be there. But there was nothing. Jesse's worries about the Westerlands, about the baby, about Esmerelda, they were nowhere to be found. He existed entirely in the moment, in the seconds ticking through his encouragement of Esmerelda's newfound courage.

Esmerelda's smile lit up the cloudy morning. "My father would have murdered me for doing this."

Jesse gestured around, grinning back. "Do ye see him? These are fresh waters, lass. No salt and sand here."

"You're enough salt and sand for us all," she teased, and they laughed, together.

Ravenna's stomach burned.

"You couldn't do this in the rivers in the Northerlands. You'd be frozen dead before you made it across to the other bank," she said, not seeing her place in this moment, but desperate not to be forgotten, either.

"That's horrible," Esmerelda said with a scandalized look. "Does that really happen?"

"Esme, careful there, you're stepping close to the drop-off," Jesse said. He moved toward her. "It's can be a bit—"

Esmerelda's scream was cut off as she disappeared under the water. Jesse didn't hesitate. He dove under and was gone. Ravenna hardly had time to make sense of what had happened. She searched for them both, eyes scanning the small white crests of the current, but they were, both of them, gone.

"Jesse!" she cried out. She dipped below the water, but the tangle of river flora obscured her view. She could see nothing but waving vines and murky gray. Gasping, she returned to the surface. She was still alone.

Then Jesse's head breached the water's surface, and Esmerelda's with it. Esmerelda's arms wound so tightly around Jesse's neck that she seemed to almost disappear into him, as if they were not two but one. His left arm folded over her back, clutching her against him as he used the other to maneuver himself through the water toward the bank. He used the branch of a nearby tree to hoist them both up to the bank, and Ravenna's breath caught to see how Esmerelda's body twined around Jesse's, all flesh and fear and the rush created by the marriage of both things.

He eased her down on the grass, but he'd forgotten her claims of modesty from earlier as he pushed her matted hair off her face, peeling the skin back by her eyes to check the color, running his thumbs over her flushed cheeks.

"I'm fine," Esmerelda insisted, but anyone with ears could hear the lie in it, and as Jesse wrapped her in his shirt, Ravenna couldn't keep her eyes from his hands that wouldn't stop moving, wouldn't stop fussing over her, searching for any signs she'd come to harm.

Esmerelda stayed his hands. "Jesse. I'm okay, I'm just... I'm a little tired now. I'm going to go in and lie down, but come tell me later, about Easlan. Yes?"

She didn't wait for his answer. She ran off toward the keep, Jesse watching her until she disappeared beyond view.

"It wasn't your fault," Ravenna said, breathing the words near his ear.

Jesse jumped. "I didnae even see you get out." He shook his head. "I should go make sure she's all right. She's full of pride, just like Ryan. She wouldnae tell me if—" He turned and the sight of her stilled his words. She hadn't redressed, and he seemed to realize that just as he remembered that, in the excitement, nor had he.

Ravenna snaked her arms around his neck once more, and this time when she kissed him, she felt his desire fight harder than his resistance. His cock throbbed against her belly, and she pushed herself tighter against him, knowing the press of her flesh would grow his pleasure beyond what he could deny himself. Jesse's hands cupped her ass, and he lifted her in a quick, sharp tug. In response, she wrapped her legs around his waist, tightening against him once more. He stumbled in the grass until they backed into a tree, the force causing them both to audibly gasp. Ravenna reached one hand down to pull him inside before he could remember all the other things more deserving of his attention, and though she, too, had imagined this, the swell of his hardness, of him, was almost more than she could bear.

Jesse reached for a branch above his head for purchase as he drove into her, holding her aloft with the force of his thrusts. He groaned his desire against her neck; sounds that were not words, but she read them anyway. *I want you. I hate you. I need you. Leave me. Please stop. Never stop.* The bark sliced at her back, but she squeezed his muscled ass in her palms, forcing the flesh to bulge through her fingers, encouraging every thrust to be harder, every stroke of his cock to last longer, to prolong her own path to what she now knew she wanted more than she'd ever imagined, for reasons beyond what she's originally designed.

He bit down on her shoulder as the pleasure rocked through him, and then she, too, felt it, the warmth of his seed coursing through her. His tight muscles spasmed, shuddering as his desire slowly drained into her, and he again, less slowly, returned to the world.

Jesse lowered her to the tall grass and stumbled away, grasping for his clothes, as he had after the fantasy version of what had now become reality. Every misstep, every failed tug of cloth against his skin was a palpable sign of his regret, which had come on so fast she'd had no time to fight back and win him to her side once more.

"Come to my bed tonight when you're home from the Mule," she whispered, kneeling beside him as he fumbled with his sword belt. She'd done what she needed to do, but now it was her own desire talking. "Properly, this time."

"Come to the back. Let's give Lord Blackwood and his seer some privacy," Easlan said, steering Jesse through the double doors leading to the kitchen. On the way in, they passed Brook, fast asleep on his cot. Jesse felt a small stab of guilt at the sight of the small boy. With all he'd had on his mind, he'd forgotten about him. At least Easlan hadn't.

"I'll pour us both some mugs," Easlan said. "Head to the very end of the hall. Kaslan is at the table already."

Jesse nodded and squeezed through the narrow hall to the room reserved for Kaslan and his son alone. It was too small for business, windowless with stale air and a meager table that seated exactly three and no more.

"That look. I'm quite familiar with that look!" Kaslan said, wagging his finger as he looked up, bleary-eyed, from his mug of tea. "That's the look of girl troubles, and I would know. Question is, which one?"

"Have ye girls in Greystone?"

"Hush. And tell me!"

"That isnae the source of my troubles," Jesse grumbled.

"It *isnae* all, but it's part, that much I can see. Quick now, tell me before Father comes and ruins the fun."

"I donnae want to talk about it, Kaslan."

"Ravenna," Kaslan guessed. He tapped the table, grinning through his sleepiness. "I knew it. Can't say I fault you, I would've made a move myself if I thought I had even half a chance. Oh, and also, you're my mate and all that."

Jesse looked around for anything that could serve as the recipient of the bile forming in his throat. He couldn't believe he'd done it. It was as surreal as one of his dreams, but it had been no dream. He'd taken her all right, against that tree, by the riverbank, and there was no waking from this one to wash away his guilt. He'd done it, despite knowing he would feel exactly as he did now. "It willnae happen again, and will ye *stop* looking at me like that. I'm not pleased with myself. I've forgotten who I am."

"You've remembered you're a man. Or did you never realize

that until now?" Kaslan teased. "You've always been so serious, Jesse. Even as a wee boy. There's no harm in some fun."

"Your Reach is on the verge of war. I see no place for fun."

"What are we fighting for, if not for that? Look here, Jesse. You like her. She likes you. Not everything has to be so complicated."

Jesse fought another wave of nausea. "But it *is* complicated, Kaslan. I have my brother's wife in my hands, and now there's a child. Esme... she really doesnae like Ravenna. I donnae know why, but it upsets her, and if she gets upset, she might get sick, and if she gets sick, then..." Jesse buried his face in his hands. "I cannae deal with the attentions of a priestess, in addition to all else on my shoulders. There's no gain in forgetting who I am."

Kaslan pulled Jesse's hands away from his face. "But was it as good as you imagined it would be?"

Jesse felt the flush deep under his skin. "Ahh, how I wish I'd hated it."

"The joy you get from denying yourself is something to behold," Kaslan said, shaking his head. "Truly. You're a man, doing what a man does, and you still find ways to punish yourself."

"I don't expect you to understand."

"Good! For I don't." He leaned in. "Now, listen. There're whispers of ravens from The Deceiver, come from Duncarrow. With some strange messaging. Some are saying they may leave room for us to strike."

"From Lord Quinlanden? What do they say?"

"Don't know. Yet. We'll talk more later. Father's coming."

Easlan entered with the steaming mugs. "Jamesan, I assume I'd be right to say you didn't come simply for the pleasure of my company, such as it is."

"No, sir. I didnae sleep well at all."

"I'll say," Kaslan mumbled, grinning.

Jesse ignored him. "I've things on my mind, things I'd like to say before the other men arrive."

"Then say them," Easlan said with a curt nod.

"You've been a friend to my father for many years. I trust in your wisdom," Jesse started. "As I know Lady Blackwood does."

"You didn't come here to puff up my pride, either."

"But no man can be without error, least from time to time, and I wouldnae be the friend you've been to me if I didnae say I think your call to war is one."

Easlan pushed his mug aside, untouched. "Is that all?"

"I'd hoped we might discuss it."

"Discuss it? What business of it is yours what the Westerlands does to protect its own, Jamesan Strong? What does the opinion of a Southerlander matter to us?"

"Father, I'm sure that isn't—" Kaslan started, but Easlan held his hand out.

Jesse recoiled at Easlan's quickness to anger. "It isnae none of mine, except that I owe ye for the aid, and I no more want to see the kingdom at war than you."

"You're hardly a bairn yourself," Easlan replied, disgust burning in his eyes. He'd changed, and Jesse saw it more now than he had, even the night before. "What would you know about it? About war? About the business of men?"

"I can count," Jesse retorted, feeling the rise of his own rare anger. "I can see ye haven't the numbers, or the strength, to go against what awaits you. I can see what others tried to say last night. Even Lord Blackwood himself."

"And what does the son of a sea trader advise?" Easlan practically spat the words between his clenched teeth.

"I didnae come to advise, Steward James, only to caution. For I've never taken wisdom from any unless I considered them a friend, and I thought that's what we were."

Easlan shoved his chair back and stood. "You owe me nothing. If Lord Blackwood values your counsel, then offer it to him."

His heavy steps pounded as he rushed from the room. When

they'd faded to echoes, Jesse turned to Kaslan. "I said what I needed to, and I'll not say another word. He's right. This isnae my fight."

"You weren't wrong," Kaslan said in a hushed tone, one eye on the hall in fear of his father's furious return. "But he'll never see it, Jesse. You don't understand. All his life, and his father's, the James name has been akin with the lost and forgotten. He's had the respect of none except Lady Blackwood. Until now, where it's Easlan James, and not one of the greater men of the realm, called upon to save us all. He's not in his right mind, and there's nothing you, nor I, can do to change that. If you'd warned me about what you intended to say, I could've spared you yet another agony of the day."

JESSE WAS REMOVING the tethers from the hitching post, lost in his own head, when Esmerelda caught him by surprise. He'd heard the hooves on the road, but assumed them to belong to one of the men.

She wore the same oversized cloak from her earlier trips into town as her hooded form looked down upon him, but he'd know the shape of her anywhere now. It was as familiar to him as his own.

"You shouldn't be here." He looked behind him. "There are too many men here now. We have to be more careful than we were before."

"I had to say something to you, and I wanted the chance to say it alone. Just you and me," Esmerelda said. The hood hung low over her eyes, but her dark lips pulled together in a light sigh. "Let's ride, but slowly."

Jesse mounted his horse and clicked his tongue to turn her and join Esmerelda.

"I have asked a lot of you, Jesse," she said at his side. She kept her face looking ahead.

"You've asked nothing I was forced to give," he assured her. She'd said this before, and he didn't like the implication. He worried he'd given her the cause to keep saying it. "And what I've given has been no burden."

"Even so, your life has been halted, for me. You should've been home in the Southerlands by now, returned to your work, and whatever else awaited you. I've never asked, I suppose. Is there someone? Someone special awaiting you?"

"No," Jesse said. "Nor does anything await me with greater weight than seeing my brother's bairn born healthy and whole."

Esmerelda made a soft sound from under her hood. "You're a good man, for believing that. That it's you who must see this done. But I'm his mother, and I've asked enough of you already. No." Esmerelda held her hand out without looking. "Please don't tell me again how it's fine. I have more to say, before I lose the courage."

"All right. Go on."

"When I met you at the cottage, on the outskirts of Warwicktown, ready to run, to hurt those who'd hurt me, I was a spoiled, childish girl who was in love with a man I wasn't supposed to have, and angry at the one who denied me of him. I saw the world through very different eyes then. It feels as if I'm talking of a lifetime ago, when it's been mere months. But I am not the same. It's not only this wee one, either." Esmerelda let one hand fall to rest on her belly. "For all my love of Ryan, which was real and true then as it is now, I didn't see him for who he was, and who I was, and how that love was selfish. It was never me who had the most to lose. Never me. Oh, how I reveled in the pity of myself in those early days in exile with you, how much I'd given up for this love, for a world that was unfair to me alone. I was angry with you for how you reduced me to a princess in your mind, never asking myself why you might carry this anger, why it might be yours to feel, to have, to own."

"I had some misunderstandings of my own, you know."

"We are both made of them, are we not? Like earlier, when I found you at the river. I think I knew what the two of you were doing, and I chose to see it for something else, anyway. I should have left you both alone."

"Esmerelda, there's nothing there between us."

"You're a liar. And I'm a silly girl for giving you cause to feel wrong for it. I'm sorry for that. I don't even understand my own jealousy in the matter, only that it's been you and me for so long that I didn't know how to handle another."

They were approaching the forest's edge. Esmerelda brought her mare to a gentle halt. She turned in the saddle and dropped her hood back. "It's time for me to go home, Jesse."

Jesse swallowed. He looked around him, at the darkness of the edge of a dead town, of the beckoning timber line. Of the world he'd brought her to, after what felt like years together.

"If Ryan survives, he won't know where to find me. No matter what my father does when he finds out what I've done, I owe Ryan my courage, not my cowardice. The first face he sees if they let him out should be mine, and then that of his child."

Jesse lowered his head. He'd not expected her words, and he wondered how long she'd been considering this. But though it was her decision, she was making it without knowing all he did, and while she talked of owing Ryan, he owed her as well, for she was a part of it, whether or not she knew it.

How many times had he almost told her? Almost broken the Sacred Vow, for her?

He would break it now.

"There's something you need to know," Jesse said. "About what Ryan is really doing in the Wastelands."

18

TEMPESTUOUS NATURES

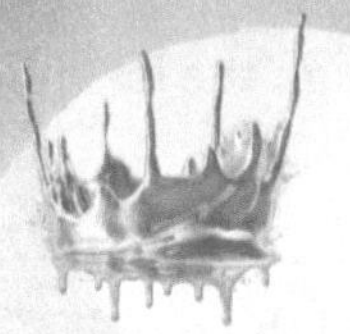

The incessant pecking of the bird against the tree at the base of the cave ripped Asherley from the best sleep of her life. At first, she thought it was another Ravenwood. They were the bane of her exile, perched in silent judgment as the long days turned to long nights. Saying nothing. Doing nothing.

She'd had some of the most wonderful dreams of her life, though they veered dangerously close to actual memories. Playing with the children and Byrne at Wildwood Falls. Standing at the shore with Byrne, toes buried in the cool sand, wondering what lay beyond the horizon. Her mind had encapsulated the happiest moments of her life, and then played them for her, reminding her of why she had taken this path.

Asherley groaned as Byrne's smiling face faded to the sharp icy wind of the Northern Range and the desperate neighs of the restless horses. She tried to shake the remains of her dream off, for there was no good living in the past, but when she attempted to sit, she was rooted in place. Her limbs felt weighted to the cold rock of the cave floor, as if she'd slept days and not hours.

Her next thought was a question. How long *had* she slept? It wasn't only her limbs fighting her. Her head was split open from the throbbing as she tried again to sit, like when she'd consumed too much of her favorite wine. She felt more rested than she had in years, but was overcome also with the terrifying sense she'd missed a great deal while she was out.

Hobbled steps called her attention to the darker side of the cave. She turned her head. Assyria.

"They're gone."

Asherley winced through the inexplicable pain, pushing herself forward. "Who? Who's gone?"

"Would I care if the Dereham and Warwick lads had left? *Stefan* is gone! With Anabella and the scholar." Assyria kicked something. It bounced off the cave wall and landed in a thud several feet from where Asherley struggled to rise.

"It seems we've slept through the best part of the morning. They're probably out hunting. Wyat has been teaching Stefan."

Assyria snickered. "No, Lady Blackwood, they are not out *hunting*. Their bows are gone, yes, but so is everything else. Their bedrolls, their sacks." Her rush of anger continued as she kicked the boys from their bed and launched into demands of them. "Do neither of you have anything to say? What did you see? What do you know? Did they tell you they were leaving?"

"We don't know anything!"

"Leave them be," Asherley said. She could sit now, so she bit back the rest of her stiffness and rolled forward, pulling herself to her feet. "Assyria," she said again, when she saw the princess had Pieter by his neck. "Leave them *be*."

Pieter cried out when Assyria dropped him. "They must know something. Isn't that important to you? Finding them?"

Asherley's head was a whirlwind all she knew and didn't. It seemed Assyria was right. They'd left. She didn't even need to ask herself why, for it was obvious to anyone with eyes to see and ears to hear. They'd left to get away from the sparring women and their tempestuous natures. "If I were Anabella... I'd go south. To my husband." She said it more to herself, but Assyria jumped quickly on her words, storming over.

"Did you know, then? That they were leaving? Did you help them?"

Asherley narrowed her eyes. "I know nothing more than you."

"Did you even see what I kicked over to you?"

Asherley looked down. "A bowl. So?"

"Smell it!"

Without taking her eyes off Assyria, Asherley knelt down. She met Assyria's eyes as she brought it to her nose. She inhaled and then sighed with recognition. "A sleeping draught."

"Now do you understand? This was *planned*. They put us to sleep and then slipped away in the night." Assyria leaned in. The energy radiating off her sent a sickness to Asherley's belly. This woman was a danger. She'd always been a danger, but this was something else. Something more.

"They couldn't have gone far, not yet," Asherley said. She sounded calm, but her heart caught in the back of her chest from the force of the beats. She put all her focus into proper breathing; into not inciting whatever bloodlust burned so hot in Assyria she could hardly contain it. She didn't know what had happened to Anabella and the others, but she was certain they didn't want to be found, and Asherley was slowly coming around to the understanding that the mother and son might be better off without the two women who had decided their fates. "Our plan has changed. We need simply to amend it."

"Simply amend it, you say," Assyria repeated. The bitter disgust rolled off her tongue. The spittle dotted Asherley's cheeks. "You have no appreciation for the years I spent caring for that woman and child, preparing them for what they would need to do to save all of us. You have no comprehension of all I've given up, for this, for them!"

Asherley reached down in instinct for her sword, but it was propped against the wall. "Perhaps my inability to appreciate this lies in your lack of willingness to explain yourself. To explain why *you* should care which Rhiagain sits upon the throne, when your standing in this kingdom is the same either way." The last of her sleep was leaving her, and now her own anger burned to the surface. "Or why you needed me to see it done."

Assyria laughed. She sounded like those creatures that lived high in the woods beyond Longwood Rush; the ones the children were afraid of. "You pride yourself on knowing so much, being so *cunning*, and yet you know nothing, do you? You know nothing!" Assyria stepped closer. Asherley backed away, toward the cave entrance and the morning light. From the corner of her eye, she saw Assyria's hand fall upon the hilt of her sword.

Asherley looked past the princess to see the boys scampering toward the back of the cave. That was good. She didn't know if she could keep them safe from what was coming. "You cannot wound me with your words, princess. For, you may be a 'good' Rhiagain, but you're still a Rhiagain, and who could respect the words of a bloodline that had to *steal* its throne to rule?"

Asherley ducked right as she heard the metal release from Assyria's sheath. She rolled to the side and retrieved her own sword, just in time to feel the princess' steel connect with the cave above her head.

"Lady Asherley!" Pieter cried out.

"Stay back, Pieter! Ransom! This is between us women, right, Assyria?" Asherley wielded her sword with both hands, out to the side, at the ready. It wasn't The Betrayer, but it would answer to her.

"I'll send their heads to their fathers before I let you stand in the way of what needs to be done, Lady Blackwood." Assyria swung her sword, and Asherley met it midair with her own.

Assyria pressed down upon her, and she stumbled back into the snow.

"And why must Anabella answer to us? Why can she not decide what is best for her own son?" Asherley grunted as their swords connected again, and then again. She'd forgotten the weight of steel in her hands, which was so much more intense when putting it to use. Men trained for years to do this, and she was already weary of the exchange. She saw the same in Assyria's eyes, but the fire burned hotter than her exhaustion, and Asherley had to find the same within her or she would lose everything on this mountainside.

"Anabella is a fool! Darrick is a fool!" Assyria cried. Her hair had come out of her plaits, dancing around her face in haphazard snarls. She looked like a madwoman as she held her sword out to the side once more. "They know nothing of what my father worked against! And he was a fool for not telling his sons what his daughters knew. For now, it falls to us, and Correen was never going to be the one to rise and meet this challenge. Never. It was me, always me."

Asherley met her attack once more and pushed their swords down to the side with a groan. Panting, she asked, "Do you know how you sound? Like all those you claim to be against, Assyria! Like you've lost your mind! I am *not* your enemy."

"Anyone who does not work to halt the awakening of The Four Sorcerers is my enemy!"

Asherley's arm was on fire as their steel connected once more. "What are you talking about? What sorcerers?"

"My father knew. He knew and tried to stop them," Assyria said. She swung her sword so hard Asherley lost her footing again. They were too close to the edge. Snow and rock crumbled off the side of the mountainside, disappearing beyond. "He imprisoned two, and then Eoghan, the fool, he *gave* one to Quinlanden. Now that he's seen Mortain's work, he'll do the same with Oldwin, and when the other two return from hiding, there will be nothing to stop them anymore. No one in this kingdom knows what's coming. And they won't, not until it's too late."

"You make no sense." Asherley went to block another hit when her sword flew from her hand. They both watched it land in a pile of snow, too far for her to reach. She sighed as she looked up to receive the next blow, but Assyria had lowered her sword.

"Mortain's submission of the Medvedev. Eoghan's attempt on Darrick's life and Eoghan's ascension to the throne. These are no accidents. The sorcerers have served us only to bide their time, and though they cannot kill us, and we cannot kill them, they can devise our undoing. They have, and they will. Not only Rhiagain. Not only Ravenwood. Not only Medvedev. Not only man." Assyria inhaled the cold air and then snapped her sword up, pressing the point into Asherley's neck. "And you thought this was all about who sits upon the throne. You silly, useless woman."

A loud caw sounded above them. The Ravenwood spies had become part of the background, but it was so close now she couldn't help but look up, and as she did, just as the tip of Assyria's sword pierced her flesh, she could hardly believe what she was seeing.

The raven dove in and swarmed tight circles around Assyria's head, confounding her. In the confusion, she dropped the sword and batted her hands around her face to be rid of the strange assault.

Asherley stumbled to the side just as the raven drove Assyria Rhiagain off the cliff and into the abyss.

Gasping, Asherley crawled through the heavy snow to the cliff's edge. She peered into the emptiness of snow and the bottomless chasm, but there was no sign of the princess. Of anything.

She looked up, searching for the raven that had done this, but in its place was a man.

"Who are you?" she managed through ragged breaths.

He answered by raising his hands above his head. Then Asherley was consumed in fresh darkness.

"Go! Run! Faster!" Ransom called behind him. He scrambled through the snow, half running, half climbing, as they pushed up the path away from the cave. "Forget the horses, just go!"

"Did you see that? Did you see it?" Pieter yelled.

"We're next if we don't get out of here!"

Pieter cried out, so Ransom turned to retrieve him. Though they were cousins, he hadn't known Pieter Dereham well at all prior to being imprisoned together, and now even the thought of being without him left him feeling sick in the belly. No one but Pieter could understand all they'd been through, and that bond was for life.

Pieter smiled gratefully as he took Ransom's arm. Ransom moved slower now, but he wouldn't leave without Pieter, even if that meant the strange, aggressive raven came for them next and drove them to the same death as the princess.

Had that really happened? Ransom had watched in muted horror as Princess Assyria had Lady Asherley on her knees. His father, Lord Warwick, always said that *you didnae put a sword to a man's throat if you didnae intend to push it through*, and this seemed a universal truth, not belonging only to the Warwicks. He'd decided then he would save Asherley, and was fumbling with an arrow in the quiver when the raven swooped down and changed everything.

"She's dead, right? The princess? She must be," Pieter said, panting as they struggled through the endlessness of the snow. Ransom didn't understand how Pieter and others lived like this. The Northerlands was covered in the stuff for most of the seasons.

It stifled him. Made him long for the briny air of Warwicktown and the burning sand between his fingers.

"I donnae know. I cannae see how she'd survive that." Ransom paused for only a moment. Before, he was certain they'd been on the path, and now he couldn't see the delineation at all. It was all white, all blinding and terrifying.

"And Lady Asherley?"

"I donnae know, Pieter. I know no more more than you." He turned to look behind him, but there was no one coming. Yet. "We need to find the trail again. I think we've lost it."

Pieter pointed. "There. That's the tree where Christian and Aylen stop to take the horses off the wagon. It's just off the path. They walk them the rest of the way to the cave."

"Are you certain?"

Pieter nodded.

Ransom groaned through every grueling step. The pass should have been cleared, but there'd been no one traveling in the past days. Anyone coming after them would see their boot prints and know something was amiss. But did it even matter anymore? The others were gone. Princess Assyria dead. Lady Blackwood...

What *had* happened to her? Who was that man?

Lord Dereham would know what to do. But they had to find their way to him before they, too, met their end on this mountain. It would've been much easier with the horses, but there was no power in the kingdom that could make him turn back.

Pieter pushed on ahead, aimed toward the tree with a fresh burst of energy. Ransom struggled to keep up. He was exhausted already. The rush of fear was wearing off, and now he was confronted with the stark understanding that both of their lives were in his hands.

Pieter had reached the tree. He half hung from a branch, grinning with pride. "Come on! There are pearapples on this one! It's like the trees in the Wintergarden that bloom and bear fruit all year." He took one from the tree and sank his teeth in for a generous bite. "See!"

Ransom smiled through his exhaustion. He *was* hungry, had been since he'd awakened to the fight between the women, but he'd forgotten it amidst the bedlam. With a bit more energy, he climbed the last of the hill, toward Pieter.

Pieter moved around to the other side of the tree. Ransom dropped his head, pulling his hood tighter as a fierce wind ripped through the pass.

"All right, grab one for the road, but no stopping. We gotta move, Pieter. This looks like a fresh storm on the horizon."

Pieter didn't respond.

Ransom peeled his hood back and looked up.

Pieter had vanished.

19
THE FOUR SORCERERS

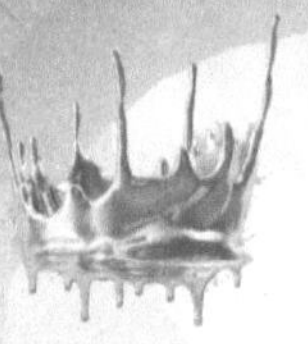

Lisbet had every intention of helping Eavan prepare the morning meal, but that was before. After the exhausting episode Yseult had led her through, she no longer had much of an appetite. She struggled to imagine food ever tasting good again, or the enjoyment of a fresh wind off Icebolt mountain filling her lungs with the air of home. Even if she was wrong, any experience she had from here until the end would be different. Everything about her was changed.

She tried to sleep, but her mind whirred so fast she nearly fell off the bedroll in a bout of dizziness. Eavan didn't even ask her what was wrong. She seemed to be purposely avoiding her, for once deciding she wasn't entitled to know what was on the mind of another.

But Lisbet wanted to share this time! She *needed* to talk about it, and Yseult had cut her off just as she was pulling closer to whatever this *awakening* was that had happened to her. She knew it was there, could feel it even now, but she didn't understand it. She couldn't read it, couldn't access it, not without help, and now she was left feeling as if they'd placed her at a table of rich delights and told she could partake of none of it.

An awakening, Yseult had said, but she wasn't speaking only of whatever was happening to Lisbet. What else had she said? Something about the Four Sorcerers?

There was one other here who might know. The one who seemed to know everything, though he was supposedly no one, from nowhere.

Lisbet slipped out of the small hut where the women slept and went off toward the one housing the two men.

"DRYSTAN?"

Eavan held her distance. She didn't know if Drystan's skill with a sword had improved, but he was likely to send it right into her, he seemed so focused on his strange, wild swings.

Drystan straightened his posture and turned. "Sorry. I didn't hear you."

"What are you doing? I thought you were tending the meat before it rots?"

"I've already finished. Now I'm practicing what Valen taught me," he answered before sheathing the sword.

"I'm surprised they gave it back to you, being a prisoner and all."

Drystan grinned. "It isn't as if I'm much of a threat with it now, am I?"

Eavan dropped her eyes. His playfulness reminded her of other men who had been the same to her, and she could not reminisce about the good ones without the painful recollection of the ones who had hurt her. This was her life now, a game of all the seemingly benign ways she could fail to escape the inescapable, whilst a prisoner of a world that had once been a place of friendship. "What are you practicing for?"

He first checked to see that they were alone. "I want to offer my services to Yseult. For when they march on Whitechurch and free the Saleen."

Eavan looked up again. "You *what*?"

"I don't want to die here, Eavan," Drystan said, moving closer, dropping his voice. "Do you?"

"Of course not, but—"

"Have you asked yourself why we're still here? After all this time?"

"Of course I have! I ask myself every day!" Eavan fought a wave of nausea. "But I don't see what you offering your service, in something you have no experience at all in, has anything to do with that."

"I understand why you're confused. So was I," Drystan said. He looked so serious that she felt suddenly uncomfortable. "But it all makes sense now, doesn't it? They could've killed us. They could've freed us. Instead, they leave us here, waiting. But maybe it isn't us who are waiting but them. Waiting *for* us. For us to stand up and pick a side."

"What does Valen say?"

"Valen says whatever he pleases, but it's never what I need." A flash of anger passed across Drystan's hard gaze, but it was gone as quick as she noticed it. "If he knew the answer, we'd be free. But he doesn't. He doesn't know everything, no matter what he might want us all to think."

"Drystan, I still can't see how you came to this conclusion."

Drystan touched her shoulder, giving her a soft, faraway look. "I just told you my purpose in being here. When you understand yours, you will know it, too."

Ash liked the old oak. He thought he remembered it from before. Not his second time in the Hinterlands, the one he'd told Drystan and the others about, but the first. The one that, even now, felt like remembering was akin to walking on clouds in a dream. Sometimes he wondered if it had even been real. Any of it. The magic. *Her.*

"I have questions, and if you have answers, you *will* give them to me," Lisbet demanded, breaking through the lovely respite. "I won't leave until you do."

Ash looked up. "Fair morning to you as well, Lisbet."

"Tell me what you know of The Four Sorcerers?"

The smile forming on his face quickly died. "What did you just say?" He noticed now the charged flush in her cheeks, the wild look in her eyes. He jumped to his feet. "Lisbet, what did you say?"

"You heard me!" she hissed at him, though it was hard to tell precisely where her anger was directed. She'd been radiating with it long before she found him. Now that he could see her more closely, he wasn't sure it was even anger at all, but a frenzy of confusion. Fear.

"Can you tell me what happened, what brought you to this?"

Lisbet's eyes darted around. "Where's Drystan? Are you expecting him?"

"He's tending the meat from our morning hunt," Ash said. "No, I'm not. Not for a while."

"Good. Good." Lisbet's feet wouldn't stop moving. "I don't want him to hear this. Or Eavan. Or anyone. I don't even want *you* to hear it, but I'm rather short on options, would you not say?"

Ash kept replaying *The Four Sorcerers* in his mind, though there was no way that was what she said. Was it? If so, it would be the second time in recent days that someone had asked him about the sorcerers, and that couldn't be mere coincidence. "It's hard for me to speak on your options when I don't know what you want from me."

"First, I won't call you Valen. Tell me your real name."

So Drystan hadn't told her any of it. Was he ashamed? Did he doubt Ash was his father? "Ash. It's not my birth name, but it's what I've been called all my life, and I don't answer to anything else."

"Except Valen."

He nodded. "Except Valen."

"Ash." Her mouth cringed as it formed the name, though Ash doubted she even realized it. Her distrust of him ran deep. He couldn't blame her for it. Though he would take an arrow to the heart for her, she'd never believe it until the last of his blood had drained into the cool earth. "I thought Yseult was your friend."

"As did I," Ash replied. He quickly amended this to, "I still believe she is, and that our friendship stayed her hand." He waved his hand around. "Why we have all we have, and not the prison given to us on our arrival."

"She no longer thinks we had anything to do with the treachery against the Saleen. I thought that's why she kept us, why she *keeps* us, but it isn't, is it?"

Ash shook his head. "She can read our hearts, Lisbet. It's why you've returned each day, to the same questions, over and over. Because she has read what is deep within you, even if you haven't."

"Well, I have," Lisbet answered. "I've read it. I read it today, and then she kicked me away before I could attempt to understand it."

This surprised Ash, but it explained her disheveled appearance. "I remember when that happened to me. She did the same when I was here."

"And?"

"And what?"

"And when did she explain it to you?"

"She didn't," Ash said. "She continued to push me until I understood it without needing explanation."

Lisbet chewed at her bottom lip. Her eyes still darted around, unable to focus on one thing for long. "Tell me about The Four Sorcerers."

"Where did you hear that?"

"From Yseult. She said it. Said they'd been awaiting this moment for hundreds of years, and they were returning now."

Ash's breath caught. "She said this?"

"Tell me what it means!"

"Lisbet." Ash held his hands out. "I know what you're going through right now, and will continue to go through as you come to these revelations about yourself. But working yourself up like this will only make it harder."

Lisbet grunted. "Just tell me. Please."

Ash shrugged. "I don't know as much as you think I do. The Four Sorcerers that Yseult mentions are the four Rhiagain sorcerers that came to our kingdom with Carrow Rhiagain when they ship-wrecked upon the shores of Duncarrow. Only two of them have ever been confirmed, but I have, more than once, heard tell of four. Who knows what the truth is?"

"Came with them?" Lisbet laughed. "Hundreds of years ago? Right."

"You asked me, and I'm telling you. It seems hard to believe, but that doesn't mean their immortality is myth. Many have borne witness to it over the years. It's been written about. Sang about, though few still know the songs. Some even say there were more than four, though if so that's a truth that has faded beyond memory or knowledge that exists today."

"And where are they? These sorcerers?"

"Two were imprisoned at Duncarrow. The others disappeared long ago. It was said they went into hiding when King Khain imprisoned the first two, but I've heard nothing of them since. Perhaps they're dead. Perhaps they found a way to return to their own kingdom. Perhaps they never existed at all."

"No one can sail beyond our shores. Everyone knows this."

"And yet, the Rhiagains found themselves here, years ago. What do we know about Beyond, other than others insisting its unobtainable? It could be miles from us, or a distance farther than we know how to measure."

Lisbet scoffed, shifting, signaling her growing impatience. "But what does it mean, about them returning? The sorcerers?"

"I don't know," Ash said, and he could see she didn't believe him. This seemed to be the nature of their relationship; she would seek him out for his knowledge and then dismiss his answers outright. "But if it has space in Yseult's thoughts, there's a reason for it. She doesn't concern herself with matters of the kingdom unless she has no other choice."

"Lisbet! There you are!" Eavan huffed as she jogged up to them both. "Valen."

Valen nodded.

"What's the matter?" Lisbet asked.

"It's your brother, the fool! He's swinging his sword around like he's practicing for the Knights of Duncarrow!"

Lisbet shot Ash a look that placed the clear blame on him for this. "Well, Drystan is no warrior. No risk of anyone being confused about that."

Eavan shook her head. "He said he's going to fight for Yseult. That he's going to be part of the assault on Whitechurch, for some great battle he seems to have created in his head!"

"Some great battle," Lisbet whispered before she passed out. Ash caught her before she hit the ground.

"Lisbet!" Eavan cried as Ash eased her down. "What did I say? What's wrong with her?"

Ash sighed, gathering Lisbet into his arms so he could take her back to her hut. "Everyone looks to me for answers, Eavan, but there's more going on here than even I know."

"Will she be all right?" Eavan prodded, right on his heels.

"She'll be fine."

"And Drystan? What do we do about him?"

"Leave Drystan to me."

Drystan mopped at his sister's forehead with a fistful of damp moss. She could wake if she wanted, but she was stubborn. More than anyone he knew. More than his mother. More than himself.

It didn't matter. Awake, asleep. She'd tell him nothing. Since their arrival here, she'd largely avoided him, and the reason was obvious. Lisbet was afraid for him, and she had no comforting lies to offer. It had always been Lisbet looking after him, and not the other way around, as it should have been. She was the one who'd concocted a plan to leave, when he was frozen by inaction. Drystan knew she would've married the king, unhappy or not, but it was fear for *his* life that pushed her over the edge, leaving her with no choice but to flee and find another life where Drystan and Ravenna could love openly.

Drystan would not magically become the man worthy of this devotion. He was exactly who he was, no more or less. Even if he succeeded in his plan, which was becoming more formed with every moment, he would still only be himself.

He missed his sister. What he wouldn't give for even one more late night by the hearth, baring their hearts in safety and love.

Valen paced outside the tent. He wanted to talk, he said, but he could wait. Drystan needed to be here, with his little sister, coming to terms with what he must do in the days ahead so that he could make this world safe for her once more.

20

THIS TIME IS DIFFERENT

Lysanor kicked sand over the remnants of the fire as the last slice of sun disappeared behind the mountains. Though it was unlikely anyone would spot the flame, way out here, they could never be too careful. They hadn't survived this long by easing their measures.

Isdemus slept most days and was awake most nights. Something was brewing in him. It was always like this, when he was nearing something important. She had a feeling he might share it with her tonight and, though exhaustion had crept in and settled upon her, she'd stay awake as long as she needed to hear his words.

A pink and purple haze painted the sky. Lysanor had always loved this transition to evening, this brief flash of dusk that lingered only long enough for you to wonder at its beauty. Her eyes threatened to flutter shut as she leaned back, watching the colors dim with the rest of the world, preparing for night.

Isdemus twitched in his sleep. He cried out, a low keening moan. Lysanor walked to him and pulled his blanket tighter over him, as she had when they were children. It was all she remembered of a childhood that was long enough in the past to have been many lifetimes for a man. The years behind her reminded her of all she was, but her fading memory was a cooling, staying hand, there to show her she was not infallible, either.

Dusk faded to night. Lysanor sighed and laid her head back on the bedroll. If she closed her eyes, she could sleep, but she had a feeling about tonight, and Isdemus. So she instead gazed up at the sparkles dotting the sky. In the White Kingdom, they called them Guardians. The Rhiagains had seized upon that as a font of their power, appropriating something that was pure and turning it to a basis of control. The Rhiagains. She didn't loathe them, as the others did, but neither could she respect them. Their behaviors in a foreign land over the last few centuries did nothing to earn more esteem in her eyes; if nothing else, it solidified her understanding of them, and what she would soon have to do.

Isdemus cried out once more. She reached over to lay a hand at his brow when he shot forward. He was so utterly still it caused her own breath to catch. He was no longer crying, no longer in distress. He was as calm as the lake beyond the ridge.

"Lysanor, you've been so patient with me."

"Brother." Lysanor sighed into her smile. "Patience is all that separates us from beasts and man."

"I hope to reward it now." He rotated his head only. He was looking at her now. His eyes glowed. "It is time. They are awakening."

Lysanor's heart skipped, but only briefly. Time was a curious construct to one who was immortal, but that didn't mean the years had not been long. It hadn't kept her mind from creeping toward doubt; doubt that they'd not done enough to counter what had been laid by the others. Never doubt in Isdemus, though, secretly, she'd wondered if he'd ever have this vision. "Would you like to break your fast first, or should I begin?"

Isdemus patted his robe. "I've enough for the journey."

Lysanor nodded. She pulled herself up with the help of a nearby branch. She indulged herself in one last glimpse of the barren valley they'd called home for too long. They could have moved elsewhere, but it was always here they would have to return, and it would've borne too much risk to venture too far, and not be ready when they were called. The stream beyond the foothill had provided their water, and the scattered trees and bushes bearing edible flora, their nourishment. They were beyond the point in their lives where they longed for large banquets, or filled bellies. Food was a means to sustain them. Their fulfillment would come in another form.

Lysanor closed her eyes. She didn't have to. The magic required nothing of her, not anymore. But there was a reverence in this, a blind trust as she surrendered herself to something that was within her, but was also bigger than her, bigger than them all.

She felt the warmth of the veil opening even before she'd opened her eyes to confirm it. Isdemus gathered the last of their meager belongings as she finished her work.

"Will they sense it? When we return?" Isdemus asked. He'd asked her this the last few times, though she wasn't surprised he'd forgotten. His mind was often split into two halves.

Lysanor nodded. "They may. Before, when we passed through, we never lingered long enough to find out. This time is different."

"This time is different," Isdemus agreed.

Lysanor stretched her hand out to the brother who had entered the world only moments behind her. "Shall we?"

Isdemus looked back only once before taking her hand and, together, they stepped through the veil.

An Awakening Across the Kingdom

21

BIGGER THAN FAITH, BIGGER THAN MAGIC

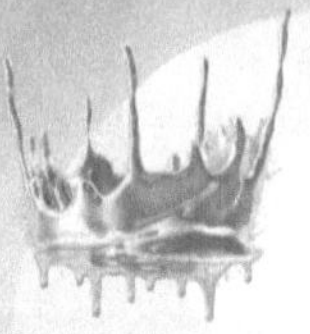

Wyat waited for the Head Magus to speak first.

He hadn't expected a celebration upon their arrival, but was surprised when they ushered him not up into the grand spired tower of the Sepulchre, but into a small sitting room, that smelled as if it belonged to the stable hand. He tried to tell himself this wasn't a sign of disrespect, or a manifestation of the longtime enmity between the Reliquary and the Sepulchre. He didn't really understand it, anyway. There was a place for both magic and theology in the kingdom, and to exist in harmony would benefit the people more than the distrust and campaigns to malign the reputations of one another.

Wyat had some magic in him. It was a secret he'd kept almost all his life, even from his mother and father. When he was old enough to enter into service in the Reliquary, at thirteen, he did so with eagerness, choosing this over the Sepulchre not because he was in denial but because he hoped, through the Guardians, he might understand himself better. If the Guardians were the source of all, of good and bad, of night and dark, then they must also be the architects of magic. This was also why he'd chosen the scholar's path.

But he was no closer to understanding magic at all. The Rhiagains had tried to bottle the mystique of the Guardians, creating a church and a clergy to organize it, but that was antithetical to who the Guardians were, and what role they played. Most serving the Reliquary knew this, too, even if they feared saying so.

Still, there was something about being in the place where magic was celebrated and studied that made Wyat's heart race in a new, exciting way. Even if he was only allowed in a room at the base that reeked of hay and shit.

"I have read in your mind that you are prepared to give me a story that is not your own, Scholar Edevane," Head Magus Tymagen said. He twisted in the hard chair; it was clearly not what he was used to in his tower office. "I implore you to remember where you are before you do so."

Wyat dropped his eyes. Shame bloomed in his cheeks. "I require asylum, but what I ask is no simple matter, Head Magus."

"No indeed. My seers know you travel with a woman and child. She is not your sister, for your notation in *The Book* indicates you are an only child, nor can a scholar take a bride. Mistress, then?"

Wyat didn't answer.

"Scholar Edevane, you would not be seeking asylum if you or your traveling companions were not in some danger. You're a man of the clergy. You have nothing to fear, not even from us. So it must be the woman or child who this is for."

"Both." His voice cracked. He cleared his throat. "It is for both of them."

"Then you will tell me who they are."

"My apologies, Head Magus, but I cannot."

The Head Magus stood. "Then I cannot help you."

"Please." Wyat jumped to his feet as well. "I beg of you. I have nowhere else I can take them."

"Nowhere else? In all the kingdom?"

Wyat shook his head. "If I told you, it would place them in even deeper danger. This is bigger than you, or me, or the institutions we serve."

"Do you know the oath I've sworn?" Head Magus Tymagen waited for Wyat to nod before continuing. "As part of my oath as Head Magus, I am obligated to protect not only the bodies but also the secrets of any seeking sanctuary within the Sepulchre. Whatever you tell me, I cannot tell another."

"It isn't my secret to tell."

"Should we bring them in, so they can tell me themselves?"

"No," Wyat said quickly. "They need their rest. They've been through enough."

"The terms of my offer to extend asylum are what I've said they are." Head Magus Tymagen tried to smile. "Whatever it is they've done, it cannot truly be that bad, can it?"

"It's not what they've done, Head Magus. It's who they are."

The Head Magus laid a hand upon Wyat's shoulder. "When we accept an asylum seeker, it must be done with a heart laid bare of secrets. Not because we are fishwives looking for gossip, but because we need to be fully aware of what threats may land upon our doorstep, should it come to that. You can trust that we will defend them if they become our protected guests."

Wyat closed his eyes and sighed. There was no other way. No other escape. The Sepulchre was the only place in the kingdom where the king's jurisdiction didn't extend, save the Hinterlands, and they would not be welcomed there. "The woman I travel with is Anabella Weatherford Rhiagain, and her son is Stefan Rhiagain. Prince Darrick's wife and son."

Head Magus Tymagen took a step back. "Darrick Rhiagain was never married, Scholar Edevane."

"I married them myself, under a cherry tree in the Wintergarden of Wulfsgate. Not long before he was murdered."

"I don't understand. If Prince Darrick was married, then why was no one told? Where have the wife and child been all these years?"

"They were prisoners of Eoghan Rhiagain," Wyat answered. "And will be prisoners again if he discovers where they've gone." He pointed toward the other room, where Anabella and Stefan rested. "In there is the true heir to this kingdom, Head Magus. Stefan Rhiagain is our rightful king."

"Some of my seers believe Darrick himself is not dead," Head Magus Tymagen said.

Wyat said nothing.

"So it is true, then. What they've seen. And if my seers have seen it, the Rhiagain sorcerers have." He nodded toward the door. "As they will eventually see who you've brought to our doorstep."

"There are fewer Magi among the Rhiagain than there are here," Wyat countered. "There are only four sorcerers, but there are thousands of you."

"Do you know there are Rhiagains in the Sepulchre?"

Wyat gaped at him. "What? Here? Why?"

"They fall under the same laws as others in the kingdom, where magic is concerned, though you can imagine not all hold themselves to that, and most practice it outside the law with no consequence. Some have come here, though. Spies, as you can imagine."

"Why allow it?"

"Refuse and draw their ire? Their eye upon us? Scholar Edevane, without offense, we don't want to become like the Reliquary, beholden to the crown. We are independent of everyone and everything, and we serve all, not a king alone. Anyway, it is better for us that we know who and what they are, then it is for them to find more subversive ways to spy on us."

"The enemy you know," Wyat mused. "Do they possess magic? Or is that part of their ruse to draw eyes upon you?"

"Rhiagains have married into this kingdom for many years. Women and men of no consequence, they say, but even simple farmers can possess magic within them. For all their mystique, I'm not aware of the Rhiagain blood itself having even a drop of magic."

"I see."

"I told you your secret would be safe, and it will be. What I know will die with me when at last my promise is spent. But what you have brought to us puts me in a situation I've never faced before. I let you stay, and I bring the eye of the Rhiagains upon us when either their Adherents within or their sorcerers on the outside learn who lives within our walls. Or I tell you that you cannot, and I violate our most inviolate law."

"I understand the difficulty I've brought upon you," Wyat replied. "But some things are bigger than our faith, or our magic. Some things are bigger than us all."

"Yes," Head Magus Tymagen said. "You can stay for now. We'll move you into the tower, to keep the mother and child safe. But in return, you must plan your next move, Scholar Edevane. There is no longevity in hiding them here forever, not for our sake or theirs. If you didn't have a plan before your arrival, it's time to make one."

ANABELLA DIDN'T NEED to hear the words said on the other side of the door to understand what was happening. Wyat was desperate. The Head Magus was scared. She blamed neither of them for feeling either thing.

She was scared and desperate, too.

Before, she'd struggled to even imagine what life would be like beyond the sky dungeon. She hadn't dared even think it, for she knew hope would kill her faster than thirst, quicker than starvation. All these weeks since the escape, she'd failed to land on how she felt to be free, because she wasn't really free, and neither was Stefan. She was accepting they might never be.

"Mama?"

Anabella had been mindlessly brushing his hair off his face when Stefan spoke up. She paused her ministrations. "Yes, darling?"

"When are we going home?"

"You mean the cave?"

"I miss my sticks. And I want to see the ships again."

Anabella's heart dropped. She'd never considered that he might long for the only home he'd ever known; that he might, even, have been happy. "We can't go back there, darling. It's not safe for us."

"Why? Did the tower fall down?"

"It's hard to explain, Stefan. When you're older, you'll understand."

Stefan frowned. His bleary eyes regarded her with confused innocence. "I don't like it here. I want to go home."

Anabella leaned in, pressing her lips to his forehead. "These are good people. Honest people. They'll take care of us. And when the time is right, we'll go home, darling. I promise."

"You said we can't go back."

"Not there," Anabella said. An idea came to her, suddenly. The Sepulchre sat at the eastern coast of the White Sea. Perhaps there were ships there. She would ask Wyat. It would be all right. Stefan would learn to love real toys, and not the makeshift ones he'd created in their cell. He'd appreciate the fresh air, and what it was like to run more than a few meters. He'd, perhaps, even find friends.

"Where, Mama?"

But though she'd soothe him, love him, ease him through this, she would not lie to him. "I don't know, darling. I wish I did, but I don't."

. . .

JESSE DREW another hard swallow of the ale. He usually preferred something weaker, but he'd asked Kaslan for the worst of what he had, the kind of swill that would make a man's teeth fall out, he drank enough of it. Kaslan had smiled his knowing smile, all but winking as he passed the tankard. But this had nothing to do with what had happened with Ravenna. Nothing at all, though she might be the one person he could talk to about it; the only one who might understand if he tried to put word to experience. Joran might, too, but Jesse didn't trust the old fool.

For all he knew, one or both of them was behind it.

The strangeness, as he'd come to calling it, just over a week ago, when he'd abruptly awakened in the middle of the night and was pulled straightaway into the sensation that something significant had changed. Within him. Beyond him. There was nothing precise about the feeling, nothing that would help him understand it. He'd tried to go back to sleep, but the tingling in his fingers and toes made relaxation a faraway dream. He finally passed out from exhaustion just as the sun was rising.

On the second tick of the sun, he had no choice but to wake and face the day. In his fatigue, he tripped coming down the stairs, but instead of falling outright, he'd *floated* down, landing neatly on his feet at the bottom. He'd looked around to see if anyone else was there and had seen it, but he was alone. *This is why men need sleep,* he'd thought, assuring himself none of it had happened, and tried to put it behind him.

The day after, he'd ridden into town and come upon a stray ass reared and ready to drop down on little Brook, who'd been sent to pick berries. Brook was splayed against the road, his pail off in a ditch, as he gaped up in horror. Jesse, heart racing in his chest, was too far away to intervene. He screamed at Brook to move, but Brook was frozen in his fear, yet before the moment could switch to a new one, one where Brook was gravely injured, a pause fell over it all. The ass' legs hovered in midair, suspended in time. Brook gaped, blinking, at the sudden halt in his fate. And Jesse... Jesse knew he'd caused it somehow. That it had something to do with the night before, just as his incident on the stairs did.

"Go!" Jesse yelled, and this time Brook rolled away. Once he was free of the danger, the ass' hooves dropped to the ground. The beast looked only slightly dazed as it ambled off into the field, its quarrel with the boy forgotten.

And though he was now on his third mug of ale, it wasn't Kaslan who'd refilled it. No one had. It had refilled itself.

Jesse decided the most plausible explanation was that he'd lost his mind.

Kaslan dropped into the chair across from him, breathless. "A scout just returned. We're expecting more visitors within the hour."

"Good. If your father intends to lead a war, you'll need more men," Jesse muttered. He'd not spoken to Easlan since their disagreement. Both men averted their eyes when they passed at the Mule.

Kaslan leaned in. "Jesse. It's Lord Warwick we're expecting."

Jesse jerked his head up. "What? What did you say?"

"With two of his top men. Rutland and Law. You know 'em?"

"Of course I know them," Jesse said, but he could hardly look at Kaslan now. The spots forming behind his eyes burned hot, and the tingling in his fingers and toes was back.

"Another man, too, though they didn't give a name. Not a steward, anyway."

"What are they doing, coming here?"

"Come to help, scout says. It's all I know. But, Jesse..."

Jesse nodded. "I know." He pushed away from the table. "I have to get back to the keep. Esmerelda isnae safe. I donnae know where to take her from here. I hadn't given it enough thought. I never expected..."

Kaslan whistled through his teeth. "Well, we could put Warwick and his men up in the abbey. It's smaller than the keep, but nicer. Father uses it for hunts, for when his mates come down. I know what you're thinking, our forests aren't the Whitewood, but we've beasts none else have."

"I wasn't thinking anything."

"You're thinking of leaving."

"What choice do I have?"

"She's still safe at Dungarde Keep. No one has business there but you."

"How? Even if you put them up at the abbey, as you say, there's nothing keeping him from venturing up to the keep, is there? At least the other men here have never seen Esmerelda in the flesh before. But a man will know his own daughter, Kaslan."

Kaslan's head moved to the side, to look past Jesse. He started to slowly stand. "I hope you weren't planning to keep yourself hidden as well, for they're here."

Jesse turned right as the door opened. Khallum, Law, and Rutland walked in with a fourth man, flanked by some Westerland men that he recognized but didn't know their names. The Southerland men wore the damp humors of those who'd been on the road a spell, both in appearance and stench, though Khallum looked ready to start a war himself from the fire in his eyes.

"At least your father isn't among them," Kaslan whispered and then went to join Easlan in welcoming them.

Jesse watched in a daze as Khallum and Easlan exchanged embraces, as the men, nervous, laughing, unsure, measured each other's intentions. He couldn't believe Lord Warwick was here. The one place in all the kingdom where Jesse had thought he could tuck Esmerelda safely away was the one place he chose to come to. He didn't believe in fate, but this might just change his mind.

"Is that Jesse Strong?" Khallum's booming voice carried across the half-full tavern.

So much for slipping away. Jesse drained the tankard, and, wiping his arm across his mouth, went to meet him.

"Aye, it is!" Khallum was grinning, but the suspicion in his eyes was as clear as the skies outside. He watched Jesse carefully as he draped an arm over him in a haphazard embrace. "This wasnae a surprise I expected at the end of our journey."

"Indeed," Law chimed in. "And I'll ken Hamish doesn't know his son is here, either, or he would've mentioned of it."

Jesse looked back and forth between his lord and his lord's top men. He should say something, but what?

Easlan broke the uneasy tension. "Lord Warwick, if you please, Kaslan and I will get Law and Rutland settled in while you catch up with young Strong."

Khallum nodded. He seemed to barely hear him. "Aye. We've some catching up to do." The seconds ticked into immeasurably long moments as Khallum, eyes fixed on Jesse's, waited for the men to leave them.

"Want some ale?" Jesse asked. One of his hands started to tremble. He shoved it into his vest.

"Aye. None of the shite James serves to travelers, either."

Jesse smiled through his nerves. He turned, eager to be free of Khallum's intense gaze even for a moment. He recovered his breaths as he slipped behind the bar and poured two fresh tankards. Khallum accepted both and moved to a nearby table.

Khallum had emptied his before Jesse could sit down. He shoved it aside with a belch. "I ken you're a long way from Rush-wood, where ye told yer father you'd be."

Jesse nodded. He didn't dare touch his own ale. He was afraid it might refill itself again, and that would be one more thing he'd struggle to explain to the lord of his land.

"Nor is Greystone Abbey a waypoint on the return to Sandycove, unless you've made an enemy of the Guardians, or have never acquainted yourself with a map."

"No, Lord Warwick," Jesse said.

"But a Strong man? He knows his maps, I ken. He knows them better than any."

Jesse sighed and looked down. He had always appreciated a simple life, and a lie was the perfect disruption to that. It would complicate everything. But he had no choice. The last few months of his life had been one long fabrication, and he'd never shake it off, no matter where the days ahead took him. "It wasnae my intention to mislead my father, Lord Warwick. I knew he wouldn't understand why I came to the aid of the Westerlands."

Khallum leaned back in his chair. He crossed his arms. "Nay, nor can I. What care have you of the fate of the Western Reach?"

"It isnae so much that as my care for the men within," Jesse said carefully. "Easlan and Kaslan James are friends of my father, as they are yours. And they were the only men beyond the Souther-lands who offered to send aid when you called for it."

"Aye, and a lot of good that was, all five of 'em," Khallum muttered, but some of his suspicion had faded away. "You're wrong about your father, I ken. He'd understand. I've never met a man more loyal than Hamish Strong. Loyal to a fault."

Jesse raised his tankard to that, but put it back on the table, untouched.

"What scrapes me, Jesse, is why you'd leave when ye did, knowin' what ye did. About your brother, and what he was after."

"I expected I'd be back before he was out." Jesse held his breath. A heavy realization fell over him. Khallum might have news of Ryan, and with these words, he'd all but asked for it.

"You expected wrong." A dark look passed over Khallum's face. "I'm not prepared with the right words, seeing as I didnae expect to see ye here. But your brother, Ryan, he *is* out, lad. He carried out his task with near perfection. And the man he went in for? Free. Alive. We have him somewhere safe, for when the time comes."

Jesse noted Khallum didn't call Darrick by name. A handful of men knew of Darrick Rhiagain's fate before Ryan was sent to the Wastelands. He wondered how many knew it now.

Whatever the number, they could add Esmerelda to the list. He'd had no choice but to tell her when she'd come to him with her intention to return home. It had worked in staying her energy for the idea, but she'd kept to herself since, hardly saying a word to anyone. If he hadn't been consumed with his own troubles, namely the strangeness, he would've tried harder.

"I knew he would do it," Jesse said, finding his words. But there was a reason Khallum hadn't said anything about Ryan's own health. He couldn't delay and live in this moment of intentional ignorance, either. "And Ryan?"

Khallum hung his head. "He's alive, but he's nay gained consciousness. Hamish is with him, at his side. There he'll stay, until Ryan wakes or I call for him to deploy my men for war."

Jesse had no choice but to take a hard swig from the ale or risk launching the bile in his throat across the table. "What do the physicians say? Do ye have healers with him?"

"We cannae risk a healer, but he has Rutland's wife tending him. One of her nurses, anyway."

"Rutland's wife is hardly a nursewife!"

"Rutland's wife is the only one not already leaving him to a promise spent, young Strong."

Jesse grimaced. He swallowed his anger, though he preferred it to the pain tickling at the center of his belly, threatening to spread. "And what does Rutland's wife say, then?" he asked through clenched teeth.

"Tha' there's naught much she can do, other than keeping broth in him and his sheets clean."

Jesse laughed to fend off tears. "But she doesnae know Ryan.

Not a force exists that can keep him down forever. All she has to do is tell him to sleep, and he'll wake, just for the chance to be contrary."

Khallum nodded. He didn't look convinced. "Let us hope so. Ryan has done a great service to this kingdom. He deserves to live to see it through."

Jesse realized then that he'd never prepared himself for this possibility. In his mind, there was no outcome that didn't have Ryan emerging victorious, sporting the self-sure grin that had gotten him in more than enough trouble, and the confidence of a man twice his rank. He found he couldn't even conjure the image of his brother convalescing in bed, riding the line between life and death.

"There isnae a day that passes where I donnae miss my Esmerelda," Khallum continued with a hard sigh. "But this? This woulda broken her heart. I denied her in life, perhaps the Guardians will grant her wish in death."

"No. One day, but not now," Jesse said, shaking his head. "As you said, Ryan deserves to live to see what he's done for all of us. And he will. I know him."

Khallum shoved his chair back and stood. "It isnae for me to say, and I willnae order you to do it. But one man in the Westerlands can do little. One man at yer father's side may do everything. Especially if I call him to service for this kingdom." He turned behind him. "Now, where did James take them?"

Jesse felt as if he had the entire kingdom on his shoulders as he stood. "They're at the abbey. I'll escort you."

Jesse looked more disheveled than usual when he walked through the door. Ravenna was surprised to see him at mid-morning. Usually he left at sunrise and returned just as the last of the day's light slipped behind the forest, in time to reheat dinner over the dying fire. Sometimes he conversed with them. Often, he preferred to be alone with his thoughts and the silence.

His eyes widened in relief when he saw her. That alone perked her suspicion.

"Ravenna, thank the Guardians it's you," he said, looking around the room, searching for something. "Where's Esme?"

"Resting. She was up half the night at the privy." She pointed at her belly.

He stopped. "Is she all right?"

"I understand women expect this, when they're with child," Ravenna replied. Her words were a recitation of things she'd heard from her mother and grandmother. She hadn't experienced this, and would not now anytime soon. Her belly was shrinking. She'd read all the signs wrong. There was no child growing within her. It may have been as simple as the change in her diet since fleeing The Rookery. She might never know, but she'd been wrong. Horribly, painfully wrong.

But the damage she'd wrought upon matters at the keep was done and could not be undone.

Jesse nodded with an absent look. "Better that she's resting if she's unwell. This might make her worse."

"What might?" Ravenna moved closer, careful to keep the distance between them. Each second she spent in his presence only deepened her regret at what had happened in the river. He hadn't come to her bed later that night, or the next, either. He wasn't in love with her. He wanted her, but that wasn't the same. Jesse wasn't a typical man, following his lusts. He followed his loyalty. Something she had shown herself to be absent of at every step of her journey. "What happened?"

He stopped pacing and looked at her. "The last thing I ever expected. Khallum Warwick is here. He's come to the aid of the Westerlands. *Here,* in Greystone Abbey."

Ravenna's mouth parted. "Esmerelda's *father?* Is here?"

"The very one." His mouth drew into a loose frown. "And she *cannae* know this, you understand? The distress might cost her the bairn's life." He moved around the room again, this time collecting things, piling them in his arms. Esmerelda's scarf. Her house shoes.

"You possess a lot of fear over that baby's life."

"It might be all that's left of my brother."

"It's more than that."

"My mother... she lost a few that way. I know what stress can do to a bairn."

"I think you may underestimate Esmerelda. She has a right to know."

"Maybe you're right. But what if you're wrong?"

"What, then? You cannot hide this from her, or him, forever."

"Aye, but I can for now, just as I'll not tell her that Ryan is finally free of that wretched prison camp, but isn't expected to wake."

Ravenna gasped. "Jesse! I'm so sorry."

"I cannae think on it now. It's more important than ever that his son and wife are protected."

"Are we leaving?"

"Not yet, but soon," Jesse said. "Soon as I know where the feck to take her."

"I wish I had a helpful idea, but I don't know this kingdom at all."

"I donnae need your ideas, but..." He regarded her with fresh curiosity. "Tell me about your magic."

"My magic?"

Jesse nodded in impatience. "Aye, aye, what can you, ye know, *do*?"

"I can heal those who are unwell or have come to harm," Ravenna replied with a sigh. "I can lay minor protections. Obfuscations, meant to confuse those who would intend us harm." Sometimes this was her only consolation to all she'd done. She knew that without the magic she'd lain to keep the men of Wulfsgate off their trail, Drystan and the others would never have made it to their destination. They would've never made it farther than Torrin's Pass.

Yes, but they were led the rest of the way as prisoners. And you did nothing.

"Ravenna?"

"Sorry?"

Jesse pointed his finger, moving it in a circle around him. "We need one. Here. At Dungarde Keep. To keep Khallum and his men from wandering in."

"I can do that, but... you know, she sometimes ventures into town. She can't help herself. It's hard being here, alone, all the time."

"Your job is to stop her."

"She's more stubborn than I am!"

Jesse rolled his hands. "Use your magic, or something."

"I don't have the magic to do that." Ravenna sighed. "Maybe she *should* know. I know how you worry about her, but she's not fragile. She's not even a little fragile. She's stronger than I am."

"Esmerelda is my responsibility. Bringing her here... she's changed. Strong she may be, but she's waning, and I donnae know how to stop it."

Ravenna bowed her head. "I'm afraid at least some of that is my fault."

Jesse shook his head. "I donnae know what you're talking about."

"I owe you a great apology, Jesse."

He glanced toward the stairs. "For?"

"I didn't send the dreams intentionally," Ravenna said. The confession was coming now, and it felt good. It felt right. He deserved to know the truth, which was perhaps its own form of loyalty. It was his truth, as much as hers. "But I may have, inadvertently. I may have, in my desperation."

"You're not making any sense."

Ravenna laid a hand on her belly. "When I came here, I thought I was with child. Drystan's child. And, though he's run off, Drystan is still the heir of Wulfsgate, of the whole of the Northerlands. Any child of his would belong to them, not to me. They would hunt me from coast to coast, north to south. His mother, especially, would not rest until the babe was with his father's brood. I would have no means to fight them, an outcast of my own people, no allies of my own to protect me."

"But how... how would they have known? Drystan himself didnae know, did he?"

"There are magic practicers among the Derehams. Seers. I needed there to be a cause for doubt about the father."

Jesse at last comprehended. A dark understanding passed over his eyes. "*Me?*"

Ravenna nodded. She still couldn't meet his eyes. If she did before the words were out, she'd lose the courage. "But, now I know, there is no child. I was wrong about that. As I was wrong to confuse you so. To cause harm to the closeness between you and Esmerelda. To deceive someone who's done nothing but help me."

Jesse fell back in the chair behind him. He stared blankly for several moments and then pitched forward over his knees, dropping his face into his hands.

"Please speak. Say something," Ravenna pleaded. "Anything. Even your anger I would welcome."

He peeled his hands away and looked up halfway. "I couldnae fathom why my own will was so weak. But it was never me. It was never me at all. It was you, all this time, and though I asked you, you denied it. Do ye know how many nights, how many *long* nights I questioned my own measure?"

Ravenna slowly nodded.

"Of course, you know. You were there each time I'd awake, spent from dreams I didnae ask for. You were there, at the river, to give to me what I couldnae understand wanting. And for... for *nothing*?"

"It wasn't nothing. I didn't know it was nothing."

"Why not just *tell* me, Ravenna? I would have protected you! I would have lied, as I've done for Esme, as I now do every day of my life, to keep that from happening to you! Can ye not see my entire life is a lie now? What's one more?"

"I couldn't have known how you would react."

Jesse laughed. "What must the men of Midnight Crest be like, for you to look upon someone who's given you aid and see an enemy?"

The tears flowed. She couldn't stop them. "The men of Midnight Crest are no men. Drystan was the first man who showed me the meaning of kindness." She wiped at her eyes, straightening. No, this would not do. She was apologizing, not seeking to wind him even further around her finger. Perhaps she couldn't undo the damage done, but she could prevent more from happening. "I was wrong. About you. About many things. I would say I was wrong to leave Midnight Crest, but that would be to create yet another lie. I didn't belong there, and I don't belong here. My fear is that I'll never know where I *do* belong. That I'll never know why I couldn't do as the women before me did and rise to the honor given me. To know my role. But that isn't your problem, Jesse Strong. It's mine, and I was desperately wrong for seeking to make it yours as well."

Jesse pushed himself to his feet. He moved to her, raising his hands. They hovered at the sides of her arms, debating whether to land. At last they did, and for a moment, he looked as if he might kiss her. Not the hard press of passion by the river that had stolen her breath and her resolve, but something softer. He dropped her arms and stepped back. "When I laid eyes upon you in the Hinterlands, I was in love with ye then, Ravenna. Guardians help me, I couldnae explain it, not for the life of me, but I was. And I fought against it with all I had, until…" He looked again toward the stairs. "But I can never know what was me, and what was you. And as I think about it, now, perhaps that's best. For if I thought I could love you without the sway of magic, I wouldnae be able to do what I need to do, for her. For Ryan."

Jesse reached for the pile of Esmerelda's belongings and handed them to Ravenna. A palpable relief had replaced the darkness. He seemed now a man unburdened, of her, of all that had passed between them, and if that was the price of honesty, then she must bear it. She couldn't tell him she'd done nothing in the Hinterlands. That whatever he felt had been his own. She wouldn't tell him this, for in releasing him from his obligation to his feelings, she was freeing him in other ways, too.

"I accept your apology," Jesse said. "And in return, I ask you to aid me in protecting her. Just long enough for me to get her away from her father, once more."

LADIES OF THE MOUNTAIN

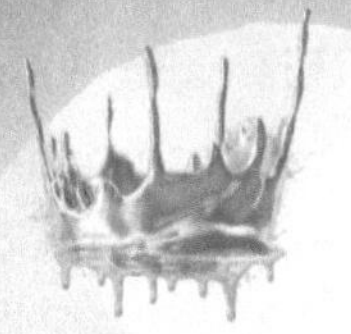

Asherley's gown was crafted of pure alabaster silk. Even to someone who had never denied herself anything, this was an indulgence. The winter fruits left in her bowl while she was sleeping were another, as were the rich stews of tubers and squash prepared and slid into her room. There was no meat. Their abhorrence to it was another piece of information she had stored somewhere, for when it might matter. As it happened eventually with most of these things, the time of mattering had arrived, though she wasn't sure her diet was as important as the reason she'd been brought here.

She couldn't say whether Midnight Crest was as she expected, because she'd not been allowed outside the small but well-appointed room. There was no lock, at least not of the physical kind, but the magic was stronger than anything man could build with their hands. That she slept full nights was another kind of magic, and though this loss of control was maddening, the restfulness was grudgingly welcome. She couldn't remember a time in her life where she'd ever slept so well.

After the first day or so of screaming and banging on walls, on the ivory door, she'd adjusted to the idea of being their prisoner and decided that the loss of her peace would not join the loss of her freedom. She had no magic more powerful than theirs with which to best them and free herself, so waiting was all she could do. The absence of anyone passing anywhere near her proximity thwarted her attempts to read whispers. If there'd been a block, the kind thrown up by magic wielders in the presence of other magic wielders, she could've sensed it, but there was simply nothing. She was well and truly alone.

Asherley maintained this calm, knowing that if they desired her dead, she would've been thrown from the mountain like Assyria. They either wanted her, or needed her, and she could use that.

She wondered if Anabella and the others had made it somewhere safe. She desperately hoped so. Had it been her plan, and not Assyria's, she would've given the power to Anabella to begin with. Why should it not be Anabella with the choice to decide the fate of her son and herself? But Assyria wasn't a mother. She couldn't know what it meant to sacrifice everything for your child. To give up even your freedom so that they could find their own.

Thinking of her children was the only thing that threatened Asherley's resolve. Emberley was in Wulfsgate, and for that she was grateful. But she'd had no word of Brandyn or Gabi. She still felt them, as if even way up here at the top of Icebolt Mountain, their energies carried, but this was only an ephemeral confirmation of their survival. For all she knew, they could be in a prison of their own.

The door opened. Through it walked a man. The same man who had stood before her on the mountainside and who was responsible for what happened to Assyria.

She spoke before he could. "You murdered Assyria Rhiagain."

The man's mouth curled into a bemused grin. "I did *not*."

"I saw you."

"I did not murder Assyria Rhiagain, for I cannot murder Assyria Rhiagain."

"It was your raven form that swarmed her and caused her to fall. I saw no others. Only you."

"Ahh. Well, yes, it *was* I who swarmed her, as you say, but I didn't cause her to fall. She fell because she lost her footing."

"Your commitment to semantics is noted, but murder is murder."

"Yet the distinction is important. I cannot kill a Rhiagain, just as a Rhiagain cannot kill me. Whether my actions influenced what choices she next made, well." The man held out his hands. "Sometimes fortune *does* smile upon us."

"Why?" Asherley asked. She moved closer to him, but he didn't recoil from her nearness. He tilted his head to the side, studying her. "Why would you want her dead?"

"I had no great motivation to see Assyria Rhiagain dead. But it seems to me she wanted *you* dead, and so I was left with no other choice, really."

Asherley narrowed her eyes. "Who are you?"

The man bowed. His dark robe swept the white marble floor. "High Priest Argentyn Ravenwood. We share a common ancestor, as you know."

"Argentyn." Asherley let the name sink in, musing over it. She knew next to nothing about him. It was his wife who mattered in their monastic world. "And why should you care whether I live or die?"

Argentyn wound his hands behind him and regarded her with an unreadable look. "Do you have what you need? Are you comfortable? Does the food agree with your constitution?"

"Why won't you answer me?"

"You'll be safer here, as things go," Argentyn replied, looking around. "Now that events are in motion."

"What in all the Guardians are you talking about?" She gestured around her. "Safer here? Where I'm a prisoner?"

Argentyn balked. He looked offended. "You're not a prisoner."

She laughed. "Then release me."

"You'll be safer here," he repeated. "How is your magic?"

Asherley was aghast at his deliberate effort to be obtuse. "I'm sorry? My magic?"

"Is it stronger, now that you are more near the source?"

"I'll give it a try if you let me out of this prison cell."

Argentyn's eyes swept the room. "I see no prison cell, Lady Blackwood. Only ardent attempts at hospitality."

"Let me go."

"I can release you in another way."

Asherley launched forward, but in an instant his hand raised, and she was halted, midair.

"Try it with magic next time, and I may allow it," Argentyn said, stifling a yawn. "There is more freedom in knowledge than in movement. Your allies in Wulfsgate have been denying you a powerful truth, one that is not theirs to withhold."

"I already know my daughter is dead," Asherley said through a clenched jaw. "You cannot hurt me further by repeating it."

"My condolences," Argentyn said. "For your Hollyn. But also for Byrne."

Asherley's blood cooled so fast her knees buckled. "Byrne?"

"Murdered, by Lord Quinlanden, in an ambush. As he was preparing to turn in for the evening, I hear," Argentyn said flatly. "Lord Quinlanden is now the Lord of the Westerlands as well, they say, though he hasn't been seen since he procured your husband's head in a box and presented it to the king. The Westerlands, as I understand it, has been thrust into utter chaos."

A thousand tiny lights died behind Asherley's eyes until there was only darkness and the cool welcome of the floor.

• • •

*H*E *FELL THROUGH THE AIR*. *The air took him.*

Ransom Warwick had arrived at Wulfsgate the night before, and before he collapsed, he'd managed nine words. *He fell through the air. The air took him.* As they'd laid him in bed, Gretchen succeeded in also getting a nod out of him when she asked if he meant Pieter, before he fell into a long rest. Once he was out, no one could wake him again. Whatever he'd been through demanded sleep.

They'd speculated themselves into a flurry while he rested. What could he mean about Pieter? Had he fallen? Fallen off the mountain? No, Gretchen decided, it couldn't be that, for she'd know if her little cub was dead, wouldn't she? But where were the others? Asherley and Anabella? The princess? Little Stefan and the scholar?

Holden insisted they stop talking about it until Ransom could answer their questions. The guessing, he said, only ushered them to terrible conclusions, and there must be a rational explanation. Gretchen countered that nothing good could've brought Ransom Warwick, alone and frost-eaten, by foot, to their doorstep other than catastrophe. Christian and Aylen blamed themselves for not pushing harder to travel to the pass more frequently. Alric insisted, in that strange desperation he radiated with when he had a strong feeling about something, that he knew exactly what Ransom meant. That Pieter had fallen through the veil, just as he once had.

In a huff, they'd all gone their separate ways at the keep.

Gretchen was there at Ransom's bedside when he woke. With the same maternal ministrations she'd applied to her own children when they were unwell, she pulled Ransom's truth from him, slowly, and then eased him back to sleep with a light draught. Ransom was old enough to be the lord of the Southerlands, but his experiences had reduced him again to a young boy, in need of a fiction to replace a terrible reality. Gretchen couldn't do that, but she could give him some peace. She could do it for Gwyn.

Gretchen called the others together to share what they learned. She knew immediately how they'd respond, for it was how she had, though she'd now had more time to let it settle over her.

"Ransom has been through a great ordeal, and I would ask that none of you go to his bedside demanding answers he doesn't have. He has told me what he knows, and there'll be no more." Gretchen turned to Aylen. "You asked me earlier about healing him. When we're done here, you can go to him, though most of his physical wounds are superficial. He's had a long journey by foot. None of his hurts will surprise you."

Aylen nodded.

Gretchen settled back against the old wood of the dining table. She didn't dare sit. The flames from the hearth warmed her, but they didn't soothe her. Her feet twitched with nervous energy as she searched for the right words. The ones she needed to hear as much as they did.

"I have some troubling news. Anabella, Wyat, and Stefan slipped off into the night before anyone could stop them. Lady Asherley and Princess Assyria are dead after some kind of fight between them. A fight that seemed, to Ransom, to be about the others leaving. Assyria fell from the mountain, and Asherley was assailed, by a man."

Earwyn gasped. Both hands clapped over her mouth. Gretchen couldn't find the words for her. Not yet.

"A man?" Holden asked. "He's certain he saw a man? Who?"

"He's in an awful state, but he said he and Pieter both saw this man and Asherley exchange words, and then they saw him... this is where Ransom is unclear. But she fell to the snow. This is when the boys ran. They ran for their lives, back up the snowy pass. They searched for a trail, and eventually found one. When they were certain that whoever had harmed Asherley was not behind them, they stopped, and—"

Ember appeared in the doorway. "My mother is not dead."

"Ember," Gretchen said gently. "Darling. I was coming to see you next. Please, let us find the answers, which we are all desperate for. We, too, want to believe she's still out there."

"No, I don't want to believe. I know. My mother *is* alive," Ember said, lacking any of the emotion Gretchen expected from her.

Earwyn stood, but didn't rush to her niece's side. She wore a helpless look as she watched her.

"Emberley. Go on, now," Holden said. "Let us finish and then we will decide what to do about Lady Asherley."

Ember rolled her tongue around the inside edge of her bottom lip. "Do that. I'll already have a plan by the time you're done." She turned and left.

"She's a curious child," Holden muttered.

"She's a bold and brave young woman," Earwyn countered, voice quaking. "One whose mother trusted her with the fate of the entire Westerlands. She is my sister's daughter, through and through. She has a right to be here."

Gretchen nodded. "Ember is no child. Not anymore. But if Asherley is alive, she would've taken the pass and returned to us, as Ransom did." She paused. "I'm sorry, Earwyn. I hope I'm wrong."

Earwyn bowed her head. "Unless she's injured and cannot."

"I can have a search party organized within two ticks, once you release me," Christian said.

"We'll need one. For Asherley. And for Pieter." Gretchen finished telling Ransom's tale, though she'd come to the hardest part. *He fell through the air. The air took him.* "What happened to Pieter is even less clear. Ransom claims they came upon a fruit tree. Christian, he says Pieter recognized it as the one you and Aylen stop at, to remove the horses from the harnesses and carry the goods by foot."

Christian exhaled. "Yes, it's... it's a rather large tree, and it makes for a fair landmark, for it's out of place amongst dense pine and fir. There're no others around it. It stands in a light clearing, and the leaves are so dense that there's hardly any snow beneath it. Pearapples, I think, like the ones that grow in the Wintergarden."

"Christian and I have discussed its strangeness more than once," Aylen said. "If I'm being truthful, it's always made me nervous. It doesn't belong there."

"It's there for the veil," Alric said from the corner, sounding suddenly weary of the topic. He sighed. "A protection of sorts. I could never make sense of it. I always wished I'd met someone who could explain it to me better."

"Alric, darling. They've lost their son. This isn't helpful," Earwyn said. Gretchen felt sad for her, and not only for the news of her sister. The great beauty and cunning of Earwyn Blackwood was wasted on a half-wit like Alric. One of the many tragedies born at the Rhiagains' hands two decades before.

"Or why I've never been able to return," Alric continued, oblivious to his wife's humiliation. "Dozens of times I've been back to that spot, and not once have I been allowed to pass back through."

"This isn't the time for this nonsense," Holden said. His frustration with his brother had been brewing most of their lives, but had hit a crescendo when Holden became lord; for now, Alric was not only his brother, but also his burden. "Pieter is lost in the pass. He's a clever boy and will know to find any cover available to him. He knows how to find and prepare his own food. If we make good time, we can be there before he needs us."

"You would know it isn't nonsense if you'd been there," Alric said, and Earwyn looked as if she might turn to a puddle in her chair. Gretchen couldn't blame her for sending her only son to Oldcastle for an education. "And if you want to save Pieter, you'll stop treating me as if I've been kicked in the head by a horse too many times."

Holden shot Gretchen a knowing look, and she had to stifle an inappropriate laugh. This had once, a lifetime ago, been her prime guess as to the cause of Alric's state of mind. Holden evidently hadn't forgotten her words. And she, in this strange fleeting moment of a shared joke with her husband, remembered how she'd once loved him. How much fun they'd had in the early days.

"Lord Alric, if what you say has happened to Pieter is true, our search party will discover this," Aylen said with a sweet smile. "Now that you've made us aware of this possibility."

"It's no mere possibility, Lady Aylen. There is no cliff to fall from anywhere near that tree. No hole to sink into. There is only one place a man can disappear if he's standing at the pearapple tree at the final bend in Torrin's Pass."

Christian stood. "If you feel there's more to discuss, by all means continue, but I'm going to assemble the party so we can leave while there's still light. Mother?"

Gretchen nodded just as her husband said, "Good, Son. Count me amongst the men."

"I will, Father."

"Uncle Alric, I could use your aid," Christian said. The older man puffed in a swell of pride and followed, hobbling behind him.

"Forgive my husband, Gretchen. He's been even worse since Ransom arrived, talking about falling through the air. He's not himself."

"Earwyn, think nothing of it," Gretchen said. "He should be more sensitive to the news you just received. And besides, we spend far too much of our lives making excuses for the men."

"I'm still sitting right here," Holden said.

"Yes, and?" Gretchen replied, but she was smiling. She couldn't explain it, for it was both ill-timed and counter to her more recent feelings about her husband. All she could do was add it to the list of all the inexplicable things that had happened to her in the past few months. "Aylen, you, Earwyn and I will stay behind with the children. That all right?"

"I'll tend to Ransom, in case his needs are greater than we realize."

Earwyn nodded with bleary eyes, unable to speak for the sob rising in her throat. She left the room.

Gretchen turned to Holden. "There will be no joy in this world if you and the men don't return with both the missing."

"If what Ransom said about Asherley is true…"

Gretchen nodded. "Then you must return with enough evidence of the deed to put the matter to bed, for everyone. For if she is dead, then we have the next Lady of the Westerlands under our roof, and we will bear even more responsibility in seeing that Emberley's land is restored to her."

"Emberley? What of the son? Brandyn?"

"He may be her stated heir, but it was Emberley who Asherley chose to lead the children away from danger, and to know what to do once they were clear of it." Gretchen reached forward and grabbed his hand, surprising herself. "Haven't you learned, the hard way, to discern between what a lady says and what a lady means?"

EMBER RAN to the clearing at the center of the Wintergarden. It was here that he often came to her, perched upon the branch of a nearby tree, watching. Always watching. Judging. Whether or not she wanted him to; no matter what she said to get him to leave.

Well, now she had need of him.

"Alasyr!" she cried. "I know you're out there!"

She spun around in circles, scanning every branch as she searched for him. Fresh snow dotted her face. It landed in her eyes, blurring her vision. She ignored it. He was there. He had to be. He was *always* there.

"ALASYR RAVENWOOD!" she screamed so loud her voice cracked. The howl that followed got lost in a fierce wind.

"Ember." Marsh's breath warmed her neck. His arms slid around her from behind. "What are you doing?"

"He can find her! He can cover so much more in flight than the men will on foot, and *faster*."

"All right. But what aren't you saying?"

She tore herself away, stumbling back into the patches of snow. "I shouldn't *need* him to do this for me. I'm a Ravenwood! And I don't believe that my blood is tainted, or less than, simply because I'm also a Warwick. I need a teacher, Marsh. Someone who knows who I am." Again, her eyes performed the search of the branches, darting with quickness to each one. "Someone who knows what's happening to me, and how I can use it to save my mother."

"Not him." Marsh shook his head. He took a step, but something stopped him from coming closer. "He would kill you if he thought he'd get away with it. You know that, don't you?"

"No." Ember's head flew back and forth. Her eyes couldn't stay focused on any one thing, one branch, one possible place he could be, watching. "He doesn't want me dead. He's afraid of me. Of what I mean."

"What you mean?" Marsh sighed. "You're not making sense. Honestly, Ember, you haven't been making sense for a while."

"It's not my job to make you understand."

"I *love* you, Emberley."

She stopped spinning. Her panting escalated as she caught up to the moment. "If you love me, then you love all of me. Even this." She tapped her chest. "This *need*. Something has changed in me since I came here. I *know* you can see it. Maybe you can even feel it. It isn't fair to expect me to bury it, for your comfort."

"For my comfort?" Marsh looked ready to cry and laugh at the same time. "I wake up every day wondering if I'll ever see my home again. My mother and father. Jonah and Lyria. And then I roll over, and I look at you, and I know that home is wherever you are." He took another step. "Emberley, I don't want you to bury who you are. I just don't want to lose you to it."

Ember looked again at the sky. "Then help me find him before that happens."

Christian sent two men to assemble the search party with haste. He issued an order to the kitchens to prepare enough provisions for a fortnight. When he was done, he and Alric went to the stables to ready the horses for the ride.

"Uncle Alric," Christian said, as he stood before Sun. "Tell me more about the veil."

Alric dropped his hands from his pony's saddle. The beast was old and worse for wear, but looked at his master with pure adoration. "Your father has given me enough grief. Now you, too, Christian?"

"I'm asking you because I want to know."

Alric scoffed. "No one wants to know. I made that error years before, when I returned. I thought the kingdom would want my story, but instead I was met with jests and derision."

"People diminish or fear what they don't understand," Christian said. "But I've spent most of my life at the Sepulchre. I've seen things no one here would believe, but that doesn't mean they weren't real."

"Perhaps I did imagine it. I never could find it again," Alric said.

Christian approached his uncle. "All these years, you've held fast to your version of things. That happens only when someone's belief is strong."

Alric dropped his eyes. His uncle looked so old. Christian realized he'd always thought of him as old, despite that he was only halfway through his third decade. He wondered then what his uncle had been like before he'd been through this ordeal that had shaped the whole of his life and renamed it. Had he ever known joy? Pleasure?

"For once, I fear speaking about it. For it isn't enough to know, is it? If that knowledge cannot save Pieter?"

Christian clapped his hands over Alric's shoulders. "You returned. So he must be able to, as well."

"But I don't know how I returned. I don't even know how I was able to step through. I only know... the bear, it had me by the foot, and when I pulled it back, oh what a foolish thing to do, it was as if a great fire had spread through me, but I had no choice but to ignore it and persevere, or die. And then I crawled forward, beyond the pearapple tree, and... disappeared. The bear no longer had hold of me. Where there had been snow, there was now desert. And warmth! Warmth unlike any I'd ever known in the Northerlands. I couldn't stand; my foot was mangled beyond recognition. From where I lay, all I could see was white sand, as far as my vision could stretch. All except a tree. Like the pearapple, it seemed out of place, like it couldn't possibly have grown there under any natural circumstance. It had these low, bowing branches, and on them dangled fruits that looked like oranges, but they were bright green, and twice the size. I tore one of my shirts and used it to wrap what was left of my foot. It was then I passed out from the pain, and when I awoke, nothing had changed. I was still in this strange desert, still lying beneath the tree. I had this pull... this over-whelming sense that if I could stand, if I could make my way farther from this tree, there'd be a whole world for me to explore. A whole world awaiting me, if only I could again find myself able. The ache in my foot had subsided some, but I knew the damage was beyond what could be repaired, even without looking at it. I also knew that if I didn't find my way home, I would lose that foot and with it, perhaps, my life. My son was only a baby, and Earwyn needed me. I kept saying that, aloud so I would mean it. My family, they need me."

"And then?" Christian prodded.

"And then..." Alric closed his eyes, inhaling a breath of icy air. "And then I crawled back the direction I'd come from, and the desert was replaced by the familiar pierce of the icy snow. I turned and could no longer see the white sand or the tree with fruit like oranges. There was nothing at all, except the shock of cold and the smell of my blood, which had settled into the snow nearby. The bear was gone, as was my horse, but the pony who'd traveled with me, carrying my supplies, he'd waited for me." Alric smiled at the old beast. "Imagine he doesn't have too many years left. He deserves a hero's send off, when his time comes."

"You said you returned later and couldn't find where you'd crossed over."

Alric ran his hands down the mule's mangy pelt. "I walked all over that area by the tree. I camped beneath it. I begged the Guardians to show me once more what they'd shown me before, but I could never do it again. And so no one believed me." He pointed at his foot. "But that bear would've killed me dead, spent my promise in the next few seconds, had I not crawled into the desert of another world, Christian. That I know. Maybe the Guardians sensed Pieter would die if he remained where he was and did the same for him. It would all be a guess, with so little I know. How many other men have been lost in the pass, never to be recovered? Is it coincidence? Who could know? But I know what happened to me. And I'm all but certain it happened to your brother."

Christian nodded, letting his thoughts wander as he absorbed all his uncle had said. He'd keep this conversation to himself, for now. It was probably nothing. It might be something.

But if he could keep his mother from losing yet another son, he'd not dismiss the possibility that Alric Dereham had, once upon a time, stepped into another world and returned to tell the tale.

23
HALF-TRUTHS

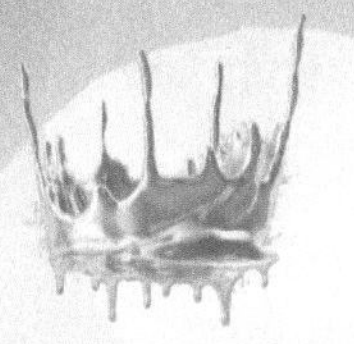

Kian led Lisbet through the forest, taking a path that was now so recognizable that she didn't need an escort, despite that she'd never be allowed without one. She'd come to think of this place as home, in a way. The vivid emeralds and sapphires of the forest, that once reminded her she was far from where she should be, had become familiar and welcome, a relief from her tempestuous emotions. Even these daily jaunts through the trees and undergrowth gave her a sense of routine, something she hadn't realized she'd missed until she had it again.

She was happy Kael hadn't escorted her since the early days. Despite the terrible dressing down she'd witnessed Kian give Eavan when they arrived, she thought of Kian as light and Kael as darkness. It wasn't that simple. She knew that. Nothing was. But where she was intrigued by Kian, she was afraid of Kael, and her mother had taught her to always trust in her senses when it came to others, for they were given these warnings for a reason.

But even Kian hadn't come for her for almost a fortnight. Not since Yseult had pulled something new and strange from Lisbet.

Until today.

They entered the same hut where they'd taken Lisbet after she'd passed out. Yseult wasn't inside, and neither was Kael. Kian gestured for Lisbet to sit. She pulled herself atop the platform they'd laid her on that day. That now, with fresh eyes, resembled an altar more than a table. Kian eased himself into his mother's seat across the small room.

"Where is Yseult?"

"Have you considered what you saw in here?"

"Is she coming?"

"Have there been further visions?"

"I want to talk to your mother."

"She sends me to continue your instruction."

"My instruction." Lisbet frowned. "Where is she? Did something happen?"

A small crack appeared in Kian's resolve, and she could see he would answer her questions if she kept at him. He was not his mother. Not yet. "She is unwell. Tell me about the past few days, Lisbet."

"Unwell? She's sick?" Lisbet's heart sank. Yseult *had* seemed off, but Lisbet assumed this to be weariness born of the current circumstances facing the Medvedev, of knowing she must prepare to lead her people to war to help the Saleen.

Kian stared forward. He looked past her. "You knew better than to ask questions of my mother. Yet you ask them of me."

"She's not here, or I would ask her questions, too. After the last time you brought me here, I deserve answers. What happened to me then? When you brought me here?"

"You are awakening, with the rest of the kingdom, as my mother told you."

"You say this to me, knowing it confuses me, knowing I will not understand."

Kian drew his lips in a tight line. His familiar peeked into the hut and then returned to flight. "My mother's wellness is linked to our people. She has been fading since the sorcerer enslaved the Saleen. Her recovery is tied to the matter's resolution."

"And how will the matter be resolved, Kian? My brother speaks of going to war. Valen says the Medvedev must unite now, despite their differences. Is that your plan? To fight? Is that why you brought us here? To join you?"

"I will take over your instruction," Kian said again. His voice dropped an octave, an attempt at authority. "And the only questions now will be mine. Have you experienced further visions?"

Lisbet watched him closely. He was very serious, but there was a kindness beneath the surface that he couldn't completely shield. She wondered how much he'd changed since Eavan had loved him, years before, whether he was the same Kian or someone new. He was the eldest, so it seemed reasonable he was trained to be his mother's replacement one day, something further supported by him being here now with her, but she didn't know how long they lived, and how they passed the mantle of power down through their people. And if Yseult truly was sick, did that mean she was dying? "No," she said. "I have not." She folded her hands over her lap, wringing them until her fingers were a pale white. "The truth is, I'm afraid to be alone when it happens."

"Why are you afraid?"

"Of course you wouldn't understand. You've had these gifts all your life."

"You think we do not have to work for our gifts?"

"I think you don't keep your truths from each other."

Kian stretched his arm out. His familiar soared into the hut, landing in the middle of his forearm. "You want truth. We are all linked. To our familiars. To one another. You want to know about Mother being unwell. She has severed one of these links so that we do not experience her pain, our pain, the pain of the Saleen. This is the truth of our gifts. My mother is dying to give us life."

Lisbet swallowed a gasp. "Is she... will she truly die, Kian? Do you mean that?"

"Time," Kian replied. He slipped into a parlance more natural for him. "Cannot know. Time. Runs. Reveals." He frowned, as if realizing he'd slipped into his natural way of speaking. "That is enough for today."

"We only just started!"

"That is your lack of patience speaking, Lisbet. Nothing more."

"You did this to me. And now you leave me dangling in the dark, confused and alone."

"There is no blame to be found, only the inevitable outcome you find yourself dangling in, as you say. Did you know Eavan is carrying the child of one of the men who harmed her?"

Lisbet paled. Her mouth, ready to rebut anything but this, closed. "What?"

"She keeps this from you. You could know this, if you were not afraid of what you are awakening to. This is not the only secret in your circle." Kian stood. "Your brother will be gone when you return."

Lisbet stumbled as she dropped off the altar. Her mind was still gathering around Eavan's truth, which put a sharp and terrible end to an already horrific experience. And now he'd dropped another revelation on her? "What do you mean, gone?"

Kian didn't answer. He gestured toward the door. "If you had quarrels with him, they will remain so."

"Kian! I'm not going anywhere until you explain what you mean!"

He closed his eyes. She felt the air around her change as he spurred her to action, summoning her forward.

"All right!" Lisbet cried. He released her from the magic. "But I don't understand you, or your mother. I don't understand why you speak in riddles, and half-truths."

"You are still awakening," Kian said, moving aside so she could exit ahead of him. "Your full truths would destroy you to see them now."

"Jesse Strong, right? Hamish's son?"

Jesse finished tightening the saddle on his horse and turned toward the sound of an unfamiliar voice. The face he recognized. He'd come in with Khallum and the others from the Southerlands, though was clearly no Southerlander himself.

The stranger held out his hand, and Jesse took it, still sizing him up. "Aye. And you are?"

"Godfrey," the man said. He didn't offer a family name. As he stepped closer, the moonlight illuminating his face, Jesse could see he was not much older than he was.

"You know my father?"

"We were recently acquainted. He's a good man."

"Everyone says as much," Jesse replied. No, not a Southerlander, but he wasn't a man of the Westerlands, either. He sounded both from everywhere and nowhere. "Where did you meet him?"

Godfrey hesitated in his answer. He glanced back toward the Mule. "At the bedside of his son, who's recently returned from Camp Atonement."

The blood drained away from Jesse's face and hands. "Ryan? You saw my brother?"

Godfrey nodded. He again looked behind him. He seemed anxious. "Jesse, Lord Warwick may have told you that Ryan is poorly at the moment. That he's not expected to make it." He stepped closer and leaned in to whisper, "But you and I both know he has every reason to live."

Jesse searched for a response, but was struck dumb. This man, this stranger, couldn't have made the implication it seemed he was making.

"Aye! Godfrey! Horses are ready!" Rutland called from several yards away.

"Tell me what you mean by that," Jesse said, afraid to follow, afraid not to. "Who are you?"

Godfrey tipped an invisible hat, smiled, and went to join the others.

DRYSTAN WAITED until Lisbet was gone with Kian and Eavan, off with the younger girls, to collect food for their morning meal. He'd already said too much. He never should have told them he was going to fight for Yseult. All that had done was invoke those long, heavy looks of concern, followed by sighs. He knew the sighs well. He'd heard them all his life. *Guardians bless the boy,* came alongside the sound, more than enough for him to understand what they meant.

They surely thought they were protecting him. The reactions were born of love. But they didn't know what it was like to be him, to have been raised with everyone around you knowing you were *such a sweet boy,* but nothing more. Nothing useful. Possessed of none of the qualities needed for the life of service awaiting him. He heard these things often enough to believe them. They were facets of his identity.

His time in the Hinterlands hadn't felt like prison. Not really. He didn't say this to the others, not even Valen, but for once he understood what was meant by the word freedom. He thought he'd found it in his dangerous love for Ravenna, but he was beginning to understand what she must have when she left them. He'd simply needed to leave, in order to know who he was. It was not who they all thought him to be. He knew that much.

He also wasn't who he was when he'd left Wulfsgate. This

wasn't some philosophical transition born of his journey, but something else entirely. It started nearly a fortnight ago, when he'd felt as if he'd birthed something within him. Even if he'd wanted to share it, the others would have thought him completely mad!

He first knew he wasn't imagining it when his knife fell in the rapids of the river, and he thought he'd lost it forever. But then he looked to his left, on the riverbank, and there it again was. Not lost. Dry. Ready for use.

He'd thought maybe he was tired. Valen had him rising with the sun, thrust directly into action upon waking, with no time to adjust to the morning. There was always work to do. Drystan thought Valen was just trying to keep himself busy so his mind didn't linger too long on what had happened to them, but he did as the older man asked.

Later that same day, he'd seen Gabi trip over a log. He heard the snap before he saw her ankle, pointing in the complete opposite direction than it should. He dreaded having to ask any of the Medvedev to see to it, and, just for fun, just to see if he *could*, Drystan laid his hands on the howling girl and in his mind he saw her healed.

Gabi had stopped howling. Her screams faded to a confused whisper. She pulled her leg away from him, now fully healed, and ran off before he could ask her if she was okay. When he tried to talk to her about it later, she pretended not to know what he meant.

That had been the catalyst. The moment he *knew* he'd come here for a reason. It wasn't to wither away as a prisoner of the Medvedev, but to find within him the power to aid them. His mother always said the Medvedev had no need of men, and Valen had repeated this very same thing, but it was now men who had hurt them, and it was up to men, the good men, to undo this hurt.

He'd misjudged things. The Medvedev weren't going to war.

They were waiting for him, and perhaps others, men, brave men, *awakened* men, to solve this.

Drystan ran deeper into the forest. He wished he had his horse, but he had a strong feeling that if he stopped to ask the Medvedev for anything, the spell would be broken. He had to do this on his own, with his own feet carrying him, and the weapons he could bear. It wasn't weapons he'd need when he got to Whitechurch, though. These he brought to secure his meals, so he could keep his strength for the task ahead.

"Drystan!" Valen called from behind him. How long had he been there? He hadn't sensed him at all.

Drystan slowed but didn't stop. "Leave me alone, Valen!"

Valen caught up to him and wrestled his arm until Drystan stopped. He was stronger and faster, despite being twice his age. But Drystan had something he didn't. "Where do you think you're going?"

"I'm leaving."

Valen laughed. "Leaving."

"You can laugh long after I'm gone."

Valen reached a hand to check Drystan's forehead and cheeks. "You know we cannot leave. Nothing has changed. What's gotten into you?"

Drystan recoiled at his touch. "*Everything* has changed."

Valen dropped his hands away. He watched him, a dozen thoughts passing over his eyes as he did. "Some days past. That's what you mean."

Drystan's ire eased. "Do you mean... you noticed the change, too?"

Valen nodded. "And I believe Lisbet did as well. Remember when she collapsed?"

"Yeah."

"She saw something. A vision. She wouldn't tell me, of course, you know Lisbet. But then she asked me something, something she had no reason to know."

"What did she ask you?"

"She asked me about the four sorcerers."

"The who?"

Valen shook his head. "It's as we talked about, the Rhiagain sorcerers... I told her I don't know much about them, only what's been rumored. She was angry at me, she thought I was holding back, but I would have told her what she wanted to know if I had the answers." His gaze grew more intense. "Tell me what changed for you."

"You first."

"All right, then. Little things, mostly. The air warming when I feel a chill. A fresh energy rippling through me when I've noted that I'm tired. Do you remember when it stopped raining abruptly the other day? I had just thought to myself how inconvenient the rain was when we needed to hunt and, though it had been pouring for hours, the rain cleared in an instant; the sun broke through the clouds. There were other things, too. By themselves, I would've thought little of them, but together, they're harder to ignore. Something has changed for me, and it seems for you and Lisbet as well."

Drystan shifted his bow to the other arm. He remembered its heft now that his excitement had died away. The pull of his sword at his waist was almost unbearable. He didn't want to feel this; it was akin to how he'd felt his whole life, as if he wasn't *enough* for what was required.

"I have to go," Drystan said. "And you're wrong. We can leave. I know it, and I will prove it when I pass beyond the barrier."

Valen slowly nodded. "Very well. Then I'm coming."

"I haven't even told you where I'm going!"

"It doesn't matter to me. You're my son. You could tell me you meant to swim to the Beyond, and I'd be right by your side."

Drystan narrowed his eyes. "You say you're my father. The trouble is, I'll never know if you speak true, Valen."

"Ash," Valen corrected. "I'd never expect you to call me Father. That name is reserved for the man who reared you. But I don't want the deception of a false name hanging between us anymore. My name is Drystan Sylvaine, but I was Ash to your mother, and Ash I've been since. Ash is who I am."

"Ash," Drystan repeated. "Well, I don't have any designs to swim to the Beyond, but I do intend to kill the sorcerer Mortain and free the Saleen, so you can either step aside, or join me, but you won't stop me."

A strange look passed over Ash's face. Surprise fading to pride. "I would not deign to stop you, Drystan. But I would welcome the chance to aid you."

Drystan turned again toward the forest ahead. The barrier was close. He could feel it. He knew it would open for him and allow passage. "I only visited Whitechurch once, as a small boy. We went the long way, traveling via the Compass Roads. But I've seen the maps. Whitechurch isn't so far from here, is it?"

"No, it's not so far."

"You know the town."

"I know it well."

"You can't return for your things. Lisbet, Eavan, they can't know I've gone. Not until it's far too late to do anything about it."

"There's nothing I need that we don't have right here."

Drystan flushed at the strange way the words made him feel. He'd wanted to do this alone. Something within him had insisted it be this way. But he couldn't deny the fear of all the things facing him he couldn't predict, all the things he didn't know about his adversary or the land he occupied, and Valen—Ash—was the bridge that could connect him to these things.

He was also, probably, his father.

"Right. We ready then?"

Ash nodded. "After you, Drystan."

Drystan started again through the forest and, as they approached the invisible barrier dividing prison from freedom, Ash slipped his hand through Drystan's. Drystan didn't look down, nor did he look back, only forward, and as he crossed the barrier, he felt, for the first time in his life, that he was aimed true.

24

THE SLITHERING SHADOWS

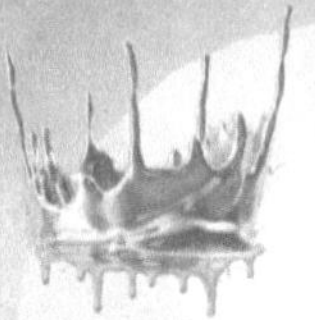

Correen was the only one who wasn't afraid of him. She didn't cow in his presence, even when being dressed down before her peers, which happened often enough that she should hate him. Her eyes never lowered when delivering news she expected to enrage him, even when it did, even when his reaction was enough to drive regret.

For that, Eoghan preferred her.

But she was not the mastermind Assyria had been. Assyria loathed him, but she'd been a force at court, always knowing precisely what needed done and seeing it through with unfeminine expediency. Their father once jested that she was clearly intended to have been born a male, but at the last minute her cock forgot to drop and the matter was concluded another way. Eoghan didn't find this as funny as Khain had, because if Assyria had been king, so very much could've been different.

And now, the semi-reign of Assyria was ended forever, for she'd revealed herself a traitor. Eoghan would have to make do with Correen, and her refreshing directness, that nonetheless lacked wisdom.

"Be swift," Eoghan urged. "Oldwin will arrive for his report any moment."

"Then one can hope he will also share with you what I'm about to," Correen said. "For when I tell you I'm troubled, it's only because I lack a more powerful word to describe my current state."

Eoghan rolled his eyes. "This is why women do not rule, sister. If you have news, share it. Without also transferring to me your emotional burden."

"It should trouble you, too," she said. "I've received these reports not from one, but several of our men along the southeastern peninsula."

"Your men, you mean."

"My men *are* your men. I would never see you caught unaware of anything in this kingdom, brother."

Eoghan nodded. "And?"

"It seems your briefings from the Wastelands have been falsified, and for some time," Correen said in a rush. "Specifically, that... that they've been fabricated to cover up the fact the camps are getting orders counter to the ones issued by you from Duncarrow. They are no longer mining for our precious resources, but disposing of the men in the camps, one by one. My sources believe whoever is giving these orders means to shut the camps down, though to what purpose, they cannot say."

Eoghan gaped at her. "Your sources are *wrong*, Correen. No one but I can give orders to the Wastelands. No one there would dare follow orders from someone other than the king."

Correen twisted her wrinkled mouth together. Her eyes never left his. "I thought the same when I received the first report, almost two months past. I even had my man executed for spreading falsehoods." She sighed. "A waste, that. He'd been a good source until I felt he was playing false. Turns out, with word from three other men, he was not."

"Four men have told you this?"

"Four men who have never met and have no means of comparing tales."

Eoghan scoffed, aghast. It was impossible, what she was suggesting, and yet he could find no plausible explanation for the reports she'd received. "But even if this were true, *who* could give orders that would be taken with more seriousness than those coming from the king himself?"

"I know not. And neither did my men. But the situation grows dire, Eoghan. There are massive graves all around the foothills of the fiery mountain to the east of Camp Atonement. What few men remain are starving to death. The end will come swift, and decisive, if nothing is done."

"We send food weekly!"

"It is no longer being distributed."

"Why? To what end?"

"That is my concern." Correen stepped closer. "That there is some great force working against you, and we have to find it *now*, before this treachery extends throughout the kingdom."

"Aiden is already my prisoner," he mused. If not Aiden, then who?

A page knocked and stuck his head through the door. "Your Grace, Lord Oldwin is here to present his report."

"Send him in."

"Wait, there's one more thing."

Eoghan held his hand to the page. "Hold him a moment." He turned back to Correen. "How can there be more?"

"This last thing, I'm much less sure of, but I can't *not* tell you, Eoghan." Correen lowered her eyes. His heart sank. She was afraid. "Some say Darrick lives."

Eoghan's spirits were immediately restored. "You silly woman. Darrick's life ended here, at Duncarrow. At my order. At the hands of my men. There is no question of his death. These things you hear are the work of bored fishwives."

"They aren't fishwives," Correen said in a low voice. "But yes, I understand. I hesitated to tell you this, but you have always trusted me to guide you, as best as I can. To keep this from you would go against that loving fealty."

Eoghan waved his hands, dismissing her. "Yes, yes. Pay no mind to it. It's only dreaming from those who would see my head smiling down upon them from the pikes of Duncarrow. As to the Wastelands, I'll put Oldwin on it." He paused. "No. I'll see first what he tells me." He leaned in. "For now, I leave it with you, and you alone. Yes?"

Correen nodded. She bowed as she backed away. "Your Grace."

"CIAN, GO BACK TO YOUR MOTHER," Yesenia whispered, as loudly as she dared. He was afraid of her, as men often were, but to raise her voice, or her hand, would be to draw the very attention she needed desperately to avoid.

"I want to help." Cian kept pace with her, slinking tight against the walls as they moved deeper down the hall. They had no good reason to be here. No explanation would be enough if caught. These halls had once housed the honorable men of the Quinlanden Guard, and now, traitors lived in these rooms, ate their food, helped themselves to their women. If even one of her own trusted attendants had been left with her, she would have sent them, but they were attended now by men handpicked by Mads Waters. Spies and traitors. There was no one to trust.

Yesenia paused. The air was thinner, headier here. Sweat rolled down her face, into her eyes. "You're the only one of us that Waters won't touch, Cian. But that changes if you're caught committing treason."

"It isn't treason when this is our home!"

"I know, dear boy, but something very wrong has happened

here, and if we don't discover it, your home may become something you never again recognize."

"What are you looking for? I can help you find it!"

"No," Yesenia insisted. Footsteps sounded at the turn at the end of the hall. Men paced, but none, so far, had come this way. But they would. "Cian, please. Your mother needs you to keep out of trouble."

"My mother has abandoned me. No one has seen her."

"What? Abandoned you?" Yesenia *had* wondered why Maeryn had gone scarce, but there were plenty of reasonable explanations. "Surely that cannot be true?"

"Gone, Aunt Yesenia. She's left. Us. Me."

Yesenia sighed. "If we're caught, you lie. You say that you followed me because you were curious. Tell me you understand."

"It wouldn't be a lie," Cian replied. His breaths were excited, heavy. He was a good boy. More like his Uncle Corin than his father, and Yesenia hoped, one day soon, to see him take his father's place.

Yesenia trusted no one but her husband. Not even Maeryn, who she knew to be on their side, but had so skillfully handled Aiden over the years that Yesenia didn't doubt she'd practiced it on her allies as well. She was a slithering shadow, one you wanted on your side, but not all the way. And now, Cian was right. She had slithered her way out of matters altogether.

It made no sense that she would leave her son and heir to an uncertain fate, but nothing made sense anymore. The king's claim to place Corin upon the seat of lordship in the Easterlands was an interesting one, especially with Cian alive and well and ready to do the same. Their guards had eased some as promised, but she couldn't take the words of a traitor king to heart any more than she could Aiden, or Mads. The missing piece was knowing the contents of the communication that was given to Mads by this same king. They had to know, and there was only one way to find out.

"Mads Waters' room is at the end of this hall. He would have received a raven from Duncarrow recently. I need to know the words written upon that vellum," Yesenia explained. She didn't tell him about the king's words, or that because of them, by all rights, she should be able to walk down this hall without hiding. That she knew better, because trusting no one was the only way to survive this game.

"I'll go on ahead."

"No. Remember what I told you. *You* followed *me*."

Cian seemed troubled by it, but he nodded and pointed for her to continue on. Yesenia moved like a cat, silent, smooth. Corin had wanted to go, had all but begged her not to do it, but only a woman could make it as far as she had. She was more warrior than any man here, but she was not a man. She was not the potential next Lord of the Easterlands.

They paused once more, as the footsteps approached the edge of the hall. The guard's shadow loomed into the hall ahead, grotesquely lit by a single sconce. She waited once more, and then, when he resumed pacing, she pushed ahead.

They approached Waters' room. There were no windows to the outside on this level. It was the only part of the keep not built into the trees, but at the base, dug halfway into the ground, close enough to the sea that the water threatened to swarm it and erase the whole thing from existence. She couldn't see the sky to read how much time had passed. Mortain would finish his morning ritual soon, and Mads would return. It had to be now.

Yesenia rolled against the door and gently pressed inward.

"SEND HIM IN," Eoghan commanded the page. The young man obliged, fearful for reasons beyond Eoghan's comprehension. Eoghan had never harmed this one. He had red hair, so was probably a Rhiagain, which was enough to spare him. Sometimes he failed to understand why *any* of them feared him so. Most had never seen his anger up close.

Oldwin entered. He held his head high, wearing a confidence that made it difficult for Eoghan to remember the slouched, defeated man he'd pulled from the sky dungeon. At times, he missed Oldwin as he was, for back then Oldwin had at least feigned a reverent respect for Eoghan. And while he still had the sense to affect it now, his newfound power had given him a boldness that left a sick, sinking feeling in Eoghan's belly. He couldn't define it yet, but it was there, and he couldn't ignore it forever.

"Your Grace."

"Go on, then."

Oldwin folded his hands over his robe. He beamed. "You will be pleased to hear that all reports from the kingdom are exactly as expected, with no uncomfortable surprises. In the Westerlands, the Quinlanden Guard have eased their actions against the citizens, per your request, and things are returning to a sense of orderly calm. In the Easterlands, Mortain continues his work with the Saleen, but Corin Quinlanden will be ready to take up his brother's mantle once we give the order. The Northerland borders are yet closed, both land and sea, but I expect once they see that the threat of war has waned, they will relax as well, and then we can renew efforts to apprehend Assyria, and the other prisoners. Whatever their plans, they cannot be to waste away in the Northerlands, can they? They'll be on the move once they deem it safe. Ah, and the Southerlands are always restless, but we have seen no signs they intend to turn this anxiousness to action."

This all seemed far too easy for Eoghan, but if there had been further unrest, Correen would have mentioned it. He nodded. "And the Wastelands?"

"Your Grace?"

"They are part of this kingdom as well, are they not? What is your report of the camps?"

Oldwin's mouth smiled, but his eyes looked dead beyond. "Of course. There is nothing new to report. Your mining efforts continue with increasingly fruitful results. More men are sent every day, and production increases in kind."

"No trouble there, then?"

Oldwin's smile deepened. "No. Why would there be?"

"Lady Yesenia," Mads said. She heard him before she saw him. His low, gravelly voice carried, bouncing off the damp stone walls. "I had a feeling it would be today. I can't quite explain it, though I *felt* it. In my bones, you might say. I may not have the gifts of Mortain, but we all have our senses, would you agree?"

Yesenia's heart skipped around. She wanted to turn and warn Cian, but it was too late. He'd entered behind her, gasping lightly at her back as he came to an abrupt halt.

"And Cian! What a gift. I sometimes forget how you resemble your father. It's as if he'd never left. Though, I cannot say he ever humbled us with his presence in the guards' quarters. Then again, I once had a much nicer apartment."

"I..." Cian's words failed him.

Mads pulled something from his vest. A scroll. He held it out, only far enough to tempt her. "This is what you're after, is it not? Funny, for I was thinking the same thing. How I would love to know the words the king sent your husband."

"I've done nothing wrong, being here. You would have received the orders that Corin and I are to be left alone. We are to have free rein of Whitechurch, same as we always have before the mess you made. We happily await the restoration of our staff and freedoms."

Mads nodded slowly. He peeled himself away from his corner desk. "The words were clear enough. Their writer? Less clear."

"They were orders from Lord Quinlanden. You would do well to heed them."

"So they say," Mads replied. "And so others will accept, without question."

Yesenia narrowed her eyes. "If I were you, I would be very cautious with your next steps, Steward Waters. For if your lord were to return and see you've gone against his wishes, you and I are both acquainted with his especial definition of mercy."

Mads laughed. "You and I also both know Aiden Quinlanden isn't returning to the Easterlands anytime soon. The question is why."

Yesenia paled. He'd come to the same conclusion she had. "If this is true, then your next lord stands behind me."

"Oh, yes. I know." Mads tossed the scroll on the floor. "You wish to the see the words badly enough to come here for them? Go on, then."

Yesenia's breath caught. He had her where he wanted her now. There it was, the answer, but at a price. Kneel and surrender to whatever fate he had prepared for her. Step away and be free.

"Your hesitation is not becoming of a Warwick."

"You know nothing about me. You know nothing that Aiden hasn't allowed you to know."

Mads' grin faded. "I know these are not his words." He kicked the scroll away. It landed in a dark corner of the room. "And I know he would not wish for me to follow them."

Yesenia flexed her hands at her sides. Many years, it had been, since she fought with a man, and she had only her fists and her quickness now. She could go for the sword at his side, but he'd expect it, and be on it before she was halfway to the task.

Mads laughed. "Cian. Arrest your aunt."

Yesenia could feel her nephew's shock behind her. "What?"

"Arrest your aunt. If you are your father's heir, then it falls to you to continue the work he started, and the values he held close. Would he allow a foreign woman to snoop around the chambers of his most trusted servant, searching for ways to sow division?"

"My father would never want Aunt Yesenia to be a prisoner."

"You would be wise to call her what she is now, Lord Quinlanden. A traitor."

"Cian, do as he says," Yesenia urged. "He's right."

"See, Cian? Even your aunt knows a treasonous snake must be dealt with."

Cian fumbled behind her. He was not his father's son, but nor was he his mother's. He was more like Corin, full of honor, lacking in the deviousness required to feign a position he didn't agree with. He should have turned back when she ordered him to. Now, for his hesitation, he would pay alongside her.

Mads reached for his desk and felt around for a piece of rope. He tossed it to Cian. "If I have to do it, you'll be joining her."

"Do it," Yesenia whispered through gritted teeth, burying her mouth into her shoulder. "Now."

Cian fumbled with the rope. He whimpered, loud enough only for her to hear. Her heart ached at the sound. He was the same age as her own son, Torquil, who was safely tucked away at university in Oldcastle. She beseeched the Guardians that Mads would forget this, as he'd seemed to forget Aiden's other sons studying there. If the adults failed to stop the darkness descending over the kingdom, it would fall to the children, as it had two decades before.

Yesenia held her hands behind her. She winced as Cian tightened the rope, though poorly. No one had ever taught him how to bind a man. She could easily escape this, but for his sake, she would not.

Mads called for the guards. Two appeared in seconds.

To the first, he said, "Lady Warwick is my prisoner now. See that she's taken to a cell, far from prying eyes. Once you've secured her, her husband will join her. And be wary of this one. She's wily."

The rough handling of the guard jerked Yesenia into action. Cian flashed her a terrified look as she passed. She had no time to say anything to him, to give him a sign that would ease him. And what had she to give him now that would not be deception? Maeryn was gone. His father was likely dead. His aunt and uncle couldn't help him now. Cian was alone, with only his guile and men who would use this.

As she stumbled into the dim hall, she heard Mads issue his orders to the second guard.

"Send word to our commanders in the Westerlands. Sack the Great Cities. Begin in the north and work your way south. Leave nothing, leave no one."

"Sir?"

"Your head, in exchange for further clarity."

The man shuffled off.

"Let it not be said," Mads called after him, "that the men of the Eastern Reach were idle when it was action demanded of them."

Mads dropped into the chair at his desk, releasing a breath it seemed he'd been holding since before breaking his fast that morning.

Maeryn had told him Yesenia Warwick would visit his chambers. And she'd been right.

Yet Yesenia's boldness in the act left him unsettled. She'd been secretive enough to not want to be caught, but met his gaze with confidence she'd be allowed to walk away without punishment.

Why?

A shadow appeared at the door of his chamber. He glanced up with a start, shocked to see Mortain.

"What are *you* doing here?"

"You arrested Lord Quinlandèn's brother, and sister-in-law."

"Spies, you mean. I caught Lady Yesenia in the act myself."

"Spying is a matter of perspective. If Lady Warwick's choice to move about freely in her home, then what must we call Lady Quinlandèn's slinking about in the shadows with you?"

"Without Maeryn, I would've been blind to the treason brewing in this very keep!"

"And yet, where is she? Gone. Slipped away in the night. Those loyal to no one are greater foes than those clear in their intentions."

"Why are you here?"

"You forget the words issued by your lord himself. That Lady Yesenia and Lord Corin are to be left alone. You have overstepped your authority here."

"I haven't forgotten the words. I know they didn't come from my lord, and I answer to no one but him."

"Your bold assumptions will end poorly for you," Mortain answered.

"Will they? And what if you're the one who's wrong?"

"You've also sent men to the Westerlands against his orders. You intend to start a war, when neither your lord nor your king desires for one."

"I don't answer to you, Mortain."

Mortain's face was lit by the flickering sconce. He seemed to be smiling. "Ahh, and yet you can no longer be sure who you answer to, can you?"

25

NOT TONIGHT, BUT SOON

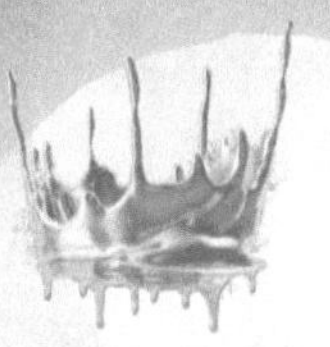

Khallum licked his lips. Crazed energy rolled off him as he scrutinized the small group of Brandyn's trusted Blackwood Banners. "Aye, well, I came here to aid men with courage." He reached between his legs and squeezed. "This all ye do then? Sit around *talking* about war, and never doing it?"

"A man with sense," Easlan chimed in. A few of the others murmured in spirited agreement, namely Khallum's own men. "A man who isn't afraid to fight for what others would take from him."

"This is the Westerlands we stand upon, not the Southerlands when last I checked the signs." Blackfen shook his head, sharing a look with the Grand Minister, Tyndall.

"Does that make ye better?" Khallum challenged. "That you've nay been where my men have, ready to die before allowing their lands and spirits taken by a king with no right?"

"Your quarrels with the crown are different from ours," Tyndall said.

"Aye, they *were* different, till the craven ratsbane sent the bootlicker's men to show ye a new one."

"And how did standing against the crown work for you last time?" Blackfen challenged. "An entire peninsula, gone. Taken. Property of the Rhiagains."

"It didnae have to be so, had the courage of the kingdom risen beside us, as it should have been! As it once *had* been, before the Rhiagains raped our shores and claimed this kingdom for themselves! And now they've done the unthinkable to the Saleen? Do ye even care about that, the lot of ye? When will it be enough?"

"Not every fight is won at the end of a sword," Blackfen countered. "And once drawn, steel cannot be re-sheathed."

Rutland snorted. "Says the bowman."

Jesse hovered in one corner, watching, Joran perched in the other. Brandyn valued their words, but it seemed they would both keep their counsel today.

Brandyn folded his hands, waiting patiently for his turn to talk. He could feel Khallum's annoyance from across the room, laced through a nervous, volatile energy that was almost scary. Khallum and Brandyn's father had been brothers, but the two men were on different ends of the same sword. Byrne had been the cooling hand of the Westerlands. Khallum was the swirling, chaotic center of the Southerlands.

Still, he needed him. Needed his men. His leadership, too, though this was where the boundaries were undefined. This was Brandyn's land, and his mother would have never bent her knee to a lord of another Reach.

"Thank you, Lord Warwick. Uncle," Brandyn said when there was a break in the rousing words of war. "For answering our call, when others didn't answer yours."

"Aye, well, I know what others didnae. One falls, we all fall."

Brandyn nodded. "You're right. It's time for us to take action." He paused then, not for the effect of his prior words to settle, but because he didn't know how to find the ones he needed to say next. "Enchanter Joran and I have both received visions, separate of one another, showing the same thing. Quinlanden's men *will* move to destroy our towns, unless we can stop them."

"Then why do I sense you are hesitant to move, Lord Blackwood?" This one, Samuel Law, reminded Brandyn more of the men his mother would have taken counsel with. Calm. Rational. He needed men like that.

"I'm not hesitant to move. I'm hesitant to make the wrong move," Brandyn said, confessing the words aloud. If his mother were here, she'd chide him for his transparency. But Brandyn couldn't follow anyone he didn't himself trust, and trust started with honesty. It's why he'd taken to Christian Dereham right away. Christian always spoke plainly and true, even to a young boy like himself. "I'm recommending we move on Whitechurch."

"Whitechurch!" Khallum exclaimed. "But the ratsbane's men are here, on *your* lands."

"Yet their orders come from Whitechurch. And without the orders, the attacks on our lands stop."

Blackfen stepped forward. "There's reason in this, as we've talked about before. Sever the source, the blood dries."

"These men are cowards and traitors," Rutland said, sliding his ale across the table in a rush of anger. "Death is the only language we all speak that conveys consequence."

"Punishment will come after we stop the enemy from further damage," Brandyn said reasonably. "We will deal with these men. I assure you. For what they've done to my people. My own father. But we can do this without causing further destruction to our people and their land."

"You cannae let them see you as weak, Lord Blackwood. Your father would have understood this," Khallum pressed. "Byrne knew an enemy could be dealt with in one way only."

"My father *is* who instilled in me a sense of caution," Brandyn retorted. He could feel his defenses forming; the heat rising. He had to squelch it or be lost to the moment as the men older and better than him were preparing to do.

Khallum snorted. "Bowing to your mother, no doubt."

"My mother," Brandyn said through clenched teeth. "Is the greatest warrior I know, and my father loved and respected that."

"Ye nay know many warriors then, lad?" Rutland quipped. He turned to Khallum. "Seems we're needed here more than we realized. Just take the lead and be done with it."

Storm dropped a hand to her knife. "Try it and die."

At this, Easlan began to look concerned. "Come now. Lord Blackwood may not have the wisdom of our years, but he is our leader here. Our lord. We are here to counsel him, not take that from him."

"There's still one with greater authority than any lord," Khallum muttered.

"My lord," Law cautioned. "Now?"

"If Lord Warwick has more wisdom he'd like to share, he's welcome to his words," Brandyn said.

Khallum's brows knitted in mounting consternation. He seemed both angry and afraid, his foot tapping in frenetic staccato, tongue rolling around the inside of his mouth as if preparing to wind up and unleash. He looked at his two stewards, and then at the other man, the one known only as Godfrey. Fingers twitching, at last, he looked up.

"Aye, well, there is one, as I said, with greater authority. One we donnae look up to because we must, but because we so choose." He ignored the wariness coming off Law and Rutland as he continued. "I didnae come only to aid you, nephew, though I would see that done as well. I came to light the spark that will end the madness that came over this kingdom when Khain ascended the throne and laid an even darker pall at the rise of his son. The *wrong* son."

Easlan emptied his drink and slammed the mug on the counter in agreement.

Khallum pointed at Jesse. "The Strong men are some of the most loyal to all the Southerlands. Jesse. His father. And now, Ryan Strong, who we sent into the Wastelands not to punish but to retrieve Darrick Rhiagain, who'd been hiding as a prisoner for five years."

Brandyn's breath caught in concert with the collective gasps chiming around him. Had he heard right?

"Aye, your hearing doesnae need adjusting, men. Eoghan Rhiagain ordered the death of his brother, but there were others in Duncarrow, less eager to see this deed done. He was instead sent to languish in prison, in secret, contrived by none other than his sister, Assyria."

"It's not possible," Blackfen said, breathless. "A secret this big could not have been kept this long."

"A secret kept safe by those who knew what it could mean," Khallum pressed. "Aye, it's easier kept than ye think. It was Assyria who came to me, judging I would be the proper man to see Darrick freed and restored. She was right, I ken, for that's Darrick Rhiagain standing to my left, alive as ever."

"No," Brandyn whispered as his eyes, as with those of every other man present, fell upon the young man sitting off by himself. He looked like Jesse, Brandyn thought, dark and serious. But there was something else about him, something Brandyn, in his youth and inexperience, could not define in words. Something that killed any shred of doubt that he was who Khallum Warwick said he was.

The man Khallum had called Darrick Rhiagain slowly stood. His dark eyes were glassy, but no tears fell. "It's true what Lord Warwick says. Eoghan ordered my death, and Assyria stayed it. But I have to confess to you all that I lost hope, long before Ryan came for me. I never expected to stand before any man or woman in this kingdom again, and so I have no speech prepared for you. I'm still adjusting to the reality that I'm here now, a free man. That my wife, who I never had a chance to share with all of you, yet lives, as does my son." He turned to Khallum. "Words fail me even now, as I know I must find the means to express my gratitude to all who have sacrificed to retrieve me from my prison. For I know the Rhiagains have been responsible for greatness but also terribleness, and every one of you would be in the right to want to see us thrown aside for something better."

Easlan fell to his knees. Slowly, one by one, every other man in the room followed suit. Brandyn lowered himself, shaking.

"No, please," Darrick said. "Please, I ask of you not to come to me with your reverence, not now. We have work to do, and I'm here to aid you in this, however I can."

"As ye can see, this isnae about a battle for the Westerlands. Nay anymore. Tis a war for the future of this kingdom," Khallum boomed. He looked satisfied, as he should, but Brandyn remembered something his mother once said about his uncle. *Khallum Warwick is a proud man, but even he knows it is the false pride of a man who has not yet earned it.* It seemed to Brandyn that Khallum knew he was earning it now.

"Your Grace," Tyndall whispered. "We never... I thought..." He lowered himself again; then, remembering Darrick had asked him not to, fumbled back to his feet, wiping away tears. "Can it be? Truly?"

Darrick approached him, taking the man's hands in his. "You are a man of the Reliquary, are you not?"

Tyndall nodded. "Grand Minister Tyndall, Your Grace. My king."

"I'm not your king yet," Darrick said. He released him and turned to the others. "I would like a word alone with Lord Blackwood, if that's all right."

Brandyn caught Jesse rushing out of the tavern from the corner of his eye.

Khallum flashed a meaningful look at his men. Brandyn could read it well enough. He thought the prince could speak sense into him where Khallum had failed, but Brandyn could read the prince, too. And that wasn't what he saw at all.

The men filtered out, leaving Brandyn alone with Darrick Rhiagain.

Darrick had been told that Brandyn was a child, little more than a decade of life in him. He could see it, of course, for Brandyn was a small boy, perhaps even for his age. But age was more than how tall you stood next to men. In the young Blackwood lord's eyes, Darrick saw what the men following him failed to. To them, he was their next in line, and for that, their last hope. But for that to be all he was, would be to gravely underestimate him.

"I'm sorry about your father, Brandyn."

Brandyn regarded him with that solemn stare he'd used when speaking to his men earlier. Darrick could almost read his thoughts; the boy was mulling, now, what had happened before Darrick dismissed the others. Was he still the leader? Did he still matter? Was Darrick, in fact, who they said he was?

"Did you know him?" Brandyn asked, without breaking his gaze.

"I met him once. Not long before the kingdom believed me dead. I met your mother, then, too. She's an exceptional woman."

This elicited a small smile from the boy. "She is. Hers are hard steps to follow."

"A leader doesn't aim to follow the steps of those before them, but to honor their path while making their own way."

Brandyn shook his head. "It doesn't matter, anyway. She'll be back soon, and then I'll return to the Sepulchre, and all of this will have felt like a dream."

"I told myself this when I was sent to the Wastelands," Darrick mused. "In the beginning, I believed it. Then reality proved my hope false." He watched him from across the table. "I don't say that to scare you, Brandyn. I hope your mother does come back, for you're still a boy, and you deserve to be that until you cannot anymore. But you should lead these men as if her time is done. Until you have reason not to."

"How? Lord Warwick has all but taken over. And now... and now... you're here. And who am I now, but the youngest child of Asherley Blackwood?"

Darrick grinned. "You are so much more than a child, Brandyn. But no matter what Lord Warwick may believe about what is best for your Reach, it is still *your* Reach. This war hasn't spread to the kingdom yet, which means it isn't mine to lead, either. What has your instinct been telling you? You say you saw yourself in Whitechurch?"

"It's more than instinct. I'm a magic wielder. A seer," Brandyn explained. "Like Joran, who was my mother's soothsayer. She trusted him, and so I must, for I know my mother trusts almost no one and never does so easily. And we've *both* seen ourselves in Whitechurch. We have both seen the castle in the trees, the Medvedev milling around the forests, mindless. I know why Lord Warwick wants to lead the war here in the Westerlands. Maybe he's right. Maybe my vision isn't what should be, but what could. Perhaps there's more I haven't seen that would spell disaster if we do it my way."

Darrick leaned back in the rickety chair. "Has life blessed you with a true friendship? One you can count on, no matter what?"

Brandyn looked toward the back room where the men had disappeared and nodded. "Storm Wakesell. She saved my life. More than once. I think the friendship is fairly one-sided, though. I don't have much to offer her in return."

"Probably more than you know," Darrick answered. "I saw the way she looked at you. Protecting you gives her a sense of purpose.

I've also known true friendship, more than once. Most recently, with Ryan Strong. Your friend Jesse's brother."

"The one who saved you."

"Yes. But what Khallum didn't tell the men about was Ryan's sacrifice. He has yet to wake up since our rescue." Darrick looked off to the side. "Even all the way across the kingdom, his wisdom lives in me." He raised his head. "When Ryan found me at the camp, I was a broken man. All I had been, all I had known, had been reduced to the sand under my tired, blistered feet. He pushed me. He wanted to *know* me. Wanted to know what I'd buried deep within, what I no longer felt was worth giving voice to. But though I didn't know it until later, I was wrong. Ryan was right. If you have something to say, say it. If you have something that can help another, you don't hold it in, where it's no good to anyone. This may be why your mother trusted Joran so. He shares when he needs to."

Brandyn twisted his mouth. "Sometimes. He's a cagey old thing."

"I'm going to tell you what I know about the sorcerer, Mortain. And you can use this information however you choose, Brandyn, but I give it to you knowing it should be part of what you use to make your decision, about how to lead your men."

"You know him? Mortain?"

"I remember him," Darrick said. "I can't say I ever knew him. My entire life at Duncarrow, he and another sorcerer, Oldwin, were imprisoned in the sky dungeon by my father. When I was about fifteen, I learned why.

"Oldwin was the first to be thrown into the prison. There was some bond that had been broken between him and my father when he failed to see something very important. Something that drove my father to madness. But, you see, my father knew something about these sorcerers. He had always known, but as long as they were of use to him, he ignored these warnings. The lure of such power is strong, as you might imagine, and the Rhiagain sorcerers, as most call them, have powers beyond anything you've ever seen or known in this kingdom, even at the Sepulchre. To have two at your side... well..."

"Joran says the sorcerers aren't Rhiagains at all, but something else," Brandyn said.

Darrick nodded. "Joran is right. Did he also tell you they were immortal?"

"Yeah, but that's impossible."

"Here, in the kingdom, it is. Where they come from, it's a way of life. You may have heard the term, the four sorcerers."

Brandyn nodded.

"There are four here, in the kingdom. But there were more than that, where they come from. Ilynglass."

"Ilynglass. That's Beyond?"

"It's one Beyond."

"What happened to the others?"

"No one knows. But they say only four made the journey with Carrow Rhiagain, hundreds of years ago. All four survived, but as the Rhiagains who journeyed with them died off, and time passed, the truth of the sorcerers remained within their ranks alone. What lingered in my ancestors were whispers, tales passed down, the kind that usually take different shape and form the more they are repeated. But the one thing my father did know was that they were exceedingly dangerous. That they serve us now, but the time will come when they no longer have to, and when it does, all as we know it will end."

"What does that even mean?" Brandyn asked. "All as we know it will end? There are four of them, and many thousands of us."

"I know his fear was real. And I know he failed Eoghan by never telling him these things. How do I know he failed? Because Eoghan, though cruel, would not have been foolish enough to free one and give him to a man like Aiden Quinlanden. I suspect he's freed Oldwin as well, seeing the opportunity to have such a crea-ture at his side."

Brandyn traced his finger along the grooves of the wooden table. "Why tell me this?"

"Because all of this, all your troubles, began when Mortain arrived in Whitechurch in 'service' to Aiden Quinlanden. But have you asked yourself why Aiden isn't the one directing these men? Why he has gone conspicuously absent?" Darrick leaned in. "I don't know what Mortain's aim is, what motivations lie at the core of his desire to see this kingdom at war. But I know it begins with him. And if it begins with him..."

Brandyn's fingers stopped moving. He looked up. "It ends with him."

"For now, anyway," Darrick said, nodding. "For there are still three others out there, biding their time."

"Esme, wake up. We need to talk."

Esmerelda hadn't been sleeping at all. She slept much less than they assumed she did, likely because she spent a fair amount of time in bed. But lying wasn't sleeping. For her, it was the only time she could be sure to be alone, where she could think without disturbance.

She turned to see Jesse's troubled expression. He sat on the side of the bed, keeping the same odd distance he always strived for between them, while also looking as if he might take her in his arms if the wind blew the wrong way. She was as confused by this, she thought, as he was.

"Jesse." She yawned, because it seemed like the next fair thing to do, keeping up with his belief that she was always tired. Not that she wanted to lie to him. But he fussed after her so much that it kept some of that, at least, at bay, which also gave her some needed peace.

She finished rolling around, and now she could see it wasn't only his face, but all of him, in distress. He was truly agitated, wringing his hands, hardly able to stay still. She almost reached for him, to ease him, but then thought better of it.

"There are things I need to tell you," he said. "I should have told you before, but—"

"My father is here," Esmerelda said. Watching him like this made her tired. Physically. Mentally. More than she had been, and that was something. "I already know."

Jesse stopped tapping his foot. "You know? How?"

"I heard you talking to Ravenna."

"But you were sleeping."

"I wasn't," Esmerelda said. "And I heard you. It's fine, Jesse. I know already."

"But..." He had a question, he just didn't know what it was.

She tried to smile. For him. "Ravenna was right. You misjudge me and what I can handle. Being with child doesn't make me weak. I've never been so strong."

Jesse touched her arm. "I didn't think you were weak, Esmerelda."

"You did," she said, now smiling fully. "But I know it was a misunderstanding born of love for Ryan."

He looked down. His hand remained, though he couldn't quite decide what to do with it.

"And I don't care, about you and Ravenna. It's a waste to trouble yourself over it so."

"If you heard us, then you know what she..." He shook his head. "I will own my part in it all, but I was relieved to hear her confess about the magic."

"Your protection of me doesn't prohibit you from being a man," Esmerelda replied. "Or from having a man's desires. I saw how you looked upon her from the very first time, in the Hinterlands. Magic or not. You only deny yourself for my sake, and I've no concern on the matter at all, beyond wanting you to be happy, as my brother."

Jesse flushed a dark red. "It doesnae matter. I've other priorities, and my desires aren't one of them." He seemed to realize his hand still grazed her skin, and he pulled it back, recoiling at his oversight. "But there's something else I have to tell you, and I donnae know how."

"Is it Ryan?"

"How did you know?"

"What else would have you so troubled?" Esmerelda pulled herself up so she could meet his eyes.

"When you heard Ravenna and me talking, you didnae hear what I told her about Ryan, then?"

"He's dead, isn't he?"

Jesse took a sharp intake of breath. "Even to hear those words aloud, I... no, he's not dead. But he isnae well. He has yet to wake, and Lord Warwick, your father, thinks perhaps he will not. You remember what I told you? About why your father sent him to prison?"

Esmerelda laughed. "How could I ever forget such a thing?"

Jesse didn't join in her laughter. "Darrick Rhiagain is *here*, in Greystone Abbey. He came with your father. I talked to him... last night, though I didnae know who he was. Not then. He said the most curious thing, about Ryan, but now his words make sense." He aimed an even more concerned look upon her than the earlier one. "Did you hear me, about Ryan? That he hasn't awakened?"

"Yes. I heard you."

Jesse reached for one of her hands. He folded it into both of his. "Perhaps you're in shock."

"No." She released her hand, patting his before pulling it back to her lap. "I've been preparing for worse. If he sleeps, there's yet hope."

"You were right before, when you wanted to leave. We cannae stay here."

"I know."

"Give me time. A week. A fortnight at most. I'll have a plan for us."

"Okay, Jesse."

"We will go to Ryan. Darrick will tell me where he is, if I ask. He knows about you. And he cares for Ryan. They became friends in there."

Esmerelda nodded. "I would like that."

"Are you sure you're all right? Can I get you something? To drink, to break your fast?"

She shook her head. "You can stop fussing over me."

Jesse smiled, shaking his head as he looked away, around, anywhere but at her. "Aye. Right. I'll go talk to Darrick, and I'll make peace with Easlan. We'll be on our way before you know it."

It made her happy to see him with purpose once more. He'd been so dark, so aimless and unhappy, since his quarrel with Easlan. Looking after her had also become a darkness in his life. Not because he saw her as a burden, but because of the confusion she stirred in him. It wasn't unlike the confusion Ravenna had caused in him, but it was worse. This one had no magic to blame.

She knew this confusion, because it lived in her, too.

When he was gone, Esmerelda slipped from the bed. She checked her knapsack, making sure once more that she hadn't forgotten anything.

Not tonight, but soon.

26

THE SEARCH

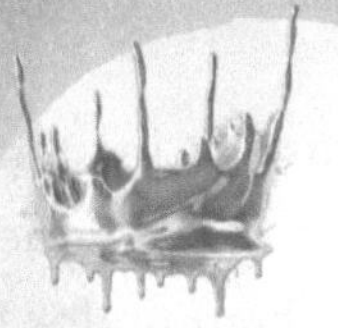

The snow was blinding. A fresh storm had rolled off the mountains the night before they departed Wulfsgate. It would have passed over the town by now, but it lingered in Torrin's Pass, where the cold air trapped it and bade it stay longer. These were not the conditions in which they could easily find anyone. But every day Pieter and Asherley spent here brought them further from safe recovery.

Christian kept Ransom close to his side. It wasn't anything clear, but he'd had a sense about the boy, a sense that stopped just short of a vision. Even all these years later, with all his training, Christian sometimes struggled to parse a feeling from a sense. Whether he was experiencing the protectiveness common to all men, or if it was something more.

Christian wanted to leave Ransom behind, but Holden insisted he come. He'd nearly bullied Aylen into declaring him fit for travel. Ransom was the last person to see Pieter and Asherley both, Holden said. His sparse memory might bloom in returning him to where it all happened.

The boy rode solemnly at Christian's side, having both receded and aged overnight. Nineteen years, Gretchen had said. He could have been nine or ninety now, and both would have been believable, but a young man on the verge of having his own family, old enough to step up and be the lord of his own land, this seemed out of reach for the boy riding beside him.

"We're close." Ransom muttered the words. Measured against the wind, only Christian heard them. The wulves they'd brought to aid with the search howled behind them, sounding their cries into the gusts.

"Bannermen! We're close!" Christian called ahead to the men. Fifteen of Holden's most trusted. None had balked at the orders when they went to round them up for the call to arms. More had volunteered, but Christian gently refused their aid. The pass wasn't big enough for more, and they wanted to find Pieter and Asherley, not bury their trail underfoot.

Holden pulled up beside him. "Pieter first."

Christian nodded. "I'm sending two men ahead to scout the mountainside near the cave. Once we find Pieter, we will join them."

Holden reached a hand across the space between them and proffered a quick squeeze to Christian's arm. "Good."

Christian heard Alric several paces behind him. He knew it was him because the pony had a different gait, and a soft snuff he sounded every few steps. The beast was old, but it was determined to serve until its legs caved atop its hooves. Likely it had served beyond its capability already and existed now on devotion alone.

He'd shared the Alric conversation with no one. He didn't know what he believed, but he was certain *Alric* believed what he was saying. Whether it had happened as he remembered, only the Guardians knew, but Christian felt bad for his uncle. He wasn't a liar or an idiot. Only changed by what he believed had happened to him, and the subsequent loss of respect from his family and peers.

"Be wary of indulging your uncle," Holden said. "His intentions are good, but his words will drive you to madness with him."

Christian wondered if his father knew he'd talked to Alric about the veil, or was only heading off the possibility. "I can discern the difference, Father."

"He thought he could as well. You see him now, what he's become."

"I see a man who feels shunned by his own family, for something beyond his control."

"Then you believe him."

The outline of the pearapple tree broke through the fog of snow. Ransom instinctively picked up pace, pulling ahead.

"I believe he believes," Christian said. "And that is enough for me to treat him with kindness."

"Kindness can be a cruelty when administered to those requiring a firmer hand."

"There." Ransom dropped from his horse. He approached the tree. "He was there, he was... he came around the backside, here." Ransom danced under the overhead branches, darting here, there, in erratic fits and starts. "He looked at me, and I looked back, to see if we'd been followed, and when I returned to him, he was gone."

Christian paused his horse near where Ransoms crouched. "Here?"

"Aye."

Christian shot a look at Alric, to search his face for even a flicker of recognition; but a daze had passed over him.

"Right," he said. "Bannermen! Fan out, using this tree as the center of your efforts!" To his father, he said, "We'll take a couple of wulves. You and I can search for signs of him here, see if he can find where his trail went cold."

"And me." Alric dropped from his mule. "I know this tree well."

Holden grunted into his cloak, but the sound stayed trapped in the dark fur.

"All hands are welcome," Christian said and clapped his uncle on the back.

EMBER FOUND Aylen in the infirmary, a small building to the back of the keep, near the medicinal rows of the Wintergarden. The silver-haired woman was checking inventories of cloths and medicines, scribbling her results in a tattered notebook. Ember liked her already, and this seemed another reason to. There were others who could and should do these things for her, but Aylen would do them, anyway.

"What are you doing?"

Aylen turned. "Oh, Ember. I didn't see you there. It's time someone did an inventory here. I don't think they know *what* they have anymore."

"You'd rather be with Lord Christian."

"I suppose I would, yes. I know he promised you a trip over the pass. You've likely deduced that won't be possible now."

"I no longer need to go over the pass if my mother will be returning here."

Aylen dropped her eyes. "Guardians willing."

"I knew they'd ordered you to stay back with the women, but I thought it was to tend to Ransom," Ember remarked.

Aylen flashed a quick smile as she jotted her note. "Lord Dereham felt he was well enough to travel and more useful there besides."

"What did you feel?"

Aylen set her notebook aside. "Physically, he's well enough now."

"Because you healed him."

"Yes."

"But you cannot heal the mind."

"Healing the mind is beyond the power of any healer." Aylen

dusted her hands on her gown. "Is there something I can help you with, Ember?"

"I hope so." Ember stepped farther into the small room. The sharp scent of tinctures and herbs overwhelmed her senses, but Aylen didn't seem to notice. "My mother isn't dead, Aylen. I know what others think, but I know, just as you knew you could heal Ransom."

Aylen studied her. "You mean you can sense her with magic?"

"All Ravenwoods are connected," Ember said, and though this was supposition, a guess, it felt right and true. "It's how Alasyr knows his sister still lives. Why he won't give up on her, though others have."

"If he knows because of this connection, then so would his parents. But haven't they given up their search for her?"

Ember shook her head. "They know she's alive, and they don't want her back. She's a traitor to them now, and they'd rather she die than return. Alasyr is different. He cares more for his sister than for their traditions, and he'll never give up searching for her."

"Wow. I see." Aylen leaned back into the table. "And for this reason, you believe your mother still lives?"

"I didn't expect you to believe me. Only to help me."

Aylen sighed into a smile. "I never said I didn't believe you, Emberley. Much of mastering magic lies in trusting instinct. There's no place for doubt in magic, only the lingering question of what's yet unknown."

"It's stronger for me now that I'm here," Emberley went on. "It's as if being closer to Midnight Crest, or even other Ravenwoods, intensifies what I had before, makes it bolder, but also more... more volatile. I shouldn't even be telling you this. No one is supposed to know about Blackwood magic, or we'd be executed for practicing it outside the Sepulchre's purview." Ember laughed. "And you, from the Consortium. I must be a fool, but you can see how desperate I am."

"I'm a Magi, not an agent of the law," Aylen said. "Last time we spoke of this, you denied it. Why tell me now?"

Ember fought back the tears. "Something is… changing inside me, and I don't know what to do about it. I have no one to talk to about it. No one to help me understand it."

Aylen nodded. "I saw the mess you left in the forest."

Ember gasped. "You saw that?"

"I suspect many did, but only another magic dealer would have attributed the work to you."

Ember's eyes blurred. How she hated to cry. Her frustration pushed at the back of her eyes, the tips of her fingers, demanding escape. "I didn't mean to do it."

Aylen stepped forward and rested a hand on her arm. "I know. And I know you've come to me for aid, and I'll do what I can to help you, but I'm a healer. I teach young healers. I know next to nothing about the magic inside you, and if it comes from your Ravenwood blood, I know even less. I don't have to tell you their magic is different, or that we've never had a Ravenwood in our halls."

"Magic is magic, right?"

"We've had no opportunity to study the magic of the Ravenwoods, so I cannot say."

"But you *can* help me?"

Aylen tucked a stray hair behind Ember's ear. "I'll do whatever I can, but in return, you must promise me something."

Ember nodded furiously. "Anything."

"Nothing again happens like what happened in the forest," Aylen said. "If you want to try something, to practice, we try together. And for the love of the Guardians, Ember, please don't do anything foolish without consulting with me first."

Ember grinned, heart racing. "I can agree to that."

"We found a sword, sir."

Christian ducked under the branches of the pearapple tree and moved back toward the path. He took the sword from the man and turned it over in his gloved hands, regarding the hilt and guard. "See the etching of the crossed swords, Father? This came from the Rhiagain armory."

Holden took the sword in his own hands. They bowed under the heft. "Would this have come with our friends when they fled Duncarrow?"

"It's possible. I know they had steel with them when they got here, though I never got a close look at it. We only brought them bows, for hunting."

"Too large for a woman's hands."

"That doesn't mean a woman wasn't wielding it," Christian countered. To the man who had recovered it, he asked, "Was there anything else?"

"Remnants of a camp in the cave. Blankets. Clothing. Some provisions. Two bows."

"Signs of trouble? A struggle?"

"It would seem they left in a rush. But I see no other signs beyond the discarded sword and the disturbance in the snow near where we found it."

Christian nodded. "Thank you."

"Have you seen him yet? Your brother?" Holden tapped his head. "You know what I'm asking."

"I haven't had any visions," Christian said. "It doesn't work that way, as I've told you. We get what we need, the elders say, not what we want."

"We must find your brother."

"And we will, Father."

"We cannot return to your mother without her son."

They both turned at the sound of deep, harrowing sobs. Alric knelt at the base of the tree, face flushed dark with emotion, howling his words.

"Why? How? What must we do to understand your desires? What must I give for you to return our Pieter? I have already given you everything!"

Holden closed his eyes and grunted. "Get him out of here."

"The men know to ignore him when he's like this."

"Well, I cannot. Have one of them escort him back to Wulfsgate."

"I FEEL terrible not going with the men to the pass," Marsh moaned. He was splayed in his chair, watching her change to her nightclothes. "I was the only one who stayed behind."

"You could've gone," Ember said. She tossed her filthy clothes in a corner pile. She'd been wearing them nigh a week, and it had been a few days too long, according to the stench wafting off them and her. She sniffed twice, scrunching her nose. Well, Marsh didn't seem to mind, anyway. "No one stopped you from going but you."

"I won't leave you."

Ember scoffed. "Please. It's never been like that with us. Let's not let it become so."

Marsh leaned forward, dropping his feet to the floor. "Like what?"

"You know what I mean."

"Maybe you should tell me, just to be sure."

She didn't want to feel this way about Marsh. Like he was an annoyance, and only in her way. He'd said he loved her, and maybe she loved him, too. She didn't know. She was unclear on how one would even identify such a thing, and for it to happen now, of all times, meant she was even less capable of recognizing it. She had nothing more to give him. Not when her mother was missing, her homeland was in turmoil, and her own internal conflict was raging unabated.

Ember pushed herself to speak calmly, though the urge to take his head off was about as strong as any other urge she had toward him. "I only meant that I don't need protection, not here." She waved her hands around. "Look where we are. I'm safe in Wulfsgate. If you wanted to go, you should have gone."

"You're safe from some things, but not others. What if Alasyr is only waiting for me to leave?"

Ember laughed. "And you think I cannot protect myself from Alasyr Ravenwood? That *you* have more ability to do so?"

March recoiled, wounded. "You think so little of me. I know I wasn't always the strength you needed, on our journey here—"

"It wasn't your *strength* I needed! I had enough of my own, thank you." She could see in his darkening expression these had been the wrong words. Ember knelt before him. "What I needed was your companionship. *You.*"

Marsh looked off to the side. "I know you're tough, Ember, but I'm not nothing."

"Did I say you were nothing?"

"I said that I loved you before. You said nothing then."

Ember dropped back on her heels. "I suppose I assumed you said it in the chaos of the moment. I was upset, you were upset."

Marsh snorted. "I would never say such a thing to you if I didn't mean it."

"Okay."

"Okay?"

"Thank you."

"*Thank you?*"

"What would you like me to say?"

Marsh jumped to his feet. He lifted his hands over his head, winding them through his hair. He regarded her with one purple eye and one green one. "Nothing you don't mean."

"I... uh..." Ember fumbled her words. What could she say? Not the truth. That while perhaps she did love him, her love would have to wait, and no, she couldn't say for how long. She had too much on her mind, in her heart, that took precedence.

He laughed. "Right. Why am I even here? There's a war brewing in the Westerlands, and instead I spend my days and nights pining after you, wishing for... for..."

Ember knew she should say something. Anything! Anything at all, to change how he was feeling, to refute his fears. She reached for him, to touch him, to hold him, a language she understood far better, anyway. "Marsh."

He pulled away. "Don't hurt yourself, Ember. You've told me how you feel, in the absence of what's so hard for you to say."

"I don't know what you want to hear!"

Marsh wrapped his hands around her arms. "I don't want you to tell me what you think I want to hear, Emberley! I want... I want *you.* I want to be at your side, for whatever terror faces us next. I want to be strong for you, even though I know good and well you don't need it and never have." He pressed his forehead to hers. "I want you to let me be there for you as you grieve your father, and worry after your mother."

"I've been... I've had too much on my mind to grieve my father properly," Ember confessed. "If I think on it too long, I'll go mad. I can't talk about it. Not with you. Not with anyone."

Marsh kissed her. "We don't have to talk. I just need to know what you need from me."

Ember dropped her head. "I don't need anything from you. I mean... nothing else."

Marsh lowered his back to the chair, nodding. "Okay, then."

27

THE MIDNIGHT GOAT

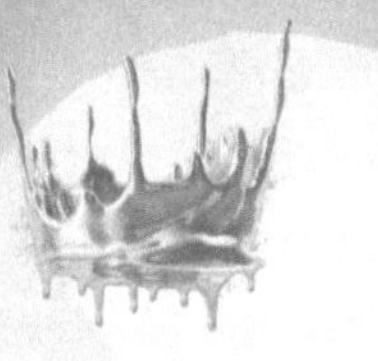

Alasyr heard her call. He'd heard all her calls over the preceding days. Every last tortured one. He didn't even have to be near her to hear them. He suffered the agonizing desperation of Emberley Blackwood all the way from Midnight Crest.

He hadn't left The Rookery, not since the night he witnessed his father, and maybe another, apprehend and abscond with Ember's mother. Asherley Blackwood was locked away in an apartment that had once been reserved for dowager high priestesses, but had, for years, been collecting cobwebs and coldness. The path there had crumbled away, leaving the only means of access a short flight across the gap of broken balustrades.

But he found he couldn't face the half-blood with this knowledge burning inside him. He felt no loyalty toward her, and yet... it was *inexplicable* to him; this sense of betrayal. She was nothing! Nothing to him, nothing to the Ravenwoods. Just a girl, with powers she didn't understand, and not enough wisdom to comprehend her role in the world.

"Have you seen Father?"

Alasyr stiffened. He hadn't even heard Ryandyr come up behind him. He'd grown lax, and there was nothing more dangerous.

"No," he lied. He didn't look back the way he'd come, for fear she'd see the truth in his eyes. Not only was their father harboring an outsider in The Rookery, Alasyr was fairly certain he was the only other one who knew about it. "He may be at the temple."

"I checked there. Mother is looking for him."

"What does Mother want?"

Ryandyr peeked back from under her velvet hood, her face flushed. She was still more child than woman, and he struggled to imagine her being ready for the Langenacht in two short years. She hadn't been as closely watched as Ravenna. Ryandyr had been allowed to play—as much as any Ravenwood not destined for the scepter—and to eat and drink as she pleased. She could wear what she wished, and no one measured her waistline daily. Until now. The sweet childish plumpness in her cheeks had already receded. "I don't know, Alasyr, but she seems cross with him."

Cross? Now, this was intriguing. Did she know? "What did she say?"

"Only to tell her should I find him."

"Nothing else?"

Ryandyr shook her head.

Alasyr leaned in close. "You'll need to learn to read what others would prefer you didn't, if you're to be a successful high priestess."

Ryandyr dropped her gaze. "Yes, brother."

Alasyr reached gently for her chin. He tilted her head back. "You don't answer to me, Ryandyr. Nor anyone. Not even whoever wins your hand at the Langenacht."

Her violet eyes implored him. "Will you cast your lot for me, as you did for Ravenna?"

A wave of bile rose to the back of his throat, unwelcome. He didn't answer; he turned and left her standing there, burning holes in his back with her confusion, and when he was halfway down the corridor, he turned his pace to a sprint.

Asherley didn't turn toward the light click of the door closing. She had no energy for conversation with Argentyn, especially not the riddle-filled kind he favored when he visited. He'd ripped the last thread of her strength from her with the revelation about Byrne, and since that day, she'd failed to weave it back to life.

She didn't understand what was happening to her. She hadn't even mourned her beloved Hollyn to this depth. Her children were everything to her, and Byrne was... he was...

He was just a man, she tried, and failed, to tell herself. Asherley had attempted over the years to cull any excess pride she possessed, for she knew it would eventually be her undoing, but she couldn't ever let go of how swollen with purpose she felt at never having needed a man. She loved her husband, she told herself, but that was a choice. It was not the same as needing him.

Oh, what a lie that had been. There was more than one kind of need. More than one way to complete a life together.

Though she spun her grief to rage, it was a powerless fury. She could imagine her hands at the throat of Aiden Quinlanden, but she could not actualize it, not from here. Not when Argentyn Ravenwood had taken that from her.

"Your meals have been satisfactory?" he asked, and she nearly laughed. Her meals! Was he truly asking her this?

"Your plants are tasteless. It's as if your cook is affronted by the very idea of seasoning."

"We eat only what we can produce. We rely on none but ourselves."

Asherley did laugh at this. "No? Is that why you hide up here, under the protection of the Northerland lord?"

"The arrangement is mutually beneficial. We have provided

much in return. Lord Dereham's own wife would not be alive to see these times, if not for Ravenna's skill and aid."

Asherley sat up in her bed. "And how proud you are of Ravenna! Your shining jewel. Your beloved heir, symbol of hope and prosperity. Your... oh, yes. Forgive me. She's in exile now."

"A path she chose."

Asherley shrugged. "If given the choice between an orgiastic act of sexual slavery with my closest known relatives and a life of freedom, I would've chosen the same."

Argentyn scoffed. He folded his hands over his velvet robe. "And you wonder why we don't welcome outsiders to our world. They understand nothing about our way of life. That, too, is a choice."

"You revile choices that don't align with yours, while pretending that leaves a choice at all."

"Your attempt to simplify what is not simple at all is a function of man, one we have no use for here," Argentyn countered. "We grieve for Ravenna. Not only for what she has left behind, but what she runs toward. She doesn't know the danger she's in. That all who bear Ravenwood blood are in."

Asherley stood. She enjoyed his mingled look of fear and disgust as she stepped toward him. "My kin and I have borne Ravenwood blood for generations, living far from Midnight Crest. We have thrived with it. Whatever danger you've envisioned, it doesn't exist."

"It *didn't* exist," he corrected her. "It does now. The sorcerers are awakening. As was foretold."

"What sorcerers?" she asked, willing her face to stay her thoughts from surfacing. This was the second time someone had mentioned the sorcerers to her, and as a threat.

"The ones you call the Rhiagain sorcerers. But they aren't Rhiagains. And where they come from, they have never served a Rhiagain."

"Are you going to tell me, or leave me here to enjoy more of your tasteless stews for days?"

Argentyn leaned into the table behind him. He no longer wore the self-satisfied look of the one wielding the whole of the room's power, but instead looked troubled. He seemed weighted with something. Asherley didn't know if she wanted this burden, but she had nothing else to look forward to in this colorless, lifeless room, and perhaps not beyond it, either. Of all the things she had learned in life, knowing the value of living in the moment, of embracing what was given, even if not what was wanted, had served her the best.

"Argentyn," she pressed. "I can do nothing from here, anyway. I'm at your mercy. Why not put me to use and unburden yourself, as you so clearly want to?"

"You're right, you can do nothing."

"You are here for a reason. And I'm here for a reason, even if you refuse to share it."

"Varinya doesn't even believe the tales passed down. Why would a half-blood?"

"I have no reason to believe or to doubt, beyond the words you choose to share. I have none of your history, your perceived truths."

Argentyn turned his head to the side with a light scoff. "You're right. You have none."

"Why am I here?"

"For your safety."

"Safety from what?"

"How little you know."

"*Tell me!*" she yelled. The sound startled them both.

"There are no written records among the Ravenwoods," Argentyn said slowly. "Only what is passed through oral tradition. The chosen women are given visions of the past, while the men receive these tales by moonlight from other men who have been relegated to the fate prescribed us. We are there to aid our High Priestess, to see her purpose fulfilled. Never to rule her, no matter how foolish her choices."

"And you believe your wife to be foolish?"

Argentyn balked. "There is nothing foolish about the High Priestess. Even if she does not share my concerns."

"Maybe she didn't see it after all," Asherley replied with a light shrug. "This vision."

Argentyn's mouth parted, a tiny rage building behind his eyes. "You dare say such a thing. You dare defile the High Priestess of Midnight Crest with this blasphemy."

Asherley wanted to roll her eyes. Thought better of it. "Go on, then."

"Do you know where we come from? The Ravenwoods?"

"Beyond, like the Rhiagains. So they say."

"Beyond. Yes. Though only the women who have experienced their vision know what Beyond means to us. The men... we rely on the distorted tales passed through one another. What we know lacks the clarity of what the women have *seen*. Do you understand? The High Priestesses, current and former, are the only ones who have ever seen our past. And so they are the only ones in possession of its truest form."

"Why does the past matter to you so much?"

"The past dictates the present. Without the past, Ravenna, all of us, would not be in peril. This Beyond you speak of has no name for me, like it does for the chosen women. But it was there that the Ravenwoods came to life. There that the Rhiagains came to life. And there that the great sorcerers, too, came to life."

Asherley had been wearing a mocking grin for most of this exchange, but it faded now. What Argentyn had just told her was the first thing that built upon her knowledge, rather than confusing it. "You all come from the same place?"

He nodded. "A place where Ravenwood and sorcerer were

equals, and Rhiagain... ahh, they were no kings there. It was the Rhiagains who served *us,* the wielders of magic. They were nothing if we did not say they were."

"They don't serve you here," Asherley countered. "It is the Rhiagains who rule, and the Ravenwoods who cower in the shadows."

"Yes," he agreed. "But not for much longer. The sorcerers are awakening, and once they do, nothing will ever be the same again."

"Why? Because they want to kill you?"

"They cannot kill us, as they cannot kill a Rhiagain. As we cannot kill them, either." Argentyn's head cocked to the side. He closed his eyes. "Varinya calls for me. I must go. She cannot find me here."

Asherley snaked her hand out and grabbed his arm. "You can't leave it like this. We're not finished."

Argentyn wrenched his arm away. "I've already given you more than you deserve." His eyes passed around the room, landed on her once more, and then he spun and left.

ALASYR CAME to a stop under the silver arches of the Courtyard of Regents. A heavy relief settled over him as he saw he was the only one there. He shouldn't step another foot forward. It would be blasphemy. The Courtyard of Regents was for the present and dowager High Priestesses alone, and their husbands, should they allow them. He was only an eldest son, which meant nothing at all in the world of the Ravenwoods.

There was no reason not to turn back. If he wanted to be alone with his thoughts, there were many such places in The Rookery, none of which would bring upon him the punishment this place would if discovered. But as he was pulled back the way he came, his eyes landed upon the silvery trees swaying in the east wind, the midnight goats milling about the dewy grass, born of magic alone, this high in the mountains.

Alasyr took one step forward. Now, he'd broken the rule; the punishment, for which, was unknown to him, as most Ravenwoods were ardent disciples of law.

He took another step. His heart soared, leaping into the back of his throat, but he took another. He'd never violated any rules before. Never wanted to. He'd tried to sneak Ravenna food when her parents were starving her to bring her down to her proper size, but he didn't quite think that was the same. It was not the type of thing considered in the spirit of the laws crafted, which were designed for uniformity and conformity, in a world that would collapse without either.

Alasyr moved inward toward the center of the great circle. He'd been here as a very small boy, with his mother, before he could walk far. Once he could cross the circle on his own without tottering over, his mother stopped bringing him.

Icy rain peppered the surrounding ground. He stepped under one of the silvery oaks, watching from safety. There was nowhere else in The Rookery more exposed, but the tall wooden chairs where the women sat were out in the open of the circle. There was a lesson here, he thought.

Several goats pressed past him, moving swiftly to join other goats who were circling something at the edge of the circle. Alasyr followed with curiosity, and as he stepped closer to where the goats all settled, restless, he saw one of them lying on its side, in a pool of blood.

Alasyr gasped. He couldn't help it. The vibrant crimson was a shocking mark against this carefully curated world of silver and white. What had caused this?

He'd so loved the midnight goats as a boy. He pouted when he could no longer go to the courtyard to see them, but his mother couldn't be swayed. *The courtyard isn't for you, Alasyr. Not yet. One day, if you join your sister, or even her daughter, you'll see them again, should their kindness allow it.*

But these goats will be dead, Mother. They will be new goats.

The midnight goats are immortal, darling. These same goats you so love now will await you when your time again comes.

The caw of mountain vultures sounded above. They swirled to and fro, awaiting their moment.

A terrible sadness gripped Alasyr suddenly. The dying goat blinked, regarding him through bleary eyes as its life waned away. The other midnight goats bleated, rolling their silver fur toward the sky to sing their song of grief.

He looked behind him, toward the arches, once more. No one but Alasyr, and the melancholy goats preparing for their funereal moment.

Tears rolled down his cheeks and dropped to the icy marble beneath him. Rain joined them, blending his sorrow with nature. As the frozen rain picked up in intensity, some of the dying goat's blood washed away, inward, where it would seep into the ground and provide sustenance for incoming life, a gift from the outgoing.

None of it felt right. Not the dying goat, or those mourning him before he was gone. Not this courtyard, this castle, this world, this life.

The last of the life drained away from the goat. The air around him filled with the grieving cries of those who were left.

Alasyr wrenched his mouth wide and released a silent scream that rolled from the depths of his belly. As it pulsed forward, away from him, he fell to his knees at the side of the goat and hovered his trembling hands just above the mangled fur.

"This should not be how it ends for you, immortal friend," Alasyr sobbed. A great white light traveled from his hands, one he'd never seen before. He nearly fell back at the shock of seeing it, but just as swiftly was overcome with the realization that though this was new, it was not to be feared. Alasyr trembled with this new power, smiling through his tears now, and with delight he watched as the wound at the goat's side closed. The goat's blank eyes again surged with life, white turning to a brilliant blue, as if a cloud passing away to reveal the sun. A knowing bleat passed among the other goats, and he felt small mouths nestle into him from behind, the sides, as they all gathered around him in gratitude for what he had done.

And what had he done?

He had raised the dead to life. A magic that was believed to be no longer.

Alasyr fell back on his palms, breathless.

28

A DECLARATION OF WAR

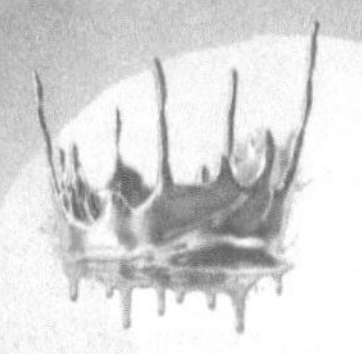

The howl that came from young Storm Wakesell when she learned of her father's murder was the worst sound Jesse had ever heard.

The news arrived courtesy of a man named Stirling Oakenwell, one of Quinlanden's top men and the steward of Oak Hill. Lord Warwick had a sword at the man's throat before he could even cross the town boundary, but Brandyn was just as quick, stepping alongside the flash of steel between the men to remind them who was at the helm.

An eye for an eye, young Lord Blackwood. This man is complicit in your father's murder!

He wouldn't be here, alone, if that were so.

Jesse thought if Brandyn were anyone but Byrne's only son, Khallum would have taken over by now; perhaps had the boy under strict counsel until he was older. But those who had known Byrne would see him in his son's eyes. He was more Warwick than Blackwood, at least to look upon him. Jesse hadn't met the boy's mother, but from all he'd heard, she was the one quick to temper, and probably better matched to Khallum than Byrne.

From Oakenwell, they learned that Quinlanden had sent word to both Oakenwell and Waters to stand down in their sacking of the Westerlands. Neither man believed the words had come from Quinlanden, but if they hadn't come from him, then they'd come from the king himself, which was baffling and curious all at once. While Oakenwell rode from town to town to carry out the orders, Mads defied them, crafting his own instead, ramping up the attacks on Westerland villages and towns in frequency and cruelty.

Starting with Whitewood.

"Mads' men have razed it, killing any man whether fighting or fleeing. Burning homes, with women and children inside," Oakenwell said. His cheeks flushed with the burden of the hard ride he'd taken to reach them, and the horrors he'd left behind in Whitewood. "He chose to start there because—"

"The Seven Sisters isolates them from the rest of the Reach, preventing quick aid," Brandyn finished for him. He closed his eyes.

"And my father?" Storm raced forward, grabbing the man by the arm. "My mother?"

"You're the Wakesell girl?"

"Steward Wakesell is my father. Tell me!"

Oakenwell dropped his eyes. He couldn't make himself look at her. "Your father was murdered. Your mother... I cannot say. If the Guardians possess mercy, she made it away, with the few others who fled."

Storm dropped to her knees and sounded a keening cry into the dim tavern walls. Brandyn went to her side and held her close to him as he looked over her shoulder at the men who watched him, hovered in quiet desperation as they awaited their lord's response to these atrocities.

"Steward Oakenwell, we thank you for this news, however hard it was to hear. We appreciate the risk you have taken in coming to us. That there has been a split amongst Quinlanden's men helps us. We can use this to our advantage."

"This is a declaration of war!" Khallum boomed. His energy had escalated now to a place where it consumed everyone around it. As he moved about the room, those left in his whirling wake were stirred to his same passion, rallying around it. "I donnae care if the words are from the bootlicker or the ratsbane, or who defied them and who followed them! Do any of you?"

Storm jumped to her feet. As she wiped the last of her tears away, she seemed to shrug off the weight of her grief with it, like a second skin, becoming again a warrior. "I don't! Politics didn't kill my father, and they'll not save other fathers!"

"It's time, Lord Blackwood," Easlan said. He was less animated than the other men now, and the seriousness in his eyes seemed to give Brandyn pause. "We've waited long enough for the moment to arrive. It is here."

"Here? Aye, we've missed the moment and now we're chasing it!" Rutland boomed.

Brandyn nodded. Jesse could feel the boy's conflict from across the tavern. He knew what he needed to do, but feared he would not know how.

Even Jesse understood the need for the Westerlands to go to war now, but he would not be joining them.

Brandyn looked upon the small group of men gathered. Not a boy, but a man. His voice shook, but he did not. "The Westerlands will no longer abide the Quinlanden treason on our lands. We will answer it, swift and decisive. We will spare none, for they have not and would not spare us. And when we are finished with them, if there are any left, they will look upon the last day of this war as the day their world ended."

Though there were few men gathered, the cheers were deafening. This was what they'd wanted to hear from him all along. He would be judged later, when his story was read in *The Book of All*

Things, for waiting until another great man of his realm had been executed, but these men would follow him to whatever end, no matter what.

"Will you join us, Steward Oakenwell? Will you be able to leave behind your service of the Easterlands? To be branded a betrayer?"

Oakenwell knelt before Brandyn. He held his sword aloft. "I have served my Reach since I was a boy, and my fathers before me have served, with unyielding fealty, a Reach that doesn't belong to one man, but all men. I betray no one. To do nothing is the betrayal. To allow Quinlanden to do what he has done harms all in the land he claims to love. So yes, Lord Blackwood, I will join you so that order can be restored to both the Westerlands *and* the Easterlands, where so many watch and wait for the same end as you."

Brandyn nodded. "I think we understand one another. We will harm no one that does not stand against us. You have my word."

"Those who donnae stand with you *are* against you, Lord Blackwood," Khallum countered.

"I won't harm those who cower in their homes, fearing the wrath of both Reaches. None of them asked for this," Brandyn replied. "Uncle, have we still your men?"

"Aye, you've had my men. They thirst for direction. What shall I give them?"

"Send half to Longwood Rush, to force the red and gold from our city. If Longwood prevails, the Reach will not fall."

"And the rest?"

"They will meet us in Whitechurch, where this war will be ended."

"Us?" Khallum turned to his men, then back to Brandyn, but his nephew had already moved on.

"Blackfen, I have need of your riding skills. I need you to guide the men who have come to us here in Greystone from across the Reach. Prepare them for swift and hard rides home."

Blackfen nodded. "The Rush Riders, too, are ready for aim, my lord."

"When they reach their homes, they'll do so carrying an important message. The men of the Westerlands must know it is time to rise, to whatever end, and that they have their lord and lords of other Reaches ready to rise with them. It will be upon them to defend the Westerlands while we keep more war from their doorsteps. Send these men as swiftly as you can to cover as many towns and villages as possible. Assure them that the flags of Longwood Rush will fly again once more, and that they are to stand proud for the Westerlands, for the kingdom stands with them. Tell *no one* where the rest of us are going. Our enemies will know soon enough, but we need to prolong that for as long as we can. If we lose our surprise, the enslaved Medvedev will outnumber us, and we'll be walking into certain death. It will be a rout." Brandyn paused. "I would like for you to deliver a message to Wulfsgate personally. To Lord and Lady Dereham."

"What shall I tell them, Lord Blackwood?"

"Tell them the Southerlands have joined us in retaking our land, and we call for their aid. Before you leave, we will have our strategy decided, which you will take to them. They will require it in exchange for their men. It's what they've required from us all along." Brandyn lowered his voice. "I also ask you to order my sister to remain in Wulfsgate, where she's safe. For if..." Brandyn didn't finish.

"I understand. I expect she'll fight your order."

"Yes. But in the end, she'll comply. She gave up everything when my mother asked her to. This isn't so hard in comparison."

Blackfen nodded.

"Lord Warwick, will you join me at the war board for strategy? For the rest of you," Brandyn went on, solemn in word and expression, "eat and drink well this afternoon, for tonight we ride."

• • •

JESSE HAD JUST MOUNTED his horse when Brandyn stopped him. Darrick was with him.

"Your Grace. Lord Blackwood." Jesse turned his horse to face them. He looked at the prince. "I didnae see you in the room when Lord Blackwood stirred the men to war."

Darrick shook his head. "I needed a moment alone with my thoughts."

"Aye. I see. Well, I willnae be joining you men on your ride to war. If you're still engaged in this when I've done what I need to do, I'll come back and give what aid I can."

"I've appreciated your counsel," Brandyn said. "You're not like the other men in there."

Jesse laughed. "I'm nay sure you mean that as a compliment."

"I do," Brandyn insisted. "They are either lusted for blood, or incapable of seeing the full view of what awaits us. And as I lack the experience needed to address either argument, your perspective has been an aid to me."

"I cannae claim to see the future either, Lord Blackwood, but that is why I have advised caution. Your most beloved resources are your land and those who live upon it, and war protects neither. Yet I would ride with you, at your side, if I didnae have my own responsibility to tend to."

"I understand. My cousin is fortunate to have you."

"Your cousin?" Darrick repeated.

Jesse turned to look at him. "When you came to me about Ryan. What you said about Esmerelda. You know, then, that she..."

Darrick answered with a solemn nod. "He told me your plan to take her to your mother's people. It's not my business how you ended up here, after."

"We weren't welcomed there. I suspect they're vigilant against outsiders because of Quinlanden's treachery. So we came here."

Darrick looked past him, toward the woods that led to the keep. "She's here, then?"

"Easlan offered us use of his keep. I thought she could be safe here, but there isnae safety in hiding, no matter the stones above and around you, is there? Then the men began arriving, and... it doesnae matter. There's no safety in hiding. Esmerelda realized this before I did. If I can get her to his side, he'll wake. I know it."

"I feel the same," Darrick said. "The memory of her kept him going, day after day. She kept him alive, against the crushing defeat the Wastelands settles over all men who are sent there. You'll tell her, won't you?"

"Aye, I will." Jesse reached forward. He laid a hand, briefly, on the prince's forearm. "Ryan knew what awaited him here. But he also knew what awaited him in there. He was proud to serve his lord, and you."

Darrick met his eyes. "Ryan Strong is the truest friend I've ever known. And now, I'm honored to call his brother friend, as well."

AFTER JESSE HAD RIDDEN AWAY, Brandyn looked at Darrick. "I saw myself."

"Another vision?"

"I was face to face with the sorcerer. Though I've... I don't know him, I knew it was him. I knew it, same as I know you and I are here, having this talk."

"What else did you see?"

Brandyn dropped his eyes. "Nothing. But I know that's where I'm to end up when we arrive in Whitechurch."

"To confront him."

"I believe so, yes."

"Then I will aid you."

"I wouldn't ask that of you. I only wanted you to know, because you're... you're the king, or should be."

Darrick chuckled. "If I'm ever going to be king, then I will not be one who hides in their keep on an island while others do what they will not. Oakenwell will tell us where to find him, and how to get him alone."

"You believe him, then? Oakenwell?"

"He isn't the only one in horror of the choices their lord has made on their behalf. He came here to aid us against his own men not because he's a traitor, but because a traitor has ordered them to do things that go against their conscience."

"We must free the Saleen, Your Grace."

"Yes."

Brandyn didn't voice aloud his secret hope; that if they were met with victory, and the Saleen were again free, perhaps he could convince the Medvedev who held Gabrianna and Meadow prisoner to release them.

"We have no choice? But to go after Mortain?"

Darrick nodded. "If we don't, then our ride on Whitechurch will be futile, for Mortain will finally send his Medvedev slaves to battle. We can probably defend ourselves against the meager Quinlanden Guard remaining in Whitechurch, but not against the numbers he's rumored to have amassed with the Saleen."

"I don't understand," Brandyn said. "Something has been bothering me since I learned what they did to the Medvedev."

"What is it?"

"Why enslave them only for them to sit idle in the forest? Why has he not deployed them yet?"

Darrick sighed. "And this, Brandyn, is the question that stands between me and restful nights."

JESSE DROPPED his sword belt on the chair. He didn't bother hanging it. A strange thrill passed through him as he hurried through the house, searching for Esmerelda. It was, he thought, a ripple of purpose, such as he'd only believed he'd known before now. Ryan was alive. He was free. Esmerelda was carrying his child, and they deserved to be a family, just as they'd wanted. As they'd endured all of this for.

Jesse was the one who could link these worlds.

He flew up the stairs, calling her name. "Esmerelda!" Breathless, he ducked into her room. She wasn't there, and her bed was made. This was curious, as she rarely bothered to make it anymore with how often she was bedridden. He started to leave, to search the next one, but his eyes locked on how orderly everything was. Her clothing was no longer laid out on the bench in the corner. The tables were clear of her hairpins and other things Jesse had teased her about not needing.

"Esmerelda?" he called out the door. He leaned over the railing, eyes scanning the lower floor. The situation was the same. It no longer had the lived-in feel he'd come to find welcoming when returning each evening from the Mule. The floors were pristine, the furniture smooth and ready for new tenants. Even the coals had been removed from the fire, and the hearth dusted.

"Ravenna?" Jesse forced himself farther down the hall, where he found Ravenna's room had also been stripped of the signs of recent life. Her satchel, too, was missing.

"Guardians," he whispered, moving to his own room, which was untouched from how he'd left it. The only living space that betrayed anyone had been here recently at all. He sank down on his bed, bowing over, thinking. So they'd left. But why? And to where? It made no sense that they'd gone anywhere together, given the animosity between them. Yet they were both gone.

Esmerelda had decided to return to Ryan on her own. The idea came upon him suddenly, and once it did, it seemed obvious. But he'd promised her he would take her, so why go without him? Why, when she knew the path would be dangerous and was afraid to be alone? Had Ravenna promised her protection that Esmerelda didn't believe she could get from him?

Jesse quickly gathered his own things. He didn't have time for the extra touches the women had taken to tidy the space, but Easlan would have to forgive him. If he moved swiftly enough, he would catch up to them within a day. They couldn't be far ahead. He'd seen them here just that morning. Their trail would still be warm enough to follow.

He secured his bag to the saddle. It was then he noticed two of the horses were gone, something he hadn't seen when he'd arrived home. He wondered how many other signs he'd missed over the preceding days. Signs that could've helped him to see this coming and prevent it.

Jesse rode swiftly into town. He couldn't leave without telling Easlan why they'd disappeared in such a rush. But as he neared the Mule, the rush of frenzied energy from all the men gathering, saddling horses, checking steel, overwhelmed his senses. Horses neighing, leather buckled and strapped, skins being refilled and ales emptied. The men were abuzz, come to life with the promise of war, and the uncertain temptation of victory. Their blood was hot now, but they didn't think of how quickly it could cool. They thought only of fulfilling within them that pull that was both sacred and innate; a man's right to defend what is his, against any foe, against any odds.

"Jesse." Rutland rode forward and nodded at him. "Where's your armor?"

"I'm not joining you."

"No? Your father is. Lord Warwick has already sent the scout. Steward Strong will lead the army that'll ride north into Whitechurch."

"So Lord Warwick isnae gonna fight him on it, then?"

Rutland shrugged. He looked back toward the whooping and hollering men. "I suppose he sees some wisdom in the boy's way. The Warwick Guard is strong. It will draw Quinlanden's men back to the Easterlands when they see they've left their own land open for the taking, and will allow us a proper defense should the sorcerer deploy the Medvedev. Nye and Bradford will have their own men coming up from the south through Greystone to aid in dispersing the red and gold from the Westerland cities and villages. If the Northerlands answer our call, they'll be spread along the border to decide things before the red and gold can reach either side."

Jesse nodded. "A fair plan, from the sounds of it. I'll join you, when I can. I have something I must attend to first."

Rutland's face creased with suspicion. "Something more important than a war for the future of the realm?"

"I... I can't explain it right now." Jesse tugged on the reins and spurred his mare back to action. "Please, tell Easlan! I'll come back when I can!"

Jesse pressed his horse into a gallop and rode away from the Rutland and the Long-Trodden Mule.

29
DAIN

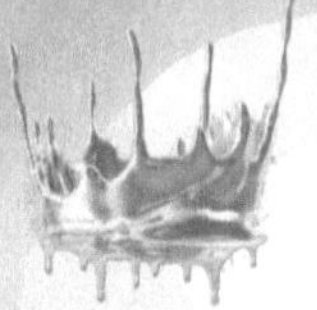

"Lisbet, we must find calm in order to find answers. I'm sure there's a rational reason for all this," Eavan said, using the same obnoxiously soothing tone Lisbet's mother employed when everything was wrong and she wasn't ready for her children to know it.

"Drystan and Valen are *gone*. We have already searched the entire boundary of our prison. They're not here. Days they've been missing, days we've been searching. They couldn't have gone far, as we're still *prisoners*. So where are they?"

Eavan dropped onto the fur-covered cot. "I don't know. But your insinuation that Kian or Yseult would hurt them is unfounded. They would never do such a thing. Never."

Lisbet snickered. "It would not be the first time you underestimated your so-called friends."

Tears glistened in Eavan's eyes. "They *were* my friends. And I curse my father for taking that, too, from me."

Lisbet softened. "Things have changed. Yes, you can thank your father for them changing, but that doesn't mean they haven't changed." She pointed toward the flap in their tent. "You understand that, don't you? That they've probably taken my brother and Valen? Kian *knew* Drystan would be gone, and he was. He knew that because they've taken him."

Eavan gazed down at the hands in her lap and nodded. "Much *has* changed. Including something I haven't had the heart to tell you."

Lisbet softly sighed and joined her on the cot. She gathered her cousin in her arms and pulled her close. "I already know, Eavan. I didn't want to make you speak of it if you weren't ready."

Eavan's hair shook as she buried her head further into Lisbet's shoulder. "I'm not ready now."

"Okay." Lisbet kissed her forehead, brushing blond hairs aside. "When you are, we'll talk about what needs to be done."

Eavan looked up. "What needs to be done?"

"I see no men here to tell us. So it will be you who decides, as it should be." Lisbet unwrapped herself from Eavan and stood. "Kian has ignored me for days, but he needs something from me. He and his mother both do. He'll come for me again, and when he does, I intend to find out what they've done with Drystan and Valen, or die for the effort. But I will not return here without answers."

"What can I do?"

"Keep Meadow and Gabi calm about this. I can't bear their tears and fear right now, and neither can you. Maintain the lie, for as long as we can. They've gone on an extended hunt. That's all."

Eavan wiped at her eyes, nodding. "I don't know what I'd do without you here. You're so strong, Lisbet. In ways I could never be."

Lisbet softly smiled. "Nonsense. We are all given the strength we need, when we need it. You're sitting here because you found yours when something unspeakable was happening to you. And when your days are dark, Eavan, you only need say so because I'll remind you of this truth until my breath runs out."

. . .

THEIR STEPS WERE SLOW. Drystan knew their pace would not be what it was before they arrived in the Hinterlands, without their horses to carry them, but now he endured the grueling desperation of knowing he should be farther along than he was. They hadn't crossed into the Easterlands and he was afraid to ask Valen how long before they would, because the answer might dishearten him. He could abide nothing to dissuade him from the stirring in his heart that prompted him onto this path.

Ash incessantly cast anxious glances over his shoulder, or to the left and right of them, eyes darting in search of any number of unseen dangers. He didn't believe Drystan, not all the way. Not yet. He still expected the Medvedev to come accost them and return them to the invisible prison in the Drumain lands.

But though he'd had no one to tell him this, he instinctively knew they were past Drumain lands now, and into Saleen. A pall of sadness hit him when they'd crossed the unseen barrier. At first, he'd worked to shrug it off, for he could have nothing holding him back. Then he remembered it was the Saleen he was doing this for. The Saleen and all Medvedev who wished to live in peace. Once he embraced this, he was further emboldened with each lift of his worn boots, and his journey became at least somewhat easier to bear.

"Do you have a plan?" Ash asked. His eyes still darted out into the forest, waiting for something to stop them. "For when we get there?"

"I'll get Mortain alone and kill him."

Ash wanted to laugh. Drystan felt it. "You make that sound as if it will be easy."

"I don't expect it to be easy. I expect you to help me navigate Whitechurch so I can craft a plan to get him alone."

"Even if you do, Mortain is more powerful than anyone you've ever encountered before. You cannot simply poke him with the sharp end of your sword."

"Are you mocking me?"

"No, Drystan, I—"

"You are," Drystan said, quickening his pace. "And if you are my father, as you say, then your ever changing behavior toward me is all the more confusing."

"What do you mean by that?"

Drystan laughed. His breath unfurled in small clouds before him as he huffed. The weather had grown colder as they neared the coast. "One moment you're teaching me, nurturing me. The next, you treat me no better than you would an annoyance. A flea, landing upon your arm, lacking the intelligence to know you'll take its life in the next moment."

"I don't think of you that way at all. I do think your mother would have my head if I let you walk into Whitechurch without knowing precisely what you're going to do when you get there." Ash stopped moving. "There's something else I wanted to tell you. It didn't seem important before, and perhaps it isn't now, but as you already think I keep things from you, I won't keep this."

Drystan halted without turning. He closed his eyes, sighing inwardly. "Another secret, then."

"It's not a secret, though few know of it."

"Then say it, so we can get on with things."

"I'm a Sylvaine only in name," Valen said. He stepped closer, so he was now beside Drystan. He looked at him. "Steward Sylvaine and his wife took me in, when I was very young. I remember nothing before them, and I've never met my birth family. They were probably indigents, without a coin to their name and not a lick of means to rear a child. Children are born all over this kingdom who are unwanted or to parents who can't care for them every day. I only know Stewardess Sylvaine was barren, and my father came home one day with me. When I was older, they told me the truth, for they both were darker featured, and I, with my reddish hair, was a clear standout. But they loved me as their own, and I was happy in their home, as their only son. I would have contentedly taken my father's place, as the Steward of Rushwood, had circumstances not drawn me down another path."

"Why did you think I should know this?"

"It's your truth, too. You deserve to know it."

"Fine. I know it, now. Can we continue?"

Ash looked sad as he pointed his hand forward. "After you, Drystan."

"Have you considered what you saw in here?"

Lisbet jumped off the small altar. She enjoyed Kian's confused recoil as she approached him on his mother's throne. She'd waited for him to settle into their routine. If she'd confronted him in the forest, he would've had more of his defenses ready, or sent her back to wait even longer.

"It's my turn for answers, Kian."

"So you have seen more?"

"I don't care about the magic right now! I want to know where my brother is. I want to know what you've done with him!"

Kian cast a nervous glance at the door. "Ah, this is too soon. You were meant to see this, not be told."

"See what exactly?"

"The truth."

Lisbet snickered. "You and the truth aren't well acquainted."

"It is not for someone to hold or release the truth of another. The truth of an individual must be found within themselves."

"Mother's blood! Do you know how that sounds? No one would ever know a thing if you were king of this world. Now, tell me where Drystan is!"

Kian bowed his head into his hands. "You were supposed to see it. I do not know why you haven't yet. Perhaps your worry has clouded your awakening? I cannot say. But now that Drystan has departed us—"

"Departed? What does that mean?"

"He is gone. Not here. And the time is now. On that, Mother was clear."

"Time for what?"

"For you to leave." Kian looked up. "Sit. I shall tell you, though it is not the way. Not our way."

Lisbet had another bitter remark loaded, but what she wanted more than to sting him was for him to tell her about Drystan. Had she heard him right, that he wanted her to leave? It was almost funny, a gaoler telling a prisoner to leave, but nothing about what was happening—that terrible, sad look in Kian's eyes, what appeared to be genuine pain at what was coming—seemed worthy of laughter.

"I'm listening," she said through clenched teeth.

"Your brother left for Whitechurch. Ash joined him. They intend to take the life of Mortain, the sorcerer. We allowed them to leave. For this was why they had come, even if they didn't know it when they arrived."

Lisbet gaped at him. "They *what*?"

"Your brother and Ash are awakening, as you are. And you are not the only ones. Drystan's awakening will take him to Whitechurch, where he will attempt what I have already told you. Either way, he will die. If he is given his truth, the truth of who he truly is, this distraction will lead him to failure. If he dies in ignorance of this truth, he will succeed."

Lisbet's breath caught high in her throat, so high she almost choked on it. "No. I don't believe you. Drystan could never hurt anyone, not even a man of great evil like Mortain. He would..." Her breath released and now she struggled to return it. "He can't *die*. He's not even a man yet. And what do you mean, who he really is?"

"Your brother kept a secret from you," Kian said coolly. "When you were first taken by my mother's guards, Valen revealed to Drystan that he was his blood father. Not Holden Dereham. That Valen's true name was Drystan Sylvaine, known as Ash by most, and also now by you, and that he had loved your mother against nature and law, and Drystan resulted from this forbidden love."

Lisbet couldn't help but laugh. "That's mad. My mother wouldn't have done that to my father."

"Drystan was still a babe when Ash pretended to take her herbs and die upon her floor. Except he did not die. Only to her was he dead."

Lisbet gasped. "The blacksmith's apprentice who died in her chambers?"

"Yes."

"What a load of wulf shit! My mother didn't even know that man!"

"You can flail in your acceptance of it, but Drystan is Ash's son. Drystan himself has already accepted his truth. If not on the surface, then deep down, where the truths of all of us live. But what Ash did not tell him, for he could not, was the deeper truth of who both men are. Ash is not a Sylvaine. He was ripped from another childhood and placed with the steward and his wife, where he grew in ignorance."

"It doesn't surprise me that the man is a nobody."

"Ash Sylvaine is Dain Rhiagain."

Lisbet paled. She felt, even, the blood leave her lips as she attempted to speak. "Dain Rhiagain is dead. He died as a boy. Everyone knows this."

"Khain ordered his son's death, but words were not enough to compel a man to commit such an act, even from a king. Dain was quietly placed with the Sylvaines, who were not told what child they were taking. The lie nearly died with the king's chancellor. He at last confessed it, on his deathbed, and that truth was carried first to Khain, and then to Eoghan. Khain may be dead, but Eoghan is not, and he knows Dain is alive. His very survival threatens Eoghan's."

Lisbet fought back a wave of stinging tears.

"But Khain was also not Dain's father. It was a sorcerer, Isdemus, who spelled Khain's wife and saw that it was his seed that proved strongest when it came time for her womb to quicken. Ash is the son of a creature capable of magic greater than any in this kingdom, and also the son of a Rhiagain, through his mother. He and his three children are in grave danger. If this kingdom stands, it will be because the four of them prevailed in their destiny. If it falls, it will be because they could not."

Lisbet could make sense of this later. For now, she needed her questions answered, before Kian decided he was no longer keen to do so. "But Valen... Ash... Dain..." She shook her head in frustration. "Ash. Who are his other two children?"

"I will tell you the identity of one of them."

"All right, then."

Kian nodded. "You, Lisbet. You are his daughter."

"No." Lisbet shook her head, setting her mouth in a firm, hard line. "No. I am my *father's* daughter. I look just like him."

"I do not think even Ash knows it," Kian went on, ignoring her protests. "Or your mother, for it happened years after his 'death,' when he came to her as if a ghost, though very real."

"No!"

"And now, you are free to leave." Kian stood.

"I'm not leaving here until I understand why you would say such things!"

"You have the choice where you go. You could even choose to follow Drystan and tell him what I have told you," Kian said. "But know that if you do, he will fail, and he will still die. You cannot save him. He will die no matter what choices you or he make from here on. Some things cannot be changed."

"You have just told me Drystan is a *Rhiagain,* a Rhiagain! And the true heir to this throne!"

"Yes."

"And that... that... I'm a Rhiagain as well? That we both share the blood of our enemy? No. No."

"Yes, Lisbet."

"They would've married me to my uncle!"

"They did not know."

"It cannot be true. It cannot. Why, why would you lie to me? Tell me such things, and then tell me... tell me that my beloved Drystan will *die* and that I should do nothing? Just let it happen?"

"You were intended to see this for yourself." Kian sighed, lowering his head. "Your belief of it would have come much easier."

Tears poured down her face unabated. "If what you say is true, I have to see him! I never even had the chance to say goodbye, and you tell me I'll never see him again? That he'll die, no matter what?"

Kian nodded. "You say I am not acquainted well with the truth, but I would not lie to you. I have never lied to you. I have said only what I was allowed to say."

"I don't believe you."

Kian looked at her sadly. "Yes, you do."

"What am I supposed to do with these terrible 'truths' you've given me, Kian?" Lisbet sobbed. "What good are they to me, when my brother is going to die, my father is... is..." She buried her face in her hands. Kian's heat swirled around her as he approached. He didn't touch her, though she felt he wanted to.

"I cannot say, for they are your truths, not mine," Kian said. "But it is time for you to leave. Today. You, Eavan, the others. You may lead them out of our lands, unmolested, and your destination is your business. You need not tell me." He half-grinned. "I'll see it, anyway, eventually."

Lisbet drew a hard breath. She squeezed her eyes shut. Where would she go? In all her desperation these weeks in the Hinterlands, she'd never considered where they'd head if they found themselves free. She had no news of the outside world. Was the kingdom at war because of what she and Eavan had done? Could she go home? Was Wulfsgate even her home now?

"Starcaller awaits you," Kian said. "I kept my promise."

"What if I'd rather stay?"

Kian didn't look surprised by the question. "You cannot."

"Why?"

"This is not your home."

"It didn't stop you from imprisoning us!"

"You were never the prisoners you thought yourselves to be. I thought you might see that now. You were here so you could, all three of you, come to the moments you each find yourselves in now."

"Ash and Drystan are meant to kill Mortain, but what of me? You tell me who I am, but now what I'm supposed to do!"

"You will know when you know."

"Agggggh!"

"Frustration harms only you," Kian said evenly. "We must go now."

"Wait. You didn't tell me who Ash's other child was?"

"I will not. For they have not yet come upon that truth themselves."

"But you know?"

"Go on, Lisbet. You are free. Choose your path now, in this freedom."

Lisbet realized then that she would miss Kian. She would miss all of this, even the maddening daily interrogations. She would miss the colors in these woods that she'd never see again anywhere in the kingdom, and the simplicity of her day.

More than that, she would miss the veil of obliviousness she'd lived in until only moments ago. She would regret asking the questions. Regret leaving. Coming here. If she'd only told her mother to intervene in Drystan's affair with Ravenna, they could've stayed home, safe. Their blood wouldn't have mattered, for no one ever would have known. Lisbet would have married her uncle, but in ignorance, and Drystan's life, though ordinary, would not soon be ending.

"That was never your path. To stay," Kian said. He didn't apologize for reading her mind.

"No," she agreed, as she stole a greedy gulp of air.

Kian's hand hovered over her arm. She knew he could hide his sadness if he wanted to, but he didn't, for her. He would never say the words, but she read them, in his eyes, in his beautifully curved mouth.

"What would you do, if you were me?" she whispered. "I ask you as a friend."

"I would go forward. I would never look back."

30

BREWING CHAOS

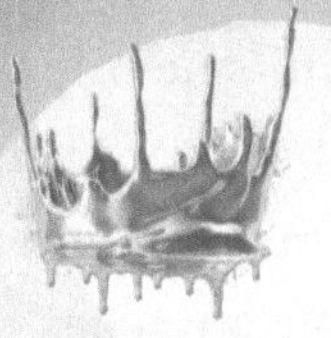

Stefan kicked the bundle of straw down the hall, pretending it was a ball and that he was preparing to win a game he had never played before, much less defined. It barely resembled a ball at all, haphazard straw bound with leather scraps, but he was no stranger to imagining things as he wished them to be, not as they were.

One of the Magi had rolled it together for him. He couldn't remember her name, but she was very nice, smiling as she noted that a little boy should have toys. He happened to agree. He wanted to tell her that anything in the world could be a toy if you were inclined to think of it that way, but he didn't know how to talk to adults who were not his mother. So he'd grinned in delight and accepted her handcrafted gift with gratitude.

"Careful, young one," a Magi said as Stefan nearly ran smack into him. They were always patting him on the head, or tongue-clicking at him. They weren't mean to him, but he could tell that they were not used to someone his size at the Sepulchre. He asked his mother if he should be a better boy, and she answered that he could be more mindful—of course, everyone could—but that he was already the best boy and there was no room for improvement there.

He felt better after that, and more confidently kicked the ball down the hallway, which was so long he was afraid to find himself on the other end. He was better at dodging the tall people in their silver cloaks now, too, and it seemed they'd stopped realizing he was even there! Mother would say they'd grown used to him, but Stefan knew he'd just become a better boy after all.

The ball rolled toward the top of the stairs. He gasped inwardly, willing the ball backward through space. For a moment it looked as if his unseen magic might work, and then it teetered over the stone, making soft crunches as it bounced down to the floor below.

Stefan twisted his lips, running his teeth over them. This was a dilemma. He wasn't supposed to leave this floor. His mother made him promise, and Wyat, too. He liked Wyat, because Wyat would play with him, but he hadn't been around lately to play. He was off on a quest, Stefan's mother said, which sounded very exciting, but at the moment, unhelpful. If Wyat were here, he'd know what to do about the ball.

Stefan looked down both ends of the hall. He was alone, for now. No one to see him disobey his mother. But her words lived in him nonetheless. *You must behave even when no one is looking, for that is when it most counts.*

He groaned, then stopped himself when it started to sound too much like he was crying. No matter what he did about this ball, he would *not* cry about it. He wasn't a baby.

Stefan decided to go for it. He was, after all, only going to grab the ball and run back up the stairs. There was no trouble in that.

He darted toward the staircase, spiraling down. His mother complained that the Sepulchre was nothing but stairs, but Stefan thought she might like them better if she was allowed to play on them. They were almost magic themselves, the way you could see no more than several steps ahead and had to just *believe* that there would be more stairs with each corner you rounded.

Aha! He spotted the ball lingering on the third step from the bottom. Sucking an inward sigh of relief, Stefan gingerly moved down the remaining steps and reached for it. If it had rolled out and into the hall, he might have been spotted. The Guardians were on his side today.

Stefan paused when he heard voices. He recognized one of them, as it came from one of the few people he'd talked to more than once here. The Head Magus. It was then that Stefan remembered what his mother had said about the floor beneath theirs. *I am told this is where the elders reside, their private quarters. You must never disturb them, Son. It is no place for either of us.*

He reached for the ball, slowly, but he saw his shadow looming into the stone hall when he moved forward. He jumped back. "Mother's blood," he whispered, using the phrase his mother employed when she was frustrated.

"We cannot afford a war at our doorstep. You know this," the one whose voice was unfamiliar to Stefan said. He sounded like what Stefan imagined a bear would sound like.

"Nor can we break our sacred vows, Elder Thorsen. Once we are possessed of a truth, it is ours to keep, not to spread," said the Head Magus. "I should not need to remind you of this."

"What are vows if we are no more?" asked The Bear.

"You speak in the riddles of a philosopher, not the practicality of a leader," the Head Magus snapped. "And this isn't suitable conversation for a hallway. Shall I even ask you how you came into possession of such information when it was only I who knew it? Knew of them?"

"Tymagen. Come on. You are new to your rank, but even you know we cannot keep the child of a fugitive prince here forever."

"Nor will we."

"The Rhiagains will know. Soon. If they don't already."

"A secret that I should trust you to keep, not spread."

"You know I will not. Have not. But it is known just the same. What will we do when the Rhiagains send their guards here?"

"We shall tell them we do no more than honor our laws of sanctuary. We did not invite this. It landed upon our doorstep, as is the way for all those seeking sanctuary. These laws are inviolate, even to them."

The Bear laughed. "You think they will care?"

"They have respected our way for hundreds of years. They don't want a war with us, either. Especially one we will not fight with swords."

The Bear dropped his voice. "Spread the word. Draw their eye away, to where it belongs. To the prince."

"I will not."

"Then I will."

"No!" the Head Magus yelled. The sound echoed off the stone, and Stefan nearly fell back. He was breathing so hard now that he was sure they'd hear him, but they didn't. He wanted to leave, but he couldn't without the ball. If he didn't retrieve it, they'd know what he'd done. He had no choice but to wait.

"Where is your loyalty, Tymagen? To a crown or to us?"

"I cannot be loyal to us without being loyal to who we are, Thorsen. As an elder, I would expect you to know this, and to see this truth honored, not reviled. If we violate the trust of ones who have come to us in the vulnerability in sanctuary, then we're no better than the Reliquary, swaying to the wind of convenience and expediency. I will not. And if you do, I'll see you excommunicated."

The Bear gasped. "You are choosing outsiders over your own elders, Tymagen. You will live to regret it."

"I will live safe in my conscience," the Head Magus answered. "And in knowing that this is why some of us are meant to lead and others are not."

Angry footsteps sounded next, and they slowly disappeared

down the hall. The Bear lingered a moment until he, too, stormed away, moving in the opposite direction. He passed the stairs but didn't notice Stefan cowering in the shadows. Stefan exhaled his relief.

Quickly, he grabbed the ball and raced back up the stairs. When he reached the top, he again checked to ensure he was alone, and then returned to kicking the ball. This time, more carefully. More mindfully, as his mother would say.

But his heart wasn't in it anymore. He didn't understand the strange exchange between the Head Magus and The Bear, but it troubled him just the same. It left a dark feeling in his belly that took all the fun out of whatever playtime remained to him before supper.

Suddenly, he knew why he felt so afraid. He had no choice but to tell his mother what he had heard, but to do so, he would also reveal that he'd gone to the forbidden floor.

Stefan picked up his ball. He felt like crying, for reasons he didn't understand. But he knew he was done playing for the day. He had to find the courage to confess to his mother what he'd done, so he could tell her what he'd heard.

Maybe tomorrow he'd feel like playing again.

"Tell me why your womb has not quickened with my son," Eoghan demanded. "Are you burdened by the thought of your father in my prison? Has that interfered with your fertility?"

Assana was frustrated, but not by this. "No, Your Grace. He belongs in prison."

Eoghan almost smiled. "Yes, he does. I've given it some thought, and I think I may let him die there. What do you think?"

"I think there are worse fates for a man like my father."

"And the Easterlands? What would they say?"

"Some men follow other men because they're called by inspiration. Others follow for fear of losing their heads. He has perhaps one or two who are driven by the former motivation. As for the latter..."

"I will put your uncle on his seat," Eoghan said with a pleased look. He seemed to admire his own ideas as he paused. "I hear they love him."

"My uncle Corin is loved. But the people will expect my brother, Cian, as he is next according to tradition."

Eoghan's grin faded. "You're suggesting I chose wrong?"

Assana shook her head. The king's ever-shifting moods were exhausting. *He* was exhausting. Even watching him try to move his frail body left hers laden by an invisible weight. "Only sharing with you my knowledge of my homeland, Your Grace."

"Hmm," Eoghan grunted. "If not your father, then what? Do I not fuck you enough?"

If Assana had been attracted to him in the slightest, this comment would have elicited a flush in her cheeks. A boy she'd once believed she'd marry had used this word with her, not so long ago, and it had been all she could do not to tell him about the burning between her legs at his frivolity with her. With Eoghan, the words produced a dire need for her to control the bile forming in the back of her throat.

"I don't know why I've disappointed you in this, Your Grace," Assana replied, affecting her best version of humility. "If my mother were here, I believe she would have counsel for me on the matter that may prove useful."

"Your mother?" Eoghan looked directly at her for the first time. His sad eyes focused only on her. "Do you miss her?"

Assana looked down and nodded. She did miss her mother. No one had known the limits of Aiden's cruelty as Maeryn had, but it hadn't slowed her from her duties to her children. Assana's anger at Eavan for thrusting her into this world hadn't waned, but her acceptance of her circumstances had leveled out. With that had come the realization of all she missed at home, and that was true of nothing or no one more than her mother.

Eoghan rolled his head to the side, still watching her. "I could send for her. Would you like that?"

Assana brightened as she looked up again. "You would do that for me?"

He shrugged. "Not for you. For me. Oldwin will arrive in a moment to either lie to me or tell me there's chaos brewing in the kingdom. There will be no relief from that until I have an heir." When Assana clapped her hands over her mouth to hide the beaming smile, Eoghan sighed. "Go on, then. Leave me."

"Thank you, Your Grace. Your kindness humbles me," she said as she bowed, backing away.

"Yes, yes." Eoghan waved his hand. "Oh, there is one more thing. Your mother. Has she any younger children?"

"Your Grace?"

"Little ones! Of the age that still consume her milk."

Assana shook her head. She tried to look confused by the question, though she understood it well. All of Duncarrow seemed to know about his strange proclivity. "No, Your Grace. My youngest brother is twelve. And she never nursed her own children. My father wouldn't allow it."

"Pity," he answered. "This may prove painful for her, then."

Corridyn Ravenwood was dying. Alasyr hadn't been well acquainted with the old man. He'd been old when Alasyr was born. Unlike the series of deaths a female Ravenwood experienced, it was a true death, their only death. As they lay upon the ceremonial bed, their last, they were given their own Final Death rites.

Alasyr struggled to understand his exact relation to Corridyn. He thought the old man was an ancestor of his grandmother Adynora's uncle, four or five generations back, which would make him quite old, though some lived longer than that. There were Ravenwoods still walking the halls of The Rookery with over two centuries behind them.

It was the men who attended the bedside of the dying man. It was not required. Alasyr hadn't planned to visit Corridyn's bedside at all, until he heard others whisper that he'd had no visitors, and would die alone. This sparked a pang of sadness in Alasyr, not only for the old man, but for all of them. Could it truly be that a Ravenwood could live so long and still die alone?

Alasyr made his way to the chambers that were set aside for this tradition. The Perch of the Final Death it was called, though there was nothing inside resembling a perch or a cage. Only a small bed in the center of the alabaster room, surrounded by candles.

He found Corridyn was alone, and as he entered, Alasyr questioned his choice to come. If he didn't know the old man, the old man would not know him. Would it only emphasize that his loved ones had failed to see him?

"Alasyr," a gravelly voice said from the bed. "Son of Varinya. How unexpected. How lovely."

Alasyr swallowed the lump in his throat and slowly approached the bed. As he came close, he saw something that only happened to Ravenwoods as their Final Death loomed near. The smoothness in the man's face was a sea of wrinkles. Dark spots dotted his pale cheeks. Some said it was magic leaving a Ravenwood; that it was magic which produced their beauty and held it fast for so many years.

"You know me?" Alasyr asked. There was no chair, so he knelt.

"In the same way you know me, I suppose." The man's words took twice as long as they should to finish. He drew out every letter, as if each pained him. "How kind of you to come, when no one else would."

"Can I get you anything?"

"There is nothing I need now."

"All right." Alasyr sat back on his heels, lost for how to continue the conversation.

"Would you like to know why no one else has visited me?"

"If you... if you would like to tell me."

"It is my inclination to tell which has left me alone in my final hours," Corridyn said with a sly smile. "I sometimes wonder if the magic didn't leave me earlier, for this. But it hasn't left me entirely, has it?"

Alasyr watched the old man in silence.

"I have made many mistakes, Alasyr. But none more terrible than upholding the falsehood that provides the foundation for our world."

"What do you mean?"

"Have you not detected it yourself? No, you are very young yet. You have years ahead of you, still, in careful, joyous ignorance before you, too, begin to question."

"I know not everything is as they'd want us to believe," Alasyr said, and almost immediately regretted the words. Dying or not, a confession of this type bordered on treason. The wrong ears would make it so.

"You know that, do you? Good." Corridyn closed his eyes, nodding. "You knew it way before I did, then."

"I don't *know* anything," Alasyr replied, and was overcome by a short swell of anger as he said the words. "I only see that there are truths being kept from me."

"From most," Corridyn said. "For there can be no order in chaos."

"It wouldn't need to be chaos."

"It would. Without the lie, chaos is all that's left."

"What lie?"

Corridyn rolled his head to the side. Now, Alasyr could see how deep the man's eyes had receded into his sockets; how his skin hung, no longer fully attached to bone. "It is all a lie. The passing of memories. The chosen one. There are no memories. There is no one of us better than another, not due to the order of their birth, anyway."

Alasyr scoffed. "But my mother has had her memories. My grandmother. And they're both very powerful women."

"All Ravenwoods are powerful," Corridyn answered.

"They wouldn't lie."

"They would, to protect themselves, and their daughters. They would, for fear of being cast against the mountain for the failure of it."

Alasyr softly gasped as the man's words settled into him, into every bone, every drop of blood coursing through him. "But... the Langenacht. It always reveals the chosen High Priest. Always."

"The reigning High Priestess chooses who her daughter will marry. It is she who blesses her daughter's womb, and the seed of the man who she believes will best honor her. She does this without knowing the women before her have done the same, in love, of protection of their daughters. In fear that her daughter's womb will not quicken, and they'll cast her out, as is the way." The old man's words took longer the more he spoke. "Ahh, but you are still young. You are possessed of doubt, but haven't yet been driven by it." His bony hands reached for Alasyr's. Alasyr gave them over. "You are a kind boy, to visit a dying man. Pay no mind to me. I feel the last of our ancestors leave me, and I would sleep now."

Alasyr nodded. Hot tears burned at his eyes, and he didn't know why they were there, or what they wanted of him. He didn't know how to make sense of the words, or whether he should. The man was, after all, dying, and it was known one on the edge of life and death was prone to nonsense.

Still, it left a sourness in his belly as he left the chambers, making his way to his own room. He thought of his father's secret jaunts. His mother's hushed words. Ravenna, lost in the world. The midnight goat. The dying man that Alasyr could return to life, with his hands, he now knew, but feared what would happen if he did.

The old man was right. There was chaos.

It had taken domicile in Alasyr, and he feared there was no way to be rid of it.

"Your Grace, it may be time to deploy the Knights of Duncarrow."

Eoghan turned his face away from the sorcerer. There was never a moment he didn't feel he was under the intense scrutiny of Oldwin, the result of which he knew he'd experience in ways too soon to predict. "You told me the ravens would be enough to quell tensions."

"It was, until Mads Waters decided not to heed his own lord's advice."

"Are we to believe Waters is acting against Aiden's wishes or that he has seen through the words as belonging to someone not his lord?"

"One simply cannot say for certain."

"No," Eoghan said in disgust. "This is the work of one man, not many. We will deal with it as such."

Oldwin stepped forward. His dark, wide eyes were all Eoghan could see when he looked up. There was death beyond the blackness. He thought this every time he looked upon the sorcerer. "One man has defied the order, but he has prompted many men to action. It cannot be allowed to continue."

"I didn't release you from the sky dungeon to advise me in matters of war, but to scry the future. Yet you've given me no divinations. No visions. Instead, you tell me I should go to war, when I have told you that will *not* be my legacy!"

Oldwin kept his cool despite Eoghan's rattled constitution. "And if I told you I'd seen war?"

"If you told me that now I'd have your head for not telling me sooner."

Oldwin grinned. "Then it is just as well that I've seen nothing."

"For you," Eoghan grunted. "Not for me. What good is a seer who sees nothing?"

"I *have* seen something," Oldwin answered with a slow drawl. "Something you will appreciate. But can we first, Your Grace, put the matter of Mads Waters to bed? He's imprisoned Lord Corin and Lady Yesenia. He's already sacked Whitewood, and by the time we receive another raven, there will be more left in his wake. What orders shall I give?"

"Mortain was a gift from the Rhiagains. He answers to us, does he not?"

Oldwin hesitated. Nodded.

"Order him to deal with the matter of Waters. Swiftly, before more damage is done. He will then spread the word that Waters acted alone, against the wishes of his king and lord, and will put an end to the chaos spreading across the Westerlands. All men who wish to be spared will lay down their arms and do as commanded."

Oldwin bowed. "Your Grace."

"Also, send for Maeryn Blackwood."

"Lady Blackwood? You mean for her to come here?"

"Yes."

"But why?"

"You do not question me, Oldwin. I have my reasons."

"Lady Assana," Oldwin muttered, and Eoghan knew the sorcerer meant for him to hear it. He wouldn't give him the satisfaction of reacting.

"I'm weary. Tell me your vision and go."

"Ahh, yes. You will soon be less troubled about lacking an heir, Your Grace."

"Have you seen Assana with child?"

"Not Assana," Oldwin said. "Your next wife."

31

A CALL TO ARMS

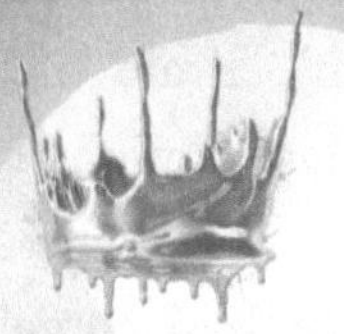

Hamish read the words on the vellum three times. The raven had been whipped about in the strong wind coming off Leecaster Bay, making it just in time to stand before him and die, having completed its final task. Hamish had no especial soft place for ravens, but he very much wished that he could've healed the poor little beast that had given his life to deliver this message.

If nothing else, it seemed like a terrible omen. He'd never seen a messenger raven drop dead on delivery.

It was time. Khallum had said it would come, and yet Hamish hadn't spent near enough time preparing himself for this moment. He'd done more talking than he had in all his life these past days and weeks. Sharing with Ryan the stories of Yanna, of how he'd discovered her, and then, his love for her, which had been less of a discovery and more, a powerful thrust of the Guardians. *I loved her before I knew her name,* he'd said, smiling at the memory. Yanna de Medvedev. His tragic beauty with the swollen belly and a fear unlike he'd seen in any man or woman before. It was just as well she refused to give name to the ratsbane who'd done it to her, for

Hamish couldn't have rescued her if he was in the crown prison camp.

When Jesse had come whispering into the world, Hamish forgot he wasn't the boy's father. He forgot this truth at most points in Jesse's life, seeing it only in the glimpses of how Jesse was so different from most Strong men. In the eyes, mostly, was where he saw it. His cooler, easier behaviors could be explained away to the differing natures in all men, but behind Jesse's dark eyes, the truth lived. Hamish wasn't afraid of the truth; only that Jesse might discover it, and that it might cause him to question his place.

But Ryan... when Ryan had come, Hamish had nothing to forget. Ryan looked like his older brother, but he also looked very much like his father; he had Hamish's sandy blond hair and pale blue eyes. He was a Strong, through and through, though had thankfully inherited his mother's more delicate looks as well, for where a woman would grudgingly marry Hamish Strong for his title and money, one would eagerly marry Ryan Strong for his nature and beauty.

One tried. And she'd paid the price, as had Ryan.

"I'm 'fraid it's time, Son," Hamish said to his sleeping son. He closed Ryan's hands into his swollen fist. "What I'd give to be 'ere when you wake."

Hamish looked again at the words. *I lead the men here to deal with the matter where it began. It is time for you and Garrick to lead the men of the west half of our Reach to Whitechurch. We must draw Quinlanden's men away from the Westerlands and take the war to his own land.*

Hamish bowed his head and sighed. "Ye deserve the chance to fight, too. A fierce warrior, ye'd be. I know it."

"Sir?" Missy's small voice appeared in the doorway. "I've come to change his linens. I can come back."

"Nay," Hamish replied, wiping his hands over his eyes. He

didn't lean down to embrace or kiss his son. That would imply a goodbye, and he would see him again. The Guardians hadn't allowed him to linger this long to take him later. "I must take leave, lass. I donnae know when I'll return. I can trust ye? To look after him?"

Missy affected a light bow. "Stewardess Rutland wouldnae have me behave any other way, sir."

Hamish moved toward her, leaning in. Her eyes widened at his closeness. "If he dies, I'll scorch this kingdom till there's nay a blade of grass to remind us of what it was."

Missy swallowed her fear of him and met his eyes with the same intensity. "Then I know my task."

Gwyn's tears blurred her view of the vellum curling into the flames and disappearing. That Khallum had bothered to send her a raven at all made everything worse, somehow. He never told her anything when he was away. He'd never seen the need in it, no matter how she'd begged for news of his exploits. He couldn't know what it was like to be the one left behind; the one to assuage the fears of the children, when her own fears ran relentless.

"Mother?" Niall's hands gripped the back of the chair. "What's wrong?"

Little Garrick appeared in the doorway. "Has something happened?"

She turned and looked at them both, one by one. Gwyn saw no point in hiding her tears from them anymore. Niall was now their heir, if Ransom didn't return. At fifteen, he was ready for betrothal and she'd already been in talks with Stewardess Nye about one of her daughters. And though she still thought of her youngest as Little Garrick, he was twelve now and closer to being a husband than a bairn. When their father was that age, he was already training for a war his own father promised but never delivered.

Khallum had sent for them both in Oldcastle, brought them home to her. If Oldcastle wasn't safe anymore…

"Your father is calling the Southerlands to war, my sons."

"Why? Where?" Niall asked.

"To the Westerlands, where the most terrible treacheries have happened and must be put to bed before they spread to the other Reaches and bring a darkness that will not be so easy to slide off. To the Easterlands, where it began."

"Is that where he's been all this time?" Garrick asked, frowning. "I thought you said he had business in Blackpool."

Gwyn shook her head. Her red hair fell from its plaits and she didn't bother re-pinning it. "I cannot say if he's been in Blackpool, or elsewhere. I cannot even tell you where he is now, or where he's going."

Niall came before her and knelt at her knees. "I donnae understand. Father has always had enmity for the other Reaches. They've never come when we called. Why does he go when they do?"

"Your father sees what others cannot. That a war against one Reach is a war against us all."

"Then I should be with him! At his side! Why else would he call me home from study if not for that?" Niall cried. "Other men of my age will be called, so why not his own son? Why should I be given special treatment?"

Gwyn gathered his hands in one of hers and opened her arms for Garrick to join them. "How I wish I had answers for you boys. I only know that he keeps these things from us out of love, nothing more or less. Esmerelda is lost to us. If Ransom returns to us, he will not be the same young man who left us. The two of you are the hope and pride of the Warwicks now, and if that's what guides him to stay your own hands from involvement, then I cannot say I would do any different, were I him."

Garrick laid his head against her leg. "Father says we should fear nothing."

Gwyn ran her hands through his hair. "But you are afraid, aren't you?"

He nodded.

She kissed the tops of both her son's heads. "Aye, your mother is afraid, too. But you know who should be more afraid? Whoever finds themselves on the wrong end of your father's ire. For that person, fear will be the last thing they know."

AYLEN WAITED until the other men were marching toward the Gates of the North before slipping away to the armory to piece together a set for herself. Her sword, Witchwind, was always with her, even in the infirmary. It was never far from her hand. This, her father had taught her. But she'd left for the Sepulchre before they could fit her for armor, with her siblings. She'd never even watched a man put it on, so she wasn't sure if she'd know the right order, the way it should fit. She didn't know if the blacksmith would have made anything for someone her size, but she supposed a children's cut would work.

The armory had been picked clean. Weapons, mail, plate, all of which had been crafted in the weeks leading up to use. Christian told her that before recent events had forced the blacksmiths back into perpetual work, some of the swords in the armory of Wulfsgate had been rusted. All who had needed a sword carried one already, or had their ancestral steel mounted somewhere as a display of pride. None had seen use.

But she was in luck, for though some men had taken their sons, they'd conscripted few children to respond to the call to arms from the Westerlands. She saw this collection piled in a corner, and, with a glance back at the door, knelt to sift through and find what she could for herself.

You know I never ask anything of you, Christian had said as he headed to the armory himself, hardly a tick of the sun past. *But I beg of you now, stay with my mother. Bar the gates of the keep if you must. I cannot lose you, Aylen.*

There are other women going to fight. Women with half my skill at the sword. Do you not think all strong hands are needed?

He'd turned to her with a great sadness in his eyes. *Aye. I think that. But I'm going to be selfish now, so that my reason for life still has hers when I return.*

It was unfair, and Christian knew it, but he said the words anyway, not appreciating what would happen to her if he didn't return. This was why they couldn't fail in their aid. This was why Aylen snuck away after her husband had departed for the border-lands to find her own armor and join them.

Her only regret was not following through on her promise with Ember, to practice with her. But she would make true on it when the war ended. She would put it before all else.

"Daughter."

Aylen froze. Gretchen.

Aylen stood, straightening her spine. "Lady Gretchen. I was... I..."

"Tidying up?" Gretchen stepped across the dirt floor until they were side by side. "I would do the same, if I didn't have the children. Even a year ago, I might have gone, when all my babies were still here. But now, there are two. And I cannot lose them."

Aylen clasped her hands. "Someday, you will have them all here again with you."

Gretchen squeezed Aylen's hands and dropped them. "I believe they're out there somewhere, Aylen. But I'm not so foolish as to hope for them all here again. That is not the world we live in. Not anymore."

Aylen sighed. "This is why I must go."

"It will not be me who stops you," Gretchen replied. She

dropped her eyes to Aylen's belly. "Is there any chance?"

Aylen shook her head.

"Are you taking something, then?"

"An elixir I learned to make at the Sepulchre."

"You want them. He doesn't."

"That's close enough to the truth, I suppose."

Gretchen nodded, surveying the wreckage left from the men who'd whirled in a short time ago. "Christian says a lot about what he doesn't want. He has his reasons, and they are his own. He's certainly never shared them with me. Yet, now that he's home, he's becoming precisely the man he believed he should not." Gretchen exhaled. "And so, you must both return to me, Aylen, for the homecoming of my son and his wife has given me a hope I thought was lost forever."

"He has been different since coming back," Aylen agreed. "But I would caution you against hanging hopes on him resuming the mantle of heir, Lady Gretchen. He is a man called to service, and at present, he's serving his Reach. But when his banishment ends, he will be called to serve the one place he feels he is home."

Gretchen's smile was glacial. "We'll see."

"I HAVE TO GO, EMBER."

"You say that as if I'm stopping you."

Marsh tossed his satchel over his shoulder. "I know you're not stopping me. How could you? I'm fighting for *our* Reach. Yours, if your mother does what everyone expects her to and names you heir in place of Brandyn."

Ember looked up. "Is that your way of saying I should come and fight?"

Marsh rushed over and knelt before her. "*No.* You heard what the Rush Rider said. Blackfen. Your brother has ordered you to stay here, where you're safe."

She laughed. "My brother is eleven. Twelve. He cannot order me to do anything."

"He's not wrong, Ember. If something happens to him, it all comes down to you, no matter what your mother did or didn't want."

"Pfft." Ember looked away. She'd been torn between two worlds since Arturo Blackfen arrived with the call to arms. The Northerlands were being asked to defend the borders between east and west, to contain the battles to each side. At last, the Westerlands had direction, and it was Brandyn leading them. Brandyn! He had help, of course, from their Uncle Khallum. That was good. Khallum was competent and would not be afraid to do whatever was needed to end this.

This *was* her fight. A battle for her own lands, her people, everyone she had ever known or loved. And yet, she was drawn here, eyes to the north, to her origin. Though she couldn't explain it, she felt strongly that the two were inextricably tied together, and that she couldn't ignore what was happening to her here without also causing harm to the future of the Blackwoods and the Westerlands.

Where Marsh fit into all of this, she didn't know. Or if he even did. But she couldn't leave things like this. She might never see him again, and he deserved better than her confused indifference as he marched to war and an uncertain future.

Ember reached for him, fighting the thoughts and desires pulling her away from this moment and into another. With a small huff, he accepted her embrace and with his arms wrapped tight around her, she whispered the words he most needed to hear, despite not knowing whether they were true or not. "I love you, Marsh Tyndall. Be safe, and be brave."

Marsh melted in her arms. Her heart sank. She hoped she'd done the right thing.

His kiss brought her back to him in his final moments in Wulfsgate. "I'll come back to you, Emberley, I promise. And when I do, I'll be worthy of asking the question you know I most want to ask of you."

"One thing at a time," Ember said, forehead pressed to his. She felt like crying, but equally felt like running until her legs gave out. A scream trapped in her throat.

"Will you be here? Do you promise you'll stay in Wulfsgate?"

Ember tried to smile. "I can't return to the Westerlands until you settle that matter, now, can I? Where else would I go?"

Marsh didn't return the smile. His eyes looked north. "Not all answers are good for us," he said.

KHALLUM EASED his warhorse to a slower pace. The beast was meant to run, and run hard. It was used to a master who was all too happy to indulge this.

It was the snapping symphony of the two standards catching the wind that kept him from darting forward. On the left, the green banner bearing the Westerlands' providing mother, arms spread; on the right, the dark orange of the Southerlands and the crested waves. Farther north, the blue fabric bearing the jagged mountain would be heading their way, though their paths would not cross unless something went wrong. The seer, Joran, advised against displaying their banners so openly, but they would discard them for secrecy soon enough. Until they crossed into hostile lands, they were one, and they were proud.

How he, his father, and his father before him had fantasized about this. A kingdom united, marching against the line of kings that had turned this realm broken. He pushed down the niggling anger at how it had taken the Westerlands crying for help; how none had come when a Warwick had called.

Aye, but ye have never had a reason for them to fight. A king worth following, and a hope to go with it.

Darrick fell to the middle of the pack, riding with the other men led by Law. None but those most trusted to Khallum and Brandyn as yet knew his secret. They'd keep it from Duncarrow as long as the Guardians allowed, and not all men who started with them on this journey would end it with them. The time would come to reveal to the rest of the kingdom what he, Khallum Warwick, had known and done. With that would come the respect the Warwicks deserved but had never harvested.

"Ye reckon Hamish has them all headed north yet? And Nye, west?" Rutland asked, from his left.

"Aye," Khallum said, squinting against the noonday sun. It was unseasonably warm, even for the southern part of the kingdom. Beads of sweat cut down the filth on his forehead and cheeks. "They would've left the moment the order reached them."

"We'd never know if they failed. Least not until it was too late."

"Hamish willnae fail. Nor Nye," Khallum said. "Byrne told me once that Asherley had a clairvoyant in her employ. One who could share and read thoughts across the kingdom. No mere seer like that swindler riding with us."

"Hogwash. Do ye not think that if such a magic existed, we'd know? Think of the advantages. Wars would be over before they started."

"Aye? Byrne wouldnae lie about it. 'Tis possible the magician embellished their skills."

"And the Northerlands? Will they come?"

Khallum inhaled a mouthful of the fresh breeze passing over. An image of Gretchen, hair catching the wind, face fierce with a power no one could take from her. She would have joined his war in Termonglen had he a plan then. Holden, too, maybe, though he had no kind thoughts to spare for the coward.

And she had his Ransom. His heir. He trusted her to do right by his boy, and by their alliance. "Aye. Tis no longer a lost cause in their eyes."

"Even if we deal with Quinlanden's men, and the sorcerer holding the Medvedev in sway—"

"When. When we deal with them."

Rutland sighed. "Aye. *When*. Then we have the Knights of Duncarrow and the Rhiagain Guard to contend with."

"And?"

"And no one knows their true size, Khallum. Do ye not think this to be intentional on the king's part?"

"First, ye can call me Khallum by a fire over ale, but not when my men are armored up and ready to fight at my command, aye?" He waited until Rutland nodded. "Second, I donnae care about the size of the ratsbane's army. I've sailed near the Isle of Belcarrow. 'Tis not so large an isle that it could house the number of men required to take on a kingdom. A Reach? Aye, perhaps. But it cannae stand against the all of us."

"There are rumors that a new army is being raised. In the Wastelands."

Khallum laughed. "The waning, failing men working the mines? Poor lads couldn't swing a sword any higher than their waist."

"No," Rutland said. "You remember, Kh—my lord. The rumors? That they were killin' the men off? And then, our... friend, Godfrey, he confirmed it for us. There's not many left. Maybe the camps are for something else."

"Hmph." Khallum dismissed the conversation, but Rutland's words stuck with him. It'd made no sense, what Darrick had said about the men dragged from their beds, the pits of the dead. Diamonds, the king was mining there, which was no great surprise, but if they'd ceased operations, there must be something more valuable than the most rare and precious rock in the kingdom.

Whatever it was, it could wait. It had to.

The task ahead required all of them.

32

AIMED TRUE

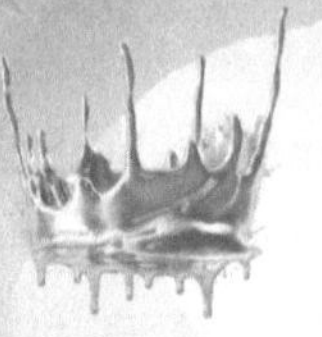

Alasyr waited until he was certain no one had followed him, and then he quietly slipped into the room.

Asherley's voice made him jump. "Who are *you?*" She approached him so quickly he almost tripped. "What do you want?"

He held his hands out, bidding her to lower her voice. "My name is Alasyr. I am the eldest son of Varinya and Argentyn. And no one knows I'm here right now."

Asherley regarded him with hard suspicion. "You answered one of my questions. Now you'll answer the other."

Her commanding manner took Alasyr back. She was quite confident for a woman who was a prisoner, with no reasonable means of escape. But he could see Emberley in her. In the high swell of her cheeks as she held her head aloft; the burning darkness behind her eyes. Both women had learned to turn their fear to power. Emberley thought she could learn from Alasyr, but this he would like to learn from her. He imagined it could prove quite useful.

"I've met your daughter. Emberley."

"And are in love with her, I can see."

"No!" Alasyr exclaimed, disgusted. "I am not *in love* with her. I would not even call her friend."

"I've read your whispers. You would do well to hide them from others who would do the same."

"You've *what*?"

"Why are you here, Alasyr?"

"I wanted you to know that I'm going to tell her you're here and let things happen as they will."

"Why would you do that?"

"The Derehams believe you're dead. Ember knows you aren't. It drives her to madness."

"So now she's Ember to you, and you have a care for the state of her mind."

Alasyr shook his head in frustration. "Stop attributing words to me I have not said!"

Asherley shrugged. She looked half as calm as he felt. A storm raged within him, and he hated this woman, that she could see it and he couldn't stop it. But it had been raging far too long. Since before he was aware of it. And now it could not be quieted.

"Very well. I'll ask another way. Why betray your family for a girl you claim isn't even dear enough to be called friend?"

"How are you so... so like this? So unafraid?" Alasyr challenged. His eyes burned hot with tears that he'd use every bit of his power not to spill. The words of Corridyn flamed high in his mind.

"I wasn't always," Asherley said, her voice kinder, less defended. "Unafraid, that is. But the greatest skill one can learn is to surrender to that which is beyond our control, and then to search for that which is. As you're well aware, I'm powerless to leave here. So thinking on it, dwelling on it, is a wasted energy better spent elsewhere."

"She is much like you. Your daughter."

This elicited a smile from Asherley. "She's most like me, of all my children."

"She's coming into powers she doesn't understand. She nearly spent the entire forest in her rage."

Asherley's smile died. "Why are you here, Alasyr?"

"As I said, I'm going to tell her you're here. She deserves to know."

"No. That is not why you're going to tell her."

Alasyr ground his tongue into the roof of his mouth. "My reasons are my own."

"I sense revenge in you. Ire. And if this is what guides you, you will falter, and you will take down those you love with you."

"I lost the only one I loved," Alasyr said. One hot tear escaped, and he smacked at his eyes to stop others. "My mother and father have lied to me all my life. My siblings will do as tradition demands and never question it, just as I would have! I *would* have. I cast my lot for my own sister not only because I loved her but because it was expected!"

"Would you like some wine?"

"What?"

"Your face is flushed so red I fear you'll pass out," Asherley said. She stood, and, sighing, went to the table in the corner to pour him a glass. "What did they lie to you about?" she asked as she handed him the glass.

Alasyr just stared at it and then set it aside. But he was no longer crying. Perhaps that had been her aim, to redirect him, to allow him to collect himself. "Everything."

She nodded. "Lies weave this entire kingdom together. Why should Midnight Crest be any different?"

"We *are* different. This is why we're feared."

Asherley shook her head. "You're not feared. You're protected, by these mountains. By the men at the base of them. The kingdom doesn't fear Ravenwoods, it only lacks the means to come and take them."

"That isn't true."

She lifted her shoulders.

"Emberley deserves to know you're here."

"Your life will be forfeit."

"My life?" Alasyr laughed. "I don't even know what my life is. But I understand Ravenna a little better. I cannot stay. I cannot leave. I cannot do a thing except live in this misery, wishing I hadn't let the illusion fade so I could live in the unwitting bliss all other Ravenwoods spend their lives in."

"Take me to her instead," Asherley said.

He shook his head. "There's only one way off this mountain, by flight. I couldn't take you safely. Not on my own."

"Your father brought me here on his own."

"No," Alasyr said. "I don't believe he did it on his own."

"Oh?" Asherley's eyes widened in interest. "So there are others who have joined him in his strange treason?"

"I don't know who they are. But I saw at least one other watching you, when you were in the cave."

"You were watching us, too, then."

"I was watching my father. I wish now that I'd left it alone."

"If he finds you here, there'll be no words or magic to get you out of the trouble awaiting you," Asherley said. She stepped to him and touched his shoulder in a gesture that was almost motherly. "If you cannot stop yourself from sharing with Emberley what you know, then the least I ask of you is that you tell her something for me."

"What?"

"That she must not attempt to come rescue me. It would mean certain death for her."

"You're still alive."

"I don't trust your father," Asherley said. "And neither do you."

• • •

"WYAT. Please listen to me. We cannot stay here."

Wyat paced the small room. The deep worry creasing his brows, spreading out to his stiff, tired limbs, hurt Anabella's heart. Once again, she was reminded of the burden she and Stefan had become, which was what she was, no matter how he objected to her thinking this way.

"Perhaps Stefan heard wrong. He wasn't even supposed to be on that floor."

"He told us why he was. He may not have understood what he was hearing, but it scared him, more than the consequences of being where he was not allowed. He had no guile in him when he shared this with me. He doesn't understand the implications of what he heard."

"There is nowhere *to* go, Anabella!" Wyat's anger faded immediately to sadness as he melted against the wall. "If only there was. There is nowhere else in this kingdom where I can keep you safe. This was it, my only idea. I've spent our time here searching for answers that simply do not exist."

"This isn't your fault. But we aren't safe here, Wyat. The Head Magus cannot protect us from the elders who would see the trouble swept from their doorstep."

He tilted his head at her, regarding her through bleary eyes. "Perhaps it is time to go to Darrick, then."

"To Darrick?" Anabella's breath caught. "Do you know where he is? Precisely, I mean?"

Wyat nodded. "One of Lord Warwick's scouts slipped when delivering a message. He's in Whitecliffe, at the pauper's surgery run by Stewardess Rutland. Christian Dereham caught it. He told me."

"But... why would Christian tell you?"

"He reminded me we were allies, not prisoners, and that we deserved to know. That *you* deserved to know."

"Then why are you only telling me this now?"

"Because I knew you'd want to go to him, and taking you there was not safe." He bowed his head. "Perhaps it should be Darrick who decides. I couldn't live with myself if something happened to you or Stefan under my watch."

Anabella wanted to reassure him, to remind him that no one had been more loyal to her husband, that Wyat was her brother in all ways that mattered, that they would make it, safely, and all would be well. But the words felt too heavy on the tongue, and so they died there.

"Get as much rest as you can. We'll leave tomorrow," he said and left.

"Do they all live in the trees like this?" Drystan asked as they moved through the woods at the edge of Bythesea. Ash had steered them farther off course to avoid detection, but even this deep in the forest they encountered the scattered home or two.

"Only those with great wealth," Ash explained. "The higher in the trees, the more sprawl, the more money a family possesses. Their castles in the trees are the biggest display of wealth they know, and this is where their gold goes. Bythesea is known especially for such wealth, as the most prominent port town in all the Easterlands."

"I thought that was Briarhaven?"

"They've slowed commerce through Briarhaven in recent years, as the Magi complained about the sorts that would come to port. Harassing their Adherents and Magi and worse. These days, the taxes to trade through Briarhaven are prohibitive for all but reputable traders."

Drystan waved his hand around, gesturing at the sporadic homes in the branches. "Seems odd to want to live so far from the town, out here."

"Does it? I've never considered it before, I suppose. Isn't that the way of things? What is ordinary to you is unusual to another."

Drystan pulled to a stop. "You must know. I'm certain of my purpose, Ash. I won't change my mind. Nothing will stop me from killing the sorcerer and freeing the Medvedev. Even if it costs me my own life."

Ash shook his head. "It won't. I'll be there, with you."

"I don't think you understand what I'm saying. You seem to want to protect me. But if you cannot stop that instinct in Whitechurch, then you should turn around now."

"Drystan—"

"I'm serious, Ash. If I survive this, and the task is not done, it will be as good as death for me."

"Son, why does this matter so much to you?" Ash asked. "Where does this passion come from, for a cause that has nothing to do with you?"

"Have you ever been called to purpose?"

"I believe so."

"No," Drystan said. "You would know so. You would be so utterly certain that everything else you ever held dear as a truth would be called into question."

Ash slowly nodded. "Very well. I promise not to intervene, if the task is not yet complete."

"Or to do it for me."

"Does it matter, who slays the dragon, if the dragon is felled?"

"Dragons aren't real," Drystan said and spurred himself back into action. "But sorcerers are."

"We don't even know the way!" Ravenna yelled.

"I didn't ask you to come with me," Esmerelda called back, breathless, as she rode hard through the forest. She wanted to ride harder, but she had to think of her child. Riding at all right now was a risk, but she couldn't stay any longer or she'd not be able to travel until after her child was born. Ryan needed her. He was waiting for her. If the Guardians punished her for answering this call, then all hope truly was lost.

Ravenna struggled to keep pace with her. She supposed those northern sorcerers had no use for horses, flying about the mountains as they did. "I won't let you do this alone!"

"You won't *let* me?" Esmerelda laughed, hair flying behind her. She no longer bothered to cover it. Whatever happened, happened. "Seems you couldn't keep up to stop me if you tried."

"I *am* trying. But not to stop you."

"Then what, Ravenna?"

"I'm trying to *help* you!"

"Like you helped me in Greystone Abbey?"

"I've already apologized for that, Esmerelda. I'll keep apologizing if there's forgiveness at the end."

"To offer you that, I would first need to care," Esmerelda snapped. She realized, though, that she didn't mean the words anymore. She did care. She didn't hate Ravenna. She envied her, for her freedom, for her confidence, and the easiness in which she wrapped Jesse, and probably all men, around her finger. Esmerelda had been told her whole life she was beautiful, but had rarely been given compliments about anything beyond the surface of who she was. She was useful, that's all. A pawn for a good marriage and more money for her father.

"We don't have to be friends," Ravenna called, narrowing the gap between them. "But I will see you aimed true. Let that resolve matters between us, once and for all, so when we part, we can do so with no further enmity between us."

Esmerelda pulled to a sudden stop. Ravenna kept on with her prattling, but Esmerelda raised a hand, cutting her words to a halt. "Do you hear that?" she whispered.

Ravenna started to say no, but then her head cocked to the

side. Listening. She reached behind her, for her bow. Esmerelda touched the dagger strapped against her thigh.

"Horses. A dozen, or more," she responded, dropping her voice so low Esmerelda had to read her lips. "They've stopped."

A meaningful look passed between the two women. There was little chance they could win a fight against men. But they could run.

Esmerelda nodded. Ravenna returned it.

Esmerelda was the first to spring into action. Her horse launched forward, Ravenna's right behind. The horses lying in wait in the forest came to life, a cacophony of powerful thuds against dirt and brush as they quickly closed in on them.

"Harder!" Ravenna cried. "Harder than you've ever ridden in your life!"

"They're right on us!"

"Go! Ride!"

Esmerelda was several paces ahead when she realized Ravenna was no longer behind her. She tried to look over her shoulder, to spot her, but there was nothing. Some of the horses giving chase had also fallen off.

She twisted to look and saw that Ravenna had surrendered herself to the assailants. Her panicked, resigned face nodded feverishly at Esmerelda to go, keep riding, go on. Panting, Esmerelda kept her grueling pace, but she couldn't get the image of Ravenna's strange expression out of her head. It slowed her, and she eventually stopped.

Before she could turn, powerful arms looped around hers and she was pulled from atop her horse with a rush so hard she saw stars.

"No!" Ravenna cried out.

Esmerelda's feet dragged the ground as she wrestled for footing. She grunted and thrashed in their arms, but these men were strong. She struggled for breath through their rough handling. "You... are... hurting me!"

"Struggle, and you'll really know pain," a deep, hard voice responded. To someone else, he called, "Pass the rope!"

"Let her go!" Ravenna cried. "I'll go with you willingly!"

The soldier jostled Esmerelda over his shoulder. "You'll come, willingly or not. We're taking you both."

"I'm with child, you oaf!" Esmerelda grunted as the air was knocked from her chest.

"Our orders were to bring you in alive. As long as you can still be properly plucked and fucked, I imagine he won't care about the condition of your arrival."

Orders. They'd been hunted.

At last she caught the standard etched upon their armor.

The crossed swords.

Duncarrow.

The king.

EMBERLEY ASSEMBLED scraps from the armory. There wasn't much left. All the men, and even many young boys, had taken everything crafted. She found some cuffs and a slink of mail that was only slightly too large. The last helmet, lying bereft in a corner, was made for a man even larger than her father. It fell off her head before she could adjust it.

She'd had to sneak past Ransom to do it. He was furious with Gretchen for ordering him to stay behind with the women. Ember understood his anger. Her cousin was the heir apparent of the Southerlands, and after all that had happened across the Reaches, this seemed important in ways that had been purely theoretical before. But the reasons he should go were the same reasons he should stay.

Why are you siding with Lady Dereham? Father would want me there, Ember!

Ransom. Your father has lost his daughter and brother, all so quickly he hasn't properly mourned either. He wouldn't handle well losing you, too.

Your mother has lost a spouse and child, and yet your brother leads his army to war.

If she were here, she'd be leading it herself, and Brandyn would be safely tucked away with the other magic dealers of the realm.

I donnae expect a girl to understand.

Then perhaps don't whine to me about it.

That had been enough to get him to leave her alone.

She'd always preferred being alone. It was a part of her she tried to hide, for most around her believed it to be unnatural to spend so much time with one's own thoughts. Her mother understood this about her and never made her feel bad for it. She accepted it wasn't that Ember didn't wish to share her time and space with others, but that she felt others would not want to share that same time or space if they understood her, truly. She couldn't say the things that came to her mind aloud. She couldn't express them with words even if she tried. It was easier to live with the inexplicable feelings and sensations that were a part of her, than to put voice to them and be judged.

And now her mother was gone. Emberley had held fast to her hope that her mother would return, but the search of the pass had dulled everyone's spirits. She was almost grateful they were all gone to war now, for she was weary of all the talk. All the speculation. No one knew *anything*, but they had no shortage of opinions on the matter.

Emberley knew one thing. If her mother wasn't returning, then she must go and fight for their Reach in her name.

"You aren't really considering going to war in *that*?"

Ember jumped back, tripping over scraps of metal. "Alasyr!"

"You are? You're going?"

"Why haven't you come?"

"You really intend to do it, don't you? You little fool."

Ember flushed, straightening what little she assembled for herself with a small measure of pride. "The Westerlands is my home. Marsh was right, though not for the reasons he meant. I must defend her. My mother would not want me sulking in the snowy shadows." She narrowed her eyes. "Why are you here, anyway? I called for you. You didn't answer."

"I'm here about your mother."

"My mother?"

Alasyr's steps crunched and then softened as he stepped from the snow into the dirt and hay. "Yes, Emberley, your mother. Lady Asherley."

Ember's breath caught. Her mouth parted. "You found her? You went to look for her, after all?"

"I didn't need to look for her," Alasyr said slowly, carefully. He stepped closer. As he did, a paralyzing nervousness traveled through Ember. Something was wrong.

Ember took a step back, but she didn't drop her eyes. "Where is she?"

Alasyr smiled bitterly. "Secrets will kill a man, if he holds them within too long. I watched a man die a few days ago. He was fit, healthy, and then he wasn't, and it was the secrets, his truths, that got him."

"Alasyr, you're not making any sense. What does this have to do with my mother?"

"I have a secret. And, as your mother so wisely said, if I share it, my life is forfeit."

"My mother? You *talked* to her?"

"Oh, yes. Because your mother didn't die against the cliffs like the Rhiagain princess. She was unharmed in the fight, and was taken, by my father, to Midnight Crest, where she has been his prisoner ever since."

Ember gasped. "No. You lie."

Alasyr lifted his hands. "I have everything to lose with the truth, and nothing to gain in deception." He laughed. "What does it even matter? What does any of it matter? Do you think Ravenna asked herself this same question when she ran off with the Dereham boy?"

"I... I don't know," Ember managed. Her mother. At Midnight Crest. It wasn't possible, was it? She saw no lie in Alasyr, despite her desperate accusation. And how she wanted to believe it... how she needed to. Her mother was alive! "I knew she didn't die on that mountain."

"She'll die on another mountain if you don't save her."

"What does your father want with her?"

"I don't know. Nothing makes sense to me anymore. And you're asking the wrong question, Emberley Blackwood."

"What question should I be asking then?"

"Ask me how. How you will get to the top of a mountain that neither man nor horse can scale."

Ember shook her head. "All right. How?"

Alasyr leaned in and whispered next to her ear, "You fly."

JESSE HAD BEEN FOLLOWING their trail for hours. Neither Esmerelda nor Ravenna had bothered to cover it, and he only lost it once, after crossing a stream and finding they'd changed paths. He shook his head as he navigated the alteration. They were so off course they'd be dipping into the Easterlands in a day if they didn't correct.

He'd never understood the point in reliving past moments or conversations, but he couldn't help wondering if there was some word, some turn of phrase he could've used to prevent Esmerelda from leaving without him. He'd done all he could to convince her she was family now, no longer a burden. Whatever other purpose his life would serve, for now the one that involved protecting her was all that mattered. He wasn't done, even if she'd decided he was.

Fresh horse dung told him he was narrowing the gap. But what concerned him were the new tracks he saw coming from the south. Six, perhaps seven horses. His apprehension deepened when he saw them merge with the tracks from Esmerelda's and Ravenna's horses.

Jesse's own horse drew up in fear. He saw it, too. Two horses, not tethered, but not running, either. They shifted about, afraid, listless, as if they'd seen something terrible and couldn't decide what to do. Jesse clicked his tongue to ease his mare and slowly approached the scene.

He recognized Esmerelda's pack in a bush; the contents spilled. To the left, Ravenna's was in a similar state.

"Guardians," Jesse whispered, scanning, searching, for any other signs; anything at all that might prove out another outcome than the one that seemed most obvious.

But there was no denying it. The women had been taken. Whoever had taken them had been hunting them, perhaps for some time.

The trail was not yet cold. He could still catch them.

Jesse quickly dismounted to collect the packs when a curious sensation filled his chest. It was as if air was being pumped into him, and as he looked down, to examine the cause, he found his feet had left the ground and he was suspended in the air, looking down at the remains of the Esmerelda and Ravenna's fate.

"What foul nonsense is this?" he hissed, flailing his arms, willing himself back to the ground. This wasn't like the other strangeness surrounding him of late. He didn't need this, or ask for it. He desperately wanted it to go away, and that should have been enough to end it, but it wasn't.

Two figures stepped into his view from behind the trees. A man and a woman. Deep within him, he knew those words didn't describe these creatures, though. They might appear as such, but they were more. They were—

"Jamesan Strong. We've come a long way for you," the woman said. Her smile terrified him.

"Are you doing this? Let me down!"

"You can let yourself down," the man said. "There is nothing I have done to you that you are incapable of doing yourself."

"That's horseshit." Jesse grunted, trying again. "Release me!"

The woman raised a hand, and Jesse fell to the ground. He rolled toward the bush, reaching for his sword as he came back up.

But it would not release from the hilt. He struggled, yanking as he hobbled to his feet.

"I told you, Lysanor. I told you we should subdue him."

"No," Lysanor said, stepping closer to Jesse, still desperately working to free his sword. "I will not harm him. Nor will you. If you did, you'd be sore about it later. I know you, Isdemus."

Isdemus sighed. "Yes, yes. But look at him. He will never come willingly."

"Was it you? Was it you and your friend who took the women?"

"No," Lysanor said, smiling sadly. "But we know who did."

"Yes, we know who did, and you'll be very angry with us, but we will not be following them."

"Are ye feckin' mad?" Jesse demanded, incredulous. It was as if he was in the throes of a fever dream from which he couldn't wake. "Who are you, anyway? I've heard tales about the disgraced Magi. Is that it, are you on banishment?"

Lysanor laughed. Isdemus joined in.

"Banishment, yes, of a sort," Isdemus said. "But the Magi of the Sepulchre are babes in the woods. They know nothing."

"Not *nothing,* Isdemus, we've been over this. Their magic is different, that's all."

"It's inferior."

"*Different.*"

"If ye two are quite done, you can tell me who has my friends. I donnae need your aid, just aim me true," Jesse said. He'd given up on the sword and made for his horse. If only he could get some distance, he could be free of this profane magic and the peculiar creatures wielding it.

Lysanor sighed. "I hate when you're right. Catch him, will you?"

"Anything for you," Isdemus replied.

Before Jesse could make sense of their strange exchange, a darkness filled his vision, and he was falling, falling.

FOR DEATH, FOR LIFE, FOR VICTORY

33

HELP FROM OTHERS

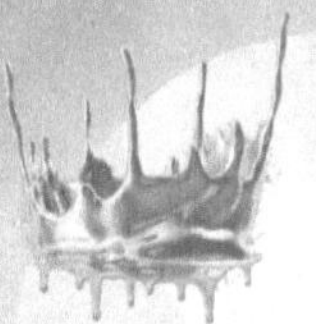

They weren't far from Whitechurch now. Khallum had wanted to cut through the Gap of Ever to bisect Fionn's Pass, but Oakenwell insisted there'd be more men to the south of Whitechurch in anticipation of that, and it was the men led by Strong and Garrick who were better prepared to distract them. If Lord Warwick and Lord Blackwood wanted to maintain their secrecy in position, Oakenwell said, they would have to add a day and cross where the pass eased at Rushwood.

Khallum hadn't made up his mind about Oakenwell. The man's earnest defection was written plainly upon his face. But when he tried to envision one of his own men doing the same, the raw discomfort this produced created a twinge of doubt. He both admired Oakenwell, for standing strong against tyranny, and also feared the very idea of him. What if Law, Rutland, or the others decided Khallum was a tyrant? Would they then also be the heroes in their tale, and he, the villain, as The Deceiver was in Oakenwell's tale?

They camped just beyond Rushwood, setting up in a spot where the homes gave way to forest, and the foothills provided some cover. They were small in number, Brandyn's Bannermen and Khallum's few trusted men, but if Hamish and Garrick came through, this wouldn't be a factor in victory. The might of the Southerlands could best the whole of Quinlanden's army with some luck, but most of Quinlanden's army was in the Westerlands. It would be a bloodbath.

Unless they deployed the Medvedev.

"Turning in, my lord," Rutland said with a nod before disappearing into his small tent. Law waved from a few paces down, doing the same. The others had already retired, except the prince, who was off on a walk by himself, something he did most nights. He'd never hear of anyone joining him. Khallum supposed he understood. The man had been alone with his thoughts for five years. Wasn't so easy to share them now.

Khallum started to kick dirt over the remnants of the fire when he heard his nephew come up behind him. He knew it was him by the soft sound of his steps against the undergrowth of the forest floor. Twelve was too young to be leading an army.

"Lord Warwick?"

Khallum turned. "We're kin, Brandyn. No need for formalities, unless the men are present."

Brandyn nodded. He looked down at his feet. "I can't sleep. I thought maybe you were having the same trouble."

"Aye," Khallum lied. "Sit. We'll enjoy the last of the embers and pass a tick."

Brandyn smiled in relief and settled upon a rock one of the others, Storm maybe, had brought over for them to sit on while they prepared the evening meal. "I know I've been to Whitechurch, but I don't remember it. I was much younger."

"A strange place. They live in the trees."

Brandyn laughed. "My mother says this is so they can lord over the less fortunate."

"I donnae suspect your ma is wrong in that."

"You know my mother, don't you? Were you friends?"

Khallum whistled through his lips. "I wouldnae say friends, but I respect her. She's tough. Tough as any man, I'd say. More than some."

"Like my father."

"Your father was salt and sand, through and through."

"Can you tell me about him?"

Khallum took a swig from his wine flask. He passed it to Brandyn, who shook his head. "Byrne? You spent more time with him than me. Been twenty years or more since he called the Southerlands home."

"I know who my father was. He was good and kind, and made more time for us than would be expected of a man," Brandyn said carefully. "But he was more than that. I'd like to see him through your eyes, Uncle."

Khallum chuckled, his breath turning into a small cloud in the cool night air. "Aye, well, Byrne was a funny lad. Ye have to know, most Warwicks are serious, as it goes. We're tough. Yesenia was the toughest of all. She'd smack us around if we even looked like a tear might spring into our eyes. When we were quite little, I mean. Tell us we were weak, due to the tiny cod flapping between our thighs, and she, who was born to bear children into the world, was tougher than the gems we sprang from the mines."

Brandyn giggled. "She said that?"

"Oh, aye. And Byrne, she'd tell him to harden up. Remind him that salt and sand had no soft edges, ye ken? It should cut ye, not soothe ye. But one day, she stopped fussing him. She knew he wasnae like she and I, and she accepted it, I think, in her own way."

"Did something happen that made her change her mind?"

Khallum nodded, looking off into the dark woods. "One day... t'was raining, that's what I remember clearest. The rain. Enough for a month, but in hours. Mud pooling everywhere, men getting their boots stuck in it. Byrne was hunting. Hated it, he did, but

Father made us all do it, even though we had men to do it for us. Said men provided, from kings to clothiers, and if we were men, we provided. Was a simple thing to him. Not to Byrne, who loved all things, two or four legged."

Brandyn smiled softly. His eyes glassed over as the dying smoke passed by. "He still did. I remember that most of all."

Khallum nodded. "Aye, well, he loved them then, and my father, he didnae catch it in time. He never understood his youngest boy. And I ken neither did Yesenia and I. But that day, he came back with his arms full of birds. Sparrows, little things. Not even birds among the wiser of them, but there were dozens of them. Dead, all of 'em. Not a speck of blood, so no struggle with something bigger. Just dead. Yesenia and I told 'im he'd be sick, he played with 'em too long, but he dropped to his knees and cried. Scattered the dead birds around him and lay in the middle and sobbed. Yesenia began in on him, but something stayed her. She turned to me and said, 'donnae let Father see this,' and we kept Byrne safe from him for that night. And then in the morning, he wasnae lying in the center anymore. He was sitting. And the birds? They were alive as day, swirling and chirping around his head as he laughed and laughed."

Brandyn gasped. "They returned to life? Did he... did he do that?"

Khallum shrugged, grunting. "My brother had no magic in him before that day, or after that day. But I cannae deny what I saw. Yesenia saw it, too. And she never said another word to him about the tiny cod between his thighs, or his tender heart."

"Wow. I never knew that."

Khallum nodded. "Don't suppose he talked much about us, did he?"

"Not really. We asked him, Ember and me mostly. But he never wanted to talk about it."

"Aye, I suppose he wouldn't. I've fooled myself, all these years, believing Byrne was salt and sand, but he was always meant to wed your ma, I ken, and end up where the Guardians meant to place him all along."

"I don't know who I'm most like," Brandyn said with a long sigh. "I think my men believe I'm my mother's son, but I... I'm not so sure, Uncle Khallum. I think I'm more my father."

Khallum kicked dirt at the edges of the fire to quell the rise of emotion trapped in his chest. "There's no shame to be found in being the son of Byrne Warwick, Brandyn. He was the best of us all."

Brandyn hung his head. "Yeah. He was my best friend."

Khallum reached over and squeezed his shoulder. "Shall we go over the plan once more?"

LISBET HAD TOLD THEM EVERYTHING. All of it. Every last terrible truth Kian had tossed in her lap like a sweetmeat. She watched the faces of Eavan, Gabrianna, and Meadow as they absorbed that Valen was Dain Rhiagain, and that Drystan and Lisbet were his children. Observing this was like experiencing it all over again, but with access to her own emotions, which had been shoved aside with everything she'd ever known about herself. Through their eyes, their gasps, their disbelief, Lisbet felt it all sink deep into her marrow. No longer a story, but a reality that was a part of her.

And though they had questions, lots of questions, they all believed her. Just as she'd believed Kian. Somewhere within her, she'd always known that her truth wasn't what she'd been given these past fourteen years, and these revelations brought the gaps to a close. The puddles of doubt receded, and the sun peeked through. She wondered if they could see this in her, and that was why their own dubiousness faded as her words went on, barreling toward the shocking end.

"We can't save him," she'd told them, days ago, when they

were still under the veil of the Drumain of the Hinterlands. "I would give my life to save him, but it would be another life wasted, for he would still die."

"But you want to go to him, don't you?" Eavan asked through her tears. "Even so?"

"Not to stop him, Eavan. I... my mother always told me there are things bigger than ourselves. Things that can hurt us, to save others. I never understood it until now." Lisbet shook her head. "No, I can't stop him. I can't take this last act of heroism from him. But I can see him one last time."

"I know of this Mortain. I heard my mother speak of him, with her seer, Joran. He's a monster, from another world," Gabi said. In her eyes was a hollow, faraway look.

"I was afraid of him," Eavan said. "He's not like us."

"Kian said the same," Lisbet answered. "But he also said Drystan can succeed, as long as he doesn't know his truth, like I do. I think... I think because he would sink under the pressure of knowing such a thing."

"I always knew you were special." Eavan grinned, wiping at her eyes. "I always knew you were more than snow and ice and furs."

"I will always be Lisbet Dereham of Wulfsgate," she corrected her. "But I'm also something else, and I've been given this revelation for a reason."

"What?" Meadow asked? "What reason?"

"I don't know yet. Kian insisted I must discover this for myself."

"How convenient. How he loves his riddles," Eavan quipped. Color had returned to her cheeks. Lisbet hoped that meant the fire within her was burning once more.

"And we have to go? Now?" Gabi asked. When Lisbet nodded, she added, "I have to admit, I was reluctant to come here, terrified *being* here, but now I'm just as scared to leave."

Lisbet reached forward and squeezed her hand. "Me too, Gabi. I'm feeling all sorts of ways about all of this."

"So we can go home?" Meadow asked.

"Your home is at war," Lisbet said to her. "Your home is not safe."

"But Brook went home!"

"We don't know where Brook went. Only that he escaped."

"Lisbet is right," Gabi said. "And so was Drystan, for going to stop this madness. I know Uncle Aiden isn't a good man, but I don't think he would have done this on his own."

"But now we must decide where *we* go," Lisbet said to them all. "Wulfsgate is safe. The keep is a fortress and the borders are closed to anyone who doesn't belong. Eavan, you can take Gabi and Meadow there until this all ends. My mother will see after everyone."

Eavan shook her head. "And leave you? Not a chance."

"I'm heading straight into the lion's den. It may be a one-way journey."

Eavan shrugged. "Then we better be prepared for it. Right, girls?"

Gabi and Meadow each hesitated before nodding. "That's right," Gabi said. "I left what was safe to save my sister, and now she's gone. And my father is gone. And my home may never be the same. What's left for me, if not to help others?"

"Let's go, Lisbet," Eavan said with a small smile. "Let's go see your brother. And then, when the end has come, we will return him to your mother, and to his place among the ancestors of Wulfsgate."

Marsh rode up on his horse. "The scouts have returned from Parth. There're no reports yet of Quinlanden men coming toward the border."

"Good," Holden said.

"Is that good, Lord Dereham?" Marsh asked. "We're here because they expect them to be drawn off, toward the Easterlands. If they're not drawn off, then Lord Blackwood's plan hasn't succeeded, has it?"

Christian pulled his hood tighter around his face. It was warmer south of the Northerlands, but the winds were merciless. "I know waiting is hard, Marsh. But that's what war is. Waiting, for days, weeks, months, and then, at last, being thrust into the worst day of your life."

Marsh grinned. "Sounds great."

"They'll come," Holden said. He didn't share their humors. "The boy has Khallum Warwick at his side. He'll not miss an opportunity to draw blood."

Marsh hunkered down on his horse as another hard wind ripped off the Seven Sisters. "It's not more than a couple days ride home for me, from here."

"Your home won't be home until this war is over," Christian cautioned. "You don't know what you'd find."

"Yeah. Right," Marsh answered. He looked toward the mountains. "I only hope Blackfen passed my message to them, that I was safe in Wulfsgate. I'd like that to be their last word of me, if things go poorly for them, or us."

"It does a man no good to think of the end," Holden said. "It comes either way."

"I feel so much better," Marsh muttered.

"I know waiting is hard," Christian said. "And I know you worry about Ember, but she's safer there than anywhere else in the kingdom."

"It's not her safety I worry for," Marsh said.

Christian nodded knowingly. "Ahh. Alasyr? He ignites her curiosity, that's all. She looks for part of herself in him, for the blood they share. Pay it no mind."

"Alasyr? The Ravenwood boy?" Holden asked. "What's Ember doing with him?"

"Nothing, Father," Christian said, passing a look at Marsh. "He's dipped down toward Wulfsgate in his efforts to find his sister, is all."

"Hmph. He should remember his place. We don't venture up Icebolt Mountain, lingering near their home."

"We couldn't even if we wanted to," Christian said. "There's no way up that mountain without wings."

"Mother's blood. What is Alric saying to our men now?"

Christian turned toward where his father was looking and saw his uncle gathered in a group of men. The ones behind him were laughing and rolling their eyes. The ones in front of him wore humoring looks, inciting the ones making fun.

A sudden anger rolled through Christian as he watched their treatment of him. "I don't care what he's said. I won't condone any man treating the brother of the lord of our Reach with such disrespect, and neither should you."

Christian clicked his tongue, spurring Sun into action, and went to go do what his father would not.

Khallum drew a circle in the dirt with a long yew branch. "Here's Whitechurch." He traced two Xs to the upper right and left. "You, me, Oakenwell, Joran, will be here," he said, pointing to the westernmost X.

"And Storm."

"Aye," Khallum said, shaking his head. "And your little friend."

"I'll wager she's killed more men than you have."

Khallum ignored him. "Rutland, Law, the James men, and our friend we willnae name aloud will go west. This will keep our power divided between the camps, should one be discovered. I ken I'll have the Grand Minister ride ahead to Whitechurch, for they wouldnae dare assault a man of the Reliquary, Westerland roots or nay. There's none in a better position to assess the state of things there."

Brandyn dropped his voice. "Perhaps our 'friend' should not have come at all. Not without reinforcements."

"We have reinforcements coming from the south."

"But when?"

"Soon."

Brandyn scowled. "I don't want our men walking into an ambush."

"Do ye suppose I've not thought of that, then?" Khallum countered, bristling.

"No, I—"

"Because I've come to do more than aid ye, nephew. I intend to win your Reach back. And when the tallies are figured, it will be the Southerlands with the most numbers, the most men who showed to save the Westerlands."

Brandyn kicked his feet over the rudimentary battle map in the dirt. "Good night, Uncle."

34
WORDS AND DEEDS

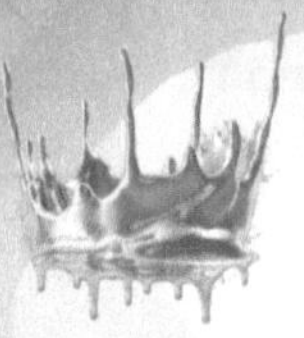

Eoghan dismissed his Master of Ships in a rage. He hadn't even known he had one. Correen told him, when he demanded she tell him why Maeryn Blackwood hadn't arrived yet.

"I have heard nothing myself, but let us engage the Master of Ships."

"Master of Ships? What does he do, exactly?"

"He would know of any vessels scheduled for port at Duncarrow, a fortnight or so in advance. A ship doesn't leave its origin port until the receiving port has approved them, so if anything was properly planned, he would have it recorded."

"Fascinating. So he would have known about the ship that carried our sister, Lady Blackwood, and the others?"

Correen set her lips tight. "Not exactly, Eoghan. That ship was scheduled to port with resources for the keep, and that was precisely what was on board. It was the departure that was done under subterfuge."

"Fascinating."

"Eoghan," Correen said. "I cannot fault you for searching for a place to lay blame. But that betrayal happened elsewhere, and it does us no good to punish those who are loyal to us. Shall I fetch him?"

The Master of Ships was useless. He had no word of Maeryn Blackwood arriving now or at any time. He offered to double-check his logs, to which Eoghan agreed, with little hope in the results, and sent him off.

When he was gone, Correen asked, "Shall I send for Oldwin? It was he you left in charge of sending for her, yes?"

"No!"

"All right." Correen folded her hands over her torso.

"Say it."

"Say what?"

"Whatever it is you want to say but are holding back!"

"Are you certain later would not be better, in your current humors?"

"Now!" Eoghan thundered.

"Very well." Correen sighed, and the sound bore the heaviness of a feeling long kept. "There's been more news from the kingdom."

Eoghan dropped into his chair and waved his hand. "Go on, then. I don't care how bad it is. I want to measure it against the words Oldwin uses when he comes in here to give his own reports."

"Word has spread of Mortain's treachery against the Medvedev. Somehow, this has made its way across the kingdom, and now there are even more stirrings of rebellion."

"Against Aiden?"

"Against you!" Correen cleared her throat. "Against you," she said again, this time with less enthusiasm. "For there is no disabusing anyone of the belief that Lord Quinlanden acted under your command in everything he's done so far."

"But he's a rogue!"

"Would you like me to spread that word?"

Eoghan groaned and slumped lower in his chair. His bones hurt today, more than usual. They felt as if they were shrinking, pulling him inward. "No, for the only thing worse than my command of his acts is my ignorance of them. Tell me more of the rebellion."

"My men have sent word of an army marching upon Whitechurch. From the Southerlands."

"Oh? Let them raze it. Perhaps that will be the satisfying end we all crave."

"Eoghan. If we know of it, then so do Quinlanden's men, and Mortain. And if they know of it, then they will meet force with force. There will be war."

"How many times have I said that I *do not want war* in this kingdom!"

Correen closed her eyes. "What we want is not always what we get. I cannot slow the hand of time, or stay what is already in motion. We should discuss the deployment of the Rhiagain Guard."

"Are you my Master of War?"

"No, but you also don't have a Master of War, as you've not replaced the one our father dismissed."

"Then who leads my armies?"

"Your generals on land, and admirals for your small naval command. From the Isle of Belcarrow. I could have them here by supper tomorrow."

"I already told Oldwin I will not deploy men." Eoghan inhaled. The dry air burned his tender lungs. "Do you know how little of this he tells me? He parcels it out, careful words with sinister smiles. He was here only this morning, and he said nothing of the Medvedev rumor. Nothing of the men marching upon Whitechurch. He speaks of little pockets of rebellion, kept down by

Quinlanden's men. And I have allowed this. I have allowed Quinlanden's men to subdue those who haven't betrayed me as he has. Is it any wonder the kingdom believes this comes from Duncarrow?"

"What would you like me to do, Eoghan?"

"I think... I think Oldwin is working against me, Correen. How could I have been so blind?"

"Can I speak honestly?"

"Have I ever asked you to lie?"

Correen sat down across from him. She dropped her voice low. "Father locked the sorcerers away for a reason. He knew they were dangerous. That they couldn't be trusted. That no matter what gain there was to be had in what they could do, what they knew, it was not worth the price. And I think you've known for a while that Oldwin works for no one but himself, but you'd hoped what he could bring you would be enough."

Eoghan buried his face in his hands. "But it isn't enough. He's given me nothing. And I fear he will take everything." He looked up. "What does he want? What does Mortain want?"

Correen shook her head. "I don't know. I don't think Father knew, either. And that scared him, as it should scare you."

"What do I do?"

"I don't know," she said after a pause. "It will not be so easy to put them back in their box."

"I could have them arrested. They're powerful, but my Knights of Duncarrow could subdue them."

"You could."

"What? You don't think I should?"

Correen glanced toward the door with a careful look. "Brother, I do not think that the sorcerers were locked up for so long because they were forced to be, but because they chose to be. Metal and stone alone aren't enough to subdue creatures who possess their power. If you put them back in the sky dungeon, this time they'll not bother to feign as if it has any power over them at all."

"Then what?"

"Did you know there are new prisoners in the sky dungeon? Has he told you?"

"New prisoners? Who?"

"Esmerelda Warwick, and the Ravenwood. Ravenna."

Eoghan gasped. He nearly laughed. "The old fool did it. He wasn't lying after all."

Correen reached forward and clasped one of his bony hands in hers. "Do not let this ease your mind on Oldwin! He's done it to distract you, Eoghan. To keep the child entertained so the father can do as he pleases."

Eoghan's smile faded. "I say again, Correen, then what?"

"For now, play his game. Be the unwitting boy king he takes you for. For the only way to win against him is to let him think *he* is winning."

THEY MADE camp south of Oak Hill, just miles from the Southerlands border. Wyat waited until he heard their breathing slow, before he dropped to his knees, eyes to the sky and the Guardians.

"Oh Guardian of the Unpromised Future, I beseech you to keep your watchful gaze moving, and to pass over the bodies of Anabella and Stefan, for their promise is yet to be fulfilled. And to you, Guardian of Anguish and Tribulation, I say, with fealty and kindness, that you have spent enough upon these two. Let your work be done." Wyat closed his eyes. The air was warmer here than it had been, and he let it pass over his flesh with gratitude. Here, they could sleep outdoors, safe from the elements. "And at last, Guardian of Rebirth and Renewal, I beseech you, most of all, to see within the hearts of Anabella and Stefan and in that sight witness their worthiness of you. Of a new life, and the happiness that comes with it. They have not endured this much in the purview of your brethren for naught."

When he was done, Wyat traced his finger along the path of the Guardians and then kissed his finger. He stood, looking down at the sleeping woman and child.

"What would you have wanted, Darrick? This? Am I still on the path you would've set me upon?" he whispered with a sigh. Too many years had passed. He no longer knew the man he'd once loved with near the same commitment as he'd given the Guardians. This Darrick, fresh from five years of hard labor, was not the same man, and he couldn't know what he wanted. Did he even still possess the same idealism? The same belief in truth and honor?

Wyat walked down to the stream that ran adjacent to their small camp. He'd do about anything to take a dip, but he'd have to be satisfied with refilling their skins. A few hours of rest, and then they needed to be back on the road. Not long now until Whitecliffe, and their next gamble with safety.

And Darrick, if the Guardians willed it.

He was in the middle of relieving himself when he heard the crunching sound. He strained to see in the dark. Nothing. But then the sound echoed, again. He finished his business and quietly buckled his trousers, dropping one hand to his sword.

Wyat stepped quietly through the forest. He could still see nothing, nothing to confirm the sounds. He heard Stefan cry out and he quickened his pace, returning to the camp just in time to see the boy being carried off.

"Stop!" Wyat cried. He released his sword from its sheath, and the sound of metal filled the cool air. "Drop the boy!"

The thief cast a quick glance over his shoulder and cried out,

"He'll fetch a meal or three! Shouldnae ha' left him alone!" The thief bolted back into the forest, toward the hill.

Anabella started to rouse. She looked at Wyat, groggy, confused. "What's happened?" Her eyes widened. "Where's Stefan?"

"You stay here!" Wyat cried, pointing the sword first at her and then in the direction the thief had taken Stefan. "Take out your dagger and stay put!"

Wyat flew through the brush, ignoring the sting of branches slapping his face. He moved faster, but it seemed the thief had twice his speed and had gained nearly enough distance to be free.

Wyat pushed harder, leaping over logs, even the dead carcass of a bear. At last, Stefan's red hair flashed under a spill of moonlight. He was getting closer, but not close enough. Not nearly close enough.

Panting, Wyat reached within himself for whatever reserves remained. He screamed out a groan and launched himself into the night, well aware his heart might explode in his chest if he pushed any harder.

Ahead, Stefan screamed. His horror tore a hole through Wyat.

As the night air slapped him, Wyat remembered the small axe strapped to his waist. He'd used it just that night for firewood, sharpening it on a whetstone while Anabella heated their stew. He reached for it, struggling against the leather strap. Years before, as a boy, he'd been the best at throwing daggers. His father thought he'd enter the Rhiagain Guard, maybe train as an assassin, but Wyat had no hunger for blood, or for war. His only desire was to learn.

But he had no choice now. It was this, or lose Stefan to the thief, whose own hunger must have been greater than all Wyat's defenses against him. Slowing only slightly, he released the axe and raised it up, dropping it behind, near his ear. He said a silent prayer to the Guardians and then, channeling the remainder of his energy into the weapon, he let sail the axe.

The axe whistled as it passed through the air. The thief must have heard it, and his curiosity got the best of him as he turned, just as the axe split his forehead in two.

Wyat ran until his legs gave out, which happened at the same time the thief dropped to his knees. A viscous stream of blood flowed from where the axe was embedded in his head, flanked by two startled eyes. Stefan rolled out of his arms, and as soon as he hit the forest floor, he stumbled toward Wyat.

"I only wished for a meal," the thief said, breathless, before falling to the side.

Stefan wrapped himself in Wyat's arms, sobbing. "It's okay, Stefan. Everything is fine, now. You're safe."

"He was going to eat me!" Stefan cried. His tiny hands made fists around Wyat's shirt.

"He wasn't going to eat you. Come, let's go back to your mother." Wyat lifted the boy in his arms and turned away from the dead man, before either of them could dwell on the horrific scene too long.

When they returned to camp, Wyat dropped Stefan into his mother's arms and went to roll his bed and pack his things. "If there was one, there will be more. We have to leave now."

"Shh, baby, easy now," Anabella said, comforting her son. "Wyat. What happened?"

"We can speak of it later. For now, we have to go."

"I won't go until you tell me." She stood, reaching for his arm. "You're shaking."

"I killed a man!" Wyat cried. He recoiled from her touch. "I've never taken a life before now. I swore I never would."

"You did it to protect Stefan."

"My reasons don't matter when a man is dead."

"Wyat, they *do* matter. The Guardians don't expect you to be idle when someone means you harm. Do we have any ale left? You need something to calm you."

Wyat stumbled away from her, flailing his arms. "I don't need ale. I don't need your words. I don't need the deed erased."

Anabella backed away. She pressed one hand to the back of Stefan's head, as if protecting him. "Then tell me what to do."

"Pack. We're leaving tonight."

"For you. What to do for you."

"Nothing." Wyat emptied his bowl from the evening's meal, shaking the remnants into the dirt, before shoving it in his bag. "I told you. I don't need anything."

"Perhaps we were wrong to leave Duncarrow when we did," Anabella said, sighing. She packed with one hand, holding the hysterical Stefan with the other. "If we'd waited a little longer—"

"You'd be dead if you'd waited," Wyat rejoined. "Correen had been growing that seed in Eoghan for months, perhaps years. There was no greater threat to Eoghan's seat than Stefan, and daily she reminded him of this. She would've had you tossed into the White Sea, forgotten to all."

"Is this better?" Anabella hissed. "We're not safe anywhere! You took a life to save my son, but that man isn't the first to die on his behalf, is he? What of those lives Assyria took to protect our secret? I cannot live like this, Wyat, and neither can Stefan. I cannot bear the burden of these lives on my conscience, nor of your own horror at being the bringer of death. Of what will happen to you if Eoghan or his men discover what you've done for us."

Wyat closed his eyes. He inhaled, filling his lungs, releasing some of the night's poison back into the air. His hands still trembled, but there was nothing he could do about that. Not now. "We'll be with Darrick soon, and he will know what to do."

• • •

"Ravenna! Wake already!"

Ravenna could hear her name, the sound of Esmerelda's voice, but both felt like they were at the end of a long hall, or part of her dreamscape. It seemed important to follow the sound. She opened her eyes.

"Oh, thank the Guardians!" Esmerelda cried. She swayed, gripping her belly, and blew out a measured breath. "I think I know where we are. I've heard my father talk of this place. The sky dungeon."

As Ravenna blinked reality into existence, she could see they were in a small room, made of stone. Behind Esmerelda was a tiny window with bars, and to her right, a desk. "The sky dungeon?"

"Aye, at Duncarrow. They put all their prisoners at the top of the tallest tower. They don't fear their escape because the only way out is death."

That sounded a bit like The Rookery, Ravenna thought, but the revelation was quickly replaced by a splitting pain in her head as she tried to sit. A tight sound escaped her as she winced. "They must have never had a Ravenwood prisoner, then. My raven form can fit through the bars. I'll go for help."

Esmerelda's face fell. She didn't want to be alone, that was clear, but she didn't say it aloud. "Right. Right! You can fly to Jesse, and he'll know what to do."

Ravenna whipped her head around to take in the rest of their surroundings. She was sitting on a bed made of straw. Now that her senses had returned to her, the putrid scent coming off bedding that had probably never been washed made her gag hard enough to clap her hands over her mouth. Beyond that, a pot for relieving. The desk from before. A pile of sticks and rocks in the corner, assembled in a way that reminded her of how Nyssa and Torrin would play with random things from the Wintergarden at Wulfsgate. And vellum.

It was better than the bottom of the rough sacks they'd been held in for days untold, but not by much.

"Someone was recently here," she said.

"What do you think happened to him?" Esmerelda asked. She had trouble being still. She shifted from foot to foot, eyes passing over the same things, over and over.

"Her, I think," Ravenna replied. "I think a woman was here. And maybe a child."

"A child? In here? That's incomprehensible," Esmerelda said. "I hope they escaped."

"Your hope would be wasted on any unfortunate enough to find themselves here."

"You should go," Esmerelda said. The words looked as if they pained her. "Quickly. Before they return."

Ravenna approached her. "Will you be okay here, by yourself?"

Esmerelda sucked in a hard breath. "I have no choice, do I? Go, before I find I'm too weak to allow it."

Ravenna hesitated, and then kissed Esmerelda on the side of her mouth. "I swear to you, I won't leave you here to suffer. I'll raise an entire army if I have to." She read the fear in Esmerelda. "Esme, I won't let you deliver this child here, in a prison."

Esmerelda dropped her eyes. "Don't promise me anything, Ravenna. I find my strength in truth, not pretty lies."

Ravenna lifted Esmerelda's chin with her finger. "I'm not your father. I'm not Ryan, or Jesse, who would speak their words with the best intentions, not knowing how they inadvertently place you deeper in the cage. If I make it away from Duncarrow, then it would take death to keep me from returning for you."

Esmerelda laughed quietly. "We were hardly friends before this, and now you talk as if we're sisters."

"Have you any sisters, Esmerelda?"

"Only brothers."

"I have sisters. I didn't choose them. They didn't choose me. But I choose you. My sister in choice."

"There are worse choices," Esmerelda said, with a light twinkle in her eyes.

They both turned in a snap toward the sound of the cell door creaking open. A man. Ravenna had never seen him before, but there was something strange and familiar about him, like laying eyes upon one sharing your blood for the first time. His eyes belied someone of great age, but he seemed no older than her own father. The lines drawing his face into hard sections confused her further on this matter.

He raised a hand and the cell door slammed closed behind him.

"Sorcerer," Ravenna whispered. Esmerelda huddled closer to her.

"Was it the magic, Mistress Ravenwood? Or had you sorted this out even before that?" the man asked. His grin sent a chill straight to her feet.

Ravenna regarded him with a hard stare.

"I've heard of your kind before," Esmerelda said, eyes narrowing. "Was this your cell? I'm surprised you were so willing to surrender the accommodations."

"Mine was down the hall, Lady Warwick. Or do they still call one a lady once they've feigned their death and forsaken their family?"

"And what do they call you?" she demanded.

"Oldwin." He affected a light bow. "I've come to arrange your marriages to the king. How fortunate you both are that my men came across you in your travels."

Esmerelda spat on the floor. "I died once to keep myself from the hands of the craven ratsbane. Donnae think I won't do it again."

"Esme," Ravenna cautioned. "I'm afraid your king will be

disappointed. Esmerelda is already married, and I'm forbidden from marrying outside my blood."

Oldwin laughed. He clutched his chest. "For Esmerelda, I believe the word you seek is *widow,* that is, if you were even wed at all, and I say you were not. Ryan Strong belongs to the Wastelands. To the king. His life is forfeit."

Ravenna squeezed Esmerelda's hand in warning.

"Will the king pretend this child is his, then?" Esmerelda demanded. "The rumor in the kingdom is he cannot function to create his own."

Oldwin's grin faded from his lined face. He blinked, regarding Esmerelda with a strange look. "Your child has no place in this kingdom. Your *child* will be cast into the sea, like Darrick Rhiagain, or perhaps smashed upon the rocks, depending on my spirits the day of its unfortunate birth."

This time, Esmerelda spat upon the sorcerer's face. "Touch me or mine and die."

Oldwin calmly wiped the spittle from his eye and turned to Ravenna. "As for you," Oldwin said, stepping closer. As he did, his full height became more clear. He towered over them, casting a shadow in body and deed. But he knelt so that their faces nearly touched. "I see no other Ravenwood here to enforce your meaningless laws. Your marriage to the king begins a new era in the kingdom, one long overdue, would you not say?"

"Is the king so desperate for brides you must kidnap them now?" Esmerelda quipped.

Oldwin slapped her so hard she flew back, stumbling against the deck chair. When Ravenna went to reach for her, Oldwin snapped her back, gripping her forearm in his bony hand. "But don't think, Ravenna, that I've completely disregarded your concern for the Ravenwood traditions. You missed out on the most important one of all, did you not? The Langenacht."

Ravenna swallowed hard. "I chose another life."

Oldwin tilted his head to the side. "But, according to *tradition*, you cannot simply choose not to! So, do not trouble yourself. When your brethren hear of this wedding, they will know we did not throw aside *all* the Ravenwoods hold dear."

Oldwin cupped her face in his hands. They were clammy, cold. "Every male Rhiagain, boy or man, will have their chance to compete against the king for the right to your hand."

35

CLEVER, SLIPPERY

Varinya knew as well as anyone, and better than some, how ephemeral a secret was. Their very existence as Ravenwoods in a foreign kingdom had been woven around the protection of secrecy, and yet as individuals it was unthinkable to keep their own.

It was not her own secret that plagued her today, but Argentyn's. Clever, slippery Argentyn, who thought so highly of his abilities that he'd never considered others might discover his behavior. It grated on her that he was partly right; he'd carried on for some time before she picked up on it. And it wasn't even her, but her mother, Adynora, which so finely underscored Varinya's own failure on the matter that it nearly cut her open.

I trust you'll deal with the matter, Daughter.

Yes, Mother.

Is that a tear? Put it away. Save it, for if you cannot tidy this mess Argentyn has created, you'll be spending it on him.

Had anyone else discovered what he'd been up to, he'd be dead already.

He was not the only Ravenwood man to think his skills superior to the women. Many of them were this way, accepting their place in the hierarchy while harboring the private belief that the females were no more than figureheads needing to be guided by the more knowledgeable and competent.

Varinya had stopped giving care to Argentyn's opinions of her when she took the veil of High Priestess. He could no longer lay his hands on her in violence, and he'd been forced into more caution with his words. Tradition didn't change feelings, but she was safer married to him than she'd been as his sister.

His behavior now, however, had left them all vulnerable. Varinya. Her children. The entire Rookery, if word spread and a discussion was had about the half-blood being kept prisoner within their walls.

Nor was Lady Blackwood the first half-blood to live amongst the stone and cold of Midnight Crest, but that was a secret she no longer felt the same urgency to protect. It was history now, like a passing storm.

She sat upon the throne in the Courtyard Regents. He'd kept her waiting, and he would pay for that as well, for the pain building in her neck from sitting so erect for so long only incensed her further. Even the midnight goats, cooing as they passed by the fabric of her gown, couldn't soften her heart today.

At last Argentyn stepped upon the ice. His hands were laced behind his back and he wore a casual look, as if he'd been summoned to help her find her missing slipper. "You called for me?"

"You called for me, High Priestess," she corrected.

The lazy grin faded away. "Really, Varinya?"

"Really, High Priestess."

He shook his head. "Very well. You called for me, *High Priestess*, and I am here. Have we an audience?"

"You better pray not, or even I cannot save you from the fate awaiting you."

Argentyn wore his concern in the lines of his brow. "Has something happened?"

"Only that which you have designed and driven into existence yourself, you foolish man." She kept her head held high, offering not a whisper of the familiarity he was so used to with her. "I should ask you why you've done it, but your answer would make me complicit."

"I'm quite lost, Varinya—"

"High Priestess! And you are *not* lost, Argentyn Ravenwood, you know very well why you are here, what you have done, and what I know. It will not be long before the entire Rookery knows!"

His breath swirled in the frigid air. He looked behind him, shifting, then gave a short laugh. "I saved her life."

Varinya was incredulous. "I'll need a better explanation than that. What is her life to you? To me? To any of us?"

"She has our blood, V... High Priestess."

"She has the blood of a traitor, Argentyn! She is *not* one of us. That may not be her fault, but nor is it our problem, yet you've deigned to make it ours, and so now it is."

"Lady Blackwood may be useful to us. If we could study her, study her magic, we might better understand the effects of mixing bloodlines, of how far Rhosyn's line has strayed from ours, of—"

"Oh, spare me your lies of selflessness and service. You don't want her here to enrich our knowledge. Even I know that."

Argentyn bristled. "If you know so much, then tell me. What are my motivations?"

This was the problem. She didn't have this answer. She couldn't see into his heart, and this troubled her. "Her time here has come to an end."

Argentyn laughed. "What would you have me do, cast her against the mountain?"

His laugh died when Varinya didn't disabuse him of this suggestion. "You? You will do nothing. I will take things from here. You are not to visit her. You are not to speak of her. You are not to even think of her, not even in your passing thoughts, or the space of your dreams. It is as if, to you, she no longer exists at all."

"What will you do with her?"

"That is no longer your concern."

Wulfsgate had never felt so still.

The bustle of travelers, shopkeepers, and smiths had died away, replaced by the occasional woman, huddled in her furs, passing down the road alone or with her small children. Even the energy of the keep had shifted; the kitchens were no longer so lively with only a handful of mouths to concern themselves with, and the absence of men walking the halls meant her thoughts were now so loud it was as if she was being screamed at, in echoes.

There were still men; those left by Holden to guard the gates, and the keep. But they were not her men.

Gretchen's place was here, despite how empty and alone she felt. She would not leave her youngest children with anyone, not now, and maybe not ever again. They were all she had left. And when Pieter returned to her—a possibility she forced herself to believe, in the same way she strong-armed her mind to imagining Drystan and Lisbet might one day return—she had to be here to welcome him home.

But the quiet was driving her to madness.

Gretchen finished the last of the jug of wine and lifted herself away from the table. Her head was woozy with drink, and she swayed on her feet, but it didn't stop her from finding the old familiar path and making her way down the stairs with the damp walls, toward the one place in all the Northerlands where she could be free.

"Ash," she whispered, breathless, as she clutched a gap in the mossy stones. She'd come down the stairs too fast, and now her head was a whirlwind. "I know what you said before. I held fast to your belief in me, I did. I swear it. But I *need* you. I need you, and if you love me, you'll come to me."

The only answer to her plea was the thump of her heart beating in her ears.

"Mother's blood, Ash, do I have to beg? Because I will! I'll drop to my knees and prostrate myself before you, and say whatever it is you wish me to say to return you to me!"

"Mama?"

Gretchen gasped. She whirled around. The light from her torch swung wildly, her eyes following suit, until they landed upon little Nyssa.

She knelt down before her daughter. "Nyssa, darling, what are you doing here?"

"I couldn't sleep."

"No?" Gretchen touched her face with the back of her hands. "You're warm. Do you feel poorly?"

"When will Father be home? And Christian?"

"I don't know, wulfling. They've left to keep us all safe. The Northerlands, and the kingdom."

Nyssa's tired eyes widened. "That sounds very important."

Gretchen nodded. "It is. I can't think of anything more important than what they've gone to do. Shall I heat some stew for you?"

Nyssa shook her head. "I'm not hungry." She looked past her mother, and, with a light gasp, pointed. "What are those?"

Gretchen turned and realized her daughter was asking about the tombs. That this was the first time she'd seen one. Neither Gretchen nor Holden had brought the twins here before. "This is where your ancestors have gone to be at rest after their promise was spent."

Nyssa twisted her face. "There are dead people down here?"

"They are only bodies now. Their souls have gone to be with the Guardians."

"Are all the people who died in Wulfsgate here?" Nyssa seemed to be calculating what accommodating such a thing would require.

"No, wulfling. Only your father's family. Like this one, see? Hadden Dereham. This was your grandfather. And with him, your grandmother, Mylannie."

"How did he die?"

"No one knows. They found him one morning, having passed in his sleep." How many times had she told this lie? Pretended that the deaths of all the mothers and fathers of the lords and ladies forced into marriage were not a gift of the crown?

"I hope that's how I die," Nyssa said plainly. She read another tomb and drew an inward gasp. "Torrin. Is that for my brother?"

"No, wulfling, that isn't for your brother. We called him Rinn, but he was your father's eldest brother. He would have been the heir had he not died before his time. But he wasn't the first Torrin, or the last. Your brother was named for many great men who came before him."

Nyssa seemed more relaxed now, her uneasiness replaced by curiosity. Gretchen took her daughter by the hand and walked her through what she knew of her husband's family history, answering what questions she could, feeling more at peace with every word that felt true. This wasn't the relief she'd sought in coming here, but the Guardians had a strange way of delivering what was needed.

At last, Nyssa yawned, and Gretchen could see she was ready for bed. "Shall we go up? You can sleep in my bed tonight."

Nyssa brightened. "Really?"

"Yes, wulfling. Come."

Nyssa planted her feet. "Mama... I have a question."

"All right."

"If all of Father's family is here, that means I'll be here, too?"

Gretchen kissed her on the forehead. "Unless your husband prefers you join him in his own family crypts. But not for a very long time. You have many years ahead of you."

Nyssa wasn't satisfied with this answer. "I like it down here. I can visit with people who are gone, like they never left."

"Yes, it can be like that, at times," Gretchen said, concerned by the look in her daughter's eyes, and where this was going. "Come, let's go up."

"I miss Drystan, Lisbet, and Pieter. Can we make tombs for them, too? So I can come down and visit them?"

Stars surged into Gretchen's vision and she had to reach for a patch of moss on the wall to steady herself. "Tombs are for the dead, wulfling."

Nyssa looked up. She gave her mother a placating look, took her hand, and nodded. "Okay, let's go to bed."

ALASYR HAD BEEN NOWHERE near Wulfsgate since he'd betrayed his family. He didn't dare dip down, even if he was confident he wouldn't be spotted. What he'd done, telling Emberley about Argentyn's crime, was unconscionable. He'd be punished horribly if his betrayal was discovered, and there was only one answer for treason.

He hovered just beyond the entrance to the Courtyard of Regents. He wanted to see the midnight goat again, especially the one he'd saved, but he wouldn't commit another crime with his recent ones lingering so fresh. Even the thought of stepping a foot into the icy rotunda sent a chill of fear through him.

Alasyr jumped as his father came barreling toward him, from the courtyard. He was so startled at his lapse in attention that at first he didn't notice his father's disheveled state. These days, he knew well what troubled his father and sent his own conscience into a tailspin.

He was more surprised to see his mother calmly follow. She paused at the entrance and regarded Alasyr with a dark smile. The bleariness in her eyes made him desperately curious about had transpired between them.

"Alasyr. Just who I wanted to see."

"Me?" Alasyr turned toward the direction his father had fled. "Is everything all right, Mother?"

"Don't concern yourself with your father. He is long past the age where he can rely on any excuse for his actions." She stepped closer and rested a hand along Alasyr's cheek. "You, though. You're still a boy in many ways. I can't hold you at fault for what you knew and did nothing about."

"I—"

"Shh," Varinya replied. "There are ears everywhere. Didn't Corridyn tell you as much when you visited his deathbed?"

Alasyr's heart soared in uneven beats. His mother knew. She knew everything. Had she known all along? "I don't know what possessed him to do it, Mother. I followed him... I..."

Varinya kissed his forehead. Her lips were icy, but he nonetheless felt the spread of warmth within. "As I was saying, about ears."

They both took to their wings, leaving Argentyn behind, fuming. Varinya soared ahead, with Alasyr in anxious pursuit. At last she landed at the base of a cave. It wasn't far from Midnight Crest, but he'd never set foot inside.

"I need to know where your father is keeping Lady Blackwood, Alasyr."

"In the old dowager quarters no one uses anymore," he blurted. "I don't know why he keeps her, Mother. I truly don't. He and I... we've never spoken of it. Not a word."

"I have my suspicions," Varinya said, turning toward the

entrance of the cave. A blizzard swirled beyond, obscuring any view. "But you're wrong. He's moved her. To where, I don't know, but when I said she was in the old quarters, he let me believe it. I'm well acquainted with your father's tics when he lies."

"I didn't know he'd moved her," Alasyr said. He couldn't help squinting in hopes for a better view beyond the cave. Argentyn could be on the other side and they wouldn't know.

"Hmm," she said. "I hear you've been speaking to Lady Blackwood's daughter. That the two of you are friends."

"I have spoken to her," Alasyr confessed. Then he lied to his mother. "But we aren't friends."

"Why speak to her at all?"

He dropped his eyes. "I thought she could aid me in bringing Ravenna back."

Varinya laughed, but there was no humor in it. He thought he heard her crying, but was afraid to look. "No one can help with that now, Son, least of all a half-blood child who has no place among us." She again approached him. "I need you to find where he has her. I cannot go searching without drawing attention to his activities, but no one will pay mind to your steps."

"Yes, Mother."

"You don't sound particularly eager to serve me in this."

Alasyr sighed. "I'm angry at Father as well, for bringing her here. But... that isn't her fault, is it? He took her, against her will, he and... and I don't know who the other was. I can't figure it out."

"There's another?" Varinya asked. She paled. "You're certain?"

"I saw another raven watching him the day he took Lady Blackwood."

Varinya nodded. Her attempt to seem unbothered by this revelation failed. It was written plainly in the soft lines of her face. "Your concern for Lady Blackwood is honorable, but misplaced. Just as your friendship is with her daughter."

"I'm not concerned for her, it's—"

Varinya held up a hand. "I agree. She didn't ask to be brought here. And now she must leave. You will help me see this done?"

Alasyr swallowed. "You'll send her to Wulfsgate? You won't hurt her?"

"I won't hurt her," Varinya replied after a small beat, and Alasyr knew she was lying.

36
DARK VELVET

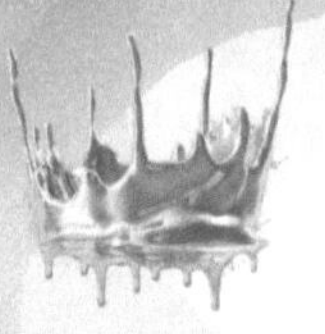

Ember once more found herself in the place where she'd scorched the earth with her desperation.

She was alone. It was a solitude that radiated. Everyone had left her. She had no ill will about it. Marsh and Aylen did what they had to do. Aylen couldn't have helped her, anyway. She'd only agreed to do so reluctantly, and with enough skepticism to melt Ember's hopeful heart. It was a foolish thought to begin with. Only a Ravenwood could help another Ravenwood, and to get to one, she had to do something she'd never done before.

She had to fly.

He'd made it sound so simple, when they both knew it would be anything but for the girl who'd been raised a Blackwood. But something had shifted in their relationship. When they'd first met, Alasyr scoffed at the idea she could do anything a Ravenwood could do. Now, he was issuing a challenge. His belief of her, *in* her, had evolved. He didn't speak this challenge with derision, but hope, and if Alasyr now saw the possibility, she must too.

Even his absence was a dare. *Come to me. See what happens. There's tea here.*

But it wasn't Alasyr she needed to find her wings for.

Ember dropped to her knees. She pressed her eyes close and pulled the energy from deep within, willing it out through her arms. She braced herself so hard a trickle of blood dripped from her mouth where she'd bitten into her tongue.

She imagined what it might look like for her to have wings. A beak. Sleek black feathers. It wasn't hard. She'd seen Alasyr transform many times. It happened so fast, in the blink of an eye, but when she watched carefully, she could see his feet draw inward to become talons. His pale, smooth flesh stretch into dark velvet. His curved mouth elongating, becoming an orange beak.

Ember focused herself so hard into envisioning this outcome that she felt something pop in her eye. When she opened them, one was hazy. "Mother's blood," she panted, bracing a root protruding from the ground to catch her breath. "Come on. I'm not the first. I won't be the last. I'm a Ravenwood, and I can do this."

She renewed her efforts, this time sending the energy into specific areas of her body. She pushed some to her shoulder blades, willing them to become wings. She opened her mouth, conjuring it outward, turning it to a beak.

At last the heat she recognized built from a well within her, and before she could harness it, it radiated outward, throwing her back into the charred brush.

Breathless, she looked around. She hadn't scorched it again, but there was nothing left for her to destroy. Nothing had changed. Not her. Not the world around her.

"You can do it," she barked. "You are not a failure, Emberley! Your mother chose you! She chose you!"

Again, she turned her mind toward the task.

Again, she fell back, spent.

Hours passed. The well of her own energy had run dry. If she intended to continue, she'd have to find it elsewhere.

A red fox peeked from behind a ruined tree. His beady eyes

regarded her. She could kill him. She wanted to kill him. To take his power and make it her own. Yes... yes, she could do this. She knew it, suddenly, as if the learning had come to her in a single moment. Whatever she took from others, she could absorb for herself.

But to take power in this way would mean surrendering herself to another. This was not why she'd come here. Why she was drawn here. Why she'd left her home, her family, two things that were forever changed for her, no matter whether she returned or not.

Her mother would know what to do, but her mother had chosen her for the same reason. She was failing her now. Failing Gabi and Brandyn. Failing Alasyr. Failing herself.

Ember laid her head down, letting her cheeks be scratched by the dead earth, and watched the fox through her tears.

GABRIANNA HUNG BACK SEVERAL PACES. She watched the easy way Eavan and Lisbet talked as they rode ahead, and it made her miss Hollyn and Emberley all the more. Emberley she might see again one day, if the Guardians were good and full of love for her, but she knew in her heart that Hollyn was dead. Dead like her father. Both of them now belonging to a past she wished desperately to crawl back into with her soft blanket and heart full of hope.

Meadow rode with Lisbet. She was afraid, she said, and so Lisbet offered to carry her on the back of Starcaller, who was no doubt an impressive beast capable of carrying them all. No one asked Gabrianna if she was okay, if she was afraid. This wasn't Longwood Rush, with her father eager to whisk her away from reality to one he'd created for her, frolicking in the forests alongside the River Rush. Out here, no one asked, because no one could fix what was broken.

She absorbed the fear of all of them. Her mother used to call this her curse. *Empaths have it the worst of all those with magic. They have to mind their own fears and tragedies while not losing themselves to the fears and tragedies of others. You can learn this, Gabi, but it will not be easy. I'll teach you.*

Asherley never did teach her. By the time Gabi came into these powers, Hollyn was already deeply sick with her strange illness. And then the king died, and the new king, the boy king, demanded his brides. Gabi was forgotten by all except her father; but her father couldn't help her. Her father was a wonderful man. A wonderful, unremarkable man.

And who else could she tell? It was treason to practice magic outside the permission of the Sepulchre, but only Brandyn was sent to study. They all had magic, though. Every Blackwood she knew had some, and one day, the kingdom would find out, and they'd be forced into hiding like the Ravenwoods. She was certain of it. She had no one to talk to about this to allay her fear and redirect it, so this belief was all she had.

But there was something else she was now sure of, something that had come to her on their slow ride from the Drumain lands toward the unknown of Whitechurch. It hadn't been fear that had made her stay with Lisbet and join her on her quest to see her brother one last time. She wasn't afraid of being alone as she had been before. She really wasn't afraid at all; her fears were more an extension of her knowledge, an almost resigned acceptance to a fate she had little control over.

She'd joined Lisbet because, for the first time since leaving Longwood Rush, she had a purpose she understood. Lisbet's needs were clear and defined, and she only needed Gabi to follow, not to lead. Gabi thought she would spend the rest of her life following, even to places she didn't want to go, if it meant she never had to lead again.

And maybe, just maybe, when they made their trek back to Wulfsgate, she'd cross paths with Emberley, and she could tell her this, and they could be a family again.

• • •

THE VISION CAME to Asherley in a dream.

Emberley. Her radiant smile and eyes like flames danced before her in such perfect clarity that she didn't know she was dreaming. But something darker would soon replace this image of Emberley. Even the air was muted of all color. A pall fell over her daughter, and the forest where she stood. Ember looked at the sky, raising her charred arms to the Guardians, sobbing.

A hard breeze whipped through the dead trees, scattering the ashes of Emberley Blackwood to the wind and skies.

"Wake," a voice commanded. But Asherley was tethered to this vision of her daughter's end. He'd told her then, this boy, Alasyr. Emberley knew, and her desperate attempts to fly into the mountains would be her end.

She had to find him, to command him to stop her. She didn't know how she'd do this, but she didn't have a choice, did she? If she had to employ whatever magic awaited her in this strange place, she—

Asherley was ripped into consciousness by a fresh shock of water running down her face. She bolted upward, off the chair, gasping.

"Do you always sleep with such commitment?" a smooth voice asked. Female.

Asherley reached for a nearby blanket and wiped her face. "You don't sound like Argentyn."

The woman laughed. "I'm not supposed to know about you. Did he tell you this?"

"He's told me many things I don't think you'd approve of."

"Such as?"

Asherley leaned back against the chaise, looking more calm than she felt. Inside, her heart raced at the lingering, terrible vision of Emberley. Oh, how she wished she were a better seer. That she could understand how to interpret what she'd seen. Joran would know, but Joran wasn't here. For all she knew, he was dead, too.

She decided she had no loyalty to the man who had locked her away here. "He doubts the veracity of your magic. Particularly, the magic of the women. The visions."

Varinya's tight smile dissolved. "Does he now?"

"Men have always lacked in the strength of faith. This isn't unique to Ravenwoods."

"And did he tell you why he brought you here?"

"To protect me, he said. From some great danger he's seen ahead."

"Hmm." Varinya turned away, examining the room. She was a lovely woman. They could drop her into any town in any Reach and she would be desired by all fortunate enough to lay eyes upon her. But she was also sad, and alone. Asherley read these things from her with little effort.

"I see you don't believe that any more than I do," Asherley said.

"What I believe is my concern," Varinya said, again looking at her. The emotions that had been so clearly etched upon her were now gone. "And at present, we have a more pressing matter than what punishment awaits my husband."

Asherley stood, so that she was face to face with the High Priestess. She rose half a foot taller, but she was used to this. Asherley was taller than most women, and often the men, too. It had worked to her advantage over the years, though she had less confidence in its effect now. "High Priestess Varinya. That is your name, right, Varinya?"

Varinya offered a curt nod.

"I didn't come here of my own choice. I have no desire to be a part of your world, or cause chaos within it. My daughter is in Wulfsgate, she's in danger, and—"

"My daughter is as good as dead to me, so you'll find no sympathy here, Lady Blackwood," Varinya snapped. "My husband was the fool who brought you here, and he will pay for that lapse, but that changes nothing about the problem facing me now. You *are* here. On outsider, in our halls, where outsiders have never been welcome. This must be dealt with. I know you, as a leader yourself, understand this."

"High Priestess, I no more want to be here than you want me to be," Asherley pressed. But she knew when she'd been bested; when the fight was won before it began. Her words meant nothing against the turmoil brewing within Varinya Ravenwood at the threat upon her world. "Aid me down the mountain and you will never see my face again."

Varinya rolled her head to the side. "Oh, darling. You'll be going down the mountain soon, but not in the way you're hoping."

A HAWK OVERHEAD SOUNDED A CRY, rousing Ember. The stiffness pooled in her limbs, screaming back at her attempts to move. She groaned as she pulled herself up, using the gnarled root for purchase.

How long had she been asleep? She hadn't meant to drift away. She'd only wanted to lie down a spell, long enough to catch her breath and her bearings.

Dusk greeted her through the gap in the trees. Long enough, then.

Ember rolled herself forward, dropping onto her knees. Wincing, wobbly, she forced herself to stand.

Then she saw them.

Rounding her in a circle, peppered amongst the embers of the forest.

Feathers.

"Mine," she whispered, dropping back down to pick them up in her arms. She ran her fingers over the soft felt, enjoying the responsiveness as she tickled the edges in the same way she did as a girl when she played her hair comb as an instrument.

She was certain they hadn't been there before, and as she held them, a deep connection stirred within, in the way she supposed she might if holding a limb that had become severed.

This had happened while she was sleeping.

Ember's mouth parted in a light gasp.

That was the answer.

It was not focus she required.

It was peace.

37
WHAT WE PROTECT

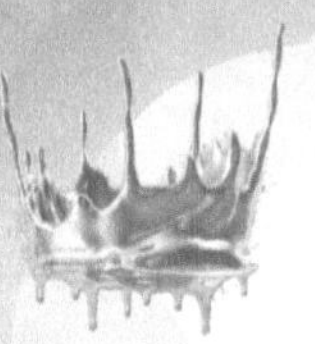

"Mother?" Kian asked when Kael emerged from Yseult's hut. He'd been waiting. Kael had been in there forever. "Resting." Kael didn't stop. He continued on, away, heading in the direction of the river.

Kian matched his pace. "Us?"

"Lost. You."

"How?"

Kael came to a stop. He inhaled roughly. "You lied. The girl."

Kian's heart leapt. There was no use in denial. "Yes."

"To protect."

"No!" Kian moved around to the front of his brother. "Yes. To protect. Her."

"Is before. Eavan."

Kian scoffed. He switched to speaking like a man. He'd grown used to it, perhaps even fond of it, since having men among them. "No. Not the same. I was young then. Caught in the web of my youthful foolishness. I am not him now."

"To speak like them?" Kael sneered. "You wish this? Fine."

"Mother has always said that we should practice this. They won't be the last here. You were not prepared this time."

"Fine, I said." Kael shoved him off. "If you are not of love with her, your choice lacks more sense than I assumed."

"They say in love, not of love, Kael. She will die as a Dereham. As the child of Dain she could yet live."

"It is not our way to mislead, Kian. I know this is not as mother taught us. Tell me why."

"Her fate does not have to be her brother's. She will search for greatness that would have eluded her otherwise."

"I do not ask of greatness. I ask why you care of the fate of a woman more than upholding our ways."

Kian looked away, toward the copse of violet and gold trees that would lead him to where Lisbet once slept; once ate her meals and tended to the others, who looked up to her as a leader. It had only been with great reluctance that he'd released her back into the world. Words within him battled this, even still. Words he could never give her. "What if it is not a lie? She is awakening, Kael. Just as the others."

"It is not only the children of Dain who are awakening. All across the kingdom. You know this."

"She has seen Drystan! Seen his destiny! Just as Mother knew she would. This is why she chose Lisbet. *You* know *this*."

"Dain left the bed of Gretchen Dereham two years before Lisbet was conceived. Impossible for him to have sired her. Your hearsay brings dishonor."

"No," Kian said. "He still came to her bed. As a man no longer living, in her eyes. What if he came to her in the flesh, and she knew not the difference?"

Kael tapped the side of Kian's head. "You have changed. For her."

"I *am* changed, but not for her." Kian narrowed his eyes and leaned in. "What we protect here is not for us. Not only us. You forget this."

"Pfft." Kael turned away. "You grow soft on man."

"Men are part of this world. Your hatred of them does not make this less so. If we fail, they fall with us."

"Would that be so terrible? We could start anew."

"You know what would happen. You know. Mother has seen it. There would be no anew. No us."

Kael scowled. "They could never come here. Not possible."

"We did not believe what happened to the Saleen to be possible, either. They can come, Kael. They will, if not stopped. Mother has seen many outcomes." Kian dropped his voice. "But there are those who would help us protect. She has seen them, too."

Kael laughed. "The children of Dain will save us, you say. But they must die to do it. It is the only way."

"Not all must die. And they are not alone."

38
RECOLLECTIONS

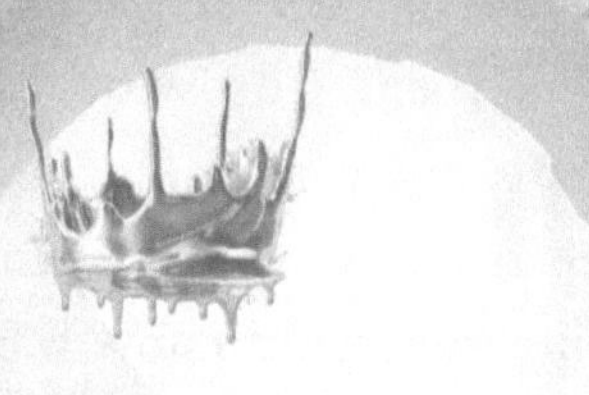

Jesse blinked through the very last of a sleep that he knew had lasted longer than he had time for. A powerful wanting, a need to move, to be free, crept into the bones of his fingers and toes as he willed them to life.

The smell of long-burning fire was the first familiar sensation. The next was the image of the strange magicians from before, whose names he may have heard but couldn't remember.

If he'd known these were the last familiar things he'd see for a while, Jesse might have returned to his rest.

"Ahh, he's waking," the female magician said. Sorcerer. Magi. He didn't know the word. He'd never bothered himself with understanding magic. It wasn't his world.

"Lysanor, pass the skin. He'll be afflicted with a mighty thirst," the male said.

Lysanor. The other's name was just within his grasp.

Jesse accepted the skin from Lysanor and took a greedy gulp. His body demanded more, so much more, but she gently peeled it from his hands.

"Slowly," she cautioned, in the same cool tone his mother used when she was teaching him something. "The water is different here."

"Not *that* different," the male said.

"It takes less, Isdemus. He wouldn't know that. We have to teach him this, as with all things."

Jesse propped himself up further and allowed himself his first glance at the strange place they'd brought him to. He didn't recognize the auburn hues of the dusty earth, or the towering arcs of the range just behind them. The wind carried finely milled sand, passing it over his clothes, their food and blankets. There were no trees; trees were his way of identifying a place, something his father taught him. You could know a place by its trees, and you could gain your bearings that way.

The moon hung lower and brighter than he'd ever seen it before. The sight of it startled him. He lifted a hand, as if he thought he could touch it, then lowered it again, feeling foolish. It was night, but the world was bright.

"Where am I?" he asked, though he trusted neither of them to give him an answer straight. Still, he had to try to make sense of what had happened to the world, to him, while he'd been out.

"He's recovered enough to ask a reasonable question," Lysanor said pointedly.

"Tell me, what constitutes a *reasonable* question in your esteem?" Isdemus countered.

Jesse felt as if he was coming into the last stretch of an old marriage, the way the two spoke to one another. But they were not old.

"Oh, go on already. He deserves to know."

Isdemus sighed. The sound was laden with the history between them, one Jesse was glad not to have been a part of, but yet felt recognizable. The sorcerer shot his hand out to the side like a child in the throes of a fresh tantrum. As he did, a small ball of light appeared. When Isdemus rotated his hand, curving his fingers inward, the ball grew, its center becoming a brilliant orange as the edges spread farther outward.

"It's lovely, really," Lysanor said. "I think that's large enough now."

Isdemus lowered his arm, but the ball of light didn't diminish. It hovered in the air, as if waiting for another command from its creator.

"Go on, then," Lysanor urged, giving Jesse a light nudge. "It's for you."

"For me?" Jesse repeated. "What am I supposed to do with... with that?"

"You have questions. Your answers can be found there."

Jesse laughed, coughing at the end as his scratchy throat demanded more water. "Into that? Nay. Not today." He pushed himself to his feet, dusting himself off. "I'd like to go now."

"Just look at it," Isdemus said gently. "Go on. Take a look. That's all."

Jesse grunted, frustrated with himself as he turned, obediently, to observe the strange ball. He started to demand something from Isdemus, but forgot his words. What was he going to ask? Was it even important? Did it matter?

Jesse stepped toward the ball of light. Yes. He should go there. He was supposed to be there. Why wasn't he there already? How could he have taken so long?

"It cannot harm you," Lysanor said, but she was far away now, and Jesse was stepping forward into the light, where he belonged.

Mortain finished his morning binding of the Saleen and then walked down to the Sparkling Beck. There was an old well by its banks, so oddly placed that there were stories about who had put it there and why. Mortain didn't have the answer. He didn't care.

The idiot, Waters, hadn't joined him today. He hadn't joined him in nearly a week. That was fine. He didn't need him anymore. He'd never needed him, though he'd proved useful in his easy acquiescence to treasonous choices. Men like Waters, they were born to hurt others, and Mortain could use that, *had* used that, but he could not comprehend a call to evil without cause. He once watched Waters crush a baby duckling underfoot, then chuckle to himself as he examined the aftermath. Mortain, who had taken more lives than he had capacity or desire to count, couldn't understand a man like that.

He didn't understand men at all, but he wasn't here to decipher them. That men had been in the one place he needed to be was an obstacle, nothing more. But not all men were like Quinlanden. Not all would bend their morals far enough to snap for the promise of power. This was why he'd chosen him, and not the lords of the other Reaches. Why he'd planted the idea in Eoghan's malformed head. Mortain hadn't even had to employ convincing on Quinlanden, who easily laid his sword at the feet of a king whose ancestors had done nothing for him.

But he was old now. He was tired. There could be no more failures. Oldwin had an endless font of energy that Mortain almost envied. He had a mind for the constant politics and maneuvers of court, and, Mortain suspected, enjoyed it more than he should.

Mortain only wanted what they'd come here for.

He leaned over the old well. The dank scent traveling upward used to turn his stomach, but he was used to it now. Though inches from the river, this well had run dry.

Mortain waved his hand, and fresh water appeared. He waited until he saw the face he was after.

"Tell me what you've seen," he said.

Oldwin laughed from the water. "Hello to you as well!"

"Tell me."

"Has it really become so bad, Mortain? That you cannot even scry for yourself?"

"Binding them takes everything from me. You know this."

"Do others know this?"

"Why would others know this? Why would others know anything?"

Oldwin lifted his brows. "They know you are the center of the war waged by the Easterlands. They come to you now to put an end to it."

"Who?"

Oldwin laughed. "Truly? You truly have seen nothing? You old fool. You never could do more than one thing at a time."

Mortain swallowed his displeasure. Not for the first time, he wondered if Isdemus, or even Lysanor, would have been more palatable to partner with, but they had aimed elsewhere, and he wasn't left with a choice. "Who, Oldwin?"

Oldwin told him. Told him about the boy, about Warwick. About the Southerlands.

But while Oldwin laughed at him, something he'd grown quite used to over the years and no longer bothered him as it once did, Mortain was somewhere else.

"You do not look as worried as you should," Oldwin said with an indignant look as his humor faded.

"We each see opportunities in different things."

"Ah! Tell me!"

Mortain looked behind him. There was no one there, but there would be.

"You want to know? Scry it," Mortain said and waved a hand over the water, drying the well.

He checked his surroundings once more.

Still alone.

Mortain stepped back from the riverbank. His slow steps crunched in the forest's undergrowth, and then disappeared altogether as his feet curled into talons, pulling inward toward the firmness of his phoenix form, prismatic ochre and amber and flame spreading into wings broad enough to cover the well.

He aimed his beak toward the sky and burst into flight.

He made his way down the cobblestone road running parallel to the wharf. The place was familiar to him, and soon he recognized it. If he were to walk another hundred paces or so, he'd see the sign reading Wayfarer's Bythesea, where he'd passed more than a few free evenings.

Rutland's ship was docked just past there. They'd taken his vessel this time, Drummond's Pride, which stuck like a thorn in Hamish's thumb, just as it would have his father's had he not gone to the Guardians long ago. But Lord Warwick said it would be so, and so it was. Hamish couldn't wait for Warwick's son to take over. Khallum. Khallum had been his best mate since they were both in swaddling. Khallum knew Hamish was loyal and would reward him for it.

Now, the day was coming back. He'd awakened in the bed of a local fishwife, chased away half-heartedly by her red-cheeked husband as if the routine was so familiar to him now that it no longer required fair effort. The night left no lasting impression beyond this, other than the dull reminder that he should take a wife. His mother had picked up the refrain when his father died, and she never let him forget it.

Aye, Ma, he would say, but a freebooter needs jus' tha' right woman, ye ken? One who willnae lose sleep o'er the long absences, nor a little dip on the side just the same.

And Ma would remind him that there were plenty of women fitting that bill in Sandycove; women built to be the wife of a trader, expecting no more or less. Strong men married young, she reminded him. They didn't wait, like other men.

Hamish didn't know why he'd waited to marry, batting away every suggestion she made with a rationale that made little sense to him even as he muttered the words in protest.

She's too shrill.

Too plump.

Too thin.

Too fair on the eyes.

Not fair enough.

None of that talked of the fear in his heart, that he hadn't enough to please a woman beyond the name.

He was a few paces from Wayfarer's Bythesea when he saw her. He might not have noticed her at all, if not for the pale green hair cascading around her face, which was covered in filth. He'd never seen hair like it in all his travels. What could even make a color like that, he wondered, as he stepped closer to where she huddled against the side of a fur trader's shop.

People walking by threw coin at her, or even spilled their drink at her feet. She cowed at their assaults. Whatever spirit she'd had was broken by whatever had come before.

Hamish, 'tis not your business, he thought, and in the same passage of the moment thought, t'would cost so little to put a hot meal in her belly and buy her a room for the eve.

He made his way through the thick crowd toward her. When he knelt by her, she recoiled, covering her face with her hands as if expecting to be struck. His heart flipped.

"There, now. Let me get a look at ye."

"That isn't my trade, sir," she muttered, still hiding her face.

"'Tis a good thing tha's nay what I'm after, then," he said gently, peeling her hands away from her face. His heart surged once more when, this time, she let him.

She was covered in scratches and filth months deep, but she was beautiful, and he could do nothing about the way he fell in love with her.

It was then he noticed the little ball of fur at her side. A fox.

"Shoo! Get!" he called, but she reached for the animal and clutched it protectively to her chest.

"He's no nuisance," she said. "He's mine."

"Yours? Now I've seen everything."

The fox purred as it snuggled under her chin.

"Name's Hamish. Hamish Strong," he said. He offered her his hand, but she only stared at it.

"Ah, look, there's Hamish! You'd suppose he'd had enough after being chased off by one husband already!" Lem Garrick called out. Hamish already knew who he was talking to. It had to be Erran Rutland.

Hamish waved a hand behind him dismissively. He didn't care about their cajoling on a good day, but right now it was a bother, and all he wanted was to know more about this strange young woman with the green hair.

"Right, well, just know we sail at sundown with or without ye!"

They continued on, their drunken laughter following them.

"Allow me to put some food in ye," Hamish said to the woman.

"I won't pay what you're asking."

"And what am I..." Hamish's eyes widened. He shook his head with vigor. "Nay. Nay. I ain't 'spect nothing in return, miss. Only to see the hunger in yer eyes die."

Her distrust didn't fade, so he reached inside the satchel he carried and pulled out a hunk of bread, flushing at precisely the moment they both noticed he'd eaten half of it. He'd forgotten about his earlier hunger when the idea came to him.

The young woman ripped the bread from his hands and shoved it greedily into her mouth, inhaling it in one gulp.

"Careful, now," he said. "Need something to wash that down." He reached for his wineskin, and this, too, she took. Her famishment was greater than her pride or judgment.

"Have I earned your name, at least?"

"Yanna," she said, so quietly he made her repeat it.

"Yanna," he mused. "Name's unusual I ken. Ye ain't from Bythesea?"

She shook her head.

Hamish pulled a rag from his satchel and handed it to her so she could clean herself off. She only looked at it before setting it aside.

"Where are your people? I could take ye to them."

"I can never go back."

"Why?"

Yanna lowered her eyes to her belly. She placed a hand upon it.

Hamish fell back on his haunches. "Is that... what happened to ye, then?"

He had his answer in her silence.

"The ratsbane! What bloody man dips his wick and cannae see after his own spawn?" The look of horror on her face tempered his words. He remembered himself. "Where is he? The da'?"

Yanna buried her hands in her face and sobbed.

He understood then.

He knew enough.

For one, he wasn't getting on Drummond's Pride that evening.

"Yanna. Look here. Look at me. Can ye tell me if t'would be too much if I said that I ken I might be the man to see after ye? Not only today but... well, I ken... for as long as ye will have me? Not for fun, ye ken, or even love, though perhaps we'll find some of that along the way."

Yanna blinked. Her fresh tears cut a ragged path through the crests of dirt on her face. Her newly revealed pale skin nearly glittered in the noonday sun.

Hamish thought this time when his heart stopped that it was for good. He'd just offered to marry a stranger; one whose belly swelled with the child of a man who had taken everything from her. She had no family. No name. Nothing but her tragedy.

But nor could he take the words back.

She stole his breath clear away when she nodded.

"He's been in there a while now," Lysanor said. The light chill in the desert air nipped at her just enough for her to dig out the blanket from her bedroll.

"He's only just begun. Be patient."

"What will it show him? Everything?"

"In time."

"You know I despise your riddles."

"The light will know."

"Ahh, you are terrible!"

Isdemus smiled, but he looked very tired. "I hope we were right, Lysanor. I hope he was ready. For if he was not…"

She nodded. "I know."

39

ON THE EVE OF WHAT WILL BE

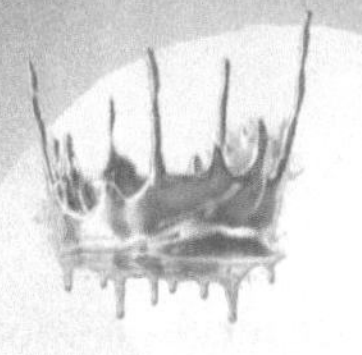

"You're restless."

Darrick looked up from the stump where he cupped the last of the evening's tea in his palms. He didn't mix his with mead as the other men did. It muted his sleep, and there were few things about his freedom he valued more. "Is that an accusation, Law?"

Law grinned as he gazed off into the forest. They all did it now, by instinct. Their camps were exposed, and there was little doubt that word had reached Waters and Mortain of their arrival, or would soon. Lord Khallum sent Storm that evening to tell them they'd move into Whitechurch just before night turned to dawn. They should move now, but the day would be long and the men needed a few hours, or they'd never last it.

Without the Southerland Guard? Rutland asked, as confounded as all the others receiving the direction. *That was not the plan, girl.*

They will be here soon, Lord Warwick says. Brandyn senses danger. That we are chasing it, not ahead of it. Until the morrow, stay quick and low, and out of sight. Maintain the high ground so you can spot them coming before they see you. When there's enough light to see the path, make for the old abbey by the sea. He says you will know it, Steward Rutland, from your time at port. We meet there.

Trading a hiding place without walls for one with? That it, girl?

Oakenwell says it gives us the best vantage point to determine entry into Arboriana.

Oakenwell.

I don't trust him either, sir, but Lord Warwick does. And Br—Lord Blackwood, as well. Until reinforcements arrive, all we have is our trust.

Why not move now, then?

Would you see the arrow coming at you from the darkness before or after it split your forehead... sir?

"Only thinking a man deserves a spot of rest on the eve of what will be," Law answered. He warmed his hands over the dying fire.

"Do you make predictions, Law?"

"I leave that to the Sepulchre and their soothsayers," Law answered, his lip curling slightly. "But I see something tickling at your mind."

Darrick nodded. He gazed down into the now cool liquid in the tin cup. "I'm caught between a desire to aid and a desire to lead. I cannot lead, for this isn't my fight. Young Lord Blackwood would give it to me, but I will not take it. And yet what aid can I proffer? A man still recovering from five years of prison?"

"Your presence alone stirs hope in the men," Law pointed out. "They see you at their side, not ruling from some crumbling tower upon an isle in the White Sea. They would follow you, Your Grace, to whatever end. But they will die for the man who would die for them."

"We could all die in a few hours."

"Aye."

"It changes nothing. We cannot delay."

"No," Law agreed. "For not only will those in Whitechurch be aware of our arrival, but word will reach your brother about you. He may already know."

"Oldwin knows. He misses nothing," Darrick mused. "If Eoghan doesn't, then it is only because the sorcerer has conspired to keep it from him."

"Oldwin relies on Mortain. Soon, we will discover the extent of this reliance," Law said.

Darrick looked up. "He will not be so easy to dispatch. He'll see any attack before it lands. He has the means to defend against anything we attempt."

"Should that change anything for us?"

Darrick shook his head. "Only something we should know."

"Brandyn is only a boy. We all worry for him," Law said.

"Lord Warwick will protect him," Darrick answered, and he could see in Law's concerned gaze that his words were not as convincing as he'd hoped. He should find the right ones, the ones that would inspire Law and the other men. But the ones tickling his tongue were hollow. They were all likely to die tomorrow, even young Brandyn, and the only consolation would be if Mortain perished with them.

He'd never again lay eyes upon Anabella, his Isa. He'd never meet his son, to see with his own eyes if the boy favored his father. And he'd not live to embrace Ryan as a free man, and a friend.

But he would perish in service to his kingdom, not rotting away in a mine. That was something.

"There are others who can and will assume command of the Westerlands and Southerlands should our lords not survive what's to come," Law began, clapping a hand on his shoulder. "There are others who can take the helm should our lords fall. But there's only one Darrick Rhiagain. Only one savior of this realm. I cannot command you to be safe."

Darrick smiled with a whimsical look. "No, you cannot. Nor would I be inclined to follow such a command."

Law chuckled. "Just the same, Your Grace."

• • •

"I CAN'T HEAR your whispers from here. What did he say?"

"That's the point of whispers."

"Well?"

Yesenia cast a nervous glance between her husband and where the guard had stood moments before, beyond the thick steel of the bars. Bars no man could sever with strength alone. Nor even a beast, or even many beasts. She recalled Aiden laughing about it over a dinner party... how hopeless a man was supposed to feel if he ever found himself imprisoned by a Quinlanden.

She stretched her face against the bars, straining to see as far as she could. The sconces lining the walls brightened her view, enough to confirm what she'd hoped. No patrol, for now. Only the guards perched at the bend in the long hall, and they'd been engrossed in their game of cross-and-pile for half the night. And why not, when there was no chance of their prisoners escaping?

Yesenia returned to the half-rotted bench where Corin gaped at her in anticipation. She dropped her voice low. "You remember the old adage I loathe so much?"

Corin half-grinned. "The one about when life gives you coriander?"

"No, no. The other one."

"Ahh. Good news and bad news? Is that it?"

Yesenia nodded. "We aren't alone, Corin. Men from the Westerlands, those who could slip through the notice of the Quinlanden Guard, are on their way, here, to us."

"But that's great news!" Corin whispered.

"No, for they are few. No more than ten, the guard said."

"One man is enough to change a kingdom, Yesenia. Think of what the loss of Darrick did to us."

"Mads and Mortain know."

The hint of joy playing at the corner of Corin's eyes faded. "Of course they do. That's how our friend in the guard knows."

She nodded. "Among them... among them is Byrne's boy. Brandyn." Yesenia dropped her eyes and inhaled, drawing a long breath. "And my brother, Khallum."

"Two Reaches standing united against treason! This is good for us. For everyone."

"They'll be walking into an ambush, Corin. Brandyn and Khallum will be executed. With them both gone, Mads and Mortain's victory over the Westerlands and Southerlands will be total. There are others... an army. My brother's. But they'll come too late."

Corin took a while before responding. "Asherley and Byrne have other children. Daughters, but it would not be the first time a woman ruled the Westerlands. And Khallum has sons. Three, yes?"

"Your idealism is beautiful to me, Corin. You remind me of Byrne at times. But it doesn't serve us now. Losing two lords would be a blow not easily or quickly recovered from."

Corin gathered his wife's hands in his. "I refuse to believe hope is lost. Can we not find someone loyal to us to deliver a message? To warn them?"

"He would be killed, and the message would die with him. The Quinlanden Guard has eyes on the camps. It won't be long now."

"Then what? What do we do?"

"I don't know yet," Yesenia said, casting another look at the torchlight flickering upon the walls beyond the bars, casting shadows. "But if Brandyn and Khallum have put their lives on the line for us, we'll be doing the same when the time comes."

Corin sank back against the cold wall. "Do you think Maeryn has something to do with this?"

"That little snake? She hasn't the cunning."

"Then where is she, Yesenia?" He waved a weary hand. "Waters might have spared her the cells with us, had she not already slipped into a shadow no one can find her in. She's left Cian alone and abandoned us."

"She couldn't have gone far."

Corin's eyes went dark in the dim cell. "Unless she had help. Unless she hasn't been on our side all this time, after all."

DRYSTAN FELT a hard tug at his neck as he flew back against the hill. Ash flashed him an apologetic look, but the finger at his lips and his wide eyes kept Drystan from crying out his anger.

"A camp," Ash whispered. "Just beyond the ridge."

"I didn't see it."

"They've been clever," Ash replied. "There are no banners. They don't want anyone to know who they are, or who they represent. To others passing by, they'd appear to be brigands, named for no one."

"You saw through the ruse easily."

"Because I know these woods." Ash looked around. "They're swept, cleaned out with frequency, making it inhospitable to brigands, or anyone with less than good intent."

"Why do you look concerned? What does that mean?"

Ash looked past him. "I suspect we've come upon the first threads of a war, Drystan. If we've spotted these men, Whitechurch will know about them, too."

"How is that our concern?"

"Who knows how many more camps like this there will be? How far the resistance spreads?"

Drystan readjusted his shirt, pausing to rub the sore spot on his neck. "Hopefully far and wide. It will make our task easier."

"No," Ash cried, spinning to face him. "Son. How can we possibly sneak into Whitechurch if they're awakened to a threat? If they're preparing for battle?"

Drystan scoffed. He looked away. All his life he'd wished for a father who showed half the concern Ash was showing now, but now that he had it, it was a hindrance. It hung about him, thick and cloying, like a coat of spiderwebs. "You choose to see it this way. I see it another way."

Ash held his hands out. "Tell me, then. How do you see it?"

"I see..." Drystan struggled to get the words out. No matter what he said, Ash would pick them apart, attempt to discredit him. He would employ his age and experience, things Drystan couldn't compete with. "Opportunity. I see a city distracted by coming war, who won't notice two unremarkable men moving about. We look like servants already, in the rags Yseult provided us. Why not become them?"

Ash's sigh split Drystan's heart in two. He recognized the sound. It was too close to the one he was so used to from Holden. "We cannot base our plans on something so flimsy."

Drystan jumped to his feet. He reattached his pack and looked down at Ash. "*My* plan. And if you don't like it, don't agree with it, then you would do well to remember that I *do not need you* and I can and will do this alone!"

He stormed off ahead, searching for an alternate route around the camp of unknown men.

KHALLUM HAD URGED the boy off to sleep, but there'd be none for himself. He'd lied to him. To himself. In a few short hours, they'd sneak into Whitechurch like assassins, an act his imagination had little trouble preparing for him. It was the return he could not see.

In his heart, he knew there'd be no return. Even if Hamish and the Southerland Guard made it on time, Khallum and Brandyn would be in the center of the beast's belly, surrounded by the promise of their death. The only hope remaining was that they could secure victory before the Guardians deemed their promise spent.

Niall would be ready to take the helm for the Southerlands until his older brother could safely return. Fifteen was almost a man. Khallum had been not much older, when he'd taken over from his father. It would only be temporary, and Gwyn would aid him, steer him true. Khallum had never thought much of women as rulers, but he'd left his Reach in his wife's hands more than once, and he'd never doubted her ability to care for it should the need arise.

She'd never forgive him for not coming back this time. Such was love, he supposed, and he also supposed that he did love her. In his mind, he compared her to the women he could've wed and bed had the king not interceded, and it was an exercise that couldn't happen without resentment for the crown, but was nonetheless laced with gratitude. She'd made a fine wife, and an even better mother. If there was another bloodline worthy of running through a Warwick's veins, the cold-bittered Derehams was it.

He'd done what he could for her. He had the best men leading the Great Families. They would know how to shape either Ransom or Niall to be their next lord, and they'd do it with fealty and love. They'd proffer the widowed Lady Warwick with the honor she had earned, and perhaps, once their new lord had a family of his own, arrange a good second marriage for her.

A soft, but high sound pierced through the night. At first, Khallum thought he'd imagined it. Then it happened a second time. Not a bird. His hand fell to his sword.

When he heard it again, it was accompanied by a single word. "Father."

Khallum turned toward the boy's tent. Brandyn was dreaming, then. About Byrne. Khallum had his share of these dreams since his brother was murdered.

He faced the dead fire again, returning to the heaviness of his thoughts. But Brandyn's cries escalated, and if Khallum didn't rouse him, the boy would wake the men.

With a groan, he heaved himself to his feet, dusting the dirt off him. He ambled toward the tent and leaned inside.

Brandyn thrashed in his bedroll, drenched in a marriage of sweat and tears. He cried out for his father, and as he did, his hand reached for something unknown.

Khallum leaned down to wake him, but Brandyn's small hand gripped his and the boy rolled toward him in soft relief. Khallum glanced into the night, then lay next to him.

When he held an arm out, the boy crawled into it, and Brandyn cried no more.

HAMISH HAD WANTED to cut north near Stone Mawr, but Lem Garrick insisted they take the northern path out of Blackpool and go east through the Gap of Ever. Hamish had countered that the Quinlanden Guard would surely be stationed there, as the only passable location along the interior of Fionn's Pass, but Garrick won. Garrick didn't have Lord Warwick around to temper his bullishness toward Hamish, and the others supported Garrick.

They'd had some trouble at the gap, just as Hamish had predicted. But no one said *aye, just as Strong said*. Because Garrick had taken the lead at some point on their way north, it was his men who first discovered and then dealt with the problem. It was Garrick whose name they passed around that evening's fire, throwing around words like "conqueror," in earnest while Hamish tore at the tough meat in quiet angst.

He tried not to think about Ryan lying as if lifeless in a bed in a tower. There was no use in it. He couldn't help his son there or here, and if they didn't deliver the victory Lord Warwick expected, it would be every son and the daughter in the Reach—the kingdom —who'd be left defenseless.

But he did think of Jesse. It wasn't like his eldest to linger long on his journeys. He should've been home months ago, but instead of worry, what Hamish felt about his long absence was suspicion. Jesse was more than capable of defending himself. There would've been word sent to Sandycove if he'd been hurt or killed. Instead, there was nothing. The absence of word. Complete silence.

Whatever trouble he'd found himself in, Hamish only hoped he knew what he was doing.

He pulled out the wrinkled map from his sack, using the splash of moonlight through the forest trees to read the faded ink.

"Garrick reckons a tomorrow evening landing," Barne Holton said, dropping onto the log beside him.

Hamish quickly folded the map and put it away. "Garrick underestimates his men. We'll be there by midday, Guardians willing."

"Ye ken that's too early, or right on time?"

"I ken we'll be lucky if it's not too late," Hamish barked, and went to give his men the last words of the evening.

40

FRIENDSHIPS BIRTHED OF DESPERATION

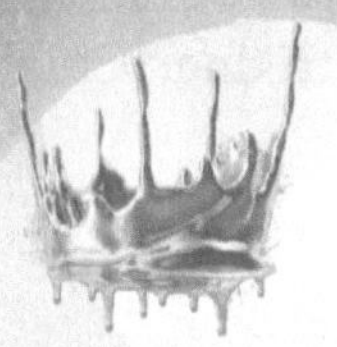

Oldwin stood before the man he was forced to call master. But that wasn't quite right, to call it forced. He'd chosen to call him such, just as he'd chosen his banishment to the sky dungeon for what amounted to half a mortal man's lifetime. Every choice he'd made had brought him to precisely this moment and would soon lead him to the one he'd done this, all of this, for.

The petulant child swimming in his raiment was making demands. Take me to my wives! I want to see them! Oldwin had perfected his magic over the many years of his life, honed it to precision, but there was no magic adequate for feigning fealty to this wretched creature. Every day he must prostrate himself before the sack of malformed bones was a day he emerged more victorious than the last.

"Your Grace. Tradition mandates we must wait until your wedding day."

"Did my father?" Eoghan volleyed, all nasally annoyance. "Did his father?"

Oldwin swallowed the bile in his throat and grinned. "Your father and his father knew their brides, for they were Rhiagains. Ravenna and Esmerelda are foreign brides. Marriages made with foreign houses must pass this final test of temptation. For a foreign bride must be chosen for what she brings, not the face she casts upon the world."

Eoghan sneered. "So you're saying they're hideous? You fear I'll take one look upon them and lose my meal?"

"They are both quite striking, actually. But that is not why you will wed them."

"Please, Oldwin, proffer me more counsel on my motivations. You offer me so much already."

Oldwin flexed his fingers at his side, buried in his robe. "Is that not why you exorcised me from the dungeon, to serve counsel?"

"Counsel in the form of visions! I never asked for anything else!" Eoghan spewed, breathless as soon as the words left him. He rolled forward, heaving in exhaustion. "And what visions have you brought me, Oldwin?"

The haggard sister, Correen, put a loving hand upon his shoulder, staying him. Correen was crafty. Not cunning, like Assyria, though. Had she been the one at his side, Oldwin would have had to play his game with more care. Correen suspected his motives, but she'd taken no action that would slow him. He'd wondered if she wasn't silently cheering him forward.

But no. She *had* shared these suspicions with her brother. Her support of Eoghan's misgivings gave him the courage to speak as he did, even knowing Oldwin's magic was more powerful than a king's authority.

Oldwin continued carefully. He would not need this child much longer. "It was my visions that brought your new brides to you, Your Grace. It was perhaps not the Right of Choosing you imagined, but only I could bring a Ravenwood to your bed."

"Only you?" Eoghan laughed. It faded to a racking cough. "Only you care about Ravenwoods to begin with. What is a Ravenwood to me?"

"Have you forgotten you share a common ancestor? That it is the Ravenwoods you have to blame for quelling the powerful magic in the Rhiagains, leaving you weak and confused and groveling?" Oldwin almost spun time in reverse to take back the words, but the flicker of fear in Eoghan's face was enough to tell him his lapse in control had struck a powerful nerve.

Eoghan looked away, flushed. "I have no care about pasts, or Ravenwoods and Rhiagains. We don't live in the past. We live now. That is what matters." When he again looked at Oldwin, he was more composed. "I wish to marry them now."

"On the morrow, Your Grace. All the festivities have been arranged. The day will prove most joyous."

"What if I don't want to wait?"

Oldwin sighed. "I suppose I could advise the court there will be no festivities."

"Why would there not be festivities at my wedding?"

"Brother, you did not want festivities at the Right of Choosing, remember? So perhaps there is no reason to wait, as you say," Correen said gently. Her eyes were daggers as she coolly regarded Oldwin.

"It would not do to disappoint the court," Oldwin said. "But... it is your choice, Your Grace. I serve at your command."

"Fine! Tomorrow!" Eoghan barked, again dissolving into a coughing fit.

"He is not well, Oldwin. Leave us," Correen commanded.

All the venom in his veins came to life as he bowed before her for what was hopefully the last time.

For tomorrow, while the king took his new brides, the kingdom would march toward chaos.

• • •

ANABELLA AND WYAT were introduced to a young woman named Missy. She flitted through her brief tour of the old keep, breathless and sweaty, giving the occasional name to one of the men lying on cots. Anabella felt bad taking her away from her service to them. She could see Wyat felt the same.

But none of these men was Darrick.

"Do you see your man? Look closely, now. A man takes on a different look when he's fallen on the hard times, least the kind that bring a man here."

"Missy, ah, I should have mentioned," Wyat said suddenly. "We are here on behalf of Lord Warwick. He had some especial guests, did he not?"

Missy cocked her head. "Were they? Special? He said they were not."

Wyat quickly shook his head. "No, not special, that's not what I meant."

"I know the men. The men in the tower," she said. "Come."

Missy rushed through the overflowing piles of men, oblivious to the stench of rot and decay, and even death, as she made for the center of the room. She lifted her skirts when they reached the spiral staircase, and though there were stairs crumbled and missing, navigated her way up with smooth confidence. Anabella stumbled several paces behind, clutching tightly to Stefan's small hand. He made like he wanted to run ahead, but she held fast to him. Wyat briefly laid a hand upon her shoulder so she knew he was there, right behind them.

Anabella was out of breath when they reached the top of the tower, and Wyat, too, seemed like he could make fine use of a chair. Not Missy, who spun around and pointed to two doorways. "Tha' one is empty, all except for some things I been storing there, like cloth for bandages and the like. No space downstairs anymore, ye ken. No one else comes up here 'cept me. Orders from Steward Rutland hisself."

Anabella nodded.

"And that one," she said, wiping her brow on her sleeve as she pointed to the other door. "Tha's where Lord Warwick has me keeping his especial friend, as ye say. There's a chair, and an extra cot, though I been meaning to take it down to the hall, for we need them somethin' desperate."

"I shouldn't have called them special," Wyat said. "I... only meant..."

"I know what ye meant. Whoever all these men are, find their way to us, they're just charges. I've no care of the name they wore 'fore comin' here, and neither do the others," Missy said with a light nod. "Go on, with your business for Lord Warwick. I've my own down in the hall, as ye might've kenned."

Wyat nodded. He looked toward the door. "You have our gratitude, Missy. It is evident your time is not without value."

"Hm," she replied.

Wyat entered. Anabella's heart was suddenly no longer in her control, skipping out of control with erratic beats. She'd known this moment lay ahead, but hadn't given it the proper thought, and now the moment was upon her. Darrick was inside. Her Darrick. And now, she would see him, but she'd given no care to washing her face, or bothering to do something, anything, with her hair. She would not be the girl he left in the Wintergarden, rosy-cheeked and so in love with him that it might have been tinged with madness.

"Mama?" Stefan asked.

"Sorry. My mind traveled elsewhere for a spell."

Wyat appeared in the doorway with a confused look. "There must be some confusion. This isn't the man we expected to see."

"There was two men, until a month or so ago. Or was it longer? I donnae ken the passing of time as you might," Missy replied with a thoughtful look.

"Two men?" Wyat stepped closer to her. "What did the other

man look like?"

"I dinnae? Dark hair, tall. Striking, that one. He didnae coalesce long. Steward Law took to 'im, they went out for runs, if ye ken. Out to Drummond's Cock. Who runs if they donnae have to?"

Wyat reached for her arm. "Where did he go?"

Missy's pleasantness faded. She ripped her arm away. "I donnae know, 'cause 'tis not my business what Lord Warwick's *especial guests* are up to."

He dropped his hand back to his side, contrite. "Apologies, miss."

"All I know, he left with Lord Warwick and the others. Steward Rutland and Steward Law."

Anabella's heart raced even faster. She would not be facing her husband this day. She'd given her hope to this, and she would pay, as she'd always paid for choosing him. The old lingering belief that she'd never see him again replaced any happiness she'd conjured over the preceding months of limited freedom.

If Darrick wasn't in that room, who was?

"The other man, then," Wyat said, voicing her own thoughts. "What do you know about him?"

"I'm not supposed to know nothin'," Missy replied, defensive. "I only know they came in together, both men. Some say from the Wastelands, but 'tis none of my business."

"That man. Is he resting?"

Missy shrugged. She started for the stairs. "Lord Warwick and the other, Lord Strong, neither liked what I had to say."

"Which was?"

"I donnae think that one'll wake again. He's just too stubborn to let the Guardians do their work."

Missy excused herself and shuffled back down the stairs.

"That's Ryan Strong," Wyat mused when Missy was gone. "The

scout said it was Steward Strong's own son they sent in to rescue..." He trailed off. Even alone, they didn't dare speak his name.

"Then he must have grown close to him," Anabella said. She watched the door. Beyond was the closest she might ever feel to her husband again. If he did wake, perhaps Stefan would like to speak to a man who knew his father. Perhaps better, even, than Wyat, for desperation birthed friendships neither time nor distance could sunder.

Wyat leaned against the stone wall, sinking into a crouch. His sigh was muffled in his hands, splayed against his face.

"What's wrong?" she asked him.

"This was our last hope, Anabella. I'm lost for what to do next. Where to take you. D—your husband, he could be anywhere. Anywhere at all."

Anabella released Stefan's hands and knelt before Wyat. She peeled his hands from his face, and when she spoke, she didn't know where the hopefulness of her words came from, only that it was real. "No, Wyat. This is where we belong. This is where he would want us to be, tending to the man who gave him his freedom. And, as for me, for Stefan, it's where we want to be, too. Wherever he's gone, whatever his reasons for following Lord Warwick, this is where he'll return. I know it."

Wyat looked up, bleary-eyed. "Then we'll need to ask Missy for more of those cots she can't spare."

Ravenna traced her finger along the thin line the moonlight cast into their small cell. Beside her, Esmerelda tried to sleep. It was no use. Ravenna had tried, too, but there was nothing there but her fear and regret.

Her magic didn't work here. The sorcerer, Oldwin, had done

something to her, or to the cell. Her raven form was useless. She couldn't fly away, as she'd planned, to find help. She could do nothing. She was effectively neutered.

Esmerelda draped an arm across her waist. "It will be okay, Ravenna. We'll find our way out."

Ravenna almost laughed. She was supposed to be the strong one. She'd determined to protect Esmerelda, and it was Esmerelda who'd broken the paralysis lingering between them. "I won't let them harm your child, Esmerelda. I swear to you."

Esmerelda squeezed her hand on the curve in Ravenna's waist. "I don't think we should make promises. Not in this place."

Ravenna turned and faced her. "You don't sound scared."

"You expect me to cry myself to sleep, a defenseless pup?"

Ravenna sighed. "I don't think you're defenseless, or a pup. You're stronger than me. I'm terrified."

Esmerelda's breath formed curls in the air of the chilled cell. "I am as well, except... Jesse would say I'm stubborn, but if he could see me now, it's *from* him I learned to find calm in chaos. He wouldn't be panicked, to be where we are. He wouldn't surrender to the fear."

"There's something special about Jesse. Something not even he knows, I don't think," Ravenna said. "It's more than his Medvedev blood."

Esmerelda nodded against the small pillow. "Aye. I suspect he knows it, too, and would like to forget it."

Ravenna smiled in the darkness. "That does sound like him."

"You care for him, don't you?"

Ravenna considered her answer. She wanted there to be nothing but honesty between them. Esmerelda was now her sister, to the end. "Not in the way you do."

Esmerelda dropped her eyes. "Right."

"It tears you apart inside. I can see it."

"It diverts me." Esmerelda caressed her belly. "It tries to keep me from what I must do."

"Must do? Or want to do?"

"Words," Esmerelda said with a sigh. "They mean nothing. What we do is all that matters. Ryan is the end of my path. The two of us and our child."

"And this is what you want?"

"It's the only thing I've ever wanted."

"I thought I knew what I wanted," Ravenna said. "I left my home, my people, everything I had ever known, to be with Drystan. And then I left him, too."

"He was captured," Esmerelda comforted. "Taken to a place you could never find on your own. You had no choice but to leave him until you could find a way."

A surge of warmth coursed through Ravenna, despite the strong chill from the sea air. She'd never had anyone she could talk to like this. "I could've tried harder. If I'd wanted to." She sighed. "The tracker I told you about. The one I gave Drystan. Do you remember?"

"Yes."

"I sensed him leave his prison. Days past. He's free now. How or why I cannot say, but he's done it, all without my help. Without me. I'd like to think... well..."

Esmerelda propped her hands under her head, watching her. "Does it help to say these things aloud?"

"Maybe."

"Then say them."

"I don't think I ever loved Drystan the way he loved me," Ravenna replied, and it was as if, for a moment in time, she was weightless, drifting. "I wanted to. I have *never* wanted anything more in my life than for my love to be true and pure, and for it to be all I could ever need for the rest of my days."

"What you describe, this love that is blind to your own needs, is exactly the cage all women are expected to climb contentedly into when they're given to their husband."

"Is it still a cage when it is your choice?"

"Just because you weren't forced doesn't mean it was a choice." Esmerelda pressed her forehead to Ravenna's. "You chose love because you thought only a man could deliver you your freedom. Just as you did with Jesse. A means to an end."

Ravenna's inward gasp startled them both. She'd never considered it in these terms, but they felt closer to her truth than anything she'd reconciled in her mind before. "Where did this wisdom come from, Esmerelda?"

Esmerelda laughed. "Do you mean, where does the daughter of a lord, who was only bred for one purpose, find such enlightenment?"

"Yes, I suppose that's what I mean."

"When the cage door opens, the mind follows," Esmerelda said after a heavy pause. "Even here, I'm more free than I was in Warwicktown, and if I die here, then I still would not have chosen different."

"Then you're further along in your enlightenment than I am. For all I can think of is the Langenacht Oldwin promised me."

"He's taunting you, Ravenna. He wants to break you, because this gives him power over you. The king would never allow his bride to be sullied this way. If you were to become pregnant from such a vile act, the paternity would forever be in question, and so would the succession."

"If he even intends for me to wed Eoghan."

Esmerelda balked. "Why else would you be here?"

Ravenna rolled onto her back. "Wondering about this keeps me awake, no matter how tired I am."

Esmerelda reached over and laced their hands together. "There won't be a Langenacht. There won't be a wedding. We'll be gone before either can happen."

Ravenna chuckled at the raw confidence in Esmerelda's words. "How?"

Esmerelda closed her eyes. "I haven't figured that out. But I know if we believe it, we will find a way."

41

THE DEMANDS OF DARKNESS

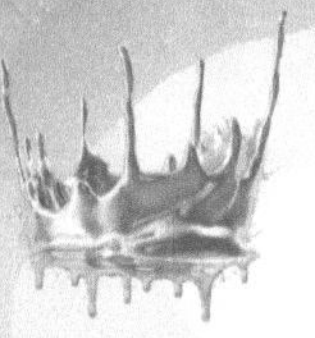

Brandyn awoke to the violent sensation of drowning. His nostrils burned as he thrashed in desperation to expel the assault, arms flailing as he kicked his feet to push to the surface, going nowhere. His lungs were on fire, but the water pooled mainly around an obstruction in his mouth. It was large enough that he couldn't close his jaw, and it tasted of filth and old cloth, and a lifetime of cleaning floors.

"I can stop," a cool, soothing voice called out. Brandyn didn't recognize it. Maybe if he didn't open his eyes, he could pretend he was still asleep in his tent, that he didn't feel the rope cutting into his flesh as it bound him to the chair, or smell the dank air of what seemed to be a cellar.

"Stop," Brandyn begged, though the word was indistinguishable from a grunt with the mass of rotting fabric wedged in his mouth, drenched in foul water.

A hand ripped the rag from his mouth. Brandyn heaved out a breath, then sucked one in. He didn't know which he needed more, to be rid of what was in him or to pull in precious air.

"Tell me how many are coming."

Brandyn pitched forward. Only the restraints kept him from falling. Now that his mind wasn't swirling wholly around the attack of water and filth, he became acutely aware of the dull, aching pains in his arms and legs. Memories to pair with these aches came back, too, but he pushed them down for later.

A hand gripped his chin, ripping his gaze upward again. Now he did open his eyes and found himself looking at a man he'd never seen before but knew just the same. He knew it was Mortain for the otherworldly sense of the creature. He looked ordinary enough, features like any other nondescript man, but it was the eyes that gave him away.

"It cannot only be the Southerlands, for I could crush them with a wave of my hand. So tell me. Who else. How many. The command order they require before they will attack the city."

Brandyn spat into the sorcerer's face.

He was promptly rewarded with the replacement of the rag. He struggled to expel it, but Mortain held it firm over his mouth.

"I won't ask you forever, Lord Blackwood. I have some patience at my age, but not enough for whatever childish heroics swirl around in your head as you struggle to make sense of this."

Brandyn thrashed against his bindings. Ember always said anyone who would dare best you should feel the pain, too. That you should never show you were defeated. If he was here, then he'd already been defeated. But he would not stop kicking, stop screaming through his bindings, until Mortain finished the job. He would not go quietly.

"Go on. Get your energies out. That's a good boy. I can wait."

Brandyn went still. His eyes burned from the strange air, but he focused on boring holes in Mortain anyway, blinking hard through the unwelcome tears.

Mortain removed the rag. Brandyn wanted, more than anything, a glass of mead or anything to clear the pungent taste from his mouth, but he dared not ask. He wouldn't be granted anything here, except a slow death.

"Now then. This doesn't have to be so terrible, Brandyn. I take no pleasure in punishing you. You might not believe that, though it's true. It is. But you have something that I need, and I will use whatever means to extract it from you. Would it not be much easier to simply give it to me willingly?"

"If you're such a brilliant sorcerer, why not take it from my mind?"

Mortain's amused confidence wavered. "You already know the answer, Brandyn. Your Ravenwood blood grants you abilities that provide some challenge to me. You keep your thoughts hidden, where I cannot find them. Not without force." He dropped himself lower so that their eyes met. "But what you have felt this far is only a taste. I will sever your fingers one by one and feed them to you, as I set a thousand rats upon you to partake in a slow but bountiful feast. And that is only the morning festivities."

Brandyn tried hard to hide his fear from the creature. He would feed upon it, and when he did, he would take until there was nothing left of him but the memories that once made him.

"You came here to take the Easterlands," Mortain said. "As they have taken what was yours."

"I came here to take your life," Brandyn answered. "But now I see you're nothing like what they said you were. You look like no more than an ordinary man, nothing to be frightened of. It will not be so hard as I imagined in my mind, in the end."

Mortain laughed. "And how now do you see yourself accomplishing this impossible task?"

Brandyn shook as he forced his mouth into a grin. "It's as you said. My Ravenwood blood."

"As weak and diluted as it is?"

"Not so weak as to give you what you want from me."

Mortain turned away. When he pivoted back, his anger was all

Brandyn saw before the fist connected with his face, sending him back to the darkness.

Ravenna pressed her hands into the fabric of her dress as she walked a pace ahead of the guards. She held her head high and back, knowing full well that any who bore witness would have certain beliefs of her, and she intended to fulfill none of them. But at this hour the halls were empty. They passed only more sleepy guards and the occasional servant.

The walk was longer than she expected. They bypassed the hall to the king's apartments and continued on long enough for her to wonder if the sorcerer's remote location was intentional on behalf of a king who must possess at least some insecurities about the powerful magician.

At last the guards flanked a set of double doors. The dark wood was inlaid with swirling patterns familiar to her, but not enough to provoke recognition.

The guards opened the doors. One put a heavy hand on her back and shoved her in, and before she could turn to address it, a gust of wind knocked her forward as the doors again closed.

"Oldwin," Ravenna said. Her hands threatened to shake, but she would not allow it. She'd made a promise, as much to Esmerelda as herself. If she didn't have the courage to see it through, then she didn't deserve to survive this night.

The sorcerer buttoned the cuffs on his blouse. He'd been sleeping, then, and had redressed for her. "You've come here to bargain with me."

"Did you read that in my mind, or is that a guess?"

"You've confirmed it now, either way."

Ravenna looked around the room. The appointments were generous, but old. Ripe with the musty scent of the forgotten. It settled into everything, all except Oldwin. She sucked in a breath, inhaling both her strength and the room's strangeness. "I've come to tell you I will submit to your Langenacht willingly, without fight. But I want something from you in return."

Oldwin grinned. "And you believe you're somehow in a position to make demands?"

"You accepted my request to come to you. You pulled yourself from sleep to do it. There must be some interest on your part."

"Don't underestimate the curiosity of an old man," Oldwin said. He regarded her with a look that chilled her. "I cannot help wanting to know what it is you ask in return."

"Esmerelda's child is unharmed. You will have royal attendants see the child born healthy, and it will be given back to the mother, where it will stay."

"You assume I have the power to grant this wish."

"I know you do."

"Then you misjudge your king and his own wishes. He will not abide the bastard child of his wife toddling about these halls."

"He is not my king," Ravenna said with a swell of pride. "Nor do I really believe he is yours."

Oldwin took a step closer to her. "He is the king of this realm, of which you and I are a part, whether we accept this or not."

Ravenna exhaled. "Then it seems I was misguided in coming here. Have the guards escort me back."

Oldwin shook his head. "That will not do, either. If you are seen leaving so soon after your arrival, they will whisper that Oldwin's cock no longer rises."

Ravenna suppressed a gasp. Of course, that's what they assumed. She was the fool for not realizing it sooner.

"Perhaps I can grant you what you wish," Oldwin said, stepping closer still. "But what I ask in return is not what you're offering."

Ravenna's eyes widened. "You knew I would come."

"It was not magic at play with that, little raven," Oldwin answered. "I see how you protect the Warwick girl. There is some guilt between you, some lingering and complicated emotion that defies conventional logic of men. Don't unfold it for me here. I have no care for any of it. The wiles of women have never interested me, but it did make clear your motivation before you voiced the words."

Ravenna would kill for a chalice of wine. For anything at all to calm her. But she was here now, in this moment, on the edge of learning her fate, and she must face it with all her wits. "Tell me, then. What it is you would ask in return."

"You must have asked yourself why I would give someone with your gifts over to a weak and sickly king."

"Would you care if I had?"

Oldwin grinned. "You'll marry the king tomorrow. After you've been passed around every Rhiagain man or boy who has reached their maturity. But the child born to you first will not be a Rhiagain."

Ravenna frowned. "I don't understand."

Oldwin's hands reached for the buttons on his blouse. "It will be my child. And if you want the Warwick bastard to live, and his mother to see them grow, then tonight you will come to my bed with gladness. Not only willingly, but enthusiastically, and that enthusiasm will be judged by me alone as sufficient or not. There will be no tears, no forlorn glances into the distance. Only you convincing me I'm the only man you have ever wanted in your bed. And when I spill my seed within you, and it quickens in your womb, bound by my magic, only then will I consider your promise fulfilled."

Ravenna fought the acrid bile forming in her throat. Somehow, he'd known. He'd known that the idea of lying with even a hundred Rhiagains would be more palatable than one night in his bed. "If your magic is so powerful, why the need for me to come to your bed at all? Why not light my womb with a wave of your hand?"

Oldwin was so close now she could smell his foul breath. "What would be the fun in that?"

WHITECHURCH DIDN'T STRIKE Drystan as a town on the brink of war.

There was the same hum of energy that ran under the surface of any town. If the roads had been covered in snow, he thought it wouldn't look so very different from Wulfsgate, other than the manors in the trees off in the distance. It had a more erudite feel than his home, every detail more carefully considered, from the carving of the eaves on each building to the craftsmanship of the roads themselves. The Easterlands had claimed home to all the important pillars of the kingdom, from religion to magic to education. He felt the shadows of this pride as he passed through.

Commerce had slowed for the evening, and what remained were the drunks stumbling from taverns and the occasional traveler taking advantage of the clear roads.

"I don't trust this," Ash whispered as they made their way down the main road, toward the gates to Arboriana. From here, the keep in the trees looked mythical, abstract, like in the tapestries that lined the halls of Wulfsgate Keep, or the great paintings he heard tell of but had rarely seen with his own eyes. "There's no way the Quinlanden men aren't aware of the men camped just beyond the town."

"For a man who once led us with such confidence, you're notably absent of it since we left the Hinterlands," Drystan quipped. He'd grown weary of Ash's doom-filled proclamations, and now found it easier simply to reduce them to jests, or ignore them altogether.

"You'll forgive me if my son's life holds value to me."

"Forgiven," Drystan muttered. He didn't know if Ash was right or wrong to be worried. What he did know was the eerie calm settled over Whitechurch was more hospitable to his plan than chaos. If the town had been swarmed with guards, they'd be subject to checkpoints and questioning. In the quiet of the middle of night, they were unmolested as they made their way slowly toward Arboriana. The eyes roaming the streets at this hour were diverted toward their own dubious intentions.

Ash was mercifully quiet as they continued on, past the high spires of the town reliquary, and then the towering arches of the guildhall. If he was home in Wulfsgate, Drystan would be treated to the lingering scents of spit-roasted boar, or the metallic taste that sometimes hung in the snowy air long after the day's smelting had finished. The call of home had never been stronger than it was now, and he couldn't help but wonder what his mother was doing at just that moment. Was she thinking of him? Had she long ago abandoned hope of his return?

He would be ashamed to face her now. *I left everything for Ravenna, and then she left me.* And even that, his wanton act of disobedience, in the name of love, felt like an act committed by a boy, in another time. He loved her still, but in the way it was safe to love a fond but distant memory, and he'd accepted that she was the necessary catalyst to spur him toward his true purpose. It was a boy who'd loved Ravenna Ravenwood. It was a man who walked toward his destiny. It would be a man who took one life so that many others could be saved.

"If you intend to enter as servants, we cannot take the main entrance," Ash said. He'd stopped advancing, and Drystan looked up to see they were closing in on a massive stone wall, with tall wooden gates marking the center.

"Why do they have gates as high as the sky around Arboriana?"

"Not what you're used to in Wulfsgate, is it?"

"We have gates, but we rarely close them. All are welcome at Wulfsgate Keep."

"I would wager they're closed right now."

"Even then it would not feel as this does."

"You stand upon land belonging to Quinlandens now, Drystan. Of which you are, even if you were not raised so. These are your people."

Drystan shook his head. "They will never be my people. I'm a Dereham, no matter what blood runs through my veins. It will be a Dereham who saves the Saleen. When it is written in *The Book of All Things,* this victory will belong to the Northerlands. Hadden's Bane ends with me."

Ash squeezed his shoulder. He looked in another direction, away from Drystan. "The guards ahead will be better trained to spot outsiders. We'll need to divert east. There's an alleyway that runs half underground. There used to be a metal grate preventing passage, but they were dissolved enough to step through. We'll know soon if they've been replaced. If it's been left the same as it was when your mother was sneaking to meet me, it will lead us in through the kitchens."

"We'll enter that way," Drystan said. "But when it is all over, we'll stand proud at these gates as we watch the Saleen return to their lands. As the Easterlands rejoice in their freedom from tyranny."

Storm's head pounded as she stumbled through the undergrowth, swaying on her feet. She ripped open Brandyn's tent, her eyes confirming what her heart already knew.

"Lord Warwick!" she screamed, drawing her sword. She backed away, turning slowly in a circle as she strained to see in the darkness. Trees, tents, supplies. No sign of the assailants who had knocked them into oblivion. "Steward Oakenwell!"

And why spare them at all? This question tickled the back of her mind, and she knew the answer mattered. But that wasn't what mattered now. "Lord Warwick!" she screamed again.

She flipped around, sword raised, at the sound of crunching behind her. But it was only Joran, a trail of blood dried upon his forehead, moving unsteadily through the remnants of a night still not ended.

"Where's Brandyn?" she demanded.

"You know this answer already," Joran replied, closing his eyes through a long, painful exhale.

"You knew? You let them take him?"

"Storm, we both know the risk we took in arriving before our reinforcements." Joran winced, lowering himself to a log. He clutched his face. "You'll find Lord Warwick deeper in the forest with the Quinlanden defector. Oakenwell."

Storm's chest heaved with the urgency driving her heart. "What are they doing in the forest?" When Joran closed his eyes, she added, "Tell me, you old bag!"

"You would do well to calm yourself, girl." He nodded at her bobbing sword. "You'll not survive ten steps going in alone. They captured one of the men from the ambush. That's why they're in the forest. Best to leave it be, so you don't disrupt your sensibilities with the business of men."

"I will not be reduced to being called a *girl* by a man who failed his order, his lady, and now his lord," Storm spat, and marched away from him and into the forest.

She didn't know in which direction to go, but quickly spotted their trail by moonlight and traced their steps. Within a few minutes, the animalistic moans of a man's desperation reached her, and after a few more paces, she saw the cause.

Khallum twisted a dagger into the arm of a man held down by Oakenwell. Oakenwell pulled his hand from the man's mouth as Khallum leaned in.

"Last chance. I'll nay offer another. Tell us where they've taken the boy, or I leave you to die with a thousand cuts. It will be a blessing if the wulves donnae getcha before the blood runs dry."

"And how to get us there, quickly," Oakenwell hissed.

"It's as I said!" The man heaved forward, but Oakenwell pinned him from more than this futile movement. "I don't know where they've taken him. I cannot get you in. They'll know... when I don't return with the others..." He struggled for breath. Khallum twisted the knife once more, and the man howled. "They'll know you have me!"

"Then show us a way in that willnae catch the same attention, you slithering scrotum."

Storm stepped forward. Neither Khallum nor Oakenwell paid her much mind beyond a brief glance of recognition. She knelt before the Quinlanden guard and stuck her lone dagger under his chin, sinking the tip into his flesh. "These men here? They're good on their word, you know. Lord Warwick, he'll leave you just as he said he will, with a parting gift on top. But me? I'll go find your wife. Do you have children? If you're fortunate I won't be as thorough in my work as I intend and there'll still be someone in the kingdom with your blood up to the task of seeing them through their dead-given rites."

"The servant's quarters! That's the best you'll find, that's—"

Storm flipped her knife to his neck and sliced him from ear to ear.

"Girl, what's wrong with you?" Oakenwell demanded. He dropped the dying man to the ground, rising toward Storm as the dead weight fell away. "Did you not see he was going to talk?"

"Oh? Is this not your land, Steward Oakenwell? What could he tell us that you'd not already know?"

"Whitechurch is not as I left it. It would be a fool who marched in, pretending it was," Oakenwell countered.

Khallum stepped between them. "Enough. I'm spent of patience. Brandyn will be dead before dawn. Our scouts were slaughtered in the night. Tyndall hasn't returned, and may very well be dead. We need to get word to Rutland and Law. They *donnae* send word to Hamish and the Warwick Guard to strike until Brandyn is safe. No matter what happens. They wait for *my* order." He turned to Storm. "Girl, you're the scout now."

"I'll suck on your mother's cock before I leave Brandyn's fate in anyone's hands but mine."

"I very much doubt ye would speak to your own mother with that filth in your mouth," Khallum retorted. "Joran, then."

"You think the Magi will take orders from you?" Oakenwell asked.

"Unless he wants both his lord and our next king's blood on his hands, he'll swallow his distaste for me and do what's necessary."

RAVENNA WATCHED Oldwin from across the room. His pale flesh glittered against the flicker of candlelight. The warmth of the light did nothing to soften him. With one hand, he stroked his cock, and with the other, he propped himself against his pile of pillows. Waiting.

This would not be like her first time with Drystan, soft and inviting. Or with Jesse, ardent and demanding. She could conjure the image of one or both of them to help her through this act, but it would tarnish what little purity still lived within her. She loved both men, in her own way. She would not leave Oldwin's stain upon either of their legacies.

She slipped out of her dress. The chill whipped her to the bone. Oldwin didn't seem to notice, or be bothered by, the cold. He needed no tapestries on his walls to trap the warmth. His blood was ice.

Ravenna stepped across the cool stones, drawing closer to the bed. It would have been a task, but a far easier one, to simply lie beneath him and let him do as he pleased with her. But what he demanded of her was far more. It was everything.

She willed her lips to curve into a seductive smile. They knew the movement. They'd drawn these lines before. Oldwin's grin in response conveyed his pleasure in the act so far. Maintaining it would be the difference between life and death for Esmerelda's child. Esmerelda had posited, just that evening, that surrendering to a path without force didn't mean there was any choice involved.

Ravenna slid up the end of the bed. Her tongue traced a slow trail over her lips. Oldwin released his hand, leaving his erection towering for her in invitation.

Her flesh brushed his as she moved up toward him, and she was not surprised it was as icy as the air around him. Her plastered smile never wavered as she moved higher, dropping her legs over his hips.

"Esmerelda can never know this bought her child's life," Ravenna said.

"Tell me what you want from me, Ravenna Ravenwood."

The burning in her chest screamed at her. It dug a pit deep in her belly. She ignored it. "I want your cock buried so far inside me that it is lost forever."

"What else, Ravenna?"

Ravenna splayed her fingers at her hips, digging them deep into the soft flesh to keep them from shaking. "For your seed to fill my womb and bear fruit."

Oldwin's smile split his face in half. "Then take it."

As Ravenna lowered herself over the sorcerer, taking him in, a part of her died.

She let this part of her go.

She no longer needed it.

It wouldn't serve her this night, or the next.

42
MAKING PEACE WITH THE MAGIC

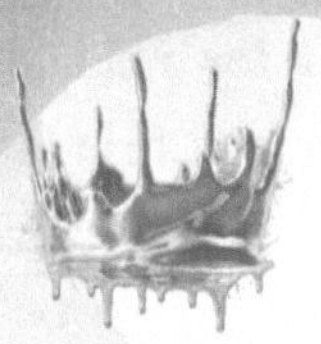

Gretchen secured the last satchel to the saddle. Her breath unfurled before her in white tufts, giving color to her doubt. She'd stopped looking behind her when she reached the barn. There wasn't anyone to stop her. All the men had ridden off to war, and Aylen, too. The thin guard Holden left for her hadn't even noticed her slip away in the dead of night.

The horse neighed, swishing its head back and forth. She didn't know this one's name. It had been left behind, picked over for better, stronger beasts for the ride to war. She was a mare, with a light gray mane and even lighter eyes. Instead of resisting the call of a new rider, Silverwind, as Gretchen now thought of her, seemed eager for whatever attentions lay ahead. She lifted and dropped her feet, chuffing softly in anticipation of the unspoken but nonetheless promised adventures the two would have.

Gretchen had left letters for Nyssa and Torrin. Oh, how she'd agonized over the words. Wondering if she'd chosen the right ones. She tried to make them understand that if it had been either one of them, she'd do the same. She had no choice.

To Earwyn she left a separate letter. *In the event I should not return.* She began with those words because they were the ones etched most clearly upon her fears. She would either return with Pieter, or she would not return at all. Earwyn had her instructions for what to do should the latter prove reality. She had played the role of second mother to the twins for years; to assume the mantle of their permanent caretaker would not be so hard for her.

There were letters, also, for Drystan and Lisbet. Earwyn would hold fast to them, as they'd all held to their hope. Should they never be read, they'd be sent for inclusion in *The Book of All Things.*

Her last letter had been for Christian. She didn't leave this one with Earwyn. She'd slipped it into his chambers. This one was for his eyes only.

For Holden, she left nothing. She'd tried to find words for him, but none came, and the night was drawing short.

Gretchen fought back the wish that she had someone to accompany her on this journey. She at first told herself she couldn't trust anyone enough to take them along, but as she packed the things she would take, deciding what would be needed to sustain life for two, she began to accept that she'd shied away from including anyone else in her scheme because it would have been unfair to them. Pieter was *her* son. She could not ask anyone else to risk their life to find him.

Gretchen Dereham rode out of Wulfsgate without resistance. No one there to stop, or, or even wave her off on her journey. No one to ask where she was headed, alone, at this time of night. None but her and a horse she'd never ridden before, and a path she'd only taken with her husband at the helm.

Gretchen leaned down to whisper in the horse's ear. "We have quite the trek ahead of us, Silverwind. Shall we get on with it?"

Silverwind snorted and kicked to life.

. . .

EMBER'S HEART raced so hard it pulsed into her fingers, her toes. It rose to her neck, radiating with warmth and promise. It rushed behind her eyes, sending dark spots circling into her vision.

She had to go back. If Lady Gretchen awoke and found her missing, she'd send out a search party, which might come at the wrong time, and then she'd have a big problem on her hands. She'd be forced to explain the feathers. Far too many to blame the birds. Those looking for her might even come in the middle of a transformation, and she couldn't hold the form long enough to stay that way until they were gone.

Yet.

But she *had* transformed. She'd done it. All she'd had to do to make it happen was find her calm. All the straining and begging of the Guardians only held her back. She had to make peace with the magic stirring within.

Flying was another thing. She could hop, but hopping wasn't enough. She couldn't hop her way to Midnight Crest and rescue her mother.

She'd get it. Eventually. But she didn't have eventually. Alasyr's warning wasn't a casual one. Fear had pushed him to betray his family. For her.

If only Marsh was here to see it. She missed him, more than she realized she would.

"Ember? What are you doing out here?"

Ember was so lost in her own head that she, at first, thought the words had come from a nearby rabbit. It seemed less strange, somehow, than coming from a child. She was shocked to see Torrin standing there.

"What are *you* doing out here in the Forest of Lycana, in the middle of the night, without your mother?"

"You didn't hear it?"

"Hear what?"

"All the birds! They all flew away, I saw... well, first I heard them. It woke me up, so I jumped from my bed and ran to the window, and then I *saw* them."

"The birds?"

"Yes, the birds! There were so many. I can't count as high as the birds I saw. They were swirling around, in a circle, above the forest. So I followed them." Torrin pointed to the sky. "Can't you hear them?"

Ember gaped at him as she looked up. There they were, just as he'd said. Thousands of birds. Not only ravens, but birds of all kinds, swirling in a constant circle, cawing, screeching.

Were they for her?

Torrin flashed her an impatient look. "You really didn't see them or hear them?"

Ember shook her head.

"Mother's blood. You must have been very busy with whatever you're doing out here to miss *that.*"

Ember crouched slightly to meet his eyes. "If I show you, can you keep a secret?"

Torrin's mouth parted in excitement. He nodded wildly.

"Stand over there. And don't close your eyes, Torrin. Not even for a second. If you do, you might miss it."

Torrin could hardly stand still. "Miss what?"

"Watch. If I told you, you'd never believe me."

AYLEN WAS NOT the first woman in the kingdom to ride to war. This she knew from studying the histories in *The Book of All Things,* which was compulsory reading in her days of attending schooling, before her father shipped her off to the Sepulchre in fear for her life. There had been a brief war that broke out just after the Rhia-gains were declared gods and placed upon the throne. At that time, the Southerlands, who had been the only Reach to stand united against the outsider kings, deployed not only every man and boy, but most women. But they were no match for the other three Reaches, who bowed to the new king and his family all too willingly.

She thought of this as she enjoyed an ale in the warm and inviting *Tavern at the Middle of the World*. It was nicer than any establishment she'd patronized in the north, despite its secluded location, which seemed as intentional as the well-seasoned food and roaring fire in not one but several hearths.

She was close, now, to where the men of Wulfsgate held camp. But that was not where she was going. She intended to ride east and join Brandyn, whom she'd once promised aid to. Fulfilling that promise mattered to her. She would not be allowed to join the men at the battle lines, but she could ride to Whitechurch to counsel, or to heal, or to whatever else he might need from her. She could yet find use for herself.

"Another pour?"

Aylen looked up to see the barkeep, Una, with her pitcher. Aylen nodded, and Una refilled her mug.

"No place for a woman tonight." Una nodded at her armor. "Even dressed as ye are."

"Why tonight?" Aylen asked.

"These men are preparing for war."

Aylen grinned, raising her cup. "As are we all."

Una shook her head. She wiped her brow with the back of her hand, then smeared it on her apron. "Nay. *Tonight*, girl. They ride for the borders, planning to surprise the men from the north." Una leaned in. "Your men, yes?"

Aylen's grin faded. "How do you know?"

"Of war or your alliance?"

Aylen shrugged. "Either. Both."

Una looked up, scanning the room quickly with her sharp eyes. "They see your armor, but pay ye no mind, for what doesn't dangle between your legs. I see yer armor, and perhaps the men sleeping in their bedrolls need not be so surprised for what's coming."

Aylen dropped her sack of coin on the table, heart racing. "How can I thank you?"

Una looked at the money and chuckled. "I ken that's enough right there."

Aylen could still hear Una laughing as she retrieved Witchwind and her bow and fled into the night.

THE ICY BREEZE burned his cheek. It whipped against his head, but his father held it firmly in place, resisting the thrash of the relentless wind.

"I've seen you skulking these halls, like a specter. I *know* you know. What have you done with her? Where is she?"

"Who? Where is who?"

"Do not play me for a fool, Alasyr!"

"Let me down before you kill me!" Alasyr demanded. He pressed his eyes closed. They were so dry from the exposure to the cold air that he feared they could leave the sockets on their own. He'd stopped resisting so hard. His father had him almost completely suspended in the sky, his hands the only thing keeping him from a hard death against Icebolt Mountain. If his father released him, he wouldn't have time to find his wings before Argentyn struck him down. "I haven't done anything!"

"We both know that's not true. We've talked about this before, haven't we? How your curiosity would lead you down a dark path. Like it did Ravenna. You've flown a line too far with this one, Son. You should never, ever have involved yourself in this."

"I don't know what you're talking about!"

"When I think of Ravenna, it is not with *sadness* but annoyance, that we now have to invest our wasted time in Ryandyr. But this is why the High Priestess must deliver more than one heir.

More than one daughter, more than one son. And you are not the only son."

Alasyr resisted the urge to look down. He knew what he'd see. The view was familiar, but he'd never beheld it aloft and floating in the middle of a budding storm. He'd never seen it through helpless eyes. "Tell me what you want and let me down."

Argentyn leaned in. "I want to know what you told your mother."

"I haven't told Mother anything. I..."

Argentyn's face peeled back in a grin. "Ah, but you have. I can see it in your eyes. In your hesitation. But you'll find no such hesitation in me, Alasyr. I would mourn you in the time it took to watch your bones shatter upon the crag below, and then I would go to find Nevyn and instill in him the same thing I once did in you, that you now seem to have forgotten. Duty. I would tell your mother, the others, that you had an episode and fell, too stricken by the tremors to shift into your raven form. You would not be the first. It happens, in bloodlines as closed as ours."

Alasyr was now certain his father would kill him, no matter what he said or didn't say. You didn't make such a threat if you weren't prepared to follow through. "Perhaps you should be less concerned with what I've said and more with what you've done," he hissed.

"What I've..." Argentyn laughed. He removed one hand from Alasyr's neck and wiped it across his own face. Alasyr choked at the loss of leverage. "So it was you."

"I thought... I thought you were searching for Ravenna, and then I saw—"

"Spying on your grandmother and me. You've known all along."

"Grandmother?" Alasyr stopped breathing. "Adynora?"

Argentyn moved his hand back to his son's neck. "And you thought your mother should know? What you *saw*? You cannot *fathom* what you've seen, and what it means. And now, she's taken Lady Blackwood. Her blood is on your hands."

"She came to me," Alasyr croaked. "I had no choice."

"Then you understand that I, too, have no choice," Argentyn said with a look that was almost sad, but Alasyr wasn't fooled. He was practicing, for later, when the others discovered Alasyr's tragic fate.

"Release him, Argentyn."

The vise around Alasyr's neck was too strong for him to turn, but it was his mother's voice he heard. And others, murmuring around her. A surge of relief passed through him. He knew he had narrowly escaped death. Argentyn might have still done it, had she been alone, but with others, his punishment for the murder of another Ravenwood would be swift and decisive.

"We were only talking, Varinya." Argentyn pulled him in and dropped him to his feet, a loving smile painted on his face as he touched his son's cheek. It was more sinister than the earlier promise of death. "Weren't we, Alasyr?"

The warning flashing in Varinya's eyes was enough to cut them both down. But it was reserved for her husband alone. "You ever touch my son again, and there will be no tribunal. No court to decide your fate, only me. And my vengeance is stronger than any magic I wield."

Argentyn laughed, eyes darting across the group of witnesses. They said nothing. They weren't there to join Varinya in the tearing down of her husband. Only to watch.

"That is all," she said, and as she walked past, she reached a hand to Alasyr. He took it, joining her. He didn't look back, but he didn't need to.

She hadn't stayed her husband's hand, only delayed it.

• • •

Torrin watched Emberley for hours. The dark turned to light, and his battle to fight off the beckoning sleep raged harder with every tick that passed. Mama would be angry when she found his bed empty, but the punishment would be worth it. Whatever it was, it would be worth it.

He'd seen the Ravenwoods, of course. Strange as they were, they were part of the skies in Wulfsgate. But he'd always thought of them as different, like monsters in the forest were different, or the Medvedev, whom he'd never actually seen, were different. It was hard to imagine being something different, when you'd always been what you were.

But Emberley, she was supposed to be like him. She was his cousin, his *family*. And now he'd watched her not once, nor even twice, but over a dozen times, transform into a *raven*. Poof went the air and flesh was replaced by feathers, feet by talons. Her small red mouth curved into a beak. He could watch this forever and notice something different each time. He had a thousand questions, but he said nothing at all, in fear she might decide to rescind her invitation.

Yet try as she might, Emberley couldn't fly higher than the nearby tree that had been cut down by lightning. When her frustration took over, she couldn't even transform anymore. Torrin perched on a nearby log, dangling over the edge in anxious anticipation each time. He would've done no better, his heart racing, stars dancing before his eyes when she'd fail. She said she needed peace, and he had no idea where to find that in himself. He was in awe.

At last, she paused, exhaling with her whole body. "Torrin, tell me about your happiest memory of your mother."

Torrin frowned. "Why?"

Ember closed her eyes. She held her arms out and started spinning, slowly. "Tell me. Please."

Torrin groaned. "You're being weird." He nearly laughed then, for her request was the least weird thing about her that night.

"Yet you'll answer me, won't you?"

"I don't know," he said, shrugging. "I guess in Wintertide when she lets me come into the kitchen and help bake for the townspeople."

Ember continued her spinning. "Oh? And what do you bake?"

"Cakes. Pies. Roulades. Bread. You know."

"Tell me more."

Torrin scratched his head. "I don't know what else there is to tell. I like rolling the dough out. It's fun to watch the edges grow longer the harder I push. Oh! And sometimes she lets me taste the custard or the filling. You know, what's left over after they go into the oven, that is. And then there's..."

Torrin had gotten lost in the telling. He looked up and saw a raven spiraling into the sky, gaining more height with each push of its wings.

His mouth dropped as he watched her soar above the treetops and into the skies, where she disappeared altogether.

43
AN HONOR TO SERVE

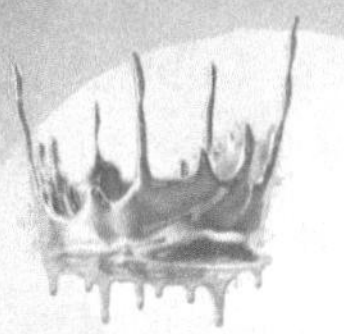

Lisbet had a sense they were coming upon others even before the man stepped into their path.

Eavan and Gabi both made for their daggers, while Meadow hung behind. Lisbet hesitated. She was immediately disarmed by the all-consuming, inexplicable sense that the man standing before them was their friend. The utter absence of malice radiating from his invisible aura—the kind she now saw on all people—startled her.

Her father would chide her for hesitating. Her mother would remind her that all strangers were dangerous, and softness was a weakness. But it was not softness that stayed her hand. It was not softness that kept the others from unleashing an attack upon him.

Lisbet's greatest lesson from the Medvedev was to listen to her instincts. Now, they told her to approach this man. That she had no choice. They were meant to meet.

She held both hands to her sides, staying her cousins. "Who are you?" she asked him.

Lisbet fell a little bit in love with him when his first question wasn't a return one about what three girls were doing alone in the forest.

"Godfrey, they call me," he said. His mouth stopped short of forming a smile. "And you?"

"Don't you dare tell him!" Eavan hissed. Lisbet smelled her fear. One more part of her awakening revealing itself. Like auras, but stronger. "No man has any fair business at this hour!"

"Lisbet Dereham," she said, and both girls behind her gasped. "This is Eavan Quinlanden, Gabrianna Blackwood, and Meadow Ashenhurst. We've come in search of my brother, Drystan, who we believe..." Here, she faltered. "We believe he's come this way."

Godfrey nodded, taking each of them in. "Three of the four houses standing before me. I feel compelled to drop into a bow."

"That won't be necessary," Lisbet answered.

"Four houses," Gabi countered, shifting her shoulders back in pride. "My father was a Warwick."

"Byrne," the man said, nodding into his understanding. "I was grieved to hear of his loss. I met him once, years ago. He was a good man."

"He was a great man. And none of us are just one house anymore, Sir Godfrey," Gabi answered. "Not since the Epoch."

"Yes, of course you're right," he replied. "It seems perhaps we were meant to cross paths. While I've not come across your brother, I travel with someone else who will no doubt interest you. Brandyn Blackwood."

Gabi cried out. "My brother! He's here? Where?"

Godfrey took a step closer. "Not here. He camps with Lord Warwick, across the ridge."

"Uncle Khallum and Brandyn?" Eavan whispered. "They're together? Here? What the Guardians has happened since we've been away?"

Godfrey looked at Gabi when he answered. "Your father's murder set into course a path for war. The Westerlands is full of

Quinlanden men, in every corner of the Reach. Brandyn is now Lord of the Westerlands, in the absence of your father, and your mother, who has escaped from Duncarrow. But it isn't safe for him. It won't be safe anywhere until this threat is neutered."

Gabi stepped forward, around Lisbet. "Mother's blood. My mother was at Duncarrow? And she's escaped?"

"She took your sister's place at the Right of Choosing. But she wasn't there long. She escaped by ship, at night, with others."

Gabi turned to Lisbet and Eavan. "Then she must be safe!"

Lisbet afforded her a quick, encouraging smile, but something was troubling her. "If there's to be war, why are you here, in Whitechurch? Is my uncle—that is, Lord Quinlanden, now truly the enemy?"

Godfrey gave her a strange look. "You were serious when you said you'd been away. Where in the kingdom could you have gone that you didn't know any of this?"

The three girls exchanged glances. "The Hinterlands," Eavan said, surprising Lisbet with how easily she'd come around to the man as well. "We were first prisoners, and then guests, of Yseult of the Drumain."

Godfrey raised both brows. "Quite a story you must have. For another time."

"For another time," Lisbet agreed. "Then you're here to confront Lord Quinlanden?"

"Lord Quinlanden is a pawn of another man, though man is a generous word for such a creature as Mortain of Ilynglass."

"My father's sorcerer!" Eavan cried. "The one who enslaved the Medvedev!"

All at once, Lisbet understood more than she cared to. "That's who Drystan has come for," she whispered to herself. "To avenge the Saleen."

Godfrey's face darkened. "If your brother has come to confront

Mortain, I hope he has come with more than his desire to do it. Mortain's magic is no trifle."

"But that's what Brandyn came to do? Isn't it?" Gabi challenged. Her cheeks were flushed with nervous excitement.

Godfrey exhaled.

"Something's wrong," Lisbet said. "I can see it."

"Only a sense," he said. "I wandered out here to catch a final moment with my thoughts, but I've been gone long enough, and I should return."

"Great, we're coming with you."

He shook his head. "There's nothing for you at Arboriana. Nothing but death."

Another man appeared in full armor. "Godfrey. Who are you speaking with?"

Godfrey waved him forward. "Steward Law. You would not believe me if I told you who has joined us."

Steward Law removed his helmet. "Children. What are you doing out here? Alone?"

"We're heading for the same place you are," Lisbet said, and this time she did touch her bow. Not in threat, but to show she wasn't afraid. "We represent the houses Dereham, Blackwood, Warwick, and those Quinlandens who would see greatness restored to their Reach once more."

"No. Absolutely not." He looked at Godfrey. "Who are these bairns? Where are their parents? Are these... tell me these are not the children who ran from their duty and started this war?"

"Two of us are," Eavan answered, holding her head high. "We refused to marry a pretender, and we'll die before it ever comes to pass. Two did die to avoid this fate. We'll avenge them both one day."

"The whole kingdom is looking for you. You are not safe here."

"We're not safe anywhere, as long as the king lives," Lisbet spat.

"I'd say there's Warwick blood in that one, if I didn't know better," Law muttered. "Foolish girls. You've walked straight into the wulf's lair, and you don't even know it."

"Godfrey told us what we will find at Arboriana. We're not afraid."

"Has he told you there's only a handful going up against a whole city?"

Lisbet's blood chilled, but she didn't drop her eyes, or show her fear. "You have three more now than you had before."

Law choked out a laugh. He ran an armored hand over his mouth. "They are not joining us, Godfrey. I won't have their blood on my conscience."

"We have nowhere else to go!" Gabi said. "My home isn't safe! The Southerlands is full of the king's men. We cannot go back through the Hinterlands, and if what you say is true, then we will fall into the hands of the Quinlanden Guard if we try to go north. I know we're only girls in your eyes, but you don't know what we've been through!"

Law gaped at her, unsure what to do with the small girl speaking so boldly.

"Law, they're no more safe here than at Arboriana," Godfrey interjected. "We don't have the means or the time to secure their safety elsewhere."

"I have never, in all my years..." Law said, scoffing as he looked at each girl. "Children. And not just any children. The future of our realm."

"If we're the future, then why should we not get a chance to help write it?" Lisbet asked.

"I said no, girl. Those are all the words I intend to waste on it." He replaced his helmet. "Godfrey, we must speak. The Magi has come with..." He glanced briefly at the girls. "Important news."

Godfrey nodded. "I'm coming."

When Law had left, Godfrey knelt before them. "He's right.

You'd be walking into almost certain death if you come to Arboriana."

Lisbet set her jaw tight.

Godfrey rested a hand upon her shoulder. "Guardians be with you, whatever you do next."

"He's stopped screaming."

Corin watched his wife. She stood at the bars of the cell, listening to the torture of their nephew. She hadn't moved for hours. When he urged her to sit, she twitched at his touch and said she wouldn't dare seek her own comfort as long as Brandyn was suffering. He tried to offer his own helpless gestures to ease her, running his hands over her aching back. She refused this, too.

"You don't think..."

Yesenia shook her head. "No, I don't think he's dead. Mortain wants something from him, Corin. He won't be satisfied until he gets it."

"What was Khallum thinking? Bringing him here, without aid, without reinforcement?"

Yesenia turned toward him. Beads of sweat cut through the grime crusted on her face. She seemed oblivious to that, or her torn dress. He had never seen such anger radiating from her, but it was a vulnerable kind, and for that, Corin himself had never felt so neutered.

"Is that what he wants?" she answered, voicing her thoughts aloud. She looked at the crumbling ceiling and paced before the bars. "Has Mortain asked himself this very question?"

"He doesn't need a boy to give him the answer."

"He does if his visions have failed him."

"But why..." Corin's eyes widened. "No."

She nodded. Almost smiled. "Yes. Perhaps."

Corin stood and joined her. He lowered his voice to a whisper.

"If this is true, then we must simply wait for help to come. It is only a matter of time."

Yesenia turned away. "Time is the one thing Brandyn doesn't have."

THEY PASSED the first couple of hours in the stables, waiting for morning light. Drystan's eagerness took some effort to temper. He insisted on going the moment they slipped through the crumbling gates of the old close. But the bustle of morning would provide better cover than the meager workers still moving around in the dead of night, and Ash convinced him his plan would work better if he was not captured and questioned.

They entered through the kitchens. The broad stone buildings hummed with life, full to the brim with workers, and it was nothing to join them, to disappear into plain sight. Ash felt his son's energy turn into something new here. Until this point, he'd held to the thin hope he might instill a sense of reality into Drystan's idealistic vision. But as he witnessed a subtle but powerful change come over Drystan, his belated fear turned to animalistic intensity, he understood Drystan had become the vision he'd created for himself. Only death could sunder this prophetic unfolding.

Ash had sworn to himself he'd return to Gretchen with their son, but the young man whose heart seized nothing at all anymore, but this new macabre purpose was no longer her son. He was no longer the sensitive boy who had loved the wrong woman by moonlight. He might never be again.

They milled around, attempting to look busy, transferring pants from one stall to another, dropping used linens in large baskets. All the while, they kept their eyes open for anything that might prove useful.

The Guardians were on their side, for it didn't take long before this happened.

"Around here, by the vats," Ash whispered, nodding toward where he witnessed two workers arguing. The younger one, only a boy, hung low with a weariness that had come from the heavy mantle of an ill-spent night. The other barked orders, indifferent to the bedraggled state of the poor kid.

"It's someone else's turn," the tired boy whined. "Been at it all night. He ain't stopping anytime soon, neither. He never tires. Never quits."

"It is an *honor* to serve the sorcerer," the boy's superior hissed. He shoved a pail at him, and the boy stumbled back several steps. "I'll fill it with your blood, you give me another word that isn't *yes, sir!*"

Drystan exchanged a look with Ash and made toward the boy. Ash followed him, but not before a woman dropped a pile of clean linens in his arms. "Delivery. Dining room. Yesterday."

Ash nodded, trying not to lose sight of Drystan. When he didn't immediately move, the woman kicked him, and he stumbled into his next steps.

"Go on, then! The rich can't eat without 'em!"

Ash had never been in the kitchens before. It was Gretchen who used them to slip away in the night to meet him. In all his visits to Arboriana, he knew only those places where the nobles of Whitechurch spent their time. This was as unfamiliar to him as stepping into Beyond.

"Are ye deaf? Dumb?" With a disgusted groan, the woman took the linens from him. "Fine, off to the pigs with ye, then!"

She'd moved her attentions elsewhere as quickly as she landed them on Ash, so he used the distraction to search again for Drystan. He caught sight of him moving into a back room with the pail boy.

With one last glance into the busy kitchen, Ash ducked into the same room.

"I said, I'll do it for you."

The pail boy's eyes narrowed in suspicion. "And then you'll tell on me, get me kicked back to the pigs."

Drystan shook his head. "I won't say a word to anyone."

"What'll it cost me?"

"Cost you? Nothing."

The boy grew more apprehensive. "Nah. I don't believe you want nothin'. No one ever wants nothin'."

Ash stepped forward. "You'll scrub the privy for the next three nights. That's what it'll cost you. Four if you don't take the offer now, knowing what's good for you."

"And who are you?"

"His father, here to keep him from being a spot too nice to someone who doesn't deserve it."

The pail boy faltered. He blinked the heavy sleep from his eyes. Drystan started to insist there was no need for reciprocation, but Ash stayed him with a hand.

"O'right, then," the boy said. He shoved the pail at Drystan. "But you tell anyone I'll slit your throat while you sleep."

Drystan nodded. "Go get your rest. And... thanks for taking the privies."

The boy grunted and stumbled off.

"He said we need wine. Knives. And more water, for this pail," Drystan said. "Do you know where to find those things?"

Ash's mouth parted. "He's torturing someone."

Drystan nodded. He looked away. "The prisoner he's torturing is Brandyn Blackwood."

"How could you know that? You weren't in here seconds before I joined you."

Drystan tapped his head. "From his mind. I can do that now, too. I just learned it."

"Brandyn," Ash whispered. "That poor child. If he survives this, he'll never be the same."

"He'll survive it." Drystan hoisted the pail. He nodded to the table, where the wine and roll of knives waited. "Seems the Guardians continue to work alongside us." He slipped them both into his satchel. "The closer we get, the more clear the signs are to me that I was meant to be here. Brandyn is my cousin. He's all alone down there, but he's *alive*. If that isn't a sign that I was meant to save him? Then I don't know what is, Ash. I don't know if anything means anything if that means nothing."

Ash swallowed. "He'll be expecting these things. Mortain."

Drystan nodded. "Do you know the way, or shall we again beseech the Guardians to guide us?"

Lisbet and Eavan hunkered in the woods beneath the cover of a large pine tree, awaiting Gabi's word that the men had left camp. Lisbet hadn't liked the idea of timid Gabi off by herself, so Meadow joined her, but that didn't ease Lisbet's nerves any. Lisbet supposed she had no more right to say no than yes, so she let them go. Meadow could read the flora, she said. Maybe there was some use to be found in it.

"Godfrey is a peculiar man, wouldn't you say?" Eavan asked.

"I don't think that's his name at all," Lisbet answered. She pulled an apple from her bag and cut it down the middle, handing half to Eavan. "Do you?"

"Definitely not. But I don't think he hides it the way Ash did, to be deceptive. I think he hides it to protect something."

"There was something very strange about the way he talked to us."

"Very strange indeed."

"And the way Law talked to him."

"Even when he was arguing with him, it was as if he was

walking upon a bed of broken shells. Afraid not to speak out of turn," Eavan said.

"Yes," Lisbet answered. She took a bite of the apple. "Exactly that. As if Godfrey were not his peer, but his superior."

Eavan's eyes widened in excitement. "What do you think it means?"

"I don't know yet." Lisbet pulled the blanket around them both as the first of the rainstorm peppered the ground in the clearing beyond the trees. It sent a chill through her. "But it matters."

"What you whispered to yourself back there, about Drystan..."

"Yes?"

"If he's come to do what Brandyn and Lord Warwick have also come to do, then perhaps... that is, maybe Kian was wrong. About what will happen."

Lisbet shook her head. She tossed the rest of the apple into the forest. She'd had no appetite since they'd left the Drumain. Forcing herself to eat was as futile as sleeping more than a few hours. "Drystan saw enough to know he must come here. But Kian? Kian sees everything. Yseult sees everything. They would have already known about Brandyn and Lord Warwick, and Law, and even the strange Godfrey who might be someone very important. They would have known, and so Drystan's... his death... well, it could be that it happens *because* there are others here. You know?"

Eavan nodded, looking down at her half-eaten apple. She threw hers away too. "Kian said that Drystan could still fail. If he does, then we should step in and take his place, shouldn't we? Finish what he started?"

The question caught Lisbet off guard. She told herself their purpose here was a final goodbye, and the return of a body that her mother could visit in the crypts. "I don't know, Eavan."

Eavan nodded as she looked away. "I think I do. I think I know. If Drystan fails, then it falls to the Quinlanden who failed to stop this before it got so bad."

Lisbet reached for her arm. "None of this is your fault."

"Maybe not, but I can't live with it, either. I can't live with this." Eavan's hand lingered over her belly, recoiling as if it was on fire. "I won't let my father's cowardice take even more from Longwood Rush, from the Medvedev, from anyone. I don't know if I have the power to do anything, but I will know. When the time comes."

Lisbet didn't know what to say, so she said nothing.

"Do you think my mother is still alive?" Eavan asked after a pause. "That she's in there, a prisoner? Or perhaps even joined with Mortain?"

"She would never join with him."

"Lisbet, people would do anything to survive."

"Then we cannot fault her for doing what she must, to live another day, to be there for her children," Lisbet said. "For you."

Gabi appeared from the copse of trees across the clearing, waving.

"We'll finish this later," Lisbet said.

44

RECOLLECTIONS, CONTINUED

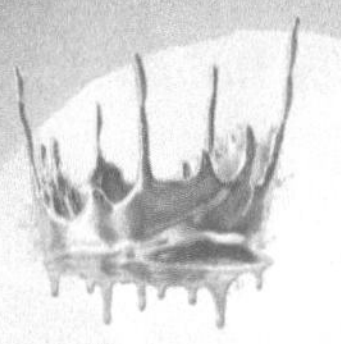

Jesse reached for his mother as she was ripped from his view, fading into the dizziness of a vision that was quickly shifting to something else, something new. He cried out, a swell of emotion trapped deep in his throat, but his voice was soundless. To see her once more, even in the terrible state she'd been in when Hamish came upon her, was a blessing he hadn't known he was so desperate for until it was cruelly taken from him.

Hamish, too, disappeared. Jesse was alone in the vacuum of darkness.

But now he was himself again, no longer his father.

He didn't dare step forward, or back. He was weightless, but also weighted, rooted to nothing and everything. Alone, but filled with the sense that he was surrounded by enemies. Called by and repelled by an unknown too perilous to explore.

The light didn't return altogether, but the darkness turned to gray. Stones. A whisper of moonlight behind a cloudy window. The chill of a room too vast to trap heat in the elaborate tapestries lining the walls.

He was in the chambers of a woman he didn't recognize. Her long *red hair fell in cascading waves down her back, curling around a cobalt gown made of the richest velvet he'd ever seen. Her beauty was as striking as her sadness, which she wore like a veil. She glanced toward her door, fearful, but upon confirming she was still alone, her anxiousness faded, replaced by cooling relief. He sensed now her thoughts. She was safe, tonight. He would not come to her bed. Her bruises could take at least one more evening to heal.*

The woman went to her dressing table, wincing as she lowered herself to the ivory bench. She ran the soft bristles of her brush through her waves, watching them in bland curiosity as they sprang in response. She wanted to cut them off; to throw them into the sea, where her husband sent so many of his enemies. She was his enemy, too, but he'd never throw her there. Not until her use was spent, and so far, she had not proved she had any.

The door opened. She suppressed a gasp, but the sharp sound dissolved when she saw the image reflected behind her in her looking glass.

"It's you," she said, dropping her brush on the table.

"It's me," a man replied. Jesse recognized this one, but the answer was just beyond his grasp. His dark hair was soft and wavy, as beautiful as the woman's, but it was his eyes that could not be ignored. Not the green, or even the flecks of amber within, but the sense that behind them one might travel anywhere. Elsewhere. Beyond.

"You know what he'll do if he finds you here alone with me."

The man pulled her strawberry hair through his fingers, letting it fall piece by piece. He leaned in, inhaling. "I know what he believes he will do."

"There you are again, saying the words but not showing me what they mean," she accused. "You don't fear him enough."

The man leaned over the top of her. He reached for her chin, tilted it high, and then kissed her from above.

"I'm more interested in what you will do now that I'm here," he said.

"We cannot. You know this."

"And I will not come unless you ask me."

"Are you not listening? Have you lost all sense? We cannot! Not until I'm carrying an heir, until the danger of it being any but his…"

The man silenced her with a kiss once more, this one deeper, more demanding. "My kind cannot have children, Decima."

She rose to meet him, her gown sweeping her hair, the floor, him. "Is this true? Or another beautiful lie?"

"Does it matter? If you believe it?"

"Should I? Believe it?"

The man lifted Decima in his arms, this time kissing her with such insisting desire she melted into the moment, folding herself around him, lost to whatever unspoken offer lingered between them now, before, and ever after.

"Just this once," she whispered as they fell back upon the fur covering her bed. "Never again."

"Once is all I ask," he answered.

Jesse opened his eyes, as if from a long sleep. He recognized the room, and the woman, Decima, but now she was abed with child, howling the pain of her birth into a sea of men with stone faces. One of them was the man from before, who had promised her he could not produce a child. He glowered in the corner, blending into the scenery. Was this his doing?

The high piercing curdle of a newborn taking its first breath filled the chambers, dulling Decima's cries. She reached for the infant, but they placed it in the arms of another man, with hair as flaming red as hers. He ignored her pleas and held the child aloft; a prize. His heir, he said, and they all took turns congratulating him, the effort solely his. Together, they departed with the infant, Decima's cries drowned out by the din of their raucous excitement for the man who at last had his heir.

The other one stayed behind. The one from before. He emerged from the shadows.

"You promised me," she accused, eyes rolling back in her head. "You promised me this could never happen."

"You think the child is not his?"

"Did you lay eyes upon him? His hair is dark, like yours. Will his eyes be green, too? Will he have your magic?"

"There are Rhiagains who are not red in hair."

"Even now, you would lie to me."

"You are dying," he said. "Now is not the time for quarrel."

"Dying?" Decima laughed.

"It is not your fault. Even a queen is not immune to the brutality of bringing a child." The man knelt at her bedside. He peeled back the blanket, revealing a bed full of dark red blood. "You see? The king, these men, they no longer need you. The midwife saw this and followed them, anyway. They would leave you to die."

Decima turned her head to hide the tears. "I would like to die."

The man laid hands upon her belly and closed his eyes. "But your work here is not yet done." He swallowed down a wave of emotion. "And I would like you to live."

"You are a fool, Isdemus," she said as her head fell to the side, surrendering to the power of the magic healing her.

When she was out, Isdemus laid a kiss upon her lips. "It was not only duty that brought me to your bed, Decima. Remember this in your final hours, which will come to you, but not yet."

Jesse watched Decima play with a small boy. She rolled a ball across the floor to him, which he caught and spun around in his hands. He watched her with wide, inquisitive eyes, but even when she asked him questions, he merely blinked in response.

"Go on then, Dain. Roll it back to me."

Dain slumped his shoulder and rolled the ball to the corner. He jumped to his feet and went to sit in the small rocker in the corner of the room.

"You have invited your own disappointment. He is not a pup to train," the king chided. Decima cast a disgusted glance away from him as he approached. But when she turned to face him, it was a pained smile she wore.

"He is a boy, who needs his father."

"He is the next king of this realm. He needs discipline."

"Then give him that," she charged. "For until now, you have given him nothing."

The king ripped her by the arm so hard she saw stars. "Beware that mouth, Decima. For you are not with child at present."

Decima fled the room. Jesse expected his vision to follow her, but it stayed with the king and the small, sullen boy named Dain. The king watched his son with such an uncomfortable awkwardness that Jesse wanted to tear his eyes away, but that was not how the visions worked.

"Dain," the king said. When the boy didn't look up from his slow rocking, he said it once more, with such force Dain was startled into looking up. "Why do you not mind your mother?"

Dain seemed afraid of the man who was supposed to be his father. The king asked once more, and Dain shrugged, flinching, expecting to be hit for it.

"If she rolls a ball to you, you roll it back. Kings do not skulk in corners, crying. Do they?"

Dain shook his head.

"Answer me, boy."

"No," Dain said in a cracking, timid voice.

"You are still a babe, but you are old enough to understand that you are a prince of this realm. As princes of this realm, we are charged with the happiness of this realm. Of Duncarrow. When your mother is happy, she comes to my bed. When she is cross, as she was when she left this room, my bed grows cold. There are others to warm it, but there can be only one queen to bear me a legacy. Do you understand?"

"No, Father."

"No, but you will. And until then, Dain? Roll the fucking ball."

. . .

"No, Oldwin. There must be another way."

The king looked as if he hadn't slept in days. His tunic hung from one shoulder, unbuttoned. The stubble on his chin told of the time he'd been in such disarray.

"There is not, Your Grace, unless you wish to see the ruin of Duncarrow and all the Rhiagains have worked for in this kingdom."

"Take Assyria then!"

"She is not your heir. She can never be your heir. So she cannot bring the destruction upon us that I bore witness to."

"If you do this, then she will be my heir, for there is no other."

"Yet."

Jesse got a closer look at this man called Oldwin. He was both old and eternally young, evidence of each reflected equally in his eyes. But he was not a man at all, no more than Isdemus.

Oldwin seemed to be in a barely contained state of glee over whatever he'd just asked of the king.

"What does Mortain say?"

"He sees the same as me, Your Grace. He sees the end, unless you stop it."

Khain's knees buckled. "And Isdemus? Has there been... word of him?"

"None. But nor would I trust the counsel of one who would leave you so easily as he has."

"Tell me the prophecy again. Speak slowly, so that I may hear the words in my own way," Khain commanded.

Oldwin folded his hands over his robe. "From you will spring a line that will undo your legacy and restore the Reaches to their own kingdoms, as it was in the time before the Rhiagains. Duncarrow will burn down to the rocks, leaving only salt and ash."

Khain drank his wine straight from the bottle, nodding through

Oldwin's retelling. Bleary-eyed, he waved the bottle at the sorcerer, brightening. "That does not specifically say it has to be a son. Nowhere does it say it must be a son!"

"What woman do you know that is capable of such mayhem?"

"Do not underestimate a Rhiagain woman. They are not like other women."

Oldwin scoffed. "I have known more than you have. Do not forget it."

"Take Assyria. Decima may again be with child, take that one."

"Do not be foolish, Your Grace. You are ruling with your heart, when a king must rule with his head."

"My heart? I have no great affection for the boy! But I have no other heir, Oldwin. Decima has not been well."

"Yes," Oldwin said with a tight smile. "Not since Isdemus disappeared."

"She was fond of him," Khain agreed, oblivious to Oldwin's deeper meaning. "He saved her life when Dain was born. She may not survive her next lying in. If she births another girl, I am lost."

"Not lost. There are many Rhiagains who would clamor to be your wife."

"I am not young any longer, Oldwin." Khain dropped the empty bottle. It rolled to the hearth.

"Age matters to a queen. Not to a king."

"He is my son."

Oldwin knelt before Khain. "Do not trouble yourself with it, Your Grace. I will see it done myself, so that your conscience can live in peace."

"Peace," Khain repeated, sniffling. "I'll never know it again."

Oldwin stood. He seemed impatient to leave, to see the task completed. "I will advise when the deed is done."

"No, not you. Give it to the Lord Chancellor. And then see him retired from court. He is old, and his time at an end in my service."

"Your Grace?"

"I can never again look upon the face of a man who would murder my son."

Oldwin bowed. "Yes. That, I can understand."

Khain buried his face in his hands, but he did not stay the sorcerer from his brutal task.

45

THE DANGEROUS BUSINESS OF TREASON

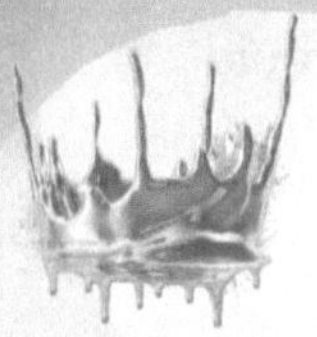

"Where is that bloody boy with my water and wine?" Mortain muttered. He kicked at the empty bucket. It went sailing into the dirt wall. The guard at the door flinched. There'd been another guard, but he'd sent him in search of the servant who'd been gone nigh one tick of the moon longer than he should have.

The boy far more valuable to him, Brandyn, slumped over in the chair, sleeping. It could not be restful. Mortain hoped it was not. He hoped the boy was plagued with nightmares of what would happen if he didn't cooperate. Nothing in his young imagination could prepare him for it. Mortain drew energy from the boy's fear. It sustained him, as wine sustained men.

Mortain intended to kill him either way. The Blackwood heir was useful now for the information he held, but he would be far more valuable dead, leaving his Reach absent of a proper lord. The Westerlands had been as stable as the Northerlands over the years, and the chaos unfolding within its borders now would spread to the entire realm soon. It already had.

But, though he would most definitely kill the child, he would perform the deed quickly if Brandyn no longer put up such a fight. He wasn't entirely convinced he could be the one to strike the death blow, for there was yet Ravenwood blood in the boy's veins, however weakened. He would enjoy it less, but if it came down to it, he'd force the guard to finish the job.

Brandyn had fire in him, like his mother. Like all Ravenwoods. He would kill that, too, before the end. In all of them, if he had the power.

He didn't, yet. But he would.

"If that servant doesn't appear before the boy wakes on his own, I'll feed your blood to the prisoner," Mortain warned the remaining guard.

The guard lowered his head with a pitiful look. Mortain despised weakness, and even more so, fear born of it. How powerless they all were here, these men who served men, who had never known real greatness. Who had no idea what existed *just beyond their borders.*

Mortain turned again to regard his handiwork of the Blackwood boy. He'd made a right mess of the kid. He'd heard the boy was twelve, but had someone told the sorcerer that the child was eight, that would have been just as easy to believe. He looked hardly old enough to be free of the teat. Perhaps he'd be doing him a favor in the end. What kind of mother would allow a baby to wander the kingdom and fall into the hands of the enemy?

Mortain didn't remember his own mother, if he'd even had one. He must have. The sorcerers were not made only of magic. His flesh and blood were not spun from air.

He started to have another go at the guard when he picked up something faint. Almost words, but no, this was something else. He strained to hear them.

They came from Brandyn. Mortain's mouth parted in wonder. So it *had* happened. The boy had slipped far enough into rest that his mind was no longer strong enough to hold the protection.

Mortain leaned in. He listened.

"Guard," Mortain barked when he was done. "Where's Waters?"

"Preparing the Guard, sir. For the city's defense."

"I need him." The guard hesitated, and Mortain would have killed him if he had time to find someone else to fetch the steward. "I need him *now!*"

Waters arrived just as a boy finally returned with the things he'd asked for. It wasn't the same boy, which was good fortune for the old one.

"The Southerland Guard is arriving from the south," Mortain said. "They—"

"Where else would they arrive from?" Waters interrupted, annoyed. "Our men are already stationed south of the city."

"Can I finish?"

Mads grunted.

"They were given instructions not to move without a very specific command. A command only Lord Warwick and Lord Blackwood possess."

Waters grunted. "Not a problem. We'll move on them."

"No. We will not move on them," Mortain answered, enjoying the discomfort spreading over the commander's face as he stepped slowly closer. "You will withdraw your men from their positions and bring them back to Whitechurch."

"I will not!"

"You will."

"Are you mad? Why even suggest such a thing? You'd bring the battle *here?*"

"You will bring your men back to the city, and then you will assume command of the Saleen. I will tell you the words they require to follow your lead, and with these words you will take them south. You will send word, using the command I give you, to Hamish Strong of the Southerland Guard, and when he attacks, I will send the Saleen to meet them. Your men will see to it that the Saleen don't veer off course."

Waters twisted his mouth into a smirk. A dim light appeared behind his eyes. "I see what you're after here, Mortain. Let's not waste our own men when we have creatures less than men to go in their place."

"Something like that."

Mads frowned. "Why issue a command to the Southerlands at all? Just set the Saleen on them when they're fat in their suppers and be done with it."

Mortain harnessed the last of his patience. He wouldn't need Mads Waters much longer, but he needed him now. "The hold I have over the Saleen has limitations. In their numbers, I can command them to move as one, en masse, but I cannot—" He grimaced. The pain of saying these words, to this creature, was unbearable. "I cannot control them each as individuals, as would be needed in battle. If I send them to battle, even the dimmest of the men fighting for the Southerlands will see they bear no swords, no armor. Not a horse between them."

"Won't they see that, anyway?"

Mortain closed his eyes. How fulfilling it would be to kill him here, now. "*Yes*, but it will not matter against a command from their lord and leader. They will not have the indulgence to avail themselves of such questions, for their lord will have decided things for them. They will be left with no choice."

"It will be a bloodbath. For us. For the Saleen, I mean. We'll be handing victory to the Southerlands."

"This battle, yes."

"And the war?"

"What war, Waters? The one here in the Easterlands I aim to prevent by redirecting the kingdom's ire toward those who would annihilate an entire race? Or the one that will spring as a result of it?"

Mads' mouth parted.

"*Now* do you understand? Have you achieved comprehension? Or will it take standing here for hours, as I break things down for you as I would for a child, before these strategies slip between the cracks of your thick skull and make landing?"

Mads turned away from him. His lips twitched, but, deciding better of whatever he thought of saying, left.

KHALLUM WAITED with Storm behind the wheelhouse. The traitor's suggestion of the servant's entrance had served them this far, but they'd not make it any farther without a plan. Oakenwell, wearing his Quinlanden armor, had gone ahead to scout for a place to slip in. He suspected Brandyn was in the dungeons, but they had no way to confirm. The only one who knew was the traitor, and he never had a chance to say before Storm unceremoniously slit his throat.

The girl wouldn't stop twitching. Raw bloodlust burned in her eyes. He recognized it well enough, but in her small body it unnerved him. Her anger lived within her unrestrained. Her loyalty to Brandyn might come at the expense of her life, and she was not only willing, but eager, to pay this price.

"Quit yer pacing," Khallum commanded. "Won't help. Save it."

"I don't need your counsel," Storm answered. She stood with her back to the wall, dagger drawn. Her free hand rested on the hilt of her small sword. It looked like the sort of thing gifted by a loving father, at the autumnwhile celebration, akin to a soft pat on the head. "And I intend to be ready, if whoever comes around that corner isn't Steward Oakenwell. Or if you were wrong about him."

"How many men have you led into battle, girl?"

"How many have you?"

He realized his error as soon as the words were out. Imagining a day like this wasn't the same as doing. He at last had the allies, but his place had come not on the battle line but skulking behind the scenes on a recovery mission.

"He's been gone long enough. I'm sick of waiting for him to betray us. I'll figure this out myself," Storm said, and started out into the open, but Khallum grabbed her back. "Let me go! You think I won't kill you, because you've got a lord in front of your name?"

"Ye won't be killing me if one of them takes you out first." Khallum held her with one arm and pointed with the free one. "Did you even look?"

Storm squirmed free, but remained reluctantly at his side. "You were wrong not to send word to the soldiers. We need them. We'll never move freely or quickly enough without them."

"The moment they move upon this town Mortain will draw his blade across Brandyn's throat. He's only valuable to our enemies now, when he can talk, and Brandyn willnae talk. As long as he refuses to give up what he knows, Mortain needs him alive. He isnae no longer so valuable when he can be recovered to lead a Reach."

"What can Brandyn tell him that he doesn't already know? If he knew about us, he knows your men come from the south."

"I donnae, girl, but if he wanted Brandyn dead, he would've had the men take his head at the camp."

"He could already be dead."

"You'd see his head lining the pikes. Prizes are for display. And do ye think he's dead?"

"No," Storm said. "But Mortain's reason for delaying the deed has as much sense as you not ordering the men to attack and end this."

"Do his reasons matter, girl? Nay, and they willnae matter more if we debate them over Brandyn's grave, neither. Once my men take Whitechurch, the sorcerer will take what he can from us before we bring him down."

"You assume too much. You assume he doesn't already have what he needs from Brandyn. We stand here, assuming, while Brandyn could be dying!"

Khallum set his mouth in a tight line. The girl was right. He'd not give her the satisfaction of the confirmation, though. "We'll find a way in ourselves, then."

"We'll never make it inside alive."

"I thought you weren't afraid of death, girl?"

Storm scoffed. "I'm not."

Khallum snickered. "Right."

Storm stepped in front of him. Her dark eyes burned hot. "I'm not afraid to die, Lord Warwick. Only afraid it will happen before I can save him."

Khallum grunted. He pushed her aside, handling her more gently than before. "Aye."

"Every moment we wait doing nothing is a moment Brandyn could be dying, alone."

Khallum said nothing.

"Do you trust him? Truly?"

"Oakenwell?"

Storm nodded.

Khallum sucked in a hard breath. "He takes off his helm anywhere near Whitechurch, he's a dead man."

"That doesn't mean he's on our side."

"He's never been on our side, girl. He's just smart enough to use one enemy to defeat another."

"We could use him."

"Eh?"

Storm lowered her daggers. "We could use him, Lord Warwick. To get in."

"Speak plainly, girl."

"Those two guards over there? The ones pacing the station? I could take them. Take their armor. For us. It will be big on me, I suppose, but will fit you fine, and we only need it just long enough to move freely until we make it to the bridge. When Oakenwell returns, I take him prisoner and use him to distract Mortain and Waters. They will want him back. They will come to see the biggest traitor in the Easterlands returned. There was no one closer to Lord Quinlanden, and his capture will grow their power when they show the people he's in their hands now."

"And me? What role do ye have me playing in this fantasy, girl?"

"You slip in, wearing their own armor, and go find Brandyn."

Khallum raised his brows. "And what of Oakenwell, then? They'll kill him."

Storm shrugged. "Treason is a dangerous business."

DARRICK STUMBLED against Tyndall as the Saleen came into view. He reached for something to steady himself, but there was nothing but his utter disbelief.

He didn't know what he was seeing, not at first. It seemed as if the forest itself had shifted; the flora becoming something unknown to him. A sea of color that didn't belong to this world, the vibrant blues and violets and greens merging into a tapestry of wonder.

Tyndall dropped to his knees. "This is so much worse. So much worse than anything I could have ever imagined in my darkest nights."

Darrick laid a hand on his shoulder. There was nothing to say. No more words for the horrors that unfolded as they looked further, into this unnatural wave of color and muted life, the endless, dazed wandering of a people more ancient than anything, man or beast, that had ever walked these lands.

Joran's message earlier that morning left a hole in Darrick's belly. On their way to the abbey, they'd caught Grand Minister

Tyndall riding hard, Whitechurch at his back. What he'd seen, he had no words for. Pale-faced, he begged them to follow.

We must join Lord Warwick and the others at Arboriana, Steward James countered, as Darrick mounted his horse.

Where we go is Arboriana, Tyndall insisted. In the woods beyond it. It's a way in. Better than any others I could find, but... but...

But what?

I have no words for the horrors, Your Grace. Only with your own eyes will you understand. For this, we have ridden across the kingdom.

They'd followed the Grand Minister to the woods beyond Arboriana, and there it all was, just as he'd said, both with the words he'd spoken, and those lingering behind his beleaguered eyes.

"We've come to end it," Law said, stepping next to Darrick. "Donnae lose yourself to what was. Look to what will be."

Darrick broke free of the other men and moved toward the mass of Saleen, swaying in haphazard unison. He ignored Rutland's call to come back. He would answer to these men in some matters, but not this. *This* had happened because he hadn't been wise enough to foresee the depth of Eoghan's jealousy, underscored by a surfeit of childish ignorance. *This* had happened because he'd let the fight be kicked out of him. Because he'd forgotten who he was, retreated somewhere he could feel contentment in surrender; where he could willfully mistake the burning in his belly for hunger and not something greater, greater than himself.

He moved down the hill, closer still. He could see now, milling with the same mindless commitment, the familiars of the Medvedev. Foxes and hawks, wulves and ravens, pacing, circling. If he were to wander down to the sea, he would witness more of the same in the crabs, turtles, and fish separated from their companions for far too long. They were not as easily subdued, it seemed, but their power had been neutered when their companions became property of Mortain.

Darrick didn't slow his pace as he stepped into the throngs of the enslaved Saleen. They regarded him with empty eyes. No curiosity flickered behind them. No thought to why this strange man was here now, among them. With a snap of the right finger, they'd turn on him, and if they did, so be it. If Mortain saw him in his mind's eye and used this moment to end him once and for all, then it was the death he'd earned.

There were no guards. No soldiers. They weren't needed here.

He looked up toward the tiered castle in the trees, Arboriana. How many had stood upon their perches and balconies, gazing into the sea of Medvedev that evil wrought? Done nothing? Said nothing?

Darrick tried to imagine Eoghan stewing in the aftermath of the terrible choices made in his criminal inexperience. He tried to stir within him some latent love for a brother who had used what little energy he had to spin hatred into ephemeral power.

The remaining threads of empathy Darrick had for his twin brother died as he regarded the hollow gazes of a hundred thousand Saleen.

They'd come back here, before the end. Free every last one, even if it took years to see the tightly wound magic unspun.

Then, all at once, the Saleen began to move.

HAMISH PUSHED THE STEW AWAY. The bowl toppled over, spilling the cooled contents into the dirt. He wasn't hungry. His hunger had crawled up into the shadow of his bowels, hiding away. This was the way of it on the eve of battle or business, and he knew, even before the messenger had come from Lord Warwick bidding them extend camp to the town border, that today they would fight. He just hadn't seen it coming so *fast*.

He stayed seated while the men around him stirred from the laziness of morning. They would strike before the full sweep of dawn, to whatever end.

"We've waited long enough. I kenned Lord Warwick'd be joinin' us, seeing as he's been awaiting this day since he was still on the teat. But if we wait any longer, we're defying orders," Garrick said, spitting a mouthful of stew inches from Hamish's boot. "A shame."

Hamish moved to his feet. The rest happened fast. He raised a hand to point, just as others all around him did the same. "Look. They... ain't even formin' a line. They're just comin'."

Garrick put a hand over his brow, squinting. "Where's the messenger? Can they not wait for the proper battle, then?"

"Go, assemble your men. Send word to the others. There'll nay be negotiation, nor proper battle today. This is a massacre," Hamish barked. He reached for his helmet and stormed away.

He felt Garrick's derision long after he'd left him by the morning fire. But they had no time for old rivalries. Hamish stepped into the row of tents, screaming, "Into formation, men! War is upon us!"

One of his top lieutenants, Lansing, ran beside him as he chanted the words. "What happened? What's going on?"

"I cannae guess, but I willnae die trying to sort it. Armor up, or we die here, today." He squeezed his arm and continued on. "This is it. This is what we've come for. War! War comes to us this day!"

All around him, men stirred to action quicker than he could've hoped. They'd come here for this, waited for it, and now were ready for it. Or so he'd thought. None were battle tested. Not even him.

Hamish pushed through the mud, back toward the front. The advancing men continued on, making no indications of pausing to form a line. There was no practiced formation that he could see. No...

"Aye, ye see that? The poor bastards are on foot. Nay a horse in sight. Are they even wearing armor?" Hamish mused as he swung his fat legs over his saddle.

Lansing drew his sword and mounted his horse. He raised it, calling his men. Down the line, thousands of Southerlanders raised their own swords in unison as each lieutenant followed suit. Hamish strained to see the end of it, and when he could not, a swell of pride, of absolute perfect joy, swirled within him. At last. It would end here, at the ends of their swords, hundreds of years bringing the Southerlands to this moment, this place.

A fear that something was wrong, very wrong, caught in his throat. He choked it down, pounding his fist three times against his armor to bring himself to the height of the moment upon them.

"Ride! Ride hard! For the Southerlands! For the realm! For death, for life! For victory!"

Hamish couldn't see who shouted the words, for he was carried forward by the momentum of thousands of horses flying through mud and grass.

He spurred his own warhorse to life and charged forth.

A Fire to Stoke or Starve

46

LANGENACHT

Oldwin hovered behind Eoghan as they regarded the young king's reflection in the looking glass. Oldwin had stopped pretending. His eyes conveyed his disdain, his smile no longer sufficient to perform the job intended. It was Eoghan now who feigned joy; who was desperate to convince the sorcerer that he could be agreeable.

How had it all changed? Eoghan asked this question of himself, of Correen, but the effort was needless, for it had never changed at all. He had never held any sway over the sorcerer, not even when the creature stood before him in chains, pathetic, awaiting freedom. The chains had never been enough to hold him. The cell was only the set of a playactor, awaiting his big scene.

Eoghan had no allies to consult. Oldwin had taken them before he could find them, dividing his kingdom in the name of the crown. Oldwin had done all these things under Eoghan's nose, often with his permission and encouragement. His smooth handling of Eoghan had been subtle and swift, leaving Eoghan to question his own beliefs, challenge their origins.

"Ahh. Look at you," Oldwin cooed from behind him. "That blue becomes you, Your Grace. You'll make a fine groom. Ravenna and Esmerelda will discover themselves the most fortunate in the realm, when they lay eyes upon you later today."

Correen appeared in the reflection, rolling her eyes. "Eoghan knows what he has and what he doesn't. Filling his head won't do at all, Oldwin. He's anxious enough."

Oldwin pretended to be aghast.

"Correen's right," Eoghan said. He set his crown aside. It was heavy; it cramped the back of his neck until the muscles seized, refusing to behave. "I am no prize as a man. What I offer is a lifetime at the side of a king." He turned to the right, where Assana sat in the corner. "Have you met your new sisters in marriage?"

Assana's face was unreadable from the shadows. "Esmerelda is my cousin. I've never had the pleasure of acquainting with any Ravenwood."

"You'll be drowning in that pleasure soon enough," Oldwin quipped.

"I look to you to get them settled and oriented. When they are moved from the dungeon to their own chambers tonight," Eoghan said. He shifted in the uncomfortable chair. Every bone in his body ached today. It was going to be one of his bad days. "As my first wife."

"Tonight? But it is your wedding night, Your Grace," Assana insisted.

"The Langenacht will satisfy my day's energy." He looked up at Oldwin's reflection. Loathed the way he inwardly cringed before he said words he knew Oldwin would not like. "I'd like us to reconsider engaging in such archaic traditions here in Duncarrow. That is not our way, and Ravenna joins our world, where she must learn to adapt, not the other way around."

Oldwin tilted his head with a thoughtful look. "She is no mere bride from the Reaches, Your Grace. She comes from another world, like us. From Beyond. If we are to join these worlds and make them one, we must give her some familiarity. Something to show her we welcome her and those things she holds dear."

"I refuse to believe that girl lost a moment's rest over not having to rut with half her bloodline in one night," Correen said. "No wonder she ran."

Oldwin flashed her a patronizing look that could've shattered the glass. "And what would an old maid know of the longings of a young and beautiful priestess?"

Correen was unfazed. "More than an old sorcerer who has likely never had a woman come to his bed willingly."

"Enough," Eoghan barked. He enjoyed Correen's bristling, but couldn't be seen to indulge it. Not anymore. "I still don't like it, Oldwin. All those men. How can I face the court with a woman who's been bedded by everyone I know? How can I face those men in the halls when I know they've lain with my wife?"

"With the pride of the king who won her hand," Oldwin answered smartly. "What they have only tasted will become your feast."

Correen made a gagging sound.

"Yes, but..." Eoghan would lose this battle. He would lose, not because Oldwin was better matched to his wits than him, but because he didn't understand Oldwin's tactic of forcing Ravenna into an orgy on her wedding day. This was not about tradition. But if not that, then what? "I cannot have a bride, Oldwin, who carries the child of another man in her womb. And we can never be certain that any child born of this ceremony will be mine."

Oldwin clapped both hands on Eoghan's shoulders, so hard the king winced. "Ahh, is that your worry, Your Grace? Never mind that. I've already blessed your seed so that it will be yours and yours alone that bears fruit on this blessed day."

"Blessed his seed?" Correen repeated. "I don't care to know what *that* entailed."

Eoghan glared at her for the implication. "And what of the Warwick bastard growing in the womb of my other wife?"

"Don't let it trouble you. I'll see that, upon its birth, it's returned to the Southerlands, where it belongs." Oldwin grinned. "In the same box Lord Warwick's head has lain rotting for weeks."

RAVENNA PACED THE CELL. It was a short, unsatisfying walk, but she couldn't make herself sit still. The guards would come for them soon. They'd come for her first. She would summon her courage, as she had the night before, and do what was required. Had she only *done what was required* in Midnight Crest, she would not be standing in the cold cell of a dungeon, awaiting the "blessing" of bedding a dozen men before marrying the worst of them.

"Where were you last night?" Esmerelda asked. She neatly folded the blanket; a gesture that conveyed her innate need for decency, even here.

"Last night? Here. With you."

Esmerelda set the blanket on the bed and approached her. "I beg of you, don't lie to me. Not you, Ravenna. Not now."

Ravenna sighed and looked away. She was a fool for thinking she could protect Esmerelda from the truth. "I went to Oldwin. To see if... it doesn't matter. I was wrong. He is no man. He already knows what he'll do. He's known all along."

Esmerelda touched her arm. "I won't make you feel any worse than you do already. What you did took courage. Your inability to find his humanity is his failure, not yours."

Ravenna looked down at Esmerelda's hand. She covered it with hers and tried to smile. "Never surrender, right?"

Esmerelda laughed through fresh tears. "We must be brave today, and all days thereafter. It won't do for them to think they've broken us."

Ravenna pressed both hands to Esmerelda's face and laid a

gentle kiss upon her lips. "What has been broken can be remade."

Esmerelda pressed her forehead against hers. "Like a phoenix, rising from the ashes of its destruction."

"Have you ever seen a phoenix?"

Esmerelda shook her head. "They're not real. Creatures of myth only, like dragons."

They both jumped as the cell door slammed open. A dozen guards swarmed in, surrounding Ravenna as they jerked her away, dragging her toward the door.

"You need all these men to subdue one woman?" Esmerelda laughed. "Perhaps you'll discover soon that even that won't be enough!"

To Ravenna, Esmerelda mouthed, *courage.*

Ravenna mouthed in return, *never surrender.*

ESMERELDA RAN TO THE WINDOW. All throughout the night she'd lain awake, listening to them build the dais upon which Ravenna would endure the unthinkable for hours. It was because of this that she'd heard Ravenna slip out of the cell with the guards, not returning until dawn.

Esmerelda believed Ravenna when she said she'd gone to appeal to Oldwin, but she knew Ravenna had hedged around the truth. To protect her, which she could forgive, but that lie limited Esmerelda in how she could protect Ravenna in return.

She couldn't protect her from the day ahead, and that failure burned deep in her empty belly. It was hard to remember a time when she'd harbored such animosity for Ravenna, jealous of her free way in the world, of her easy sexuality and confidence. Circumstances had bound them together, and there was nothing now that could sunder that bond. For Ravenna, she would not look away from the horrors she'd witness beyond her tiny window. If Ravenna needed strength, and looked up to find it, she would be at the other end of her gaze, no matter how hard it would be to bear helpless witness.

Esmerelda pulled the chair to the window and slumped in it. The child growing within her was restless, and it stole what little strength she had remaining.

Ryan would never meet his child.

Jesse would never meet the baby he'd devoted his own life to protect.

And nor would she, for there was no one here to challenge Oldwin and the king.

She reached into the bodice of her dress and felt for the small blade. She'd found it stitched into the pillow. It wasn't much, but it didn't need to be much, if it landed well.

Esmerelda closed her eyes and hummed a song her mother used to sing to her as she waited for the Langenacht to begin.

Atop the dais was a plush pile of bedding, mountains of furs and velvet, more grand even than what she had in her own lavish bedchamber at Midnight Crest. Torches stuck in the ground boasted high, emerald flames, which were not exactly as the green-light fires were high in the Northerland Range, but not that different, either. Both were created by magic.

Oldwin had crafted a careful illusion for the Rhiagains, who had left the seclusion of their chambers at Duncarrow to witness the unusual wedding festivities.

Ravenna was led down the rocky path toward the dais without restraints. She'd agreed to do this willingly and was surrounded by enemies. And how *many* Rhiagains there were! Until she'd laid eyes upon the couple hundred pale-faced redheads gaping at her in indifference and confusion, she'd assumed Duncarrow was home only to the king and his closest relations.

Oldwin awaited her at the end of her path. His flowing white robes gave the underlying feel of a man of faith, of the Reliquary. A creature like Oldwin had no faith, but from the way the Rhiagains threw him awestruck glances, he'd calculated this move well. It didn't matter who you were, only who others believed you were.

A fierce wind ripped through the gap in the rocks. She nearly lost her footing on the uneven ground as she drew closer. It was startling how little the Rhiagains had done to address the harsh aesthetics of the craggy isle. Hundreds of years and they'd only cleaned up and carved out one small, pitiful courtyard. No flowers or trees. No color, no joy. Only patches of half-dead grass.

Oldwin held a hand out to her as she climbed the two steps, joining him. The ice passed from him and through her, into her. The shock of it forced a gasp from her throat.

"It has been too long since the Rhiagains have held a ceremony within the rocks of Duncarrow. Too long since we've had the mettle to declare the rest of the kingdom uninvited!" Oldwin called out. His voice carried across the wind, echoing through the gathered. "The Right of Choosing failed not because of a wayward kingdom, but because it was not ours. Not us, here, together, celebrating on our own land, with our own people!"

Wan faces exchanged fearful glances. They didn't know what reaction he wanted from them.

Ravenna looked down to see a line of men, some of them boys, all in white robes. She counted ten of them. They shivered in the cold breeze. Had they come willingly? Did they want to partake in this? Some shifted their gaze away as she regarded them. One looked at her with aggression burning in his eyes. The violence in his irises made her a promise for later. She hoped he went last. By that time, she'd be delirious enough not to notice his cruelty.

"This Ravenwood has come a long way to join two houses that were sundered long before the Rhiagains came to this kingdom," Oldwin continued on, waving his arms over the crowd as if performing a great blessing. "To show our gratitude for this bold act of selflessness, we will grant her the one thing she has asked of us. We will grant her the tradition the Ravenwoods hold so sacred. The Langenacht."

While Oldwin explained to the gathered Rhiagains what they could expect, Ravenna chanced a look up at the tiny windows of the sky dungeon. She thought she saw Esmerelda's face peering down, but it was too far to know whether her sister was there, or if it was only her heart summoning more courage.

"One by one, each of you will take your place. You will lie with Lady Ravenna, the future wife of your great king, not stopping until your seed has spent itself. King Eoghan will take his place last of all. He will climb these steps and claim his bride. I cannot predict the outcome of this day, and which man will light the future queen's womb. But I have the greatest faith that King Eoghan will emerge victorious, and today will be the day the Guardians at last grant him an heir!"

Scattered applause greeted the proclamation. Ravenna looked among them, breathless with fear, wondering if any could see the truth written upon her face. That she had fled her home so that she could choose the men who came to her bed, grasping forward into the future of her choice, not the one forced upon her.

If any did, they gave no signs. They seemed more put upon to have been forced out in the cold.

"Gilford Rhiagain, will you come join us as we begin our sacred ceremony?" Oldwin called out.

A young man, hardly older than her, shuffled past the other robed men, eyeing his feet as he climbed the stairs. He tripped on the top one, careening into her. When he looked up, she saw the fear in his eyes matched her own. She was not the only victim on this day.

"It's time," Oldwin whispered in her ear. She glanced around once more. Was this truly her fate? To lie with ten men, and then a king, while these strange people watched, indifferent to her pain?

"Now," he urged. "Or our promise is forfeit."

Ravenna nodded through her anxious exhale, wrapping her cloak tight. But Oldwin ripped it away and nudged her toward the pile of bedding. She dropped to her knees on the furs and cried out when Oldwin yanked her by the arms, flipping her onto her back.

He held her from above and nodded to the boy, Gilford. "Don't be shy, Gilford. Pull up her dress."

Shame burned in Gilford's eyes as he shuffled closer. A guard shoved him and he fell into the furs. His mouth hung slack as he struggled with the thick fabric of his robe, pulling it up and over his head.

He crawled toward Ravenna on his hands and knees.

"You can let go of me," Ravenna hissed to Oldwin, pulling at her arms.

"I will stay with you until the end. I want to experience this with you. Feel what you're feeling."

"That isn't part of the Langenacht."

"I have some things I would like to say to you. As you take in this experience I have crafted, just for you," Oldwin purred. He snapped his fingers, and Gilford fell down over Ravenna. His hot breath smelled stale. She felt him reach down between both their legs, and after a moment, he found his way. Eyes closed, Gilford pushed into her, and when he did, his fear, his shame, drifted back into the wind. He moaned into his rhythm as he took his pleasure of her.

"Don't embarrass yourself, Gilford. Take your time, boy. You will never again in your life fuck a queen," Oldwin told him, and then lowered his voice. These next words were just for Ravenna. "I cannot kill you. Surely you know that already? Just as you cannot kill me. We are forever bound from the mortal harm of each other. But that doesn't mean I cannot destroy you."

Gilford moved faster inside her, grunting through each inexperienced stroke now. Ravenna bounced beneath him from the force of the act. She grimaced as sweat from the boy's brow landed upon her face. She was desperate to wipe it away, but Oldwin had her pinned.

"What is broken can be remade," Ravenna replied through clenched teeth. "You cannot destroy me, Oldwin, not if you made me to lie with every man and beast in this kingdom. For that is not where my soul lives."

Gilford affected a series of jerks and then fell upon her. A bitter warmth spread within her. The first one was over.

"You will regret not taking your time, young Gilford," Oldwin chided as the boy stumbled away, sleepy-eyed. "And now we call Thane forth to lie with the future queen."

This man was older and far less unsure compared to the inexperienced Gilford. He approached the dais with a swagger in his step and reached beneath his robe to grab his cock before he'd even made it to the bed.

"You're wrong about your soul, Ravenna," Oldwin whispered. He nodded at Thane, who reached down between Ravenna's legs and shoved several fingers inside. Thane shook his head with a laugh, and when Ravenna looked down at what was in his hand, she understood why.

Stars exploded in her head when Thane slammed into her. She arched her back as if it might snap if she did not, but Oldwin held fast to her. She had never known such pain as this sensation of being ripped in half. Her courage faltered as hot tears burned the back of her eyes.

"Don't spoil your experience, as Gilford did. We aren't bound by time here. The ceremony lasts until each man has finished," Oldwin said to Thane. Oldwin's fingernails dug into her flesh as his words grew more harried. "I will let them have you for days, even if it kills you. Since I cannot, I should let them do it for me. But I will not. For the child that will grow in you is mine, and so you are mine, until you give it to me."

"The child will never be yours. I will throw myself into the sea before I allow you to even lay eyes upon it."

Oldwin looked up. "Slower, Thane. Allow the queen her enjoyment."

Thane eased his pace, but this did nothing for the pain. She knew why Oldwin had chosen this one for her, and if she survived long enough to take the next man, it would be his magic alone that enabled this.

"Do you know who I am, Ravenna?" Oldwin said to her. His spittle dotted the side of her face. She couldn't see it, couldn't feel it, but she knew that he'd grown hard from seeing these men take her, from the physical connection binding them as he felt her pain pass through her flesh and into him, where he feasted upon it.

"You're a monster."

"Yes, but who am I?"

Ravenna closed her eyes and looked away from him, but he pressed his lips to hers and turned her face back.

"You have asked yourself far too many times why you were not like the others at Midnight Crest. Why you couldn't fall in line, and do as duty commanded. You may not know what sets you apart, but your mother does."

"You know nothing about my mother."

"I know your mother as only a man can know a woman."

Ravenna's heart ceased beating long enough for the pain to overcome her momentarily. "You've never left Duncarrow."

"I found her in the Forest of Lycana. Did you know that she once loved the boy who failed his father? Hadden's Bane. Holden. She'd found the courage to leave him, leave him before she gave herself to him and destroyed her future. That's when I discovered her. Only when she looked upon me, she saw the man she'd broken her heart to leave. *Just this once,* I begged of her, but it was not the begging that saddled her into my lap, was it? And when you were born, she knew what her sins had wrought. As did Argentyn."

Thane seized her by the hips, lifting her as he drove into the final leg of his turn with her. As he did, a scream was birthed from deep within her. It tore through her veins, piercing holes through every place it bounced off, snapping against the cock of the man who would have killed her if she let this continue. The sky went dark and all she could see were thousands of feathers, floating, landing softly upon her, upon the man above her screaming that she was killing him, upon the others who had stumbled away in their fear.

Ravenna angled herself toward the sky and exploded.

"You could still put halt to this," Assana pleaded as she watched her husband make jerky strides across his chambers. "Even Oldwin's power has limitations."

Eoghan stopped and spun on her. "He was your choice. *Yours*."

Assana should have cast her eyes away, but she didn't. She was done ingratiating herself to him, and fealty would not serve him, anyway. It was time for him to find courage. Real courage. "There was no one else. You needed counsel."

"What does a woman know about counsel, or what a king needs?"

"The only true counsel you've known has been from women."

Eoghan reached for her dress and clutched it in his fingers. This close, she heard the wheezing of his desperate breaths. "I should kill you."

Assana gritted her teeth and leaned down. "Then why don't you?"

Eoghan shoved with a burst of ineffective strength. She stumbled back a few steps, but it was not the outcome he'd imagined. She could almost see into his dark mind, where he killed everyone who was better than he was, or had bested him. How many times had he killed her?

He clutched the table, sucking in air. "Why don't I kill you, you say?" He left the question hanging between them, unanswered.

"Oldwin's power is drawn in secrecy and closed rooms," Assana said, approaching once more. She was no longer afraid of him. She dropped her hands onto the table, leaning to look at him; she demanded his eyes. "If you go out there now, if you call a halt to this farce, standing before your people, he cannot challenge you. He will never challenge you before them all."

"What care you of the fate of Ravenna Ravenwood?"

"You know, it's not only Ravenna's fate at stake today. If you grant this authority for him, he will take until there's nothing left." Assana scoffed. "Do you really intend to allow him to kill an infant?"

"It would not be the first time Oldwin dispatched of a child."

"Yes, but *that* child *lived*! That child is out there, somewhere—"

"Plotting, planning, ready to take my throne!"

Assana shook her head. "I don't think so, nor do I think you believe it. For, this man, if he still lives today, would be old enough to be your own father, would he not? He has had all the years of his life to come usurp this crown."

Eoghan's face was bright red and strained when he turned it toward her. The veins around his face were like worms desperate for escape. "You don't know the will of a Rhiagain. What we would do for this crown. What we have done."

Assana slid her hand over his. "You did what you had to with Darrick. He left you no choice. He would have let it all be dismantled, Duncarrow torn apart, stone by stone."

Eoghan dropped his head, closing his eyes. "There are rumors he lives."

"Nothing but!" Assana exclaimed, laughing. "He's been gone five years. Let him go! Let Dain go. It is only you now, husband, and the kingdom that belongs to *you*. There is no one else."

He nodded at her belly without looking at her. "There must be someone else, or others will seek to take the crown for themselves. We have no choice. Have you any signs yet?"

Assana smiled through her lie. "Some. We will know soon."

"Do you know what the guards told me?"

She shook her head.

"Last night, while the moon was high, Oldwin summoned Ravenna to his chambers. She didn't leave until dawn."

Assana's mouth parted in a light gasp. "What do you think... they're not allies, surely? Not after what he does to her now, in the courtyard?"

"I think he's lain with her himself."

Assana's heart raced. It thrilled her to be the king's confidante. But it came with the fear that she would say the wrong thing and lose her ground. "Do you think she went to him willingly?"

Eoghan curled his lip into a snarl, clutching his hands so tight around the edge of the table they turned a deep purple. "He doesn't intend for Ravenna Ravenwood to bear a Rhiagain heir. He intends for her to bear his. He neglected to mention that it was his seed he blessed. Not mine."

Assana took a sharp intake of breath. She should not have been so shocked. She prayed he didn't take this as a sign of weakness, of a lack of guile. "Then... then why hold the Langenacht at all?"

Eoghan shoved away from the table. "Because he *hates* the Ravenwoods, that's why. He loathes them, has always loathed them. It was always about this. How could I not see it?"

"I don't see how you could've known," Assana said, shaking her head. "It was mere chance he was even able to apprehend her, it—"

"No. It was not mere chance. He only wished for it to seem so, to me."

Assana straightened herself. "Then if this is the truth, his truth, your truth, what will you do?"

"What will I *do*?"

Assana pointed to the window. "Yes, husband. What will you do to show Duncarrow, and the entire kingdom, that it is Eoghan Rhiagain who sits upon this throne and not Oldwin of Ilynglass?"

ESMERELDA GAPED in horror as Ravenna soared up and away, a whirl of feathers and blood and fire. She didn't know where to look, what to make of what she was seeing. She'd seen Ravenna transform before, but this was nothing like that. What she'd seen before was a raven.

This was a phoenix.

Voices in the hall pulled her attention away from the window. The guards fussed with keys, and the steps drew closer. Esmerelda wiped her tears away and felt again for the dagger at her breast. She hesitated before withdrawing it. Her father hadn't taught her much in the ways of men, but he'd avowed that no Warwick would ever be caught unable to defend themselves. Not man, nor woman. She had never felt closer to him than those nights in the stables as he guided her through the quick jabs into the piles of hay.

It was her time to become a queen, but she would not go quietly.

She squared her shoulders and waited for the cell door to open.

THEY STOPPED JUST before the cell. Eoghan regarded the oversized ring of keys in his hands and turned to Assana. "If I send her back to her father, we can have peace."

Assana nodded. "You will be a hero. The kingdom will know the malevolence at Duncarrow started and ended with the sorcerer."

"Be certain," he said, splaying his fingers over her belly. "For if Oldwin kills me, it will be our child who reigns. Are you? Certain?"

Assana started to say something. Now was not the time for

confessions. In the end, she just nodded.

"Let me speak to her first. She needs to know she has nothing to fear from me."

"I'll distract the guards. They belong to Oldwin now, and they won't allow you to leave with her so easily. I will meet you back in your chambers."

Eoghan paused. Nodded.

Assana wrung her hands together and then, clumsily, leaned in to peck his cheek. "You are better than the man she will expect to walk into her cell. Show her this and let us be free of Oldwin, and of the legacy that has followed you since you sent Darrick into the sea."

THE DOOR SWUNG OPEN. The king stood before her.

He was alone.

Esmerelda had never met Eoghan Rhiagain before. She'd seen his painting in the guildhall at Warwicktown, but the artist had done their part to soften the way his limbs gnarled inwards, and the slump of his spine that hadn't happened overnight.

"Lady Esmerelda," Eoghan said. She was still recovering from the shock of his physical deformity that the small high voice, that of a boy, didn't startle her as it might have. Nothing about him seemed right. This was no king standing before her. Had *he* really caused all the mayhem now plaguing their kingdom? This pathetic creature? "This is not the way I wanted for us to meet."

"Nor I, for as you know, I once chose death over standing here before you."

"Yet I'm pleased that you live now."

"Yes, I'm sure you are," she said. The hand clutching the blade slipped with sweat. She grasped it tighter, taking a brave step forward. "For now, you've gotten what you wanted all along."

Quickness. Quickness is the mark of a woman's hand in battle.

Small, decisive thrusts, Esmerelda. Ye ken?

Yes, Father.

You are small, and can move faster than a man. They willnae expect skill from you.

"You don't belong in a cell," Eoghan said. "I've made arra—"

Eoghan's face froze as an arc of crimson streamed from his neck where her blade had swiped. He didn't immediately grab for the wound. Even as he bled out, his shock at the swift shift of the moment held him in thrall of her as his eyes asked questions his mouth could not form.

He stumbled back against the table and Esmerelda leapt forward, driving the knife into his shoulder, and then again into his neck, where it found no purchase, for the flesh had already been mangled by her handiwork. Esmerelda screamed as she buried the knife a dozen times, landing haphazardly but decisively.

"For my uncle, Byrne! For the Southerlands, and the salt and sand that will *never* be yours! For the Westerlands! For my Ryan, and my child, that you willnae *ever* lay your filthy hands on!" Her screeches blinded her. She was lost to her frenzy, to words she could no longer hear herself shrieking, to the stabbing motion of a hand that was no longer her own.

At last she climbed off him, breathless. She staggered backward. What life remained in Eoghan could be seen only in the light dying in his eyes.

Fleetingly, she wondered where the guards were. Why they hadn't come to accost her, to save their king. But she didn't wonder this for long.

"You cannot die until you know, you monster. I want you to know about Darrick. He's *alive,* you craven bastard. You lose. You lost then, though ye didnae know it. Darrick Rhiagain lives and he'll come take his rightful place on the throne of Duncarrow!"

With one last scream, Esmerelda rushed forth and jammed the knife into his eye.

47

CHILDREN AND TRAITORS

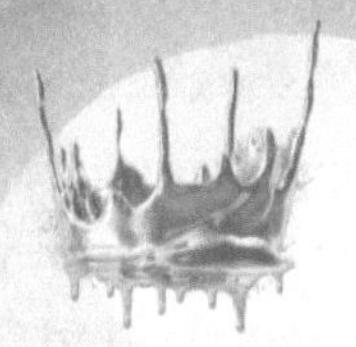

"Send Steward Waters out!" Storm yelled, planting herself at the center of the bridge. "I wish to treat with him, and I will not speak to another."

"Got a message for him, do ya? From who, girl?" a guard, who'd been standing on the other end chatting with the blacksmith, called. They both laughed and returned to their conversation. As if there wasn't a war brewing just beyond their doorstep.

Storm smirked, squaring her stance. Oakenwell's armor lay in a heap at her feet. "From Lord Warwick of the Southerlands!"

The men stopped talking. They passed their astonishment between them.

Oakenwell tensed in front of her. "What did I tell you? They'll kill you, and then me."

"As long as they kill you first, I don't see the problem. I'm fast," Storm said, voice low. "We don't need them to believe us, we only need to keep them distracted."

"Yeah? If they don't apprehend Lord Warwick before he can find Lord Blackwood, you mean?"

"They'd kill Lord Warwick without hesitation, were he

standing in my spot. You and I both know it. It had to be me who brought you in. He has the best chance of finding Brandyn now."

"And if he does? He'll be no match for Mortain. He should have called for the Southerland forces."

"Well, he didn't, did he? So here we are, you and I, and we better make the most of it." She smiled. "Ahh, here we go."

A dozen guards swarmed up, swords drawn. Storm raised her hands and kicked Oakenwell to do the same.

"Who's in charge here?" she called out.

A decorated guard stepped forward. "That would be me, but you'll find we don't mix the business of words with children in the Easterlands, especially the female kind." He nodded at Oakenwell. "Send him forth. We'll take it from here."

"It is the law of this kingdom that a messenger be treated with the respect of a lord of the realm. Put away your swords, and deliver my message, or be counted as traitors in *The Book*."

The men seemed unsure as they exchanged looks. Some lowered their steel halfway, others doubled down on their threat-filled glares.

The one in charge stepped forward, sword out, but at his side.

"Are you men? Men would not be afraid of a mere girl," Storm challenged. "Men would live by the code of honor of the kingdom and fetch the only man authorized to treat with me."

"The code doesn't extend to children and traitors," one spat.

Oakenwell stepped forward. "It is not for you to decide what I am. Call for Steward Waters and he can judge my actions in the absence of Lord Quinlanden."

"Or *I* can," said the one in charge. Several of the guards snickered.

"If you do, you will be sent to the dungeon as a traitor yourself. For your authority does not extend to a man of Great Family, and even Mads Waters would not go against a tradition so inviolate."

"Go on, then." The guard in charge nodded to others in the

back. "Go find him. We may not see battle today like our brothers but there'll be a show for us to enjoy just the same."

"I haven't seen him this morning," one said.

"That's 'cos he's in the dungeon with that sorcerer, you half-wit. Now go."

"Doing what?"

"How should I know? Ain't our business. Ask me another question and see what answer you get."

"Now what, girl?" Oakenwell said over his shoulder.

"Now," Storm said with a sigh. "We wait, and we hope it takes them longer than it should."

"You're late," Mortain accused. He kicked at the bucket Drystan laid at his feet. The water spilled all over them both. To the other man he said, "Why are you here, Waters? Why aren't you with your men, looking after the Saleen?"

Waters half-laughed. "I chose not to add bearing witness to genocide to my conscience. My men have their orders. Tepid as they are. Look after the mindless undead? They may as well catch a noontime nap."

Mortain scoffed. He looked again at Brandyn. "The wind has shifted solidly in our favor. Everything that happens now will happen as it should."

Waters grunted. He slapped Brandyn. It elicited a pained grunt, but didn't rouse him. "Why haven't you killed the little pube, already?"

Drystan pressed himself against the wall. He was too late, Mortain had said, but he'd made it just in time. Brandyn was alive, and Mortain was still here. Everything in his life had led him here, to this moment, at the precipice of his destiny. What would his father think? His mother? What would they say if they saw all he'd done since leaving home, all he'd become? Standing here, now, mere inches from the creature who would either further the kingdom's pain or at last end it, at the tip of Drystan's sword.

Mortain sighed in pure annoyance. "You ask why the boy is alive? I ask myself why I have suffered *you* to live, when your usefulness was spent long ago."

Waters dropped a hand on his sword. "You wouldn't dare. Lord Quinlanden—"

"Is a prisoner of the king, you fool! You *almost* grasped this with your dull assertion that the words coming from Duncarrow were not his, but you lack the cleverness to understand *why* they were not his. Aiden Quinlanden will never again be in charge here. Will never step foot in the Easterlands, let alone rule it. He'll die in a cell in Duncarrow, and the sooner it happens, the better for him."

Waters sputtered through an attempt at a response. "You don't know that. You are no wiser than me, Mortain."

"You don't know *what* I am," Mortain answered. "If I ever choose to show you, your life will already be mine."

"Pardon me. Apologies. Sorry. Steward Waters? You're needed. On the bridge."

Waters spun on the lowly guard. "For *what*?"

"There's a... a prisoner. A traitor."

Waters gestured around him. "Can you not see we're in a dungeon? There're prisoners all around us."

"Not just any prisoner, sir. Steward Oakenwell."

Mortain laughed. "Ahh. There may yet be fun ahead of you, Waters, in what little remains of your life."

Waters grunted and followed the guard.

Drystan willed his heart to slow. His breaths, he pushed to the shallows. Mortain hadn't yet looked his way. He was fixed on Brandyn, regarding him with slowly increasing intensity. Drystan found he couldn't look at his cousin, that his courage had brought him here, but it could not force him to behold the broken body of a child.

But he, too, wondered why Mortain had not killed him.

"What a pathetic little thing you are," Mortain mused. "Defenseless. Pointless."

Drystan knelt quietly and set the bottle of wine down in a pile of hay.

"It seems I cannot kill you after all. Your Ravenwood blood, as insignificant as it is, has nonetheless prevented me from finishing this. But there are other ways to ensure a man's death. There are wulves who would be happy to feast upon your broken flesh. Starving children who would take their crude daggers of shale and rock to you in exchange for a hot meal."

Drystan slowly lowered his hand to the hilt of his sword.

"I know I promised you a swift death if you cooperated, but does it count if I pulled what I needed from you instead of receiving it willingly? I'm not certain it does, Brandyn of Longwood Rush. I'm not certain at all."

Drystan's hand moved with controlled swiftness as he withdrew the steel from its sheath.

"I should send your head to the king," Mortain said with a light laugh. "He's amassing quite the collection from the Blackwoods. He should open a gallery. For that, I might even return to Duncarrow."

Brandyn started to wake. His astounded gaze locked tight onto Drystan, both eyes peeled so wide they seemed to tremble. Drystan shook his head in a panic, and Brandyn let his head fall to the side.

A strained sound came from the boy. Mortain leaned in to hear it better.

"What was that, Brandyn? You would like me to spare your life?"

"I said," Brandyn croaked. "Yours ends here."

Drystan sprang forward and launched himself at Mortain. The sorcerer turned just as Drystan's sword came down upon his neck, slicing clean through.

Drystan dropped his sword to the stone floor. He heaved one final pant and then stopped breathing altogether, mouth hung, suspended in his shift from disbelief to acceptance. Brandyn drew a hard, inward gasp, trapping the sound there. They both watched Mortain's head roll across the floor and land at the foot of the guard who had missed everything.

The guard screamed.

Ash hovered impatiently in the hallway. He'd grabbed a basket of linens on their way to the dungeon. When Drystan was ushered into the cell, he lingered behind, wearing an overly anxious look to show anyone wondering about him that he was awaiting the one who would give him direction.

The door to the cell was open. What a bold monster Mortain was, inviting anyone to dare challenge him. Knowing it would mean their death. Ash had never met any of the sorcerers, but he'd heard enough stories to know they were not in possession of a man's morals.

Drystan seemed to understand this, but his blood ran far too hot on the ephemeral idea of fate. Ash had seen greater men fall upon the sword of what they believed to be their destiny, and lesser men live long lives from their outright rejection of it.

Drystan could be a great man. He didn't need the head of the enemy on the end of his sword. He had the whole of the Northerlands to build his legacy upon. Sylvaine or no, Drystan was a Dereham, a man of the Northerlands, if not in blood, then in all the other ways that mattered. With Gretchen's help, he would bring hope after the generational curse of Hadden's Bane, a prophetic veil Holden would never shed no matter what accomplishments he notched on his belt.

If Drystan succeeded in doing what he'd come for, he would be the hero of the realm, welcomed home as an easy replacement for his father. If he failed, his efforts would die here with him.

There was no longer anything Ash could do either way.

The helplessness gnawed at him. He had only just gained a son, and in the most pivotal moment of Drystan's short life, Ash could only watch, his power taken, his purpose shattered, as his son approached it alone.

Two guards walked past him, pushing him farther against the wall. He dropped the basket of linens. These were men who had drawn the worst fate of the guards, working the dungeons. And yet, still, there was a hierarchy. Ash wasn't even worth the murmur of apology.

As he knelt to retrieve his basket, Ash looked toward the cell just as Drystan brought the sword down upon the back of Mortain's neck. It all happened so slowly, but yet so fast, that Ash couldn't comprehend what he was seeing. Somehow, he brought the basket back into his arms, clutching it tight, his mind still committed to the present task and not the horror unfolding before him.

The guard's scream ripped him forward. Ash threw the linens to the side and drew his sword, but in an instant was overcome by a handful of guards answering the call of the one who had witnessed the bloody end of the sorcerer.

Drystan turned to face them, assumed the stance Ash taught him. He reached for the sword he'd dropped at his feet. Ash's heart swelled with pride, but also the fear of knowing, knowing, *knowing* what came next and the acceptance he would not get there quick enough to stop it.

Drystan hardly had his sword up to block one blow when all seven guards buried their steel in him, one by one. Drystan stumbled back against Brandyn, and the younger boy reached down for his hand, which he was able to take only briefly before the blood caused him to lose purchase. Down to the floor, Drystan slid, just as Ash burst into the cell.

He had only a moment. Only a moment to see Drystan look up, bleary-eyed, to hear him say the words.

"I did it, Father."

Drystan's eyes closed.

Ash spun to face the assailants. The first he speared through the belly, and as he withdrew it, he pulled a dagger from his belt and sent it sailing into the neck of another. He bore down and howled through the windmill he made with his sword as he brought it through four more, bearing down at the resistance of flesh and bone; and then, when they had all fallen, clutching their wounds, he finished them.

The last one backed toward the door. He dropped his sword. Fear burned in his eyes.

"Please don't," he begged. "I have a family."

Ash pulled his sword free and drew the end across the guard's neck. "Then you should not have killed mine."

THE MAN who had slashed through seven guards on his own leaned in and quickly cut the straps binding Brandyn to the chair. Brandyn fell to his knees, where Drystan lay half on his side. He searched for any sign that what he was seeing with Drystan was a trick of light, any chance he might only be wounded, but there was nothing. He was gone.

The stranger pulled Drystan against him, and the sob that emanated when his mouth peeled open was so horrifying that Brandyn felt he would hear it in his nightmares for the rest of his days.

Brandyn was free, and Drystan Dereham was dead. How many others had fallen, while he'd failed to free himself from the sorcerer? How had Drystan even come to be here at all?

Brandyn's head spun as he pushed himself to weave all that had happened into something that made sense.

Mortain was dead, too, and it had been Drystan who'd done it. Brandyn walked over to the cell door, where Mortain's lopsided look of shock was wedged between the wall and a box. He wound the sorcerer's hair in his fingers and lifted him to his face to look at the creature once more. He didn't seem so terrifying now.

"Thank you for helping me. But I don't understand," Brandyn said to the man clutching Drystan. He instinctively fought looking at Drystan's mangled body, but he had to. Drystan had died saving him. Brandyn owed him a life debt he could never repay. "I don't understand," he said again.

"More men will be coming. It's not safe for you here."

"Who are you?"

The man looked up. "A friend of the Derehams."

Brandyn looked around the room at the theater of carnage. "And a friend to me now."

The man said nothing. He pressed his lips to Drystan's bloody forehead and pushed a sob into his flesh.

"You can't leave him here," Brandyn guessed. He stepped over several corpses to look out the cell door. Both ways down the hall were empty. For now. "I'll help you take him, but I don't know the way."

The man stood, lifting Drystan in his arms. Red-faced, he nodded. "I know the way. Come."

Brandyn followed the man out, allowing himself one last glance at the massacre. Mortain's headless body was slumped against the bottom of the chair, and the sight of it prompted Brandyn's realization he was still holding the head. He should drop it, kick it straight into a gutter where it belonged.

But somewhere in Duncarrow, someone had his father's head. He wouldn't release this one so easily.

Brandyn jogged behind the stranger, one eye cast over his

shoulder. But it wasn't guards who stopped his pace, but the sound of voices he knew.

Voices of *his* people.

"Brandyn! Oh Guardians, you're safe! You're free!"

Brandyn gasped. "Aunt Yesenia?"

"We have to go, now!" the stranger called back.

"Then help me free them," Brandyn said. He searched for anything he could use to unlock the cell door. He kicked over a stool, lifted a nearby bucket. His hands searched through the dust, shoving stray pieces of hay to the side. But there was nothing.

The stranger shifted Drystan to one arm, and with his other, he used his dagger's point to pick the lock. It sprang open, and Yesenia flew out, crushing Brandyn to her chest.

"You don't look well at all, little one," she said when she pulled back and examined him. "Oh, no, Brandyn, no—"

Brandyn swooned into her arms.

"We have to get out of here before more guards come!" Ash screamed.

"He's dying!" Yesenia cried. She knelt by Brandyn, who'd slipped into unconsciousness.

The man with her scooped Brandyn into his arms. Their eyes met briefly. Ash recognized him. Corin Quinlanden. The good one. The one who never would have let his Reach become what Aiden did. The man who should have been lord.

"Corin. Hold tight to him until we can get him to safety. Until aid arrives, we're the traitors here," Ash said to Corin.

Corin nodded. "I know you."

"And you know this boy in my arms who has died saving us all, and we can talk about both things when we are no longer in the dungeon of our enemy."

Yesenia's gaze passed between the two men. She nodded, exhaling. "I know a better way out than the way we came in."

BRANDYN FLOATED in and out of awareness as he bounced in someone's arms. It seemed they were climbing higher, but to where? Was he dying? Was this the final path he would take before his promise was spent? He remembered when he was a small boy, much smaller than he was now, hearing his mother tell of how her mother whispered of a great stair she would climb as she went to meet the Guardians.

He strained to see who held him, but the morning light blinded him. His head throbbed with the exquisite pain that had finally caught up and was now declaring itself. The rest of him was a broken mess. He didn't want to know how bad it was. As long as he didn't know, he could still convince himself he might live.

"There," a man said. Brandyn heard others now, footsteps along what sounded like stairs. Farther, they wound, until he was dizzy.

"What is this?" a man asked. He knew this man, even though they'd only just met. He was the one who'd taken care of the guards before they could do to him what they'd done to poor Drystan.

"You've never been up here?"

"No."

"I suppose you wouldn't have, would you? This perch is for the Lord of the Easterlands. Our father never brought Gretchen up here. He brought me, once or twice. Preparing me, in the event something happened to Aiden."

The other man inhaled in recognition. "Then I know it. But from the ground. As a citizen who gathered among other citizens to hear the lord speak."

"From here we can see the sea, to the east, and Fionn's Pass in the west."

"But how do they hear him? All the way up here?"

Brandyn's eyes opened wide enough to see the conal curve of an amplifier. It was significantly bigger than the one they had in Longwood Rush, but they didn't climb to the tops of trees to address their people there.

"Brandyn. Finally." Yesenia's worried face flashed in and out of his vision as it slowly returned. "We must find a healer."

The man holding him eased him down. Brandyn wobbled, unsteady, as he struggled to gain footing. A sharp spray of pain spread through him once more. He looked up at the man who had been holding him. Uncle Corin.

What had he heard his mother say so many times over the years? *It should have been Corin.*

"Rest him here for a moment. He'll be safe there. We've thrown the bar over the door," Corin said to the stranger, pointing at the lounger at the far side of the perch. "Ash. That's your name, isn't it? Gretchen's boy. She once loved you a great deal."

"She loved me longer than once," Ash replied, but he did as Corin suggested, laying Drystan gently down. He seemed afraid, regretful to leave him, even for the moment, as he backed away.

Yesenia took Brandyn by the shoulders and pointed. But as he followed the direction she gestured, the hand on his shoulder tightened to a vise.

"Guardians," Yesenia whispered. "What's happened?"

Brandyn leaned into the railing for support. His gaze traveled beyond the city walls, but he didn't know where to focus. Blood and flesh littered the fields between the forests, dotting the land-scape. Thousands of bodies there must be, a whole sea of them. As he strained to better understand, he saw the vibrant blues and violets and greens painting the ground in waves.

But there were men still living, too. Men bearing the orange standard of the Southerlands, wandering around in a daze, surveying the same damage.

"I understand now," Yesenia said low, breathless. "Oh, Guardians, I finally understand. He never wanted the Medvedev to fight for him. He wanted them to die, every last one, at the hands of the kingdom. To leave us this aching regret that would linger many generations."

Corin stood at Brandyn's other side. He rested a hand on his back. "You're still holding the sorcerer's head. I tried to take it from you, but even when you were lost to us, your grip never lessened."

Brandyn looked down and was once more taken by surprise at his determination to hold fast to something so vile. "I'll know what to do with it when I know."

"He can't hurt anyone anymore. We owe everything to Drystan. Poor, sweet boy."

"I'll take him back to his mother," Ash said. He didn't seem to be there with him, but moored elsewhere, to another moment, another time. "So he can be laid in the crypts with the Derehams before him."

Between Corin and Ash passed a knowing look. "You are still so loyal to Gretchen, even after all these years have passed, and she belongs to another lifetime," Corin said. He moved to Drystan and knelt by his side. He brushed his hand over the boy's face. "My poor sister. She has endured so much. This will crush her forever."

"There are some things for which rescue is impossible," Ash said. "The last consolation I can give her is that he will be buried with his people."

"The only magic that could restore him was the magic that lived within the one he killed," Corin said. "But that same magic has now laid waste to the entirety of the Saleen. It is a vile magic that has no place in this kingdom, even for the good it might have done."

"Drystan's life cannot be measured so simply."

"No one's can. But men will still try to, because it is the only way to make sense of what doesn't."

Brandyn moved to another corner of the perch. He looked down into the town at the base of Arboriana. The citizens moved with the same dazed confusion they'd seen in the Southerland men as they surveyed the fruit of their warfare; as if they had awakened from one horror, only to find themselves in another. He turned to Corin. "Where is Cian? Is he not the lord now?"

"The king named me Aiden's successor," Corin said with an uneasy look. "The Easterlands belongs to Cian, and I'll help him claim his birthright. But we must tread carefully here, until we can get a better handle on what's happened in Duncarrow."

Brandyn nodded. "Go find him, before one of our enemies does."

"What will you do?" Yesenia asked.

"I came here with others. They'll be looking for me."

"You're in no fit shape to do anything but rest, Brandyn."

"I'll rest when I find my men. We're not so far from the Sepulchre, if I need to ride there."

"Foolish and stubborn, like another Warwick I know," Corin teased.

"I'll be with him," Ash said, stepping forward. He laid a hand on Brandyn's head. "I'll help you find your men first, and then I'll take my... I'll take Gretchen's son home to her."

Corin approached him. "Allow me to take Drystan somewhere safe until you're ready to escort him to Wulfsgate. We can prepare him for the journey so his mother can still look upon him when you arrive."

Ash cast a cautious look at Drystan, and then, after a pause, nodded.

Corin met his eyes. "I promise you. I'll see to the task myself."

Ash let out a soft, shuddering sob and then guided Brandyn toward the stairs.

. . .

"Asʜ!" Lisbet cried, flying nearly into him as he stepped beyond the castle entrance and headed toward the bridge. "Where is he? Where's Drystan?"

Ash had placed his emotions somewhere safe, until he saw the hope die in his daughter's face. For, she *was* his daughter. He could see it now, even if he'd been afraid to accept it before. She was born after his "death," but when Ash learned Gretchen had conjured him in another form, he couldn't resist returning to her. In her grief and confusion she hadn't seen through him, that it was he, the Ash of flesh and blood, and not the ghost of her imagination. He had never been able to stay away for long. He left when he realized that his weakness had been the cause of her conception once more. That the cycle of hurt would never end as long as they were together.

Ash shook his head. He dropped to his knees and Lisbet fell into his arms.

"Tell me. Tell me what happened."

"I cannot find the words," Ash managed through his tears.

"But did... did he..."

"He did. He was brave, and he was perfect, and he has saved this kingdom, Lisbet."

Lisbet sobbed against his chest. He held her tight, his own tears no longer restrained by anything strong enough to hold them.

"Where is he?" she asked, pulling away. She wiped at her eyes. A subtle but powerful change came over her as she forced back her grief, replacing it with calm. She was so much like her mother.

"With his uncle Corin. He will see that Drystan is prepared for the journey."

"I hadn't thought of..." Lisbet's entire body shuddered with her sigh. "I can't think of it now."

"You came here to stop him?"

She shook her head. "Kian told me that if I intervened, Drystan would fail. That I couldn't even say goodbye to him, for the damage it would cause to his courage."

"I would like to know more about what you learned from Kian, someday, if you will tell me."

"I came here to take him home," she said. "To my mother and father."

"He's your brother, and I wouldn't take that honor from you. But he is... he is also my son, and if you'd allow it, it would mean everything to me to accompany you."

Lisbet smiled tightly. She kissed his cheek. "Of course you can come. But that means you will have to face my mother. She'll know how you've deceived her."

Ash nodded. He looked past her, at the three girls who had traveled with her. Followed her, was more like, because Lisbet was a leader, like Gretchen. They would follow her to Wulfsgate, too. They'd follow anywhere she led. "I always intended to tell her, one day."

"There was something else Kian said to me."

"Oh?"

"About..." A conflicted look passed over her face. "Not now. Maybe we can discuss it on the journey home."

"We shouldn't delay for long. Corin and Cian will work to restore order, but there are still those here who are loyal to Aiden and to the crown."

Lisbet nodded. "The girls haven't eaten much in days. Let's get food in their bellies, and we can be on our way."

Brandyn lingered behind, giving space to Ash and Lisbet's tearful exchange. He'd begun to understand something about Ash, about his unlikely connection to the Derehams, but it was not his business.

Something more pressing caught his eye as he looked into the growing sunrise.

Arms waved his way. He couldn't make out faces in the glare, but he knew it was his attention they were after. These were his men.

Brandyn quietly slipped past Ash, but before he could go to where the men had beckoned him, another familiar face stopped his heart.

"Brandyn?" Gabi's small voice was foreign, like a song from another lifetime.

"Gabi…" He had resigned himself to never seeing any of them again. He'd accepted that the path they'd been set on didn't lead back to one another.

He lifted Mortain's head out to the side, anticipating what would come next.

Gabi flew into his arms. When he groaned in pain, she jumped back. "Oh no. What *happened*? Oh, dear, you look terrible."

"I'm fine," he insisted, trying to smile. "I promise."

"You are not fine, Brandyn Blackwood!" She gaped as she looked down. "Is that a man's *head*?"

"He was no man, Gabi."

"Yet that is most definitely a head! Have you gone mad?"

Eavan Quinlanden was there too, and she laughed at them both. "Can it truly be that after the months away from one another, the first thing you two do is bicker like children?"

But there was another with them. Meadow Ashenhurst, for whom Brandyn had news she would very much like to hear.

A hard swell of hope spun up within him. Gabi had survived, Meadow had survived, Ember was safe. Little Meadow was here, too. They'd all lived.

"Whose head, Brandyn?" Gabi demanded.

"One of the men responsible for taking our father from us. I'll get them all, before it's done. Make a proper collection of it."

Gabi nodded. She bit down hard on her lower lip. "Do get them all. But... maybe not... about the collection part..."

Brandyn turned to Eavan. "You should go inside. It should be safe for you now. Your uncle has gone to find Cian and make things right."

Eavan shook her head. "This isn't my home anymore."

"Your father may be a traitor, but your mother is inside somewhere, worried sick for you."

"My mother is dead," Eavan said.

"Dead?"

Eavan waved around. "Dead. Dead to me. Dead in the ways that matter. Do you see her? Was she with Corin, and Yesenia, when you were with them? Did she come down when the sorcerer fell?"

"Eavan, she may have been in hiding. Mortain and Waters—"

"*Where was my mother when the king tried to take me?*"

Brandyn reached forward and took her hand. "We all do what we have to in order to survive, I guess. We've already lost too much."

"How is it we are all here, now, together? What nonsense have the Guardians conspired to bring us to this moment?" Eavan mused.

The sun passed behind a cloud and Brandyn saw Khallum in the distance, with the other men who had summoned him. Joran. Law. Rutland. Oakenwell.

Khallum had Mads Waters at the end of his sword.

"Meadow," he said, approaching the girl. "Brook is safe. He's in Greystone Abbey. I've seen him with my own eyes. Steward James has taken good care of him, and he left him in capable hands when we rode east. You'll be reunited again soon. I'm certain of it."

Meadow buried her face in her hands and sobbed.

"I'll be back," he said to the others.

"Oh, no, no way, I'm not leaving your side, Brandyn," Gabi said. "Not this time."

BRANDYN CLIMBED the small hill toward the group gathered under the cluster of oaks. He could see now, as the trees shaded them from the sun, that gathered were the men who had come to Whitechurch believing in the vision of a twelve-year-old boy.

Only Darrick, the Grand Minister, and Joran were missing.

"Aye, there's our little lord. Nice of ye to join us," Khallum charged with a sly grin. "While you've been busy getting the piss knocked out of ye, we got our hands on this ratsbane." He shoved the tip of the sword into Waters' neck.

"Took that many of you to do it," Waters hissed.

"Nay, just me, but all great performances deserve an audience." Erran Rutland snorted.

"Who's that, Brandyn?" Gabi whispered. "Who is that man?"

"This is the man who stood at Aiden's side when he killed our father," Brandyn answered, drawing closer. He'd thought about this moment, of course, but mostly in his dreams, where he was taller, bolder, braver. He had never faced any man in combat, and if it was just the two of them, Waters would have bested him before he could draw his sword. But Mads was not a soldier now. He was not a steward of a Great Family. He was nothing but a man at the end of a sword, waiting to die.

"My gift to you," Khallum said. "Nephew."

"And a generous one," Easlan James said. He dropped a boot into Mads' side. "The best kind."

"I only ever did as Lord Quinlanden asked," pleaded Mads carefully. The sword end stuck in his throat kept him from anima-tion. "That is no crime, to serve your lord. You know this."

"Do I look like I decide men's crimes?" Brandyn asked him,

stepping around so he could see the coward's face. "I'm not the law."

Mads must have seen something in Brandyn's eyes that stayed his relief. "I had no quarrel with Byrne Warwick."

"He had no quarrel with you. You still killed him."

"It was not me—" Mads choked as Khallum pressed on the sword.

"I leave it to you to decide what to do with him," Khallum said.

"What would you do, if you were me?"

"I am not you."

His eyes passed to the James men, to Rutland, Law, and the others. But none had answers for him. Even Storm only watched him, impassive.

"Mortain took my sword. Will someone give me theirs?" Brandyn asked.

"Brandyn, *listen* to me! Listen to reason!" Mads pleaded. "If you take my life, you will be no better than those you bear vengeance toward. I'm disarmed! There is no honor in murdering a man who cannot even defend himself!"

"My father was disarmed when you swarmed upon him in his nightclothes like cowards."

"You don't have to listen to the words of this filth, my lord," Kaslan spat. "These *lies* of a traitor."

Easlan James withdrew his sword, and, turning the hilt, passed it to Brandyn. Storm's hand fell away from her own.

"Thank you, Steward James." Brandyn set the head of Mortain aside and looked at his uncle. "Have you seen the fields beyond Whitechurch?"

"We've been busy with this one."

"Mortain has led the Saleen to slaughter," Brandyn said. "Every last one." He turned his attention back to Mads. "You are complicit. You did nothing to stop it. You aided him, protecting him while he enslaved them."

"I had no choice!"

"We always have a choice," Brandyn said, and before he could convince himself to listen to more of the creature's pleas, he swung his sword to the side and brought it down upon the neck of Mads Waters.

Kaslan James reached down and hoisted the severed head.

Brandyn kicked Mortain's head over to him. "Save them both. Gifts for my mother."

48

FLY AND FLY HIGH

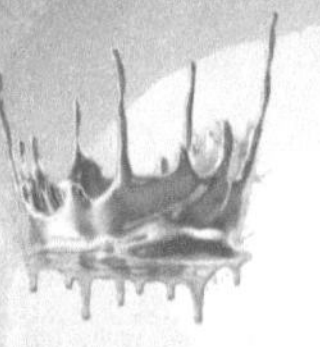

She had done it! She was *doing* it! What seemed like hours had passed, and Ember's wings hadn't failed her. She was tired, but not as much as she'd expected to be. Not so much that she needed to find ground.

In all the exhilaration of her achievement, she'd not paused her racing mind long enough to consider what it was like to be something other than what she'd been all her life.

A raven.

She, Emberley Blackwood, had ceased to have two arms, and, in their place, she now had wings. Her legs had become talons. Her scarlet hair, her one vanity, was gone altogether in this transformation, and she had no care of it. She didn't miss it. She didn't miss any of it.

An icy wind rattled the trees, and she angled her head—her small, perfectly angled scalp, her curved beak—lower to find cover. But her wings were greater protection than her arms had ever been on land. She glided over the wind like a ship riding a soft wave, and when she tried to laugh, the sound that came out instead was a trilling, excited *caw*.

She was still Ember. She was still herself, but she was... she was *more* now, more than she'd ever been or imagined she could be. The fire burning in her belly didn't belong to a raven, or a young woman, but the mingled potential of two halves having found one another, fusing together to become one, at last.

Ember was meant to be here. She was called here, and had been rewarded for answering this call with bravery.

Torrin's voice was small and distant. He was excited for her, but he also sounded afraid. It had been a while since she'd taken flight, and she'd left him all alone in the forest. But surely he'd understand? He'd do the same if he learned to fly, and fly high.

What was left now, but to fly to Midnight Crest and save her mother?

Ember braced against the ice, riding the ebbs and flows of the mountain wind. The higher she soared, the more the elements whipped her around, threatening her with certain death if she didn't push back, fight for her right to be there, which was just as much as the wind and the freezing rain driving sideways. She was one with all these things, no matter how they tried to declare otherwise.

She didn't know the way, but she'd watched Alasyr enough times to guess. Would he be there, waiting? He'd never shared the extent of his magic with her. She'd only seen him shift, never perform any great miracle, or even small ones.

Emberley had never known such cold. A thousand tiny bones ached against the onslaught. She forced herself to embrace this, as the other Ravenwoods must have for all the years they'd lived at Midnight Crest.

Ember pushed harder and higher. The peaks of Icebolt Mountain appeared behind a gap in the heavy cloud cover. She was close. But these clouds formed walls impeding her vision, and one wrong turn would send her crashing into the unforgiving crags.

She broke through the clouds, and the dark, towering spires of

Midnight Crest appeared. And ahh, it was even more incredible, more amazing than she ever envisioned late at night when she couldn't sleep for all her curiosity. How sad she felt for all those who would never see this for themselves; this beauty that was so unlike anything built on the ground.

Her approach came on fast. What had seemed so far away was now right before her, and then she saw them, too. Alasyr. Two others.

And her mother.

Mama!

They all stood behind the balustrades, animated, arms flailing, faced off in some kind of challenge. They were fighting. It had escalated. Ember had the horrible feeling she'd come upon the end of it, at precisely the right time to put a stop to whatever terrible end would come without her intervention.

Fate had brought her here right now, at this moment.

She winced and made her final descent, angling into a tailwind that helped ease her in closer without hitting the stone.

Alasyr turned and saw her. Panic colored his face deep red. He shook his head in furious rhythm. "Emberley! No!"

She tried to call back to him, but she wasn't Emberley, not in the way she needed to be, and shifting back now would send her careening thousands of feet to her death.

It's okay! I did it! I did it, just as you said I could! She screamed these things in her mind, pleading with her magic to send them to him without a voice. But the panic didn't subside, and the two sorcerers she didn't recognize both turned at the same time. The man's look mirrored Alasyr's, and he spun toward the woman, in anticipation, in fear.

The woman's mouth twisted into a grimace of blind hatred. She raised both her hands before her and thrust them forward, aiming them at Emberley.

"*Nooooo!*" Asherley cried and leapt forward just as Ember saw the source of her mother's horror. Saw the arc of lightning fly from the sorcerer's fingertips and travel swiftly across the wind. "Emberley, fly! Fly higher!"

The shock tore through her. Her wings separated from her body, and she was spiraling, twirling through ice and clouds, and white and silver and frost, and then the white was gone, and there was only—

"What have you done?" Alasyr spun on his mother, the dread pushing through his limbs, flushing his face. "Mother, *what have you done?*"

"I told you. I warned you. You did this yourself when you brought them here," Varinya replied, stumbling back against the balustrade, eyes drawn to her singed fingertips. When she looked up again, slack-jawed, it was her husband she fixed on. "You, Argentyn. You did this. You killed that girl."

Alasyr looked into the air in desperation; that he might see Emberley reemerge, soaring higher, the death bolts having missed her after all. His heart knew better. He would never forget the sight of Emberley's wings floating off into the wind as she disappeared into the storm.

He stepped forward, and his mother grabbed him by the arm.

"You will not go after her, Alasyr Ravenwood."

Alasyr tore away. "You will never again tell me what to do. Either of you. Any of you."

"If you leave here now, you leave here forever," Varinya threatened. She bowed forward, clutching her belly.

"Remember this moment, Mother. Father. Remember it as the end that it will become." He pressed into the balustrade and chanced a final glance at Asherley Blackwood. "I'm sorry, Lady Blackwood... I..."

Alasyr exploded into feathers and left Midnight Crest behind.

. . .

THE FIGURE OBSERVED the showdown between Ravenwoods old and new from the dark of corners.

They'd been there when the sorcerer lay with Varinya in the forest of man, and, later, when Argentyn brought a half-blood to Midnight Crest; when Varinya's blindness was replaced by awareness. They had done nothing—could do nothing—when Varinya spoiled herself, but they could spin the web that helped return the order of their careful world that had been disrupted.

Varinya had murdered the half-blood child in cold blood, a decision born of fear rather than reason. She was not wrong to do it, but she would pay for it, just as Argentyn would. As they both should, for knocking their world off balance.

And the child's mother... ahh, it was her they should pay mind to. The figure could see within her an emergence occurring. She was waking up, as they all did, eventually. As the rest would.

The lingering draw of sadness beckoned, but the figure would not follow its call. What would happen next was long needed. The pall it would cast across their heart would be just another tragedy needed to restore that which should never have been torn asunder at all.

ASHERLEY'S RAGE, deep from within, screamed for an outlet. It was not her who pushed it back, bidding it to wait, but something did. *Something* rooted her to the cold, damp stones as she trembled through the most acute pain she had ever known.

Varinya and Argentyn argued over Varinya's horrific choice to strike down a defenseless child. But Argentyn wasn't on Asherley's side, either. He wasn't defending her or her kin, but rather, his own strange and unclear motives, which she had never discerned and now never would.

What woman could call herself a mother and murder another mother's child?

Asherley again willed her feet to move. They didn't obey. A surge of power spread to her fingers, and down, into her toes. It scorched her neck, which, though exposed to the ice and cold, now felt as if it was burning down to ash and bone. Asherley roared her frustrations forth into the air, but no sound came out.

Emberley. The remembrances floating across her mind were exquisite torture. Sweet Emberley, climbing on her father's back in the forest as he feigned being a large black bear, ready to eat them all. Stubborn Emberley, who she'd find in the barn late at night practicing her archery when it didn't come to her naturally. Daring Emberley, who challenged the boys of the Reach to feats of strength they were not used to losing, especially not to a girl. Compassionate Emberley, who first killed the self-pity in Hollyn when her illness took hold, and then adjusted her life to be like her sister's, so that she didn't have to be alone and left out.

All these Emberleys were now gone. Snuffed out by a scared, weak priestess who couldn't see past her own fears, and had allowed herself to be consumed and driven by them.

Argentyn was telling Varinya that he would kill her, consequence be damned. And yet he only stood there, bold enough for the words, but not the action.

Asherley closed her eyes and envisioned her hands closing in on his throat, the life draining away as she reiterated the words of his wife; the one thing Asherley could agree with her on: *You did this.*

Argentyn suddenly ceased his animated but empty dressing down of his wife. He stumbled back against the stone balustrade, clutching at his neck in clawing, haphazard grasps. Varinya dropped her own anger for a moment, the rage in her eyes dying away to confusion. She tried to aid him, peeling back his hands, but her efforts availed no results. His nails dug at his neck, drawing long, bloody lines down his flesh as he barked for breath.

Asherley's fury took a pause. Was she... was she responsible? She'd imagined it, yes, but she had never possessed such a power as this, she...

Asherley imagined Argentyn Ravenwood flying upward into the air and then out, out into the abyss, his neck snapping before he could shift into his escape.

Asherley gasped inwardly as Varinya half fell over the edge, reaching for her husband, who rolled into the air and then, following a loud, satisfying crack, disappeared into a patch of clouds.

Varinya stumbled backward. She struggled for breath through her confusion. With a start, she whipped her gaze to Asherley.

"You did this."

The laughter started, and she never wanted it to stop. If she could always feel as she did now, there would never again be pain she couldn't survive. Byrne, Hollyn, Emberley. She could channel them into *this* feeling as she avenged them, subsisting on this gift of retribution that was greater than anything she'd ever known before.

Varinya moved closer and stopped. She was afraid.

"You murdered my child. I should find yours and return the favor."

Varinya's throat ebbed as she swallowed. She threw her head back. "Ravenna is more than all of us. More, even, than you, Lady Blackwood. She may not know it yet, but, like you, she will find herself when she most needs it."

Asherley grinned down at her hands. "The source is Midnight Crest. Isn't it?"

Varinya glared proudly in her silence.

"It isn't you. Or your mother. Or her mother. There's something *here,* within the stones, that gives you what you are. And as you find yourself farther from the source, the gift cannot sustain itself. Ravenna's power comes from elsewhere, and *that* is the secret you protect, isn't it? Is this why you sent her away?"

"Rhosyn may have given you a drop of her blood, but that doesn't make you a Ravenwood. You know nothing. And if you listened to my husband's theories drip from his lips, you know even less."

"If I'm wrong, my drop of blood, as you say, would not be enough to do this." Asherley pressed her lips tight, grunting as she lifted Varinya into the air with magic alone. Magic that had found her, *chosen* her.

Varinya's gown swished as her feet kicked. She reached for her neck, as her husband had only moments ago, but with none of the same vigor. "What are you waiting for, then? *Do* it."

"I wanted to see your face, to see the feral acceptance that you've entered the final moments of your pathetic life," Asherley said, and then, with a pass of her arms, she sent the High Priestess to the same fate as her husband.

Now she was alone. Her only company, the sound of the wind whipping through the stone pillars, bouncing off the empty halls.

Asherley dropped to her knees.

49
A THOUSAND TINY CUTS

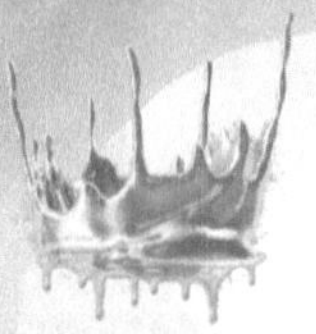

Ravenna soared high above Duncarrow. She was engulfed in flame, but it did not burn her. It hardly touched her at all. Anyone with their eyes cast to the sky would see a magnificent ball of fire, but she was only warm from it, like the hint of morning sun coming up on the horizon.

She flew in circles around the keep, signaling no intention to land. How long could she do this? Before, her raven wings could keep her aloft for hours, but now?

Ravenna closed her eyes and pointed down, toward the White Sea. She glided just above the surface, enjoying the soft briny spray tickling the underside of her wings, which were now longer, and no longer black but a fiery, vibrant orange.

She had a strange urge to dive beneath the surface. Something within nudged her, whispering that she could swim now, too. Go on, try.

Later.

Now, she had to find within her the nerve to return to the place that had nearly destroyed her. She'd been someone—something—else then, and now she was this, but the fear remained. She would shed this, as she had her raven self, but to do so properly would take time, and Esmerelda didn't have time.

With Ravenna gone, Oldwin and the king would turn their attentions to the only daughter of the Southerlands. No doubt these attentions would be born of rage at the scene Ravenna left behind in her wake.

She'd already suffered one loss born of her failure. Though she was changed—her magic, too, though the extent of these differences were yet unknown to her—some remnants of who she was remained, such as the amulet Drystan had never taken off. Not even as his life was taken from him. When that magic seeing over him died away, something within her died as well. Ravenna's life had been a series of many deaths, and she had no time to grieve them, only to use them, to turn pain to power.

Ravenna let her toes skim the sea's surface once more and then pushed back into the sky.

Esmerelda huddled in the corner of the room. The body of the dead king taunted her. The pool of blood beneath him traveled fast when he'd been more freshly dead, so fast she'd pulled her feet inward to avoid being touched by even a drop. He'd been dead long enough now that it slowed its spread as the last drops left him.

In her hand she clutched the instrument that had performed the deed. She didn't want it; it burned her flesh, searing her soul. There was no greater act of treason in the kingdom than the one she'd just done. The courage she'd summoned to take his life was all she had left in her, turned out, for she could not will herself to stand, to walk out the open cell door and claim the freedom she'd won for herself.

Why hadn't they come for her? Was it a trap? Were they waiting for her to step through the door, emboldened by false bravery, only to clap her into chains and drag her to the dais where they'd take her head?

In those long dark minutes that passed, it was Jesse whose face she saw in her mind. His rare, soft smile reminding her that everything would be fine. Ryan was there, too, but time and distance had dulled his effect on her. More than these things, maybe; everything that had passed since she'd left his side in the stables of Warwicktown.

Thinking of Ravenna struck an even deeper nerve. Oh, how naively Esmerelda had promised to free her of the Langenacht, whispering into the night like girls spending a springtide holiday together. She would forever and ever remember Ravenna's screams. She'd lied to Ravenna and herself. What a fool she'd been. She hadn't changed in the months since leaving home. She wasn't stronger, or more capable. Her assault on the king would not have succeeded had anyone else been with him; had he foreseen that a small girl who had always done as others demanded could summon the mettle to harm him.

He was not at all what she'd expected. Her mind kept returning to the strange way he talked to her, as if readying himself for apology. He hadn't come to harm her. She knew it then, even before sinking the blade into him. She knew it now. Still, she'd killed him, and it wasn't regret she was feeling over the deed, but the muddled confusion of questions that would remain forever unanswered.

Esmerelda folded the bloody knife back into her dress. She stared down the door, challenging the empty void beyond to fill with faces who would get this over with, already, so she didn't have to sit there, shaking, wondering.

Aye, and why do ye not just step through? Ye did more than any man before ever has. Why stop here?

"My strength was only what you gave me, Jesse," she whispered to the empty cell, but as the words left her, she knew they were a lie. Jesse had shown her the path, but it was she, Esmerelda

Warwick, who had taken it. Who had stood her ground with the powerful sorcerer, who might have struck her dead with the blink of his eyes. Who had faced down a tyrant king and emerged the victor.

"Esmerelda?"

Esmerelda looked up with a start, hand wound tight around the crumbling hilt of the knife. The face staring back gave her a shock. "*Assana*? Is that really you?"

Both of Assana's hands flew to her mouth as she surveyed the situation in the cell. "Guardians, Esme. You did this?"

Esmerelda nodded, swallowing hard. "I... I know he was your husband, I—"

"Hold still," Assana said quickly. She peeked back into the hall, then eased the cell door closed, leaving enough gap to reopen it. She slid shut the small window used to pass food to the prisoners. "How? How did you do it?"

Esmerelda held out the knife. "I found it in the pillow. Stitched in."

"Do you know whose cell this was?"

Esmerelda shook her head. She wanted to cry, but she couldn't decide what emotion was driving the need.

"Darrick Rhiagain had a wife before Eoghan had him killed," Assana said. She knelt by her husband's body. "He kept her here. Her and her son."

Esmerelda gasped. "A wife and child? And no one knew?"

"No one knew. Not until she fled in the middle of the night with the king's sister and Lady Asherley."

Esmerelda was stunned by this revelation. But Assana didn't know everything. She still referred to Darrick as dead, so she didn't know about the Wastelands, about the daring escape. For now, she'd keep this to herself. Her father had killed Esmerelda's uncle. Assana's intentions toward her were still unclear.

"Where's Oldwin?" Esmerelda asked.

"Fuming somewhere. Could you see the ceremony from your cell?"

"Yes, in the beginning, but..."

Assana nodded at Eoghan. "He must have been so very surprised when you sprang that knife on him. Cute little thing that you are. Did you know he'd come to rescue you?"

Esmerelda didn't respond. The knot in her belly widened.

Assana glanced nervously at the door. "Oldwin has over-stepped his authority in this kingdom, and he must be stopped. If he isn't, then this kingdom will never again look the same."

"But what about Ravenna? Where's Ravenna?"

"Ravenna," Assana said with a strange, musing look, "decided not to play his sick game any longer and turned into an orange bird and flew away."

So she hadn't imagined this.

"Let's talk when we're safe. Oldwin will be on his way for you, and for Eoghan. When he finds you've killed his pawn, he won't exercise the same restraint he did before."

Assana crossed the room, stepping over her dead husband with only a casual glance. She held out a hand to Esmerelda.

"Come, Esme. We don't have much time. Oldwin may already be on his way here."

Esmerelda hesitated. She didn't trust Assana. She hardly knew her. They'd played together as girls, but from the enmity between the Quinlandens and the Warwicks grew a chasm that eventually became too great to pass.

She looked up into the eyes of the one person who'd crossed the threshold of the cell. The one person who might be on her side. If she wasn't, there was no one else. She was alone in Duncarrow with a terrible crime that would stain her name and her family's name forever. *The Book of All Things* would not go easy on her just because the Rhiagains had reigned terror upon the realm. History had a way of softening the names of tyrants.

But the deed was done. She could remain here, cowering and indecisive, forever.

Or she could go boldly forth and accept the risk offered.

Esmerelda reached up and took her hand.

OLDWIN FELT IT. Like a thousand tiny cuts across the surface of his flesh, and one fatal wound to the heart, he experienced the precise moment that Mortain was extricated from the world.

It wasn't possible that Mortain was gone. Thousands of years wasted, snuffed out by a creature less than. For it could only be a creature less than, as there was none greater than a sorcerer of Ilynglass.

And now, he was alone. Mortain was the last of the great ones, the ones who saw the unflinching potential of possessing the great bounty just beyond their grasp, if they could only crack through the elusive magic the Medvedev used to keep them from it.

Once, there had been others who believed. Perhaps they still did, but they'd refused to leave Ilynglass; and so, Oldwin, Mortain, Isdemus, and Lysanor had gone on alone, architecting a crown from nothing but the wonders of a magic unlike anything the kingdom had seen.

Isdemus had been the first to peel away. His vigor for the cause they'd all planned together, so many years before, waned, and it was only a matter of time before Lysanor followed. The two were intrinsically linked, just as Oldwin and Mortain had been. The power of dualities had been at the foundation of their magic since the beginning of time. No sorcerer possessed precisely the same combination of abilities. Oldwin didn't share Mortain's gift of flight. Oldwin's gift of persuasion was not Mortain's. The complements in the dualities were meant to soften as much as to strengthen.

Had Ravenna known any of this, she would've grasped that it

was Mortain, and not Oldwin, who was her father. Mortain who had given her the flight of the phoenix, mingling with her innate mysticism as a Ravenwood to form something new. She was Mortain's child, through and through, in more ways even than she realized.

Mortain had been no great seer, so he could be forgiven for not foretelling his death, but Oldwin? Oldwin could see in the futures yet unwritten. He'd failed his brother in this and would not get the chance to atone for it. Mortain had the gift of restoring life to death, not him.

Did Ravenna also possess this gift of her father?

Ravenna. Had he miscalculated with her? One of his greatest gifts was the wisdom to precisely shape another into his own use. In his mind's eye, he had seen that breaking her would bring her closer. The flicker of doubt first appeared in the way she welcomed the young Rhiagain, Gilford, to his task. She would have taken them all, if he hadn't introduced the brutal Thane so early in the ceremony. He had rushed his undoing of her. He'd forced her to flee, and now she was gone, and Mortain was gone, and he was alone in his fight.

Ah, well. He'd been alone for over a generation in the sky dungeon. He was no less the magician now.

Somehow, the men of the kingdom had discerned the importance of Mortain to the darkness spreading over the realm, and they'd ended him. They'd seen through the use of the king as a scapegoat. Not one ship lingered beyond Duncarrow, waiting to strike the crown that had pushed the kingdom into war.

There would be. Though it would not be Eoghan's head they'd be coming for.

Oldwin quickened his pace as he moved through the cold and lifeless halls of Duncarrow, aimed toward the king's apartments. He didn't pause for pleasantries as the dazed Rhiagain courtesans offered their perfunctory nods, or their useless, trite exchanges about the weather that he refused to return. They whispered about the Langenacht, but that, too, would become ephemeral. As would they.

His dark blue robe caught wind as he rounded the corner to the final hall leading him to the king's room.

"Sir Oldwin. I'm afraid the king isn't here," one of the guards said. The other guard looked terrified for him. Rightfully so.

Oldwin raised his hand in the air. The guard who had spoken fell dead. The other cowered against the door in fear. "Tell me, where is the king?"

"Please don't kill me, sir!"

"Would you like to die quickly, or at my pleasure?"

"Sir—"

Oldwin slapped him. "Tell me, or it will not only be you but everyone you love."

"He went... he went with Lady Assana..."

"Went? Where?" Oldwin mocked his timid speech.

"To the sky dungeon, sir."

Oldwin groaned and lifted his hand once more. He was already on his way when he heard the second guard slump, lifeless, to the floor.

So Eoghan had gone to the dungeon after all. He'd seen this, of course, but his visions couldn't be trusted as they once could. The light had begun to die, and his gifts were failing him.

Had the rest of his vision come to pass? How lovely that would that be. For as much as he would enjoy his hands at the puny throat of the gnarled and broken boy king, he would surrender that gift to know his own yet had life in it.

There were important matters to be decided, and he would be the one to decide.

Esmerelda and Assana he would return to their homes—their heads, anyway.

And why not? He'd started this war. It was his fire to stoke or to starve.

Eoghan, he'd stick upon the pikes lining the balustrades of Duncarrow. For the Rhiagains to look upon as they slumped through the motions of their strange and banal existence. For those passing by on their ships. There it would rot, a sickly reminder of how easily the power he'd given could be taken back.

"All these gifts I've given you," Oldwin hissed as he rounded the crumbling spiral staircase to the sky dungeon. "All these things you've squandered."

When he reached the top, he was alone. No guards sitting at the top of the stairs playing their silly games, gossiping about things that didn't matter beyond their limited, insular world. None at the end of the hall. He suspected if he rounded the final corner, to where he'd lived for so long, he'd find the same.

"Is anyone there? Hello? Are we saved?" a voice called. Aiden Quinlanden. Oldwin stopped outside his cell.

"I'm here, Lord Quinlanden, but you will soon wish you did not call upon me."

"Oldwin? Is it you?"

"When have we ever been on such familiar terms, Lord Quinlanden?"

"It *is* you!" Aiden shuffled across the cell. "You came to me, in a dream. It was so clear that I knew it was no ordinary dream. It was you who coerced me to go after Lord Byrne. To take the Westerlands. You showed me a future, but it was very different from the one I find myself in now."

Oldwin had no patience for this. "Only men would commit atrocious deeds and retreat from the responsibility of them."

"But you don't deny you came to me! That you promised me a day when the kingdom would be mine."

"You have spent your usefulness to me and this kingdom, Lord Quinlanden."

Aiden approached the bars. He had the nerve to look arrogant. "I'm not afraid of you. I know what you are. I had another like you, but he was a pet. Mortain. He answered to me."

"Mortain is dead." Oldwin closed his eyes and inhaled an impatient breath. His hand shot out and Aiden was lifted into the air with an invisible hand. "Consider that I'm doing you a great favor right now, you useless sack of flesh," he snarled. He passed his arm across the air, as if throwing a ball, and Aiden went flying into the far wall, the bones in his body snapping in musical tandem as he connected with the stone. Oldwin waited long enough to watch his limp body fall to the floor before moving on.

The next cell was open. Ah, the lives that had passed time in those four walls. Anabella. Stefan. Ravenna. Esmerelda. If he was prone to nostalgia, he might allow himself to pause and think back on the power and influence that had milled around at their pleasure, alive only because they allowed it.

But he was not. And the cell was empty. He knew this before he stepped inside.

Oldwin chuckled as he knelt by the already cooling corpse of the gnarled, pathetic Eoghan Rhiagain, last of his line. Had it transpired as he'd seen in his vision? Or was it Assana? Some other shadowy assassin, who had dispensed of the guards without drawing an eye?

Oldwin lifted Eoghan into the stagnant air with magic and returned the way he came. He held his hand out, guiding a floating, dead Eoghan ahead of him, down the stairs, and back through the halls.

How he'd enjoy this part.

"The king is dead!" Oldwin boomed, as if this declaration was necessary. Mostly he enjoyed the way his voice sounded, echoing off the undecorated stone. The words were only flourish, icing atop an overly sweetened cake. "He has named the great sorcerer

Oldwin his successor! You will kneel before your king and witness his mercy toward those who serve with fealty!"

The sleepwalking Rhiagains came to life. Gasps of shock, dismay. Fear.

Of him.

Good.

"Find me the dowager princess and the Warwick girl!" The gathered Rhiagains all gaped in horror at him, rooted in place. "No... no, don't you dare linger when I make a command. *Don't you dare refuse to answer to my call.*"

One of them pointed down the hall.

Oldwin struck them dead.

"I didn't ask where they went. I commanded you to find them. And for each minute that passes that they are not in my hands, one of you will die."

The flurry of action that followed sent a welcome warmth to his belly.

He had always been exceptionally good at being whoever others needed him to be, but it would be a delight to—finally, once more—be himself.

50

THE EXCHANGE

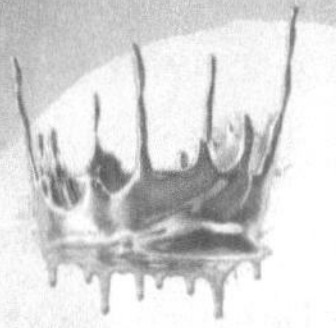

A foul wind ripped off the Seven Sisters. Even out here, east of Parth, they felt the wrath of the storm descending off the mountains. Springtide beckoned, but it seemed winter still had more to say.

Holden's men were restless. They'd had no word from east or west in a fortnight or more. The war could be over and they wouldn't know it, and the men had said as much, muttering to each other over their cups. They'd devolved to the part of the campaign where they spent more time musing about the things at home they missed rather than the bravery they'd spend when battle reached them.

That is the real business of war, Hadden Dereham was known to say, over the wintertide fires. *The battle of an idle mind.* But Hadden Dereham had never seen war; nor had any man in the Northerlands under a fair age. It was the favored topic of all men, who never let a lack of practical knowledge get in the way of hardened wisdom.

He wasn't wrong, as it turned out. Holden had first cut his teeth on some stirring speeches to stay the edginess, but when those failed—earlier than he'd hoped—he had the men run drills. But the tight organization lasted mere nights before the men were content to curl up in their tents with the handspun spirits their wives had packed.

Holden missed his own wife. She was volatile and a puzzle he'd stopped attempting to solve, but he had gained in this marriage, not lost. He often thought the opposite was true for her. Clearly, she thought so. But, in other ways, she showed her gratitude. His allowing her to act as most wives were forbidden gave her a freedom even she couldn't deny. He'd never tried very hard to stem the passion in her; that sharp demand to be in control. If he'd tried harder, Lisbet might have been the last child to spring from their bed, for it would have gone ice cold. Instead of subduing his wife, he decided to allow her happiness, and in return, she helped grow his legacy.

But he'd been powerless to stop her children from being taken from her, one by one. He half-expected to find Nyssa and Torrin had also disappeared in his absence.

Holden's belly clenched with pride every time he heard Christian speak commands to the men. He was so natural at it, in a way Holden had never been. He was meant to be the one to lead when Holden's promise was spent, but he remained insistent upon abandoning his home for a cold life with the other Magi in their sky tower.

Holden would never understand it. No matter how Christian tried to bring Holden to his side, there was no accepting abandoning the inviolate duties of a lord. Holden could have a hundred sons waiting their turn at the seat, but the task was Christian's, and there was no changing his mind. Only in death could Christian relinquish this duty.

Activity at the forest line drew his attention. At his side, Christian tensed and reached for Sun's reins.

"What is it, do you think?" Christian asked. "Those aren't our men."

"No," Holden answered. He mounted his horse just as Marsh rode up.

"No vagabonds, either. Look at the armor. That's proper issue."

"But no standard. Intentional, no doubt."

"Quinlanden men," Marsh announced, riding up. "Our scout rode in to say they'd been spotted coming south through the Whitewood."

"It's not an attack," Christian said, riding to Holden's side. "There's no more than a dozen of them."

"They aren't waving a white flag either," Holden murmured. He spurred his horse to action and moved forward. The other men had come to life and followed, falling into rough formation.

"What else did the scout say, Marsh?"

"Only that it was just the ones coming across the field now. No more were spotted."

"I don't like this," Christian said, whistling through his exhale.

"No, Son. I don't like it either," Holden said.

"Should we ride to meet them?"

"Send out a messenger, see what they want," Marsh said. "My father always told me if it looks deceptive, you can bet it is."

"No," Holden said. He squinted across the field, and what he saw caused a hitch in his breath. He'd spotted their purpose, and he would ensure Christian never did. "I'll go."

"Father?" He felt Christian's gaze from beside him.

"Alone, Christian."

"Forget it," Marsh said. "No way are you going out there alone. Sir."

"Then you come, but Christian stays here."

"Father. Two against twelve? Are you mad?"

"I'm not mad, but I am your commander, and I command you to stay. Tyndall, with me." He moved several paces forward to be sure Christian hadn't followed. "You have command until I return."

Holden pushed his mare to quicken pace, putting as much distance as he could between his son and what was ahead. Marsh kept astride of him, wearing a solemn look.

"Have you seen it?" Holden asked him.

"Seen what, sir?"

"Their reason for coming."

"I assumed it was…" Marsh trailed off. "Oh. Oh, no."

"Christian cannot know until we've settled the matter."

"Is she… do you think…"

"I know no more than you, Tyndall."

Marsh exhaled. "We should have brought more men. It isn't too late to go back."

"They didn't come here for battle. They came to parley. With me. Only me."

Marsh launched into more questions, but they died unasked. He rode the rest of the way in silence.

"Say nothing," Holden said, as they approached the Quinlanden men. "Do what you can to keep the sight of this from the camp."

"Yes, sir."

One of the guards stepped forward. "I'm Lieutenant Castle. These are my men."

"Lord Dereham," Holden answered evenly, trying, for now, to keep his eye off their prize. "But you knew that."

"We did. It's you we've come to see. But then, she was also on her way to you, was she not? To warn you?"

"Name your price."

Castle laughed. He glanced back at his men, running his tongue over his lower lip. "I'd heard you were a man of few words. But not a single pleasantry? Do you not wish to even know how my day was?"

"Name. Your. Price."

"You."

"What?"

"You," Castle said, the smile dying away. "Your life, for Lady Wynter's."

Marsh gasped. Holden held a hand up, staying him.

"How do I know she's not already dead?"

Castle snapped gloved fingers. Behind him, a man nudged Aylen, whose broken body was draped over the saddle of a nearby horse. Her silver hair was matted with blood. She moaned, but hardly moved.

"Who did this to her?" Holden demanded.

"She's fortunate to be alive at all after what she did to my men. Seven of them, she cut down, before we righted things. Are you certain your son married a woman at all?"

The men laughed.

"Why hasn't she healed herself?" Holden asked.

"She needs hands to heal, no?" Castle gestured behind him. "Triple bound. Just to be certain." He winked.

Marsh's horse made a soft sound nearby, reminding Holden he wasn't alone.

"Very well. Place Lady Aylen on the horse with my man, Tyndall," Holden commanded.

"No!" Marsh cried. "Lord Dereham, there has to be another way!"

"There is not," he said. He sounded far more at peace than he felt inside, where a tempest of dread brewed. It hadn't been born here, however. He'd possessed it in some form all his life, and now his life would end, and he'd never learned to conquer it. But not all things were given proper endings, as all Derehams knew. "Aylen was coming to warn us. There are more coming. What Lieutenant Castle here offers is not only the life of my daughter-in-law, but also an agreement to call off the attack in exchange for a prisoner of value. Am I understanding you correctly, Lieutenant?"

"Quite well, Lord Dereham."

"No," Marsh said again, but he'd already given up the fight. A man had to know when he was beaten. Marsh would learn this lesson early, hopefully before it cost him his own life.

"Place Lady Aylen on Tyndall's saddle. Once they've ridden beyond the reach of your arrows, I will surrender myself in exchange for peace along the borderlands."

Castle nodded. He waved at one of the soldiers to bring Aylen forth.

"You'll turn over her sword as well. Witchwind is her ancestral steel. It belongs with her."

One of the men groaned as he was forced to hand forward what had evidently been his piece of the war chest.

Holden turned to Marsh. He passed Witchwind to him and then dropped his voice. "When she's closer to the camp than to us, unbind her and let her heal herself."

"Yes. Of course, sir."

"For you I also have a message."

Marsh tried to hide the tears brewing in his eyes. "Sir?"

"You tell my son that Iceborne is his. It has always been his, but now it is his as the Lord of the Northerlands. He will pass it to his own son one day, Guardians willing."

Marsh nodded. He bit his lip so hard he drew blood.

"*That* is the price, Tyndall. You tell him. *That* is what I trade my life for here today. So that I can leave this world knowing my Reach is in the hands of my eldest son, where it belongs. Where it has always belonged."

Voice cracking, Marsh placed his hand on his heart and said, "I will tell him, sir."

"You're a good lad, Tyndall. I thank you for your service and release you to the command of my son." The soldier dropped Aylen in front of Marsh, who struggled to keep her from falling off. "That will be all, boy."

Marsh wiped at his eyes. He saluted him for a few moments longer than he should have. "It has been my honor, sir."

Holden finally exhaled properly when he heard Marsh's horse fade into the distance.

"All I ask is that you don't take my head in front of my son," Holden said to Castle when he could no longer hear echoes of Marsh.

"It will not be me who decides your fate, nor will it be decided here," Castle said. "Bind him."

Holden never let his eyes fall away as the bindings ripped at the flesh on his wrists. The fear swirling in his belly formed into something new then; it was no more useful, but it had evolved, and was that not all he had ever wanted, to grow? To become more?

Holden Dereham kept his head high and his eyes wide as he rode away with the enemy to the sound of his son's screams.

51

THE KING

Samuel Law kept a respectable distance from the prince. He held back at the edge of the field, close enough to intervene if trouble struck, far enough to respect the man's innate need for privacy.

This was how he'd always approached their short relationship. He had great respect for Darrick, and he supposed that feeling to be mutual. Within that respect was knowing when to give counsel, and when to hold one's tongue.

Darrick stepped through the sea of Saleen corpses with a deliberate slowness. He seemed to take the time to regard each of their faces, committing them to memory. He knelt to run his hands over the fur of the familiars who had died with them, their fates tragically and intrinsically linked.

It was hard to know what their future king was thinking, but he could guess.

Law had never beheld such horrors. It was simpler to let his vision blur as he bore witness to the atrocity stretching for what seemed miles, never quite ending. All his life he had been the one others looked to for practical advisement. The cool center of a tempestuous sea. He was relieved no one was asking for it now.

Mortain's death prevented more of this, but didn't come near to making up for the losses scored to the Medvedev. There could be no reckoning to make this right. Only a careful recalculation of the battle ahead, and a removal of the power structure that had allowed this genocide to come to pass.

Easlan James appeared at his side. "I can't help but wonder if we should have seen it. When that sorcerer left them idle so long, if we should have known."

"Would you like comfort? I have none to give." He pointed at Tyndall, kneeling, issuing emotional blessings over the dead. "The Grand Minister will spend weeks here, if he intends to bless them all. And it will do naught but for his own conscience."

Easlan's mouth twitched. "If we'd come sooner…"

"If we'd come sooner, the only thing different would be the timeline. Mortain needed Brandyn in order to send the Southerlands to attack."

"Why not just send the Medvedev on the offensive?"

"I ken his magic was strong only enough to subdue them. You heard what Hamish said. They swarmed in like wraiths. The Medvedev didn't fight. They didn't even defend. Our men would not have attacked in these conditions without that order. They would've seen it for what it was, and put a halt to it."

"Then it is our fault, no matter how we look at it."

"Our fault was in not seeing the threat the sorcerers posed to our kingdom years earlier, before it came to this," Law answered. He kept his eyes on Darrick. He didn't dare drop them lower, joining Darrick in his grim assessment of the calamity. "And there are more yet out there, Steward James. Three that we know of. And I'd say what we know has not served us so well."

Easlan frowned. "You don't speak like the other Southerlanders, Law."

Law put it on for him. "Aye? Like salt and sand?"

Easlan chuckled. Law thought it felt good to hear a man laugh, even if he couldn't manage the same from himself. If he ever laughed again, it would be a miracle from the Guardians themselves.

"I do when I'm in my cups," Law said. "Or in the right company."

"You? In your cups? I'd like to see that," Easlan said. "What will you do now?"

"Whatever Lord Warwick decides, I will follow. I suppose a return to the Southerlands to regroup on our efforts. Beyond that..." Law nodded at the prince. "There is still this matter, isn't there?"

"He cannot stay hidden forever."

"I don't believe he intends that at all."

"He's afraid," Easlan said. "As we all would be, but we aren't all kings, are we?"

"Neither is he," Law reminded him. "Not yet."

Easlan crossed his arms, once more looking out into the field of death. He whistled softly through his teeth, shaking his head.

"Are we all accounted for? All our men?" Law asked him.

"Aye."

"No losses then?" Law closed his eyes. "Among our own, that is."

"We were fortunate," Easlan said. "But we would be fools to believe this is the end of it."

"Aye," Law answered. "The War of the Westerlands has been won. The War for the White Kingdom has only just begun."

Darrick stopped trying to memorize their faces. He couldn't summon more outrage by knowing more of them. There was nothing left to mine from the depths of his regret. As Assyria would have told him, *if all you can think of is what you could have done, you will never do what should be done.*

He hoped she'd survived her escape from Duncarrow. He would like the chance to tell her how her wisdom kept him alive in those early days at Camp Atonement. After a while he'd forgotten most things, but they were coming back now, when he could again make use of them.

Law and James thought he couldn't hear them, but the silence from the dead was so deafening that their words were *all* he could hear.

He'd trusted in the counsel of better, more seasoned men. He'd stepped aside and let the Westerlands lead a fight that belonged to them. But it was not the Westerlands who would have a reckoning for the massacre of the Saleen.

Only the Rhiagains would answer for this. For bringing the sorcerers to the White Kingdom. For everything since and between.

Wittingly or no, Eoghan had unleashed this.

Only Darrick could put it all back.

"Law," Darrick called. "Could we make use of the ravens at Arboriana?"

"Of course. I can request a scribe as well. Would you be requiring a short or long distance raven, Your Grace?"

"Not one raven. I'll need them all," Darrick said. He closed his eyes as a cool breeze passed over the graveyard of the Saleen.

"I'm sorry, did you say all?"

"Every one they have, and the ravens from any nearby towns as well," Darrick replied. "I have a message that I want read in every corner of this kingdom, from sea to sea."

Law stepped forward. "We're ready to help you deliver it, Your Grace."

James whispered to Law, under his breath. "Should we not wait for Lord Warwick?"

"No," Darrick answered for Law. "I will not allow the kingdom to forget who brought us here, but it is I who must take us forward."

James dropped his eyes and nodded.

Darrick turned. "The first one will go to Duncarrow, so that Eoghan will know and will have to witness the awakening ripples through the kingdom when they learn their rightful king has returned."

"And with it, their hope," James said.

"And Law," Darrick said, forcing a small smile. "I would like my wife and son sent to me as soon as possible."

52

A PERFECT CIRCLE

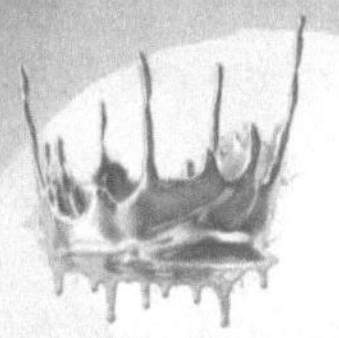

Jesse had first watched little Dain Rhiagain handed over to a man, who later in his visions he learned to know as Steward Rhiagain of Rushwood. The steward and his wife renamed him, though this new name had nothing to with his prior name or life. They were not told anything about the poor, unwanted little boy. He came to them without an identity, the childless couple becoming a new hope for his future.

So they called him Drystan, a family name of the Sylvaines. Drystan had a deep reddish hair, and striking eyes one did not quickly forget. They were a flecked gray, like the ash of a long-dead fire, and as he aged, and his baby cheeks gave way to the finer chiseling of a young man, they became his most prominent trait. Drystan's first love was a girl named Gretchen, and she declared he would be known as Ash, and in return, he called her Sparrow.

Gretchen was not just any daughter of the realm. She was the daughter of Lord Quinlanden, a man who trusted Drystan's father as his own brother. Despite this trust, the lord did not approve of the evolving friendship of Drystan and his daughter. He had other plans for her. But *if she knew it, if Drystan knew it, they did not seem bothered. Their love seemed bigger than anything—to them, at least.*

Theirs was a courtship defined by swings. Jesse followed them through passionate, near violent disagreements, which eventually faded to a tenderness that made him uncomfortable to witness, for how foreign it was to him. Drystan forgot his name and became Ash, and it was Ash who finally made the move that turned their playfulness into something more; something permanent, solid, and real that neither seemed capable of leaving behind. No matter how deep their fires of rage ran when one would fall in disfavor with the other, they never burned hotter than the flames that bound them.

Lord Quinlanden declared it would be an Oakenwell boy to secure Gretchen's betrothal. Gretchen was heartsick, hiding in her room for days, but when she emerged, it was with a wickedness in her eyes. She went to Ash and used her pain as a weapon to cause him to hurt as much as she, striking out in her pain by insisting how thrilled she was, how utterly blessed to marry the Oakenwell heir. In one last terrible blow, she told Ash she had never loved him.

This was a game they played. Of jealousy and strife, of power and pain, and ultimately love. But Ash did not rise to this as he had in the past. It was not anger with which he received this news, but a heartbreak that apology could not cure. Not this time.

Ash left Gretchen by the large dogwood in the great Rushwood, and when he did not return later that day, or the next, Gretchen knew she had extended the game too far this time.

Her pride kept her from being the one to mend the cold war between them. It was her pride that ultimately caused her to arrive too late to his family's keep, discovering from an attendant that the Sylvaines had gone to spend the season with the Medvedev. They were not expected for a month or more.

From here, Jesse lost sight of Gretchen. He flashed forward, and was again with Ash, in a forest he knew, but also did not. It was the Hinter-

lands, but a part he had never seen, and yet he understood, instinctively, that this was his mother's home, which had been denied to him.

Ash's cold eyes regarded the world from the shadows of each moment. His heart had not recovered. His mind did not understand how someone could love so deep and hate as far. His mother and father, who had no other children, fussed over him. His mother, rightly guessing the cause of her son's angst as only a mother can, coyly introduced him to the young Yanna de Medvedev, who was still rosy in the cheeks. Her pale green hair flowed freely; she had not yet come to plait it or tie it back, as she would later in life.

Yanna's sister, Yseult, chided Yanna for how she flushed when she spoke to Ash. Yseult warned her of what could happen, should she fall for a man. She would be cast out, unwelcome. Yanna had a playfulness in her that her sister, who would one day become Chieftainess, could not afford. She laughed off her sister's warnings, insisting that Ash and the others would return to their kingdom, as they always did, and nothing would change.

But Yanna underestimated the deep yearning of a heart broken in half. Of all it would do to mend itself of the pain for even an hour; a minute. Yanna's soft hair tosses and high giggles threatened to close the wound. Her light touches on his arm as she showed him her favorite trees, as she let her familiar climb over his shoulders, nearly sealed it.

Ash beheld her under a sprawling oak and thought to himself that he was Drystan here, and Ash out there. It was Ash who had crippled under the weight of his heartbreak at the hands of Gretchen, his Sparrow, but it was Drystan who could put aside those things, at least for now, and take the beautiful, glowing Medvedev by the hands and pull her closer for a kiss.

But he found he could not stop there. And Yanna's sleepy, blissed gaze she gave him when he tried to stay himself only made him lose himself all the more. She would regret this. He would regret this. Both thought this, at the same time, for their own reasons, as they made love beneath the oak, sealing a fate that neither would ever fully comprehend.

Drystan returned to his world, lovesick, but he would take that over the heartbreak that returned as he again slipped into the life he had known as Ash. The one Gretchen had colored in for him, painting every corner and edge with herself so that there could be no escape.

And when she threw her arms around his neck and blessed him with an ocean of her tears, what else could he do, but kiss them away?

He could not know of the new heartbreak burning bright in the heart of Yanna, who had come to regret her declarations to a sister who now had cause to throw them back at her. Yanna, the fool. Yanna, the traitor. She heard this and more from Yseult, who, through her tears, declared that if she wished to remain in the lands of the Drumain, she must be rid of the child growing within her. A child that could never, ever be permitted to live within their clahnn. An abomination of their ways.

And Yanna, in her youth, her unwitting impetuousness, declared that she could live nowhere that would demand such a thing of her. Yseult, in a fury, cursed her from returning; from ever having the ability to again find the doors to enter their lands.

Yseult would regret this later; Jesse saw this, too. Time was fluid where he was.

Though this regret would not happen for a long time.

Yanna wandered the borderlands of the Easterlands. She had no money. No horse, no name. She bartered with the only currency she had, herself, and many nights she lay awake wondering if the day's events had taken her child from her. But they never did. Within her womb, a son grew stronger every day.

At last, she found herself in Bythesea, a port town where she supposed she might have better luck. As a Medvedev she was skilled in everything from seamstressing to preparing meals to even smithing, and here she could find work, and make enough coin to find Drystan and make her declaration: that their love had caused this, and their love could cure all.

Instead, she found more of the same.

More cruelty.

More pain.

Disappointment unlike she had ever believed was possible.

And then, when the hope had been beaten away, when she no longer possessed the idealism that she and her child could have anything resembling a life out in the kingdom, she was taken by the hand by a young Hamish Strong...

53

RYAN

Stefan was the first to wake at the sound of a visitor. Anabella stirred behind him, wincing as the aches from spending another night on the cot when she unfolded her limbs. The hard bed gave her a glimpse into how she might feel in another decade, if she lived long enough to greet her middle age.

Across the circular room, Wyat was already at attention. He had a hand on his sword, but he looked less concerned than curious.

The hooded figure was tall, though slight in figure, like a woman. But they didn't walk like a woman. They'd entered the room with full, purposeful strides, and when they dropped to their knees, by Ryan's bedside, there was nothing delicate in that, either.

The figure raised a hand. Across the room, the door slammed closed.

Anabella and Stefan gasped in unison.

"Magic, Mama," he whispered, and all Anabella could do was nod.

The figure made no acknowledgment of them. Surely they

knew they were not alone in this room they'd entered without invitation.

The hood fell back. Short waves of violet caught the light streaming through the long windows.

"Medvedev," Wyat whispered.

The figure turned, and now there could be no doubt it was a man. Or was that even the right word? Anabella didn't know how Medvedev made distinctions of their gender, or if they even possessed a gender at all. She would ask questions about the Medvedev, following her father around as he worked to prepare his furs for sale. He told her to save her curiosity for those things, and people, who wanted to be understood, for the Medvedev did not.

"I have not come to hurt anyone. But if you come near me, that purpose will change," the Medvedev said.

"We mean no one harm," Anabella answered before Wyat could. "We're only here to help see this man back to health."

"Then we are in accord," the Medvedev said. He studied the three of them with increasing scrutiny. "Who are you to him? Not you," he said to Anabella. "I know who you are. And your son."

"Scholar Edevane. Ryan and I are not yet acquainted, though I am a friend," Wyat said evenly. It was evident he didn't yet trust the lavender-haired creature. "It would be harder to explain his connection to the Medvedev, I would think."

"Kael," the Medvedev said. "Is my name." He turned his attention back to Ryan.

Wyat laughed, shaking his head. "That was no answer at all."

"Kael," Stefan said. "We are well met, sir. I am Stefan."

"As I said. I know who you are," Kael said without turning. He seemed to study Ryan, his eyes falling over the sleeping man, inch by inch.

"How?" Stefan's eyes twinkled as he looked up at Anabella. "I don't know you."

"You'll meet your father soon," Kael said matter-of-factly. "Beyond that, I have no more to share."

Stefan practically shook with this news. Anabella pulled him tight. She would have turned her fury on anyone daring to give them false hope, but the Medvedev were said to see all, to know all. This Kael wasn't their friend, but nor did he seem to be their enemy, or intent to stir deception.

"You better not be lying to the child," Wyat warned.

"Only men do that."

"Then tell us why you've come for a boy from the Southerlands who's just barely of noble birth."

"Nobility has no meaning to me. We are all born under the same sky," Kael said. He paused his examination of Ryan. "No. I nearly lied to you, and so must correct. I come because he is the nephew of the great Yseult of the Drumain, and she will not hear of his death if it can be avoided."

Anabella and Wyat exchanged looks. Ryan was Medvedev?

"His mother, Yanna," Kael said, answering their shared but unspoken question. "She came to the Southerlands under a veil of deception. She gave Hamish Strong two sons. Neither belong here."

"Where is the other?" Wyat asked. "Should he not be here, at his brother's side?"

"Addressing his own destiny," Kael said. There was a decisiveness to his words. He was done speaking.

Kael of the Medvedev leaned forward over the still, sleeping body of Ryan Strong and, with a monstrous inhale, he rolled back against his heels, waiting.

Ryan Strong opened his eyes.

Kael jumped to his feet, replaced his hood, and fled in a whoosh of fabric catching air.

· · ·

ANABELLA WAS A NATURAL CAREGIVER. People assumed this was true of all women who were also mothers, but this hadn't been Wyat's experience at all. His own mother had gleefully turned him into the care of a nan whose idea of rearing a child included regular beatings laced with heavy doses of shame.

After they were both dead—his mother, bringing her tenth child into the world, and the nan, from too many years in her cups—Wyat's father finally acknowledged what Wyat had known all along. *I guess it's no wonder you had a yearning to understand the meaning of things.*

But the Guardians hadn't made Stewardess Edevane predisposed to turning her nose up at children, or the nan violent and unloving. Nor had they given Anabella Weatherford Rhiagain her gift of compassion. They gave men a world with which to make their choices and men become who they became.

Ryan struggled in and out of consciousness. He would wake long enough to blink a few times and take in what must have been very confusing surroundings, and then surrender once more to rest. But this rest wasn't like the rest from before. Kael had seen to that. Now when Ryan slept, it was a sleep he could wake from.

Wyat was still spinning his thoughts around what they'd witnessed. He'd read about the Medvedev at the Reliquary. He'd studied their ways, their magic—which they knew so little about—their unique speech, which Kael hadn't used on them at all, surprisingly. Nothing could've prepared him for being in the presence of one.

He had so many questions to ask, but he'd known even before Kael fled that he'd never get the chance to ask them.

Wyat was musing over this when Ryan said his first word to them.

"Water."

Anabella was on top of it. She had the water poured into a glass before he could even prop himself up. Wyat came around the other side to help him.

"The water is from yesterday. I'll have them fetch more from the stream for you," Anabella said, flushing with apology.

"Where am I?" Ryan asked. Water dribbled down his chin. He pushed her hand away.

"You're in Whitecliffe. You're safe now."

"Safe from what?"

"From anyone who would wish to do you harm."

Ryan's lip curled. "Harm? Why would anyone?" He gestured at his throat, and Anabella again fed him a sip from the cup. "Thank you. Who are you?"

"I'm the one who owes you everything," Anabella said through fresh tears. "For you delivered my husband from his terror."

"Your husband? Who's your husband?"

"Darrick is my husband. I understand he might not have told you about me, when you were in the Wastelands?"

"In the Wastelands? Darrick? Lady, I donnae know... why am I here? Where's my father, and that wench he married? Where's Jesse?"

Anabella exchanged a troubled look with Wyat.

Wyat reached forward and touched Ryan's arm. "You've been resting here weeks following your escape from the Wastelands. But perhaps more rest is needed."

The disgust in Ryan's eyes when he regarded Wyat's hand upon him caused him to rescind his comfort.

"He's confused," Anabella said to Wyat.

"He's lying the feck right here," Ryan snapped. "And he'd like to see his father and brother."

"Ryan, what's the last thing you remember?" Wyat asked.

"You, staring at me like I just ground yer mother's corn."

"Before you woke up to find us here, Ryan. What do you remember before that?"

"Aye, we were celebrating the death of the old traitor king, tha's what I remember, and I'd like to be doin' it still."

"Eoghan? Eoghan is still very much alive," Anabella said.

Ryan snorted. "Aye, I suppose he'll be king now, won't he?"

Anabella mouthed the word *Khain* to Wyat.

Wyat nodded, sighing. "So you don't remember going to the Wastelands?"

"Catch me dead before I'd go there," Ryan said with a hard frown. "Why the feck... who are you people?"

"And Esmerelda? You don't remember her?" Anabella pressed softly.

"That gold-tongued witch? Lord Warwick's spawn?"

Wyat stretched his jaw into a wince. "Right. Well, then—"

"So, you don't know where Darrick went?" The disappointment in Anabella's face, the sorrow laced into her words, broke Wyat's heart.

"Darrick who, lass? I dinnae any Darrick. Unless you mean that whorepicker comes round the tavern?"

Anabella buried her face in her hands. "We have to go find Kael. He can fix this."

"He's gone, Anabella. He did what he came to do," Wyat said, wishing the words didn't feel so true.

Ryan sat up in the bed. He looked around the room. "Which one of you feckers filched my sword?"

54

COMMAND

Christian was weary of watching his wife sleep. He hadn't left her side in the tent other than a few trips out to address the men awaiting his word on what to do next. Each time he'd linger, struggling for words, before retreating into a place more familiar to him. They'd fashioned a travel litter for Aylen while he was steadfast in his tending of her. The sight of it brought him to tears.

They'd done it as much for him as themselves. It was time to go home. The word had come shortly after Holden's capture that the short-lived war was now over. Whitechurch was back in the hands of friends, and the men deployed to the Westerlands had begun the slow retreat home. Had the men come with Aylen half a day later, Holden would still be here, leading his own men.

But then Aylen would be dead, for there would've been no negotiation to give her life value to them.

No one bothered him. Not the men looking for direction. Not Alric. Not even Marsh, who held the blame for what happened with the negotiators deep in his troubled gaze.

Yes, Christian was tired of watching his wife sleep because he hadn't looked into her eyes in so long that he'd forgotten how that felt.

He'd been so preoccupied with his horror at the condition she'd arrived in—that she was there at all! Oh, he should have known she wouldn't be content to stay behind—he hadn't immediately noticed that they'd returned without Holden. He'd sobbed into her crimson-matted silver hair, screaming at Marsh to be quicker at undoing the bindings the enemy had used to keep her from healing herself. As he'd lowered her from the horse, her arms and legs going limp over the sides and ends of his embrace, he'd reached deep within himself for any signs that he'd repressed his own healing abilities over the years. He'd begged, pleaded, and sobbed for the Guardians to intervene.

Only when he was certain she was healed beyond death's reach did he seek his father. Holden must have a plan to answer this crime. Aylen was a lady of the Northern Reach, the wife of their heir apparent. The men delivering her hadn't been fit to share a meal at the same table, let alone handle her so crudely.

Instead, he found a solemn Marsh, gathered around the men who had seen what Christian had not.

Marsh passed Witchwind to Christian, dropping the sword and scabbard in his arms.

"Not your fault, Tyndall," Alric said. "Holden has been waiting for this moment all his life. He knew what he had to do, and he did it. A hundred men couldn't have changed his mind."

"What the hell are you talking about?" Christian cried, storming from the tent. "Waiting to be taken? To give himself up to the enemy?"

"Christian—" Tyndall put out a hand, but Christian knocked it away.

"Did your father speak to his lord and commander this way?" he demanded. He tore his gaze through the other men, landing on

Alric. "For that's what he did, did he not? Leave me in command? He seems to have told everyone but me this."

Marsh dropped his eyes. "That was one command he left with me. Sir."

"Don't let me stop you from sharing the others."

"Christian," Alric warned. "Remember yourself."

"The greatest curse of my life is that I can never seem to forget who I am, Alric, so please don't trouble yourself on my account," he snapped. "Go on, Marsh. Tell us all what my father wanted for you to share with me."

"Are you sure you want me to do this here?"

Christian's laugh turned into a white cloud of fury in the cool air. "Why not? He gave them to you, a stranger, not me, his son. He's never given care to what I think or feel, even in the end. May as well share them with the world."

Marsh glanced at Alric for guidance, but Alric was no help to him, or anyone. Christian saw it now, when Alric was no longer his father's burden but his. Oh, he was beginning to see so much.

"He traded his life for Lady Aylen's," Marsh said with a guilty sigh. "He wanted you to know that... that *you* are the Lord of Wulfsgate now. The Northerlands are yours. That was the price. Those were his words."

"The price?" Christian laughed. He rubbed his gloved hands over his face. "How can he be so sure I was willing to pay? Or that I have any obligation to uphold my end of a bargain I didn't agree to?"

"Would you have preferred he leave Lady Aylen to die at their hands?"

Christian sniffed. He looked away. "No, but for the love of the Guardians, I would have been a better negotiator."

"They didn't come to negotiate," Alric said. "You know this, Christian, even if your anger blinds you to it. Aylen falling into their hands was most fortuitous. But in surrendering himself, he has saved more than just her life."

"Yeah? Is that what I should say to my mother when I tell her that her husband is the latest in her life that will never come home? You think Nyssa and Torrin will be capable of understanding the lives saved by a father they'll never see again?"

No one had an answer. This was what it meant to be a lord. Even surrounded by many, he was completely alone.

Christian threw his head back to the sky. There wasn't enough air in the world to keep his head from spinning in rage, in pure, raw agony. He sucked at it anyway, desperate to feel something else than this utter helplessness that took over control.

He looked toward the woods, where Holden had ridden off with the men of the Easterlands. The shock of the next realization hit him like being catapulted into a stone wall. Why was he still standing there when there was still time to go after them? There were only a dozen of them. They could take them with ease.

But then he let his eyes fall again on the men, seas of pale, scared faces awaiting *his* direction. They needed him to assume the command his father had left him. They needed him to set the conditions for the rest of this war. They were paralyzed in their anticipation of something they understood better than the man tasked with delivering it to them.

He'd failed them then, retreating into the tent to disappear into the same escape Aylen was in, even if she'd gone into this rest alone. But she was alive, and he was alive, and none of the rest mattered. He'd first run away from home to be with her, and then he'd come running back when the Sepulchre commanded the terms of his banishment. Could he stay, past their sentence? If she was at his side? He could do anything if Aylen was with him. She was all that had ever mattered to him.

Now it was all over. It was time to leave. To allow the men to return to their wives and children and hearths; to tend the farms awaiting their trained hands. They didn't belong here. Perhaps they never had. Every moment spent here now was a moment wasted.

Christian emerged from the tent. Marsh pulled to attention with an impressive quickness. He could see the boy had camped himself outside, awaiting a call to serve. He had known no rest.

"At ease, Tyndall," Christian said. He clapped a hand on the boy's shoulder. Other men came to life at the sight of their commander. Christian pulled back his posture, feeling himself fall into the role that already he couldn't wait to shrug off. But that would come later. "See that the wagons are packed by nightfall. We leave at first light."

A light, nervous cheer passed through the men. Alric nodded in approval.

He was happy for them. They'd return to their families, having tallied no losses of their own. Christian had lost more than his father. He'd lost his gift. Being away from the Sepulchre, his true home, had taken from him what made him special and whole, and had given nothing to fill that hole other than the beckoning promise of failure. He'd failed to see Aylen come for him, and failed to prevent his father from trading his life for hers.

And now he would return to rule over Wulfsgate, and that failure would spread.

Christian returned to the tent and his wife, and nursed the terrible hole in his gut where the uneasy future lived.

Marsh hung back as the men filled the wagons with the unused provisions. Some had even packed away their tents, too excited to be bothered with sleep that night. Others laughed and sang songs, deep in their cups, too deep to see to the morrow when they'd regret their lapse. They could afford their joy, for there had been no losses counted against their ranks in this brief war.

None but one.

The image of Lord Dereham riding away would haunt his thoughts, waking and not, forever. Since returning with Aylen, he'd been met with brotherly claps on the back, and knowing nods, even some direct words from the men that it wasn't his fault. That he was fortunate to have been chosen as the man Lord Dereham wanted with him in the end. He hadn't been chosen at all. He was the expendable one who wasn't his son.

Would a greater man have been able to stop it? This gnawed at him.

Lord Alric ambled up. Marsh had been told by nearly everyone what a strange man Alric was—addlebrained, was the word the kind ones used—but though he had heard this enough to commit it to his memory as fact, he hadn't seen it himself. He saw only a man who had been through things no one else could understand. Marsh had never felt this more himself than he did now, when no words of well-intended comfort could undo what had been done.

"There's no gain in torturing yourself, Tyndall. No man could have stopped him. No words could have changed their minds."

Marsh nodded. He took a swig from his wineskin, but the bitter liquid only made him sick. He spat it at his feet. "Still."

"Yes. Still," Alric agreed. "But there's more to every experience than what you can see before you. You'll be known as the man who saved Lady Aylen's life. When Christian comes around to the new life he has ahead of him, he'll understand he owes you a life debt. He'll see it paid."

"I don't want him to owe me anything."

"There's what you want, and then there's the way of things."

"So I'm learning."

"What will you do in the morning, then? Return to your own home? Wildwood Falls, is it?"

"Not just yet."

"Your parents will be mighty relieved to see you."

"I have business in Wulfsgate."

Alric laughed. "Sounding like a right man, there Tyndall. What business awaits you in the Northerlands, then?"

Marsh flushed. His eyes moved to his feet.

"Ah, if not me, who can you tell? A man isn't meant to keep it all inside all the time."

"I don't keep things inside. It's only that I don't know the words. I suppose I'll have time to find them, on the ride back north."

"A lady, then?" Alric's brows rose. "Lady Ember?"

Marsh grunted.

"She's a little spitfire, boy. You'll have your hands full."

"It would be my honor to have my hands full." Marsh flushed even deeper in horror.

Alric chuckled. "You're young, yet, to be asking for her hand."

"I wasn't too young to ride to war," Marsh countered. "Or to ride by her side from Longwood Rush to Wulfsgate."

"Fair enough you are," Alric agreed. He looked up at the day's fading sun, raising a hand over his eyes. "Life is as long or as short as it is. Don't let old men like me tell you what you can and cannot do."

"Do you have children, Lord Alric?"

"A son. Balfour. He studies in Oldcastle."

"What would you tell him, if he told you he had picked a wife?"

"He has a wife already picked for him, I'm afraid," Alric said. "Lady Ember will be saved for someone, too, I suspect. But with her mother and father both gone, you might find yourselves a way around it."

"Ember has never needed anyone's permission. For anything," Marsh mused, and he thought of her clever smile as he watched the rest of the sun disappear behind the forest.

. . .

Lord Warwick's men helped secure the wagon Lisbet and Ash would use to transport Drystan. She'd nestled the blankets around him, and as she stepped back to regard her work, he looked almost peaceful. It would be the last time she ever set eyes upon her brother. Witnessing him in this state was a grotesque reminder of the difference between her intentions and the outcome she was left with. She'd fled Wulfsgate to protect him, and now he was dead. When she finally saw her mother again, it would be her burden to tell her how it had all come to pass.

Did Ravenna know? She wondered this as she rode a pace ahead of the wagon. Lisbet left the necklace around Drystan's neck. He chose to wear it in life, even after Ravenna left him, and she would not take that choice from him in death. She took more than her love when she left. She could have protected him. *Saved* him.

Lisbet knew better. Kian showed her the truth. Only a child or a fool would choose to see a lie instead.

Gabi and Eavan had come, just as she thought they would. Meadow would go on with Steward James, where she would be reunited with her brother and together, when it was safe, make the voyage home.

Gabi was eager to return to Longwood Rush, but Drandyn made her promise not to come until he could be sure all traces of the resistance were stamped out. He would send for her; he swore the Sacred Vow before all of them, which Gabi made him do before she would agree to leave him. Lisbet hid her jealousy well as the siblings embraced. She had other brothers, but there'd been only one Drystan.

Her cousins rode behind the wagon, leaving her side by side with Ash. It was strange to think of how her relationship with this man had evolved. Her first impression had been gratitude, which had faded to suspicion so fast she hardly remembered how enamored she'd been with him that night he'd rescued them all. Now both these things seemed far away and unimportant. They'd lived a lifetime between that day and now. They were not even the same people.

This was why she felt bold enough to say what was on her mind, rather than awaiting the courage or the ephemeral nudge of the right moment.

"Ash, there's something I need to ask you," she said. This time, they were taking the path well-traveled. Kian had been clear: she was not to return to the Hinterlands unless by invitation. They'd bisect the land via the Compass Road, but wouldn't venture east or west of the path.

"Is this what you wanted to ask me in Whitechurch?"

Lisbet nodded. She was grateful for Starcaller's presence. That someone who loved her was there for this moment. "Kian told me about you and my mother. About Drystan."

Ash looked ahead with a blank look. "I assumed as much, when I saw you'd followed our path."

"You're angry with Kian for not telling you that Drystan would die."

"You could say that."

"That is your right. But please don't be angry with me."

Ash turned to look at her. "You? Lisbet, I... no, child. I'm not angry with you. I'm angry at a fate that took from me my right to save my son. I'm angry that it was decided before we arrived, and that, even had I known it, it would have changed nothing."

"I understand that anger. I share it."

"What is it you wanted to ask me, then?"

Lisbet didn't hesitate. "Kian said you were my father. Not just Drystan's. Do you believe that?"

Ash's face softened as he sighed. "I always wondered. I hoped. And then I didn't dare hope, because I'd already taken one child from Holden, and I never meant to cause him such pain. It wasn't his fault Gretchen was taken from me."

"Why didn't you say *anything*? You spent all that time with Drystan, training him... loving him. But you hardly acknowledged me."

"That was the love he needed, Lisbet. You needed me to leave you alone."

Lisbet looked down as she scoffed. "All men want sons. I guess I understand."

"No. That wasn't the reason."

Lisbet whipped her head up. "Then what was the reason? How did you know what I needed? You never asked! You never even tried!"

"It's not so simple, Lisbet, it's—"

"Drystan wasn't the only one who needed someone!" she cried.

Ash reached for Starcaller's reins, slowing both horses in tandem. When they'd eased to a halt, he dismounted and reached both arms up for Lisbet. He pulled her down and into his embrace before she could fight it, and had her wrapped so tight she could hardly breathe.

"I've never wanted anything more than a daughter," he whispered against her hair. "I always knew Drystan belonged to Holden, but you? Even the thought of you dulled the heartbreak of losing your mother. When she carried you, I knew I'd gone too far with her. I did the only thing I could do, and I forced myself to leave, to return to the Medvedev, so I didn't lose my strength and run back to demand my place in your life. Lisbet, you're more than I ever could've hoped for. More than I ever dreamed you would be. My distance was only my fears taking over. If you allow me to love you freely, I'll die before I disappoint you again."

The two girls hung back with the wagon. Lisbet wondered, as Ash crushed her in his warm embrace, what they made of this strange scene. She'd told them what Kian said, of course, but Eavan and Gabi had both lost their fathers, in their own ways.

Ash released her, still holding her at arm's length. "You have my love, Lisbet. And while it is your choice whether you belong to the Derehams or the Sylvaines, I will never again let you feel as if you are not *my* daughter."

Lisbet sniffed through her tears. She wiped at her eyes. Nodded. "Kian said there were three. That you had three children."

Ash's arms fell to his sides. "I'm certain Christian is Holden's son. He's the spitting image of his father."

"I don't think he meant Christian." Lisbet shifted. "He wouldn't tell me who it was, but I know in my heart he didn't mean any of my siblings in Wulfsgate."

"Who, then?" Ash touched his hand to the corner of his mouth. His eyes shifted back and forth as he searched his memories. "I cannot fathom it, there was never another, only your—" He cut himself off with a light gasp.

"What? What is it?"

Ash exhaled. "She's gone now. If she had a child, that truth never came to me."

"How can we find out?"

"We?"

"You and me, Ash. Don't you want to know?"

Ash slowly nodded. "Yes, of course. Of course I want to know."

"Then it's settled. When we've managed matters in Wulfsgate, we'll go find them. You and me."

"You and me," he repeated with a light smile.

Lisbet realized it was three men she was talking to now. Ash, her father, and Dain Rhiagain. But he only knew he was two. It would fall to her to reveal the truth of his origins, but he would need his head on straight when he faced her mother.

She would tell him. Just not now.

Eavan pretended to smile as Gabi gushed over the reunion between father and daughter. How sweet it was! How wonderful!

She wanted to be happy for Lisbet. It had always seemed to Eavan that Lisbet kept one foot elsewhere, waiting to be called, and now she could pull it back and look forward. She adored Lisbet, more than her own sisters. Lisbet deserved happiness.

But that wasn't how Eavan felt at all. Lisbet had three parents, and Eavan had none. Her father was a traitor, and her mother a coward, and even if they were here, neither could help her through what awaited her soon as the child of a brigand rapist flourished in a belly she could no longer hide.

"How long will you stay in Wulfsgate, then?" Gabi asked. Even the way she asked the question was offensive to Eavan. Like they were on holiday. Gabi had somewhere to go when all this was over. Eavan would always now be at the mercy of the kindness—or more likely, pity—of others.

"I haven't decided."

"Your brother will be the lord now? Cian?"

"So they say."

"I don't blame you anymore, Eavan, for what happened to my father. I never should have. I see that now," Gabi said. "Mine is dead, yours is a monster. My mother is lost to the world, and yours may as well be. We are both orphans now."

Eavan loathed the hot tears burning at her cousin's words. They weren't welcome. Nor was the sympathy, the forgiveness, the tenderness with which both girls dealt with her. Now Ash as well, who looked at her and saw only what had happened to her; what *he* had rescued her from, when she could not save herself. Somewhere along the way, Eavan the young woman had been lost, and now she was only Eavan the abused. Eavan the forgotten.

"Do you think my sister will be there? Emberley? Brandyn said she was before, but she's never been content to stay still for long. Oh, and how joyous Ransom will be when we tell him his father is sending him home! All these reunions..."

"I would prefer it if we don't talk anymore," Eavan said. She ignored Gabi's stricken look, gazing straight ahead as she waited for Lisbet and Ash to get moving again.

GRETCHEN HAD HEARD the men talk enough about the damnable tree where Pieter had disappeared that she had a fair enough image of it in her mind. When she found it, right where the pass veered south, it was about what she'd envisioned, down to the vibrant fruit glistening against the snow. A fruit-bearing tree in the middle of a snowy mountain pass would have caught her notice even if she'd known nothing.

Ransom had said the fruit had mesmerized Pieter. Ransom, occupied by the fear their trail was hot with those who had killed Princess Assyria and probably Lady Asherley, didn't understand this until he'd come closer. Once it was before him, he, too, was pulled in by a keen hunger, a desire baffling to him given the events of the morning had rendered his appetite dead.

Gretchen clucked softly to Silverwind. Silverwind chuffed, understanding. They were already linked forever. She'd told the mare, in her own way, to stay only as long as she felt safe. If Gretchen were to disappear, Silverwind would be the only evidence that she'd been here, but the horse's return would be what was needed to complete the story. Within the satchel hanging from Silverwind's saddle was the note she'd sworn she wouldn't write to Holden.

Gretchen stepped through the deep banks of snow. They drifted as high as her waist in some places. Even the path hadn't yet been properly packed. The season's storms were not past them, and no place knew that truth more than the great mountain passes of the Northerlands.

She wasn't here to retrace the steps of her husband and son, and the others in the search party who had tried, and failed, to bring Pieter home. She trusted their efforts had been in earnest.

Returning home with the unfortunate news had weighed heavily on them.

It was Alric's words ringing the loudest in her mind. It was entertaining, even easy, to laugh at the man's oddities. She'd been as guilty as anyone. Now the laughter she'd spent on him felt like punishment. For where else could Pieter be? If he disappeared in the same place where Alric had, that could be no mere coincidence.

And if Alric had returned, so could Pieter.

All her life, Gretchen had been patently uninterested in all the talk of Beyond and veils, and Elsewhere. It was the stuff of myths, and what use were myths to those living in the real, provable, tangible world? It seemed to her that, no matter the truth, it was irrelevant. The lure of islands beyond the waves was strong for many, but for her, it was a distraction.

Perhaps this was what made it so simple for her to shift from disdain to hope. Her contempt for Alric had been mere annoyance at his strangeness. She had no opinion either way on whether he'd traveled beyond the kingdom by stepping through a veil.

Gretchen closed her eyes. She tried to remember precisely where Ransom had said he last saw Pieter, and she stepped sideways until it felt right. No door appeared. No strange trembling filled her limbs, telling her something new was on the horizon. What made Alric and Pieter special? How had Holden and the other escaped what they could not?

Alric was special before he claimed to have stepped into Beyond. Pieter has always believed. Holden, Christian, the others, none of them expected to find Pieter. None of them had hope. They left it in Wulfsgate.

A low rumble sounded in the pass. She looked up with enough time only to see Silverwind bolt for high ground as an avalanche of snow came barreling down upon the tree. Seconds remained before it did.

The veil only opens for one in great need.

Chilled to the bone, heart soaring, Gretchen jumped sideways.

Her left leg surged with unexpected warmth.

Gretchen looked down and saw that one leg disappeared into the snow of Torrin's Pass and the other stood firmly upon the sand of a desert.

She closed her eyes. Took one last gulp of breath of the air she knew. Said a silent prayer for Silverwind's safe return.

The roar was upon her.

Gretchen Dereham stepped into the veil.

55
PUT IT BEHIND

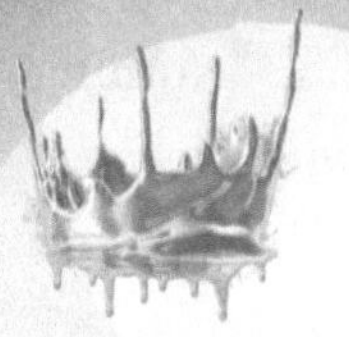

The James men hovered near the cluster of wagons, waiting. All their supplies and provisions were packed. The men had been fed, and there was no other unfinished business left untended. Cian and Corin Quinlanden were, together, cleaning up the messes left by The Deceiver, and the people of Whitechurch were relieved to follow them. Oakenwell had resumed command as the right hand of the lord, and though word had already been sent to the Westerlands for the Quinlanden Guard to return home, he sent it once more, and then sent riders to deliver the messages personally. Even a whisper of rebellion was to be put down with swiftness. The Westerlands were to be left in peace. At the proper time, reparations would be made to those whose lands and loved ones had been assailed.

Grand Minister Tyndall had departed for the Reliquary. He'd said that he wanted none to hear the news of what happened on these lands, but from one who had seen it with his own eyes.

And Joran... Joran, too, had left. He'd delivered his message to the other camp, and then disappeared.

Brandyn had some idea of where he'd gone, though.

I've seen your mother, Brandyn. I must go to her.
Where?
I'll know when I know.

These were the last words Joran had said to Brandyn the night before everything had gone to pieces.

There was now nothing keeping Brandyn now from going home.

"You look better, now that you've had a healer tend to some of your wounds," Storm said. "Nothing keeping you here now, is there? Your uncle is delaying because you delay." She nodded at Khallum, who stood alone in the distance, regarding the sky with unusual scrutiny.

"Uncle Khallum? The man doesn't know the meaning of the word. He was born with his teeth bared, sword in hand."

"He wanted war, Brandyn. The Warwicks have been awaiting their moment to turn their frustration into bloodlust since before our parents were born. He put it aside to save your life."

"I don't understand where he went when you dangled Oaken-well as bait. If you did that to get him inside, where did he go?"

"He didn't tell you?"

"We haven't spoken since... what I did on the hill. To Mads."

"He went looking for you, but he came to the dungeon too late. You were gone, a headless Mortain was heaped in the corner, and the guards that man, Ash, took care of, were laid out in a maze. He ran after you, but he didn't know your aunt and uncle had taken you to that place... the perch. When he finally made it back to land, that's when he looked up and saw you, safe." Storm chuckled to herself. "The man cried. Don't you tell him I told you."

"Oh, I could never say that to him."

"Once he knew you were safe, he seized the traitor, Waters, and bade the rest of us to spread the word of Mortain's death. We told everyone who we could find to go tell one more, two more, ten more. You wouldn't believe the relief in their eyes, Brandyn. None of them wanted this. The few who did, who fought against our promise of freedom, are in the dungeon. Cian and Corin can decide their fates. As for me, I've never been so happy to leave a place."

Brandyn turned to her. "Storm. About your parents…"

"No, please don't." Storm wrapped her hands over her lone dagger. She tapped her foot against the road in tight, jerky movements. "I've made my peace with it, but talking about it will undo it all."

"Come with me to Longwood Rush. I want you on my council." Brandyn shook his head. "No, I want you at the head of it. I want you to be the right hand of the lord. I don't trust anyone else the way I trust you."

Storm grinned from the side. "Yeah? Me? The stabby one?"

"Who else is gonna dispatch anyone who looks at me sideways?"

"What if your mother comes back?"

Brandyn's face clouded. "I've also made peace with some things, Storm. But I suppose if she does, I'd return to the Sepulchre and continue my training. I still have more to learn before I'll ever be a decent seer."

"They wouldn't let me come guard you there, would they?"

"Not likely."

Storm looped her arm through his. "Give your uncle a proper goodbye and then let's make use of the day's light."

"The ravens will have reached some in the kingdom already," Law said. "Word will be at every corner before we've crossed back into the Southerlands."

"Hmm," Khallum grunted. "I wish he'd consulted with us first."

"You don't agree with his decision?"

"Nay, I agree, but I wasnae prepared for it. We are allies. Allies work together. None of this would have happened without alliances."

"He'll be our king. Soon."

"A truth of which I'm more than aware of seeing as it was me who sprang him from the traitor's camp."

"Ryan Strong sprang him," Law answered without pause. "And the Southerlands will not forget it."

Khallum scoffed. "I've nay forgotten. I couldnae. Hamish…"

Law nodded. "You'll need to speak with him, my lord. Disavow him of the fault he's laid at his own feet for the business with the Saleen. It's false, and the man already carries enough."

"Aye. I know. I know it."

"Before we depart?"

"Aye! I said I would, didn't I?"

Law lifted both hands. "I'll leave you with your thoughts. If we depart within soon, and keep a fair pace, we could make it to Greenfen before the men give out for the night."

"Greenfen?" Khallum raised a bow. "I didnae know you were such an ambitious man, Law."

Law didn't laugh. "Just the same, my lord."

"Aye. Aye. Go on, then. Ready the men."

Brandyn stepped to his side when Law was gone. "We're leaving soon, Uncle." He held his palm to the wind, closing his eyes for a moment. "The eastward wind will give us some aid, I should hope."

A knot formed in Khallum's chest. "That was your father's trick."

"It's served me well."

"Aye. Aye." Khallum nodded away the swell of emotion. "We'll be departing soon as well. Can still make use of the day's light."

"That's exactly what Storm said."

"Wise girl. Feckin' peculiar as all, but smarter than she looks."

Brandyn chuckled. "I like that about her. She's going to lead my council."

Khallum turned a hard frown on him. "A woman? You'll name a woman to lead your council?"

"I know weaker men, but I don't know a stronger person."

Khallum snorted. "Doesnae matter, nephew, who is weak and who is strong. Your men will never follow a woman. Tisn't the way of things. Never has been, never will be."

"My mother led the Westerlands for years, and her mother before her."

"Aye, and now you're restoring things to the proper way. They'll all be mighty relieved to have a lord again, but not if ye donnae act like one."

"Then I'll fill my entire council with women."

Khallum was aghast. "Ye cannae go fillin' yer negotiating tables with bloody rags and rousing fishwife gossip."

"I can fill it with the most loyal and capable of the Westerlands."

Khallum turned away, scoffing. He looked toward the skies, where all the dead lived. "Oh, aye, Byrne, I'll be making a fair few trips to Longwood Rush, don't ye worry."

Brandyn giggled. Khallum was reminded that his nephew was only a boy, even if he was so much more than that now.

"I will, though. To check in on ye, of course, but I've also some business with the Westerlands."

"Oh?"

"Aye. My men in the Southerlands are starving. You've a shortage of minerals in your own lands. We can aid one another, I ken."

Brandyn nodded. "Yeah. Let's do that, Uncle." He took a deep breath. "I came over to thank you. For coming to my aid in Greystone, and for riding with me to Whitechurch, even if you didn't understand."

Khallum dropped his hand to the boy's shoulder. "It is nay often I'll admit I was wrong."

"Thank you for saying it now."

Khallum laughed. "Boy, did I say I was wrong?"

Brandyn threw himself against Khallum so hard it knocked them both unsteady. His small arms could barely make it around, but Khallum held him there, thinking of the last time he'd embraced his own sons. Thinking of the last time he'd seen Byrne, in Termonglen, and how he'd chided him for loving so hard.

Khallum finally ended the moment. It wouldn't do to get twisted up in pointless emotions now, or for the men to see it.

"I'll send ye some men for yer council," Khallum promised. "*Men*," he re-emphasized.

Brandyn grinned. "Thank you, Uncle. Just don't be surprised when the women send 'em packing back to their wives."

KHALLUM FOUND both the men he needed, together. Darrick and Hamish conversed at the side of one of the wagons. Hamish was in his emotions, flush-faced and waving his hands around. Darrick's calm only underscored the state Hamish was in.

"Your Grace. Hamish."

Both men paused their animated discourse to greet Khallum.

Khallum turned to Darrick. "Ride with me, Your Grace? We have much to discuss, now that the kingdom knows of your return. I'm afraid it cannae wait until we arrive in Warwicktown."

Darrick nodded. Khallum noticed he couldn't keep his eyes from wandering south, to where the Saleen met their gruesome end. Would he always turn his eyes in that direction? Would he ever sleep a full night again?

"Yes, Lord Warwick. I was telling Steward Strong here that as soon as we arrive I want to begin work on forming a council with representatives from every Reach. I have some names in mind, but would like other's opinions as well."

"To mount our offense against Duncarrow?"

"A council, Lord Warwick. Filled with men of keen minds, eager to discuss how we can unite without the need for war. Eoghan must be removed. But others do not need to die needlessly to see it done."

"He has a sorcerer, Your Grace."

"Yes, and there are two others out there somewhere. Have you wondered why they didn't join forces with Mortain and Oldwin?"

"No, I—"

"I have," Darrick said. "I've thought about it a great deal. And there can only be two answers that work properly enough to be true. Either they wish to live in peace and stay out of the turmoil, or they are foes of the ones who brought such harm to the kingdom. Either outcome leaves us exclusive of their intentions."

"With respect, Your Grace, those assumptions aren't without merit, but they render us vulnerable if we rely on them."

Darrick smiled. "We're no longer vulnerable, Lord Warwick. We are becoming, for the first time in years, a kingdom united. I don't fear Oldwin, or Isdemus, or Lysanor. I fear discord. I fear a lack of unity. Those are the scourges that tear kingdoms apart."

"So, you'll just sail to Duncarrow and ask him to leave nicely?"

"Eoghan or Oldwin?"

"Does it matter?"

Darrick sighed. "That's what the council is for. We will decide what to do next, together."

Hamish squirmed in place. The sorrow gulping upward from his insides was too much to bear. He'd spent the intervening hours between the slaughter at the south end of Whitechurch and now poring over the details of his life, searching for the crimes he must have committed to find himself here, the arbiter of the end of a race of peoples.

Even Garrick couldn't meet his eyes. They'd ridden together into battle, which was not how it was supposed to be. Garrick should have been leading his own men, but he'd stayed at Hamish's side, practically shitting himself in terror. The ripe smell of death wasn't yet upon them, but in Garrick's eyes was a glimpse, as if he was already part of a future that would come to pass faster than any of them realized.

How could they have known? The soldiers weren't wearing armor, but it wouldn't be the first run-in with savages for the Southerland men, and men didn't need mail or plate to throw an axe into the center of your forehead.

The Medvedev had swarmed in, wielding their arms high and ready to strike. The Southerland men were faster—or so they thought—and the battle was over so quickly he thought there must be another word for it. He dared not call it a slaughter, for they would never have... they would never have...

When they counted their losses, they were so few, they counted again.

And again.

They started to count the losses among the Saleen, but did the number matter when it was all of them? Men, women, children. They'd all died indiscriminately.

"They just came at us."

"There were so many. They didnae stop, or slow."

"Did ye see the look in their eyes?"

"Barbarians. Tha's what it reminded me of, yeah? Ye ken? Ye know, up high in the Northerlands, where the men don't go?"

Hamish and Garrick milled through their dazed men, picking up these scattered refrains that all said the same thing in their own ways. The Medvedev had flown at them with unslakeable blood-lust. They had answered decisively, and as they buried their swords in bellies, or drew them across necks, the Medvedev simply stopped. Their arms dropped to their sides. Their eyes took on a glazed look. And all at once, they fell. Many bled out. Others just ceased to exist.

The prince told them it was the magic that did it. The magic that bade them come streaming in, the magic that killed them. But Hamish himself had to peel his sword from the bowels of a purple-haired woman. He met Garrick's eyes as Garrick retrieved his from a small child.

"Hamish."

Hamish struggled to look at his lord. Khallum had entrusted him with the whole of the Southerland Guard, and he had used it to annihilate an entire peoples.

"Look at me, mate. There's no use in it, what you're doing to yerself. It won't do once we ride for home."

"Aye, my lord."

"Feck off with that 'my lord' bollocks, Hamish. I'm talking to you as your mate right now, ye ken? I donnae have time for the sulkin'. It has no place here."

Hamish forced himself to do as his lord commanded. There was no hiding the bleariness in his eyes, or the cause of it. "I'll do better."

Khallum grunted. His face softened. He looked conflicted about something, but before Hamish could decipher it, Khallum had him in a quick, hard embrace. "No one has ever served me better, Hamish Strong. Now, pick yerself up and be done with it. Put it behind ye. You've a son awaiting your return who needs a man capable of putting it behind him. Ye ken?"

Hamish sniffed. "I ken."

"Ain't nothing more to it. Our path is forward, not behind us."

"Aye. Aye, Khallum."

"We'll already be chasing the sun. Law's found his sense of

humor, thinking we can make it to Greenfen by nightfall. You and I both know better, though, don't we? Salt and sand."

Hamish wiped the offensive tears from his face. "Salt and sand."

Khallum clapped his hand down on Hamish's shoulder, squeezed, and walked off.

56
THE SOURCE

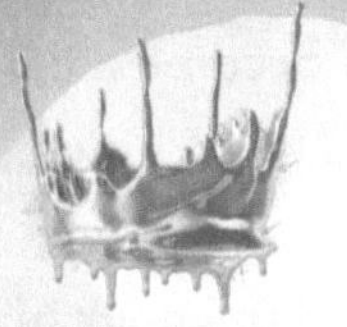

Alasyr had been scouring the hard peaks and valleys of Icebolt Mountain for hours. The mid-season storm pushed clouds in his way. Ice peppered his wings, knocking him off course more than once. It would be snow later, which was more forgiving, but there wouldn't be a later.

He never looked behind him. His mother wouldn't come after him, any more than she'd gone after Ravenna. She had lived by their traditions and would die by them. She had other children, more pliant and willing than Ravenna and Alasyr. Alasyr's one regret was not seeing it when Ravenna did, so he could have left with her. It would have spared him this new pain, more acute than any that had come before.

He found a clear patch in the sky and glided sideways, scanning the fresh swash of mountainside. There was nothing but the blinding white of snow. The same snow he'd known all his short and limited life. He'd never walked through a field of fresh blossoms, or witnessed color that was not born of magic. He didn't know the taste of venison, or the rich scents of a bustling town in the middle of summer. Until Ravenna disappeared, he'd never even stepped foot on the land of men. He'd never wanted to.

They are evil, and would lay their evil upon us, if we allowed them. His instruction on the world of men had been meager, but stark and clear. Men were only reluctant allies. Men would harm them if given the chance. Men were evil.

Ravenna understood this, but it had taken the words of this strange and powerful girl, for him to finally *see*. This girl who had been more determined to become a better version of herself than any Ravenwood Alasyr had ever known.

He entered another cloud patch, wobbling through as the turbulent winds threatened to knock him unsteady. A dozen loops he'd done, and no sight of her. But she hadn't simply disappeared. She was here, somewhere, and he would find her. He would return her to her family, who deserved to mourn her properly. Not in the hollow way Alasyr had been forced to mourn Ravenna.

Alasyr spotted something dark against the snow. His heart thrummed hard within his raven form, and he angled himself downward, never letting his raven eyes divert or even blink for fear of losing sight of her.

But as he closed in, he saw it wasn't Ember at all.

It was his father.

He supposed he should feel something about this. Sadness. Loss. Anger. But in their place was only a void.

Alasyr climbed high into the skies, once more, to continue his search.

WHEN ASHERLEY AWOKE, the first thing she noticed was that she was no longer a woman, but a well-plumed bird.

Right, then. I should have known when Emberley appeared in the skies.

Her talons stumbled for purchase. She smacked into the

balustrade like a drunkard at the end of a long night. She imagined this would look hilarious to onlookers, but she had no humor left in her. She just wanted the disorientation to end so she could take to flight and find her daughter.

She soon discovered it was as simple as moving her wings.

ALASYR WANTED to cry out her name, but had never learned to speak as a man in his raven form. Some Ravenwoods had. He'd never had use for it. When he had wings and a beak his only desire was to fly and be free of all that. Until now.

His wings ached. The weariness settled into his bones. He dropped lower, beneath the clouds, to encounter less resistance, but the wind was more animated here, and so he went lower and lower until he was nearly skimming the mountain's surface.

And there she was.

At the entrance to a small cave. The overhang had hidden her at greater heights, but as he drew closer, he could make out all the things he'd once recited in his head as flaws; her beautiful flaming hair, that strange way of dressing, in leather and cloth, wearing a blouse and pants like a boy.

Her broken body twisted unnaturally. As he landed, his talons unfolding into legs, he could see that her arms had been shattered from the force of her wings being ripped apart by Varinya's bolts.

Alasyr bit down hard on his lip and knelt beside her. Her body had cooled, her lips painted a deep blue. He had to get her out of the storm. She didn't belong out here, exposed, for a buzzard or mountain goat to feast upon.

When he pulled on her arms, they flopped back against the snow. He reached instead for the spot under them, where her shoulders met, and with a grunt he heaved himself backward. The effort was easier than he expected. She was smaller than he realized. She moved easily as he slid her inside the cave.

He was not the first one to have taken refuge here. The remnants of several campfires caught him by surprise. Only a Ravenwood could fly this high, but if a Ravenwood had been here, it could not be for any reason involving good. This was a place for secrets and hidden things.

His mother had taken him to a cave like this one, and it didn't seem as if that visit was her first. He could fill a book with all he didn't know about his people, and they'd killed any curiosity left in him to find out.

Alasyr let his hands hover over the leftover twigs and sticks from a campfire. Flames roared to life. The relief was immediate, though quickly replaced by the sight of her again.

He fell back to Emberley's side and when the tears came, he didn't recognize them, but nor did he deny them. He leaned over her and pressed his face to her chest, allowing the sobs to rip through him, here, where no one could bear witness and tell him it was not behavior becoming of a Ravenwood.

His hands spread over her broken arms as he lost his vision to the blur of angst.

"Ember, I failed you. I failed us both," he cried. The sorrow was so intense he feared he'd lose himself. He wanted to lose himself. He deserved to be lost. He had nowhere else to go.

He tried to remember how she looked, standing stubborn and strong in the Wintergarden. She'd never once been afraid of him. She wasn't mesmerized by him, either, as the men and women of Wulfsgate often were when a Ravenwood swooped down from the sky. She'd only wanted to know him, and he'd let her believe this was a desire that was not shared.

And then Alasyr imaged her this same way, but in the cave. The soft, boneless flesh of her arms snapping into formation. He pressed his lips to the edges of the hole in her belly, shrinking it away until there was no wound at all. Only the pale, unblemished skin that should be. She was cursing him for something, telling him he had it all wrong, as always, and especially about her, and—

Ember launched forward, gasping.

Alasyr stumbled back onto his hands as he watched the color return to her cheeks. She licked her dry, cracked lips with a confused look, then looked down at her forearms, turning them upside down and around.

You brought her back.

Just like the goat.

"Emberley," Alasyr whispered, breathless.

"Alasyr?" She looked down at her whole, healed body with powerful confusion.

He crawled back to her. His eyes traveled the whole of her, from face to arms to legs, moving across every fold of her flesh. He gaped at her in pure wonder. "Emberley."

She twisted her mouth. "Alasyr, what else have you been hiding from me, you odd boy?"

Alasyr's sobs turned into laughter. He reached for her hands, but decided that no, it was her face he most wanted to touch. And though he expected her to slap him away, she didn't, sliding her own hands over his, linking their fingers, her own tears coming now as if on cue.

Alasyr closed his eyes and kissed her. On the mouth, on both cheeks, on her hands. Nothing was enough. It would never be enough.

Ember reached for his hands and stopped him. She gazed into his eyes, and his heart paused.

Then she wound her arms around his neck and he was forever and ever lost.

57
WHAT HE DID NOT SEE

Oldwin leaned into the moss-covered edges of the balcony. It was so slick that one wrong move would send a man careening into the stones below. No second chances. Already, he saw the opportunities, and his reign had only begun. How many Rhiagains would get to find out before his time was done?

The balcony was small, an octagonal wonder that didn't match the design of the rest of the keep at Duncarrow. It was accessed from a corner of the apartment office, a key stronghold of the king's chambers for every king except Eoghan. Eoghan had done it all differently, not from a nuance in his style, but the raw ignorance that comes from the failures of a father.

Eoghan had adopted a policy of not cleaning what was not in active use, evidenced by cobwebs as thick as human hair taking residence in what was once the busiest room in the keep. Oldwin's new rooms had looked the same before he sent the kitchen maids to their hands and knees and promised them they would trade their life for any dust his fingers could find. He was pleased when he didn't have to order their deaths. He'd take a tidy room over the messy and inconvenient business of murder any day.

Their deaths could not come at his hand, anyway. He could no more kill a Rhiagain than a Ravenwood. Still, there were creative ways around this, as Ravenna had discovered with Thane. She'd unearthed her terror, but it had been his own fear that caused his heart to burst. He could use men as his tool, as he so often had before. Or he could simply allow the whims of fate to take their course, as he had when he'd failed to intervene in the death of Khain Rhiagain.

In his hand he clutched the vellum that had come by raven from Whitechurch. From *Darrick Rhiagain*. He wouldn't be the first pretender to rise up and make this claim, and this was Oldwin's instinct when he read the words. Another lowborn grasper in the throes of his own delusions. He'd heard the tale before. In hiding as a pauper, only to bide their time to become the king. Pathetic.

Except these ravens had flown to every corner of the kingdom, confident in their bold message. How did he know this? Because news of the one he was holding now arrived even before it did. Ravens were finicky about crossing the White Sea. They would not attempt it unless the tides were calm. By the time Oldwin had read these fated words from the once-dead prince, so had most of the kingdom.

This message comes to you from Darrick Rhiagain, rightful heir to Duncarrow. My brother Eoghan ordered my death, but allies conspired against this cowardly command, secreting me away to the Wastelands, where I have served in conditions I would wish upon no man. I am now returned, to relieve the kingdom of the terrible reign they have suffered under. I am returned, to avenge the total genocide done upon the Saleen in the name of Eoghan Rhiagain. To Eoghan, I say this: I am coming for what is mine, even if I arrive five years late to the task. And I am not alone.

Oldwin had news of his own for *Darrick Rhiagain*. He was the king now, of a kingdom that had never had but one use for him, and soon he would see that use realized. Darrick's return gave him pause, but it would not stop him.

No, what troubled him about this provocative piece of vellum in his hands was not the truth written upon it, but that *he had not seen it coming.*

He had not. Seen. It coming.

His visions had brought them to the shores of Duncarrow centuries before. His and his alone. Centuries before, the sorcerers had searched, slipping through door after door, frustrated, defeated. There were only so many worlds it could be in, and they'd been too many of them over and over, poring over what they'd missed, wondering if they'd gone about it all wrong. Over half the sorcerers born from the magic of Ilynglass perished during their searches, and some abandoned the cause entirely. By the time Oldwin saw it in his mind's eye, there were only four left still possessing the determination to see it through to the end.

Somewhere along the way, four had split into two. Isdemus and Lysanor were still thick as a band of brigands, but Oldwin and Mortain both had conditions for one another. They needed each other's magic, but they didn't need each other. It surprised him that Mortain's death wounded him as it did, but then, there was something to be said for the old ones; the last ones. Their differences were greater than their affinities, but they had survived millennia, together, and now, no more.

But he hadn't *seen* any of it.

Not Mortain's swift death at the hands of a mere boy.

Not the end of the war between the Reaches.

Not the return of Darrick.

Just as, long ago, he'd failed to see the truth of Dain Rhiagain, not once, nor even twice. Every word he whispered to Eoghan about his half-brother were pretty guesses, designed as much to deceive as to hide his blind spots. He peppered them with the small bits of intelligence he gleaned from Correen's spies, which gave them the substance of truth.

He hadn't seen Mortain's true plan for the Saleen, either, though it was brilliant. With the Saleen gone, this cleared a path that didn't exist before. A path to the end of this treasure hunt that had consumed most of his life, and once complete, would elevate it to a place far beyond his imagining.

But first, there was the matter of Darrick Rhiagain.

There was the matter of Dain and his descendants.

And there was Isdemus and Lysanor, whose bold interference in his magic would not be borne.

It was time to send his news into the kingdom.

That Eoghan Rhiagain was dead, and Oldwin of Ilynglass was now King of the White Kingdom.

"IT IS DONE. Arguing will not undo it. I must go."

"Is this why she sent me away? So that I could not stop you?"

"Now it is you, brother, who speaks in the vernacular of men."

Kael grunted. "For you. I do it for you."

Kian turned to him. "You are wrong. She sent you away because Ryan Strong is Yanna's son. He is kin. She did this for Yanna."

"Yanna was a traitor."

"None die beyond forgiveness. To hold fast to anger is not our way."

Kael curled his lip. "He has no memory."

Kian was aghast. "You left him? Like this?"

Kael rolled his eyebrows up. He moved to the chair, their mother's chair, and slid down into it. "My charge was to save him. I saved him."

"From one fate, but left him vulnerable to another." Kian sighed. "You do not learn. This is why you will never lead."

Kael gestured to the chair he was in. "Nothing impedes me from sitting here."

"Sitting is not leading."

"If Mother dies when you are gone, I will not wait for you."

Kian set his satchel aside. He didn't know when the two of them had diverted down such different paths. Kael was led by his pride, and, to what would be his downfall, an anger that Kian didn't comprehend. Kian would not exempt himself from such scrutiny of self, but he feared leaving these lands when Kael was on the edge of his volatility. Once he stepped over, he would not easily return. Who would he take with him?

"Someone must go to the Saleen lands. None of the Medvedev are protected if one is vulnerable. This you know."

"I could go in your place. I could lead them."

"Mother asked me."

"Do you always do what Mother asks?"

"I am true to her. She has led us well. She has loved us well."

"She fears what cannot come to pass. Man cannot enter our world without us. The end of the Saleen made that harder, not easier."

Kian pressed down his anger. If he engaged it, he could no longer say he and Kael were so different. It threatened to bubble up, but he was stronger than the evil. He must be. "It is our magic that keeps our borders closed. That holds the veil. There are no Saleen there now to bind it. Mortain has seen to that. Others will take his place."

"Go, then." Kael waved his hand. "How many will you take?"

"As many as she sends with me."

"She does not know everything, Kian. She says Yanna's son will save us, but she turned him from our lands when he sought us out."

"He was not ready. All things, in their appropriate time."

"Her sickness has left her mad."

"Her body is dying, not her mind, Kael."

"Her mind is no better than mine! Than yours!"

"Do not forget the oath you swore. It binds us, beyond our loyalties to one another."

Kael scoffed. "Because she says so?"

Kian took a step up and looked into his brother's eyes. He no longer recognized what glared back at him. "Because it is so. We serve her, because she serves what we protect. If you cannot do that, then may Mother have the strength to do what I could not."

He backed away, holding out a hand for his familiar, his one true friend.

"I will know, Kael. If you do not live true to your oath. I will know."

Kian grabbed his satchel and left.

58

JAMESAN

"He's not ready, Lysanor. Nothing so important has ever come as quickly as you wish it would."

"Not ready? He's been in there for so long he might not be himself when he comes out. He's been in there far too long."

"Not long enough."

"No." She shook her head. "He's the one. We designed this, we waited for it all these years, and we will not destroy him. He is not delicate, like a millennial flower that must be guarded."

"We both know there are no millennial flowers anymore. Why are you in such a rush?"

Lysanor looked toward the east, where they'd stepped through the veil. "Oldwin knows that I've interfered with his magic. That my own has protected Dain and his children, keeping his eye cast away from their truths. He knows, and now he will see us, see what we have, what we will do with it. All these years, we had nothing but time. Now, time is the one thing of which we are in great deficit."

"Are you certain?"

"That he knows? Yes. And he has rightly deduced our role in his blindness toward the return of Darrick Rhiagain, and the death of Mortain. He already knows Dain lives, and in time he will see that two of Dain's three offspring live as well. Soon, he will know about Jamesan. Once a magic has been breached... Isdemus, my protections have given way to a relentlessness that will see them all destroyed. We cannot delay."

"How do you know? Did you see it? Or are you once more guessing?" Isdemus pressed. He had one hand held toward the light, as he had for the days Jesse had been inside. His strength waned. This was the other reason they must be done with it. Lysanor had lost much over the long years, but she would not lose him.

"I saw flashes of it, and of his rage, at the moment he sundered my hold on his magic. I *felt* it, and now I feel nothing. Now he is closed to me forever. Once his all-seeing eye finds Dain, he will find the others. I cannot protect us, Isdemus. We are as if laid bare before our enemy, and now that he has dispatched of the Saleen..."

"What if he *isn't* ready, Lysanor? What if you're wrong, and he returns to us before he understands?"

"Oh, my brother," Lysanor said softly, sighing. "The light cannot make him understand. Who has ever had their truth turned upside down with such calm acceptance? No, the light cannot make him understand. Only we can, if fortune holds, and our hearts are true."

"Our hearts were not always true."

"We have corrected them. That must count for something."

"And if it does not?"

Lysanor met his eyes. "Then we will fail having first tried to save this world."

• • •

*H*E WAS AGAIN IN *B*YTHESEA. *Back to where he'd begun, where the circle had first been drawn.*

But his time here was ending. All that lay before him flickered, a light going out for the last time.

Jesse reached in clawing desperation for his mother, fast fading away. Somewhere within him he knew he'd never be able to, but it was the sorrow of every motherless boy that bade him try, anyway. Even the outcome could not erase the pain behind the intent. He would die trying, if that was the cost.

It seemed for just a moment, Yanna de Medvedev turned and saw him. Eyes locked, knowing glances passed between mother and son, the veil of life and death thin for the briefest time.

And then she was gone.

Hamish was gone.

Bythesea was gone.

It was only Jesse and the beckoning call of a blinding light.

He knew this light. This light had brought him here, and now it wished to take him away.

But once he stepped through, it was a one-way trip. He could never again return, and if he did, it would not be the same. There would no more stolen time with his mother, whose promise was long spent.

Mama, he thought, gazing back into the endless sea of nothing. Mama, why did I never listen when you tried to tell me your stories? Why did I think they were nothing? That they were trifles in my world of salt and sand? How have I let my world become so narrow that there was no room for you and what you brought to our home and hearth? That father's world was the only thing which mattered?

"Mama. I can make this right."

Jesse screamed the moment the searing light overcame him, as he was pulled, resisting, howling, into it, and then...

. . .

"Welcome back." Isdemus' voice was soothing, but was soon replaced by—

"Now do you know you who you are?"

"Lysanor, look at him. He's *clearly* in no fit state to speak. No one who returns from the light is, not for some time. Have some wine. Summon your patience."

"When I would like to know what you think of something, Isdemus, I will be sure to advise you."

"And I'm nonetheless advising you that he's in a terrible state of shock, and that he cannot be expected to rise to your unreasonable—"

"We're out of time, Isdemus! Out! There is none left. He is ready, or he is not, but Oldwin will not hesitate!"

Jesse wrapped his hands tight around his eyes, wincing as he rolled to the side to block the light. He felt the heaviness of the desert sand again, with its large round grains so unlike what he knew in the Southerlands. The sulfur in the air burned his nose. A hard wind whipped through, carrying another scent foreign to him. "Why did you pull me out? I wasn't ready! I wasn't done!"

"You were more than done. You should have been done *days* ago." Lysanor. Calm. He wanted to scream into her tranquility and destroy it, to bring her to where he was, even for a moment, so she could see, so she could understand. He was done, she said, with the even tone of a shopkeeper ready to serve the next patron. Done, she said? What did she know? What could she know? What could she *possibly* know?

"Give him time. You'll only make it worse," Isdemus pleaded with her.

Jesse waved one hand around in chaotic swats, covering his eyes with the other. He wasn't ready to open them. If he kept them closed, there was still a chance he might not really be here. "I need to see her. My mother. Please. Just for a little longer. You cannae give me that and then take it from me."

"Do you know who you are?"

"Please! I'm *begging* you. I have things I need to say to her!"

Lysanor groaned. He could almost hear her head shake. "You're a stubborn child, like the hapless man who reared you."

"I've done everything you've asked of me. I'm now asking this of you in return."

"The light doesn't work that way. It gives what it gives. It offers no more."

Jesse panted, crawling forward on his hands and knees. He didn't have the strength to stand. It had been taken, just as his mother had been. He could hardly find it within him to breathe.

"Stand, Jesse."

"I need water."

"You needed truth, and now you have that. Stand."

"I can't."

"You won't."

"I *can't*."

The air around him changed, and he at last looked up, and it was Lysanor before him. She had crawled to him, met him on his level. "You do not descend from men who cannot, Jamesan Strong."

"Why are you doing this to me? Why?"

"After everything you saw, you would ask us that?"

His vision blurred into a sea of fading worlds. He dug his hands deeper into the sand and winced to extract the tears before they could take over. "I'm a trader. I'm the son of Hamish Strong and Yanna de Medvedev. I'm known for my skill, for my loyalty, for my—"

Lysanor snapped her hand forward and grabbed his chin. "You've known your whole life you were not like your brother, or your father. Look at me!"

"Leave me alone!"

"Look at me, or I will peel your eyelids back with my fingers and pin them there for all of time."

Jesse heaved out a silent sob. He looked up. "I never asked for this."

"No one ever does. Who are you?"

"I'm a trader's son."

"*Who are you?*"

Jesse's tears came freely now. They landed in the sand beneath him as he hung beneath the strength of his shoulders, weighted by the visions. Was it true, that he had always known? No, he could not accept that. He had done what was expected of him. He'd learned his father's trade, learned it well. He would proudly inherit his title and his lands, as would his son, one day, Guardians willing. *He had done what was expected, and this was not his life!*

Hamish's gaze, loving, but with a soft, careful distance. He'd known. Not the full truth, no, but he'd known, and he'd said not one word. He loved Jesse that much.

And Yanna... did she know the man she'd loved was Dain Rhiagain? Did she know? Had she taken this truth with her as she spent the last of her promise?

Jesse gasped for breath. All at once, he remembered who he was, really was, and it wasn't this. Not what they wanted him to be.

"I need to get to Esmerelda. Oh, Guardians. She'll be long gone by now. How long was I in there?"

"Esmerelda is beyond your path now. Who are you?"

Jesse reared up and grasped Lysanor by the shoulders. "*How long?*"

Lysanor calmly extricated his fingers, one by one, and then pushed him back into the sand. He landed on the back of his heels.

"Esmerelda is beyond the help of Jamesan Strong now. Only the man you really are, the man you were born to be, can help her, but to become him, you must claim him."

"None of this makes sense. None of this. I don't know who you are, or why I'm here, or—"

It was Isdemus now who dropped to his side. He cupped Jesse's face with his palms, and a gentle peace stole over him. Isdemus had spelled him, and it had worked.

"You are the son of my son, and you will claim that birthright, here and now." Isdemus' soft handling was gone. His passion radiated from him, like a flame.

"I thought I knew who I was," Jesse said, looking back at him with a sorrowful smile.

"Say it. It must be you, child. It must be you who says it."

"I..." Jesse faltered. It was not his denial of the truth holding him back any longer, only a fear of becoming, and then failing. "I'm a son of the Medvedev."

"Go on," Isdemus urged.

"Of the Ilynglass sorcerers. Of... of the Rhiagains. Of man."

"And of Ravenwood," Isdemus said, exhaling a long-held breath. "For that blood runs through me as well."

Lysanor sighed into both hands. "Yes. Yes, Jamesan, you are all of these things. You are the only one in all the worlds who unites all five, the five who have given and taken, and you are the only one who can bring them together."

"Bring them together? How?"

"We will show you."

Jesse dropped back into the sand. He closed his eyes and willed his heart to slow. "Your magic has failed somewhere along the way. I would make a terrible king."

"King? How very limiting, Jesse," Lysanor said. She approached him once more and pressed a hand to his cheek. Her embrace this time was loving. "You're so much more than that."

Isdemus joined her. "You're the one who will save us all."

EPILOGUE

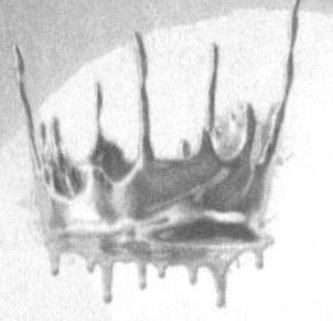

I t was Correen who found them.

They'd cleared the royal apartments, headed toward the banquet hall when Correen waved them down, scurrying over with her dress poorly hitched in her sweaty fingers.

When Assana saw her dour, fat-faced sister-in-law barreling toward them, she was certain this was the end. Correen's loyalty to Eoghan was the only thing Assana actually knew about her. She skulked around the keep boasting expressions so sour Assana had to wonder after her diet. She'd never had more than a few words for her brother's wife, all of them some form of order or admonishment.

Assana positioned herself in front of Esmerelda, as if that would stop anyone with an earnest intention to harm them. She didn't even know why she did it. Why she'd saved Esmerelda, and not simply saved herself. There was more than one way to weaponize your anger. Esmerelda's frenetic jabs to Eoghan's little broken body was one. Assana, coming to the aid of someone in need when no one did the same for her, was another.

"Ah, there you both are! I thought he'd killed you, too." Correen was doused in sweat. She waved her hands, urging them to come. "Follow me. He'll be looking for us."

"What do you mean you thought he'd killed us? Oldwin?" Assana asked as she kept pace with the princess. She wouldn't have guessed the woman could move this fast.

"Of course, Oldwin!" Correen hissed, turning her head to the side. She kept dropping her skirts as she ran, lifting them not quite high enough to come off the stone. "He killed the king! He claims *he* is the king now! Pfft! He isn't even a Rhiagain!"

Esmerelda and Assana shared a wide-eyed look. Assana took her by the hand and they ran faster.

So Oldwin was telling everyone he'd done the treasonous deed. But Assana didn't trust Oldwin's intentions in claiming the kill for himself. There was more behind it. Nothing that creature said or did was accidental. Whatever the answer, it made them less safe, not more.

Correen ushered them down a set of unfamiliar steps. She realized how limited she'd been in her short reign as not-a-queen of Duncarrow, how little she'd seen and done. This wasn't a festive court, alive with color and dance and music. It was dead with the absence of these things.

They descended in a spiral until they came to a large squarish room. Around the perimeter of the room were three doors.

"These are the storerooms. Where the kitchens keep all of our provisions. We keep enough for a year or more. We've had to, with the Southerlands and their treachery."

Esmerelda gritted her teeth. Assana gave her hand a squeeze of caution.

"Do you spend much time down here, Princess?" Assana asked.

Correen looked inexplicably proud when she said, "I am the Mistress of Kitchens."

"Why are we here?"

Correen wiped her sweat onto her sleeve and pointed to the room on the right. "That one. We'll be safe here. It's hardly accessed. It's full of dried meats. My brother... the king, that is, he never possessed the constitution for such rich food, and the cooks are forbidden from serving it in his presence."

"Yes, well, he's dead now, and everyone else likes meat," Assana pointedly replied.

Correen pulled at the rat's nest atop of her head. "You make a fair point, Lady Assana. Oh, it's too late to go back up!"

Esmerelda touched her arm. "Are there no ships?"

"Ships?" Correen dropped her hands and laughed. She looked half-mad. "You wouldn't make it past the range of the bows. Did you not hear me, girl? Oldwin is king now, or so he says. And who will stop him? Who could?"

"Ravenna could," Esmerelda mused, to herself.

Correen cackled. "That girl flew right off. Rightfully so. I hope she's found herself long gone from here."

"She'll come back, for me," Esmerelda said. Her hands fell to her belly in a protective shield.

"Then you'll both die," Correen said. "You choose, then." She nodded at Assana. "Meats, grains, or wine."

"Meat," Assana decided. "For Oldwin will let them all starve. That's more his way."

Correen bent backward to afford herself one more wary glance up the stairs and then ushered them into the most richly scented space Assana had ever entered. At first it stoked her belly, and then it was all she could do not to gag.

She regretted choosing the meat room. Before she could say so, all three women paused at the sound of boots on the stairwell.

"Down. Quickly now!" Correen whispered. They all searched for a place to hide. Esmerelda positioned herself behind a cluster of barrels, and Assana and Correen fell into low crouches behind the curing shelf.

A half dozen voices filled the corridor beyond. Guards that had once served her husband, and now served the greatest traitor this realm had ever seen. Her father had nothing on Oldwin of Ilynglass.

"Let's go," one said. "Two to a room."

"There's nothing here but food. This is a fool's task."

"You heard him. Bring him one of the traitors, or it will be our heads he takes."

"No highborn would come down here, even to save their hides, so let us go to where they would, and spare our heads another day."

There was more arguing. Assana glanced at Correen, but the princess was fixed upon the door, and the absolute gamble their lives rested upon.

At last, the sounds shifted. The guards were leaving. For now.

Esmerelda moved back over to the two women. "We can't stay here."

"Plenty of food," Assana quipped.

"You know what I mean."

Assana nodded. "Is there any other way out of here, Princess? Anything else we can do?"

"We cannot return to the castle proper. There's a way to climb deeper, to sea level where smaller vessels sometimes enter by way of the portcullis. It was once the entrance for prisoners, but many years ago one of our ancestors built the sky dungeon instead. These days it's hardly in use at all. But don't get that look in your eyes. It's not the way for us. If we did not drown at the high tide, we would freeze to death before a vessel arrived to rescue us."

Assana's patience hung by a single frayed thread. "Then what do you propose we do?"

"I got you this far," Correen said. Her scowl returned. "I could have let him kill you. You could afford to be more grateful."

"For delaying our deaths by a mere few hours, or days?"

"Ravenna will come for us," Esmerelda said again. "And Jesse."

"Jesse?" Assana asked.

"Ah," Correen said with a bitter laugh. "You mean the Strong boy, don't you? The one you traveled with when you feigned your death? Son of Dain, grandson of Isdemus."

Esmerelda's face clouded with confusion. "No, you have the wrong man."

"Sure, dear. They're only rumors anyway, just like the ones about Darrick," Correen said. She slumped against the wall, sighing. "I'm spent, enough that I could find rest in this wretched place. Keep watch for a spell."

THEY'D BEEN in the cellar for days. Or was it weeks? Months? Assana had lost all sense of time. Until she'd been denied access to the sun, she hadn't realized her reliance upon it in orienting herself to the world around her.

Correen had died at some point. They moved her to the farthest corner of the room, but this arrangement wouldn't last. The room was built to keep moisture out. She would dry up, and reek, and that scent would either drive them away or draw the attention they'd so far avoided.

They never talked about it. There were many unspoken conversations between Assana and Esmerelda in these days. There was no use in guessing how the older woman had passed. Her death seemed a mercy, and one less thing for them to factor into their own survival.

The dried meats sustained them well enough, but already Esmerelda's hue had changed. The hollows in her cheeks became more prominent. She was not only eating to sustain herself, but her child. She needed fresh foods. There was nothing here for her like that in these cellar storerooms.

And Oldwin knew they were down here. She was certain of it. He would let them wither away. More, he'd enjoy it.

"Esmerelda," Assana said, shaking her cousin to wake her. "I think we have to try and leave here."

Esmerelda nodded. The dark crescents under her eyes had grown, too. Assana reflected on how she had judged their situation by Esmerelda's appearance, but what of her own? Would a mirror be enough to recognize herself?

"Correen said we could climb down to where the small ships dock."

"She also said we would freeze to death or drown."

"It's the only way, unless we want to take our chances returning to the main floor."

"What then?"

"There must be something down there that can help us. You heard her. Shipments come in, so they must go out. There may be a vessel."

"They'll be watching for us."

"Do you want to die here slowly, or take our chances?"

Esmerelda looked down at her belly. "I don't even know if my child is alive anymore. The Guardians have forsaken us."

Assana reached forward and clasped both her hands. "The Guardians have given us a choice. If your child is lost, then it is lost. But what if it isn't? What if we could save them?"

"Do you know where we're going?"

"I saw a hall behind the stairs. Correen gestured there. That must be where we climb down to sea level."

"And then what?"

"I don't know."

Esmerelda used the shelf to pull herself up. "Forgive any weakness in my words, Assana. It's not who I want to be."

"We are whoever we choose to be. We, Esmerelda, the women who took our fates into our own hands, to whatever end. Shall we?"

Esmerelda slid her hand through Assana's. They both allowed themselves a parting, fleeting glance at the bloated corpse of Correen Rhiagain.

Assana was the first out the door. They were alone, but it didn't calm her nerves. Even the slow death awaiting them in the meat storage was not enough to quell her fear she'd steered them wrong by leaving what had kept them safe so far.

Never mind that, she thought, and darted down the long hall. Esmerelda was several paces behind. She came to the end, proud to have been right. They'd never know what respite awaited them below unless they climbed down.

Assana pulled at the heavy metal rung. It didn't budge. She tried again, and the edges of the door shifted only slightly. She stumbled back. There was no use. She wasn't strong enough to do it herself.

Esmerelda appeared at her side. She slid her fingers through the rung. "Together."

Assana nodded. "Together."

They planted their feet and pulled in tandem. The heavy door swung up and nearly knocked them both over as it crashed to the floor.

"Feck," Esmerelda hissed. "You think they heard that above?"

"Go. Take the ladder first, and I'll listen for them."

Esmerelda eased herself down with Assana's help. Assana looked past her and saw a dock built of wood and iron, but that was all she could see from up above.

When Esmerelda was halfway down, Assana followed her. After she'd descended enough for safe clearance, she reached up and gave one hard tug on the inside rung of the door. With a deafening thud, it fell to a close.

Her heart dropped. They would not be able to reopen it. There would be no returning to the safety of the smelly meat room. Wherever this led, it was where they must go now.

Esmerelda dropped onto the docks and disappeared. When Assana joined her, she saw there were iron grates all around, and at the far end, the portcullis Correen had mentioned. Esmerelda found the wheel that opened it and waved.

"Is that..." Assana pointed at a small wooden ship, bobbing in the current. The hull was hardly big enough for the two of them, and she couldn't imagine it enduring the tides once they left harbor. The rope tethering it to the pole had rotted away. It barely held on.

"Our only choice? Seems like it," Esmerelda said. "Help me with this wheel."

Assana joined her and together they grimaced through the task, turning their bodies with the wheel, their grunts escalating to muted screams as the portcullis slowly opened.

"I know nothing about ships," Assana confessed. "Beyond what oars do."

Esmerelda, bent over from exhaustion, laughed. "I know less than I should about many things, Assana, but if there's one thing this Southerlander knows, it's salt and sand and the ships that connect them."

"If they did hear the door, they'll be coming."

"Aye."

"So we go."

"We go."

Assana nodded at the boat that would either save them or end them. "After you."

. . .

Ravenna had circled the keep at Duncarrow for days, dodging the arrows of the guard now belonging to the man who claimed to be her father.

His magic couldn't touch her. That was a blessing, if nothing else was. She'd seen Oldwin on the ramparts, trying. Failing. A part of her thought she might be satisfied spending the remainder of her days like this, taunting him, serving as a constant reminder of his limitations.

But she didn't stay for him.

She'd made a vow, and she would keep it.

As the days lingered on, her hope dwindled. If Esmerelda wasn't dead, then she was a prisoner of a creature who had no use for her. Ravenna was untouchable, but she was not invincible. She could not enter the keep alone.

She'd accepted that what she needed was aid when her eye caught sight of the small brown dot bobbing against the rising current. Her hope surged once more. She didn't dare swoop in and draw the eyes of the relentless guard with it.

Ravenna carved the same path as she had all these long days, curating for Oldwin's lackeys the predictability needed to keep the attention on herself, and not on the small vessel launching a daring escape.

Was Esmerelda on board? Her heart said yes.

If Oldwin's guard caught sight of them, their warships would head them off long before they made it to the kingdom. If their arrows didn't decide matters first.

Unless they had something else to distract them.

Wings spread wide, heart pounding, Ravenna aimed herself at the ramparts.

THE KING IS DEAD; the kingdom in chaos. Several find themselves on the path to save it, but at what personal cost? Continue on with Book 3, The Hidden Kingdom.

WANT to discuss what you just read? Join The Kingdom of the White Sea Official Reader Group on Facebook for book chats, giveaways, and exclusive series news.

IF YOU ENJOYED THIS NOVEL, an honest review is always appreciated.

Northerlands
THE NORTHERN REACH

Lord and Lady:
Lord Holden Dereham & Lady Gretchen Quinlanden Dereham

Capital:
Wulfsgate

Standard:
The jagged mountaintop

Children:
Christian, 19
Drystan, 17
Lisbet, 14
Pieter, 13
Nyssa and Torrin, 10 (twins)

Greater Families/Stewards:
Aldenwood, Turick, Hardeham, Frost, Horne, Arranden, Wynter,
Haddenfoot, Claybourne, Weatherford

Key Towns:
Whitecap, Midwinter Rest, Westport, Eastport, Salthill, Darkwood Run, Witchwood Cross, Wulfshead Haven, Torrin's Pass, Dunwoode

Landmarks:
Northerland Range, Icebolt Mountain, Torrin's Pass, Forest of Lycana

Notable Northerlanders:
Alric Dereham & Earwyn Blackwood Dereham of Wulfsgate
Aylen Wynter Dereham of Witchwood Cross (wife of Christian)
Anabella Weatherford Rhiagain of Whitecap (wife of Darrick)

SOUTHERLANDS
THE SOUTHERN REACH

Lord and Lady:
Lord Khallum Warwick & Lady Gwyn Dereham Warwick

Capital:
Warwicktown

Standard:
The crested wave

Children:
Ransom, 19
Esmerelda, 17
Niall, 15
Garrick, 12

Greater Families/Stewards:
Strong, Rutland, Bradford, Clayton, Garrick, Holton, Leecaster,
Law, Nye, Thorpe

Key Towns:
Sandycove, Iron Hill, Sandymount, Whitecliffe, Stone Mawr,
Blackpool, Leecaster Bay, Hornsea, Goldthorpe, Port Worthing

Landmarks:
The Golden Coast, The Warwick Throne, Drummond's Cock

Notable Southerlanders:
Hamish and Andrija Strong, & sons Jesse and Ryan of Sandycove
Lem Garrick of Iron Hill
Barne Holton of Sandymount
Samuel Law of Port Worthing
Erran and Marie Rutland, & daughters Agnes and Esther of
Whitecliffe

EASTERLANDS
THE EASTERN REACH

Lord and Lady:
Lord Aiden Quinlanden & Lady Maeryn Blackwood Quinlanden

Capital:
Whitechurch

The Resplendent Reliquary of the Guardians is located in
Riverchapel
The Consortium of the Sepulchre in the Skies is located in
Briarhaven
The Council of Universities are in Oldcastle

Standard:
The oaken tree

Children:
Eavan, 18
Assana, 17
Cian, 16

Breandan, 13
Dorrin, 12

Greater Families/Stewards:
Oakenwell, Sylvaine, Forrest, Skylark, Rowan, Rosewood, Waters, Edevane

Key Towns:
Streamstowne, Rushwood, Riverchapel, Oldcastle, Everleigh Pike, Everhart Thicket, Greenfen, Briarhaven, Bythesea, Oak Hill

Landmarks:
Fionn's Pass, Gap of Ever, The Sparkling Beck

Notable Easterlanders:
Lord Corin Quinlanden and Lady Yesenia Warwick of Whitechurch
Drystan "Ash" Sylvaine of Rushwood
Enchanter Joran Rosewood of Greenfen
Mads Waters of Bythesea
Stirling Oakenwell of Oak Hill
Wyat Edevane of Oldcastle
Mortain the Sorcerer

WESTERLANDS
THE WESTERN REACH

Lord and Lady:

Lady Asherley Blackwood & Lord Byrne Warwick (deceased)

Capital:

Longwood Rush

Standard:

The providing mother

Children:

Hollyn (deceased)

Emberley, 15

Gabrianna, 14

Brandyn, 13

Greater Families/Stewards:

Tyndall, Glenlannan, Ashenhurst, Bristol, Blakewell, James,
Stanhope, Richland, Derry, Wakesell

Key Towns:
Wildwood Falls, Pine Bluff, Windwatch Grove, Whispering Wood,
Valleybrooke, Greencastle, East Derry, Greystone Abbey,
Newcarrow, Whitewood

Landmarks:
The Seven Sisters of the West, The River Rush, Whispering Wood,
The Whitewood, The Hidden Cave

Notable Westerlanders:
Easlan James & son Kaslan of Greystone Abbey
Griffath and Clarissant Tyndall, & children Marsh, Jonah, and
Lyria of Wildwood Falls
Glen and Fleur Ashenhurst, & children Meadow and Brook of
Windwatch Grove
Mason and Jasmine Wakesell, & daughter Storm of Whitewood
Arturo Blackfen, Rush Rider
Grand Minister Rhydian Tyndall

HINTERLANDS
THE LAND OF THE MEDVEDEV

Chieftainesses:
Yseult de Medvedev, Drumain Clahnn
Ohsmha de Medvedev, Saleen Clahnn

Clahnns:
Drumain
Asgill
Mayke
Saleen

Yseult's Children:
Kian, 17
Kael, 15

Landmarks:
Forest of All

Other Notable Medvedev:
Yanna de Medvedev of Clahnn Drumain (sister of Yseult, deceased)

DUNCARROW
SEAT OF THE RHIAGAINS

King:

Eoghan Rhiagain

Wife: Lady Assana Quinlanden of the Easterlands

Standard:

The crossed swords

King's Family:

Khain- Father (deceased)

Florian- Mother (deceased)

Dain- Brother (deceased)

Assyria- Sister

Correen- Sister

Darrick- Brother

Anabella- Wife of Darrick

Stefan- Son of Darrick

Notable Rhiagains of Past:

King Carrow the Original

King Carrick the Dreamer
King Karsein
King Fynne the Good

Known Rhiagain Sorcerers:
Oldwin
Mortain
Lysanor
Isdemus

Landmarks:
The sky dungeon, Isle of Belcarrow

MIDNIGHT CREST
HAVEN OF THE RAVENWOODS

High Priestess & Priest:

Varinya & Argentyn Ravenwood

Castle:

The Rookery

Sigil:

The raven

Children:

Alasyr, 17

Ravenna, 15

Ryandyr, 13

Ashara, 10

Nyana & Nevyn, 8 (twins)

Landmarks:

Courtyard of Regents

Notable Ravenwoods:
Adynora & Rillyn (Ravenna's grandparents)
Aryc & son Sandyr
Ailyn
Corridyn
Rhosyn (defected)

THE CONSORTIUM OF THE SEPULCHRE IN THE SKIES
THE ACADEMY OF MAGIC AND RULING COUNCIL OF ELDERS

Head Magus:

Head Magus Tymagen

Location:

Briarhaven, in the Easterlands

Adherents- students

Enchanters/Enchantresses- magic practitioners who have finished their studies and been assigned into the world. May also be called by their discipline (i.e. Healers, Seers, etc.)

Magi- Instructors of magic at the Sepulchre

Elder Magi- A position of tenure that allows access to the Sacred Halls

Head Magus- The head of the Sepulchre

Notable Magi:

Magi Christian Dereham

Magi Aylen Wynter

Elder Magi Rorric Dereham
Elder Thorsen

Notable Adherents:
Brandyn Blackwood
Esther Rutland

ALSO BY SARAH M. CRADIT

KINGDOM OF THE WHITE SEA

<u>Kingdom of the White Sea Trilogy</u>

The Kingless Crown

The Broken Realm

The Hidden Kingdom

<u>The Book of All Things</u>

The Raven and the Rush

The Sylvan and the Sand

The Altruist and the Assassin

The Melody and the Master

The Claw and the Crowned

The Priestess and the Paladin

THE SAGA OF CRIMSON & CLOVER

<u>The House of Crimson and Clover Series</u>

The Storm and the Darkness

Shattered

The Illusions of Eventide

Bound

Midnight Dynasty

Asunder

Empire of Shadows

Myths of Midwinter

The Hinterland Veil

The Secrets Amongst the Cypress

Within the Garden of Twilight

House of Dusk, House of Dawn

<u>Midnight Dynasty Series</u>

A Tempest of Discovery

A Storm of Revelations

A Torrent of Deceit

<u>The Seven Series</u>

1970

1972

1973

1974

1975

1976

1980

<u>Vampires of the Merovingi Series</u>

The Island

and more

<u>The Dusk Trilogy</u>

St. Charles at Dusk: The Story of Oz and Adrienne

Flourish: The Story of Anne Fontaine

Banshee: The Story of Giselle Deschanel

Crimson & Clover Stories

Surrender: The Story of Oz and Ana

Shame: The Story of Jonathan St. Andrews

Fire & Ice: The Story of Remy & Fleur

Dark Blessing: The Landry Triplets

Pandora's Box: The Story of Jasper & Pandora

The Menagerie: Oriana's Den of Iniquities

A Band of Heather: The Story of Colleen and Noah

The Ephemeral: The Story of Autumn & Gabriel

Bayou's Edge: The Landry Triplets

For more information, and exciting bonus material, visit www. sarahmcradit.com

ABOUT THE AUTHOR

Sarah is the USA Today and International Bestselling Author of over forty contemporary and epic fantasy stories, and the creator of the Kingdom of the White Sea and Saga of Crimson & Clover universes.

Born a geek, Sarah spends her time crafting rich and multilayered worlds, obsessing over history, playing her retribution paladin (and sometimes destruction warlock), and settling provocative Tolkien debates, such as why the Great Eagles are not Gandalf's personal taxi service. Passionate about travel, she's been to over twenty countries collecting sparks of inspiration, and is always planning her next adventure.

Sarah and her husband live in a beautiful corner of SE Pennsylvania with their three tiny benevolent pug dictators.

www.sarahmcradit.com

About the Author

Sarah is the USA Today and International Bestselling Author of over forty contemporary and epic fantasy stories, and the creator of the Kingdom of the White Sea and Saga of Crimson & Clover universes.

Born a geek, Sarah spends her time crafting rich and multilayered worlds, obsessing over history, playing her retribution paladin (and sometimes destruction warlock), and settling provocative Tolkien debates, such as why the Great Eagles are not Gandalf's personal taxi service. Passionate about travel, she's been to over twenty countries collecting sparks of inspiration, and is always planning her next adventure.

Sarah and her husband live in a beautiful corner of SE Pennsylvania with their three tiny benevolent pug dictators.

www.sarahmcradit.com